AZARINTH HEALER

Book Three

RHAEGAR

Thanks for checking out *Azarinth Healer, Book Three.*

We hope you enjoy this latest instalment of Portal Books brand LitRPG/Progression Fantasy goodness, if you haven't already, be sure to sign up to our mailing list to get access to the Portal Books Story Bundle containing over 80,000 words of FREE content from our authors.

Our story bundle is all NEW never before seen content that you won't read about in the author's novels. Whenever we add more, you'll get the updates too, absolutely free.

https://portal-books.com/sign-up

Feel free to check us out on Facebook too: it's a great place to stay up to date with future releases. We also regularly run giveaways and promotions that everyone is welcome to participate in.

https://www.facebook.com/groups/LitRPGPortal/

Happy reading!

Best wishes,

The Portal Books Team

www.portal-books.com

Contents

The story so far...

Ilea's journey led her to Ravenhall, a human city south of the Plains where the Shadow's Hand resides, a famed mercenary order whose members Ilea had already encountered a few times.

She met Trian, a noble from the capital of Lys, Kyrian, a metal and curse magic user with a nebulous past, Claire, a rune mage and soon-to-be team manager, and Eve, an illusionist and mind magic user with more than a few secrets.

They trained and soon went on missions to rid the world of creatures too dangerous for anyone but Shadows to face. Preparation, perhaps, for the crisis that soon befell Ravenhall when one of the Shadow's Elders summoned demons from the Great Salt into the city, leaving Ravenhall overrun and both Ilea and Trian stranded in a strange, alien realm.

When Ilea made contact with one of the local Mind Weavers, powerful demon variants with mind magic capabilities, they struck a deal and soon found the Elder of the Shadow's Hand, Adam Strand. The man proved too much for Ilea and Trian to handle, and he left via an ancient transportation device.

Ilea and Trian managed to escape the realm through the same device, taking the Mind Weaver, Weavy, with them.

Back in Elos, Ilea and Trian reunited with Kyrian and other Shadows before Ilea left for Virilya to inform and muster the remains of the Shadows, their city lost and crawling with demons. With plans set in motion and the Shadow's Hand united, they launched their assault on Ravenhall, ridding the city of its summoned demon occupiers.

Alongside the following clean-up and arrival of Imperial troops, Ilea found Claire in the surrounding forests, hunted by Forkspear mercenaries looking for a healer called Lilith. An alias Ilea had given herself during her exploration of her first Taleen dungeon. Ilea fought and killed the mercenaries looking for her and Alice, the young noble woman she'd saved near Riverwatch.

With different opportunities and roads opening up for the group, Ilea decided to keep doing missions with the Shadow's Hand, accompanied by Kyrian. But first, they needed to find a new home for the estranged demon mind mage they'd brought back from the Great Salt before he wound up being killed by the Imperials or an overeager Shadow.

And Ilea knew just the place to take him. A den of outsiders, necromancers, and dark mages near the city of Riverwatch...

Part I

ONE

An Inn and a Boy

Ilea spread her ashen wings, feeling the air against her skin as she flew with all the speed she could muster. She breathed deeply and glanced over at the horizon, where the suns of Elos were slowly setting. They wouldn't make it all the way to Riverwatch before night fell, and while she wasn't too concerned about being found, she knew there could still be elves and other monsters lurking in the dark.

She slowed and suggested to Kyrian that they find a settlement to take a break, their flight having already taken nearly an entire day. Kyrian agreed, and before long, the glow of torchlight in the distance alerted them to a small village.

"We could just sleep outside," Kyrian said.

"After all that demon hunting?" Ilea replied. "Let's at least see what they can offer. A bed and some warmth would be nice."

Ilea landed on the road leading to the village and summoned a hood. Looking toward the others, Weavy put up his own black hood and covered most of his face again, hiding the dark holes of his eyes and the sharp teeth in his mouth behind the cloth. Ilea had gotten used to his demonic features by now, but the same wasn't true for most everyone else.

A worn sign beside the road read 'Fenhold'. Smoke was rising from several of the buildings up ahead, and Ilea heard her stomach rumble at the thought of a hearty meal.

Perhaps a potato stew… or a barley soup.

They walked along the muddy road until they came to a small stone bridge leading over a nearly empty creek flowing through the forest. A man clad in leather armor, not unlike the set Ilea was wearing, sat lazily on one side, spear in hand and short sword sheathed. He noticed them entirely too late but sprang up when he did.

"Who goes there?" he shouted, his arms shaking a little as he pointed the spear toward them.

Ilea casually walked up and stopped two meters in front of the man. He looked much younger than she'd initially thought. She smiled, realizing he probably wasn't much younger than her.

"You should be careful who you point your weapon at," Ilea said, having identified him as a level thirty warrior. Not much of a threat.

The guard's eyes opened wide as he drew back the spear, nearly losing his grip on it in the process.

"I'm sorry, it's just that… the monsters," he started, but Ilea just held up a hand.

"It's alright, we know. We're looking for a warm meal and a bed. Ready to pay, of course. Anything like that to be had in your village?"

Her casual voice seemed to calm him down considerably. Still, he occasionally glanced toward the heavily armored Kyrian and the cloaked Weavy.

"I'm Harsh," he said, visibly relaxing. "We have that, yes. But the prices are high at the moment. Winter was rough."

"Thank you," Ilea said, motioning toward her companions to follow her.

"No worries, madam. Always wanted to meet a noble."

He blushed, but Ilea completely ignored the comment.

A noble? The boy really hasn't been around a lot.

The three crossed the bridge and entered the village. A few houses built from stone and wood, nothing more. A chicken ran across the street with a little girl following close behind, cursing like the best of them.

Ilea made for the biggest building near the center of the village and found a sign outside indicating it to be an inn of some sort. Such buildings usually were. She opened the heavy door and stepped inside, holding it open for her companions.

On entering, the cold, harsh wind outside was immediately cut off and replaced by the hearty chatter of people and the warmth of a nearby fire. The smell of food was in the air, and Ilea smiled as she closed her eyes, enjoying the cozy haven with a shiver of contentment.

She opened her eyes again. Some people were looking at the newcomers, but generally, their entrance hadn't had much of an impact on the overall mood. There were around fifteen patrons, most of them armed. Three looked like soldiers, all sporting the same crest on their gear. A crest she didn't know.

Ilea walked up to a woman behind the counter, the floorboards creaking below her feet as she saw through her Sphere that there were some rats working their way into a supply chest in the cellar, as well as two people upstairs in the middle of some rather rough sex.

"Welcome, travelers! More refugees from westward?" asked the woman, apparently the innkeeper, before she shouted at someone behind her to 'hurry up with the food'. Her stern look blossomed into a friendly smile as she turned toward the new guests again. "I do hope you have silver."

Ilea nodded and removed a few coins from her pouch, putting them on the counter. "Any rooms still free? Some food and ale as well."

"There's just one room left, the far right one," the woman said, taking the coins and putting a key on the counter.

With the key in her pocket, Ilea walked to a free table and was quickly joined by her companions. She had chosen a table close to the fire and sat down near the dancing flames.

Food and drink arrived soon after. Nothing special, but filling and hot. Ilea smiled when she saw the two men walking down the stairs and seating themselves at a table nearby, one with a little more difficulty than the other.

"So, who are the people we're meeting?" Kyrian asked, breaking the silence. Weavy perked up, obviously interested in the place he'd likely be staying.

Ilea grinned. "Bunch of outsiders. Their magic is, well, frowned upon by most," she said. "But you'll see soon enough. I don't think we're more than a day or two away if we continue at the same speed."

Kyrian nodded at that and got up. "I'll sleep for two or three hours. We can leave again after."

Ilea nodded his way and raised her mug. She'd join him in an hour or two.

"You planning on sleeping?" she asked the demon next to her. His robes, boots, and hood were deliberately positioned to make it hard to see any specific features.

"No," came the short mental reply.

"Don't murder anything in here," Ilea said, pointing a finger toward him.

"I saw what happened in Ravenhall. I'm not stupid, Ilea," the demon replied. *"Even though I don't really understand your kind yet."*

He touched the wood of the table with his bandaged hands, caressing it gently.

"You don't have any wood there, do you?" Ilea asked after a while.

Weavy glanced her way but stayed silent.

"Your friend not talking?" a drunk man called, three of his friends laughing at the not-actually-a-joke. "Cowering behind your hood like that – what're you hiding? Fucking freak, I bet. Come on, show us!"

The man didn't get out another word as his eyes rolled back and he slumped down to hit the table. The whole room quickly quieted as the man slowly slid off the table and fell to the ground.

Ilea took another sip of her ale. "Did you kill him?" she asked the demon, who was still running his fingers over the table.

"No."

"He's alive guys, calm down," Ilea said, raising her mug. "Have a round on me."

Someone cheered for the round, but the guy's friends didn't seem too pleased with the situation, though they were clearly confused as to exactly what had happened.

A little while later, a boy in his early teens came up to them, obviously nervous, as he constantly brushed away his mop of black hair from his face. He was thin, his skin pale, eyes black.

"Ehm... Miss...?" he stammered in a whisper. "That... was that mind... mind magic?"

"Ask him about that, not me," Ilea said, motioning to her companion. "Weavy, I'll be in bed. Just be around somewhere when we leave. And don't eat the boy."

She got up, walking past the nervous boy, who first looked at her with wide eyes and then at the cloaked demon sitting at the table.

"Good luck," she said in passing.

"Don't worry. I already ate," Weavy said.

* * *

A light tapping on her shoulder roused her. Ilea turned over sleepily and saw Kyrian looking at her carefully, wearing his spiked metal armor. His gray eyes locked with hers as he smiled.

"I didn't want to wake you up, but you said a couple hours was fine."

"It's fine," she said and yawned, slowly sitting up on the side of the bed. She sat there for a moment, her breathing slowing as she touched her legs.

"Are you alright?" Kyrian asked.

It would be so easy, she thought, but she'd decided not to lead him on anymore. He was far less experienced than her, and she didn't want to break his heart. Let alone take any chances with her own.

"I'll be right back. Wait outside. I'll get Weavy as well," she said and blinked outside, the fresh air quickly changing her mood.

A quick bath would be nice.

The creek was only a minute away, so she walked. The water was cold, but she didn't mind as she watched the moons reflect off the surface.

Stepping out of the water, Ilea used her Embered Body Heat to dry herself, steam rising off her skin a moment later. She summoned her leather armor and stretched her arms a little, checking her belt for Aki, the sentient dagger companion she'd picked up in the Taleen dungeon.

Now to find our mind mage.

She walked back to the inn. Weavy wasn't inside, but she picked up his scent easily enough with her Hunter's Sight. It led her to a simple house at the edge of the village. Rounding it, she found them behind it.

Weavy and the boy stood a small distance apart in the moonlight. The boy was holding his hands out toward Weavy, a rune glowing on his forehead.

"Hey, you two," Ilea said. The boy immediately jerked toward her. She felt a small tug on her mind and then a push, but it was nothing compared to Eve or Weavy. "Ah, found a teacher, have you?"

"He is weak," Weavy said to her and, based on the boy's reaction, to the kid as well.

"Yeah, of course he is. He's a kid from a village in the middle of nowhere. And now he has mind magic. Did you curse him or something?"

"I did not curse the human child. The rune helps with control. It already had an affinity. It chose to learn more. Begged me, even."

"I want to come with you," the boy said, quietly at first, then he repeated it louder.

"This is your home," Ilea replied.

He shook his head, then started crying.

Ilea glanced at Weavy before she walked over and hugged the kid, pushing healing into his mind.

"You're not from here?" she asked after a while.

"I am. But I'm alone."

Great, Ilea thought, looking at Weavy. As she did so, Kyrian landed nearby and joined them.

"What's your name?" Ilea asked.

"Eyn."

"Kyrian, can you ask someone who's still awake what the circumstances are with Eyn?"

He looked at her, then flew back toward the inn.

"You want to take him in?" she asked Weavy. "I'm sure having a disciple will make a good first impression on your new friends."

The demon looked toward her and then toward the boy. *"He does not know what I am."*

"Well then, show him." Ilea turned to the boy. "Do you really want to go with your teacher? He's not a human, and you'll have to leave your life here in the village behind. Possibly forever."

"I don't have anything here. I don't care what my teacher is," the boy said, not a single stammer in his voice now, his eyes defiant.

"Good." Ilea looked at the demon. "Remove the hood."

Weavy did so. The boy's expression turned from determined to scared, then to unsure, and then right back to determined again before he bowed in front of his new master.

"Good. You've sold your soul now, and your first three children," Ilea joked.

The boy's head jolted up from the bow, and he looked first at her and then back at his master with wide eyes.

"Your soul is yours, but the children are mine," Weavy said in a completely

serious tone. "*They taste nice when they're fresh,*" he finished, looking at Ilea. She got the distant impression that he was winking. Despite his lack of eyes.

She threw up her hands in defense. "Hey, that's between you two."

The kid knew they were joking. Probably.

Kyrian returned soon after, whispering in Ilea's ear, "He lost his parents to a monster attack four years ago. Doesn't seem he's liked in the village. I assume it has to do with his magic – he unlocked a Class far earlier than most. The other kids say he's strange. Might get exiled in a few years at this rate."

Ilea sighed. "He'll fit right in. And he'll help us sweet talk Walter before we show Weavy's face."

"Are you sure? He's a child."

"The Vultures' place is far cooler than this village, trust me."

"Kidnapping a random child from a backwater village to be trained in mind magic by a demon. I'm sure nothing could go wrong," Aki weighed in from Ilea's belt.

"Exactly," Ilea smiled.

She turned to the mind mage and his new apprentice.

"All right, we're leaving. Got anything you want to take with you?" she asked, and the boy shook his head, apparently done with this place. "Come, then."

Ilea held out her hand, her wings spreading behind her, reflecting the light of the moons. The boy hesitantly crept closer and grasped one of her arms. Weavy grabbed her other arm, and they flew upward.

The journey was mostly uneventful after that. The suns rose high, and the weather was much warmer than anything Ilea had experienced in the past four months. They rushed over forests and lakes, hills and marshes before they finally saw the mountain in the distance, towering over the landscape like a monument.

"Karth," Ilea said out loud.

"We're getting far into the west," Kyrian commented.

"First time for you?"

He gave an affirming grunt. "I'm excited to see it all."

Eyn and Weavy were training, judging from Ilea's growing headache. She glanced at the two of them. It didn't seem wise to mentally attack the person carrying you hundreds of meters in the air, but she didn't mind. A quick application of her healing magic offset any discomfort.

"I'm excited too," she replied, smiling.

Ilea had barely even started exploring these lands. A lot of time had passed and she'd grown a lot stronger, but Elos still seemed incredibly vast. Perhaps it was because of the absence of planes and the internet. If she wanted to travel somewhere in Elos, she had to fly there herself or join a caravan. Not that she planned to do the latter again anytime soon.

"We'd better cover the last couple hours on foot. I don't want anyone to follow us," Ilea said.

Once they'd landed, it took them the better part of the day to run through the thick forest surrounding Karth. They stopped at a clearing a short distance from the Calys mine, the suns setting as they neared the entrance.

It didn't look like Riverwatch had taken interest in the dungeon as of yet. In fact, the area looked all but abandoned.

"Why were there no monsters in the forest?" Eyn asked. "The elders always said not to go into the forests because of all the monsters."

Ilea smiled. "It's because *we* are the monsters."

She felt incredibly proud of her delivery. Kyrian just shook his head as she basked in the boy's admiration. *God damn I'm cool.* She winked at Kyrian.

He just chuckled. "Idiot," he muttered as Ilea led the way into the dungeon.

There were even fewer hounds around this time, fleeing just as they had before Ilea had gone to the Hand. The undead looked at her but didn't attack. They had a certain fixation on Weavy, but his magic seemed to turn them away.

"What a peculiar presence..." the demon said as he looked toward a wandering undead. "Are these the... friends you spoke of?"

"I can't tell if you're being serious or if you're insulting me," Ilea said, leading them farther into the caverns. "Let me do the talking."

TWO

Friends

Ilea had only walked a few steps into the hideout before Walter showed up, black eyes staring into hers, magic pulsing around him.

Metal swirled around Kyrian in response to Walter's sudden appearance, but he waited for Ilea to act.

Ilea stepped closer to Walter and held up her hands as she smiled.

"Walter, it's me," she said.

"With a demon," he said through gritted teeth, looking between Weavy and Ilea with hard eyes.

"Calm down. He's not like the others. Not like the one Celene summoned anyway. Look at him."

As Walter's entirely black eyes stared at the demon, Eyn took a protective stance before his teacher.

Huh, that friendship formed quickly.

Weavy didn't move, nor did he use his magic.

"He fought by our side," Ilea said.

Walter finally seemed to calm down as the black in his eyes bled back to white.

"Gods, what did you do this time?" he said, shaking his head. "Don't tell me you brought this demon catastrophe upon us?" His face was haggard.

"Ah, no. I know the man who's responsible, but he's still in the demon realm," Ilea said.

She went to rest a hand on Walter's shoulder, who was now just standing there, stunned. Indra and Harthome showed up a moment later, followed by Celene and Lucia.

Ilea let go of him and walked a few steps back before she motioned to her team.

"You guys know me, I'm a member of the Shadow's Hand now. That's Kyrian, he's in my team. That's Weavy, he's a Mind Weaver and demon we found in the demon realm, the Great Salt. That kid there is a mind mage we found in a village a while away, he's Weavy's apprentice."

The Vultures listened to all this with wide eyes.

"And I come with a request. One that might interest you as much as us," Ilea said as she sidled up to Walter again.

"Next time she's here, she's going to bring a friendly elf with her..." Walter muttered with a chuckle and a shake of his head.

"Or a basilisk," Harthome laughed.

"A demon..." Celene muttered, though she didn't sound afraid in the slightest.

"You seem to know a whole lot about this demon infestation. Why don't we discuss everything over a pint of ale?" Walter suggested.

Ilea smiled a broad smile. "That does sound like a great idea."

* * *

"You want him to stay here?" Walter asked.

"Why not? You could learn a lot from each other," Ilea said, sipping her ale.

Harthome and Celene were engaged in a conversation with Weavy. The woman was surprisingly calm talking to a demon, considering the experience she'd had summoning one of them.

"That we could, but he's nearly at level two hundred, Ilea. It'd be dangerous to keep him here."

"He's called Weavy, and maybe you should talk to him first before you dismiss him like that. As far as I knew, the Vultures Brotherhood didn't discriminate based on magic or heritage, or was I wrong?"

The man grumbled and got up before he went and grabbed some food.

"This is going to be a long night," he sighed, smiling when he looked back at her. "First you stumbled into our caverns and somehow ended up a guest, and now this." He gestured to the general situation.

"You told me I should go to the Hand," Ilea said, shrugging innocently.

"Was I wrong?"

"No," she smiled, drinking some more ale. "You weren't wrong at all, Walter."

He touched her shoulder and walked over to the demon.

"Weavy," Walter said. "Come, I have to talk with you."

Weavy looked at him and nodded before he got up and joined him. Celene gave Walter an annoyed look as the two left the room.

"Are you not scared? After what happened?" Lucia asked Celene.

The woman blinked in confusion. "Would you hate all men because one of them did something bad to you?"

"Some people do," Ilea said as she started eating. "And men don't all look the same."

"He doesn't look the same as the one I summoned. That one was bluer. And his eyes were less kind."

Ilea decided not to comment on how Weavy's lack of eyes could be seen as 'kind'.

"I stand corrected, I guess."

"Besides, you're with the Hand now, you did it! Tell us all about it." Celene moved to the next table to join Ilea and Kyrian.

"Yeah, tell us. What mighty beasts have you fought?" Harthome added, joining them, as did the rest of the Vultures. Indra had started talking to the village boy at some point, but Grandpa Bones wasn't anywhere to be found.

"That sand fish was really hard to catch," Ilea said and nodded, thinking back on it.

"Carrying it was harder," Kyrian supplied as a couple of metal spheres floated around, forming a miniature version of the support beams he had used to carry it. Ilea joined in as the monster came into existence in ashen form, floating into the support beams.

"You're a creator?" Lucia exclaimed before she took Ilea's hands in hers. "That's amazing! And ash, such an interesting school of magic!"

"You're familiar with it?" Ilea asked.

Lucia grinned. "Just know that it's closely related to death. Death and fire."

"Culturally," Harthome said from the side. "Not many who wield it. Difficult to get a Class related to it."

"What other things did you fight?" Celene asked.

"We hunted down a Queen Harpy. That wasn't much compared to the demon invasion though," Ilea said.

"I'd love to see that whale you mentioned," Harthome said. "As would most everyone in this cavern."

"I doubt it's still around. The Empire and the Hand would've been very interested in its corpse," Kyrian said, dashing the man's hopes.

"I was inside it for a bit," Ilea said with her mouth full.

"Eww, you're fucking gross," Celene said and laughed.

"Says the chick who's *into* demons," Ilea retorted with a grin, for which she got a piece of meat thrown in her face, which she promptly ate.

* * *

Weavy and Walter returned sometime later, deep in conversation. They were literally dragged back into the common room by Lucia.

"Well, I guess that's a good sign," Ilea said to Kyrian, who watched on in silence.

"It is indeed," Harthome agreed.

Walter stopped talking to Weavy a moment later and looked at the others.

"We will have a vote, but I think he should stay. With the boy."

This got a few cheers from the others.

"Can't say I'm very surprised," Walter added as he joined Ilea.

"At the level of my food consumption?" she asked, swallowing.

"That's very impressive as well. No, I mean the demon, of course." He sighed. "His magical knowledge surpasses mine in many fields. His approach is incredible, dare I say revolutionary. Incredibly archaic in other things. It's refreshing, to say the least. Indra will be pleased as well, as will Grandpa Bones."

He relaxed in his chair and sipped from his drink.

"Any news to share about the goings on in the region?" Ilea asked.

Walter shook his head. "Not much. Heard about the demons long before the first of them showed up. It took a lot of brave men and women to put them down, I hear. No more Elves in the vicinity though. And there's been an influx of refugees from the western towns that were destroyed, but most move on to go farther east. If you want more recent news, you should go to the city. We don't leave too often."

"Glad it's not been too bad here."

"There was talk of hordes…" Walter frowned.

She nodded. "Yeah. Took a while to clear out just Ravenhall."

"Destroyed the whole city?"

She nodded, deciding not to expand on it.

"Will you be staying long?" Walter asked after a moment of silence.

"No, Kyrian and I will leave again. First for Riverwatch, then back to Ravenhall," she answered. "If you need anything, let me know – gold, weapons, books…"

"We're quite fine. Your new demonic addition will add more than enough for now. The same offer is there for you, of course."

"I can't think of anything. Were the elven corpses useful?"

"Very. Their anatomy is incredible. Though their usefulness has expired by now."

Ilea promptly dumped the rest of her elven corpses. She had been carrying them for a long time now and hadn't found a use for them so far.

"How? Where?" Walter asked as he got up and shouted for Indra. The old scholar rushed toward them immediately.

"You had them with you all this time?" Kyrian asked. "Why give them out now?"

"Decluttering," Ilea said as she got up and walked to the bar. "And now we have access to the bar," she said, knowing full well that Walter was still in earshot.

She could practically feel his teeth grind as she went and stored some of his homemade ale in her necklace. It was probably a low price, considering the rarity of elven corpses, but she did love it.

She grabbed something else as well and went back to Kyrian, putting a few bottles on the table. She opened one of them and sniffed it, then smiled. He cautiously did the same.

"This seems nice," he said. "Some kind of mead, and lemon? You can heal away the alcohol, right?"

"I can." Ilea grinned and drank. It felt like energy flowed right down into her stomach. There was definitely more than just honey and lemons in this beverage.

* * *

"Come on, how are you still mad?" Ilea groused.

Walter had spent the last few minutes cursing at her in what seemed like several different languages.

"You drank all of my stamina potions. Ilea, it's..." He blew out a long breath and sighed, then he chuckled. "Ah, fuck it. I still owe you, even after all this," he said as he shook his head. "Next time, though, maybe ask."

"Sorry." She summoned a gold coin. Then she looked at his crossed arms and summoned a few more.

"It's not about the gold."

"Right. I'll check with you next time," Ilea said and summoned all the ale she had already taken. "Fair deal? Including the potions?"

He took in a deep breath and sighed. "Sure."

Ilea grinned and hugged the man. "Your ale is the best."

"I know."

"Thank you, Walter. I do appreciate it," Ilea said. "And thank you for taking in Weavy. I don't know what would've happened to him if he'd stayed alone."

"Nonsense, your decision to bring him here was sound. He fits in perfectly. We've just got to get used to it, due to recent events."

"As long as Celene is fine with it."

"That thing nearly killed me too," Walter reminded her.

Ilea punched his chest. "What doesn't kill you..."

Walter smiled a wry smile but didn't respond.

Next, Ilea went on to say her goodbyes, checking on Weavy first.

"Listen to them and don't do anything stupid. If I come back here and everyone's dead or gone, I'll hold you solely responsible. Understood?"

The demon just stood there and took in her lecture. She touched Weavy's shoulder.

"And don't get manipulated into doing things you don't want to. You're a strong, independent demon who needs no demon lord, alright?"

"I understand, Ilea. Thank you for working together with me and for bringing me here," the demon said before she hugged him.

"I'll come visit, alright?" she said, letting go. "Look at you. Only two hundred years old and you're growing up so fast."

* * *

The two of them said their goodbyes to everybody and were soon back in the caves of the Calys Mines, where Ilea had run from an elf with a group of adventurers so long ago. She remembered the battles with the hounds as they made their way out.

I could probably fight that elf now, she thought, clenching her fist. *If there's ever a chance again…*

It was raining outside when they stepped out of the cave, and Ilea pulled up her hood to shield herself against the drops. Her wings spread as she watched metal spheres land in Kyrian's hands. The two of them were airborne a moment later, bound for Riverwatch. The first city Ilea had found in this world.

The flight didn't take long, and they landed a couple of hundred meters away from the city, still hidden by the tree line. Walking out from the forest, they found only a few travelers walking toward the western gate. All of them looked like hunters or adventurers.

"Occupation and reason to be here?" the guard asked, completely unimpressed by their higher level and gear.

"Mercenaries. I'm here to visit a friend," Ilea said.

"The fee to enter is ten coppers if you don't have a permit already," the guard said. He took the money before he let them inside.

"Hey, do you know Dale?" Ilea asked. "He was a captain here around half a year ago."

The guard gave a crooked grin. "I know four Dales, one's a captain. How much is that information worth to you?"

"Ah, fuck off," Ilea said and walked into the streets of Riverwatch. She'd start at his guard station. Perhaps he was still at the same one.

When she arrived, she found a guard standing outside who was a little less greedy.

"He's out hunting with some of the recruits. I can give you directions. Ilea, isn't it?" the man said, somehow remembering her.

Ilea had to admit that she had no recollection of ever meeting the man, but he did help them out, which was nice. They flew eastward toward the supposed goblin infestation in a small settlement that had stood abandoned for several decades.

The rain was pouring but Ilea could make out faint light between the trees. As they landed, she could see it was a dilapidated house near the settlement with a fire burning inside.

Ilea stepped inside without warning and blocked the sword already swinging her way with her hand. A spear was also deflected by her Veil without doing any damage. Dale looked prepared to fight before she removed her hood.

"Damn weather. Fucking wet," Ilea complained and saw the expression on Dale's face turn to relief.

"Ilea, can you still heal? One of my men is dying."

Ilea ended her grumbling immediately.

"Where?"

Dale pointed at some stairs and Ilea rushed down them, blinking twice and seeing several men in a deep cellar a moment later with her Sphere.

"I'm a healer!" she shouted as she rushed into the room.

The injured man was tall, with a youthful face and curly red hair. Ilea could tell he was weak and had lost a lot of blood from several wounds inflicted by small weapons. Worst of all, he was poisoned. Whatever the goblins had used, if it had been goblins, it had stopped him from recovering.

The two men standing nearby were a little overwhelmed by the situation and just watched on as Ilea used her healing skill to care for the man. Dale and some of his men arrived a moment later, stopping by her side as they watched her work. Kyrian stepped up as well.

"Poison," he said as a small sphere of metal floated over the man, splintering into dozens of needles that floated down toward his skin. Some of the recruits began to push forward to intervene, but Dale stopped them. The needles dug into the man's skin, and Ilea watched with her healing as the poison was expertly removed from the wounds. At least it looked like that at first. Then she realized it wasn't being removed. It was destroyed.

"Are you cursing the poison? What the hell..." Ilea said to him as she continued to heal.

"I am," Kyrian said.

They continued for three more minutes until the man was perfectly healthy again. He was likely exhausted as he was now asleep, but he looked much better.

Dale wiped his brow and slumped against the doorframe. "Thank the gods you came. Damn goblins. Why do I always underestimate the little buggers?"

THREE

How Much We Grow

"I've never really fought goblins," Ilea said as she got up from her crouched position.

"They're nasty things, killing and feeding off anything that moves. Normally the monsters around here tear them to shreds. As do we," Dale said, sighing before leaning against the wall of the cellar. Looking around for the first time, Ilea realized it must've once been a crypt.

"Are the demons changing things?" Ilea asked. "I thought only a few managed to get this far north and west?"

"Yes, but they've destroyed entire settlements southward, and the monsters aren't being left alone either. We've had refugees, people who've turned to banditry, and monsters alike arriving in this region. It's not been easy keeping up with everything. Hence we've got a lot of new recruits. But they need to learn first."

"You need help with any of that? Seems like you're in the thick of it."

Dale smiled. "I appreciate it. But I've been doing this for more than a decade. We'll get through it. And I wouldn't want to explain the expense to my superiors. We need to deal with our own problems, otherwise our budget would go to mercenaries in the first place."

"I'd help you for free, Dale."

"I'll take you healing Henry here, but no, I'd only ask if we were desperate."

"Goblins catch you unawares?" she asked, nodding toward the curly-haired recruit sleeping on the floor.

"They did. Some were higher level than expected. It's mostly the bad weather though. Spotting traps is harder, and they're small." Dale looked at her. "I haven't even greeted you yet. It's been a while, Ilea. You've changed, as expected." He gave a meaningful glance toward Kyrian.

Most of the guards were in the crypt now, somewhat apprehensive of the newcomers, but seeing that their captain knew at least one of them made them ease up a little bit.

"A lot's happened – I joined the Hand and fought some demons. What about you? I can see you've been taking the training seriously," Ilea commented after she'd identified Dale to be at level one hundred twenty-one, considerably higher than the last time they'd met.

Dale nodded grimly. "And every week brings more reason to do so. First the elves and now the demons. I heard rumors about the Hand being involved in all of it. I do hope you're still on our side."

He doesn't seem to put a lot of faith in such rumors considering the casual way he mentioned it, Ilea thought.

"A member of the Hand was involved, but we cleaned up the demons in Ravenhall at the core," she replied. "I'm sure it's going to take a while to kill all the remaining demons, but a lot of Shadows are already moving north to do just that. Lys seems capable enough as well, at least to protect their cities."

Hearing shouts from the room above, Ilea and the others looked upward.

"Goblins?" Kyrian asked, and Ilea shrugged.

"Let's go check. Or do you want to let the recruits deal with it?" Ilea asked Dale. As she looked around, she found the eyes of young guards staring back at her.

"They've seen enough for the day. Let's finish them," Dale said, and as he unsheathed his sword, a mist-like aura of red magic formed around him.

Ilea nodded and blinked upward twice to find herself in the house's main room again with four guards. She saw a few small green creatures, most of them naked and armed with crude weapons, running around and attacking the guards, who were using their shields and weapons to keep the monsters at bay.

[Goblin – lvl 19]

Ilea punted one of the creatures aside and blinked over to a guard who'd been cornered by two of the monsters before grabbing their heads and smashing them together. There was a sickening crunch as blood splattered on her Veil and the guard before her. Another blink and a kick killed a particularly thickset goblin before the remaining ones scrambled to flee.

"Any of you hurt?" Ilea asked as she glanced at the fleeing goblins. The creatures were all between level five and twenty. Weak, to be sure, but smart enough to circle around the larger guards. They weren't stupid, which meant they wouldn't be as easily dealt with as a drake or demon spawn.

At that moment, Dale rushed into the room, sword in hand, only to find the dead goblins and Ilea looking out into the rain.

"You killed them already?" he asked, sheathing his sword. "Still like to put on a show, don't you?"

It was less about putting up a show and more about him just being much slower than her, Ilea considered, though she didn't exactly want to bring that up.

"Back to Riverwatch then?" Ilea asked instead.

Dale shook his head. "We're going to venture further north tomorrow. For now, we'll stay here. It's their first time out in the wilds for some of them," he explained as he sat down next to the fire.

"You and you," he said, pointing to two guards, who stood to attention immediately. "Throw out the corpses and clean up the blood."

The men acknowledged the orders and went about their business as Ilea joined Dale by the fire. Kyrian leaned against one of the walls and looked out at the rain. The other guards in training warmed themselves by the fire or stayed down below.

"Expedition tour for the new trainees. Isn't the experience somewhat bad if you're with them?" Ilea asked as she summoned a meal.

"Levels aren't everything, Ilea. I forget that you're pretty new to all this yourself. Despite you already being a Shadow," he smiled. "Surviving in the wild, knowing what beasts to approach and what to leave alone. Learning to track and finding which abilities you're talented in. This is a good way to start. You can always go out and kill monsters, but being as prepared as possible is key."

Ilea had to agree. If she didn't have her healing and blink abilities, she'd be dead fifty times over. Good thing she'd gotten lucky with her Class.

"You've fought demons then?" Dale said, changing the subject. "We lost three people to demons two weeks ago. Took a group of adventurers and guards four hours to hunt and kill the responsible monster. Above level two hundred. And we had to burn the corpses."

Ilea swallowed. "I'm sorry," she said. "I fought many of them, yes. In Ravenhall and Virilya."

"They even reached the Capital of Lys then," Dale murmured. "Things have been a little too busy for my liking as of late," he added. "First elven attacks, now demons. I wish we could just stick to wolves and goblins."

Ilea didn't say anything. She agreed with him on the elves and demons, thinking of all the death in Ravenhall, Riverwatch, and Salia. But at the same time, she thought that only ever fighting wolves and goblins sounded terribly dull.

"You came here just to see me?" Dale asked after a while.

"We had something to do nearby. Thought I'd check in," Ilea said as she finished her meal, making the plate vanish into her inventory again.

Dale nodded and got a ration from a nearby pack.

"I hope you get a break from all these attacks for a while," Ilea said.

"This too will pass," Dale said, eyes distant. Then he refocused and looked at Ilea with curiosity. "So, already a Shadow. Care to explain how you did that in such a short time?"

"A Taleen ruin mostly, if I'm honest," Ilea said with a smile.

His brows rose. "You fought those Taleen constructs?"

"I can heal and teleport. Makes it much easier to get out alive – and to fight alone."

Dale swallowed a mouthful. "That would do it. But it's not just that," he said, looking at her for a long moment. "You're an adventurer through and through."

"Can't say I dislike the lifestyle," Ilea admitted.

In fact, she didn't just like it, she loved it. Though, emotionally, she could have done without all the recent death. Just like Dale. Another thing her strange healing seemed to help with. Same as with not going mad in her first months in Elos.

"And I suppose you found a few kindred spirits," Dale said, nodding toward Kyrian, who was still staring out into the rain. "You two make up the entire team?"

Ilea smiled. "No. There are three more. Trian is a noble from Virilya. Lightning mage, and a capable one at that. He's young, but I think he's got his heart in the right place. Claire is a tactician through and through. I'm not sure how often I'll fight by her side now that she's taken up a governmental position. And then there's Eve."

She opened and closed her mouth, seeing the guards in her sphere. She trusted Dale, but she didn't want to share her thoughts. She still didn't believe that Eve had died during the invasion, but at the same time, she didn't know where the woman was.

"The demons put a bit of a wedge into our team operations," she concluded. "For now, it's just Kyrian and me."

"You seem capable enough as it is. I'm glad you found your people."

"And I'm glad I found you that day. If you ever need a favor, feel free to reach out."

"You saved a life tonight. I think that's favor enough. But do stop by whenever you're in the area."

"I'll do just that." Ilea looked at Kyrian, then stood up and cracked her neck. "I think it's time for us to move on. Long way back to Ravenhall."

"In that weather?"

Ilea activated her Veil of Ash and spread her wings in the cramped building, seeing some color drain from the faces of the new recruits.

"In that weather," she grinned.

Dale chuckled and shook his head. "A Shadow of the Hand. Good luck on your journey."

"It was good to see you, Dale," she said, then tapped Kyrian on his shoulder.

"Captain," Kyrian said, nodding toward Dale before stepping outside, metal already floating out of his quiver.

"He's trying to be cool," Ilea said and waved to the group inside. "See you around."

She blinked to join the already-flying Kyrian. "You alright? Didn't talk much."

He didn't reply for some time as they flew southward. Soon, they were past the rains, and the clouds opened up to reveal the moons above.

"He would've died," Kyrian said eventually.

Ilea smiled. "But he didn't."

Kyrian glanced her way with an unreadable expression before turning away again. "He didn't."

FOUR

Ashen Afternoon

It had been a long day, another one after many. Michael hadn't found sleep for a week, his magic fueling him to stay awake and aware of both his work and his surroundings. The small stack of documents and letters in front of him was nearly dealt with, the final thing he needed to complete before he'd get some rest.

Another three towns have fallen to the demons… he thought, marking them on the massive map of Lys behind him with floating pins of gold. He hadn't favored being the one to stay in Virilya, but with all the recent happenings, he found he was now enjoying the position.

His office was richly decorated, as decadent as his very image. Not many knew of his magic, so his supposed decadence gave him the advantage on his territory, at least in his personal quarters.

A knock on the door made him perk up. His butler entered a moment later.

"Sir, you've been working for fifteen hours without eating or drinking. Would you like some refreshments?" he asked.

Michael smiled and sat back. "No, I'll get some rest soon. You should too. Be back again tomorrow morning."

The butler bowed and left the room again.

A second visitor arrived sometime later. One he hadn't expected. Shrouded in shadow.

One of Helena's.

The assassin didn't speak but only left a note on his desk before they vanished again. Michael ignored the intrusion and read the note.

Prim had died. Murdered in her own home.

He sighed and stood up. More work for the night. An old promise to her father. It was the least he could do. She hadn't added much to humanity, though her indulgences and rituals had been useful from time to time. She didn't care who she killed, after all.

Still, she'd been a powerful mage. Stagnating, but a loss nonetheless.

He summoned his armor and a cloak to conceal the golden sheen and teleported out into the night of Virilya.

* * *

Michael stored his helmet as he came upon the corpse. Curse marks ran through most of her skin, originating at the wounds. Daggers, most likely. Her foe had been efficient; all the cuts were in critical positions. He wondered how the assailant had gotten so close to her.

The dead and corroded ground covering most of the cave told him that Prim had been pushed to her limits. It hadn't been an assassination but a hard-fought battle, and Prim had lost.

A single assailant, he concluded as he checked the blood around the battlefield. It was a shame for the garden. One of the more pleasing ones to look at in Virilya.

His blood magic surged once more. It didn't take long for him to find what he had been looking for. He sighed and followed the trail. Two capable humans would die tonight.

* * *

Blood dripped down from Edwin's shoulder as he slowly closed the wound with blood magic. He wouldn't be able to hide for long. Explosions of ice rang through the forest as he checked his shoulder again.

It was a good thing he had more than enough finesse in infections and poisons to counteract Kyle's downright disgusting claws, but the necromantic curses didn't help. He sighed as he meditated, regaining some of his strength.

He couldn't help but grin. He and Maria had finally located the current training grounds of the Redleafs. The same teachers who had tortured them were now gone from the world.

It was no surprise Kyle and Tiana had found them. The target had been quite an obvious one compared to some of the others. The two were some of his father's best hunters, so he'd known they would encounter them sooner or later.

The suns were already high above the horizon, and the four of them had moved deep into the wildlands of the east, their game of cat and mouse leaving a path of frozen death and blood behind.

Edwin rolled forward as massive claws ripped away the tree he was hiding behind before standing and turning in a single motion to regard the massive monster of bone, flesh, fur, and claws before him.

"I can smell you…" Kyle said in a low, grumbling, inhuman tone.

The transformation wasn't pretty, but it *was* powerful. A canine head with long teeth, two small red eyes, and three antlers. His breathing was heavy now, though. Edwin was impressed the man had managed to maintain this form for this many hours, but he didn't have his intimidating reputation for nothing. The bastard of Arthur Redleaf, another beast of their House.

Edwin could smell the monster too. He could smell the festering blood of its hastily healed wounds. Wounds inflicted from his blades. He could smell the spittle as it fell to the ground, its acidic odor corrosive to the nostrils as it burned through the first green of spring.

"I will tear you apart…" Kyle howled as Edwin rushed closer, his blades parried away by a massive arm. Yet his countless small wounds were adding up, and Kyle had become more and more defensive as the hours wore on. Edwin hadn't slipped up a single time, and he didn't plan to start now.

She's here…

He dashed backward, a lance of ice shattering into a thousand shards as it impacted the ground. The pieces spiraled and rushed toward him as he moved behind a tree, hearing the ice collide with and cut through the old wood. He teleported further away as the tree started falling.

As soon as Kyle had to give up his transformation, he and Maria would make their escape. A roar echoed through the forest as Edwin looked past the trees, seeing the bleeding monster lash out. Tendrils of blood destroyed the trees and the ground around them as a rain of ice came from above.

Kyle moved, dashing through the trees at full speed, blood magic enhancing his movements as he twisted his wolf- and deer-like head in frantic motions.

"He's transforming back. Let's move," Maria said, appearing next to Edwin and leaning on a nearby tree. "I need a break," she added before falling where she stood, yet even as her consciousness left her, Edwin caught her and started running.

His eyes narrowed as he moved through the forest, not on the ground but through the treetops, his steps improved by his blade dancer skills, leaving behind only the faintest traces that could easily be mistaken for a wild animal.

It would take Kyle and Tiana a while to follow them, though he doubted either had the required skills. Both were excellent trackers, but they relied too much on their spells. Neither blood nor silver magic would be able to locate them. Edwin had made sure of that.

They'd have to use more conventional means to find them, and Edwin doubted a skilled and more conventional tracker in the Redleafs' employ was an hour or less away. He had succeeded.

Then he winced as his magic against the festering curse in his upper arm failed. It had to be removed, or there was a chance they'd track him through it.

* * *

Ilea felt the embers tearing at her skin, the heat merely a slight distraction as she held her eyes closed and concentrated on the feeling. The ash was warm and comfortable, her Heat and Pain resistances making the torturous experience much simpler compared to the acquisition of her Fire Mage Class.

She had cut down enough trees in the forest just outside Ravenhall to make a massive bonfire. Ilea was now lying naked, covered in burning ash, as she focused on her breathing, trying to feel the magic in the elements around her.

Ilea wasn't exactly spiritual, but in this world, magic truly existed. That fact made it easier to justify her current situation and not think of herself as some crazy cult member sacrificing themselves to the gods of fire, pain, and ash. Her reduced pain made it easier for her to concentrate on the magic, on the feeling on her skin and the itching she felt that wanted her to use her Manipulation skill to connect to the ash.

It felt like the opposite to her training with fire and yet the same. More difficult as her body and mind wanted to touch the ash and move it around her, mastering the element. Yet she wanted to understand it, just as she had forced herself to understand fire. Not its chemical or scientific composition but its magical nature. Something she was now sure existed on Earth as well, just to a much lower degree.

The way she had stared into a fire in a hearth, or the way the ocean made her feel, the waves moving up and down as they crashed into the sand of the beach. The way they crashed against the boat in a fury, and—

She stopped her thoughts, focusing again on the now as she tried to catch that feeling again, the feeling that made her mana, and perhaps something else within her, connect to the very elements around her.

Ilea breathed slowly, losing track of time.

It felt stronger. The feeling of fear and overwhelming power that she felt when she looked out into the ocean was real, graspable, and true. The feeling of a roaring flame, consuming houses and living beings alike, the feeling of lightning, coursing through her.

The feeling of embers, the last sparks of life burning away, glowing in a sea of gray and black flakes. The last remaining life before it returns to nature itself. To mana itself. Flakes of black and gray as they float upward, carried by the wind.

Ilea opened her eyes, her hand moving up into the air, the ash on her body trembling at the sudden magic released by her. Not wishing to control but accepting the elements around her. Its magical nature and unlimited potential. She smiled as the particles of ash danced a little on her body.

'ding' Ash and Ember Manipulation reaches 2nd lvl 20

She stood up and raised her arms, feeling the ash around her as it moved upward, her connection with the element established as she allowed her magic to take over, to become one with the ash. She studied it with her Sphere, with the feeling in her magic as she closed her eyes and felt the vortex of ash around her intensify, speeding up and cutting her body where it grazed her.

She felt small now, as if she had glimpsed into a wasteland of ash, through a tiny window within herself, grasping at a sea of knowledge, a sea of power. Ilea understood then and there that in the long run, this would be her most powerful weapon and her most solid defense. The possibilities of her manipulation and creation skills combined meant the control of an element. Not the use of it, as with her fire magic. This meant true control. True harmony.

Time passed and Ilea felt her magic drain, allowing her body and mind to fully focus on the ash around her as it cut into her skin, the ground below, and now even the trees farther back. Everything was covered in gray and black flakes.

Finally, Ilea collapsed, her mana fully spent.

She coughed and focused on her meditation, having lost the connection she had felt until but a moment ago. The ash that had been swirling around her fell, covering herself and the ground in a sea of gray and black. There was too much, way too much, for it to have come from the amount of wood she'd burned.

The answer lay in her mind as she checked a new set of notifications.

'ding' Ash Creation reaches 2nd lvl 18

'ding' Ash Creation reaches 2nd lvl 19

Nearly there as well…

A shiver went through her. But not because of the cold. The connection to the raw magic and the element of ash was an experience incomparable to anything Ilea had ever gone through. She smiled as she held out her hands and made the ash rise once more. It felt like her control had increased more than she thought the levels should've provided.

Dale had taught her to trust in her skills more, to let them guide her. Perhaps this was similar. Still, she had refused to use her skill while she was lying in the ash, so her interpretation may have been wrong. The ash still swirled, and as Ilea lifted more and more of the element, she realized just how much there was around her.

The trees bent under the sheer weight of it all, and the snow was gray instead of white all around her, farther than her Sphere could perceive. In the midst of the gray vortex was Ilea, standing steadily as she ignored the small bleeding cuts on her body. In her hand was a small black swirling sphere of ash. More and more of the surrounding element joined the small sphere as it got darker and darker, its form solidifying more and more.

She didn't force it to become more dense, more solid. It felt as if she was simply asking it to do so. The feel of her manipulation changed from something rational and forceful to something more passionate and trusting. She felt as if the ash itself was a friend to her now. The thought was a little embarrassing, even childlike, but it was the best way she could describe the feeling.

The sphere in her hand was solid by now and could be easily mistaken for a black pearl or ammunition for a rifle. Though it was around five centimeters in diameter, so it would have to be quite a rifle. She let the sphere become as small as possible before she opened a tunnel in the vortex around her, letting the little ball flash forward.

She watched on with full attention and interest as the ball smashed into a tree with a thud. The vortex of ash around her continued to swirl as she walked forward, moving with her, keeping her in the eye of the storm. The sphere was stuck in the tree, at least ten centimeters deep and, to her surprise, still solid.

That would easily be enough to kill a small animal or an unarmored low-level human. And it was a ranged attack that used nothing but mana. No ammunition and no additional tools to fire them, like with her bow. But she needed time to summon it, draw it, and shoot it.

Now it was simply a learning process to become able to use her ash in the midst of battle. She'd try it in a bout as soon as she could. For now, Ilea felt she could advance her elemental control – or rather, cooperation – quite a bit more, even though the skill wouldn't level again, at least until she could advance it to the third stage. Checking for third-tier options left her with the expected result. None were ready to be advanced. Not quite yet.

Looking at the sphere of ash in the tree, Ilea pushed at it a little harder, causing it to start to spin. A minute later, she found it actually digging deeper, the scent of burnt wood spreading into the vicinity. It was a slow process, but Ilea managed to break through the tree sometime later, the sphere of ash coming out on the other side and floating back toward her. The possibilities felt vast.

She slowly reformed the sphere into a small spike. It was harder to reform the object as it was already rather solid. She felt this would change as her understanding grew, regardless of her actual skill level. While the potential of her manipulation was capped for the moment, she felt certain she hadn't yet reached that cap in her control.

Range was another issue, and Ilea decided to test it immediately, shooting the reformed spike forward with the highest speed she could muster right now. With her main buffs at full power and her wings spread, she followed the projectile and found herself easily able to do so. A disappointment for her ashen magic, yet a testament to her own speed.

Still, it moved for dozens of meters before noticeably dropping down and finally hitting the snow-covered ground. Ilea hovered it upward again and spun it around with the power of her magic. One thing that seemed rather cool was that she didn't have to move her hands to control her ash. Nor did she have to shout out any ridiculous-sounding skill names to make it work.

It could be somewhat intimidating, but 'Ash and Ember Manipulation' doesn't have the right ring to it…

Having decided that she'd bathe in ash again tomorrow, Ilea made her way back toward Ravenhall, planning to meet Claire.

She kept five spikes of condensed ash, but while they didn't dissolve when she removed her control, Ilea found that they were crumbling a little after traveling for a while. Storing them inside her necklace wasn't possible either, likely because they were a magically touched element.

One more thing to figure out then.

FIVE

#Economics

Ravenhall looked a little better already. It had been a few days but Ilea was still surprised at the progress. The Hand or the Empire must've put up some rather good pay to entice all the workers that busied the streets. Not just soldiers and mercenaries either. Many of them were of a level much lower than usual for the Scouts or the Shadow's Hand, their magic and gear specialized for construction, not for adventuring or war.

Ilea reached the central government building sometime later. It was busy. Much more than it had been in the past days. The square was bustling with people going about their business. Walking inside and using her Sphere, Ilea was glad to find that the Hand's leadership was still there. She blinked over to Claire's office door, knocked, and was let in.

The room was nicely furnished, with a broad wooden table, a green and gold carpet, and copious bookshelves lining the walls. In addition, there was a small lounge in one of the corners, two leather chairs, a round wooden table, and a cabinet with spirits and glasses. Sunlight shone through the single window, revealing the dust floating in the air. An oil lamp sat on the broad table in front of Claire, helping illuminate the stacks of papers.

"Ilea. Back in town already?" Claire greeted her, looking up from the documents in front of her.

"Yeah, found a new home for Weavy," she said. "How are things? Already used to the new job?"

Claire sighed. "It's a lot. I won't lie. But it feels good. Every document done is a document done,"

"You talk about it like they're monsters to slay."

"You would think of it that way, wouldn't you?" Claire said with a smile. "By the way, we finally got our badges." Claire stood up and handed Ilea a black piece of metal. "Touch it while it's on top of my hand and accept. Otherwise, you'll get burned."

Ilea did just that and got a noise in her mind in response.

'ding' Would you like to claim [Shadow Badge – High Quality]?

Yes, I would like that, thank you.

'ding' You have claimed [Shadow Badge – High Quality]

"Thanks, Claire," Ilea said as Claire slowly walked to the window.

A sudden feeling of spreading magic made Ilea alert, looking around the room and beyond as her buffs came to life.

"Don't worry, it's me," Claire said, looking out of the window before she turned around, a sly smile on her face. "Can I ask you something?"

"Sure," Ilea said, intrigued by her friend's weird behavior. She walked behind the desk and sat down on the comfortable leather chair.

I have to get one of these… looks even better than the one from Salia.

Ilea smiled as she saw Claire's mouth give a small twitch through her Sphere.

"How much gold do you have?" Claire asked, making Ilea turn in her chair toward her.

"How much gold? Why?"

"I'll tell you why if you tell me how much. The room is magically sealed. Nobody else will hear. Except for your dagger."

"I am here," Aki said.

"If there's anybody I trust with information on my money, it's you," Ilea said. "Let me check… I have forty-four gold, twenty-nine silver and a whole two copper coins…" she started, watching the smile on Claire's face flatten a little and the spark in her eyes vanish.

"…not counting the two thousand gold coins I have left from a find inside a dwarven mine," Ilea added with a dumb smile. She could see Claire getting close to throwing a runed stone at her.

Claire managed to stop herself, glancing at the documents on the table instead. "That might be enough," she murmured, her eyes darting from left to right. She took a deep breath, closed her eyes, and opened them again, a fierce stare aimed at Ilea.

"Ilea, this is just between me and you. You saw all the people outside. This city is a trove of opportunities right now, but it won't be for long. There's a complete power vacuum, especially economically. Most of the Hand's members are too occupied with finding new jobs or their funds are too far away to make deals right now, and the Imperial soldiers are simply not allowed to. Most of the rich merchants are yet to come here, and the Empire itself is too slow in its bureaucracy to allow fast acquisitions of its own. I'm sitting at the source and would be able to push through a ton of deals, but I have one problem. I lack the funds. There is so much we could do, so much we could change," Claire explained in a rush, nearly tripping over her own words.

"I won't let you out of this room without at least lending me a few hundred gold. Do you have them in your storage item, your house, or somewhere hidden? I can't squander this opportunity so please, please help me. I'd get you favorable assignments and anything else you need from the Hand that's within my power. Personal advice or work is included as well, of course, as is anything else where I can be of service. *Anything.*"

Claire stressed the last word, looking deeply into Ilea's eyes. This was a woman ready to do business – at any cost.

"We said we'd have each other's backs," Ilea smiled. "There's no need for all that." She stood up and walked over to one of the shelves. She found a large box full of documents, emptied them out onto the floor, and summoned her two thousand gold coins into the box, nearly filling it to the brim.

Claire took a step closer but stopped herself, her eyes fixated on the gold.

"What exactly are you planning with all this?" Ilea asked.

Claire smiled and started pacing. "I want to take over as much of the city as I can. Housing and business buildings. First smithing, weapons, clothing, armor, leatherworkers, and, because it's you, a lot of restaurants as well. The staff will come, and I will hire the best. It's clear that the Hand won't move anywhere else. Business will return to this city.

"The sum isn't much compared to what some nobility and rich merchants can throw around, but it's enough to get things rolling. Fast. Anything I can buy or build up. I want Cless to have the best education she can get, and I want other children to receive the same. I want the guard and adventurers from around here to be equipped well. Once that's up and running, I'll start to invest in political influence as well.

"The jobs we will offer will pay well. Better than the competition. I plan to invest this gold long-term, to have experienced staff, and to build a name for every single one of those businesses. I heard some of the soldiers and Shadows ask about Lilith. With you being the main investor, I'll make sure your name is known too. A brand, if you will. And I plan to branch out as we go on," Claire explained. "Any questions?"

Ilea looked at the gold in the box. She really didn't know what to do with it. She didn't need all that to pay Balduur, and she already had her house.

And I really like the idea of being the mysterious owner of a bunch of restaurants.

"How will this work specifically?" Ilea asked, a smile on her face.

Claire mirrored her expression and walked over to her desk.

"Everything will be co-owned by the two of us. Ten percent me, ninety you. I'll reinvest most of the winnings but will set aside some funds in case you need gold immediately. I'll set up a few sample contracts, and we can discuss it further if you agree to the terms. I'll start immediately. Come back in an hour."

Ilea watched her friend summon a set of fresh papers, her expression focused as she started to write with fervor.

* * *

Ilea sat down again in the comfortable leather chair an hour later.

"Welcome back, here's the contract," Claire began immediately, sorting the papers in front of her. "I've already prepared seventy-four purchase contracts that I need you to sign with your mana and signature."

"Isn't that a lot? I mean it's a bunch of gold, but seventy-four shops? I assume it's shops?"

"Shops, houses, inns, streets, land, including in other cities nearby and further away. It won't be enough to purchase them all, let alone run things smoothly, but give me time. Plus, not all of these will come through. This is simply because you'll be gone to who knows where soon enough and I won't be able to reach you anymore."

"Alright. Just tell me where to sign. And how to sign," Ilea said.

Claire explained everything to her and insisted on going over at least the basics of the contracts with her.

Ilea was glad when they were done.

"I'm so excited to start, Ilea. Thank you so so so so much for giving me this opportunity." Claire was brimming with joy, humming a tune to herself as she put away the signed contracts. Ilea wasn't sure if she'd just invested in a super-villain.

"Well, I hope you have fun with this. I need to get back to training. Don't forget to do that either, if you find any time. I might visit again soon. Are you looking for interesting missions?" Ilea asked.

"Come back in a week and I'll have some for you. The Hand is still focusing on organizing the city, and the Empire is still dealing with the demons. I'll look for dangerous targets in hard-to-reach places," Claire smiled.

"See you then," Ilea said and blinked out of the room, glad that was finally done. Claire would've done well on Earth. She did well even here.

Shaking her head, Ilea walked out into the busy square and stretched. With the hood of her leather armor up, she cut a rather unimpressive figure other than the identification that outed her as a level two hundred twenty-four warrior.

"That's her, I think. Different armor, but yeah, I'm pretty sure that's her," a soldier in the midst of the crowd said, pointing at Ilea. He looked away and gulped as soon as she glanced his way, likely surprised that she could hear him from that distance over all the noise in the square.

The suns were setting, their last rays breaking through the cloudy horizon as a figure in light armor and a dark hood nodded to the soldier before walking toward Ilea. She looked at the figure with interest, noting the beige leather armor and the simple short sword at his waist.

He smiled and waved. He looked to be in his thirties, with brown nondescript hair and a smile on his face as he walked over with casual confidence. A rogue at level one twenty. At least he wasn't likely to be here for a fight.

"I have a delivery to make for a black-haired, blue-eyed member of the Shadow's Hand," the man said.

"I know of at least three people fitting that description," Ilea said.

The man chuckled in response and put his hands together. "I have two additional characteristics that should set you apart. Wings of ash. And bladed blue-steel gauntlets. I need to see both to confirm your identity."

"Is this usually how you deliver things? Instead of just asking for a name?"

"I don't make the rules. I just take the jobs," he said with a shrug.

Ilea sighed and summoned both her wings and gauntlets. "Happy?"

"To have found you, yes," the man said, taking a letter out of a pouch strapped to his belt. "The seal will make the letter dissolve thirty minutes after you open it. If you don't trust me, I suggest you have it examined by a rune mage around here. Shouldn't be an issue with all the Shadows around," the man said and bowed. "Good day to you."

"And to you. Thanks," Ilea said, looking at the envelope. It felt expensive.

I kind of want to follow his advice and have this checked, Ilea thought as she looked at the rune set into the thick paper. A few blinks later, she was back in Claire's office.

"Back already?" Claire asked. "Had second thoughts?"

"No, here for a small favor. Can you tell me what the rune on this does?" Ilea asked, handing Claire the letter. She looked at it for barely two seconds before handing it back.

"High-end courier, hmm? It destroys the letter within thirty minutes of opening it. Of course, you could write it down after reading it. Most of these have a mana signature from the sender so you'd be able to tell if it was forged," Claire explained.

Quite a bit more thought was put into something like this than Ilea had assumed. Good thing she'd asked Claire.

"How do I tell whose signature it is?"

"If you've ever felt their mana, it's usually simple."

"Alright, thanks. Sorry for bothering you."

"You're going to make me rich. Come here whenever you need anything," Claire smiled.

They said their goodbyes again before Ilea blinked out of the office. She flew out of the city and opened the letter as soon as she was far enough out of town for nobody to bother her. The enchantment activated immediately when she broke the seal and removed the letter.

Dear friend

I apologize for my departure. For all intents and purposes, I am dead. I hope you don't take the risk this letter poses to me lightly.

I've come across a piece of information in regard to our common "friend" whom you call Sparky. It seems his family has made enemies in the capital, leading to an escalation and their subsequent murder. It is rare for an entire House to be removed from power with such a surgical strike. I recommend the highest caution. He himself will be a target too.

I have come across this incident on my search for the Golden Lily, an organization that seems pivotal in many decisions and happenings within the Plains. I do not suggest you follow this lead or investigate the murders in the first place, but I felt I at least owed this much to you all.

Stay safe, and my condolences.

E.

Ilea's stomach dropped while reading the letter. She knew immediately that it was Eve who had written it. She needed to grab Kyrian and go and find Trian.

Her buffs activated as soon as she came to the last part of the letter, feeling a little bit of mana within it. It had felt like Eve already, and she knew for sure now that it was from her.

Rushing over the forests, the air buffeted her face as her eyes remained steadfastly open. Her vacation would sadly have to be cut short.

Trian hadn't shared much about his family, but from what she remembered, she could tell they were the most important thing to him. She just hoped he hadn't gotten in over his head already. Ilea didn't know his family, but she did know him.

Arriving at her own house, Ilea blinked inside. Kyrian was nowhere to be found, but she did pick up his scent. With Hunter's Sight activated, she rushed outside and followed the trail.

The trail led her up the closest mountain, where she found a cave entrance. Rushing inside, she discovered an artificially created hole going deep into the stone, at the end of which was Kyrian. The man was sitting in a meditative pose, metal flowing and shifting around his body.

"Kyrian!"

He shot up, hitting his head on the stone above. He looked at her with wide eyes.

"You look worried. What is it?"

"Trian's family has been killed. We need to go find him," Ilea said, her words tumbling out in a barely comprehensible jumble.

Kyrian stood up immediately, his curse magic flaring out. "What do you mean? Calm down, explain it."

Ilea slowed her breathing and told Kyrian what she had read in the letter.

"And you're sure it's from her?" he asked when she'd finished.

She nodded. His hands balled into fists before he looked at her, eyes narrowed.

"Let's go, then. The Alymie family have their seat somewhere in or around Virilya. We'll start there," Kyrian said, his voice steady as they hurried outside and took flight.

I knew I could trust him.

She gritted her teeth, thinking of Claire and of getting her involved as well. She was part of the team, just like Trian and Kyrian. Just like Eve. Yet she had found a foothold in Ravenhall. Leaving now would be disastrous. After everything she had been through recently.

I'm lying to myself. I just don't want to see her get hurt as well. And if all of this is true, I don't want her to be part of this.

She knew it was selfish, feeling the knot in her stomach, but she thought back to the earlier meeting they'd had, the joy she'd seen, all the work piled up. This would wreck everything again. Still, she felt herself warring with the decision. Taking in a deep breath, she focused.

Let's find out what happened first, see what we can do. Then I can think about it again.

"Do you know where their estate is?" Ilea asked as they rushed over snowy forests and mountains.

"No, but the city guard will know. The Alymies aren't without influence."

Ilea wanted to speed up, but Kyrian was already going as fast as he could.

"Sorry, Kyrian. We have to move," she said as she positioned herself behind him, grabbing him around the chest as she sacrificed health to overcharge her State of Azarinth.

He didn't complain as their speed increased noticeably, Ilea wincing a little every time she sacrificed more health to keep it up. Her healing was working to restore the lost health, and Ilea kept an eye on her resources so as not to suddenly burn out halfway to Virilya.

It was a long way, but if she had anything, she had stamina.

* * *

Night was falling over Virilya as Xaver looked out over the plains before the city. Fields of newly planted grain and small walled-off farms lay in the distance as the wind pushed at him. It was colder on top of the high wall, but he liked the calm and security the post brought. Aerial monsters were rare, at least in these parts, and patrolling the city wasn't exactly safe.

He watched a group of wild dogs stalk the road beyond, their figures illuminated by the last light of the suns. They would be left alone. Engaging them was too dangerous and expensive for the guard. The night outside Virilya's walls was not meant for humans, not even so close to the Imperial capital.

The guard sighed as he looked around the wall, the torch next to him flickering in the wind, before he slowly opened a large pouch on his belt and took out the book from within. Another good thing about the wall was that on normal nights, few officers would come to check those on duty, being busy with their own work and not exactly eager to come up where the winds were cold and harsh.

Legend of the Soul Forge – Ancient Mysteries Volume Six

Xaver opened the book where he'd left off and started reading. Perhaps the next chapter would be a little more reasonable. Souls of dwarves fused with machines made entirely of steel. He didn't mind some ridiculous ideas and made-up magics, but this one was the most outlandish so far. At least it wasn't as poorly written as the last one.

A sudden thump behind him made the man whirl around. He focused his magic, a spark gathering around his left hand as he grabbed his sword with his right. The book clattered to the ground as Xaver took in the sight of two people armored in black plate.

"H… Hand?" he asked dumbfounded, unsure how to proceed.

"You're lucky we're not elves," one of them said, a woman, stepping a little closer to him. "Where is the Alymie estate?" she asked, flashing a silver coin that suddenly appeared in her hand.

* * *

Ilea held the silver coin in her hand, but the guard didn't react for a full five seconds. She would've used gold just a week ago, but silver was enough for something so basic. Finally, he grabbed it and started talking. A guard so lax about his job, reading at his post, was a good target to get information quickly. Ilea's suspicion had proven correct.

"Their estate isn't in the city. It's eastward, two hours on a horse. Just follow the main street. After coming out of the first forest you'll encounter, you'll see it. I've never been there, but it's on the map," the man said, bending down to grab the book.

By the time he straightened, Ilea and Kyrian were already gone, rushing eastward right below the outer wall, most guards likely not even noticing the flying duo. The forest came into view sometime later and they passed over it. Ilea hoped they weren't too late.

She didn't know for what exactly.

The road through the forest was visible from above, but the last light of the suns disappeared long before the two reached the estate. The mansion came into view a while later, Ilea letting go of Kyrian as they slowed down a little.

Only faint light could be seen coming from inside the large house. Behind it, Ilea could see a large pile of what she simply knew was ash. No smoke was rising from it. No torches were lit around the estate, nor were any guards or other people visible.

She landed on the gravel courtyard and rushed to the door. It was closed, so she blinked inside and opened a window nearby for Kyrian to enter. Concentrating, she could hear voices coming from the floor above. The ground floor was dark, but she could navigate easily with her Sphere and enhanced sight. It smelled of blood. And fire.

The two made their way upstairs, following a wooden staircase. The many rooms following the long hallway upstairs were all open, light coming only from three of them. The voices were clearer now, and Ilea felt a weight fall from her shoulders as she recognized one of them.

"The traces are too muddled for me to work with… I'm really sorry. You'll get the money back, of course," an unknown woman was saying as Ilea burst into the large room at the center of the hallway, where she saw Trian alongside a woman clad in red light armor. Both looked at her immediately but she didn't stop moving, rushing at Trian and hugging the man.

"I'm so sorry," she said, holding him as Kyrian came into the room as well. Ilea let go of Trian and locked eyes with him. "We came as soon as we heard. How can we help?"

Trian looked confused at first but then just shook his head, sitting down on a chair.

"Leave us," he said to the woman in red, who nodded and walked out quickly. Trian didn't say anything else as Ilea and Kyrian looked around the room.

"Is she gone?" Trian asked after a long moment.

"She's below us, not moving. But it's hard for me to make her out," Ilea said, seeing the woman react downstairs through her Sphere, though she stayed where she was. "Who is she?"

"Hired adventurer. Make her leave, though I doubt she has anything to do with it," Trian sighed.

Ilea nodded and blinked downstairs, right next to the somewhat shrouded woman, grabbing her neck with a quick move and pushing her up against the wall.

"He told you to leave. If you're not gone in ten seconds, I'll kill you," Ilea said simply, throwing her a few meters away.

The woman tumbled onto the floor before she got up, a little off balance, fear in her eyes as she dashed toward the front door, jumping through the window Ilea had opened.

Ilea rubbed her temples. *Calm yourself. Breathe.*

"None of them can find anything," Trian murmured as Ilea reappeared in the room.

"I got a letter from Eve. Is it true?" Ilea asked. Thinking back to the pile of ash outside, she knew, but she wanted to be sure.

Trian gulped and nodded slowly, holding a closed fist to his mouth. He stood up and pointed to the two of them, his arm shaking a little.

"I'll pay you. I'll give you e… everything I have left. Help me find them," he said, fire in his eyes as sparks scorched the wood and floor close to him.

"Why the fuck would we need payment? Right, Kyrian?" Ilea said, looking at the other man, who nodded.

"We're with you."

Ilea didn't know what else to do for now. Trian was in pain, that was for sure. He was angry, and she shared his rage.

Ilea looked out the window and into the night while Trian regained his composure. When she turned back toward him, he looked tired, exhausted, and angry, all of it more so than she had ever seen him.

"You need rest. And you need to eat. Here," she said, summoning a meal and something to drink, putting it on the table next to him.

"I don't need shit, Ilea. I need to find whoever did this," Trian said, shoving the food off the table and sending it clattering onto the carpet, joining the dried blood.

A loud *clap* cut through the silence in the room. Trian stumbled backward and fell into the chair he had previously sat in. Ilea let her hand fall and summoned another meal.

"You're out of it. Do you think you can fight anyone if I can hit you so easily? Focus."

Trian's eyes narrowed somewhat. He took the meal and started eating quietly, blood dripping down his cheek as Ilea healed his broken jaw, the bone cracking back into place as he continued chewing.

"My… my family. They're all dead. Someone came here and murdered everybody. I only found corpses, ripped apart by magic, swords, arrows, and beasts. This was nothing small. And I have no fucking idea who did it…" he said, throwing the empty plate on the ground. As he looked at Ilea, tears joined the blood on his face.

"Then let's find out who did," she said, activating her skills.

SIX

Estate Investigation

"Kyrian will be right there. I think you should try to get some sleep," Ilea said, helping Trian into a bed. One of the few that wasn't soiled by dried blood. He looked pale and hardly reacted to her guidance, his eyes unfocused.

How long have you been here alone? Looking for clues amongst ash and long-dried blood?

She covered the man in thick blankets and sighed as she stepped out into the corridor, unsure what else to do.

Trian had burnt all the corpses, which left only the house itself as a reference for their investigation. Not that she was experienced with anything a situation like this would require. Fighting monsters was one thing, but the large-scale elimination of most of a noble House near the capital of a large Empire? That was something entirely different.

"You don't have investigation skills or anything, right?" she asked Kyrian.

He only shook his head.

Ilea could tell he had retreated back into himself, as he was prone to do in uncomfortable situations. She didn't blame him. Part of her just wanted to grab Trian and leave immediately. Still, they had to at least try and find out more, right?

"I'll see what I can do," she said, smiling a little as she noticed Trian's breathing fall into a steady rhythm in the room behind her. "Can you stay with him? It's possible that whoever is behind this wants him dead as well..." she added, glancing warily down the hallway. Kyrian nodded.

Ilea began her search by looking through the room they had talked in, her Sphere, Hunter's Sight, and enhanced senses working together in an attempt to find something. Anything.

She could tell that a battle between two or three warriors had taken place in the office, scrapes on the walls suggesting at least a few slashing weapons. There was dried blood on the carpet and some of the windows. Likely someone had been working and the attackers had taken them by surprise. They had tried to fight back but lost in the end. There were strange smells lingering in the air that she couldn't quite place. Poison, perhaps, or something else?

And it's already been a while. The trail is cold. Eve's letter must have traveled for days, or even weeks, before it got to me.

None of what she could sense led in any direction, all of it too faded or isolated. She searched the other rooms but only got similar results.

What the hell would even warrant such a massacre?

The main stairwells leading to the ground floor didn't show anything special, and neither did the rooms on the ground floor. Most of the fighting seemed to have happened upstairs, likely because most of the bedrooms were on the upper floor. If the attack had happened at night, most of the family would have been sleeping in their beds.

She found the atmosphere tense and overbearing, walking around in the dark, quiet mansion, blood still scenting the air. Ilea knew she could trust her skills and power, but Trian had been just as capable as herself the last time she'd fought him, and whoever had done this had wiped out his entire House, people very likely to be at a higher level and much more experienced than the young noble she called a friend.

Ilea made her way downstairs, opening a wooden door in the large kitchen that led to a cellar. She held a lantern to see with her eyes in addition to her Sphere. There were many crates down here, housing different foods and other goods. Some were already starting to rot, judging by the smell, but she couldn't make out any monsters or rodents trying to get in. Perhaps enchantments were still keeping them away.

She could feel her focus drawn to one of the walls in particular. A slight tugging sensation in her magical senses. Nothing suggested to her that it was special in any way, nor did her Sphere show anything behind it.

The second stage of my Sphere, then? A hidden path ahead?

Blinking blindly into the wall, Ilea found she was no longer in the same cellar. She hadn't triggered any traps, it seemed, but now she couldn't look back into the old cellar. A spell, rune, or something else was keeping her perception inside the new room, illuminated by the lantern she held. There was a door on the far side and a stairwell leading down.

Now what's this all about? Some secret vampyr training facility?

Ilea's steps echoed through the silent stairway until, finally, she came out into a new room. A bigger room than any of the previous cellars, stone brick walls with a simple design. She couldn't see the other side through her Sphere so she simply continued forward, the hall long enough for her torchlight not to reach the far end.

Four steps later, Ilea noticed a very faint tapping sound. It was quick, and it was closing in on her. She activated her spells when she saw a massive spider enter her line of sight. Of course, this spider had scythes for legs. Her surprise at its near-silent approach, considering its metal appendages, was short-lived as the beast rushed forward and attacked.

Two blades flashed horizontally at Ilea. She crouched, both weapons passing above her head before she took a single step forward and punched with her free hand, striking the spider's skull. She both heard and felt a crunch before the monster was thrown backward several meters.

'ding' You have been poisoned by Toothnick Spider, -10 Stamina per second for two minutes, movements are slowed by 10%.

A Toothnick? Ilea thought, remembering the name from one of her monster classes. Not a particularly dangerous beast, as far as she remembered. The spider looked disoriented by the punch but started to circle Ilea again, considerably more carefully now.

[Toothnick Spider – lvl 153]

Looking down at her hand, Ilea found a tooth shallowly embedded in her finger. The reason for the poisoning for sure. She pulled it out and flicked it away, glaring at the arachnid monster as it approached her again, this time rearing up and using four blades to attack her.

Ilea smiled to herself. Compared to the Taleen machines she had fought, the creature moved slowly, its attacks unoptimized and wild.

Then she jumped a few meters back as she saw a new source of light appear at the far end of the hall. Two children, one holding a torch and the other wielding a beautifully crafted curved sword.

As the two came closer, Ilea realized the bigger one wasn't a child at all, just a petite teenager. She was vaguely familiar, with high cheekbones and an angular nose, and her clothes looked expensive. The smaller one did appear to be a child though, a thin boy with dark hair and darker eyes.

"Toothie, back!" the older of the two yelled, and Ilea watched in amazement as the spider quickly made its way back to the humans. She didn't move to intercept the creature.

Toothie?

"Who are you?!" the older child yelled as Ilea walked a little closer. The girl held the curved blade in a stance that suggested significant training and skill, similar to some of the warriors Ilea had seen.

Beside her, Ilea could see a faint glow of red magic as the small boy prepared a spell in his hand, stretching out his slightly shaking arm as he peered at her.

"Who are you?" Ilea said, identifying them.

[Mage – lvl 131]

[Mage – lvl 42]

Ilea raised her brows. *One thirty-one at her age? She looks maybe sixteen? Nobles, I guess. Probably have tons of staff to help them train.*

The girl frowned. "I asked you first! Who are *you*? You're intruding on our cellar!"

"I'm here with Trian, if you know him. If you tell me your names, I'll tell you mine. Sound fair?" Ilea asked, trying to keep her voice as friendly as she could.

"Trian? He's here..." the girl said and lowered her sword, before narrowing her eyes and raising it again a second later. "You're lying," she said, her eyes getting teary. "Everyone died. I don't trust you."

Ilea suddenly appeared right in front of the girl, grabbing the sword by the blade and ripping it out of her hands. She blinked back to her original position with the sword.

"Would I have let you live just now if I was lying?" she asked, throwing the sword up and catching it again. "Your pet is injured. I can heal it if you let me. How does that sound?" Ilea continued, throwing the sword up again as she slowly walked closer, catching it by the blade. She stopped two meters in front of the pair and held out the weapon, handle first.

The girl stared defiantly into Ilea's eyes but then she nodded. She walked forward and grabbed the sword with suspicious eyes.

"Toothie, come," the girl said, and the spider approached. "Sit." The spider crouched down immediately, its fifteen eyes focused on Ilea.

Holding out her hand, Ilea took small steps toward the animal until she touched it. Other than a low hiss, there was no reaction. Right until she started healing. Ilea never wanted to hear a spider imitate a purr *ever* again. She shuddered as she finished treating the injuries she had caused and even a couple of smaller ones that weren't her fault.

The monster class hadn't mentioned anything about domestication.

"She's fine again," Ilea said, stepping back.

"Can you heal people too?" the small boy asked.

Ilea nodded. "I can. Are you injured?" she asked, looking between the boy and girl. She looked at least sixteen, maybe even older. The boy couldn't be much older than eight.

"Is Trian alright? Where is he?" the girl asked instead.

"He is. He's upstairs, but I don't know how safe it is for you there. Your names?" Ilea asked again, locking eyes with the girl.

"I'm Aurelia Alymie, and this is Samuel. We have someone injured, but I don't know if you can heal him," Aurelia said, sheathing her sword.

Ilea nodded. "Let me see if I can help. I'm Ilea, a friend of Trian's." She motioned for the kids to lead the way.

Aurelia still didn't seem completely sure, but she walked toward the exit whence she and Samuel had appeared, the torch and lantern light flickering on the stone walls of the dark room.

"Did you hide down here during the attack?" Ilea asked after a couple of minutes of silence. Without her Sphere, she would've long since lost her orientation in the complicated layout of the cellar. It was akin to a labyrinth, but the kids navigated it with sure steps.

"We... we hide here often," Aurelia said but didn't say anything further as they reached a worn wooden door. Behind, Ilea could see a bed with a man lying in it. The girl slowly opened the door.

"Orthan? Are you awake?"

She stepped closer to the bed, grabbing a towel from a small bucket on the ground. The water was dirty, that much was visible even in the faint light. Samuel stayed near the door with the torch, perhaps to keep the man from waking.

"Can I have a look?" Ilea asked, moving closer to the man. The smell of blood and sweat permeated the room. Not the best sign.

"He's not awake," Aurelia said.

Ilea stepped up and touched the man's brow. A strong fever, that much she could've guessed back on Earth. The old man was bald, his build wiry. Only burnt tatters of his shirt remained, and his leather pants were covered in blood.

And still, she felt he wasn't as weak as his appearance might suggest. His level was below two hundred, but not by much.

[Mage – lvl 192]

Activating her healing magic and moving her lantern closer, Ilea searched his body and found a nasty cut near his stomach. Pus had formed, but it looked like the girl had tried to clean it somewhat.

There were other injuries and what looked like an infection or curse. Ilea lifted the man's shirt, asking Aurelia to look away for a second. The smell of the wound was bad, but she'd seen much worse since arriving in Elos, including on her own body.

Touching the injury directly, she started using her healing skill, grabbing the towel from the girl with her other hand. She cleaned and healed the wound slowly. It didn't take long before the man's stomach looked as good as new.

No scars either with healing magic.

He stirred a little, and Ilea started focusing on the infection, carefully pulling away what remained of his shirt. She laid his shoulder bare and looked at it. His flesh was burnt in a circle and in the middle was something black. It moved slightly, and not with the same beat as his heart.

"Any idea what that is?" Ilea asked, pointing at the injury.

"Poison or a curse," Aurelia said. "Cutting it out would be best, but I wouldn't be able to stop the bleeding afterward."

"Are you sure?" Ilea asked. When she tried to affect the area with her healing magic, it seemed to resist.

Wouldn't want to get hit by something like that myself.

Through her healing, the effects she felt were similar to what she knew from Kyrian's spells. She was glad to have her Curse Resistance.

"Cut it out. I'm sure," the girl said. "I've seen something similar before."

Ilea grimaced. "I'll do it. Do you want to wait outside? I don't think this will be pleasant for him."

Aurelia didn't respond. Her gaze was focused. She glanced at Ilea and handed her the curved sword.

Ilea nodded and took the blade, then started to cut carefully into the man's flesh, holding his chest down with her other hand. She could see exactly how deep the curse had penetrated his body via her healing spell, but after a while, his legs started thrashing.

"It's alright. It'll be over soon," she said. "Hold his head," she said to Aurelia, who reacted quickly as Ilea continued to cut.

The man moaned in pain as she finally cut out the piece of infected flesh. She dropped both the sword and the chunk of flesh to the ground before she used both hands to heal him. It was quite a rough operation, not something he likely would've survived without her being a decent healer.

But I am a decent healer, she thought with a slight grin. *And he might've gotten a level in Pain Tolerance too.*

Suddenly the man gasped, pushing against Ilea's hold as his eyes shot open.

"Aaaah!" he exclaimed, magic activating as his arm shot out toward Ilea, a bladed weapon of some sort at the end of it. She blinked backward and saw that Aurelia had stepped back too.

"Orthan! Orthan! Stop it!" the girl yelled, her voice stopping the older man immediately. He looked around bleary-eyed and confused, his hand shooting toward his previously cursed shoulder as he tried to get up.

"How...h..." he managed to croak before a cough doubled him over.

"Someone came to help us," Aurelia said, walking up and grabbing the man in a hug. Ilea watched on as Orthan put his arms around Aurelia as well. She watched on in fascination as the bladed weapon, which looked like bone, moved back into his arm.

Gross but effective storage, I suppose.

"I'm glad someone survived," she said.

SEVEN

Silver Lining

"Who are you?" Orthan asked, looking at Ilea with suspicion. "The Shadow's Hand by the look of it. I must say I've had it with mercenaries. Who paid for this job?"

"I just saved your life," Ilea said, folding her arms.

Orthan sighed as he let go of Aurelia. "Look, girl, I don't care who you came to save. I certainly didn't pay for it, and I want you gone from this property."

"I'm here with Trian."

The room went quiet for a few seconds after that.

Eventually, Orthan grunted. "The boy was with the Hand. His team, yes. He survived, then. The demons weren't a good sign." He mumbled the last part of the sentence.

"He did, and he's here. Let's go see him," Ilea said. "We could use any information you have."

Orthan glared at her and touched his shoulder, glancing at the piece of bloodied flesh still on the ground. "Is the estate safe?"

"We haven't been attacked yet."

"Then lead the way"

Samuel took the lead with the torch, and Ilea was a little unnerved by the spider following on the ceiling above, but she kept that to herself.

"What was that curse?" Ilea asked.

"One of their mages," Orthan grumbled. "I managed to take his head, but the curse stayed. Damn near killed me."

"Who were they? Who attacked?"

"I have no idea. Capable people, that's all I can say. Barely one below level two hundred. They were quick, had several areas of the house covered in curses, blinding spells and traps before most of us were even awake. Rooms filled with poisons and enchantments to counter our own."

He shook his head and sighed. "They knew about everything, countered both heads of the House and their strongest abilities. Vast preparations and resources would have been required. Another noble House or someone outside the Empire. If they were from the capital, then I suspect House Carter or House Birmingale. We underestimated their resources, but to think they would go to these lengths... The risks... with Alyris. For now, we must protect what has remained."

She had no clue who the families he'd mentioned were. She was just glad Trian hadn't been here when it had all happened. And she was glad she'd found some survivors.

Nearly all above two hundred. Which means even our team might not have been enough to stop them.

Ilea thought of all the monsters and machines she'd fought. Some had shown an inkling of intelligence, sure, and their instincts were well-honed, but they remained monsters. Preparations and coordinated efforts like these were something she hadn't really considered.

Would the Forkspears do the same to me if they found me? Just to get back at Alice?

Would she be able to survive such an attack if it came down to it?

The stone walls felt colder suddenly, and Ilea tightened her grip on the lantern.

* * *

A metal needle flashed toward her but stopped just in front of her face.

"It's you," Kyrian said from his meditative pose on the ground.

She gave the still-sleeping Trian a glance. "I found some survivors," she said.

The others entered the room carefully, but on seeing Trian, Aurelia rushed to her brother's side immediately.

"Trian! Trian!" she exclaimed, hugging his slumbering form until he stirred.

"Aurelia," he whispered, jerking up a moment later before he grabbed her in a tight hug. "You're... you're real, aren't you?" he said, tears in his eyes.

Ilea leaned back against a wall and smiled ever so slightly. Looking around, she saw Samuel was still standing near the door, and Orthan only moved a little closer to the bed.

"Orthan, you old goat. You actually survived," Trian said, looking at him as he kept embracing his sister.

"And here I thought you might be some illusion. Master Trian, I'm truly sorry," he said and knelt down in front of the bed. "I have failed in my duty."

"You haven't failed anything. Stand up. I can't bear to see you this way." Trian slowly moved his legs off the side of the bed. "We have a lot to discuss."

"We do," Orthan agreed. "But not here. It isn't safe, and we cannot let whoever is responsible know that you are here."

"There are no more survivors, are there?" Trian asked. His tone betrayed a slight flicker of hope.

Orthan looked at him with wet eyes, then shook his head. "Of the twelve members of the House of Alymie I was sworn to protect, only yourself, Aurelia, and young master Samuel remain. I am so very sorry."

Trian was silent for a long moment before Orthan reached out and touched his shoulder.

"There is a safe house a few hours from here," Trian said. "It should be safe enough for us to plan the next steps at least. I checked it out already. Nobody made it there."

"But we don't have horses, and you're the only one with a flying skill."

Trian looked at Ilea.

She gave a slight smile. "I can carry two of you. Kyrian can take one as well," she said as she opened the window, a cool breeze rolling into the room. "Come on." She held out her hands to the kids. Each of them grabbed one arm as her Ashen Wings spread behind her.

* * *

The flight was low and fast, and the group tried to stay as well-hidden as possible, even flying through the last stretch of woods instead of above it. On arrival, the safe house appeared to be nothing more than a hidden cave, but when they entered it, a rather spacious and nicely furnished room revealed itself.

There were supplies, weapons, and two beds. There was also a big map of the Empire on one of the walls, their current location near Virilya marked with a pin.

Orthan, Aurelia and Samuel spent the next hour explaining what had happened in the mansion, forming at least part of a picture. Poison, paralyzing spells, curses, and an incredibly fast and efficient attack that took out more than half their forces before most were even awake.

The attackers had brought fighters and mages with specialized Classes ready to counter the strongest of the House's mages while capitalizing on the chaos and the fact that most of the older members of the House had tried to protect the younger generation. Orthan had been the only one to succeed.

"Father tried so hard to keep our relations peaceful," Trian said. "Why now, of all times?"

"There is something brewing in the capital. Murders and disappearances," Orthan said. "I fear that our House won't be the only one targeted, but I cannot be sure any of it is connected. We should've moved farther away from the capital when the refugees from the west started to reach Virilya. Coupled with the chaos brought upon us by the demons, it provided ample opportunities for many to strike. Now it is too late."

"It is." Trian remained quiet for a while. Finally, he sighed. "I want neither you, Aurelia, nor Samuel out here. Do we still have gold somewhere in the capital? I've checked the family vault already. They took everything."

"The family has small deposits with various banks and guilds in Virilya, mostly for business expenses."

Trian frowned. "They would need to be accessed by a member of the family. I'd have to prove my identity. Might be too risky. It would tell everyone who cared to know where I am and that I'm alive." Trian rubbed his chin. "But it may get them to show themselves."

"What do you intend to do?" Ilea asked.

He glanced at her, sparks dancing in his eyes. "They killed my family."

She hesitated, then nodded. "I know. It also means they're dangerous. We could go look for Eve. She sent the letter, and I have an idea that she'd know what to do."

"She found out about it. You mentioned the letter. What was she doing here?"

"I don't know, but she knows something. And if anybody could help us with finding someone, it's Eve. I'm sure her... background and her skills would come in handy. If she's willing to help, of course."

For all intents and purposes, I'm dead.

She remembered the letter, but would Eve really refuse them if they asked for her help?

What is the Golden Lily? And why were you looking for them?

"She warned us not to investigate," Kyrian said.

Ilea nodded. "We know it will be dangerous."

Trian glanced between them.

"We will try," Kyrian said. "We've hunted monsters together before, right?"

Right, Ilea thought.

"Besides, Eve is with the team, isn't she?" Kyrian asked, a sphere of metal hovering above his palm.

I hope so.

"We'll have to find her first," Ilea said. "And we can inform Claire as well. Maybe she has some insights. Plus, I'm sure she could help us hide the survivors somewhere in Ravenhall. They'll be safer in another city. Unless you have another idea."

"I agree," Trian said.

Orthan gave Trian a long look. The old man seemed tired. He'd ushered the two kids toward the beds and then sat down, resting against the stone wall, his eyes closed.

Ilea wondered how he felt. He hadn't interrupted them, nor had he said he wished to join whatever Trian planned to do. Perhaps he simply wanted to leave the decision-making to others – it was often easier that way.

* * *

The three Shadows talked in whispers, the three survivors now asleep. They were sat at the small table in the hideout.

"You two don't have to do this, you know?" Trian said. "I doubt we can take on whoever wiped out damn near my entire family. Father and Mother were powerful mages. And they are— were experienced too," he said, glaring at his slightly shaking hands.

"You don't have to talk about it now," Ilea said, leaning forward and putting a hand on his shoulder.

"You would find and face them one way or the other, would you not?" Kyrian asked after a period of silence.

Ilea noticed in her sphere that Aurelia's breathing wasn't as steady as the others, but she chose not to say anything.

Trian sighed. "I would. Even if I died trying."

The girl stirred a little but stayed quiet.

"What about Aurelia? She's your sister," Ilea said.

Trian looked at her thoughtfully, then shook his head.

"She's strong. More talented than I ever was. Orthan is a good teacher, and he knows the family. The two of them must survive. Me? Yes, I'm her brother, and I'll try my damn best not to die, but I can't leave this as it is. They killed my *parents*." He said the last word very softly. "Would you stand by and do nothing, Ilea? Kyrian?"

The candlelight flickered as it moved in the wind, illuminating the three of them only barely in the dark room.

Ilea couldn't even imagine such a situation back on Earth. Would she simply trust the police to act? This world was different. She wielded power here, enough to do something. Even knowing that her parents hadn't been particularly involved with her life, she would at least want to know who was responsible.

Kyrian stayed quiet.

"I'm not asking you to come with me. This is... personal. The danger is incomparable to any of the missions we've done before," Trian breathed.

"We were in the demon realm together," Ilea said. "How much more dangerous can it get? We are Shadows, after all."

Ilea balled one of her fists. She wasn't sure if she really believed it, but she couldn't bring herself to stop him, and she found she didn't want to abandon him to his quest either.

"We are. And we're a team," Kyrian added and smiled a little as he looked at Trian.

There was a long silence before Trian gave the faintest of smiles.

"You damn imbeciles. How did I ever end up with you?"

Ilea winked. "Must be your luck."

The moment hung softly for a few precious seconds before his smile faded.

"I just want you two to know what you're signing up for."

"We can still flee if we fuck up or get the wrong people hunting us down."

"It might not be that simple—" Trian began.

"Then we better make sure we don't fuck up," Ilea grinned.

EIGHT

The Next Steps

Ilea woke from her meditative state as a fox darted into her Sphere, rushing through the underbrush in its search for food, unaware of the hidden safe house among the bushes and rocks.

The others were still asleep. After what they'd all been through, it wasn't surprising.

Quietly stepping outside, Ilea found that she felt tired too. In a way, she hadn't felt this emotionally drained since the Taleen dungeon and her return to Salia. She was wrung out. Hollow.

Found a team to have a break from all this conflict. I suppose that's the price you pay for getting close. She sighed. *But what's the alternative, never get close to anyone? Just hide away?*

She looked up at the dark sky, a cold breeze flowing through the trees and rustling the leaves.

Here I am, feeling sorry for myself when my friend has lost damn near his entire family.

She felt guilty. A knot lodged in her stomach. She didn't feel angry or frustrated, just overwhelmed.

"You're already up?" Trian asked as he joined her in the forest.

She nodded, and the two of them sat quietly for a long while. She didn't know what to say.

"This is shit," Trian finally said. "I was so excited to get back to them. To take over more responsibilities. I feel like I learned a lot in my time as a Shadow. And now..." He shook his head. "Now it all feels pointless."

"You survived. You're here. But yes, it's shit."

She walked over to Trian and sighed. His shoulders were hunched, he had bags under his eyes, and he looked pale. She hugged him.

"I can't imagine what you're going through. And I'll be honest, I don't know what to do. So let's get them to safety first and then talk to Claire. One step at a time."

Ilea let go of him. He looked at her and nodded a few times.

"One step at a time." He wiped at his eyes. "I'll go wake them up."

* * *

Ilea remained quiet throughout their preparations to leave. They stayed low in the first section of their flight, light rain soon starting to fall from the sky.

She gritted her teeth and kept on flying, holding on to both Aurelia and Samuel, the wide-eyed kids gripping her arms with all the strength they could muster.

The rain got stronger throughout the day, and Ilea had to start using her healing on the three survivors from the Alymie estate, and their pet spider, to help with the ill effects of the cold.

"Ilea, we should rest!" Kyrian shouted over the winds, making her blink her eyes.

She didn't know how long it had been, but the sky looked darker still. She would've preferred to keep flying until they reached Ravenhall, but it would've been cruel to put the two kids through that journey without some rest. They were already shivering, clutching her with pale, wet hands, eyes closed and noses sniffling.

"Over there," she said, nodding toward a patch of forest she could see in the distance. "We'll make camp there."

The group soon landed between the trees. The rain was still falling, though lighter here than it had been closer to Virilya.

"We should build some shelter," Kyrian said as metal hovered out of his quiver, forming blades that cut into a few of the nearby trees.

Ilea activated her buffs before she went and helped, lifting entire tree trunks with her bare hands and moving them to where Kyrian indicated. They built a simple triangular structure with broad logs, pushed into the earth with her strength and secured at the top with Kyrian's flowing metal.

"Should we make a fire?" Kyrian asked.

"They're freezing," Ilea said, nodding, and she started collecting smaller branches from where they had felled the trees.

"Someone could be following," Orthan said. "As long as we have a healer, we won't die."

"If they follow, we'll have someone to interrogate," Trian said as he helped Ilea build a fire.

With Trian's lightning, the fire soon provided a little warmth in their wooden shelter. The tree trunks were still wet and wind blew in through the opening they required for the smoke, but with fresh clothes and blankets, the survivors soon stopped shivering.

Ilea shared food with them from her necklace, and they all remained quiet, eating and resting. Until Samuel started crying. Trian moved over to hug both the boy and his sister.

"It's okay," he said, repeating the sentence from time to time as they sat around the fire.

Ilea finished her meal having barely noticed the taste.

She didn't sleep that night.

* * *

The weather was less harsh during the rest of their journey, and the group arrived in the mountains overlooking Ravenhall on the following morning. The destruction from the demon summoning and the siege were still visible, but the outer walls had already been repaired and travelers were entering through the open gates.

"I'll go check with Claire as we discussed," Ilea said and flew down the mountainside. They didn't know who had attacked the Alymie estate, and they didn't know how far their influence reached. The only person Ilea was sure she could trust was Claire.

Ilea remained covered in her ash, entering the city by flashing her Shadow badge and quickly making her way toward the office Claire had been given.

She raised her hand to the door and hesitated. Then she knocked.

"Come in," came Claire's muffled voice.

Ilea stepped inside and closed the door behind her.

"Ilea. Back so soo—" Claire paused as she took in Ilea's expression and bedraggled appearance. "You... don't look well." She set down her pen, standing up before she walked over. "What happened?"

* * *

It took less than half an hour for Claire to organize cloaks and passage for their group without going through the city gates.

Ilea followed the assigned guard back to Claire's office, noting that the armored man didn't wear Imperial colors, nor was he at a high enough level to be a member of the Hand. He simply grunted to usher them all inside, where Claire stood waiting near the window. She turned and smiled, her expression strained.

Toothie skittered out from behind Aurelia when the door shut, and Ilea could sense magic flowing through the walls. Her Sphere was cut off now, and she could no longer hear anything from outside.

"The enchantments here are some of the best I have available, and I trust the guards. It should be safer to talk here than anywhere else," Claire informed them.

Trian walked over to one of the armchairs. "Thank you, Claire." He sat down and started tapping his knee with his index finger. "I… I don't know where to start."

"The Alymie estate was attacked. Ilea already told me. I understand that you lost most of your family. I'm sorry."

Trian stared at the floor as Aurelia walked over and grabbed his hand. Orthan sat Samuel down in one of the armchairs before he too sat down. Ilea and Kyrian stayed near the door.

"I wanted to ask if… If you could hide and provide shelter for Orthan, Aurelia, and Samuel," Trian said.

"And their spider," Kyrian added.

Claire glanced at the monster and blinked. "Of course. I will talk to William and Dagon to have something set up in Viscera. If, that is, you do not suspect either of them, or the Hand, to be a part of this conspiracy?"

Trian shook his head. "No. It wouldn't make sense. The Shadows were here while this happened."

"Not all of them, but I agree. I'll still make sure no other members learn of them," Claire said. "So, what will you do?"

"I'll find out who's responsible," Trian said, then looked up to meet her eyes. "And then I'll kill them."

Claire looked at him for a long moment, a slight frown forming on her face. She walked over to the bar next to the armchairs and opened one of the fancy-looking bottles. She filled a glass and walked back to the middle of the room. She looked at Trian and sipped from the dark, near-golden liquid.

"And here I was, thinking you had justifiably been exempted from tactics classes. I would have expected a statement like that from Ilea, no offense, but not from you."

"Offense taken," Ilea said and walked over to the bar. She pointed at the bottles, and Claire gave her a slight nod.

Trian scowled. "What other choice do I have? Sit back and do nothing? I know the risks, but I won't sit here while they thrive with Alymie blood on their hands. While they spend what they plundered from my family." He wiped his face.

Claire's frown deepened. "I didn't suggest you do nothing. And I wouldn't question your resolve. We all survived the demon summoning, but this is different, and you know that. Whoever is responsible is not a monster you can simply slay. Your actions will have consequences, and if not well planned out, you will die. Everyone involved will die."

Ilea took a sip from the same liquid Claire had poured. It had a smokey taste to it.

"I'm sorry," Claire continued. "I will already say right now that I won't be traveling with you to Virilya. There is too much at stake for me to risk my life. But there are resources I now have access to that will be useful, and I can help you prepare. For now, only those who will travel with you should remain here. I will take the rest to Viscera. The less they know, the better."

"Trian," Aurelia said, the grip of her hand tight around his.

He stood up and hugged her, then knelt down and looked into her eyes. "You have been strong. So very strong. I will find out who did this, and I will come back to you."

Aurelia started crying and then hit his shoulder. "Don't you dare die, you idiot." She wiped at her face and glared at him. "I will be mad if you do."

"I would be mad too," Trian said. "You can trust Claire. Work on your skills and learn what you can here. It should've been a few more years until you joined the Hand, but I suppose you may as well start already." He glanced at Claire.

"Apprenticeships and access to classes can be arranged, I'm sure," Claire said. "Orthan will be a little more difficult to find something for, but I'm sure we'll figure it out."

"I am fine with a bed and food," Orthan said. "And I will continue to teach these two as I have before. I will stand with House Alymie, until my time comes." He stood up and grabbed Samuel's hand, then touched Trian's shoulder.

"Your father would've been proud. He knew you would return from the Hand not as a boy but as a man, Trian. I know he would have advised against a reckless retaliation like you are considering, yet I knew him well. He would stand here doing the same if he were in your position. I will pray for your return and your success."

Trian hugged the man. "Thank you. For everything, Orthan. Take good care of them."

"I will," Orthan said as the two separated.

Ilea watched them stare at each other. This was a farewell. They both knew it may very well be their last.

"Good luck," Aurelia said as she hugged Trian as well. "Fight well."

"I will," Trian said and held her close, then let go. He hugged Samuel too before the three humans and their spider left with Claire.

"I will return shortly. Don't mess up my office," Claire said before the door shut and the three Shadows were left alone.

Ilea sat down in one of the chairs. She sipped from her drink, glad that they'd made it back without any attacks or major issues.

"Can you get me one of those?" Trian asked.

* * *

Claire returned in what felt like less than an hour. She closed the door and sat down at her desk, summoning a set of books before she started going through them.

"Did everything go alright?" Trian asked.

Claire didn't look his way. "Of course," she said. "Your suspicion of this being a targeted attack from another country is dubious. Alymie-owned trade and commodities rarely make it out of the Empire, nor would removing your House's known military might be even a minor blow to the capital or Lys itself, no offense." Her tone was neutral.

She looked up from the books. "Orthan's suspicions of Birmingale or Carter are well-founded, and I'm also inclined to suspect one or the other House. With how damaging the blow was, there is really no use for foul play by any other major House. It was a surgical strike at a time when the Empire is faced with potential aggression from Baralia and the aftermath of the widespread demon attacks. There will be little resources spent on finding evidence, and a few well-placed bribes will likely leave the perpetrators without tangible short-term consequences." She sighed. "I'm impressed. Well, somewhat."

Trian leaned back and clenched his jaw.

Claire stood up and started pacing. "Neither of the suspected Houses should have the sheer might to execute such an attack without outside help. That means there will be weaker links in all of this. And that means that there will have been mistakes. Like their failure to find Orthan and the other survivors. Like their failure to have you killed as well. Both suggest once more that none of the largest Houses nor an organized outside force should be responsible. And this also means that even a single Shadow team should at the very least be able to figure out who was responsible."

"I'm listening," Trian said.

"If they're smart, they will be on their guard. But based on what I saw when I met you for the first time, well, I wouldn't have thought any House in the capital would've deemed you even a minor threat. Knowing that the others survived and that you could take your time burning corpses near your estate – a very stupid move, by the way – confirms that the responsible party either has no further resources to spare on this or simply don't care."

Ilea gulped. They could've all walked into a trap. Trian could've been dead if they'd just left a few assassins at the estate.

"What if they just don't know about him?" Kyrian asked.

"No. He is one of just two children. Samuel, being an adopted ward, holds no claim to the name so could be ignored, but had they cared, they would definitely have gone after a direct descendant. They do not care or do not have the resources. Either way, it is a mistake that we can now exploit," Claire said. "I will use my position and my connections with Dagon and Sulivhaan. My work with them has already allowed for considerable leeway and preferential treatment." She glanced at Ilea, then turned back to Trian. "Information brokers in the capital will be able to at least point the way. So, Trian, I ask you this. What is your goal? Specifically."

Trian opened his mouth, then closed it. He sighed. "I want them to pay for what they did."

"Not specific enough. Say it was House Carter. You go in, kill the ruling head, Varina Carter. I doubt you three could do that without a fight. She has five sons, all near your personal power. They will be there, or they will seek to find who was responsible. They will fight you, even if perhaps they weren't directly involved. The same will be true for any of their family, spouses, and allies."

"That is their choice to make. I don't wish to kill anyone who wasn't involved, but I will fight them too, if I have to."

Ilea crossed her arms. "We should focus on those responsible and then get the fuck out and hide."

"You can see the issue then," Claire said. "No. What you will do instead is find evidence. Or attempt to find evidence."

"We need to find out who is responsible anyway," Trian said.

"I'm not talking about the word of an information broker or a letter pointing you in the right direction. I'm talking about the transfer of gold, signed letters detailing the job, and witnesses willing to confirm what happened. Enough that the Empress is forced to rescind the status of the noble House responsible in front of the Empire's nobility."

"How would we get any of that? And even if we do, Alyris of Lys would not have those responsible executed. They would be exiled at most, their businesses taken over by other noble Houses. They would simply flee, and their personal power would easily be enough to prosper in another country."

"There is always a trail. Sometimes it is considerably more difficult to find, but so far, our opponents have not proven to be beacons of experience and caution," Claire said. "And concerning your second fear, the goal of evidence is not primarily to cause damage but to dissuade any response from those who survive your strike. They will know what their family members have done. They will be exiled. And they won't have access to the same resources that they once had."

Trian sighed. "Right. I see."

"Have you done anything like this before?" Ilea asked, surprised at how quickly Claire had addressed the situation.

"I read a lot and I've been well educated. Striking at a notable noble House adds a few more variables to the mix, but if anything, that makes analyzing and planning such a strike more exciting. Besides, I won't participate in the fighting or gathering of evidence myself. Only a mad woman, or man, would take such a risk."

Ilea glanced at Kyrian and Trian. She sighed.

Claire stopped her pacing. "I trust in your abilities to fight, all three of you, but I suggest you find help when it comes to getting information. Finding Eve would be your best bet, given that she sent you that letter."

"I thought about getting her help as well," Ilea said.

"I'll start the preparations immediately," Claire said. "We will set up primary and secondary inns within the capital. I don't have contacts myself, but I will consult with Dagon and Sulivhaan to find a suitable set of places for your base of operations while you conduct this mission. I suggest you do not use your real names or anything identifying you as Shadows. Wear nondescript armor and pretend to be adventurers from the west making their way east because you heard of the demons and wanted to see if there were jobs to hunt them down. I will send letters to the inns with enchanted seals that can be broken with this coin."

Claire made a black coin appear in her hand and handed it to Trian. "They will be addressed to James Horrington, a common name in Dawntree and Salia. I will find your inns. Rest if you need to. Otherwise, I suggest you prepare to leave."

"Claire, I…" Trian said as he stood up. "I don't know how to thank you for all this. I would've just stormed in there…"

She just nodded. "We are a team. Thank me by surviving."

* * *

Ilea rested in one of the armchairs in Claire's office whilst twirling Aki in her hand. Kyrian had grabbed one of the books from Claire's bookshelves and sat nearby, reading.

"What's this word?" Kyrian asked, glancing over at Trian as he pointed at a section in the book.

"Extortion," Trian said.

Kyrian took the book back, then glanced at Trian. "What does it mean?"

Ilea was glad they could at least provide a slight distraction for Trian. She wasn't sure if Kyrian was doing it on purpose or if he too wanted to distract himself. She smiled ever so slightly, realizing that she could certainly use the distraction herself. They were about to go to Virilya and try to find, then attack, an established noble House. She wasn't sure what was more stupid – exploring a Taleen dungeon by herself or this.

She definitely knew what she would rather do. And still, she was here. She supposed she couldn't help it. If Mark had asked her to help fight some goons back on Earth, she would've probably done that too.

No. She would've most certainly done it.

Killing should've been another question, but it didn't feel consequential anymore. Not after everything that had happened with Alice, Roland, and Earl. She didn't think about it often anymore. The humans she had fought and killed blended in with all the monsters and creatures she had fought. All of them had made their choice, and so had she.

"What do you think about this plan?" she said, looking at the dagger in her hand.

"I would've intervened if you'd gone to the capital without consulting Claire," Aki said. "Other than that, I don't have anything further to add."

"Reasonable. So, do you want to stay here or come with us, by the way?"

"I... would not demand anything. I am a dagger. My wishes do not matter. Where would you have me stay?"

Trian frowned and looked over. "You were with us in the Haven and on our missions. And you were even there in the Great Salt. As far as I'm concerned, you're part of the team."

"What he said," Ilea added.

"I am sorry for your loss, Trian," Aki said. "I... felt it insensitive to speak up earlier. And your words... they mean much. Thank you. If you would accept it, I would wish to be there. To see where your actions lead, though I cannot affect them."

"You could perhaps distract someone," Kyrian said. "You do have a voice. It's unexpected for a dagger."

"It is, isn't it?" Ilea said, turning Aki around. "We should probably find Balduur and Iana too. Dagon let me know he's in the capital. My armor is pretty fucked up anyway, and if we're supposed to not look like Shadows, he could set us up with new armor." She frowned. "Though I don't know if I could pay him."

"I still have a sizable amount of gold," Trian said. "It's all that's left, but you three are helping me, so I'll pay for everything in this mission. Until I run out."

"We'll see if it'll be enough, but otherwise, we can probably find more reasonably priced craftspeople to get some armor. I do feel like he might be inclined to help anyway."

The door opened at that moment and Claire entered, and as she closed the door behind her, the enchantments reactivated. She stepped behind her large table and summoned a map.

"Join me."

Ilea walked over, holding Aki up so he could see the entire map. It depicted Virilya, with dozens of colored marks with numbers and correspondent descriptions at the top of the paper. They denoted sectors of the city, dozens of information brokers, potential hideouts and safe houses, the Carter and Birmingale estates, and locations of assets they were known to own, including warehouses, workshops, stores, and even boat docking locations on the lake bordering the city.

"Dagon came through," Claire said. "I have your inn locations too, but they're not marked."

"What did all of this cost you?" Ilea asked.

Claire smiled. "I agreed to work with the city for another two years. Securing my employment and setting you up with information. Two birds with one stone."

"He did that on purpose," Aki said.

"Probably. But he might consider it the same. He does not want to be known to give out information for free. But of course, the price is for him to decide."

"I wanted to visit a smith I know as well, for new armor," Ilea said.

Claire frowned. "It will be a risk to show your faces to anyone."

"I trust him," Ilea replied.

Claire glanced at Trian, then looked back at Ilea. "Your choice. The most prominent smithing districts are marked. I suggest you are not seen with him. Or anyone, for that matter."

"We're not assassins."

"That's what I'm worried about. Now let me show you where to go and who to contact first."

NINE

The Crouching Bear

Ilea, Trian, Kyrian, and Aki left Ravenhall before nightfall. They knew which inn to use as their base of operations and which information brokers to find and contact first. A lot was still unknown, but Ilea felt better about the whole ordeal now that they had a few specific places to begin their search.

Their first goal, besides getting some nondescript non-Hand armor, was to obtain information on Eve as well as the perpetrators of the attack.

Ilea still felt the weight of what they were about to do and the weight that rested especially on Trian's shoulders, but it felt a little less overwhelming, knowing that they were doing all of this as a team.

On their flight to Ravenhall, she had felt lost, something only underscored by the shellshocked survivors they had brought back with them. Now, they were a team of Shadows. And they had a mission on their hands.

They didn't rest during their journey, flying low and fast over the vast landscapes of the Empire. Ilea breathed deeply when she saw the walls of Virilya rising in the distance.

Night was falling as they arrived after their long flight. They switched to nondescript leather armor and equipped weapons none of them knew how to use before they made their way to the gate, entering the capital with other groups of adventurers, merchants, and caravans.

They were admitted without obvious distrust, likely due to their high level, tired expressions, dust and debris-covered armor, and quiet demeanor. They were due for some rest. That much wasn't a façade.

Lanterns and magical lights illuminated the streets in a somewhat dim light. The sound of music and the smell of food pushed through the wet cobbled streets. Just another night, it seemed.

The three of them walked through the city for a while until Trian nodded toward a tavern built into the cellar of a large house made of wood and stone. The entrance was a little hidden and the door low-set. Moss covered most of the building's side, and someone singing could be heard from within.

A sign indicated this was The Crouching Bear, the primary inn they would be staying at during their mission. Their hideout. The next morning, they would go to find a smith.

* * *

Ilea woke up as if only a mere moment had passed. She felt tired and cold. The muffled music and conversations from downstairs were gone, and outside the single murky window, it was still dark. Kyrian was still asleep, but Trian was sitting at the simple desk in the dark.

"What time is it?" she whispered, getting out of bed. She hadn't changed her clothes, nor had she taken a bath.

Trian didn't react.

"Trian?" Ilea said.

He shifted and glanced her way. "I don't know." He paused. "It's dark out."

"Are you..." She stopped herself. Of course he wasn't alright. "Do you need anything?"

He shook his head.

"I'll get us a bath up here. We'll go look for Balduur soon." She touched his shoulder as she passed.

Ilea closed the door behind her and sighed, finding the stairs and walking down. A single patron had passed out with his head on one of the tables. Though the door to the inn was open, cool air coming in from outside, the smell wasn't great.

She hadn't noticed the low ceiling when they'd arrived, nor the slightly putrid smell that seemed to permeate the entire place. This wasn't an inn to write home about. She found a young man sitting on a chair behind the counter. He was thin, his face slightly sallow, hair greasy. He glanced at her for a split second before he looked back to the book he was reading.

"Morning," Ilea said. "A bath?"

"Ten copper," he said. "There's tubs in the back and enchantments for water and heat." He didn't get up from his chair and pointed.

"Right," Ilea said, seeing the supposed tubs through her Sphere. They weren't baths really, more like large barrels cut in half. Still, they would comfortably house most adults. They reminded Ilea of small wooden hot tubs.

She walked over to them, touched one, and poured mana into one of the enchantments, causing water to flow out of a tap.

"How do I heat it?" she asked.

"The black stone with runes on it. Hold it inside the water, runes down," the man answered without getting up.

Ilea found the stone and held it in the water, pouring mana into it before she felt heat emanating from the runes.

Even a run-down place like this has this kind of convenience.

She replaced the stone when the bath was warm, grabbing the tub before she activated her buffs and carried it up to their room.

"You should bathe too," she said to Trian when she entered.

He tapped the table with his hand.

"Come on," Ilea said. "I'll help you."

She heard him grunt and walked over. "Get up and store your clothes."

She stood there and waited for a long moment before he finally stood up and walked to the tub.

Wordlessly, he turned around and stored his clothes and leather armor before he stepped into the bath, his muscular body barely fitting into the large wooden tub.

Ilea grabbed a brush and helped him clean and dry off. When she went to change the water, she saw how much blood and dirt had come off as she dumped it into a gutter out in the alley.

It was still dark outside, and she couldn't see a single person walking down the narrow path. Returning to the room, she found Trian back at his desk, dressed again but still just staring at the wall.

She let him be and bathed herself, then changed the water again and woke up Kyrian.

With all of them at least somewhat clean, Ilea put her cloak on and pulled her hood up. She saw Kyrian do the same.

"We should find Balduur now for some armor or a smith contact," she said. "Trian? You don't have to join if you don't feel up for it. But I don't think it's good if you just stay here."

He stood up and summoned his cloak. "I'm sorry, it's..." He shook his head.

"It's okay. There's no rush. You still want to do this?" Ilea asked.

He breathed in and balled his fists, then looked up and met her gaze. His eyes were bloodshot, with dark bags hanging below them.

"Yeah. Let's move. We have a lot of people to talk to today."

* * *

The larger streets of Virilya already had plenty of people going about their business in the very early hours of the morning. Ilea identified the people around them and made sure to stay vigilant with both her Sphere and occasional glances behind them when nobody else was looking their way. Their high levels would stand out, but she knew that most would only see question marks rather than a more definitive impression.

It didn't take them long to find the major smithing district. Smoke was rising above many of the buildings, but the telltale sounds of steel hitting steel were yet to be heard. Ilea checked through the smithies with her Sphere, asking for Balduur in a few stores without luck until they found a massive and well-furnished inn at a prominent location bordering a large square. She invested a single silver coin to get a location. At least someone knew Balduur, even here, or perhaps the old innkeeper simply knew more than most.

Ilea turned into a side street, lanterns illuminating everything but the smallest alleyways in the Imperial capital. They came upon a massive square stone structure with large windows set into the higher sections. A workshop, she presumed. It was the one Balduur was supposedly at.

"Well, he didn't lie about it being big..." Ilea said to herself as she looked up at a side entrance. In big lettering, she read a sign saying "Imperial Smiths" and then noticed a sound in her mind.

'ding' Elos Standard Language reaches lvl 6

Now of all times, she thought but ignored it, instead looking into the building with her Sphere and checking the various workstations. She couldn't find Balduur, but a slight smile came to her lips as she saw a familiar face.

"Iana is here," she said to her companions.

There was an Imperial guard standing at the door. *I suppose I can't just go in,* she thought. Still, the guard didn't seem particularly attentive, nor particularly awake.

"I'll have a chat with her quickly. Wait here," she said to the others and made her way toward the stone wall. Checking again to see if the guard was looking, she used her Sphere to point herself at a large furnace inside the building and blinked.

It was much hotter inside, and she could hear various people chatting and stacking crates or bundles of metals. Glancing past the furnace, she thought about how to get Iana's attention and unsheathed Aki.

"Can you tell her I'm here?" she whispered.

"You're going to throw me, aren't you?" the dagger asked.

Ilea allowed herself a slight smile and did just that, hiding behind the furnace when the metal clinked to the ground near Iana.

The young enchantress looked at the dagger and walked over a moment later.

"I'm over here," Ilea said in a quiet voice.

Iana's eyes were wide, and she spoke in the barest whisper.

"Ilea. I'm... glad you survived." She fidgeted with a small piece of metal and eyed Ilea apprehensively.

Hiding in the shadows tends to make people nervous, I guess.

"Sorry for sneaking up on you. I'm glad you survived as well. I was looking for you and Balduur."

Iana shifted, glancing over her shoulder and trying to look casual. "He won't be here for another hour. But we don't live far from here. What's going on?"

"Maybe we can talk at your place then?" Ilea whispered. "If you have time. I don't want to impose."

"No, it's fine. I can come back later," Iana said, finally appearing to relax a little at the mention of leaving the crowded forge. "Should I meet you outside?"

"Let's do that. Thanks, Iana. It's good to see you."

Iana tilted her head and tugged on a strand of hair. "You're acting serious. It's starting to scare me," she murmured.

Ilea smiled ever so slightly. "Just looking for some equipment, don't worry. And I wanted to check in on you anyway. Didn't have much else to do, the food here sucks." She winked, trying to channel her pre-parent murder personality.

Iana's expression brightened a little, and she smirked. "Typical. Okay. I'll meet you in a minute then."

"Sure. Oh, just so you know, I'm not alone. But they're friends. One of them you know already," Ilea said before she vanished again.

They didn't have to wait long. Iana joined them a few minutes later. She gave the two men a furtive glance.

"Kyrian, good to see you."

"And you, Iana."

Ilea had introduced them a while back. Ilea and Balduur had helped with his armor design, but Ilea also knew that Balduur had only agreed to that project due to the uniqueness of Kyrian's metal magic.

Iana led them through a few streets and into an alleyway lined with old houses. She stopped in front of one, opened the door, and ushered them into a block of apartments.

"Care to tell me what's going on now?" Iana asked.

"We're looking for people. Someone was killed," Ilea said.

"Murdered," Trian said. He hadn't spoken up to that moment.

Iana's face fell. "I'm sorry."

Ilea followed in silence as Iana led them up a narrow and damp wooden stairwell to the door of a cramped apartment. Ilea used her Sphere to see inside. She found she recognized a few of the people in the dwelling. Survivors from Indur, people she had only seen in passing, forced to flee here due to the demon summoning. There were more than a dozen in the first single room beyond the door, and still more further in the apartment. The assembled refugees continued beyond the reach of her Sphere.

All because of Adam. At least the people here have their lives.

Iana knocked on the door. "I'll get him. Wait here."

Ilea sat down on the stairwell. A tiny window provided at least a tiny bit of morning light.

"Are you sure we can trust him?" Trian said.

"He's not from around here," Ilea said when she saw the massive smith in her Sphere, the man somehow avoiding the people playing cards or sleeping despite his bulk.

Balduur opened the door a crack and peeked out. He glared at the three people before him, then he grinned and opened the door fully, moving out onto the stairs. Iana joined him before he closed the door behind him.

"Ilea – and crew, I suppose. You I know," he said, nodding at Kyrian. "What's with the gloomy mood? Someone summon more demons? Could've at least warned me about that, by the way. Was it the Hand?"

Ilea nodded. "One of the Elders. Ravenhall has been cleared out, and I think the region is safe again."

"You think?" Balduur said in a dry tone.

"Yeah. We're looking for some people, or information, I suppose, but that's not why I wanted to come here."

Balduur narrowed his eyes. "In a pinch, eh? Looking for a capable smith, are ya? Thought you could hit up your old pal Balduur and he might even work for free?" he said, his tone becoming increasingly dangerous.

"I went back to my family home," Trian said, "and found everyone murdered. Ilea says you're a capable smith. We need armor, something that wouldn't identify us as Shadows. Nothing extravagant but something solid that will hold up should a fight catch us by surprise. I can pay you, and if you're not interested, perhaps you could refer us to someone else we can trust." He said the words with no trace of emotion, all businesslike.

Balduur looked at Trian for a long moment, then sighed. "I'm sorry for your loss, boy. We lost a few as well on that first night. Unfortunately, I'm not supposed to do any work besides what the Empire orders, and they've been ordering a lot."

Ilea raised an eyebrow. "Didn't think you'd want to work for a city."

"I don't," he said, glaring at her. "But turns out it's illegal now to be a smith not signed by the city or the guilds, and the guilds aren't signing more right now. They're stockpiling weapons and armor, preparing for something. Word is it's not just demons anymore. People have gone missing in the past two weeks, more than is apparently usual in Virilya. If I could be certain that Indur was safe, I would take my people and return right now."

"They wouldn't let us go," Iana said with a resigned sigh.

"You asked him?" Balduur said.

Iana nodded and glanced at Ilea. "One of the smiths at the workshop, Mauran. He's from Riverwatch. He wanted to leave with a caravan but was stopped at the gate. Imperials said no craftspeople are allowed to leave."

"Not a great sign," Balduur said drily. "We shouldn't have come here."

"You should've left with the Shadows," Ilea said. "I have a contact in Ravenhall. And we could maybe get you out."

"Ilea," Trian said sharply.

"What? We can help each other, and he's a friend, just like you."

Trian looked at her for a moment, then broke eye contact.

"What's this about a contact? You mean in the Hand?" Balduur asked.

"An administrator in Ravenhall," Ilea said. "I can write a letter for you to give to her. She could set you up with a more comfortable place to stay, far away from here."

He grunted. "I'll think about it. Now take off your sorry leathers, I need to take measurements."

Ilea smiled.

"What about your orders?" Kyrian asked.

"My current second-rate employers wouldn't know how to use my skills if their lives depended on it. I'll get you your armor. The most well-made, durable, yet boring-looking sets that you could hope for. How heavy do you each want them?"

"It will depend on the cost," Trian said.

"Three Shadows asking for help," Balduur grumbled. "Find us a way out of this city and you can consider that your payment."

Iana looked at Ilea and winked. "I'll add enchantments too."

* * *

They had their measurements taken and left after being gruffly told to return in the early afternoon of the following day.

Ilea was already considering possible ways to get the craftspeople from Indur out of the city. There were six in total. Getting them through any of the city gates would be impossible without a fight, and while most of the guards weren't at a level that Ilea couldn't handle, even on her own, it would defeat their entire purpose of coming here and staying concealed. She also wondered who would show up if a fight with some guards escalated to the point where they couldn't handle it on their own.

They didn't go back to their inn, instead seeking out the information broker contacts provided by Dagon. Trian handled most of the talking and negotiations. The first contact was an old man in the back room of a seedy underground bar, the second a middle-aged woman in a brothel reeking of perfume, the third a violin player in a renowned city orchestra, trading in information as a side job it seemed, or simply as something exciting to do.

In all, they saw twelve. All the contacts were difficult to find and would've been impossible for them to reach without Dagon's instructions. They didn't ask about anything related to the Alymies, instead focusing on questions about Eve. If their goal had been to find out who had been responsible for the attack on Trian's family, then perhaps one or some of the merchants could've pointed them in the right direction, but Trian had agreed to Claire's plans. They were looking for hard evidence, and without Eve, they weren't confident about how to proceed.

The first day didn't yield anything useful in regard to Eve, but Ilea learned a few things about smuggling people in and out of the city, past the guards, or with the help of bribes. The brokers were worth the gold, providing specific routes and names, all paid for by Trian, the sum far less than their three sets of armor would've cost.

Their second day yielded even fewer results. It was a montage of frowns, shaking heads, and blank faces. No one had heard of anyone matching Eve's description, and they already had everything they needed for the escape. By the time the afternoon and their meeting with Balduur arrived, they had learned nothing more they could use.

Ilea could feel Trian's frustration as they made their way back to Balduur. On the one hand, she was glad they had the distraction of getting new armor, but on the other, she wondered how long he would keep to the plan if they continued to find nothing of substance.

Balduur fulfilled his promise. Half-plate for Trian and near full-plate for Ilea and Kyrian. Dull silver metal without any markings or engravings and closed helmets with only two holes for the eyes.

[Armament of War Helmet – High Quality] Enchantments [Durability 2 / Weight Reduction 2]

Ilea's set had no gauntlets, leaving her able to use her fists freely or to switch in the weapons Balduur had already made for her. The plating was less cumbersome at the joints, allowing her to move them better at the cost of slight vulnerabilities.

She said her thanks and gave Balduur the letter for Claire that she had prepared, asking her to help Balduur and his people.

"Found a way out yet?" the smith asked her before they left.

"I know the guard change shifts on a few sections of the wall," Ilea said. "It will probably be easiest to get you out with flight when the weather provides some cover at night. We should be able to manage six people in a single go, with everyone who isn't a crafter leaving beforehand and waiting for us along the road south."

"And we have to fly?"

"All the other options are far more complicated and far more costly. This is the only way without hiring someone. Not many can fly, let alone carry a man as heavy as you are."

Balduur grunted. "Fair. Then we wait for bad weather. I'll send the non-crafters ahead now. They've already been packing up. Then we can leave at short notice. Questions will be asked if we don't show up, and I don't want the others to be stuck here."

"Works for us, right?" Ilea said, glancing at her team. "We'll come get you when the weather looks right."

* * *

It rained that evening. Dark clouds hung above the Imperial capital of Lys. Balduur's people had already left, their warriors comfortable with protecting the group from stray demon or other monster attacks as they set up camp near the road leading south from Virilya.

Ilea could hear thunder rolling above the tiled rooftops as rain rattled against her helmet. The streets were downright abandoned.

She felt tense as she walked next to her teammates. Trian hadn't spoken much today, and Kyrian was wordlessly going along with their plans. They still hadn't found a single clue as to Eve's whereabouts.

Ilea wondered if they could hire another Shadow to help them. Someone who specialized in the kind of work they needed. But she dismissed the thought quickly, knowing they couldn't trust anyone they didn't know.

What's the alternative?

Then she saw a single figure rush over the rooftops nearby.

We're not the only ones using the weather for some plans, eh?

She kept a watchful eye on her Sphere as they walked through the wet streets of Virilya.

"Something's going on," Kyrian said when they were standing in the stairwell outside Balduur's apartment.

Ilea knocked on the door, seeing Balduur and Iana preparing with everyone else who hadn't been allowed to leave through her Sphere.

"What do you mean?"

"The city. You can feel it in the air."

"You're just not used to it," Trian said.

"Maybe. But I learned to trust my instincts in the wilderness. The only difference here is that the monsters are humans."

Balduur opened the door. "We're ready."

"Good, then let's get you out," Ilea said, leading the group outside and through the streets.

Trian helped her navigate as they made their way toward the south-eastern part of town. She had gotten a tip to start her flight a few kilometers away from the wall to get enough height to avoid alerting anyone. Still, they planned to wait for the guard change to actually fly over the walls.

They stood in a dark, unremarkable alley, mostly covered from the rain. They heard the water pattering onto the overhanging roofs above, flowing onto the road and into the gutters.

Ilea turned her head as she heard a screech. It was distant, muffled, and lost in the weather. She shook her head and focused after not hearing anything else for a handful of minutes.

Kyrian freaked you out. Calm down and focus on what you have to do.

"Guard change in ten minutes," Trian said. "You should prepare to fly."

Ilea nodded and spread her ashen wings, reaching out her arms for Iana and another craftswoman to grab onto. Balduur didn't question her as he stepped in front of Ilea and held on, his arms going around his daughter and the other craftswoman.

Ilea activated her auras and flapped her wings, finding the weight of the three people considerable but manageable. She wouldn't be able to maneuver in any efficient manner, but she wouldn't have to if everything went according to plan.

"Ready?" she asked, looking over at Kyrian, who had linked his metal so that the other three people could hang on. Trian would wait for them inside the city – his lightning wings were far too visible to join this endeavor. They would meet again in the same alley once the others had returned.

"I'm ready," Kyrian said.

"We leave," Ilea said, moving her wings. She checked the surrounding rooftops but found she could only see a few streets ahead, the rain and wind obstructing her view beyond her Sphere. She hoped the weather would have the same effect on the flying squads they'd spotted here and there since arriving in Virilya. Slowly, she rose with her passengers hanging on for dear life. Higher and higher she went.

Ilea froze when she heard an explosion from below. Had they been spotted?

"It's far down," Iana said. "Not meant for us."

Another explosion rang out soon after.

"A fire, several houses, but it's too dark to be sure. I can only see specks of figures moving around," Iana continued.

"Someone graced us with a distraction," Ilea said.

"They may actually be more vigilant on the walls as a result," Balduur murmured.

"We'll try it either way," Ilea said and braced against the wind and rain, flying the group higher until they had passed the wall, and then higher still. Then she started flying forward in a straight line, neither too fast nor too slow, keeping their speed steady to make it more difficult to be seen. She only checked behind them when they were far past the city walls.

Nobody had followed. Nobody had seen them. Or nobody who had seen had cared.

They kept flying and soon landed, Kyrian and Ilea escorting the six craftspeople from Indur to the road until they went into the forest bordering Virilya and found the others' camp.

"It's us!" Balduur called out to the torch-wielding guards, two large men and two large women, all armed and armored.

"They made it out," one of the men said, setting down his two-handed axe with a wide smile behind his beard.

Balduur turned to Ilea. "You were true to your word. Thank you."

"Of course, Balduur. Thanks again for the armor."

He gave her a look, then looked past her and in the direction of the city. "You sure you want to go back in there?"

Ilea smiled. "I'm not, no. I'd much rather be in Ravenhall, or anywhere else, but our friend needs us."

He nodded. "Don't bite off too much. And come back alive. Would be a shame for all that gear I made you to be lost."

Ilea grinned. "Someone will loot it, don't worry."

He laughed, then offered his hand. She gripped it and let go.

"Don't lose Aki," Iana chipped in.

"I'll try not to. Good luck on your journey back. Let's hope it's free of monsters."

"It never is," one of the nearby warriors said, though it didn't sound like he saw this as a problem.

"Come pay a visit when you're back," Balduur said.

"Will do," Ilea said.

"You too," Balduur added, looking at Kyrian.

Kyrian's reply was a silent nod.

"Stoic," Balduur said appreciatively. "Why can't you be like that, Ilea?"

"We wouldn't make a very interesting team like that, would we?" Ilea said, shaking Iana's hand. She then turned to leave. "Ready to go back?"

Kyrian gave her a nod.

She waved her goodbyes to the group and spread her wings, flying back toward the road, where she landed once more.

"Let's try to fly in the same way that we came from. If anyone stops us, we have our story."

"Lead the way," Kyrian said.

Ilea did just that, the two of them flying high before they slowly approached the city through the storm. Her wings pushed against the wind and rain until they reached the walls and flew past.

Nobody stopped us, Ilea thought, nearly doing a double take when she saw several fires in the streets of the city.

They started descending and soon landed in the same alley they had left from, where Trian stood waiting.

"Done?" he asked.

"Yes. It all went smoothly. Almost too perfect," Ilea said. She checked behind her, expecting some guard captain, ready to attack the intruders, but there was nobody there.

She squinted, then looked at her companions. "We should go find out what those explosions and fires are about."

"It won't have anything to do with why we're here," Trian said.

"But we're here. I'll go alone. I won't wear the new armor either. Can't hurt to get more information. I'll meet you two back at the inn."

"I'll go as well," Kyrian said. "We should split up, and if any major problems arise, we go and meet at the inn."

Trian cursed. "People might recognize me if they see my magic. I'll return now. Don't overextend."

Ilea gave him a nod and blinked up, spreading her wings before she flew up and blinked again, spotting one of the fires. It looked larger now that she was closer to the ground. She sped up as she saw magic flare in the streets and a line of fighters pushing a group of people back.

Not people, Ilea thought as she got closer. She moved into a dive and equipped her bladed blue-steel gauntlets. In front of the line of Imperial guards, she saw several demons.

She flashed past the first one, her steel slicing through its neck, severing its head before she hit the next beast. Her blade slammed into its skull before she ripped it to the right, her left gauntlet vanishing into her necklace before a single punch whipped the monster's head back.

She turned right and closed the distance to another beast with her wings, and a wide swing of her bladed arm left the demon cut in two. Next she blinked and slammed her fist into the back of another monster's head, killing it instantly.

Ilea was ready for more when she looked around, expecting a horde of demons, her pulse racing as she considered what it meant for the city. A city of hundreds of thousands, the largest settlement she had seen in Elos.

But there were no more demons, and the fire she'd seen was a few streets away.

"You there, adventurer!" one of the Imperials called out as their unit advanced, stabbing the corpses as they went.

Ilea turned. "Why are there demons here?"

"We don't know," the guard said, only his eyes visible behind the visor. "There are people trapped near the fires."

She nodded and flapped her wings, flying fast to close the distance to the flames.

Ilea checked her Sphere, then blinked into the burning house and checked for survivors. She found only corpses, shouts coming from nearby, and more magical reverberations coming from ahead.

She flew up and joined in, killing four more demons before the surroundings calmed once more, fire and water mages arriving to extinguish the flames. But when she checked her messages, all she found were demons below level sixty.

Did one of them arrive here and infect others?

"What's going on? Why are there demons in the city?" she asked one of the nearby mages.

The woman glanced at her. "You're not with the military. You should find shelter, there may be more out there."

Ilea ignored her and found another guard. "Do you know why demons showed up?"

"I don't know. The walls should make it impossible for them to get in. I suspect someone smuggled them in here," the man said as he walked past her. "You should sign up with the city if you want to help."

Ilea nodded and spread her wings, flying off to find more fires, but other than one far in the distance, all the others had already been extinguished.

They're not letting craftspeople leave, explosions are going off, and now there are demons in the street. Fucking hell.

TEN

Crash

When Ilea stirred in her bed the next morning, her eyes snapped open and she looked through her Sphere through the rest of the inn they now called home. She couldn't see Trian at his desk but calmed when she saw him in his bed. Kyrian was sitting on the floor of the same room, metal bits and pieces floating around him in slow circular patterns. He had taken the last watch.

Ilea sat up and rubbed her face, then stretched. She summoned her new armor and noticed the smell of blood.

Demons, she thought, walking over to the window before she opened it to get some 'fresh' air into the stuffy room.

"Morning," she said to Kyrian. "Good for sleep?"

Kyrian stretched and grunted. "Yeah. Could you get me something to eat if you're going downstairs?"

Ilea summoned one of Keyla's meals and set it down at the table.

"That's way too expensive," he murmured.

"You know why we're here. I don't think the cost of food is high on our list of issues. If you're bothered by it, I can get you something cheaper from downstairs, if they have any food left over from last night."

He considered for a moment. "Is it really fine for you? I don't want to feel like I'm taking advantage."

Ilea smiled. "You asking that is even more reason why it's fine. Don't worry, I have plenty of food stored away, and Keyla's alive as well. She's supposedly somewhere here in Virilya." She raised her brows. "Maybe we should've found her and gotten her out too."

"With her abilities, she'll have found a nice place to work, I'm sure."

"I really hope so. Maybe we can ask around," Ilea said, then left the room to fill up tubs for a bath.

It had become part of her morning routine, and she more or less forced her two companions to clean up too. Kyrian had enjoyed living in the wilderness, though she didn't know how often he had taken baths in various lakes and rivers. He didn't complain. Trian, on the other hand, had always been well-groomed and clean, at least since she had known him.

With everything that had happened, Ilea wasn't surprised that he had difficulties taking care of himself at the moment. She was glad she and Kyrian were here to help him out where they could, besides making sure he wouldn't immediately rush off to his death in his quest for revenge.

She scrubbed herself clean and used the same water to get rid of the blood on her leather armor. There wasn't too much. Then she silently helped Trian and offered him a meal as well.

"I don't feel like eating," he murmured.

She leaned against the wall next to the table. "I know. You should eat anyway. I'll wait."

He just sat there.

"Or I can spoon-feed you and make bird noises. Want me to make bird noises? I haven't tried before."

Trian glared at her and chuckled. "You're the most annoying shit I've ever met." He started eating.

"Doubtful. More information brokers today?"

"We still have quite a few on the list," Kyrian said.

Trian sighed. His eating slowed, eyes looking haunted once more.

"We could also take a break," Ilea suggested. "Find out what the demon stuff last night was all about. Maybe we can help out a little, kill a few of them. Might do you good, Trian."

"Maybe. But the risk of someone recognizing me is real, especially if I throw my magic around. No. We stick to the plan and we contact Claire again if we don't know how to proceed."

Good choice.

"We stick to the plan then."

* * *

Bells tolled as the group left the inn, finding soldiers in Imperial armor decorated in gray and red patrolling the streets of the capital. Most of them looked tense. Clenched jaws and hard eyes. Ilea suggested they stick to the alleyways and side streets after the first few suspicious glances.

Avoiding the guards and soldiers while searching for the various locations of the information brokers wasn't easy, but with her Sphere and their high stats, they could make their way through the city without further issues.

There was talk of demons on the lips of most passersby, and smoke still rose from a few sections of the city. Occasionally they saw entire groups of soldiers running to and fro.

They had been lucky with Balduur and his group. After the attacks, it had apparently become even more difficult for ordinary folk to leave and enter the capital. By now, it was clear that the attacks hadn't come from a central place, nor had the walls been breached by the monsters.

Ilea wondered who had set the demons loose and why. Had there been new summonings, or had demons been smuggled inside? Given how easy it had been to get Balduur out, she could only assume that others in their level range or with specialized skills could easily get things in.

There were hundreds of guards and soldiers on the streets and manning the walls, but Virilya was absolutely massive. The walls were extensive and high, and the streets provided thousands of hiding spots and ways to avoid security. Hell, even the sewer system was large enough to walk through.

She wondered how anyone could hope to find invaders or assassins in this maze. She just had to trust that the many contacts provided by Dagon would eventually lead them to Eve.

* * *

The suns were already high above the horizon when the group was let through onto a large roof terrace strewn with crates from which plants and herbs were growing. Tables and chairs had been set up between the crates, and a bar stood in one corner. A few patrons were present in the afternoon light and a band lounged on a small stage, glancing at the newcomers before returning to their conversation.

Using the description provided, they found Dagon's contact. A blonde woman wearing a red hat, smoking some kind of handmade cigarette and drinking a leaf tea with a blueish hue. She went by the name of Kariah.

Introductions were quick, the parties labeling themselves merely as buyers and sellers. Ilea and her companions were wearing their new armor to cover their features. Trian did the talking.

"We're looking for a rogue above level two hundred, blonde hair when we last saw her. She's hard to track and even harder to see. She should've been in the capital these past months."

Kariah raised her brows and took a long drag on her cigarette before stubbing it out. "That is terribly unspecific. Any particular weapons, gear, clothes, or skills?"

"Two daggers, light gear, possibly a mask. Illusion and mind magic."

Kariah slowly opened a little box on the table and took out another fancy cigarette, lighting it with a plain-looking flint lighter. Taking a puff, she exhaled toward the group before she spoke. "Anything else? Don't waste my time."

Ilea could see Trian considering. He glanced her way. She nodded.

"Mind magic through humming. Her daggers are cursed," Trian said.

Kariah smiled. "That's better. I know of three who get reasonably close to that description, but my information on their skills is limited. I'm reasonably confident that one of them has not been in the capital for a while. Of the two others, I know for sure that one has been here. She even paid me a visit. I want five gold pieces before I give you further information."

She was here? Ilea thought as Trian stacked five gold coins on the table before he invited the woman to take them. The coins vanished somewhere below the table, and Kariah nodded approvingly.

"She was wearing plain leather armor, cheap and worn. Short red hair. I felt a strange pressure while she was here, around two weeks ago. Mind magic, and subtle too. Not often you meet an expert like that. She has certainly changed since the first time I met her. And so have her questions." Kariah puffed on her cigarette. "Questions that I will not share with you for any price."

Ilea used her Hunter's Sight to try and detect anything in their surroundings. If Kariah was telling the truth, Eve had been here two weeks ago. Much too long for any reasonable trace to still be here, especially with how hard Eve was to detect already, but she would try anyway.

"Do you know where she is now?" Trian asked.

"Another five gold. I might have an idea."

Trian summoned five gold coins and placed them on the table. "Go on."

Kariah made the coins vanish and adjusted her hat, glancing at the band as they started tuning their instruments. She turned back to Trian.

"I've heard a woman has died. A dangerous woman with a rather unpleasant hobby, though, I suppose, in many ways not too different from the one whom you seek. Stab wounds from a dagger, cursed, veins of black running through the corpse. I do not know the name of this woman, but I know where she resided. The entire estate burnt down last week, and with it, the secrets held within. A few voices in the know have talked and were quickly silenced, but not before this news reached me – and doubtlessly some others. Do you have a map?"

Trian summoned one onto the table. Kariah gave him a long glance, though nothing in her demeanor suggested she knew who he was.

"Here," she said, tapping the butt of her cigarette onto the paper. "But a word of advice. And this one is free. You should not get involved in this kind of business. Death comes to those who seek this path."

Trian marked the map and made it vanish.

They left without another word. Ilea watched Kariah smoke and eye them as they left before she turned her attention back to the musicians.

* * *

It took some time to avoid all the guards and soldiers, but the group eventually arrived before a burnt plot of land in the middle of the city. Where previously there must've been luscious gardens, only ash now remained. The fire had been controlled, burning only to the very edges of the estate. What remained of the house was burnt out as well, the rest collapsed and destroyed.

Ilea connected with the remaining ash out of habit as the three of them sneaked into the ruin. Bells tolled once again in the distance, and light rain was still falling.

They searched the burnt estate and the house itself. Ilea was sure people had been burnt inside. The ash felt different. Little remained beyond a husk of ruined timber and stone. The underground cave they found didn't help them much either, as most of it had collapsed.

"We should check the surroundings," Kyrian said. "They burned everything inside. Perhaps there are clues where the fire didn't reach."

Ilea agreed. Walking back, the three of them checked the streets and houses surrounding the estate.

On the last side street, Trian's head suddenly shot up and he walked across the road. The others followed and watched him stop and touch a wall.

"What've you found?" Ilea asked, checking the surroundings as well. She couldn't find anything abnormal.

"Blood. It's a week old, at least. I'm not the best at blood tracking but this feels… familiar."

She was injured then? What were you seeking here, Eve?

Ilea looked back at the fire-ravaged plot of land. A dangerous woman had died here. Ilea knew why Eve had come.

She swallowed hard. "Can you track it?"

* * *

Trian soon found the next spot where blood had fallen. And then the next.

Ilea couldn't detect what Trian saw with the blood magic of his vampyr Class – not at first, at least. She could soon see the faint remains of a different texture where Trian could sense the blood, but it wasn't enough for her to find another spot easily.

The trail led them to another district nearby, where it suddenly stopped. Completely. They searched the various streets and houses nearby but found no more blood.

"This does feel like her, doesn't it," Ilea murmured. It reminded her of the early bouts she'd had with Eve, the way they'd both adjusted and learned to hide and detect.

"Her hideout is somewhere here," she said, walking up to the wall of a house and touching it carefully. She tapped it with her fist and raised her brows. Something felt off. What she saw with her Sphere didn't feel quite right when she focused on it.

"It's in here," she said, stepping away from the wall. Trian looked around and charged a spell, his electricity flowing into the wall and spreading over it like a disturbed nest of ants. The magic revealed a simple wooden door.

Ilea rushed toward the entrance, a sinking feeling in her stomach as she pushed into the small room. Once inside, she could see that the enchantments that had concealed the place were broken. The den was only a single room, with a desk stacked with papers on one side and a bed in the far corner.

The smell of rot and blood filled her nose as she blinked to the bed and flung away the cloth placed on the body. She could feel her lips quiver and knelt down, touching Eve's hands, which were gently placed onto her stomach, covering the grave wounds inflicted on her.

Ilea used her healing, but her mana just flowed uselessly through her own body.

She was dead.

Ilea could feel her hands starting to shake as her breathing came in fits and bursts, barely filling her lungs. Her vision started to blur, magic surging through her body in a rush.

"We c… came to look for you," she said, her voice cracking slightly. "We came because Trian… someone killed…"

Someone touched her shoulder. She didn't react, wiping at her face. She couldn't see with her eyes.

But her Sphere was there.

Her Sphere was there, and so was her friend. So was Eve. Her face. Her hands.

"I'm sorry," Kyrian said.

Ilea sobbed, grinding her teeth before she took in a sharp breath and staggered to her feet. Kyrian caught her as her legs wobbled. She pushed away and met his eyes.

"She's dead."

It was all she could manage to say.

"I'm sorry," he said again.

"There… there has to be some kind… is there magic? Can we bring her somewhere? To get her back?"

Trian had a vacant look in his eyes, and Kyrian shook his head.

"Why?" Ilea asked. "Why didn't we know? If we'd known, I could have healed her. I—"

She turned, feeling her shoulders slacken as she looked at Eve's still body.

Wasn't Eve supposed to help them find whoever had attacked Trian's family? Wasn't she supposed to begrudgingly agree with a few insults and a rough laugh? Wasn't she supposed to get angry that they'd ignored her letter and come to look for her anyway?

Wasn't she supposed to be alive?

Ilea felt empty.

Weren't we supposed to be a team?

"I don't think the wounds killed her," Trian said.

Ilea saw him raise an empty bottle. He sniffed it.

"Health potion. She came here to recover, but someone found her," he said. "Likely she was too badly injured to fight or escape."

"There are marks on the wall that suggest she fought back. But her daggers are gone," Kyrian said.

Escape, Ilea thought, her mind racing.

"What if it's an illusion? What if she somehow—"

"She's dead," Trian said. "I'm sorry, Ilea, but this is her. We know what her magic can do. This isn't it. She went to kill someone and succeeded, and then..."

Ilea shook her head, then she laughed. A hollow sound.

Too injured to fight or escape?

She could've healed those wounds in mere minutes. They could've fought together. Eve didn't have to have died.

But she had.

Ilea stood there as Trian got up and started searching the small hideout. Ilea started to hear a ringing in her left ear that soon spread to her right one as well.

She wasn't angry. She wasn't frustrated. She just felt a tight knot in her stomach. She didn't want to be here, didn't want to see her friend like this.

More than anything, she felt helpless. They were too late.

There was nothing they could do.

There was no longer a way to stop whoever had done this. There was no longer a way to convince Eve to join them, to fight demons, to go on missions together.

"More enchantments," Trian said.

She glanced toward him and saw a small section of the wall open up to his lightning. A hidden storage alcove. There were letters and documents inside, but Ilea soon turned back to Eve, kneeling down again next to the simple bed in her hideout.

A hideout. What were you doing? We were supposed to get stronger together, weren't we?

She could feel tears rolling down her cheeks.

Why did you leave?

Kyrian quietly joined her at her side and held her hand.

They were quiet for some time.

"Short red hair," Kyrian said. "She really did change it."

"These are letters and documents from high nobles of Virilya," Trian said, looking through the files in the cache. "Whatever she was doing, it was as high stakes as it gets. This is all evidence of corruption, murder, treason…"

"Ripping it all out, root and stem," Ilea murmured, thinking back on one of her conversations with Eve.

This is what you meant, isn't it? This is what you've been doing. Why join the Hand? Just to get the badge? To lay low? To hide? To get stronger? Did you ever plan to stay with us? Or was this always how it would've ended?

She breathed in deeply and wiped away her tears. She saw Kyrian do the same.

"Why did they leave her?" Kyrian said after a while. "Are those really her documents? They burned down the estate where her supposed target had been killed."

"We'll find out when we check everything," Trian said. He paused. "Her eyes were closed, her hands joined, and she was covered as well. Perhaps as a sign of respect. Who knows."

"Either way, we shouldn't leave her like this," Ilea said.

"No," Kyrian said, standing up. "We should burn her."

"Yes. But not here. Not in this city," Ilea said.

* * *

They were quiet as they snuck out of Virilya, flying eastward. Ilea carried Eve in her arms, gently landing in a meadow when they were far enough away from the capital.

It was dark, so Trian lit a torch that he summoned as soon as they had landed. Kyrian cut down two nearby trees, moving the pieces of wood into a pile and creating a pyre for their lost team member.

Ilea shivered. The body in her arms felt heavy.

She breathed in, feeling the cold air in her lungs before she stepped toward the pyre and gently set down her friend.

A spark from Trian struck the wood and started a blaze.

Ilea waited and watched the flickering flames dance through the wood. The fire soon took hold, crackling and consuming the wood as the other two stood by. She stepped close, ignoring the fires licking at her arms as she touched Eve's hand one last time. A last moment together, and soon it passed. She stepped back out and joined Trian and Kyrian.

It hurt now, she found. It hurt in her stomach. It hurt because someone had killed her friend. And it hurt because Eve hadn't trusted her enough to ask for help.

Lightning crackled and lashed out toward the sky, soon fading into nothing. Trian unleashed three strikes as Ilea sent the ash from the pyre upward and out into the winds and forests of the Plains.

* * *

Ilea felt numb when they returned to The Crouching Bear. The food she ate that night didn't taste like anything.

"This sucks..." she said to nobody in particular, hitting the dirty wooden wall behind her with the back of her head. She sighed and refocused on the letter in her hands. One of many they'd recovered from Eve's hideout.

Ilea found it difficult to concentrate, but she didn't want to try and sleep either. The evidence they'd found was real, all the notes written by Eve. Her handwriting, her vocabulary. And yet, everything they'd found painted a picture of a woman that Ilea hadn't known. Not really.

Eve, not just a teammate she'd trained and fought with, no... an assassin, a huntress, a murderer. Personal notes about her exploits, successes, and suspicions. Everyone was a suspect, everyone a potential target. Ilea remembered how Eve had made comments about Trian's nobility. She was sure now that Eve would've tried to kill him if he'd been from one of the other Houses. Some of them came up more than a few times.

And Eve had connected all of it to some shady organization called the Golden Lily. But her reasoning and evidence didn't really point anywhere. At least based on what she'd written down and what they'd found. A name overheard, a name found in a few letters. To Ilea, they just looked like other targets.

The next monster to defeat.

But these were people. Humans with their own lives. Humans who chose to do horrible things.

Ilea felt sick looking through these letters, the notes that Eve had taken. There was no mention of her team. No mention of Ilea. No mention of the Hand.

Just the next target.

Ilea set the letter down. She felt tired but didn't want to sleep. She felt filthy but didn't want to bathe.

"Maybe we should take a break," Trian said.

She looked over to where he was sitting. It was the first time since they'd found him at his family's estate that he looked truly himself, truly present.

"A drink, maybe," he said when the other two didn't speak.

Ilea nodded. "Yeah. I could use that." She got up while Trian collected all the documents and put them back into his ring, then followed him out and down into the inn's common room.

No fire burned in the hearth tonight, nor were there any musicians. Two hooded patrons sat at a table in one of the corners and spoke in quiet voices. Two oil lamps provided a bit of warm light to the large room. None of the other lamps were burning. To one side, the thin man still sat on his chair reading. It was late now.

"Nightshift?" Ilea asked him when he glanced her way.

"Always," he answered, glancing at the hooded Trian and Kyrian. He closed his book and grunted, then stood up and grabbed a few cups. "A drink?"

"A drink."

"Something strong?"

"Something strong," Ilea confirmed.

He grabbed a bottle from a shelf and pulled the cork out, poured three drinks, looked at their faces, then at the bottle, then set it down alongside the cups. He gave them another glance before he sat back on his chair and opened his book once more.

"Thanks," Ilea said, grabbing everything before they went to the far corner, opposite the other patrons. Trian lit a nearby oil lamp before he sat down.

Ilea looked at the liquid in her cup. It was a murky color, difficult to see in the dim light. It smelled of alcohol and not much else.

She breathed in and looked at her companions. "Glad you two are here."

Trian smiled, though it didn't reach his eyes. "I'd be dead already if not for you two."

"We're a team," Kyrian said.

Ilea closed her eyes.

We are, aren't we?

It had meant something to her. What they'd experienced in that village. Her conversations with Kyrian. Being stranded in the demon realm with Trian. Seeing Claire with her mother.

It had meant something to her when they'd sat in Ravenhall after they'd retaken the city with the Shadow's Hand. When they'd shared their next steps. It had felt hopeful.

"We're a team," she said, and she breathed in deep, then breathed out. "And we'll do this together. I'll have your backs whenever you need me."

"I will too," Kyrian said. His voice was firm, his eyes steady. Ilea found comfort in his simple stoicism.

Trian looked at his drink. "If we somehow survive this, the same goes for me." He paused, then raised his cup. "Today we lost one of ours. And we drink to her."

"Even though you never liked her," Ilea said.

"She trained with us, fought with us, and maybe I learned one or two things from her as well," he said, giving a crooked smile. This time, his eyes had regained a small measure of their usual light and intensity.

Ilea wanted to say something but she didn't know what. Everything she could come up with didn't feel genuine. Eve's death felt meaningless. Unnecessary.

If she was here, I'd have a lot to say to her.

But she wasn't.

Ilea looked at Trian instead and raised her cup. "To your family and your parents. I didn't know them, but they raised you well. May they find rest."

He faltered slightly, then nodded.

"To those we have lost," Kyrian added, raising his own cup.

Ilea touched the other cups and downed her drink. It tasted awful and burned her throat. She poured another and downed that one too. Her abilities would prevent her from getting too drunk, and while she could heal all the after-effects anyway, she didn't plan to do that tonight.

They sat there for a while, all three lost in their own thoughts. Ilea felt awful, but she was glad that the others were there. She had discovered a world full of possibilities. Full of magic. Still, she supposed that this was part of it too.

She could feel her lips tremble, tears coming to her eyes. She wiped them away and poured herself another drink.

"You don't look so good," Trian said drily.

She smiled. "Perceptive. I've thought the same about you recently."

"Yeah, no, I feel awful."

"We should all get a bath, then sleep," Kyrian said. "I'll take the first shift."

"You're the one giving advice now?" Ilea asked.

Kyrian glanced at her before he looked down at the table and smiled. "S… seems that way, doesn't it?"

ELEVEN

Beasts and Beasts

"There are many names in the documents," Trian said. "The question is if they have anything relevant to our cases, let alone how hard it will be to get information out of them if they do."

Ilea had found at least *some* sleep. She remembered waking up a few times.

The sky over Virilya had cleared now, though the suns were still low and yet to travel above the high-reaching walls as the city woke to another morning.

The three Shadows had decided to get some fresh air and were now sitting on top of a cathedral roof, looking over the vast capital.

"Other than the Golden Lily, there are other targets and people she seemed to be looking for," Trian continued. "One rogue who used the dark element, apparently. Eve didn't seem to have a lot on him, but she did know a lot about his fighting style and magic. A few mentions of a woman called Helena. Another man she planned to find was Edwin Redleaf. He was— do you know him?" Trian asked, interrupting himself as Ilea drew a sharp breath.

"I've met him on my travels, yes," she said, deciding to be careful. "Go on."

"Eve found rumors that he'd returned to the capital. And he's been busy. Killing dozens of more or less influential nobles. Eve wrote that several investigators and hunters from the government were looking for him, as well as… other parties."

He's killing nobles?

"Why was Eve looking for him? From all the rest we found, I thought she was here to do pretty much the same thing as Edwin."

"Perhaps because she assumed the man knew something about her targets or about this Golden Lily. And perhaps, having a similar goal, she assumed he would cooperate with her."

"This could extend to us, no?" Kyrian asked.

"How well do you know him?" Trian asked.

"He will at least listen to what we have to say. But I'm not sure if he'd help us," Ilea said.

"Still seems like the best lead we have right now, to get more information. If he's hunting down nobility, he should know a thing or two. You don't think he was involved with my family, do you?"

Ilea thought about it for a moment. "According to what I learned from Dagon, he fled his home and kidnapped his sister. But that's only what the official story says. He left to get his sister out. And to get himself out. If he's here killing nobility, it has to do with his past, I think, and with his House. If your family didn't have business with him or his House, I don't really see the connection."

Trian nodded. "Yeah. Just wanted to ask. Eve's documents suggest he doesn't have the connections or resources to launch such a large-scale operation. But you never know."

"So how do we find him?"

"There are recent murders linked to him. We could investigate the locations, but I don't think we'd get further than whoever else is looking for him. However, there's a bounty on his head. And we're a group of high-level adventurers. It won't raise too many eyebrows if we simply go and ask for information."

"More brokers?" Kyrian asked.

Trian shrugged. "We have the contacts. Let's use them."

* * *

This time around, they were far faster in finding an information broker in the know. It seemed quite a few people were interested in the Redleaf situation and watching it, wondering who Edwin's next target would be. They heard he didn't work alone either, but Ilea already knew that.

They learned the most recent attack was on a Redleaf estate to the northeast of Virilya, but the Redleafs had delayed Imperial investigators. The broker assumed there was incriminating evidence in the estate that the Redleafs didn't want to be uncovered quite yet.

Ilea and her companions didn't have the same restrictions and soon snuck out of the city to continue their search.

It was a sunny afternoon as they sped over the plains and small forests, the wild lands of Lys. The group reached their destination after nearly an hour, all of them landing at Trian's signal, their boots digging into the muddy meadow a couple of hundred meters before a massive estate.

The house looked ancient. Built of old money and able to stand the test of time even out here in the countryside. It was a sprawling affair with narrow towers rising up toward the sky like gnarled fingers. It was expensively ugly. Well taken care of, but there was something about it that made Ilea apprehensive.

She checked her Sphere. "Traps in the grass. Steel spikes and enchantments to power them."

"To keep monsters away," Kyrian said before he walked up to one of the traps. "Actually, they're too small for that. They seem more targeted against humans. They didn't want anybody intruding."

"Or escaping," Trian said with conviction as he walked a little closer. "Ilea, your Sphere and teleport are best suited for this. Think you can investigate without alerting anyone?"

"I can try," Ilea said. "Can't guarantee there won't be a fight though."

"Come back here if you're spotted. We might be able to talk or retreat. We'll move in if you're not back in ten minutes."

Ilea gave him a nod and vanished, rushing over the terrain and blinking from cover to cover as she checked for any signs of life. But other than the insects under her boots and the birds flying by, she couldn't find anything in the estate's gardens. She considered the birds being part of someone's personal magical entourage a possibility, but she didn't meet with resistance.

Ten seconds later, she reached the main building. It had a rough stone wall with windows starting two meters further up. Metal bars prevented people from getting either in or out. Combined with the traps, the place seemed more like a prison.

Using her Sphere, Ilea saw people inside. Butlers and maids, based on their clothing and the tasks they were performing. Cleaning and preparing food. She couldn't see anybody else.

Blinking up, she checked part of the first floor. Here she found some people asleep and still others cleaning. Blinking into an empty room, Ilea continued to look around. Given the size of the estate, it would take some time to look through it all.

* * *

There were many targets she could've grabbed and interrogated, but Ilea stopped when she saw two people in her Sphere who weren't dressed in the same servants' garb as everybody else.

The first was a rather plain-looking man who was strapped to a bed with metal chains. He wore damaged leather armor, with dozens of gashes visible on his body. Enough, Ilea thought, to kill any normal man. She even saw buckets placed below the bed to collect the dripping blood.

Nearby sat a woman dressed in a set of armored robes. Her hair was up in a bun with several needle-like hairpins sticking out of it. Her arms were bandaged. Ilea heard them engaged in a muffled conversation. The woman said something about rest and patience. Ilea got down on the floor and pressed her ear against it.

"Don't lecture... me," the man said.

Ilea could tell how tense the woman was, her back straight as a rod and her mouth pulled down in a frown. What she saw put Ilea on edge too. Something in her gut told her these were no ordinary adventurers. She could *feel* the heavy pressure of magic in the air.

Having fought with so many Shadows, she could now tell how different trained killers were in their movements and behavior. These two were veterans. Dangerous ones. They weren't Shadows either.

I shouldn't be here, not alone, Ilea thought, trying to stay silent as she waited and listened. If the two were even close to her level, or worse, trained to deal with someone like her, things would get dangerous quite quickly.

She heard the man's groans more clearly now. The wounds must've been painful, maybe cursed or something else. Though, while he sometimes winced, his facial expression suggested annoyance more than pain. Ilea could see some of the wounds rip open again and again after they had started to heal a little bit.

High regeneration? Or is he using some kind of skill?

"They won't heal if you move that much," said the woman, whose clear voice Ilea heard through the floor.

"He has... lear... ned a thing or two," the man said and laughed, wincing again when more of the wounds opened up from the motion. "A true blood," he said, sounding disgusted. "I will be ready again by tomorrow. Any more reports, Tiana?"

"They should still be around Fort Keenshill. The rogue is killing all the hunters and trackers who get too close. We should stop wasting resources and get back to it personally as soon as you're ready."

The man groaned. "That's all they're good for. Send everyone we can find, keep them busy."

The woman tensed further, her fists clenching. Ilea thought she saw a few of the hairpins move.

"I'd rather send for more healers. Your arrogance has caused this delay, Kyle," Tiana said, and Ilea watched as his hand flicked her way, a small projectile flashing toward the woman, who eyed it casually. The projectile was stopped right before her face by a thin material or magic of some kind. Ilea couldn't tell what it was.

"Stop it. Focus on healing your wounds," Tiana said before she looked up, right at Ilea. Her face tilted a little to the side as Ilea blinked into another room, keeping the two in her Sphere's radius.

She saw the man glance at Tiana, then up to where Ilea had been. Neither teleported or moved, however.

Did she sense me?

Ilea had heard enough for now, and she could hear her heart beating in her chest. Facing monsters was one thing, but those two just felt unsettling.

Probably wouldn't feel the same way if I wasn't skulking in the shadows. A head-on fight is far better than this.

Edwin had attacked this place, and it seemed the two of them would likely go after him and his group tomorrow.

Hurrying back to the others, she explained what she'd seen and learned.

"It could be misdirection if she noticed you sooner than it seemed," Trian said. "But I don't see the point in that. It was lucky you learned anything at all from their conversation."

"Maybe she saw you from the start," Kyrian said, "and maybe she thought if someone else is hunting this Edwin, talking of his location would get you to leave. Ideal with them both in an injured state."

Ilea raised her brows. "Shit. You might be right."

"Or it's a coincidence. Did it feel like they were acting to you?" Trian asked.

Ilea stopped to think. "She seemed tense and focused only on this Kyle. I don't know."

"Either way, we have a location to check out. Fort Keenshill you said? Let's hope the woman didn't notice you and we're not walking headfirst into a trap. And if we don't find anything, we can always return here and ask nicely."

* * *

Flying north to the only marked settlement in the vicinity on Trian's map, they soon came upon a small walled-off village. The locals seemed rather keen on directing the visiting adventurers far away from themselves as they explained exactly where Fort Keenshill was. An old ruin overtaken by monsters several decades past with no owner, nor any other interested party, to retake it.

Another flight later, Ilea could see the ruined fort in the distance, surrounded by tall trees. She could tell it had once been an impressive structure, standing defiant in the wilderness, yet nature had reclaimed it now, roots breaking through walls and ivy growing into the broken windows. She couldn't hear or see any monsters, but Ilea felt tense.

They landed near the outer stone wall, most of it mere rubble at this point. Ilea activated her Hunter's Sight and Sphere to check for any tracks or signs of human life.

"There are tracks. Look like a wolf's but bigger and bipedal. Something similar to the blood beasts we fought maybe?"

The comparison made her think of their missions for a split second. She took a deep breath and refocused.

She's gone.

"Let's try not to alert anything," Trian said.

They walked along the broken wall, the trees around them high and thick, seemingly much older than the fort itself.

"There's a corpse," Ilea said sharply. The group stopped and prepared for a fight as she walked closer to the half-eaten, torn-apart body.

"Looks like a monster got him," Kyrian suggested as Ilea checked the corpse.

"His heart is missing. It's like someone ripped out a sphere from inside his chest. Any monsters we know that can do that?"

Neither of her companions spoke up.

"A monster likely got to him, but I'm not sure if that was before or after he died. But why rip out the heart with a targeted spell and then rip into him with claws and teeth?" She looked up. "There are tracks over there. Human ones."

"I've never heard of something that can rip out hearts like that," Kyrian said absentmindedly, touching his own chest.

The suns were lower now on the horizon as the group followed the tracks. After a while, they stopped, but Ilea's Hunter's Sight showed her a path where the tracks had been removed. The ground looked ever so slightly more disturbed, enough for her skill to pick it up.

'ding' Hunter's Sight reaches 2nd lvl 8

Willing the notification away, Ilea continued following the path. It led them a little away from the fort and toward a fenced-off part of the estate. A small gamekeeper's hut could be seen behind a couple of trees. It had a rotten straw thatched roof and wooden walls with misshapen windows cut into them. She saw movement within.

"Someone's in there," Ilea whispered. Next, she felt a strange sensation in her chest. Moving to the right instinctively, a sudden surge of magic erupted inside her arm.

She gritted her teeth at the dull pain and started healing immediately, checking the wound and finding that a part of her bone and flesh had simply vanished.

"We're under attack! Keep moving, they can rip out parts of your body," Ilea said to the others as she vanished, reappearing ten meters ahead, her skills running overtime.

Hunter Recovery worked on regrowing the missing parts of bone and flesh as Ilea decided to move closer to the hut. Another weird feeling spread down her back right before she blinked away. A split second later, Ilea heard the suction of air from where she had just been standing.

Close but not quite, she thought, scanning her surroundings.

As Ilea's teammates jumped over the fence to follow her toward the hut, a woman appeared a couple of meters to the left of the wooden structure. She had light leather armor, gray hair, and purple eyes.

[Mage – lvl 231]

"You're not attacking on sight?" she asked in a tired voice. "High-level hunters but none of you is a rogue or tracker." She paused. "Why is the Hand here? If you've been paid to hunt me down, maybe we can talk," she added as Trian and Kyrian joined Ilea at her side.

"We're here for Edwin. I know him," Ilea said.

"We're not here to hunt you," Trian said, trying to defuse the situation.

By now, Ilea's arm was healed, and she flexed her fingers as she looked at the woman.

"Nor are we here on a paid job. We're looking for information. Perhaps we can come to an arrangement," Trian added.

"I'm not looking to trade information, and I can't trust—"

The woman was interrupted by the door to the hut opening, and Ilea breathed in sharply as she saw a familiar figure emerge.

"Felicia," she said, locking eyes with her. She could see the bags under her eyes, and it looked like she'd lost weight. "Long time no see."

Felicia gasped. "Ilea, I..." She gulped, then looked between the purple-eyed woman and Ilea. "I... Maria, she's... a friend."

"You don't seem so sure about that," Maria said, her eyes still focused on the group.

"She's the battle-healer who helped us through the Taleen dungeon," Felicia said.

Maria changed her stance, the look in her eyes still suggesting suspicion but no longer aggression.

"Past level two hundred already," Felicia breathed in surprise.

"You said I should explore and fight all the things that I could. I did."

Felicia smiled. "And you got stronger, as you said you would."

She looks conflicted...

Ilea got it now. With everything she'd learned from Dagon and with everything she'd experienced in the past weeks, she understood why Felicia had been conflicted about leaving her in the Taleen dungeon and why she now felt conflicted about Ilea finding them.

"I did, but I didn't just come to find you," Ilea said.

Felicia's yellow eyes evaluated Ilea before she glanced at Trian and Kyrian.

"Ilea, was it? You were a healer, weren't you? Can you still heal?" Maria asked.

"I can."

"Edwin is injured. Maybe you can speed things up."

"That works," Ilea said and made for the hut.

"Wait. Before we continue any further, you said you didn't come just to find us. Why are you here?"

Ilea glanced at Trian.

"We're looking for information," Trian said. "And we're looking to hunt some people, likely nobility. I understand your group is somewhat experienced with that kind of... work."

Maria looked at him. Her eyebrows rose before her grin widened.

"Oh, you poor boy." She shook her head. "Follow me inside."

Ilea walked over to Felicia. "It's good to see you alive. You don't look too good though."

Felicia smiled weakly. "You neither," she whispered, then followed Ilea inside.

The wooden hut reeked of blood and death. The small space was occupied by an old bed with a man lying on it. Edwin. His black eyes were flickering open and shut, and his dark hair was slick with sweat. His shoulder looked like it had been eaten from the inside out. Blood-red lines spread across his whole body like he'd been infected, and he convulsed from time to time.

Aliana was sleeping in a corner of the room. The brown-haired water mage looked a little thinner than Ilea remembered. Ilea returned her gaze to the man she'd wanted to fight again when she reached his level of power. The goal didn't seem quite so important anymore.

"Blood magic infection," Trian said. "Someone powerful did this."

Ilea tried using her healing but found her magic was countered by the infection – not completely, but progress was grindingly slow.

"It would take days to heal this, but we don't have that. Can you do something?" Ilea asked Kyrian, whose needles already floated above Edwin.

"It's not a curse, nor a poison. I could try, but I don't think it's a good idea."

Ilea nodded and touched Edwin's shoulder. Moving him would worsen his condition, which left her with only one idea.

"I'll destroy whatever's in there," Ilea said. "And then I'll heal him back. I did it recently with something similar."

Maria stepped close, but Felicia touched her arm.

"I trust her," Felicia said. "We should trust her."

They stared at each other for a long moment before Maria sighed, relented, then nodded at Ilea.

"Help me hold him down," Ilea said. When the others were in position, she pushed her reversed healing into Edwin's shoulder, destroying everything in its path as she observed both his health and his reaction.

Edwin coughed up blood while Ilea tried to localize her attack, watching the infection get removed along with the man's vitality. Stopping before she actually killed him, she started healing the area again. Both the infection and her healing worked to reclaim territory.

Contrary to the infection, however, her resources would regenerate. She could tell as much already via her healing.

"It's working, but it will take an hour or two," she said as she continued to destroy and heal Edwin's body. The blood magic had spread nearly all over him, and she couldn't weaken him too much as that seemed to worsen the infection's spread.

* * *

'ding' Azarinth Reversal reaches 2nd lvl 16

The healing had been arduous, the infection fighting back almost like a living organism. Ilea had had to exert a finer control over her abilities and expend a lot more mana than usual before finally snuffing it out.

Still, the experience had been worthwhile, and she'd learned some things about her healing magic despite the skill already being at its current maximum level.

"I'm done," she said.

Maria moved closer, then lightly slapped Edwin's face. She stopped when he started groaning and then coughing.

"What is—" he started before coughing again.

His eyes opened, and he looked around the room, locking eyes with Ilea for a long moment. Confusion turned to recognition before he started laughing. His amusement was interrupted by another bout of coughing.

"You surpassed me," he said weakly. "This quickly."

[Warrior – lvl 222]

You were dying literally seconds ago, she thought, wondering why – of all things – he was focused on her level first.

Felicia rushed to her brother and hugged him, and Maria gave Ilea a slight nod.

"I'll get some fresh air," Ilea said, stepping outside, where she found Kyrian sitting on the grass, meditating. He turned his head to look at her.

"Are you alright? Any history with them that we should know about?" he asked.

Ilea considered. Sure, there was some history. She smiled, thinking back to the Taleen dungeon. It had felt good to meet people willing to fight in a similar vein to her own. And she had learned a lot from the bouts with Felicia and the others. But she'd since met a lot of Shadows, fought by their side, and joined their Order.

Compared to her team, she didn't like Edwin all that much – and this

'Maria' seemed equally dickish. All of Edwin's fighting had been focused on his mission. It had felt like that had always stood in the way, and while Felicia and Aliana had gone along with it, the group had left Ilea behind in the end because of it.

Even now, it seemed they were still consumed by it. Edwin and Maria were hunting and murdering nobility in the capital of Lys. Ilea breathed deeply.

What are we getting ourselves into?

But what other choice did they have? They needed help. Eve was dead, and she knew Trian wouldn't drop this until he at least knew who was responsible for the attack on his family. And she wouldn't abandon him either.

She stopped next to her friend and smiled weakly. "Nothing major. Nothing that matters right now."

A few minutes later, the others stepped outside as well, Edwin being supported by Maria.

"So, the little battle-healer has managed to come this far… and with the Hand as—"

Maria interrupted him. "Shelve it for now. We need to move as fast as we can. Their trackers will know we're in the area."

"Would these 'trackers' be Kyle and Tiana?" Ilea asked. "He was still bleeding heavily, said that they would come for you tomorrow, but I suppose they could've been lying."

"How do you know that?"

"I listened to them talking. In the old Redleaf mansion. Now, in exchange for healing you, we require some information."

She would've healed him anyway, but after her conversations with Edwin back in the Taleen dungeon, she assumed that favor for favor was the way to go with him.

Maria whispered something in Edwin's ear. Edwin listened and nodded, then looked at Ilea for a long moment.

"Very well," he said. "I'll give you the information you need for saving my life. If we have it, that is. So, what do you want to know?"

"My name is Trian Alymie," Trian said, stepping forward. "My family has been murdered. I'd like to know by whom."

TWELVE

Tracks

Edwin nodded. "I see. I'm sorry for your loss. I heard of the attack. Would've assumed that they pinned that one on me. We've recovered a lot of paperwork since we arrived, and I believe your family has been mentioned in some of it. Feel free to look through it. Aliana has everything."

"She's still asleep, I'll go wake her," Felicia said, her face unreadable as she left.

"How can I be sure it wasn't you?" Trian asked.

Maria stepped a little closer to Edwin, keeping eye contact with Trian.

"I'm sorry for what happened to you," Edwin said. "As far as I can tell, the Alymies never came up in any connection to our own family. Did you see the bodies? Know anything about the attackers or how many there were?"

"A group, likely more than ten people. Different causes of death."

"It was always just me and Maria. I know you just have my word, but I'm sure you'll find more in the evidence we've recovered. We have no qualms with your House."

"That's not all," Ilea said. "A friend of ours was murdered too. She was investigating an organization called the Golden Lily. Maybe if we find them, we can figure out what happened."

Edwin looked at Ilea for a long moment. He glanced at Maria and then huffed. "From adventuring to the Hand, to looking for the Golden Lily."

"You know them?"

"Just one member. Our main target," he said and groaned as he straightened up. "Ilea, and Shadows. You seek information. You seek those who have orchestrated the fall of House Alymie. What will you do once you find out who is responsible?"

"Find them and kill them, and have our evidence brought to the Empress," Trian said.

Maria chuckled.

"Are you backed by anyone else? Or is it just the three of you?" Edwin asked. His tone didn't suggest he was mocking them. His gaze was focused.

"Just us," Trian admitted.

Maria sighed and crossed her arms. "Three lost Shadows. Hasn't your Order bled enough from your Elder's folly?"

"We've slaughtered thousands of demons," Ilea said, looking at Maria.

"Killing monsters is one thing, and I don't doubt your ability to do so. But high-level humans? Nobility hiding in their enchanted homes? Guarded by specialized mercenaries and military units? It's a different skill. Where you can bleed and track a monster, here you will have to be perfectly prepared. Timing is everything, and you will have mere seconds to strike. And to kill. Your abilities aren't suited for that. You haven't even found out who was responsible for such a massive and sloppy massacre."

"You know what happened?" Trian said.

"As Edwin has shared, we have documents that might help you. Other than that, we've heard quite a lot in the time we've been back in Virilya, and we can surmise what we don't know for sure."

"You are willing to fight and die for this?" Edwin asked.

"I am," Trian said.

"Good, because the chances are high that three Shadows won't be enough. Maybe you will succeed, but I would bet my money on at least one of you three dying. Your chances would look better with a few more people involved. People experienced in this kind of work."

"Why would you help us?"

"Because we both lack information, and while I'd like to say that our chances with our targets are better than yours, I can't state that with full confidence. And even then, I still nearly died from Kyle's wounds."

Maria balked at that. "You would consider working with them? They're inexperienced. They're *monster hunters*, Edwin."

"They are Shadows. More fights will be inevitable. With Ilea, we can heal, and with all three of them, we can risk more direct engagements."

"They are unknowns, and he is driven by emotion—"

"*I* am driven by emotion," Edwin said, his words a calm and simple statement. "We will work with them. If you don't like it, leave."

Maria ground her teeth, then sighed.

Ilea watched them, wondering if this was the right decision. But she couldn't argue with their experience. They needed help – both of their groups did, it seemed – but they would get involved in far more than they'd bargained for.

The next target. Will you stop, Edwin? Once you've killed him? Will she stop?

"What are the specific terms?" Ilea asked.

"We help find and kill your targets. And you do the same for us," Edwin said.

"Sounds fair, where's the catch?"

He grinned. "The catch is that you're looking at hunting down some second-rate impoverished House willing to murder an entire family and their staff to claw their way back to relevancy.

"My target is Arthur Redleaf. While he has neglected our businesses and has poured far too much wealth into his research, he remains well-connected and far wealthier than whoever was likely responsible for what happened to the Alymies. Our fight will likely be far more dangerous."

Ilea glanced at Trian. She found he looked determined.

Felicia joined the others with Aliana in tow, and the latter nodded at Ilea with a smile when she recognized her.

We're all desperate, it seems.

"If you two are willing to help," Trian said, "then I'd like to agree to this arrangement."

"Why do you want to kill him?" Ilea asked. "You never told me."

"And I won't. Arthur will die. He must. This is what I will offer. Nothing more, nothing less."

Ilea saw Felicia looking at the ground, and even Maria looked tense, her eyes focused on their group.

"He deserves it," Felicia said in a whisper. "Trust me, Ilea. On this, Edwin is right."

Ilea nodded. "Alright. I'm in too. Kyrian?"

"I will fight by your side," Kyrian said.

"Then it's settled," Edwin said.

"When did you say Kyle and Tiana would resume their hunt?" Maria asked. Her gaze had been drawn toward the trees behind Ilea's group.

"I don't think that's them," Ilea said. She turned around and found something in her Sphere near the fenced-off property. "I think we might've alerted whatever left those tracks."

"What tracks?" Maria asked before they all heard a growl coming from the trees.

"Looked like a big wolf, bipedal," Kyrian supplied as they all prepared for a fight.

Ilea's eyebrows shot up as she spotted a fast-moving furry creature going up and into the trees before it rushed back down – right at Trian.

Ilea stepped slightly to the side, intercepting the creature as all her skills were activated and a Veil of Ash formed around her. The impact sent her flying, but Trian managed to teleport away. The smell of pine needles and dirt filled Ilea's nose, her body rolling on the ground after smashing through several thin trees before her spinning world came to an abrupt stop.

Getting up quickly, she found lightning and metal in the air, the smell of singed hair joining the more natural scents around her. It really was a bipedal wolf, something like a werewolf, she thought as she rushed back toward the hut.

The monster was a little over two meters tall on its hind legs, lean and muscular. Its claws slashed through the air, creating a whistling sound with the sheer speed of the attacks before they were deflected by Edwin's twin swords. Despite his clear advantage of skill and range, he couldn't do anything but defend.

[Beastwolf of Krak Duun – lvl ???]

Three, which means this thing could be as strong as the demon whale that attacked Ravenhall but condensed into a much smaller, faster form.

She couldn't see Maria anymore, but all the other mages had got some distance from it, flying high in the trees and sending projectiles toward the monster.

Ilea raced toward the creature's back. Her fist landed, and a bit of mana left her as both Destruction and Wave of Ember rushed into the black fur of the beastwolf.

The monster's arm moved backward, making her blink away a couple of steps before she advanced again. Using her ash to distract the creature didn't seem like the best idea as it would obstruct the mages around her as well as Edwin. She had a feeling that it might not be much of a hindrance to the beastwolf either.

She hit with her fist again, but Edwin was sent flying backward at the same time, blood spurting out of his mouth from a powerful kick from the creature. A lightning bolt flashed toward its maw as it turned toward Ilea, crouching down slightly to dodge the attack before its claws shot toward her. They dug into her Veil, causing her to step backward to dodge as closely as possible, trying to get hits in between the flurry of claws.

Her eyes focused only on the enemy's movements as she took one step backward after another, magic attacks raining into the creature from behind, sometimes dodged and sometimes simply ignored as its bloodshot eyes focused on its prey.

Her fist hit the monster's chest right before one clawed paw nearly skewered her. Blinking left as the creature followed up its attack with a kick, she managed to get in one more hit before the beastwolf's elbow smashed into her chest. All the air in her lungs was ejected as she slid backward two meters. The beastwolf advanced, not giving her time to adjust, leaving her with no other option but to blink up and away.

The wolf turned and looked at her as her ashen wings spread behind her. Back to full health after a couple of seconds of healing, Ilea watched as the beast moved rapidly, jumping into the air and using the trees as stepping stones to get to her.

"Kyrian, get Edwin and the others up in the air. It's best if we get out of here!" Ilea shouted. Her friend nodded and flew off toward the hut as the beastwolf continued rushing toward Ilea, who lazily blinked backward time and time again, leading the beast on as lightning magic singed its fur.

After five blinks, the beast stopped as it clung to a tree, its claws digging into the wood, making it creak and splinter. The beastwolf looked up at the sun above, snarling at it. And then it howled.

You have heard a mighty beast's howl. You are paralyzed for two seconds.

'ding' Veteran reaches lvl 3

Two seconds was just enough for the monster to jump off its tree and slash at Ilea with one clawed paw before she was able to move again.

Ilea gritted her teeth as she sensed the deep gash via her healing magic. She spun in the air as she sent healing magic through her own body. Her ribs had been cracked by the hit, and Ilea considered herself lucky that the beast hadn't decided to grab her and rip off her head.

Wings spread again, she blinked upward as the beastwolf descended, crashing through several trees as Ilea flew up and out of the forest. Seeing all the others in the air as well, Edwin's group grabbing onto metal rods created by Kyrian, she continued toward them.

"You're bleeding," Trian said to Edwin as Ilea arrived. Edwin had indeed taken many heavy blows, blood seeping from a number of nasty gashes and claw cuts.

"You still can't fly?" Ilea asked as she tended to the man's injuries, looking over at the floating Felicia and Maria. Mages seemed to have a higher chance of getting a flying skill, it seemed.

"Sadly not. Maybe at two fifty, if I ever reach it," Edwin answered, looking down to the forest from where they heard more howling.

"How long were you paralyzed for?" Ilea asked, looking at Kyrian and Trian.

"Four seconds," Kyrian said, and Trian answered with seven. Nodding in return, she was glad the beast had focused on her. Otherwise someone might already be dead.

"Aren't we in the human plains, surrounded by cities and adventurers running around? How is a high-level beast like that just strolling around here?" Ilea asked.

"The wilderness is dangerous everywhere and for everybody. Something as dangerous as a beastwolf is rare in these parts, sure. But far from unheard of," Trian said. "Where should we go? I have the location of three more of my family's safe houses. One isn't too far off, but perhaps you have something better?"

"I'd say yours are the better bet," Edwin answered and left it at that.

"Alright then, follow me," Trian said and sped off.

Ilea looked back, though she was unable to make out where the beast-wolf was in the forest. Perhaps it would follow them, but if she remembered correctly, they usually had a territory and would only leave if no prey could be found.

"We should get higher," Felicia said as she looked back too, carried by eddies of magical rushing wind. The group followed the suggestion without comment as they rushed through the clouds above.

* * *

The new hideout was more spacious than the first one Trian had taken them to, comprising three rooms built into a small hill covered by a meadow and a single oak tree. A hidden enchanted hatch led them inside. Ilea guessed they were about an hour's flight away from Virilya.

They settled in, then both groups shared the documents they'd recovered so far. Edwin, Maria, and Trian quickly went over the various suspects simply based on economic interests. They came to the same conclusions as Orthan, Claire, and Trian had back in Ravenhall. It was definitely either House Carter or Birmingale, though they still lacked definitive proof.

"There's a lot more to get through," Trian said as he looked at the crates Aliana summoned from her storage ring.

"Then we'd better start," Felicia said, sitting down on one of the simple chairs in the makeshift study, dimly lit by oil lamps hanging from the stone walls.

"You said that Arthur is part of the Golden Lily," Ilea said after they'd worked for a while. Aliana was setting up cold cut platters in another room. "What do you know about them?"

Edwin set down the piece of paper he'd been reading and stood up and stretched.

"Not much, to be honest. Arthur mentioned them a few times, and I found a few letters likely corresponding with other members. From the little that I've learned, it sounded like a group of powerful individuals sharing economic interests, perhaps more, but compared to a few other cults and secret societies we've stumbled upon or eradicated, there never seemed to be a common goal or threat. However, it's true that the name itself is shrouded in a lot of mystery. They don't want to be known. You say your friend was looking for them?"

"Yeah. Among plenty of other targets, as you saw," she said, pointing to the stack of documents they'd recovered from Eve's hideout.

"Her methods were good," Maria said. "A lot of what you have here is of high quality. But I can tell she got overconfident. Always happens."

She continued reading, her facial expression not revealing anything else.

"What do you mean by that?" Kyrian asked. "That it always happens?"

Maria glanced at him. "Caution leads to success, success leads to experience and confidence. Either these kinds of people stop what they do, or they meet their match."

"What about you?"

Maria grinned. "Could happen to me too, but I'm not quite like this late friend of yours."

Ilea wondered what she meant, but she could tell the woman was done talking.

"Arthur is in hiding," Edwin said. "Or he's simply conducting his research in a secret location. But compared to any other possible sources, he's probably your best bet when it comes to finding out more about the Golden Lily."

"Nothing indicates that it was the Golden Lily, other than her looking for them," Maria said. "Your best bet is finding out who the dead girl was that your friend hunted and killed, then finding out who would be connected to her. If it was the Lily, though, any trace of her connection to them will be long scrubbed clean by now."

Chasing shadows, Ilea thought, leaning against the stone wall. She crossed her arms and sighed.

"What's this research that Arthur's conducting?" Trian asked. "You've mentioned it a few times already."

"He's trying to study and recreate the Taleen teleportation gates," Edwin said.

Trian arched an eyebrow. "Others have tried."

"Others have failed," Edwin retorted. "I agree that it is a lofty goal, but as far as goals go, I don't think it's impossible to imagine the ancient dwarven technology could be imitated. And if he succeeds, it wouldn't just propel House Redleaf to become the most powerful noble House in Lys."

"It would change everything," Trian said, tapping the table with his hand. "Has he made progress?"

"I don't know. And I don't care. It won't matter once he's dead."

"I think I've found something," Felicia said, turning the leatherbound book she had before her around and pointing at a few entries. "Payments made to the Haim mercenary group. The sums are suspicious for the listed protection service, and the dates would overlap."

Maria hissed. "How badly can you cover something up?"

"It took you an entire afternoon to get a copy of that book," Edwin said.

"That doesn't change things. Nothing should be documented in the first place for a job like that."

"I don't disagree. Do we have personnel lists?"

Maria stood up. "No. Not yet. I'll talk to a few of them too, they'll be happy to brag about something as big as that."

"You're going alone?" Ilea asked.

She watched as Maria's posture and facial expression changed in a single moment. She looked scared, vulnerable. She even had a slight limp.

But her level would be—

[Mage – lvl 122]

"You can fool identify," Ilea murmured.

Maria grinned, all the joy gone from her face a split second later.

"I'll be back in the morning."

Ilea watched her go, the others exchanging glances before the hatch to the hideout closed again.

"How common is that ability?" Ilea asked.

Edwin looked up. "Changing your perceived level? Rare, though I assume a lot of assassins and thieves have something similar at their disposal. Most of them can't fool anyone at their own level or far above, but Maria is good. Let's continue here while she's out. We'll want a few more targets for her when she gets back."

"She enjoys it, doesn't she?" Trian asked.

Edwin smiled.

Fooling people? Or killing them?

* * *

The rest of the day was consumed by reading through the mountains of documents. Eve's collection did get Edwin a few more targets, but by the time night fell, Trian had several pieces of evidence pointing at the same group.

House Birmingale.

With each piece of the puzzle that they found, the picture became clearer.

Edwin looked through the last set, a list of payments made to silence guards, sold to an information broker Edwin and his group had already talked to who wasn't on Dagon's list.

"Berserker, pyromancer, wood mage, poison rogue, and beastblood warrior, each leaving the city on the day of the attack. At least they split up, but it's impressive how careless they were," Edwin said, opening another book. "The classes match Ronan, Bale, Graham, Petra, and Wallace Birmingale. It would be too much of a coincidence for them to leave the city on the same day. Now we can investigate the details. A few servants will talk, given the House's obvious economic distress."

Trian leaned back and shook his head. Ilea walked over and touched his shoulder.

"They had debts, but to do something like that… Why didn't they find another way?" she asked.

"People often choose the easy and fast route rather than the difficult one, even if it hurts others," Felicia said.

They were quiet for a while.

"Debts," Trian murmured. "All because of some gold. They killed everyone."

"Is this enough to convince the Empress?" Ilea asked.

"Possibly," Edwin said. "Birmingale is a small House. Exiling them would be an easy choice if the evidence can't be ignored. Depending on their connections, it might be more difficult, and with tensions brewing with Baralia, Alyris might choose to keep them close and have them redeem themselves in battle. She's keener on stamping out corruption and infighting than other rulers, but there's always a line. The Alymies are gone, but the Birmingales can still prove useful."

"And what if we strike first?" Trian said.

"Not an easy operation, but with us working together, we can try. I don't have a personal stake in this, Trian Alymie, but your family was known to be honorable. I think it would be a shame if Ronan Birmingale and his House remained largely unscathed for their choices."

Trian looked at him.

"As for repercussions…" Edwin said, looking at Felicia, who closed the book before her.

"If the evidence is presented on the same night as our attack, any consequences for that strike would remain minimal. There may be one or two assassins, favors or connections from any survivors, but Alyris and the nobility of Lys wouldn't move against you. More issues will come up if you return to claim the titles granted to your late father, however."

Trian was quiet for some time before he spoke. "I can think about that in the future. If we survive."

* * *

Ilea yawned. She was glad that they were safe for now, but the hideout was starting to become both boring and depressing.

"Anyone up for a bout?" she asked, looking at the solemn group of people poring over dusty books and scraps of paper.

"We should focus on our work," Edwin said.

"We've been working through the night. Half of you haven't even slept. I need a break, and I think everyone else does too. We can just leave for a while, find a spot in the forest, and beat each other to a pulp like the gods intended."

"Why would the gods intend such a thing?" Aliana asked.

"We did get all of these magical abilities, didn't we? I didn't actually mean that literally, Aliana. I just want to spar a bit. I've grown a lot since we last fought back in the Taleen dungeon. Come on Edwin. You're interested, aren't you?"

He glanced up from the letter he was reading, then looked at her for a few seconds and sighed.

Ilea raised her brows. "Just a few hours," he said, a slight upcurve to his lips. "The air in here is getting stuffy."

Ilea blinked over to the other room where Trian was reading through another set of documents.

"How are you holding up?"

He looked at her, eyes bloodshot.

"We're going out for a break to punch each other. Would do you good to get some exercise in. You look dreadful."

"We don't have time for that," Trian said. "I've been reading the same half a page for the past fifteen minutes. Doesn't want to stay in my head."

Ilea smiled at him and waited.

He sighed and threw the parchment back on the table. "Alright, I'll join you in a minute."

* * *

The group left a little while later to find the nearby forest coated in a thin layer of mist as the morning suns started peeking through the leaves. They found suitable woodland after a short flight, far enough away not to lead anyone to the hideout.

Ilea looked at the group. "Edwin, this has been a long time coming." She cracked her knuckles. "Try not to hold back."

"You're far too inexperienced to be that cocky," he said and charged at her without another word.

Ilea dodged the first few strikes, then found an opening and threw a fist into his side, blinking away before his sword reached her.

Edwin stumbled slightly from the blow. A fire lit in his eyes.

"Alright then. Gloves off."

Ilea grinned.

THIRTEEN

Blood Magic

Edwin's swords slashed through another tree as he tried to attack Ilea. She blinked away, dodging the blood magic coating his blades.

Both Ilea and Edwin focused more on speed than anything else, but considering he'd already taken several of her punches directly, he was tougher than she'd expected.

"Your armor is good. Care to share the smith's name?" Edwin asked before he teleported closer.

"I think not," Ilea said as she sprinted at him, dodging another flurry of attacks, though some of the blood magic slipped through her defenses, even managing to singe her flesh. Nothing a little bit of healing couldn't take care of, but she found the small injuries much harder to heal than more severe wounds in the past.

Blood magic.

Her arms flew out, batting the man's hands aside and pushing his swords away before she delivered a headbutt to his chest. The hit landed, and Edwin staggered back and into a bush before he vanished again into the morning mist.

Ilea quickly followed him through the use of her Sphere and Blink skills, not giving him pause as she continued to push further and further, activating more of her skills as they went on. At first, she hadn't used her Destruction and Wave of Ember, but now she delivered them with each blow.

Ilea didn't plan on killing the man, but she did want to know if she could. Perhaps he felt the same as his attacks got stronger and faster to match hers.

Ilea delivered three punches in quick succession, hearing a slight crack from the third one as Edwin stumbled backward. Before he reacted, the others caught up, watching them fight like it was a day out at the circus.

"Don't get too far away from the area we started in," Felicia reminded them in a motherly tone.

Edwin spat out blood before red flames gathered around him. Then Ilea heard a crack and saw his shoulder shifting, indicating a broken bone had been mended.

His blades appeared before her, too fast for her to dodge, so she blinked behind him, moving her hand just in time to nudge his sword upward as it threatened to cut into her helmet. Her hand was on fire immediately, her flesh burning below her armor with a pain that was distracting even to her.

Turning off her pain perception, she used her healing spell against the red flames enveloping her hand. The fire didn't expand, stopped by her Hunter Recovery, but neither could she remove it.

Blinking into the trees when the next blade rushed toward her, Ilea ripped off her gauntlet, summoned one of her remaining Taleen swords, and hoped the blade was strong enough to do the trick. With all her strength, she slashed at her wrist. The bone was only severed halfway, but a second hit did the trick.

Healing again, Ilea found the wound now completely normal, and she put on her gauntlet again just as Edwin appeared in front of her, glancing at her as she regrew her bone and flesh below her armor.

"Nice flames," she said, honestly impressed at their destructive potential, though she couldn't help but say it in a mocking tone.

"Let me know if you're close to death," the man said with a very slight grin.

"Same goes for you," Ilea said, activating State of Azarinth's third stage before she ran at him, now focusing on his limbs instead of the blades.

Not being able to touch the flaming metal made the fight more even. She found that while the flames around his body did injure her, they were much less dangerous than those enveloping his curved short swords.

Ilea moved her body left and right, appearing and disappearing, trying to get into range for her fists while Edwin tried hard to keep her at his blades' distance. His weapon sliced past her right side as she delivered a punch to his gut, the full force of Destruction and Wave of Ember entering him before she appeared behind him.

Edwin teleported away, and Ilea followed a moment later. They stared at each other, Ilea waiting to give him time should the attack have been a little much. Edwin was panting, sweat on his brow glistening in the sunlight of the meadow.

He raised his blades again and Ilea nodded, appearing before him. His right blade flickered as Ilea turned her body to push her back against his chest as she grabbed both of his arms, pumping destructive mana into his body as he struggled to get away.

She felt a sudden heat in her right shoulder before it literally exploded, making her stumble, but thanks to Azarinth Reversal's second stage, she could continue to attack the man while she mended the nasty wound.

"Stop," he said, before adding in a whisper, "I'm getting dangerously low..."

Ilea disengaged, feeling her shoulder reconstruct under her armor. The way he'd just ignored the metal of her armor to mount that attack made her understand why so many people wanted enchantments that protected against mana intrusion. Not that she wanted to restrict herself in such a manner. She'd just have to make sure her defenses were sufficient to justify an absence of such enchantments.

Stepping toward Edwin, she started healing him as the flames left his form. He held his blades limply in both hands as he panted and leaned against a nearby tree. Ilea was quite aware that he could've targeted her heart or head with that last attack, which could've led to a different result entirely. She could certainly recover a shoulder, but not having tested actually losing her head, she didn't know how exactly that would pan out.

'ding' You have learned the General Skill Blood Magic Resistance – lvl 1
The arts of blood manipulation can be deceptive and dangerous to both ally and foe. You have stood against the old magic and lived. Next time, your chances of survival will be even higher.

'ding' Blood Magic Resistance reaches lvl 2

'ding' Blood Magic Resistance reaches lvl 3

That will come in handy, she thought and continued healing as she heard clapping from Kyrian. Felicia gave her an approving nod, and Aliana was whooping and cheering.

"Who's next?" she asked, smiling when she saw Felicia raise her hand. She approached and rolled her shoulders.

"That looked pretty intense. Are you sure you want to fight more?"

"That was just the warm-up," Ilea said, winking at Edwin, who'd sat down on a fallen tree trunk.

"We'll have to give you a handicap though, otherwise the fight will be over in less than a minute. You're an ash creator, right?"

"Yeah," Ilea said, summoning a cloud of the element above herself.

"Perfect. You're only allowed to use ash then, that's the deal," Felicia smiled.

Ilea blinked backward to make some distance, landing in the grass.

"Agreed," she said, ashen spheres forming around her, a veil of it protecting her body.

"Try not to hurt me too badly. My second class is Arcane Berserker, meaning I'll probably fight longer than I should."

"Arcane Berserker… do you lose control?"

Felicia shook her head. "No, not completely. Even if I'm close to death. Level two hundred helped me there. Just… if the fight is exciting, I can get a little overconfident."

"Go wild then. My Wind Resistance could be higher, you know," Ilea said and gestured for Felicia to start.

Felicia's yellow eyes started glowing slightly as she levitated, the grass pushed aside by magical pressure alone before the air around the woman turned chaotic, cutting into the ground and the nearby trees as Ilea moved back a little further to avoid being attacked already.

Yellow lines formed around Felicia's eyes before she opened them. "Ready?" she asked in an almost ethereal voice.

Ilea nodded and saw a blade of air moving toward her. It was so dense that she perceived it with her eyes alone, but her Sphere gave her a bit more of an insight, telling her that there were dozens of smaller blades coming her way as well, covering different possible paths of escape. A blink toward Felicia was the most reasonable thing to do, so she advanced.

Appearing behind the blades of wind, Ilea watched Felicia advance with frightening speed, her arms reaching out before cones of air were released from them. Ilea dodged both attacks with a jump, assisted by her wings before another wind blade smashed into her armor, making her tumble through the air before she landed on her feet, skidding on the grass for a couple of meters.

"You're really something. Half a year ago that would've halved you," Felicia said as she slowly approached.

Ilea moved her ash then, spinning black spheres toward Felicia, who was protected by a tornado that spun up around her. The spheres were torn apart, but Ilea was already forming fresh spikes, making them spin before she shot them out. This time Felicia dodged the projectiles, her tornado moving her body as if it was controlled by a puppeteer.

A cloud of ash formed around Ilea but was quickly blown away by a stream of wind.

"You're not gonna obscure my vision," Felicia said, sending more air blades toward Ilea.

Ilea dodged more defensively, not getting too close to the wind mage as she formed new projectiles, this time aiming for a much bigger area.

Even with her constant dodging, one of Ilea's black spikes managed to cut through the tornado and hit Felicia on her shoulder. It didn't pierce her skin, but the speed and weight still stunned the woman slightly.

"Creation really is something else. I could simply trap and crush you with air if I had such a skill."

"Can't you do that with your air manipulation?" Ilea asked, dodging backward and into the woods as air blades rushed through the trees, cutting deep into the bark.

They paused, facing each other.

"No, the extent of manipulating existing elements is limited. While helpful, it takes time to infuse it with mana and use it more freely. Your metal mage friend does it that way. You seem to be completely in control of your ash immediately upon creation."

"I can barely pierce your defenses though," Ilea frowned.

"Hmm, I let that one pass to see how it would fare against my armor. You don't have any skills that enhance your ash, do you? Mine are basically all about making my air blades more damaging."

"Hence they cut into trees like butter."

"Exactly," Felicia said as more blades cut through the forest. "Though not quite through you yet."

"Something's nearby. Let's stop for now," Ilea said, sensing something and turning around. Felicia landed next to Ilea. Her eyes still had yellow lines around them, but the tornado was absent.

"You think we overdid it?" Felicia asked, but Ilea shook her head.

"There it is," she said, pointing to a bush and tensing for a fight.

A bunny hopping out from behind it.

Ilea identified the creature just to be sure.

[Bunny – lvl 3]

"You never know," she murmured and started walking back toward the clearing. "Anyone care to help me work on some resistances?"

"Some more blood magic resistance will help. You do have that second tier of Pain Tolerance," Edwin said and stood up. "I'll ask Maria to help you as well, once she's back."

"What kind of magic does she wield? It did feel like something I've not faced before, back where we found you."

"Void magic," he said, his tone serious.

"Another one to add to the list," Ilea said with a smile.

She glanced over to see Aliana and Kyrian facing each other with their spells active. Their faces were flushed with excitement, and they seemed to be chatting a fair bit as they fought. Trian hadn't joined in quite yet, but Felicia was talking to him off to one side.

Good to get used to each other's abilities before we fight anything together. Let's see how much these two can help me with my resistances...

* * *

The next few days passed in a similar manner. The training breaks became more accepted and soon something everyone seemed to look forward to.

Maria joined in a few times as well once she'd returned. Today was one of those days.

Maria watched as an explosion of flesh and blood splattered red goop onto both Ilea and Edwin.

"Damn, that's nasty," she said from the side as Ilea's destroyed arm started reforming. "Good thing you have Pain Immunity."

"It's less effective against blood magic," Ilea said. Then she turned back to Edwin. "Does me being able to heal it bother you?"

"I'll be honest. It does a little," he replied.

"Still rips off my arm quite easily."

"No, there's threads still hanging. Here and here," he said, pointing to specific pieces of flesh. Ilea saw he was right. Soon he wouldn't even be able to rip off her whole arm anymore.

"Not sure if I like the idea of making you even harder to kill," Maria said before her void magic manifested inside Ilea's other arm. Maria was better at reducing the area of attack, which meant Ilea didn't have to regrow her right arm all the time, just heal the insides.

"I've been wondering. Can you do that inside my head? You'd be able to kill anybody with a single strike," she said.

Maria grimaced. "Sadly not. Using my void abilities is harder against more vital spots. I think it's because of the mana density. It's a form of mana intrusion, so that always made sense to me. It's easier to rip off two legs than a heart, anyway. People can tell the attack is coming, and at higher levels, they can tell even earlier."

Ilea wasn't convinced. She could see the reason in what Maria had said, but she could also see the reason in her lying about the extent of their abilities. For now, she'd just assume that either of them could destroy her brain if they wanted to.

'ding' You have learned the General Skill Void Magic Resistance – lvl 1
This mystical magic, usually used to enchant high-level items, can be applied as a form of combat magic. It's as deadly as it is silent. How exactly you survived is unclear. Perhaps the caster willed it so. Next time, it might work against a true enemy.

Ilea could tell immediately that she could perceive the incoming attack faster. The damage was noticeably lessened as well.

I need to get more of these abilities. Perhaps some exotic animals and monsters would provide—

Before she could get lost in thought, her arm was ripped off again.

'ding' Blood Magic Resistance reaches lvl 4***

Nobody attacked them out in the woods, nor did they see anybody pass by.

Even so close to the capital, Ilea felt like she was stranded far from civilization. She supposed the wilderness or, more reasonably, the monsters that were supposedly around put most people off. Local monsters proved rather absent. Perhaps it was just a coincidence, or maybe it was because their team was far more dangerous than any of the nearby wildlife.

Ilea had managed to raise her void and blood magic resistances even further while also working on lightning, wind, water, curse, health drain, mana drain, and heat resistances. Felicia's and Aliana's magic was especially useful because they were around most of the time, and her base resistances were low to start. Heat Resistance was not, as the name suggested, a resistance against warm temperatures, only against fire. The naming didn't make much sense, she thought, but boiling water wasn't exactly fire, so she gladly accepted the additional usefulness.

One way she had come up with to counter Aliana's scalding magic was to use her Embered Body Heat as it seemed increasing her own temperature marginally helped to lessen the damaging effects of the super-heated water. That meant she'd kept the skill active constantly, pouring much more mana into it than usual. Which had produced unexpected benefits.

'ding' Embered Body Heat reaches 2nd lvl 1
Regulate the heat in your body to protect yourself against harsh climates or even blend in with your environment.
2nd stage: The Embers run deep. Your blood boils and the ash around you singes, should you will it.
Category: Body Enhancement – Ashen Magic

'ding' Heat Resistance reaches 2nd lvl 1
Ignoring the warnings of your parents and friends, you refuse to not stand in fire. This skill will help lessen the damage and pain a little.
2nd stage: You've been burnt and melted again and again. Through extreme exposure, your skin, muscles, and bones become much harder to burn and melt.

She'd continued to level that one a few more times after it hit tier two. Aliana had been… enthusiastic about helping her train.

'ding' Your Water Resistance reaches 2nd lvl 1
Over time, you've learned many things. One of them is that water pressure is not a joke. This resistance helps a little with reducing the damage.
2nd stage: You've taken so much damage from water-based attacks that it might be good to check that you're not actually on fire. Getting more used to

it, your body and armor magically redirect the pressure to lessen the burden on you.

'ding' Wind Resistance reaches 2nd lvl 1
The elusive magic of wind can cut from any side. You've learned that it might've been a good idea to become a void mage. This skill helps you resist the power of wind a little more.
2nd stage: The mana flow inside you has acclimated to the air around you, making you more aerodynamic.

One benefit of her new skills was that she could take even hotter baths now and heat them up herself.

Definitely the best use of such high-level skills…

She had also managed to increase her State of Azarinth, Ashen Warrior, and Ash Creation skills. Checking her stats, she wasn't sure what to think.

Name: Ilea Spears
Unspent stat points: 0
Unspent 3rd-tier skill points [Azarinth First Hunter]: 0
Unspent 3rd-tier skill points [Inheritor of Eternal Ash]: 2

Class 1: Azarinth First Hunter – lvl 224
- Active: Destruction – 2nd lvl 20
- Active: Hunter Recovery – 2nd lvl 20
- Active: State of Azarinth – 3rd lvl 2
- Active: Blink – 3rd lvl 5
- Active: Azarinth Hunter Sphere – 2nd lvl 20
- Passive: Body of the First Hunter – 2nd lvl 20
- Passive: Azarinth Fighting – 2nd lvl 20
- Passive: Hunter's Sight – 2nd lvl 8
- Passive: Azarinth Perception – 2nd lvl 20
- Passive: Azarinth Reversal – 2nd lvl 16

Class 2: Inheritor of Eternal Ash – lvl 220
- Active: Veil of Ash – 2nd lvl 20
- Active: Form of Ash and Ember – 2nd lvl 18
- Active: Ash Creation – 2nd lvl 20
- Active: Embered Body Heat – 2nd lvl 1
- Active: Wave of Ember – 2nd lvl 12
- Passive: Ash and Ember Manipulation – 2nd lvl 20
- Passive: Ashen Wings – 2nd lvl 14
- Passive: Eyes of Ash – 2nd lvl 19
- Passive: Body of Ash – 2nd lvl 16
- Passive: Ashen Warrior – 2nd lvl 16

General Skills:
- Elos Standard language – lvl 6
- Heavy Archery – lvl 4
- Identify – lvl 7
- Meditation – 2nd lvl 17
- Veteran – lvl 3

- Arcane Magic Resistance – lvl 6
- Blast Resistance – lvl 12
- Blood Magic Resistance – lvl 8
- Corrosion Resistance – lvl 3
- Crystal Resistance – lvl 6
- Curse Resistance – 2nd lvl 2
- Dark Magic Resistance – lvl 1
- Earth Magic Resistance – lvl 5
- Fear Resistance – lvl 2
- Health Drain Resistance – lvl 17
- Heat Resistance – 2nd lvl 4
- Ice Resistance – lvl 7
- Light Magic Resistance – lvl 2
- Lightning Resistance – 2nd lvl 5
- Mana Drain Resistance – lvl 18
- Mental Resistance – 2nd lvl 10
- Mist Magic Resistance – lvl 1
- Pain Tolerance – 2nd lvl 4
- Poison Resistance – lvl 17
- Void Magic Resistance – lvl 7
- Water Resistance – 2nd lvl 1
- Wind Resistance – 2nd lvl 1

Status:
Vitality: 650
Endurance: 233
Strength: 182
Dexterity: 193
Intelligence: 596
Wisdom: 584

Health: 6500/6500
Stamina: 1492/2330
Mana: 5138/5840

She had made some progress with the team, but it didn't feel the same as when she'd been out there fighting drakes and Taleen machinery. She'd long since realized that she'd been stagnating. While it was true that she'd learned a lot in the past six months from her lessons in the Shadow's Hand and working together with her team, it had become much harder to both find and kill enemies that increased her levels and skills.

She thought back to some of the monsters she'd learned about and wondered when she could get back to facing wildlife instead of people. Things were a lot simpler when your opponents simply wanted to tear you to shreds. She shook her head and refocused on the documents set before her.

One thing at a time.

* * *

The next day came and went, Maria delivering more specific info and first-hand accounts from two warriors of the Haim mercenary group before she left again with more targets, both related to Arthur and the Birmingales. The others were mostly left to wait at the safe house. Not even Edwin joined Maria due to the heightened state of alert in the capital.

Ilea didn't like the idle hours, her thoughts going back to Eve time and time again. She also wondered if anyone was hunting them already. Working with Edwin and his group provided them with what they needed to find and potentially strike at the Birmingales, but it also made them enemies of who knew how many powerful people and groups out there.

She stood up. "I'm going to get some fresh air."

"Just get some distance from this place once you're out. We don't want to attract any attention," Edwin said.

"Sure," Ilea answered and blinked out.

The suns had set by now, the group having worked through the documents for most of the past night and day. Coupled with the heavy training the day before, she had only slept for a few hours, dreaming of the hairpin woman and the bloody man from the Redleaf estate.

She spread her wings and chose a random direction, blinking again and flying for a few minutes before she found a nice spot between a few copses of trees. There were no paths here, no buildings, no fields growing crops. Just grasses, flowers, trees, and the stars above.

She sat down on a small hill and looked to the east when she heard the sound of rushing air. She saw Felicia in her Sphere, and the woman landed in the grass a dozen meters away soon after.

Felicia walked over and smiled faintly. "Mind if I join you? Or do you want to be alone?"

Ilea thought for a moment, then shook her head. "I don't mind. Just wanted to be away from those stuffy rooms and all those documents."

And the people in there.

Felicia sat down and hugged her knees. "I get it."

They were quiet for some time, Ilea enjoying the light breeze and the stars. She had never seen such a broad and bright night sky. There was a chill in the air, but with her stats, it hardly mattered.

"I wanted to apologize," Felicia said eventually, breaking the silence.

Ilea glanced at her.

"For how we left you back in the Taleen dungeon," Felicia added.

"Edwin made his poi—"

"I'm not Edwin," Felicia cut in, her voice tense before she took a deep breath. "I'm sorry. He's..."

"Obsessed?"

"Driven. He does what he thinks is best for us. I understand why he didn't want to take you with us, but it didn't feel right how we did it. I wasn't even sure why at the time. But I understood later. We took away your right to choose, and I didn't stand up to him. I wanted to apologize for that. And I guess I'm sorry as well that, in the end, I thought his decision was right."

Ilea smiled and laid back in the grass. "You wanted to protect me."

"I did. But you didn't need that."

"Who knows. Maybe you saved my life. I could've been here with you all, not yet close to level two hundred. And I don't know if I would've wanted to join your hunt, even if you'd explained it."

Felicia smiled, but her eyes were sad. "No, you would have. It's what you're doing now, after all."

"Because I'm naïve?" Ilea asked.

"No. Because you care about people," Felicia said. "Because you're willing to fight for them." A sob went through her after she spoke.

Ilea sat up and looked at her. Felicia's shoulders bobbed lightly before she took a sharp breath and shuddered.

"Sorry, I... I didn't mean to..."

"It's okay," Ilea said, moving a little closer. She reached out and touched Felicia's arm. They were quiet for a while until Felicia broke the silence again.

"I didn't fight for you, even though you fought with us, even though I thought you were my friend," Felicia whispered.

"I didn't expect that from you. Though it did hurt when you all left, just like that."

"It did, didn't it? It hurt me too. I felt guilty, but Ed had always been the one to decide. I'm just... I don't know."

"What's going on?"

"He's been... keeping us safe, me and Aliana, but we've been working hard, hunting monsters, training. I'm at level two hundred. I can fight, but he hardly involves us. The closer we get to... Father... the more it feels like he's keeping us hidden away." She shook her head. "I'm sorry, this wasn't supposed to be about me. I just came to apologize."

"I accept your apology," Ilea said. "And you can talk about what's going on. Looks like the past months weren't too easy on you and Aliana."

She shook her head. "They weren't. But I read what I could, learned about Virilya and its nobility. Ed has started asking me for advice on various laws and Houses. It's—"

"What do *you* want to do?" Ilea interrupted.

Felicia was quiet.

"When I was alone again in the Taleen dungeon, I explored, fought the machines. Found a storage necklace," Ilea said, showing it to Felicia with a sly smile. "I also made quite a few friends and got to two hundred, though it all ended in a fucked-up battle with two large Taleen machines. Praetorians. They killed most of the expedition, and when we got back to Dawntree, elves had attacked."

"It sounds like your time wasn't easy either," Felicia said.

"Some of it, sure. But there was a lot of cool shit too. I got wings. I fought and killed a bunch of elves with the help of a Shadow team. Just wish I'd got to Salia before they attacked. But I can't change that now."

"You joined the Hand. Was your friend… I mean—"

"She was in our team, yeah."

"I'm sorry. I'm sorry she died."

"Yeah," Ilea said. She wiped at her eyes before she smiled. "She was a fucking idiot though."

"Really? How so?"

"She could've asked for help. She died, alone in her hideout, after killing God knows who. I could've healed her."

Felicia hugged Ilea's arm. "I'm sorry your friend was stupid. I guess she was obsessed too."

Ilea opened her mouth and closed it. She could feel tears rolling down her cheeks. "Yeah. It's just, you know, I thought she would trust me."

"I know."

A few minutes passed with Felicia holding onto Ilea's arm. It felt nice. She'd tried to keep her shit together around Kyrian and Trian, but with Felicia, it felt different. Maybe she was afraid that Kyrian wouldn't be able to handle it. And Trian was dealing with his own shit.

Or maybe those are all excuses. So much for trusting your friends, Ilea.

"I think I want to finish this," Felicia said. "Not just for Ed but for me and Aliana, and for Maria too, I suppose. For all of us. And for those who didn't survive. Elia, Varn, and Domenik. I want him to be gone. I don't want to kill him, and I don't want to fight him or anyone who works with him. But I want him to be gone."

"And what then?"

"What then?" Felicia looked up at the stars. "I don't know. I'll think about it after," she said, nodding, then looked at Ilea. "What about you? After this, I mean? If we don't die," she added with a laugh.

"I want to make sure Trian is safe, but... with everything that's already happened..." Ilea sighed. "I'd like to know what happened to Eve, but I can tell it'll be difficult to find out, and even then, I don't think I want to go and kill someone. I enjoyed exploring, fighting monsters. All of this is exhausting. Complicated. Monsters are simple. I want to get strong enough to go and destroy those Praetorians, and I want to get strong enough to protect my friends, to make sure I could stop an entire horde of demons if another summoning like that ever happens again. And to get strong enough so I could fight Strand."

"That's a lot of things to fight."

"I guess," Ilea smiled. "An adventurer by heart, I suppose."

"I think you have a lot to fight for," Felicia said. "And that's nice. Maybe..." she started, then fell silent and let go of Ilea.

She stood up and smiled. "Thank you for the talk," Felicia said, walking a few steps away. Then she glanced back. "I hope we're still friends."

"Of course," Ilea said, and she was warmed by the smile she received in response.

Wind flowed around her armor before Felicia ascended and flew back in the direction of their hideout.

A lot to fight for, Ilea thought, forming a bit of ash above her palm. Right now, she could really go for a fight – just for the sake of a good fight.

FOURTEEN

Plan and Execution

Ilea formed a sphere of ash above her palm. She pushed her magic to make it denser and then let it all float away.

She was nervous. Their attack would happen soon, and all their preparation, all the information they had gathered, just made her think of all the things they could've missed, all the things that could go wrong.

Maria and Edwin had kept them informed about the state of Virilya. There had been more attacks. Demons released into the city, craftspeople murdered, and arson attacks on inns, storehouses for food, and even boats. The culprit was well known by now – the neighboring kingdom of Baralia.

Tensions had been building over the past years, and while many in the high nobility pushed for open war, Empress Alyris remained stoic. Or paralyzed, as some suggested. Her unwillingness to start a war was seen by some as weak and as strong by others.

For Ilea's group, however, the situation in the capital and the Empire at large presented both problems and opportunities. If a war did break out, any high-level individuals would be highly coveted, even more so if there was a chance of them defecting to the enemy.

Finding the Birmingales, let alone striking at them, would become far more difficult if they were involved in a military campaign. And any evidence as to their attack on House Alymie would likely just present an opportunity for them to redeem themselves during the war, with more dangerous missions given to them as a way to repent. That was the consensus shared by Felicia, Trian, and Maria, at least.

On the other hand, any chaos in the city and even open warfare would present ample opportunities to strike, at least initially. Timing would be of the essence.

Ilea didn't like it. The conflict was too complex, and there were too many variables to consider. She knew it would become messy either way. Things were much simpler when the only planning needed was 'punch the bad thing until it stops moving'.

"Brooding in the treetops," Kyrian said as he floated up next to her. "Doesn't suit you."

"Are we going?" Ilea asked, ignoring the comment.

"Trian is ready to explain the details. We're just waiting for you," Kyrian said and flew down again. Ilea followed behind with a blink, her wings spreading right after to stop her fall as she rushed behind her friend.

They soon reached the hideout and joined the rest of the group. Ilea sat down on a chair, looking at the papers pinned to the wall. At the center was a floor plan of the Birmingale estate, rudimentary sketches of their targets surrounding it.

Ilea crossed her arms and glanced around at the others. Edwin, sitting on a chair and leaning forward, looked calm but focused. Maria looked disinterested as she leaned against a wall, purple magic appearing and disappearing between her fingers. Aliana wasn't present, while Felicia was staring at the table, her jaw clenched.

"You're here," Trian said, nodding her way. He had lost weight, she could tell, and there was an edge to him that scared her.

"Maria heard rumors of another set of attacks coming in two nights. Far more extensive than anything before," Trian said. "That's when we will strike. Right when the suns set. Afterward, at dawn, I will deliver our collected evidence and a written statement in the name of House Alymie to the Halls of Eternity."

"You're sure about that?" Maria asked. "They might hold you there."

"There are still nobles in the city with honor. My father and mother trusted them, and I shall trust them too."

"Who are you thinking of?"

Trian was quiet for a long moment. "Josefin Anderson."

"A scholar. Why would she help your cause?"

Ilea had heard enough of Maria's snide remarks by now to know that this Josefin was likely trustworthy. If she had anything negative to say about anyone, she said it.

"I know her personally," Trian said. "But all of that will depend on our success in our attack." His tone changed as he pointed at the map. "We're going in and out quick. There should be guards at all the entrances, inside the gardens, and in the mansion itself." He marked the spots on the map.

"Maria will leave earlier to check on their movements, but as we know, they shouldn't be above level one fifty. Likely not much of a threat with their low numbers. Still, it's paramount that we stay silent and get to our targets before they can group up," Trian continued.

"We move in past the east gate. There are trees in this section once we're past the gate. If possible, we go over the walls. Otherwise, we have to deal with the guards. Distraction or incapacitation. I'd prefer it if nobody other than our targets is killed. But if anyone stands in our way, don't hesitate.

"As soon as we get closer, I'll use my lightning magic to disable any defensive or alarming runes. We'll have a minute or two at best for this, and should I fail, all the people who can teleport will go inside the mansion regardless. We focus on our main targets if Ilea or someone else can spot them. If we can't, we move past the entrance, then right up the stairs and to the master bedroom. Ronan and Bale should be there at that hour.

"Move and kill together to make sure each target is dead before we go on to the next one. If their resistance is overwhelming, we flee, but otherwise I want to deal as much damage as possible before we retreat. It will be more difficult to find and attack any surviving members afterward.

"These are the main targets. First, Ronan Birmingale, acting head of their House," Trian said, pointing to the first sketch. A man in his fifties with long black hair. "He took part in the attack on my family. He's supposed to have surpassed the mid two hundreds, and with his Berserker and fire enhancer Classes, he'll be one of the most dangerous targets. If you find him, focus on him with everything you have. Based on what we know, he cannot be left to fight for longer than a single minute or it will become difficult to even injure him. Anybody who challenged him directly in the past ten years, whether part of the family or outside it, has been found dead."

He pointed to another sketch. "This is Bale Birmingale, Ronan's wife and matriarch of the family. The sources differ, but if anyone orchestrated the attack on my House, I think it was her. She was a high-ranking officer in the Imperial army with a lot of pull. Make sure to take her out or we'll have specialized military scouts or even worse hunting us before the night is over. She's a mage specializing in large-scale fire spells. If Ilea's perception ability works, she'll point out these two targets so we can focus on them first. I'd count the operation a success even if we get only them."

Ilea looked at the picture of the smiling woman, a middle-aged motherly type, not someone she'd associate with what had happened to the Alymies. Then again, appearances could be deceptive.

Trian pointed to the next sketch, depicting a younger man with short hair and a scar on his right cheek.

"Graham Birmingale, the oldest and only son of Bale and Ronan. He was there and didn't just target my family. He killed our staff as well."

"The mercenaries didn't speak highly of him," Maria said.

Like father, like son, Ilea thought, glancing at Edwin. Of course, it wasn't always true, and unlike this Graham, Edwin had chosen to run away and find his own way in the world.

"Graham is a wood mage and a creator too, so be careful when you face him directly," Trian said.

A wood creator, Ilea thought, remembering what she'd learned at the Hand. It would be easier for the man to call upon his element than for a non-creator, and he'd be able to use it far more freely too.

"An arrogant boy with a powerful Class," Maria said. "He won't be much trouble."

Ilea didn't miss the looks Maria gave the trio of Shadows, but she didn't take it personally. By now, she assumed Maria just disliked most people.

"Next is Petra Birmingale," Trian said. "Information on her is scarce, but we know she uses a poison-coated sword and has magic to conceal herself."

"Their assassin," Felicia said.

"Yes," Trian said, but he didn't elaborate. "Ilea, if she's there, you're likely the best bet to take her out."

Ilea gave him a slight nod. She breathed deeply and thought of Eve lying still on her bed.

This is different.

She wasn't entirely sure she wasn't just lying to herself. They would find and kill these people. She steeled herself.

They murdered your friend's family. This is justice.

"The last Birmingale confirmed to be present in the attack on my family is Wallace Birmingale," Trian said, pointing to the last sketch. "He's a close combat hand-to-hand fighter specializing in strength. I'm unsure as to the danger he poses, but we shouldn't underestimate any of the Birmingales, nor any of the members who weren't present in the attack or their guards."

"You should take them all out," Maria said. "If you don't, they'll be after you, just like you're after them now."

"I know," he said after a long pause. "But I'm not Ronan Birmingale. We'll kill only those we know are responsible."

"Your honor will be the death of you," Maria said. "And us, if we participate in this," she added, looking at Edwin.

"It will make a better case to Alyris," Felicia said quietly. "She will be more inclined to side with the Alymies, especially if the evidence reaches her."

"Let them know what we're capable of," Edwin said. "A direct assault. We will only kill who Trian tells us to kill."

"You want to send a message with this?" Maria asked.

Edwin smiled. "We're also honoring our agreement."

Trian gave him a slight nod. "I'll present every other member of their House now and what we believe their magic and abilities to look like..."

Trian continued explaining the plan after they'd all checked out the roster of notable nobles in the family, as well as possible escape routes and plans for regrouping in several different places both in and out of the city.

Even with all the preparation, Ilea knew everything would quickly devolve into chaos. She looked through the notes and tried to memorize the different names and possible abilities.

Is this what it was like for you, Eve? Ilea thought. *Hunting monsters?*

* * *

The next day came and went, the group preparing their gear and soon making their way to the capital. Felicia and Aliana didn't join them. The weather was in their favor, with dark clouds hanging over Virilya and the surrounding countryside and rain starting to fall. That meant flying in from above while avoiding the individual flying squads patrolling the far-reaching city was made much easier.

The tension in the city was tangible as the five landed. An attack from Baralia was expected and feared – that much was clear to Ilea, but she didn't know the specifics. Edwin's operation, combined with their own tonight, wouldn't help anybody feel any safer. And they surely wouldn't be the only ones seeing this as an opportune time to cause chaos.

They rushed silently through the streets, vanishing into empty houses or side streets whenever they saw lights approach. Some of the patrolling groups were soldiers, but few of them were higher than level one twenty.

No scouts or other special units...

They moved on, avoiding several encounters with patrols. Security had certainly been increased, and as they approached the noble district, they even found stationary guard posts on bridges and vantage points. Maria led them through parts of the sewer system and narrow streets to avoid them, every one of her steps quick and without hesitation.

Ilea was getting a little worried about the flying military officers and soldiers above. If they reacted quickly to the attack, they'd have a problem. Especially with the matriarch being strongly connected to the military.

Ilea quietly opened the door to an empty apartment close to the estate's western entrance, the rest following her inside. Maria had found the place a few days prior, giving them a close location to strike from.

It was hard to defend against an attack in the midst of a city. It helped that in Virilya, most of the nobles didn't build massive forts but lavishly expensive-looking mansions instead. Ilea had seen a few more defensible structures, but the Birmingales hadn't invested in one for one reason or another.

More guards were patrolling, as Maria had reported they would be, and two were standing near the entrance, a closed metal gate placed in the two-meter-high stone wall surrounding the property. Torches to each side of the gate lit up the otherwise dark street, and rain drummed on their heavy sets of armor as they waited with spear and two-handed sword in hand respectively.

"Armor," Trian said, and the set made by Balduur appeared on his body.

Ilea switched as well before both she and Trian helped Kyrian into his set. She gave the former a look but found him entirely focused.

"If we can't make it, we retreat," she said, but he avoided her eyes. "Trian. We're not losing anyone else in this team."

He gave her a quick glance and a nod.

She grabbed his arm when he turned away. "Trian."

"I heard you," he muttered.

She let go but kept her eyes on him.

"Based on the guards' placements, the gate and walls are likely enchanted," Maria said as she moved away from the window to join them.

Edwin stood leaning against a wall with his blades sheathed and his arms crossed. "Streets are damn near empty other than the city guards. It feels like the city is holding its breath."

Trian nodded. "We go for the guards at the east gate, closest to here. Incapacitate if we can. Then through the garden and up into the mansion. Ilea, Kyrian, this is your last chance to turn back."

Ilea stepped up beside him. "You're a madman, Trian. I got you through the Great Salt. I'll get you through this."

Kyrian joined them and gave a single nod.

"You two ready?" Trian asked, glancing at Maria and Edwin.

Unlike their group, Ilea couldn't sense a shred of doubt or fear from the two as Maria grinned and Edwin touched the handle of one of his swords, then nodded.

Trian made his way toward the window.

"On three, then," Trian whispered as a patrolling set of guards moved on, leaving only the two at the gate. "One..."

Ilea thought of Aurelia, Samuel, and Trian. She steeled herself and took a deep breath.

"...two... three," Trian finished, and Ilea vanished, reappearing behind the guard with the sword and grabbing his helmet, pulling backward and covering his mouth. Edwin did the same to the other one, and Trian's lightning surged through their armor and into both the guards, Ilea, and Edwin.

They could neither teleport, nor could they scream. Ilea healed herself when she felt Maria's void magic flare, the hand of the guard Ilea held onto ripped away before he could reach a set of runes embedded in the perimeter wall.

Maria gave Ilea a look and checked the street as Trian's lightning finally dealt enough damage to down the two guards. Ilea slowly set the guard down and healed both Edwin and herself. She stabilized the guards but checked her reflex to heal them further. They were burnt up pretty badly, but they were alive. They would survive.

Kyrian rushed toward them as Trian touched the gate, sparks of lightning flashing up as enchantments fizzled out, and moved a molten metal sphere into the gate's lock. There was a click, and the group rushed through the open gate, Ilea and Edwin taking the injured guards inside before they set them down close to the wall. Kyrian closed the gate when everyone was inside.

Lights from the mansion illuminated a luscious garden, flowers and small trees blooming even this early in spring. No guards were immediately visible, and they rushed toward the entrance.

"Someone's coming out. A maid," Ilea whispered just before the door opened and a woman stepped out with a bag in her hand. Her eyes widened for a split second as Trian teleported and grabbed the woman's throat before her body fell down limply a second later. Ilea saw she was alive.

Ilea moved on and checked her Sphere, her eyes wide when she focused on the master bedroom. They were both there.

"Top floor, third room at the back, master bedroom. Ronan and Bale," Ilea said.

"Wait until they're close to each other," Edwin said.

Kyrian moved his metal so he'd be ready to fly.

Ilea watched the two Birmingales. She opened and closed her fist, ready to activate all of her spells. Ronan walked close to his wife and embraced her, saying something that Ilea couldn't hear.

"Go," she said.

Ilea saw through her Sphere that at least one person in the house had noticed them, getting up from their chair and walking to the door of their room. She activated her magic and sacrificed a large chunk of health to power up her aura, gritting her teeth at the sudden rush of power before she vanished and appeared next to the couple.

All of the group bar Kyrian appeared at the same moment. Edwin's blades, wreathed in blood and fire, bit into the sides of the Birmingales' necks as Ilea felt void and lightning magic course through them.

The two were separated by the magic, and Ilea quickly grabbed Bale's two arms at the wrists as fire magic enveloped her. Ilea felt the heat and pulled the woman closer with both hands before smashing her armored head into Bale's skull.

She heard a crack as more and more fire rushed past her, burning her flesh beneath her armor even as her healing magic fought against it. Another impact and the magic flared to the side, flames engulfing the large bed and the wall beyond. The deep cut on Bale's neck was bleeding profusely, her skull fractured by Ilea's repeated attacks, reversed healing coursing through her.

Ilea heard Kyrian break through the window as more fire engulfed her. She ignored the heat and held on to Bale, whose eyes were now unfocused, her nose broken and her face bleeding. Ilea pulled her head back and snapped it forward again, her intrusion bursting forth into her enemy, her helmet crashing through fire and bone with her enhanced strength. She felt the woman go limp, a message in her mind confirming the kill.

Ilea didn't stop, moving toward the rest of her group. They hadn't been quite as successful as her. Ronan had two bloody axes in his hands and was whirling them around wildly, bleeding from at least seven deep wounds as he gargled, unable to scream with his throat cut.

Ilea appeared behind him and kicked at his legs, one of his axes slamming into her arm as he whirled and stumbled. Edwin moved close and drove his blades into the man's neck once again, deeper this time.

Ilea ducked under another axe swing as Ronan's chest sunk inward, Maria's magic taking effect as another bolt of lightning flashed through the man. Ilea ripped out the axe stuck in her arm, the weapon having punched straight through her armor. She stepped close and grabbed Ronan's arm, summoning one olvor gauntlet into her free hand before smashing it down onto his skull, sacrificing more health to hold back his arm.

Blades cut into his neck and chest as void magic ripped out chunks of his torso and two cursed lances punched through his knees. Her second punch with her gauntlet cracked his bones, and another burst of lightning coursed through Ronan's head and burst from his right eye. Ilea felt the strength in his arm leave when Edwin's next strike finally severed Ronan's neck.

His body fell, propped up by the two metal lances, as his head tumbled to the floor. Ilea staggered back, and as a kill notification appeared in her mind, she healed the deep wound that would have cut off her arm were it not for her armor. She breathed hard, seeing more people approach in her Sphere. They hadn't been quiet.

"More coming," she said, sacrificing more health to improve her body enhancement spell.

This is far from over.

FIFTEEN

Murder

Maria vanished. Edwin flicked the blood off his swords and twirled his weapons. Red lightning crackled around Trian as he stepped next to Ilea. Kyrian stood behind them, metal spears splitting into needles and moving to circle around him.

Ilea braced herself, the wound on her arm closing just as the door to the master bedroom burst open.

Bright barriers flared to life in front of a young woman with a clean-shaven head. She wore white robes, and her eyes shone with magic. Another woman wearing light metal armor rushed in behind the barrier mage. Her blonde hair flowed down to her shoulders, and she glowed with a faint golden light. A healer.

Next to them appeared a tall man in heavy steel half plate, his joints free of armor, his empty hands raised in a defensive stance. His limbs were thick, and he carried the ton of metal he wore easily. His eyes went wide as he spotted the bodies and the group of fighters responsible.

[Barrier Mage – lvl 189]

[Healer – lvl 203]

[Warrior – lvl 210]

Behind them followed four uniformed guards, and another three appeared near the windows of the large room in a flanking maneuver. They had various classes and armaments and were all close to level one hundred.

Ilea looked at the immense man in plated armor. Wallace Birmingale, she knew, the brawler. And one of their targets. She took a deep breath.

"What have you d—" the man started to say as Ilea felt a presence in her Sphere. Not Maria, but something else. Someone who had rushed past the newly arrived fighters, who were still standing there, wary of the intruders. She saw this new presence go for Trian, saw the blade before she appeared in front of him to intercept.

Steel struck steel, a blade scraping against Ilea's armor and past her shoulder, missing the lightning mage behind her by a hair. Ilea punched but saw the near-invisible figure in her Sphere flash backward as the room exploded into movement. Wooden roots broke through the floor and magic flashed from both her team and the enemy, but Ilea stayed focused on the near-invisible figure, intent on not losing them.

Ilea dodged low past a set of roots, stopping in her tracks when a surge of fire flashed in front of her. Lightning and metal flew past her from her allies and struck the barriers protecting the enemy. She saw Edwin rush past, sword in hand, but stayed focused on the form in her sphere. It flowed upward, to the side, to the ceiling, then down, aiming at Kyrian.

Ilea jumped and intercepted with a tackle, feeling the heavy impact as she tried to grapple the formless figure. They tumbled to the floor before a thick root struck Ilea's side and made her roll away, still clutching the figure. She pushed reversed healing into the assassin before she punched down.

Though the impact was soft, her intrusion broke the shrouding spell, revealing black leather armor, dark, near-orange eyes, and a curved sword that slashed upward and between Ilea's shoulder pieces. She twisted, and the blade struck her armor instead. The movement made her let go of the woman, who pushed herself back and kicked against Ilea's knee, jumping up as her shroud formed around her once more.

Ilea leaped aside and summoned her ash as more roots broke through the floor. Windows to her right shattered as a streak of red lightning exploded into them. She kept herself steady as the floor gave way and she saw Edwin's body crash through one of the walls, thrown by Wallace, who followed with fast and heavy steps. Ilea focused on the shrouded rogue, debris, magic, and metal shrapnel pushing back the lower-leveled guards, the barrier mage, and the healer.

She saw the rogue appear in a dining room below, so she blinked down right next to her. Ilea moved to kick when she saw the woman shift away and turn, her blade angled so its point was aimed at Ilea's chest. With a flash of magic and movement, the woman rushed past Ilea's kick and struck her enchanted armor head-on, the blade punching through with the screeching cry of rent metal.

The strike was deflected just enough to miss Ilea's spine, but it still drove Ilea backward across the floor, her chest pierced by the blade. The blade had struck clean through her, puncturing her armor on both sides. She coughed blood into her helmet, feeling the poison already taking effect.

'ding' You have been poisoned by the Whispering Flow, -92 health per second for three minutes

"That was your heart," the woman said, her voice neutral.

Petra Birmingale. Nice to meet you.

Ilea reached up and grabbed the blade before the rogue could rip it out. She held it fast and sacrificed some health to boost her auras. She could feel both the poison and her own healing battling for supremacy, her power surging as she stepped forward, pushing the blade deeper until she could grasp the hand that held it.

Got you.

She squeezed and pulled the invisible woman close, slamming her helmet into the head of the shrouded form, the impact once again breaking the spell.

Then Ilea felt a pulse flow through her. Something was wrong.

The blade.

She couldn't feel the pain, but she could feel her muscles tense as the poison continued to spread.

Burning more health to push her aura, Ilea grappled and fell with the woman in her arms, reverse healing flowing into her. She screamed.

They fell with a dull thud, and the blade was thrust even deeper into her, its hilt now pressed against Ilea's armor. She raised her right arm to block the left hand of Petra, whose arm was shaking as she held the dagger.

Ilea held on to Petra with her legs and punched down with her right hand, magic surging into the rogue as Ilea struck her in the face from point-blank range. Another strike, and her hand came away bloodied.

The third strike broke the woman's jaw, magic being driven into her enemy as Ilea felt her own body going more rigid, the poison slowly paralyzing her, doing more than just wiping out her health, only stopped by her aura and healing.

More.

She sacrificed further health and grabbed the woman's head with her left hand. Petra summoned another dagger into her right hand and tried to stab Ilea's arm, but the weapon scraped fruitlessly against the well-crafted armor.

Ilea squeezed Petra's right hand, breaking bones before she grabbed one of the daggers. She set her jaw, tasting blood as she turned the weapon and pushed more of her dwindling health into her aura.

Screaming, she slammed the blade into the woman's head. Petra's right arm went slack at the same moment, and her movements stopped as her eyes looked up at Ilea in a panic. She twitched for another second before she lay still.

Ilea sat atop her and leaned back, seeing two of the guards from the fight upstairs break into the dining room. She gripped the blade still jutting from her torso and gritted her teeth, wheezing from her pierced lung.

[Warrior – lvl 121]

[Mage – lvl 134]

She pulled the blade out to the harsh sound of metal scraping against steel, throwing it aside with a clatter as she pushed her healing and aura into her body to get rid of the grave wound and the poison.

"I don't n... need a h... heart," she gasped before she locked eyes with the guards. One of them grasped a two-handed hammer, the other had six spheres of water hovering before his chest. "You d... don't w... want... this fight."

Impacts and shouts echoed from both the rooms above and outside the house as well. The two guards eyed Ilea for a few seconds before the warrior tapped the mage's shoulder.

"Noble business. This is beyond our pay grade. Let's get the city guard."

The other man nodded and they slowly retreated, keeping their eyes on Ilea before they shut the door behind them.

Ilea took an appreciative breath as the hole in her lung closed up. Her heart started beating again a moment later, and then she felt the poison finally take over.

She moved away from Petra's corpse and fell to the ground, breathing hard before she locked up entirely. She focused on her health and healing, clenching her jaw before she sacrificed newly recovered health.

She stored her armor and summoned Aki into her hand, then cut into her own chest. Bit by bit, she sliced away her own flesh where the poisoned blade had infected it, and then she healed again, all the while watching her surroundings with her Sphere, listening to the impacts. The mansion shook, sending old oil paintings and a nearby vase crashing to the floor.

Ilea's breathing became less ragged as she cut away the last bit of infected tissue that she could reach, pushing with her healing and aura against the rest. The poison still burned in her chest and would demand more health than she had to remove it. It would be safest to wait it out, but her friends were out there fighting.

"Sorry, Aki," she said, glancing at the blade.

"Talk later. Focus now," he said, and she stored him in her necklace.

Ilea blinked outside into the garden, finding smoldering streaks in the grass and sizzling red lighting burning wooden roots that were moving fluidly to ensnare and attack. She saw the wood creator, Graham Birmingale, rise up into the air with long twisting roots extending from his arms and legs. He reached up and lashed a wooden limb down against the flying Trian, who teleported to avoid the strike.

"You dare attack us?" Graham screamed. Spittle flecked his lips, and his eyes radiated fury.

Ilea spread her own wings and flew toward the fight as Graham moved the wood around him to protect against the storm of needles that harried him. Ilea prepared to blink close.

Then, just as he opened his mouth to scream, his entire head imploded with a strange sucking noise. His twisting wooden arms and legs flailed as his form staggered and fell to the ground. From somewhere in the garden came a scream, and Ilea looked for their last target.

The mansion of the Birmingales had caught fire and part of the upper floor had collapsed, yet there were no Imperial guards nearby, no soldiers arriving to interrupt their fight. It was dark, yet Ilea thought that she saw smoke rising in the distance. From more than one place.

She blinked closer to Trian and landed in the grass where the man had fallen to one knee, touching his shoulder. His armor was dented.

"I can't heal right now, how inj—" Ilea began, but she cut off when she felt the ground shake. She looked at the sky and saw glowing spheres of fire descending down toward the distant districts of the capital. "What's…"

"Artillery magic," Edwin said when he appeared next to them. "You're injured."

"I need a moment if you need healing too."

"Our situation is changing. Only one target left."

"You *monsters*!" came a scream from near the mansion.

Ilea saw the barrier mage, Ania, the youngest of the family, rush toward them before the tall man, Wallace, caught her arm.

"Why?" Ania screamed. She staggered as Wallace pulled her back, her face tear-streaked and glaring at their group.

Ilea couldn't see Maria with her eyes or her Sphere. But she could see that Wallace wasn't focused only on their group, his stance tense and his eyes darting from side to side. His left arm was limp, but Hera, their healer and another of the sisters, was standing at his side. A dim warm glow emanated from her form and eyes. They were the only three left. The guards had fled. Or they'd died. Ilea didn't know.

Another tremor made the ground shake ever so slightly. The night sky lit up as a bright red beam of arcane light seared into the distance, evaporating near a dozen spheres of flame falling down on the city.

What was that?

Ilea could feel the pressure of the arcane magic in the air itself and raised her arms instinctively.

"We chose a good night for this attack," Edwin said as he glanced up at the sky, then turned to Trian. "Ready to finish this?"

Trian stood up and staggered slightly as red lightning flickered around him.

Ilea watched Wallace step before the two young sisters. She saw the determination in his eyes, the fear and terror in the eyes of Ania and Hera. Two young sisters caught up in this mess. Ignorant. Innocent.

"Fight me, just let them go," Wallace pleaded.

"You... killed them all," Trian said, his voice trembling. His body was awash with surging red sparks.

"It wasn't my choice to make," the tall man said, resignation in his eyes.

"What are you talking about?" Hera asked, touching the man's arm. Her voice shook with fear and confusion.

"Why did they come?!" Ania screamed. "They killed mother!"

Ilea could see the look in Wallace's eyes. She could see the guilt. And she saw Trian take a step toward them, his lightning building as Edwin prepared his blades. Kyrian glanced her way.

She reached out and gripped Trian's arm, stopping him. "This is enough."

He looked back, his eyes bloodshot, his face streaked with sweat and viscera. "No. It is *not*."

"It is," Ilea said, feeling him tug at her grip, but she only held on harder. Ilea could feel the power of his lightning reaching a crescendo, but she pulled him closer, putting her arms around him and hugging her friend. "This is enough."

Kyrian joined them and put a hand on Trian's shoulder. "We're here."

Trian screamed, and two bursts of lightning shot in violent arcs from his arms and hands into the ground around them, tearing furrows in the earth. His body went slack before he sobbed.

Ilea held him close. She looked past his shoulder and locked eyes with Wallace. There was hope there now, and a begrudging respect. She saw Hera's wide eyes and Ania's slack-jawed gaze. They had no idea what was happening, nor why. Unlike Wallace.

"What will you do?" she asked him.

Wallace was quiet for a moment as more distant explosions shook the city. Ilea could hear screeches too, not far off. Demons. Summoned or brought into the city to spread chaos.

"My brother and his wife have died for their choices. Our House has honor no longer. I offer my life for the lives of my nieces. They had nothing to do with it," Wallace said.

His jaw was tight, his stance resolute. Hera sobbed, pawing at her uncle's armor. Ania froze.

"Just go," Kyrian said.

Ilea nodded.

Trian said nothing. He wiped blood from his face and gazed out at the ruined estate.

Wallace hesitated for just a moment, then grabbed Ania and Hera and threw one over each shoulder before running toward the wall and leaping over it, vanishing into the night. The last three surviving members of House Birmingale.

Maria appeared on the broken section of the burning mansion and jumped down, landing right where Wallace had stood a moment prior.

"They will hunt you. It would've been better to end it now. A mercy too. For everyone."

"We didn't ask you," Ilea said, still holding Trian. He had stopped sobbing.

The poison's effects finally faded. Her health was low, but she checked Trian first, finding the right side of his chest in tatters, with internal bleeding and six broken ribs. She helped him sit down in the grass and started healing.

"Is he alright?" Kyrian asked, metal spheres still circling him.

"He'll survive."

"That armor didn't exactly help, did it?" Maria asked as she walked over, nodding at the damaged section of Ilea's chest piece.

"It did, actually."

"What poison did she use?"

"Whispering Flow."

Maria whistled. "You killed her? Where's her corpse?" She turned when another section of the mansion collapsed, the flames now ravaging the first floor and attic. "Never mind."

"That concludes our part of the agreement," Edwin said, having cleaned his blades before he sheathed them. "You were right," he said to Maria.

She grinned. "The timing was impeccable. Not a single soldier in the vicinity."

"What's happening?" Ilea asked.

"War," Edwin said. "Or, to be more precise, a siege. I suggest you three leave the city as soon as you can. We should meet up again at the hideout in a few days' time."

"What about you two?"

"The night is still young, Ilea, and war brings a lot of opportunities. I hope you three don't forget your promise."

Ilea gave him a nod and turned back to Trian.

"I thought for sure one or two of you would die. Well done," Maria said. For once, she sounded sincere.

As Ilea watched them leave, Kyrian said, "We should get out of here too. Before any guards arrive."

Ilea nodded. She saw the dark clouds above flash with color from time to time, the fires still burning in the city. She felt dull tremors and breathed in deep, then crouched down.

"Trian, we need to leave." She waited for a few seconds, then just threw him over her shoulder and flew out of the garden into a nearby street, Kyrian following behind.

Ilea landed and ran through several streets, skirting between many other large mansions similar to the one they'd attacked. She saw dim lights from many of the windows. Some were open, revealing people peering out into the night.

The streets themselves were deserted, but when they entered a less affluent part of the city, she saw a few people rush past. She stopped and checked for soldiers, finding a group flying in the distance but nobody on the streets.

More people were looking out of their windows here, and the shouts were becoming more frequent as the ground continued to shake from time to time. She heard distant explosions and continued onward. They ran for a few more minutes before Kyrian spoke up.

"We should get inside," he said, pointing farther down the road.

Ilea saw where he meant – an inn with a dozen or so people standing outside, their faces turned toward the distant magic above the westernmost part of the city.

"Down that alley," she said, pointing and rushing into a small gap between two three-story structures. She checked in her Sphere but found no pursuers following them. Breathing out, she set Trian down and stored her bloodied and damaged set of plate armor, replacing it with traveling clothes and a cloak.

Couldn't stop Petra's attack. Even with my ash and Balduur's fine work.

"You two should change as well," she said, checking on Trian again. He was leaning against a stone wall, his eyes unfocused. "Trian. We're not out of this yet. Look at me."

He glanced up, took a breath, then shuddered. His armor was replaced in the next moment with a similar outfit to hers.

"Can you give me mine as well?" Kyrian asked, looking at Trian.

"Yes. Have this too," Trian said, handing Kyrian a ring. "We'll check the contents later. Ronan carried it."

"A storage ring..." Kyrian said. "W... why? That's..."

"I have one already," Trian shrugged.

Ilea gave Kyrian a nod. "I have a storage device too. Probably good if you don't flash it around. Someone might recognize it."

It was a broad golden ring with three sapphire stones set into it. She preferred her necklace. Seeing Kyrian's hesitation, she explained, "Claim the ring, then focus on your armor and store it."

Kyrian nodded. His armor vanished a moment later, and he received his clothes and cloak from Trian.

Ilea crouched down next to Trian. "How are you holding up?"

He glanced at her, then looked away, shaking his head slightly. "I don't... I don't know. I... need time."

"Sure," Ilea said, rubbing Trian's shoulder lightly. "We're here, okay?"

He looked at her and breathed in.

"Ready," Kyrian said, pulling his cloak up and over his head.

"Good. Let's move at a brisk pace and find out what's going on with this siege."

"Shouldn't we leave the city?"

"Maybe. I don't know."

"Try the inn for now," Kyrian said.

Ilea smiled slightly and went to the end of the alley. Glancing out, she could see a few more people running now. Others had gone outside and were now simply standing and watching the distant spectacle.

They're just standing there, watching...

She waved to her companions and started toward the inn. Their group didn't attract a lot of attention due to the magical bombardment in the distance.

"What's going on?" a middle-aged man said to another as they passed.

"We're safe here, right?"

"Of course, this is Virilya. Half our military is here."

"Right, but who would be foolish enough to attack then?"

"Think it's elves?"

"So far east? No, probably bandits."

"Bandits? Are you kidding me? You see those spells, right? And they're using the central district defenses, the cannons!"

Ilea stepped into the inn. There were a few people inside, but most had gone out into the cool night air. The innkeep was gone, so she just checked the keys behind the counter, took one, and looked for the room it belonged to. She'd pay later. Leaving coins on the counter seemed like a bad idea.

The room was cramped and stuffy, containing a single bed, a small dresser, and no windows. On the dresser was a small lantern that she held out to Trian. He lit it with a spark of lightning as Kyrian closed the door behind them.

Trian sat on the bed and brushed the bedding with his hands. He had an unfocused expression again.

"What should we do?" Kyrian asked.

"I don't know," Ilea said. "Edwin said we should meet them at the hideout in a few days' time."

"I don't think leaving now is a good idea. There will be a lot of soldiers near the walls and gates."

"Right," Ilea said. Then she heard a scream outside. "I'll check that. Can you stay here with Trian?"

Kyrian glanced between them.

"It's fine. I can teleport and fly," Ilea said. She saw him nod, then vanished.

She reappeared in the street, where the people in front of the inn were scrambling to get back inside, a single form barreling down the street and toward them.

Ilea heard the familiar moan of demon spawn and rushed to meet it, one of her bladed blue-steel gauntlets appearing on her right arm as she jumped and twirled, dodging its claws and slicing through its neck. She landed in a crouch and was already storing her weapon as the creature toppled over.

She took the chance to check her messages.

'ding' Your group has defeated [Eternal Pyromancer – lvl 230 / Catalyst of Fire – lvl 222]

'ding' Your group has defeated [Unyielding Berserker – lvl 248 / Fire Wielder – lvl 241]

'ding' Azarinth First Hunter has reached lvl 225 – 5 stat points awarded

'ding' Azarinth First Hunter has reached lvl 226 – 5 stat points awarded

'ding' Inheritor of Eternal Ash has reached lvl 221 – 5 stat points awarded

'ding' Azarinth Reversal reaches 2nd lvl 17

'ding' Form of Ash and Ember reaches 2nd lvl 19

'ding' Wave of Ember reaches 2nd lvl 13

'ding' Eyes of Ash reaches 2nd lvl 20

'ding' Body of Ash reaches 2nd lvl 17

'ding' Ashen Warrior reaches 2nd lvl 17

'ding' You have killed [Blade of Whispers lvl 241 / Claw of Rot lvl 221]. For killing an enemy fifteen or more levels above your own, you receive bonus experience.

'ding' Poison Resistance reaches lvl 18

'ding' Poison Resistance reaches lvl 19

'ding' Poison Resistance reaches lvl 20

'ding' You have killed [Beastblood Warrior lvl 210 / Pure Enhancer lvl 203]

'ding' Inheritor of Eternal Ash has reached lvl 222 – 5 stat points awarded

Seeing the messages for killing Ronan, Bale, and Petra made her tense up.

We killed them. Murdered them in their own home.

She breathed faster and faster, almost hyperventilating before circling healing magic through her head calmed her nerves. It had been one thing to plan everything, and she had come here to support Trian. But now it was done.

"She killed it! She killed the beast!" one of the people looking out from a nearby window shouted, cheers filling the air.

Ilea slowed her breathing and focused. *You're here now. Focus on what you can do, on what you should do.*

She said the words to herself, but it didn't work. Instead, she closed her eyes and focused solely on her healing, on the magic flowing through her head.

They killed Trian's family. What you did was justified.

She saw Petra's vacant eyes as she lay there on the floor of the dining room, a dagger jutting out of her head.

Ilea felt her right eye twitch. She nodded to herself and turned, ignoring the dead low-level demon before she walked back into the inn.

"Who's the innkeep?" she asked, summoning a silver coin. "We took room number four."

A large bald man with a mustache stepped up, a large plank of wood in his hands.

"You killed that demon?"

She nodded.

"The room's free."

She glanced at the impromptu weapon in his hands and gave him a nod, blinking into the room upstairs.

"Just me," she said as several metal spheres splintered into needles and pointed her way.

"What's going on?" Kyrian asked as Ilea looked down at Trian, who was sitting in the same position as before.

"Demons. There are demons running around in the city. Just a single one here, but I heard more before. Near the estate. I think… demons… demons I can fight. I should help. I can heal as well. I can find out exactly what's happening. See how the city plans to respond."

"I'll stay with him. He was murmuring something before. I don't think he's well," Kyrian said, nodding toward Trian.

Ilea checked him quickly with her healing. "It's probably just been a lot."

She circled some healing mana into his head, but Trian reached up and touched her hand.

"Don't. I don't want that. I need to… feel it."

She stopped. "Okay. Rest. I'll be back soon."

"We'll be here. If not, we'll try to get to the hideout," Kyrian said. "Be careful."

Ilea gave him a nod and vanished. Once outside, she spread her wings and checked the street, then flew farther up.

What are you doing, Ilea? Are you a hero now?

She saw dozens of bright spells in the distance. Many were raining down onto the city, others were flying up or flaring in the hundreds of streets of the capital. She saw people rushing over rooftops, others flying. She heard shouts and explosions.

It felt like Ravenhall, down in the Haven. But here she was alone with Kyrian and Trian. And she knew from Edwin and Maria that this wasn't a demon summoning by a single mage. It was an attack from a neighboring kingdom.

She gulped and clenched her fists. Part of her wanted to go back into the room, to flee the city, to hide away, but wasn't she a Shadow now? Didn't she have magic that could heal? Wings that let her fly? And enough strength to do… something?

She wasn't sure what she should do, but the thought of going back to see Trian the way he was right now made her stomach tighten. Out here, at least, she could do something.

Find injured people and heal them. Kill the demons. Simple.

The thought grounded her and she flew off, turning in the air to make sure she memorized where their inn was located. Another bright beam flashed out from the central district, the structures surrounding it lighting up in the night.

The entire central district looked like a fortress in the center of the city. Without the attack and the powerful arcane magic emanating from somewhere within, it may have even looked bland compared to some of the other far more embellished large temples and structures in the city, but now it looked towering and imposing, even with the massive city walls in the distance.

Ilea heard more screams and followed them, finding another single demon swinging its clawed hands into a wooden door. She landed and sacrificed a bit of health, punching the monster in its spine. She heard the crack and saw it sag, the level fifty creature dead before it hit the ground.

"It's dead," she called to the people holding the door shut from the other side.

But Ilea didn't wait for a response and flew on, finding more creatures now, all of them alone. Getting closer to the magical detonations, she started to see more soldiers in the streets, squads running toward the battle site. She saw mages flying above, nearly all wearing the gray and red of the Empire.

She glimpsed something in her Sphere and instinctively blinked down and into an apartment, just in time to stop an assassin from sinking his blade into the back of a man looking out of his window.

[Rogue – lvl 152]

He wore dark red leather armor. The colors, she knew, of Baralia.

The assassin struggled against her hold, grabbing a second dagger and stabbing at her chest.

When Ilea caught his arm with her other hand, the assassin kicked at her leg. She felt the impact but ignored it.

"What are you doing? Why are you here?"

She saw the assassin's target scream and stumble away, fleeing from the room.

"You are not with the Empire," the assassin said.

Ilea saw another figure appear in the apartment below, slashing their short sword at the people standing near the windows. She heard screams and let go of the assassin to teleport down, where she found another man clad in dark red leather armor.

She shoulder charged him, the impact sending him crashing into the stone wall before she reached him again and punched. He ducked, and her fist splintered the stone before he vanished.

The assassin above was gone now as well, so Ilea turned to the people moaning and sobbing around her. Pushing a man aside, she touched an injured woman lying on the ground.

"I'm a healer," she said, using her magic to take care of the injury.

What are they doing?

She ignored all the pleas and questions of the people around her. A moment later, she heard a heavy impact and felt the walls shake as a ringing came to her ears.

"They're hitting closer!" someone shouted.

Ilea checked the others for injuries, then blinked outside. A set of houses on the opposite side of the road had started collapsing, fires burning on several roofs and parts of the road. More screams rent the air.

Ilea swallowed hard. She checked her Sphere and rushed into the first home, finding three people trapped below a half-collapsed wall. She sacrificed health and felt her aura strengthen, sliding in with her back to the wall before she pushed and raised it up.

"Get out!" she shouted, and the people clambered out and ran toward the exit. She blinked up and outside, looking for the assassins when she saw three more meteor-like spheres descend onto the buildings nearby.

Are they targeting the people living here? Those assassins…

She turned around and rushed back to the house she'd just been in. She used her Hunter's Sight to track what she could, blinking through several homes before she found them.

Four people lay dead, including one of the assassins she'd been tracking. The other one had his longsword angled toward a fighter wearing half-plate armor with a short gray and red cape. He could barely stand on his injured right leg, but his spear was keeping the assassin at a distance.

Ilea didn't wait – she rushed the assassin and grabbed his arm, punching his head twice as he failed to slash at her with his blade. The first strike broke bone. The second killed him. She let go and checked the warrior, slapping aside his spear before she started pushing healing mana into him.

[Warrior – lvl 138]

"Who are you?" he asked through strained breaths.

"Just a Shadow passing through. Why were they here? What I—"

She broke off as the house trembled, a wave of heat bursting through the windows and flashing past Ilea as more screams joined in the chaos.

"They're striking at our people, killing randomly to create fear and chaos. I'm afraid it's working," the warrior said. "Shadow, thank you for the help, but there's more to do."

Ilea nodded his way as he made for the door and then blinked outside, where she saw people running through the streets, away from the city walls and the fiery spheres reaching closer and closer to the residential areas. She saw flashes of magic in the sky, squinting and seeing fighters meeting each other in battle.

Ilea breathed deeply and went toward the next house. She didn't want to get involved with the fighting. She didn't want to face and kill soldiers and assassins from a distant kingdom. She didn't want to be here, but she knew she didn't want to just let people die either.

Ilea felt her hands shake. She steadied them and flew toward the next collapsed house.

SIXTEEN

Evacuation

Ilea lost herself in her task of rescuing and healing people trapped below fallen debris. She didn't encounter any more assassins, but she saw three more demons. The destruction was extensive. Dozens of homes were destroyed or burning, the fires spreading as the battles in the skies continued.

She was carrying two more people out of the flames of what had once been a bakery when a group of soldiers intercepted her and began to aid the survivors.

"Adventurer, stay close," one of them said. At that moment, a distant bell tolled. Shortly after, more joined in. These were closer and more numerous.

Another soldier raised his sword. "Evacuate the people! Retreat to the central district! Take the people west and through the gates!"

Ilea looked at the soldier before launching herself into the air. High above the rooftops, she saw more troops making their way west, giving up their positions. Civilians ran from their homes in droves and soon joined a throng of people moving in a singular direction, shouts telling them to evacuate toward the west.

They're losing…

The battles in the skies were still raging on. She didn't see a massive invading army, but what she saw were continuous spells raining down onto the many homes of the people of Virilya.

Ilea flew above the throng and blinked down to help up those who fell in the stampede. She turned when she saw a spear of blood cut through three elderly evacuees, glancing up to see a mage in red robes teleport to the other side of the road, then start charging another spell.

She blinked toward him but was intercepted by another man, who wore blood-red armor and a helmet that hid his face. A heavy hammer struck at her. She raised her arms before her and felt the weapon's impact against her ash. All the air was punched from her lungs, her arms broken as she was sent flying backward.

She steadied herself in the air and started healing as a third person in dark red armor appeared, slashing at her with two curved swords. She only saw the focused eyes behind the helmet, blinking back when the hammer wielder appeared again. Both were above her own level, but not by much.

Ilea dodged a spear of blood sent her way and saw three Imperials rushing the two red-armored fighters she'd been facing. But rather than providing aid, two of them were dead in the next moment. The third fled.

She narrowed her eyes and breathed out, raising her arms and rushing back in. She barely saw the sword wielder twirl, tearing several cuts into her arms before her neck pulsed with magic. She dodged aside as her shoulder exploded in blood and gore. Another Imperial squad rushed toward them. She saw more enemies too, red shadows over the rooftops.

She attempted to heal her wounds but found her magic wasn't working well against the cuts left by the blade wielder. She was losing blood, and the pair were closing the distance once more.

Ilea raised her arms and summoned her blue-steel gauntlets, but then she saw the hammer wielder stop and shout something before vanishing. She could feel pressure from behind and above her.

A monster.

The Baralia blade wielder disappeared just before rushing air cut into the ground and split the stone. Ilea saw the blood mage above jump back, but he was still ripped into three pieces by invisible blades of air, his remains twirling in the air before they started falling.

Ilea turned and looked up to see a slender form hovering some distance above her, surrounded by moving winds, her long white hair reflecting the moonlight. Ilea glimpsed a white and silver mask on the woman's face before she shot into the distance in a wave of wind and magic.

"Adventurer, move with us, protect the people! We will take them to the western gate," a nearby soldier said, ordering his men in the same direction. "Calm and steady, for the Empire!"

Ilea turned and flew above the soldiers, joining the growing throng of fleeing people. She was glad the woman had shown up. The nearby Imperial soldiers would've likely died without her help, and Ilea would've likely had to flee herself. The wounds on her arms and chest were healing but still not closed, and her clothes were wet with her own blood.

She gulped but couldn't help contain her smile. The power she'd felt, the calm in the woman's slight movements, and the magic when she'd rushed away. She'd felt the same way when she'd seen wings of fire for the first time back in the Riverwatch tournament.

Ilea was running now, the same as with the Praetorians, but that woman, masked in white and silver, didn't need to run. Ilea knew that, one day, she wanted to be the same.

* * *

Ilea helped where she could, mostly healing those who tripped and were trampled by other fleeing citizens. More soldiers were present now, either flying above them or running beside them.

Everything slowed a few minutes later, as the streets were overfilled with people shouting and crying. They carried heavy packs, bundles, and various belongings. Some carried way too much, others were without even their shirts.

Suddenly, the soldiers shouted instructions to organize the people and formed defensive lines. Ilea saw a flash of magic and flew into another street, finding three assassins facing a squad of soldiers, but the Baralia men vanished as soon as they met resistance. She landed and turned to the one injured soldier, his eye cut out, blood running down his face.

"Halt!" one of his companions shouted.

Ilea raised her hands. "Adventurer, healer," she said, summoning her Shadow badge to drive the point home. She healed the man as soon as the others let her pass, then flew back into the sky again.

The streets were packed now with hundreds, no, thousands of residents making their way westward toward the high walls of the capital and out into the relative safety of the countryside beyond.

Ilea felt small in all of this. She heard the bells tolling, saw the beams of magic blasting out from the central district. She knew this chaos was the reason why their plan had succeeded without interference.

She'd known attacks had been planned for tonight, and she'd known that the tensions between Baralia and Lys had built to breaking point. But an attempted siege and an evacuation of the entire capital was far beyond what she'd expected.

She kept her breathing steady and stayed with the line of soldiers, with many other adventurers and even a few Shadows joining in as they helped the people along amid the explosions reverberating through the city streets.

* * *

Ilea stayed with the Imperial soldiers, whose numbers swelled from a few dozen at the start to hundreds, their formations protecting the slowly moving crowd of people. The attacks continued, but they were less frequent now and quickly dealt with by the prepared soldiers.

Soon, she felt redundant, seeing healers moving with the soldiers now. She flew to the edge of the throng of people, still more civilians running to join it, as squads of soldiers guided them along. A blink brought her into a cellar, and she teleported from one empty house to the next until she saw fewer people in the streets above.

Flying low, she made her way back to the section of the city where she knew the inn was. By the time she arrived, the road before the inn was deserted but the sounds of bells and magic remained, though mostly more distant now.

Ilea found the inn itself deserted too, with chairs lying on the ground and a wet puddle in the hearth, still steaming, where the fire used to be. She went upstairs and knocked on the door, seeing both Kyrian and Trian still in their room.

"It's me," she said, blinking inside.

Kyrian stood up from the bed, eyes wide. He gestured for her to explain, so she did, quickly telling them what she'd seen and done.

At some point, Trian shook his head and looked at her. "Why aren't they counterattacking?"

Kyrian turned toward him. "Overwhelming forces?"

"No, Ilea said there are only a few fighters and assassins in the city."

"That's just what I saw, there was fighting in the sky as well," Ilea said. "But yeah, they were targeting civilians. Maybe that's why the Empress is evacuating."

"Maybe," Trian said, but he didn't look convinced. "The evidence..." He stood up, eyes widening. "We need to get to the central district and deliver it before it's too late."

"Too late?" Kyrian asked.

"They might give up the walls, but no enemy has ever set their boots into the Halls of Eternity, into the heart of this city. If they're evacuating, soon there will only be soldiers here. We should move fast, then leave the city with everyone else," he said, suddenly animated as he made his way to the door. "I can do it alone, but it may be safer..." he said and paused, looking at them for a long moment. "If we go there together."

"We go together," Ilea said.

Kyrian nodded.

There was the barest flicker of a grateful smile on Trian's face. Then he turned to the job at hand.

* * *

The way toward the central district was chaotic, but the three moved fast and used their Shadow badges to get past a few groups of soldiers without much trouble. When they reached the thick walls of the central district, they were stopped, however, as the soldiers weren't letting anyone in without good reason and verification.

Ilea could feel the dense magic pulsing in the walls, far-reaching enchantments more powerful than anything she'd ever seen or felt before. Beyond the guards and broad stone stairwell leading up, she could see the center of the Empire's power: the walled-off central district with massive stone structures jutting out beyond, built mainly to be defensible. Stone stairs led up toward heavy iron gates, Imperials moving in and out.

Trian managed to pay one of the Imperial messengers to go and fetch Josefin Anderson, the woman he'd chosen to give the evidence to, before rejoining the others not far from the stairwell. It was protected by near level two hundred warriors wearing full plate armor and vigilant mages, some of whom were watching their group with suspicion.

"We should circle toward the southernmost stairwell. She'll meet us there," Trian said, and they moved.

Ilea could hear her heartbeat as they waited in one of the streets, soldiers rushing by constantly, most of them heading toward the central district. They didn't have to wait long, a hooded figure soon finding them. She walked at a brisk pace, her face and hair hidden.

"Friend," she said in a quiet voice when she reached Trian, hugging him. "I'm sorry. I wish I'd known."

He nodded, breathing sharply before he pushed her away slightly. "I came to deliver this to you," he said, a package appearing in his hands. "It should be enough to convince even the Empress."

"Who was it?" Josefin asked.

"Birmingale," Trian said.

She was quiet for a short while and then nodded, taking the package. It vanished from her hands. "Did you come for this alone?"

"It's already done."

"I see," Josefin said, breathing in deeply. "I will do what I can with this. You should leave the city. The central district will soon be locked down."

"Locked down? The Empress is abandoning the rest of the city?"

"Yes, for the time being. Baralia is here for her, the high nobility, and Virilya itself. The death and destruction are intended to draw out the highest-level defenders. By evacuating the citizens, the Empress deprives the invaders of their leverage."

"Can we not fight back? Our armies…" He glanced at Ilea and Kyrian, then shook his head.

Josefin moved a little closer and talked in a whisper. "There is more at play here, Trian. The Empress must've known that tensions were growing, that Baralia would soon make their move. This was planned, as were the evacuation and lockdown of the central district."

"Thousands will die. Many must've died already."

Josefin glanced behind her. When she looked back at Trian, her mouth was a thin line.

"I know, but she must've taken everything into account. Remember, if the battle were to be truly joined in the city streets, the fallout would result in far greater casualties than we are seeing tonight. You all must know only too well the collateral damage high-level fighters can cause. I'm not sure exactly what she's planning, but I trust her judgment. She has argued for the people and their safety many times before, and her policies reflect it. If this attack is what the people of the Empire must endure, then it must be so."

"They'll die in the wilderness."

"Not with much of the army escorting them. Coordinated and thousands strong, no common beasts will dare get close."

Trian furrowed his brow. "And Baralia will not pursue?"

Josefin gave Trian an appraising look as he puzzled it out.

"The central district, and its occupants, remain here. Alyris is presenting herself as bait," Trian whispered. "They won't pursue because everything they want is right here."

Josefin nodded. "I hope so, Trian, and I hope they do not move their troops to intercept the populace. It is dangerous to plan when the arrogance of your enemy has such a vital part to play, but their uncoordinated attacks so far suggest our information is correct. This is a last effort by the High King Baron to keep his kingdom from falling apart." Josefin paused. "I need to leave. Do take care and find me again when... if... things are different."

"I will. And I trust you," Trian said.

"I will do my part," Josefin said and bowed her head, then glanced at Ilea and Kyrian. "Shadows," she said, before she turned and walked away at the same brisk pace.

As Trian stood and watched the woman go, Ilea touched his shoulder.

"Let's go. Leave the city and go to the hideout."

He didn't react for a long moment, then blinked his eyes and nodded.

SEVENTEEN

The Island

Ilea, Trian, and Kyrian separated from the throng of people evacuating the capital soon after they passed through the outer walls. The large number of Imperial troops coupled with all the adventurers and civilians moving out of the city broke through the southern side of the Baralia siege with ease, the enemy army having attacked mainly from the north. Some of their units were even retreating northward or going back into the city, either looking for easier targets or simply being uninterested in the evacuation.

Ilea would've been concerned about monsters attacking the mostly low-level refugees, but there were thousands of soldiers and mages accompanying them, and given how fast and efficient the evacuation was, it was clear they had trained and prepared for such an event. There were hundreds of spells floating around, and fast-moving enchanted wagons pulled by horses and other beasts made up the center of the massive formation. By the time a new day broke, she assumed they would have already traveled a reasonable distance from the capital.

The trio reached the hideout before dawn, Ilea knocking on the hatch leading into the hidden structure before she opened it. She saw the others in her Sphere. Felicia was sitting at the table, a book open before her, but her eyes were closed. Aliana slept on a bedroll nearby.

"It's us," Ilea said before she blinked down, waving at Felicia, who opened her eyes at the noise. Felicia smiled, standing up and looking at Kyrian and then Trian. She frowned slightly at their haggard appearance, worry lines creasing her face.

Ilea finally switched out her bloodied clothes and cloak, cracking her neck.

"Looking for your brother? They're still in the capital. Wanted to use the opportunity."

"What opportunity?" Felicia asked. "How extensive were the attacks?"

Ilea saw Aliana stir, raising her head and rubbing her eyes.

"Baralia has laid siege to the city. Lys is evacuating the entire capital," Ilea said. Felicia drew a sharp breath, an intense look in her yellow eyes before she went back to the table and sat down, turning the pages of the book. She started writing, paused, then sat back.

"We should rest," Kyrian said.

"Food first," Aliana said. She went to a pack nearby and started removing things. "Can't sleep on an empty stomach."

"A siege," Felicia murmured. "Evacuation." She shook her head. "Your mission, how… how did it go?"

Ilea breathed in deep. She saw both of her teammates sitting at the table, Aliana already placing mugs and plates in front of them.

For the next half an hour, Ilea and Kyrian recounted the events to the others before Trian left to sleep in another room. He hadn't touched his food.

A few candles burned on the table beside their empty plates as Felicia wrote in the book before her. The strokes of her pen were deliberate, Ilea noticed, slow and smooth. The pages filled up with what she assumed to be the events they were describing.

"Are you documenting what we did? I'm not sure if that's a good idea," Ilea said.

Felicia looked up. "No. I'm detailing what's happening in the capital, every little thing you mentioned. And I'm writing down theories and my thoughts. Evacuating the capital due to this attack obviously seems excessive, but with everything Maria and Ed uncovered in the past weeks, it wouldn't surprise me if Empress Alyris is using this invasion as an opportunity."

Ilea felt tired. The food was nice, despite it all being various types of meat and meat-based dishes. There had even been beef in the dessert for some reason. She didn't miss that Kyrian asked for seconds anyway, and she saw him and Aliana exchanging shy glances from time to time. Perhaps if her day hadn't been what it was, she would've thought it endearing. As it was, she couldn't muster the energy to care much about anything.

"You can tell me more about your theories tomorrow, except if it's really important for me to know right now," she said.

Felicia looked at the book, smiled ever so slightly, then looked back at Ilea. "No. Of course. You should go sleep. It's not immediately relevant. Except maybe to Ed… and myself." She whispered the last words, almost like a realization.

"Good," Ilea said and stood up, then stretched. "Wake us up if anything comes up. Or if you want to change guard."

"It's fine. I'm glad you three made it back, safe and alive. And… it's good that you were successful."

Ilea went into the other room, not commenting. Was it good that they'd been successful? Of course it was. They'd killed a bunch of murderers.

Still, as she lay down on the bedroll and moved her back against the wall, Ilea felt exhausted and empty. They'd found and killed those responsible, fought and bled to bring them to justice. And yet it didn't feel like things had changed. Eve was still dead. Trian had still lost his family. She just hoped it would give him some closure. Perhaps now, or once they'd found Arthur Redleaf, Trian could grieve.

She fell asleep shortly after, her thoughts on the different assassins in the capital. Ilea was glad, in many ways, not to be in Virilya anymore. She hoped that in their quest to help Edwin, they wouldn't have to go back there.

* * *

When Ilea woke up, the room was dark. The air was stuffy and cool, the bedroll hard on the stone floor, but she didn't feel any discomfort from having slept on it. Trian was still asleep, she saw, and she didn't know how much time had passed. Kyrian and Aliana were sitting at the table, talking. Felicia was asleep as well.

Ilea didn't feel like sleeping anymore and blinked out into the largest room with the table, landing on her feet. Kyrian jerked when she appeared, but Aliana just smiled.

"Morning," Ilea said.

Kyrian looked at her. "Manage to get some sleep?"

Ilea sat down at the table. "A little, yeah. How are you holding up?"

He shrugged. "Not the most pleasant mission we've been on so far."

"Yeah. Feels like it's been ages since we went on our first one together." She paused. "We should go on a simple hunt once we're done with this shit. Just the team, or whoever wants to join, and a bunch of monsters to fight."

"I'll join. I'll want to take some time off after this. Somewhere nice," he said, glancing at Aliana. She met his eyes, and he looked away, scratching the back of his head. "I should probably sleep a little too, before everyone else gets up."

"You should, probably," Aliana said.

"How long was I asleep?" Ilea asked.

"I'm not sure to be honest," Aliana said, watching Kyrian leave and sighing.

Ilea raised an eyebrow. She felt a little less exhausted, but the air down here was bothering her.

"Mind if I pop out for a while? Back in a bit."

"Of course," Aliana said. "Oh! If you find any creatures, kill them and bring me their corpses."

Ilea stretched her arms. "You could just ask me to hunt something, like a normal person."

"Says the woman who went into the capital of Lys to eradicate a noble House," Aliana countered with a smirk.

"I'm not particularly proud of that one. Maybe call me 'the woman who dove head-first into a flying demon whale to cut it up from the inside'?"

Aliana peered at Ilea with her large brown eyes. "Demon whale? Sounds made up." Then she pouted. "Also, don't mention that if you don't have any of its meat."

Ilea rolled her eyes, waved, then vanished.

She reappeared in the meadow above and had to shield her eyes against the sunlight. It was past noon already.

They talked until now? After everything we did in the capital?

Spreading her wings, Ilea flew out into the forest, basking in the sun and breathing in the fresh scent of the grass and trees around her. It felt good, as if she was absorbing the energy she'd lost in the dark streets of Virilya, in that burning mansion, among the soldiers and people fleeing from the magic raining down from the sky.

"You don't look so good there," Aki said.

Ilea was surprised to hear him, but she didn't quite jump.

"Yeah."

"Anything I can do?"

"No, but I appreciate the offer. How about you? You've been around through all this."

"It's… a change. Not the kind of adventure I enjoy, but I can tell at least that you feel the same," Aki said. "But I'll stick with you, for now. Just don't want to make a scene, being a talking dagger and all. But I'm here."

Ilea smiled. "And I appreciate that, friend. Do speak up if you need anything, or if you want me to take you somewhere."

"Here is good. Focus on your mission for now. We'll talk again when it's over."

Ilea nodded, patting the sheathed dagger before she moved on and landed.

Once we're done helping Edwin, I'll go on a fucking month-long vacation. Just me, maybe the team, the wilderness, and whatever monsters want to kill me.

She hoped there'd be a lot.

Walking through the forest, she thought of the various creatures she'd learned about in her classes at the Shadow's Hand. Her smile faltered as these thoughts led her to memories of Eve, but she tried to stay focused on the moment. On the trees, the light filtering through the leaves above, the birds chirping.

It would've been nice for you to have been here, for all this. Could've used your experience. Could've used another friend.

She breathed deeply, closing her eyes for a moment. She heard an animal call, opened her eyes, and smiled.

Time to hunt.

* * *

Ilea sacrificed more of her health as she ran alongside the stag-like creature she'd found. Its antlers were made of some type of crystal, and its fur was a dark green and rough to the touch. She'd decided not to kill the harmless creature, dodging another one of the crystal spears it conjured from thin air and sent in her general direction.

It was way too cute to punch. Looking into its deep brown eyes made her feel like the forest itself was staring back at her. At first, it had run from her, but the creature didn't seem quite as stressed out by her presence now.

[Hereviir – lvl 38]

She didn't blink but slowed when the creature slowed. Ilea grinned and walked closer, reaching her hand out to touch the beast again, causing it to summon a set of crystal shards that exploded straight into her ashen armor.

Ilea felt the impacts, but none managed to penetrate her veil. She watched the hereviir gallop away and sighed.

Guess I wasn't supposed to befriend you.

She would've liked to try for a bit longer. It was possible that the creature would've grown more used to her in time, but she felt she needed to get back. She assumed Aliana hadn't slept much either.

On returning, Ilea found Felicia was up, while Aliana was asleep again.

"Your hunt wasn't successful?" Felicia asked.

"Didn't want to kill the wildlife," Ilea said, summoning two meals and pushing one toward Felicia. "Not exactly a need for it either."

"Are there vegetables in this? Aliana will be disappointed," Felicia said, grabbing the plate. "Thank you."

They ate in silence for a while until Felicia spoke up once more.

"You look better. Better than last night, I mean."

"I feel a little better too." Then Ilea saw the smile on Felicia's face, along with a hint of melancholy. "What's going on?"

Felicia made to speak, then hesitated. "I just… I've been thinking a lot, since we talked. It's…"

She shook her head.

"You don't have to share if you don't want to," Ilea said.

Felicia nodded. "Just… thank you. I think."

Ilea raised her spoon in an acknowledging gesture. She finished her plate and summoned another meal. "So. You said last night that you'd figured out some things in regard to the siege?"

Felicia seemed glad for the change of topic. She nodded. "Just theories. I mean, why would Alyris, the Empress of Lys, Lys, with its dominant, well-trained, and well-equipped military, allow a kingdom of slaver cities to lay siege to her capital? They could've rallied their troops, gathered the most powerful nobles of Virilya, and destroyed any invading forces. It would've been bloody, yes, but there's no doubt in my mind that they would've emerged victorious."

"So why didn't they?"

"Because Alyris knows about Baralia. I don't. Lys would've won one battle before the walls of Virilya and would've then been dragged into an extensive war. A war that perhaps they didn't want. With such a brazen attack, I don't think the same was true for Baralia. High King Baron must've speculated that an attack on the capital wouldn't be ignored by the proud Empire. He wanted to draw Lys into a protracted war.

"Instead, here we are, with Lys prioritizing its people and using its military not to strike back but to evacuate. Baralia will loot and destroy, and they will try to breach the central district. They will lay siege to it. A target presented by Alyris – and a play for time. Time which, I think, King Baron is running out of."

His name is still confusing. King and Baron, what are you? "Why is he running out of time?" Ilea asked. Politics wasn't really her thing, but Felicia seemed to be having fun explaining.

"Hmm. A lot of potential reasons. Baralia isn't nearly as united as, say, Kroll, nor is their power centralized, as in Lys. Their cities are far more independent, as are those holding power in said cities. And there have been disputes, many in the last few decades, more so in the last few years. Many vie for power, more territory, other cities, or perhaps even the entire kingdom itself, and High King Baron's rule is no longer as secure as it once was. I suspect this invasion is an attempt to show strength to his nobility."

"Why not attack someone else then? If the Imperial military is as powerful as you say."

Felicia grinned as if she knew something that Ilea didn't.

"Well, I imagine there would've been other targets, but what then? They go to war, take more territory and more people, meaning new war lords might emerge, more potential challengers to the High King. With Lys, he knows the Empress wouldn't take such an attack lightly, and his lords know that only a united Baralia could even stand a chance.

"It's pride and arrogance. Perhaps a last effort by High King Baron to stay in power, and his lessers have no choice but to go along with it or lose their own positions to someone more eager to prove themselves. It's a risky move for sure, and it could well splinter his own kingdom. Alyris must know this too and has thus decided to wait it out for the time being."

"Even if it meant many died in the attacks? And I'm sure more will in the evacuation."

"What other options were there? If the Empire attacked preemptively, it would be faced with a united Baralia. Or if the Empire fought in Virilya, many would still have died in the battle within the city. So she chose to evacuate and fortify the central district. Perhaps the evacuation could've been executed earlier, but then Baralia would've had time to prepare and react, so luring them into this exact scenario would've become far more unlikely. Though I suppose you're right. In any scenario, there would've been many who died, soldiers and civilians alike, but those choices aren't for us to make."

"I'm not sure what to think about all this. I'm just glad I'm not the Empress," Ilea said. Making these kinds of choices was a shit job.

"I know what you mean, but all that is just my interpretation. I'm not in the know when it comes to the intricacies of Virilya's nobility and what kind of conflicts are happening internally. If the corruption in the capital is running as deep as Ed thinks, this could be an opportunity for the Empress as well. Any Lys nobility will have no choice but to remain in the central district during the siege, and the Empress' oversight will be far more present.

"I'm sure there will be some restructuring in this period, and if she isn't overthrown, which I doubt will happen, she should come out with Lys being more united than it's been in her lifetime. What that will mean for Baralia and any other power in the Plains is difficult to say."

"You're certainly invested in all of this," Ilea said.

"Maybe I shouldn't be. It's just that... my family was once a respected House in Virilya. Until Arthur took power. But I shouldn't talk too much about it. We have more important things to think about right now."

Ilea looked at her for a long moment and smiled. "Sure." She looked at the ceiling, then back at Felicia. "I saw a white-haired mage with a white and silver mask. I think she used wind magic, like you. Really powerful too. Was that the Empress?" She assumed the ruler of Lys would have to have great personal power to stay in such a position.

"I don't know," Felicia said. "Could've been a noble."

Ilea nodded.

* * *

Edwin and Maria arrived in the late afternoon, both of them exhausted, the thick smell of blood and sweat filling the air around them. Ilea didn't have to ask if they'd been successful, not after seeing Edwin's self-satisfied smirk.

He summoned a stack of documents onto the table, took off the storage ring that Aliana normally wore, and went to the other room.

"I will sleep. When I wake up, we leave and head eastward toward the ocean. To the Isle of Garath."

Ilea locked eyes with Maria, who gave her a glance before she went to join Edwin.

Felicia started to go through the documents a moment later. Trian was sitting expressionless at the table. He'd slept longer than any of them but still had dark bags under his eyes. Kyrian had left with Aliana to hunt. Ilea assumed there was more than just hunting going on, but who knew? Maybe they just shared a deep interest in the local wildlife.

She chuckled to herself, leaning back in her chair until it touched the stone wall. *Maybe it's totally innocent and this is just me being horny.*

Though she didn't feel particularly horny right now. She'd bathed in a river earlier but the hideout still reeked, and she felt downright chained to the promise of helping Edwin out. She wanted to be done with this responsibility. The only reason she didn't hate it was because Felicia was involved.

The Isle of Garath.

"I don't suppose either of you would like some fresh air?" she asked.

"I would, but I want to know what they found first," Felicia said.

Ilea looked at Trian. "Trian?"

He glanced at her, closed his eyes, and sighed as if she'd asked a great favor of him. "What difference does it make?"

"I'll be in a better mood." Ilea stood up and walked over to him, then helped him up. "And you will be too."

"I doubt that," Trian said softly, but he didn't resist. He teleported outside, and Ilea followed.

"There's a nice pond a few minutes in this direction," Ilea said, pointing eastward. Trian didn't react but followed when she started flying.

A brief time later, they landed near the pond. Its surface was a dark green, though sadly there were no incredibly dangerous creatures lurking inside. Ilea had checked.

Trian leaned against a tree and glanced at the water.

"Not exactly the lake of Virilya," he murmured.

"Just a pond, yeah," Ilea said. She grabbed a rock and flung it into the water. "How do you feel? Fresh air good?"

He smirked ever so slightly. "The air is good, yeah. Better, but the pond smells too."

"It's not poisonous, sadly," Ilea said.

He puffed air out of his nose. "I know you're trying to help. I appreciate it, Ilea. I just think I need time most of all. Things don't really make sense right now."

"You're up for helping with this mission?"

He nodded. "I gave my word. I'll fight… but afterward? I don't know."

"Aurelia, Orthan, and Samuel are in Ravenhall."

"Yeah. I know. I'll probably join them. It's just..." He looked at the pond. "I know this is what I wanted. But nothing has *changed*..."

Some of the tension seemed to release as he said the words. As if he'd been holding them in, as if they'd been weighing him down.

Ilea smiled, then grabbed another stone and flung it into the water. "I know."

They were quiet for a long while, Ilea throwing a few more rocks before she sat down and leaned against a tree trunk.

"Thank you," Trian said.

Ilea glanced at him.

"For stopping me when you did. I..." He shook his head.

"Easy to get lost in it all. I'm glad you're not angry."

"I was. For a while," he said. "Yeah." He paused. "Sorry, for all this. For what happened to Eve. For what I felt I had to do. Thanks for being there. For helping out."

"I'm sorry too. And hey, that's what friends are for."

"Hunting down a noble House in the capital of Lys?"

Ilea smiled. "Yeah, that and getting stranded in a realm of demons with. Retaking a city overtaken by said demons, hunting down sand creatures in the southern desert. Friend activities."

"Friend activities," Trian murmured before he crouched down and touched the earth. He took a stone and closed his hand around it, then threw it into the pond.

It landed with a dull plopping sound. It hadn't bounced.

* * *

They were ready to leave in the evening. Edwin and Maria had found recent documentation on enchantment equipment bought in Virilya and delivered to the east. They knew the equipment was connected to Arthur's research based on the type, the quantity bought, and the price paid.

They flew east for a long while before, finally, Edwin motioned for them to land after night had fallen. The last stretch would be traveled on foot. The weather was clear, so it would be simple for even an average guard to spot them in the skies.

Their group moved quietly and quickly over the fields toward the ocean to the east. Ilea could hear the waves crashing against the cliffs. She smelled salt in the air and saw the others in her Sphere. All of them had come.

A group of boulders stood near the cliffs overlooking the body of endless water, illuminated by the moons above, the only cover for hundreds of meters for the group of high-level fighters.

Or assassins.

Ilea appeared near one of the rocks and sat down, stretching her arms before resting her back on the stone. Kyrian sat beside her as Edwin walked toward the edge of the cliff, his eyes focused on the distant islands barely visible to them. One of those small dots would be their target – or at least, they hoped it was.

"There's more than one," Maria said as she stepped beside him.

"And that's very good for us," he answered. "You and Ilea will fly out to see if there's a good base for us there, perhaps check for villages, towns, or castles nearby as well."

Maria nodded and looked at Ilea. "Coming?"

"If you ask nicely."

Maria scowled while Ilea stood up.

"I guess I did agree to help."

"Please, don't kill each other if you can manage it," Edwin said.

"I'll try," Ilea said, opening her arms.

Maria rolled her eyes and walked over. Ilea grabbed Maria and jumped off the cliff, neither of them making a sound before her wings spread at the last moment, the two of them speeding up tremendously as they glided silently over the waves.

The flight wasn't long, and the two of them landed on a rocky beach a couple of minutes later, quickly running for cover. The island itself looked mostly barren. Long rocky beaches, broken boulders, and scraggy trees. Not the kind of place Ilea expected to be inhabited.

"That rules out an army defending the whole group of islands," Ilea said as they stopped running behind an outcrop of rocks without hearing any cries of alarm.

"Or they're leading us into a trap," Maria said in a quiet voice.

"Or that, sure," Ilea agreed.

The two of them walked over the barren landscape and scanned their surroundings for movements or any signs of life.

"You don't seem convinced. Arthur isn't a fool, and I doubt he'd be here alone," Maria said as they climbed one of the island's higher hills.

"Costs money to hire people. If he's not paranoid then I don't think they'd watch all of these islands. What are they doing here anyway?"

Maria shrugged. "His research. He never took the time to explain any details to his little soldiers and assassins. Probably a Taleen ruin somewhere out there."

"Little soldiers and assassins?"

Maria didn't reply.

They reached the crest of the hill and crouched. There were lights in the distance on a different island. It looked like a small village with a port, fishing boats bobbing in the dark waters.

"I don't think that's our target," Ilea said.

"No, but they might know where it is. I want you to stay here and wait for me to get back. Is that agreeable?" Maria asked, locking eyes with her.

"Sure you don't want someone to have your back?"

Maria shook her head. "I'll need a quick lift if someone discovers or attacks me. Can I trust you to be here when I come back?"

"I told you, I agreed to help. How long do you need?"

"At that distance, about an hour. If I'm not back by then, report back to Edwin."

Ilea nodded and sat down on a nearby rock, watching Maria disappear.

How am I supposed to know when an hour has passed?

* * *

Maurice spat on the ground as he stepped out of the tavern to take a piss. Looking around, he saw only a few people still awake in this shithole fisher village he had found himself in.

The pay was good, of course, second to none he had worked for so far. At least considering the risks involved. Or the lack thereof. And with Zoy in their team, he didn't even have to worry about seeing a single Taleen machine get close to him. The damn things were terrifying.

"But that doesn't matter to you guys, does it?" he asked the raven sitting on the stone next to him. "Nah, didn't think so." He pulled up his pants and looked into the distance. "Fucking shit village."

He turned around and headed back to the tavern, looking to get more mead. He wasn't on duty tonight, which allowed him to roam freely around the group of islands.

"Come on," he said to the raven, which hopped after him happily before it fluttered onto his shoulder.

"Maurice. Come back for more?" Tammy said with a sly smile as she tapped the very silver he'd paid her earlier that evening on the wooden table. She had fiery red hair and an enormous bust. Money well spent, in his opinion. But he wasn't in the market for another ride just yet.

"More mead," he said simply, going to the bar. *Decent whores for a backwater place like this,* he thought. The mead, on the other hand, wasn't anything special, nor were the fighters. He could probably wipe out half the damn village on his own before anybody even noticed.

"The Shadow's back, I see," one of the resident drunkards said, pounding his mug on the table. "Mysterious as always, no words for the common folk, hah!"

"I'm not one of those damn Shadows," Maurice replied. "And I swear if you say that to me one more time, I'll have this bird rip out your eyes before I shove them down your bloody throat."

"I meant no offense… crow man…" the drunkard said and cackled.

Wearing black makes you a Shadow now, Maurice thought as he downed his mug of ale.

He hoped the Redleaf would be done with this ruin before the month was through. Now that spring had come, it would bring some life back into the nearby cities. And a lot of work for a mercenary like him. Work that paid less but was more fun than guarding a worn-down castle.

"Heard the Empire of Lys is at war again," someone said, Maurice's ears picking up the line in the myriad of conversations.

"Ah fuck off, news like that reaches us every other month. Nobody can take the Empire. Not Kroll, not Baralia, and not the damn elves. If they even exist," another man said, bringing an end to the interesting rumor.

War was always a great opportunity to make money… and to purchase a castle or two for rather low prices. Lys had some nice ones, after all.

"Elves are real, saw one myself…" another voice proclaimed, but Maurice had lost interest already. Had the man seen an elf, he wouldn't be here to tell the tale. Even Maurice wasn't about to face one of those monsters himself. That was most of the reason he was working so far east.

He finished his second mug of mead.

Time to get the boy.

EIGHTEEN

The Baker

Maria followed the high-level mercenary out of the inn. He was the only one here who could be working for Arthur. She followed him through the village until he knocked on the door of one of the wooden shacks, smoke rising from its chimney.

She held her breath and waited, seeing the mercenary glance behind him before he knocked again.

A chubby man opened the door. He looked at the mercenary and smiled. "Maurice!" he shouted and stepped out. He was large, both tall and broad, both fat and muscle. He wore simple, loose-fitting linen clothes, and his expression was one of joy. Maria saw no wit or cunning in the man's eyes or expression.

"Seems like you had a good evening, Popi," 'Maurice' said. The one she'd been following was a typical mercenary. All scars and brooding looks. He wore light armor and carried himself like a man who'd seen his fair share of true warfare.

'Popi' nodded before he smacked his belly. "I did. New cakes. They all liked them." He looked toward the inn and smiled. Maria stood completely still, all her cloaking skills active as she watched the two men before her.

Maurice was at level two hundred and ten, and Popi was at one ninety. It might be possible for her to handle them alone, but she had no clue about their abilities.

"Cakes again? Popi, if you spend all your money on baking for free, you might as well stop..." Maurice started before he spun around.

"Did you find a new birdie?" Popi asked.

"Maybe," Maurice said and cracked his neck before he whispered something into Popi's ear.

"Sure, can do!" Popi said as his shirt and pants were replaced with heavy red armor adorned with tubes.

Storage item.

Maria stood her ground, waiting for something to happen. Maurice looked in her direction but not directly at her.

Keen senses.

The temperature around her suddenly rose. Magic surged from the armored man as hot air left the tubes on his arms, her surroundings heating up to a scorching degree near instantly. Fires sprung up around her as the foliage caught flame. Sweat started forming but evaporated instantly as her skin started to heat up, then burn.

The damage was manageable though, and she wasn't about to expose herself. The mission could be compromised if she moved to avoid the ability and, with her second stage of Pain Tolerance, Maria could endure this for quite a while.

Her vitality and heat resistance were relatively high as well. She just had to make sure the flames moved naturally around her so that she didn't stand out in the area of the spell. An old trick she'd learned long ago.

Popi continued his spell for another few seconds before he stopped and looked at Maurice next to him.

"Are you sure there's something there? It's all burnt now," the mage said.

Maria watched as Maurice scratched his unkempt beard, his near-black eyes staring at a point very close to her.

"Guess not," he said.

Maria was just breathing a sigh of relief when two blades sprung from the bracers of Maurice's light armor, the tips reaching his hands and ending near his shoulders. He rushed toward her and spun in the air, leaving Maria with no choice but to teleport away, making the barest whisper of noise as she landed. Maurice looked at her and smiled.

"A little hunter in the wild. Now, what are we looking at here?" he said before a swarm of ravens appeared from thin air, the birds advancing on her position as she turned tail and rushed toward Ilea as fast as she could.

* * *

Ilea watched the tranquil village on the other isle, sitting on her stone and enjoying one of Keyla's creations.

I do hope she made it out in all that chaos. Should've looked for her when I helped Balduur, she thought when she heard a noise.

Summoning her damaged armor, she checked the surroundings with her Sphere, and, sure enough, someone entered it just a moment later. According to the shape, lack of visual, and the fact she knew where Ilea was meant it had to be Maria. The two people she spotted following Maria let Ilea know that something had gone terribly wrong.

"You alright?" she asked as Maria's skills deactivated one after the other. Her skin was a complete mess, cracked and blackened. "Flee, fight, or talk?" Ilea asked. There was no answer, so she started to heal. Either her face was too messed up to talk or she just didn't want to. The damage wasn't serious, but it certainly looked that way.

A bunch of ravens advanced on the two of them and started dive-bombing the pair, talons and beaks sharp as swords. Ilea waved at them with one arm while healing Maria.

One of Maria's followers had already reached them. The one who controlled the birds, as far as Ilea could tell. *They already found her. Better to talk than fight, I guess.*

"Hey, raven guy, stop for a minute, will you?" Ilea shouted as she grabbed one of the birds out of the air, looking at it closely.

Rabid ravens or what?

The attackers hesitated at her words. One had blades on his arms, similar in design to her blue-steel gauntlets but broader and reaching all the way past his shoulders.

Suppose Balduur's design wasn't unique. Or maybe this is his work too?

The second man was still quite a distance away, his huge form lumbering toward them on the one land path that led up to the cliff side.

"Don't touch my fucking birds," the blade-wielding man said. "Or I'll cut the invisible one apart and shove her down your throat."

"Piece by piece?" Ilea asked drily.

"Yes. Piece by fucking piece. Let go of my bird, alright?" he said, some of the tension gone in his tone.

Ilea shrugged.

"If you promise not to be such an aggressive little shit," Ilea said and let go of the bird.

The man grunted. "Good. But I won't promise anything. Now who the hell are you, and why was that one spying on us?" The man pointed at Maria just as the second man arrived in very heavy-looking armor made of red metal and what looked like glass or plastic tubes going from his arms up to his shoulders. There were more on his back. He stopped, breathing heavily, putting his hands on his knees as he recovered from his run.

"Here on a job, Shadow's Hand. She's a... we met on the road. We had common goals, but she likes to spy on people. Rude, I agree. Who are you?"

[Mage – lvl 210]

[Baker – lvl 190]

Having identified them, she didn't give either of them time to respond.

"What's a baker doing out here? Are you like a high-level delivery service?"

"No, we're—" the man started, but Ilea interrupted him and instead addressed the baker.

"Can I buy some bread or a cake from you? Food's been rather boring lately," Ilea lied.

The baker's helmet vanished instantly, revealing grayish hair, green eyes, and a chubby face. The fact that his size suggested he liked to enjoy his own creations made her even more interested.

His face lit up at her request, and he summoned both bread and a piece of cake. The cake was bright yellow and looked perfectly browned around the edges.

"I do, I do. You can try it for free even. I like to share," he said excitedly, laughing as he finished.

Ilea grinned, saliva forming in her mouth at the sight. She glanced in Maria's direction.

"That's crazy. I think I love this guy." She turned back toward him. "That's very nice of you, but you'll never earn money like that. I can pay you. That cake looks delicious."

Ilea finished healing Maria, who had activated her cloaking skills again but was still standing next to her, nearly completely still.

The bird mage scratched his head and sighed. "Look, fuck, can we first clear up why you're here and why your friend spied on us? After that, you can buy all the cake you like."

"First, again, that's not my friend. And second, she's just very shy. And curious. She likes to follow interesting men around." Ilea summoned her Shadow badge and threw it to the man, who caught it. "I'm with the Hand. Heard something about a Taleen dungeon, but I usually don't check the details. I just like to fight the machines," she said, most of it true. "So, why are you on this island anyway? And you didn't answer my previous question, who are you two?"

Ilea advanced on the baker as non-threateningly as possible, accepting the piece of cake he was holding toward her. She smiled and bowed her head, then inspected the cake. A cheesecake variant, yellow with red berries and, now she looked at it more closely, a thin cream topping. It certainly looked rich. She hoped it was poisoned as she took a bite.

It wasn't, but it *was* good. It would've been too sweet for her tastes, but the tartness of the berries balanced it out well.

"This is good. Really damn good," she said, taking another bite. "Do you do poisoned cakes too?"

"Poison kills people," the baker said, tutting. "We're just here to guard the castle," he added with a smile. "You should come visit us sometime. My name is Popi."

"Nice to meet you, Popi. My name is Lilith, and I'd love to come visit you," Ilea replied as she devoured the rest of the cake.

"Popi, I told you not to talk to strangers so openly. What if they've come to attack us?" the mage asked.

"I'm sorry for burning your friend. He told me to do it," Popi said to Ilea, then looked down at his feet.

"It's fine. She's going to be alright. Look, we meant no offense, okay?" Ilea smiled.

"For fuck's sake," the mage said, scratching the back of his head. "I'm Maurice. We're guards from nearby. You should tell her not to spy on people. And I'm afraid the Taleen dungeon has been cleared out already."

"That's a shame. Doesn't matter too much, though. Got a few more jobs in the region."

"May I ask who paid for that Taleen ruin job?"

"No clue."

"Right. Look, I don't like you here, so you should leave," he said, turning away. "Come on, Popi, we're supposed to be back in two hours."

"Before you go, Popi, do you have any more of that cake?" Ilea said. "I'm willing to pay you twenty coppers for each cake. Actually, how much do the ingredients cost? I don't want to rob you."

"Lilith, forget about the fucking cake," Maria hissed.

"Already healed I see. You're full of surprises," Maurice said.

"You should try the cheesecake before you complain," Ilea said.

Popi summoned the rest of the cake and handed it over. "No need to pay. I like baking."

"I can see that," Ilea said, taking the gift. "Thank you," she said with a wide smile. "Popi, I'll remember the name."

He smiled.

Maurice sighed and tapped Popi's arm. "Come on, big guy."

Ilea watched them leave. Maurice's birds fluttered around them, and the man glanced back a few times before they were gone beyond the treeline that started down the slope.

Ilea spread her wings before she grabbed the near-invisible Maria and ascended, looking in the direction of the two mercenaries she'd likely have to face in battle in the following days.

I do hope I won't have to kill them, she thought as she sped up, though not to her full speed so as not to reveal anything. She didn't fly toward the others, instead taking a massive detour to throw Maurice off.

Was Popi just playing the fool? She wasn't sure. Part of her wanted to believe he was as innocent as he'd acted, but then she remembered Maria's quick performance back in the hideout. There were actors out there with magic to help them fool anyone.

"That went better than expected," Ilea said when they landed.

"I'm not sure you fooled him," Maria said.

"Either way, they likely know we're coming," Ilea said.

"We could've forced a search or held them hostage," Maria said as they walked back to the others.

"You got literally *baked,*" Ilea said. After talking to the two, she didn't really want to fight them, not that she'd say that to Maria.

She'll know anyway.

They soon reached the others and explained what had happened. To her surprise, Edwin didn't care much about the mercenary encounter.

"He's really here," he said after they'd finished, thinking out loud as he got a notebook from his pack and started to write. "So, he has one mercenary team at least. And you already seem on friendly terms with them. I understand that none of you three came here to fight and kill mercenaries, but I won't shy away from doing that if it's required. But I also won't dismiss other options.

"Ilea, you'll distract them while we attack. They might be less inclined to fight you. If you can hold back two or more of them, it will be worthwhile. I'd assume the team is four to six people. Let's hope for fewer.

"We'll find the location of the Isle of Garath in the village. Then Maria will scout again, this time alone and from farther away. No risks this time. We know they have ways to find you now. Ilea, do you think you could take the two of them in a straight-up fight?"

Ilea shrugged. She didn't feel great about leaving Trian and Kyrian to fight without a healer, but if their other option was a direct battle against Popi, Maurice, and whoever else was around, it may very well be the safest one.

"No idea. How much gold do you have? If they're mercenaries, maybe we can convince them that way," Ilea suggested.

"I doubt my father would hire easily bought people. Still, with your connection, it might be an option. You may offer up to five gold pieces per person for them to abandon their duty."

"Edwin… are you sure?" Maria asked, but he just waved her off.

"We have to use whatever means we can."

Whatever means, Ilea thought.

"When do we move?" she asked.

"As soon as the suns are up. We'll be able to better scout the isle then."

* * *

Ravens spread out to scout the surroundings as they crossed the last hill before the Isle of Garath.

"Here we are. Piss poor boring shit island," Maurice said as he took a deep breath. He wasn't sure if he was ready to face his team, not even after an easygoing night out.

The suns wouldn't be up for another couple of hours, but the torches could be seen from afar. Their isle was small and technically more like half an isle. While not connected by land, a narrow stone pathway led to it from the closest other isle.

Guess that makes it one bigger isle, doesn't it?

He looked around to find Popi a dozen meters further back, looking at something under a rock that was entirely too heavy to lift.

"Found something?"

"Spring," Popi said and smiled, picking a little flower from near the rock before he let go of the massive thing.

"Spring," Maurice said before he laughed and shook his head. "Spring is when we're finally done with this job – and these people."

He walked toward their island. The ruined castle at its center gave the place an eerie feeling, just like most things that led to a Taleen dungeon. A good thing this one had been empty and small.

Rare for the fucking dwarves.

"I like Zoy," Popi said in a happy tone.

Maurice didn't reply. He found the girl creepy, almost as much as the Taleen dungeon. She hardly ever talked, and her only drive seemed to be fighting more of those killing machines.

He sighed as they crossed the pathway to the rocky terrain of the Isle of Garath. Certainly not the worst foundation for a defensible position. Looking down, however, he saw the dark waves of the ocean. It made him shiver.

Why out here?

"Zoy's nice," Popi argued, likely interpreting Maurice's silence as disapproval.

"Sure. Just don't get too close. She won't come with us after this is over," Maurice replied when they got to the platform on the other side.

Like most nights, Welk was playing his harmonica. Having gotten to know the man, the sound put Maurice on edge more than anything else.

"Welcome back. How were the whores?" Welk asked, stopping his playing. He continued right after, not listening to Maurice's lack of a response.

The fire was still burning, giving off some heat in the cold night. Though it was spring, as Popi had apparently just found out, being so close to the ocean, it was still rather cool at night. Not that anybody at their levels would be bothered much by that. Still, the fire kept away creatures and some of the isles' inhabitants, human and otherwise.

"Anything to report?" Welk asked, and Maurice looked at him.

"Met some people. Shadow's Hand," he said as he sat down, glancing at Zoy, who was sitting in silence, her pale white eyes staring at nothing.

"Shadow's Hand?" Welk stopped playing. "Why are they here?"

"On a mission," Maurice said, opening his pack and getting out some bread and dried meat.

"Yeah, I could figure that one out myself, smartass. What mission? Anything to do with Mr. Redleaf or the Taleen dungeon?"

Maurice just shrugged. "Couldn't tell ya. If they come here, we'll ask. The girl seemed more eager to try Popi's baking," he said, thinking back to the weird encounter.

He'd definitely met a bunch of eccentric high-level people, but most Shadows had been less than talkative and mostly professional. Which was why he'd never thought about joining the fuckers. That and them imitating his style.

And three hundred gold is far too much to pay for their lackluster services.

"Popi's baking? You should've found out more and interrogated them. What if they're our enemy?" Welk asked as he got up and started pacing.

Maurice grunted. He could certainly see how the two supposed Shadows were here for something related to Arthur Redleaf, but he didn't exactly care. He was here to fight anyone who attacked, help with any monsters, and guard the expedition team, not start an investigation into anyone who showed up in pissing range.

NINETEEN

Engage

"We can't have Shadows appearing on this island and not interrogate them at the very least," Welk complained as he walked to the castle, likely to tell his lord about what Maurice had reported.

Maurice ignored most of the bald man's words. Self-important people liked to talk a lot when they felt righteous, even more so when they felt like their even more self-important masters were the ones who had been slighted.

Maybe we'll lose this job earlier than expected.

Maurice smiled at the idea. He could do with a change, but the money had been a little too good to ignore.

"Any news from inside?" he asked the silent Zoy.

There was no response or reaction at all.

"Nothing, then. Well, I'm sure they'll get us if they find any of those killing machines."

Again, she remained impassive as if the thought were no different to any other.

"How do they not scare you?" he asked in a joking manner, finishing his meal as a couple of guards walked by, armored in red and gray.

"They are just machines," Zoy said, gracing them with her voice. Popi perked up and summoned a cupcake.

"I made a new one. You said you didn't hate lemon," Popi said, shyly walking over to where Zoy was sitting. She didn't look at him but didn't prevent him from setting the cupcake down next to her on the stone.

"Thank you, Popi," she said before she placed her hand near the cupcake, moving it a little until she finally found it.

Don't have to fool us, lady, Maurice thought, but he'd had that talk with her several times already. Maybe he would've believed it before he saw her fight.

"I'm gonna catch some sleep. Wake me when something interesting happens," he said and lay down on his mat.

"I will wake you up. Dream of good things. Like food," Popi said.

Maurice grumbled to himself, but he couldn't help but smile.

Really can't leave that guy alone or he'll be taken advantage of in all kinds of ways. Too nice for this world.

* * *

Ilea saw the first light of the suns on the distant horizon. Dawn was finally breaking.

She looked at the isle before her and saw the remnants of a small campfire before the dilapidated stone bridge. There were three people there, two of whom she'd met before. On the other side of the bridge stood the ruins of what would have been called a typical medieval castle on Earth. It had four crumbling outer walls made of stone, complete with ramparts and watchtowers, though most were cracked and ravaged by age. In the middle stood a massive hall with a sloping roof that towered above the walls and an open courtyard in front.

At least fifteen guards in the castle itself. And mercenaries to guard the only direct path. Are they trying to keep people out or in? Maybe Arthur doesn't really trust the mercenaries?

The others would strike at the ancient ruins directly, flying in from the ocean side. Her goal was to distract or dissuade some of the highest-level adversaries from participating in the battle. According to both Maria and Edwin, the Redleaf guards would mostly be around level one hundred to one twenty. The mercenaries – at least, the two she knew already – were around two hundred.

Time to put on my nicest face.

Ilea glided down to the tiny stone bridge that connected the two islands. She smiled as she made her way over the walkway, not trying to hide herself in any way.

Two Redleaf guards at the top of the stairs leading to the castle pointed at her but didn't do anything yet. The third person sitting near the fire was a woman in white metal armor with short blonde hair. None of them reacted before she shouted and waved at them.

"Hey Popi!"

"Lilith!" Popi answered, smiling back, kicking at the third person, who had been soundly asleep. Maurice grumbled and sat up, looking skeptical.

"The Shadow girl," he said with a scowl. "The invisible angry one here too?" he asked, a little apprehension clear in his voice.

The woman in white armor hadn't moved at all yet. Her eyes were white, and she stared into the distance.

"She didn't feel like seeing your faces," Ilea said, looking at the woman.

Is she blind?

Ilea tensed her body slightly, turning a little toward the woman. Her Sphere told her enough. There was a slight twitch in the woman's fingers, and her breathing slowed down a bit.

Ilea laughed. "I knew it," she said, relaxing. "Popi, how are you doing? Thought I'd check in before I left this place again. Maybe buy a few more cakes while I have the chance."

Ilea smiled at the man as she sat down next to him, opening her pack and getting her pouch.

"Guardian hunting going alright?" Ilea asked, just to make conversation.

"You speak as if you are familiar with the machines. Are you?" the woman in white asked, speaking for the first time.

Ilea noticed the two guards from the stairs walking toward them.

"What's the meaning of this? Who is this person?" one of them asked.

[Warrior – lvl 131]

[Warrior – lvl 118]

Just like Edwin predicted.

"Fuck off, she's just here to buy cake," Maurice said.

Ilea wasn't sure he really believed that, but her smile grew wider.

"What do you mean she's just—"

The guard was interrupted when the woman in white held up her hand.

"The machines. Speak," she stated in a quiet yet intense voice that even the guards seemed loathe to interrupt.

"I explored a Taleen dungeon a while back, fought a bunch of Guardians. What about it?" Ilea said as she gratefully took a cupcake Popi handed to her.

"What kind?"

"Guardians, sword and ranged variants, the ones that shoot slugs, Centurions," Ilea said, looking at the cupcake before she bit into it. She thought of the glowing green eyes, the mace, and the scythe. She chewed as she looked into the milky white eyes of the tense warrior before her.

[Warrior – lvl ??]

Which means she's higher than two fifty at least.

Ilea debated how to handle this interaction. The girl seemed far more concerned about the machines than Ilea herself.

"Where was the dungeon?" she probed.

"Maybe I'll tell you if you tell me your name," Ilea smiled, taking another bite of the cupcake.

Mmm, lemony.

The guards looked at each other and shook their heads before they went back to their posts, seemingly entirely out of their comfort zone.

Not interested in dealing with the mercenaries either. That could be why they're camping out here in the first place.

"This cupcake is fucking delicious," she said.

"Zoy," the 'blind' woman said after a while.

"Zoy… Interesting name. The dungeon is inside the massive mountain Karth. I wouldn't recommend going in though, there are two Praetorians waiting."

As Ilea finished the cupcake, she didn't miss the sudden increase in tension in Zoy's body. She moved her head for the first time as she looked up at the sky.

"You fought them?" she asked after a while, returning her gaze to the same nothingness before her. "Did you destroy them?"

Ilea shook her head. "No. I was cursed and had to flee. They were three marks. I'm not sure I could face them even now."

"You really are something," Maurice said as he sat forward and put something that looked like coffee into one of the pans above the campfire, filling it with water from a flask. "Never heard the mute talk this much."

"Means she's not mute," Ilea said, smiling when Maurice scowled at her. "Got bloody mauled by them," she continued, turning back to Zoy. "Centurions are one thing but Praetorians… They seemed… intelligent. Dangerous."

"Do you fear them?" Zoy asked. She appeared to be holding her breath.

Strange lady.

Ilea gritted her teeth, thinking back to the two machines decimating the expedition.

"Yeah," she said. "I do."

She hadn't been able to do anything back then. And she doubted she could do anything now.

"And that's why you want to face them again," Zoy surmised. "You think you could win?"

"No. Not yet."

Ilea saw Zoy's lips twitch upward ever so slightly. "Then I will leave them to you, Huntress Lilith. I hope you do not meet your end."

"I hope the same for you."

"She's talked more just now than she has all week," Maurice murmured as he stirred the brew he'd set down above the campfire.

"Smells nice, can I have some?" Ilea asked.

"If you pay me. One silver for a cup," Maurice answered with a grin.

"You're overcharging me. Five copper."

"Eighty."

"Ten."

"Seventy-five."

"Twenty," Ilea said. "Not more. His cakes are better."

"Twenty it is for the Lady Lilith," Maurice said, pouring her a cup of the brew.

It smelled and tasted close to coffee. It wasn't that she missed it particularly, but it made her think of Earth, of hanging out in a cafe with a friend, of enjoying a peaceful summer day while the birds chirped in the background.

But flying was better.

Though I probably wouldn't have to deal with distracting a bunch of mercenaries.

Ilea sighed as she drank from the mug. She closed her eyes until she heard a dull explosion from down toward the ocean. Opening her eyes, she stood up and followed the others, who rushed over to see what was going on.

Chunks of rock were falling down toward the ocean, dust and debris rising from the side of the castle ruin. A large part of its outer wall was now missing, and shouts from the guards could be heard.

"Shit," Maurice muttered as magic gathered around the three mercenaries.

"Wait," Ilea said. She took a sip from her mug and looked at the three. "A few friends of mine. They're here to kill your employer. Arthur Redleaf."

"You... of course," Maurice said as he turned toward her. Strangely, he wasn't scowling. Zoy was standing beside him with her swords sheathed, entirely calm.

"My friends offer five gold coins for each one of you to leave your post and leave this be. You know Arthur better than me, but from what I hear—"

"He's had it coming," Maurice shrugged. He looked over at the falling debris, then glanced at Popi. "It's more than he's paying us. Still, we've got a reputation to consider. Then again, fuck this island. The whole place is shit. Popi, you make the call."

"Lilith is nicer than Mr. Redleaf," Popi said. "He doesn't like cake."

Maurice actually chuckled. "Your lucky day, Shadow. Any other employer in the past years and I would've put you in the ground."

Ilea smiled slightly. *Is this really what will decide how many people try to stop us? Liking cake? Guess I'll take it. Cake is dope.*

"What about you, Zoy? Will you stop me if I go help them?" Ilea said.

"I will."

"For Arthur?"

"The Taleen network. He will find a way to activate the gates here."

"I see. You won't reconsider even if I share the location of the dungeon below Dawntree?"

Zoy shook her head as more shouts came from the ruin.

"Guess there's no other way. It was nice meeting you," Ilea said.

Zoy grinned slightly. "*Var nakuun,* Lilith."

She vanished, reappearing closer to the castle ruin.

Ilea summoned ten gold coins and handed them to the remaining two mercenaries. "You two should leave. Here's your gold."

"Pleasure doing business with you," Maurice said. "Enjoy the brawl."

Ilea smiled and jumped off the stone bridge. She spread her wings and flew out and around the castle until she was looking into a large hall where Edwin was in the midst of combat, his blades clashing with the greatsword of a heavily armored woman. She was one of the most muscular women Ilea had ever seen and screamed incoherently with each strike. A berserker, perhaps?

Landing in the hall behind him, Ilea's ash spread out around her as her skills activated all at once. As she glanced around, she saw Kyrian's metal spheres floating nearby and Trian's lightning lighting up the room. There was also a middle-aged man with a bald spot and unimpressive physique, his face seemingly set in a permanent frown. His cloak was finely made, rose gold inlays glinting in the light. Next was a Viking-looking guy with no hair at all except a long-braided beard. He wore rough leathers, and his green eyes were focused. Last was the angry chick with the greatsword. She had unkempt strawberry blonde hair and bloodshot eyes. There was also a bunch of uniformed Redleaf guards rushing into the hall.

Surprise attack officially failed.

Ilea couldn't see Maria, Felicia, or Aliana.

Perhaps Edwin told them to stay back?

The ash surrounding her was blown away by a strong wind that originated from the middle-aged man, who lifted his hand to stop the approaching guards. While he didn't look impressive at first glance, Ilea could see now that his eyes pulsed with barely restrained energy. A powerful mage.

Hello, Mr. Redleaf.

"Son! You disappoint me," he said, glancing at the three Shadows in turn. "The Shadow's Hand? Not even revenge could you manage on your own."

The hypocrisy of his words wasn't lost on Ilea as she watched the guards take up positions around the man, aiming their bows, swords, and spells at Edwin and their group.

"Doesn't look good," Kyrian whispered to her.

"Your entry gave us an easy way to escape though. Let's see what he does," Ilea whispered back.

Zoy stood to the side of the enemy group, two short curved blades in her hands.

"You're right, I'm not alone," Edwin said as he pushed away the muscular woman's blade and slashed one of his own across her armor. She started screaming, in pain this time, and Ilea remembered his ability to inflict damage with his blood magic even through armor.

"Take him down," Arthur spat, his frown deepening into a scowl.

Then the chest of a guard next to him exploded, splattering blood and guts over both him and much of the stone floor.

Ah, there she is.

Ilea vanished. She felt the familiar feeling of a curse on her immediately when she reappeared among a small knot of guards who she identified as mages. The effect seemed much worse on them than on her as she punched the first one, sending him into the wall behind him like a rag doll, breaking several bones with her attack.

Ash spread again, but this time it wasn't washed away as she blinked to the next mage, a younger man who frantically sent beams of light at her like machine gun fire before her fist smacked into his chest. His energy shield broke with the first punch before her second caved in his chest. The third punch didn't land because a blade came dangerously close, and Ilea had to dodge. The blade shimmered white in the dark ash around her. Two blades, actually.

"Are you sure about this, Zoy?" Ilea asked. Her answer was two quick slashes that Ilea dodged by swaying backward. She was unwilling to engage her just yet, using the guards around them as cover and targets at the same time.

Maria used her magic from somewhere hidden, one guard after another dropping dead or screaming from missing limbs as Ilea blinked between them. Zoy's white glowing blades flashed through her ash as she followed. Ilea continuously spread out her ash wherever Zoy appeared.

Kyrian's curses were affecting her and the enemy wherever they stood, his metal spikes and needles flying through her ash and the hall itself. Then a blast of wind sent some of her ash, several guards, and Ilea herself flying into the air. She spread her wings before she blinked away, avoiding the mercenary's white blades as she spotted Arthur sending a massive blast of wind her way.

Blinking away again, she looked up at the ceiling and saw that part of it was no longer there. Instead, a jagged circular hole exposed the sky beyond. Chunks of rocks and bricks were visible around the edges of the hole over a hundred feet above, and debris was still falling. It was impossible to tell if the damage had been caused by a friend or foe.

Her ears popped, and a sharp pain went through her head as a wave of strange magic passed over her, originating from the intense green-eyed man next to Arthur.

Sound, she thought as she watched him play a rune-covered harmonica. She activated her second stage of Pain Tolerance and blinked closer to the two of them, coming to a stop only to be engaged by Zoy again.

The berserker woman screamed and charged at Kyrian like an enraged bull. He flew out of the castle to avoid her.

Zoy rushed at Ilea and she dodged right, parrying one of the white blades with a bladed gauntlet that she summoned just in time. She punched with her left fist, the impact leaving the woman slightly off-balance before a blast of lightning slammed into her and sent her skidding over the floor. Ilea jumped aside to avoid a blast of air coming her way before she spread her ash around and heated it up as much as she could.

Zoy closed the distance again, Ilea summoning both her bladed gauntlets now as a flurry of slashes came from her adversary. Ilea dodged, weaved, and parried where she could, but it was clear that the warrior was far more experienced with bladed weapons. Ilea had a few cuts on her arms that were already healing.

Ilea moved in, letting Zoy strike against her sides, her wings moving out from her back to slow the blades. Ilea sacrificed a few hundred points of health and kicked the warrior just as the blades cut through her ash and reached her Veil and armor. Zoy stumbled back, turning the momentum into a roll to avoid a bolt of red lightning that instead burnt into the floor.

Ilea raised her arms as another wave of sound washed over her. She clenched her teeth and pushed against the wave, looking at Arthur and the sound mage before the former threw out his arms. All the air around her was pushed backward in an instant, sending Ilea crashing through the wall behind her and out toward the ocean. Zoy and an unfortunate guard had been hit as well, the latter screaming as he fell toward the water.

Stabilizing quickly, Ilea healed the damage to both her ears and the rest of her body, recovering from internal bleeding in several places and even a cracked rib from the wind alone.

Zoy teleported back to the castle in intervals, using the ability in a similar fashion to Ilea's own blink, but her wings and blink combined got her there much quicker than her adversary. She accelerated as much as she could and flew back through the wall the wind spell had knocked down.

Turning slightly, she crashed her whole weight into the bald sound mage, who was preoccupied with sending magic out toward the flying Trian. He turned a little at the last moment to avoid critical damage, but she still sent herself and the man flying through the wall behind him and into another courtyard with a single punch.

She heard a noise so loud her ears ruptured immediately. Ilea felt her vision blurring, the taste of blood in her mouth. She healed against the spell, her head thrumming. All she could do was hold down the mage as she steeled herself against his spell.

She sacrificed more health before it was too late and saw that he was bloodied as well, one of his arms mangled. She gritted her teeth, summoning her olvor gauntlets as she felt the power of her aura flow through her, then smashed her fists down into his face. The first impact sent a shock wave back that nearly sent her flying, but her wings pushed against it and her fists came down again, cracking through whatever barrier he'd put up.

She felt another wave of sound thrum through her, but her next strike hit his face, bone breaking as his magic dissipated. The next strike cracked his skull. Finally, both fists smeared the remainder of his skull and brains into the ground.

Ilea took a ragged breath, her arms sagging to her side before she stored her gauntlets. She couldn't see with her left eye, and breathing felt strange. Several messages popped up in her mind as she healed the extensive damage to her body, starting with her head and eyes, then moving on to her chest.

She stumbled to her feet when the worst of it was gone, nearly falling again, her vision spinning as she blinked her eyes. A sword hit her in the shoulder, the force sending her to one knee as she used her Sphere to see the enemy. One of the guards.

He raised his sword again and brought it down as Ilea vanished, reappearing behind him with a scream, her fist slamming hard into his leather armor and her intrusion flashing out into his back. She fell to one knee and saw him fall as well, his weapon clattering to the ground before she forced herself to stand up once more.

As soon as she stepped back into the hall from the courtyard, a blast of wind sent her right back out. Her wings did enough to prevent her crashing into the stone outer wall, and once she'd slid to a stop, she blinked into the main hall.

Some of the guards were moaning in pain and parts of the room were covered in ash, some of it still floating in the air. One of Edwin's swords was stuck through the greatsword wielder's neck. He pulled it out slowly, letting the corpse drop to the ground. Arthur and Zoy were nowhere to be seen. Kyrian and Trian landed nearby a second later.

"Where's Maria?" Ilea asked.

"On the hunt," Edwin said before he ran to a set of stairs leading down.

TWENTY

Old Friend

The ancient stone stairs led down for quite a while. Some of them were covered in blood and one or two corpses of Redleaf guards. Finally, the exit opened up into a broad white corridor, Arthur standing at the end of it near a set of runed marble pillars.

"Edwin!" he shouted with arms spread wide. He now wore a heavier black and red robe, cuts and damage showing on parts of it. His face was bloodied, his eyes narrowed.

"Arthur," Edwin said and spat on the ground.

"Years of research ruined because of your petty revenge. You're just a mistake I made decades past," Arthur said. His voice sounded tense. "You're here now. Let's finish this."

Ilea braced herself as Arthur raised his hands, a cone of wind rushing through the corridor. She dug her hand into the ground, but her Veil was unable to absorb the damage completely and she was pushed backward. Edwin and Trian had been hurled back toward the stairs, but Kyrian stood next to her, his metal forming a barrier before him that split the wind.

"Begone," Arthur said, touching one of the rune-covered pillars.

Ilea could feel the air change in an instant. Her blink failed to activate. She moved her wings when she saw Zoy jump in front of her, her back toward her.

Ilea turned in the air and saw Edwin and Trian getting back up and Maria appearing next to them before white light and then darkness enveloped her.

It only appeared dark to her eyes though, as she saw the ground below her through her Sphere. Yet the sounds of battle had vanished, and everyone else was gone.

Teleported somewhere else. Who else did he get?

There was nobody else in her Sphere, not even Kyrian or Zoy, who'd been closest to her.

Zoy wanted to be there. She knew what was about to happen.

'ding' You have entered the Iz dungeon

A dungeon?

Something at the border of her Sphere moved closer. Something large, though it barely made a sound. Ilea held her breath and blinked to the side again and again until she found a large chunk of rock for cover.

She stayed as quiet as she could, her Sphere not delivering any more information than the fact that she was standing on an even floor next to a natural rock with space to hide. Her healing took care of the injuries Arthur's wind magic had caused.

He activated a Taleen teleportation device.

Then she heard clicking. Metal on stone. She looked toward where the noise had come from, and her whole body went still. Her eyes widened when she saw the familiar green eyes scanning the dark. The eyes turned to face her before they went up and up. She knew what it was before Identify confirmed it.

[Taleen Praetorian - ???]

She saw it step into her Sphere, raising its scythe as its glowing green eyes stared at her.

"Intruder," it said.

"Fuck," Ilea answered.

Her stomach plunged. That memory of chill gripped her. She could feel her breathing pick up. She took a single step back before she stopped herself.

Get a grip. It's just another monster to fight.

Her trembling stilled and her mind cleared.

'ding' Fear Resistance reaches lvl 3

No Kyrian, no Zoy. No Arthur, Trian, or Edwin. No one to get hurt.

"Just you and me," she said to the machine.

A smile began to creep onto her face. She slowed her breathing, the hairs on her neck standing up as she watched the large Praetorian advance toward her. She would have to find a way back, but for now, the Praetorian was in the way.

All of her magic flared to life, her third-tier State of Azarinth activating as she sacrificed a chunk of health. The scythe rushed over her as she slid under it, ash spreading around her to distract the machine.

She blinked and found the blade waiting for her, crossing her arms with summoned olvor gauntlets as it smashed into her and sent her flying. Her gauntlets were scraped and a little dented as she slid to a stop, the Praetorian advancing even faster than the speed at which she'd been sent flying backward from its previous attack.

Ilea blinked farther away, flying as fast as she could through the seemingly endless dark corridor, but the machine kept up, its scythe slashing through the air with relentlessly precise strikes. She tensed her jaw and turned. Then she screamed into the darkness, right at the green eyes of the machine.

Again, the blade whipped out at her, but this time she blinked toward its head at the last moment, her fist landing on the slightly shimmering barrier that protected the green metal of the Praetorian's body, her destructive mana flowing into the forcefield as she flew back.

Ilea saw the scythe coming down again in a wide arc as she landed on the ground. She breathed out and moved her hand upward as she ducked slightly, sacrificing health and striking the broad blade with her palm, sending it over herself as she moved closer. She delivered a kick to one of the machine's large legs, more mana burning into its shield, and avoided its counterstrike at her back with a swift twirl to the right.

Ilea breathed fast, watching her mana sizzling against the shimmering barrier, a small section of green steel already exposed as she stepped to the side to avoid the scythe that was scraping a furrow into the stone. She moved close and kicked again. The impact sent shock waves through her leg before she blinked close again.

That's right, just another monster. I'll deal with you, then find a way back.

Ilea delivered attack after attack against the same leg, her whole being one with her skills, all of her consciousness focused on destroying the enemy. She was making progress, she could feel it. Then a burst of magic sent a burst of arcane energy out in a sphere around the machine and made her stop and skid back.

Her Veil was destroyed, quickly rebuilding as Ilea blinked in again, past the moving scythe. Her heart was racing as she flew and dodged the massive blade she knew could punch right through her armor and deliver a devastating curse to prevent her healing.

Another kick pounded the leg of the Praetorian. Ilea laughed, feeling the air pressure when the scythe rushed over her.

You're just bigger than the others.

She jumped and blinked backward when the Praetorian advanced.

Still just a machine, she thought, staring at the green eyes as she watched its many legs and scythe within her sphere. Then her eyes widened when she spotted another set of green eyes advancing through the corridor – and there were more behind.

Shit. Can't even destroy one of them. Two is suicide. Even I'm not that crazy… yet.

She swore under her breath and retreated, dodging the first Praetorian's blade whenever necessary. It was fast, definitely, but with her Sphere and knowing them a little better by now, she felt confident to show her back as she flew off. She finally found the end of the corridor, her wings taking her upward and away from the monsters lurking in the dark. It turned out they couldn't fly, nor did they climb the walls to follow.

Farther and farther she went, forced to dodge the scythes flying at her even a hundred meters in the air. Metal spheres from turrets and machines invisible to her shot out and joined in the attack as she rushed and blinked through the dark space.

There you are, she thought, flying toward a wall and smashing through one of the turrets with her fist before she continued her way up. *I have to get back to the others.*

She felt her hands shaking after the encounter below. She glanced down a few times, forcing herself to take slow breaths as she kept flying, but a wide smile was plastered on her face.

I fought one of them.

'ding' Fear Resistance reaches lvl 4

Ilea reached the top of the wall and glided over it, the bullets behind her ricocheting off the stone she now knew to be white, and looked out over the space beyond.

It's… huge.

Her small form was lost in the vast space of green and gold she had found herself in. Bright crystal light shone down from above. Far above, too far for her to make out what produced it.

Still, she knew she was underground. Before her spread a city, more expansive than any settlement she'd seen in Elos before. Definitely Taleen in nature, but nothing like the ruins she'd visited so far. There were more varied structures here, buildings reaching nearly a hundred meters in height, as well as domes and cathedrals. There were finely decorated walled-off mansions and contrasting structures reminding her of brutalist architecture. All of it was gray, black, and green, with a little gold showing here and there.

At the city's center, she could make out a floating golden sphere. It was difficult to ascertain how large it really was, but she was sure it was bigger than the demon whale she'd fought above Ravenhall.

There were no voices or music, nor did she see a single person moving in the hundreds of cobbled roads she saw. Instead, she saw thousands of Guardians standing motionless. Fields filled only with machines, many of them as large as a Praetorian or even bigger. She saw lights in the streets and lights floating above. Some of them even looked like they were coming toward her.

Move, Ilea told herself.

She gulped, hoping Kyrian hadn't been teleported here as well. Finding him in this expansive city would be near impossible.

More so with all of those machines.

Seeing most of them simply standing still felt eerie. Were they guarding something? Were they inactive? She didn't want to find out.

I need to get out of here.

She sped up, going to the first set of houses she found that weren't swarming with Guardians. There was only one inside, its eyes starting to glow green when her fist smashed into its torso, denting the metal inward, and its green lights extinguished again.

If anybody knows where I am and how I got here, it's Arthur.

Ilea looked outside and saw a sea of green light in the distance.

A new type.

They were flying machines that reminded her of upside-down scorpions with mechanical arms and floodlights that searched the surroundings. Guardians and worse were hanging on their bellies.

What the hell is this place?

She walked around the fully furnished room, a thick layer of dust on top of everything.

It's too big and probably too dangerous to search for a single person. If Kyrian really was teleported, then I have to get back to Arthur, back to whatever he used to teleport me here, find out where Kyrian went, and go there. Or force Arthur to bring him back.

The plan was a gamble, of course, but the others were likely still fighting, Trian was likely still fighting, and she had yet to defeat a single Praetorian in battle, let alone ten. Or a thousand.

I have to go back. Now.

She sat down and activated the third tier of her Blink ability. *Let's see if this works.* The skill charged up, and her mana flowed into it. As more and more of it entered it, she started to become anxious. It took a long while to charge up, and she was pretty sure she'd have to restart if it was interrupted. She soon saw lights floating by, more with every passing minute.

Most of the runes had appeared, and her spell was thrumming with magic when she heard a machine move right beside the house she was in. It crawled on the walls outside for a minute before it reached the floor she was on.

[Taleen Guardian – lvl 150]

The machine turned toward her, green soulless eyes staring at her, the opening on its chest letting her know that it was one of the ranged machines. Her wings, ash, and Veil formed as she continued to funnel mana into her teleportation skill.

The Guardian fired its first slug, crashing through her hastily built wall of ash before it was stopped by her Veil, falling down before a second one hit. More noises came from outside, and soon the tapping of metal against stone was all she heard.

The room was flooded in greenish light a moment later, and Ilea was nearly blinded by the flying machine hovering right outside the house. A sharp noise drowned out the metal tapping as glowing red energy gathered in its core—

The world went white again and Ilea fell on her back, hitting the wooden floor of her home, her breathing erratic. Her helmet vanished into her necklace as she stared at the ceiling.

'ding' Fear Resistance reaches lvl 5

"What the actual fuck was that?"

The question hung in the room as she let her Meditation take care of her adrenaline-filled body. A minute later, she stumbled to her feet and went to the table, summoning some of Walter's ale and pouring herself a cup with shaking hands. Then another one.

"Found the fucking motherload didn't I? First demons, then Taleen, what the fuck is next?"

She poured herself yet another cup. Meditation was still working, mostly to get the vast amounts of mana that she'd used for her third-tier Blink ability back.

Ilea took a deep breath.

Back to that isle now.

She hoped Trian, Kyrian, and the others were still alive. At least she was pretty sure Zoy had been teleported away as well, which would've removed one of Arthur's strongest allies. Arthur was standing alone now.

She spread her wings as she appeared outside. She could simply follow the coast and would find the isles eventually. And this time, she wouldn't have to hold back on her speed.

Ilea sacrificed a hundred health, which was near-instantly replaced by her healing skill, and with red runes visible on her face, she blinked northward, reaching her top speed quickly. More and more health was sacrificed to keep her speed at its maximum. She'd have to stop at some point to recharge, but seeing how little mana she had to use to keep both her blink and healing active made her smile. A good thing she'd invested so much in Wisdom.

Still, it would take several hours to reach the Isle of Garath. She tried to push away the worry she felt for her friends and checked through the messages in her mind, hoping they would distract her.

'ding' Your group has killed [Harmony Mage – lvl 225 / Blood Enhancer – lvl 218]

'ding' Your group has killed [Barricade Berserker – lvl 205 / Blood Berserker – lvl 183]

...

'ding' You have killed [Taleen Guardian – lvl 150]

'ding' Azarinth First Hunter has reached lvl 227 – 5 stat points awarded

'ding' Inheritor of Eternal Ash has reached lvl 223 – 5 stat points awarded

'ding' State of Azarinth reaches 3rd lvl 3

'ding' Form of Ash and Ember reaches 2nd lvl 20

'ding' Ashen Wings reaches 2nd lvl 15

She immediately thought about the third tier of her second class. With five skills at the end of the second tier, there would be options available. A broad grin spread on her face despite the circumstances.

3rd-tier skill points available [Azarinth First Hunter]: 0
Skills available for 3rd-tier advancement in [Azarinth First Hunter]:
None available

3rd-tier skill points available [Inheritor of Eternal Ash]: 2
Skills available for 3rd-tier advancement in [Inheritor of Eternal Ash]:
- Veil of Ash
- Ash Creation

Only two. For now, the choice is easy.

Ilea selected Veil of Ash, one of the few defensive skills she had available and the skill that, together with Blink, had saved her life just a few minutes prior in the Taleen dungeon. Considering what she'd seen, it was currently at the very bottom of her list of places to go to. Still, now that she knew about it, it *was* on the list.

'ding' Veil of Ash advances to 3rd tier

Active: Veil of Ash – 3rd lvl 1
A thin mist of ash forms around you to protect you and attack nearby enemies. You are in full control. The veil greatly increases your resilience.
2nd stage: The strength of your Resistance skills also benefits from the Veil of Ash.
3rd stage: The density of your Veil of Ash increases and is now affected by your Ash and Ember Manipulation. It increases the defensive capabilities of all ash and ember you control.
Category: Body Enhancement – Ashen magic

So, the walls of ash I create might actually do something other than look cool.

The change didn't feel as tangible as her third tier of Blink or State of Azarinth. She quickly activated her Veil in flight, just in case anything changed so drastically that it would surprise her as soon as she was back in a fight.

The ash formed around her a little more quickly than it had before, hovering a little closer to her armor and more visible due to being darker than before. She couldn't see herself, but looking at her arms, the ash didn't cover her body completely, instead swirling around it and moving to give the impression of a living element.

Checking her third-tier advancements again, Ilea found the expected result.

3rd-tier skill points available [Inheritor of Eternal Ash]: 1
Skills available for 3rd-tier advancement in [Inheritor of Eternal Ash]:
None available

Since she'd advanced one skill, she now only had four skills in her second Class at the highest level of the second tier. That meant she had to advance another skill to level twenty before she could choose her next third-tier skill.

Seems like Ash Creation is the only one available for now anyway.

Ilea kept up her speed as she looked through her stats.

Status:
Vitality: 650
Endurance: 233
Strength: 182
Dexterity: 193
Intelligence: 601
Wisdom: 599

She had enough Vitality to face down nearly everything she'd been confronted with so far. It was her highest stat – and for good reason. She thought of the sound mage she'd killed with just three attacks. Not something she wanted to happen to herself when someone of a similar level attacked her.

Although both the sound mage's and Arthur's magic messed me up pretty badly. Without my healing, I'd have had issues continuing the fight. It might've killed me. It made sense to an extent why it seemed like a lot of mages put most of their stats toward attack power. *But they don't have healing. At least, not those I've faced so far.*

She sped over the landscape, watching the ocean waves as she sacrificed more health and blinked time and time again. For her fighting style, Endurance was nowhere near as important as Wisdom. She'd rarely experienced stamina exhaustion before her mana ran out, despite her Wisdom being far higher than her Endurance. Strength and Dexterity helped her move better and strike harder, but her main damage still came from her auras and magic intrusion abilities.

She found that a combination of Strength, Dexterity, and Endurance was necessary to allow for efficient fighting, at least given the necessity of moving around and getting in close, compared to shooting a bunch of laser beams from your hands or forehead while standing still. Her focus would remain on Vitality, Intelligence, and Wisdom – while also keeping Endurance, Strength, and Dexterity high enough to keep her fighting style effective.

For now, she put her newfound stat points into Intelligence and kept on flying.

TWENTY-ONE

Hunters and Prey

Several hours passed with Ilea flying at her highest possible speed, though she had to slow down from time to time to recover her mana and health a little. Finally seeing the island group in the distance, she slowed and observed the situation, her Meditation skill working quickly to recover her lost mana and in turn health as her Hunter Recovery took care of the sacrificed life force.

No massive fire or any spells could be seen in the distance as she moved closer, her health and mana reaching acceptable levels to take part in a fight once more. The busted wall of the castle made the large hall they had initially fought in visible. A few people were standing near one of the walls. People she knew.

Ilea sped up again and landed casually next to the injured Edwin. He was slumped against the wall, a large amount of his own blood pooling underneath him. He barely acknowledged her as he bit into a pastry.

A man in dark armor and another in red stood nearby. Ilea couldn't help but smile at the sight.

"Didn't think I'd see you again so soon, Maurice," Ilea said to the man in black armor. "Hey, Popi," she added as the baker handed more pastries to Edwin.

Maria was hovering nearby as well, nearly invisible but breathing hard.

"Come back to fight after all?" Ilea asked the mercenaries.

Maurice grinned. "No. Observed from a distance. Chose to come and help the obviously affluent invaders."

"Popi is healing," Popi said. "The opposite of poison."

Ilea raised an eyebrow at this but just nodded. *Healing pastries. Why not?*

"Where's Trian?" she asked.

"Ilea..." Edwin said, gulping down his food as he focused on her. He tried to get up but winced as a wound on his stomach opened again.

"So that's your name," Maurice chuckled. "He's probably trying to say that the wind magic girl that followed Arthur out is in danger. Went that way. The lightning mage too," he added, pointing toward the mainland.

"Wind magic girl? Felicia?" Ilea asked. Then she blinked out, not waiting for a response as she sacrificed health again to speed up. The girl hadn't listened to her brother after all. She was proud and worried at the same time. The woman wasn't at the same level as Edwin and Maria.

Ilea reached the mainland less than a minute later, looking around only to find much of the vegetation destroyed and dead. Following the destruction and disturbed earth, she finally spotted three people who were huddled together in a clearing, evidently created by a large blast. Aliana was there with Trian and Felicia. Injured but alive, all of them.

She landed close to Trian and started healing him, looking down at Felicia. She was kneeling down in front of the burnt corpse of Arthur Redleaf.

"Felicia," she said quietly. "You did it."

Felicia turned to her, brushing away tears before she nodded. Ilea went over and hugged her, healing her injuries as the woman sobbed into her shoulder.

"Are you injured, Aliana?" Ilea asked as she healed the deep cuts, the bruises, and the broken shoulder Felicia had suffered in their fight.

"Nothing serious," Aliana said as she looked at Arthur's body.

"Is Kyrian here?" Ilea asked, knowing that he was likely trapped in whatever Taleen dungeon he'd wound up in. Hopefully, he hadn't been transported to Iz as well.

"He vanished with you and the warrior we faced before," Trian said. "He's not with you?"

Ilea shook her head. "We didn't arrive together."

Trian frowned. He made to speak but shook his head instead, his eyes staring into the distance. "Him too..." he said after a long moment.

Ilea glared at him. "He's not dead. He's out there, somewhere in one of those ruins."

And she would find him. In time.

With Arthur dead, she didn't know if anybody could give her the necessary answers to Kyrian's location or the teleportation gate used, but perhaps there was still something left in the castle. She was glad at least that the others were alive and that they'd gotten their revenge. Perhaps now they could finally find some closure.

"Come on, let's get you to the others and heal up everybody," Ilea said before Felicia spoke, pointing toward a spot in the distance.

"Someone's coming. Fast."

Ilea checked out the people approaching. "Two of them," she said, spreading her wings and grabbing Aliana and Trian. "Let's regroup, if they're hostile, we'll have a better chance together," she added before launching into the air.

Once they reached the others, Ilea immediately went to Maria, checking her injuries and healing them as quickly as she could, focusing on the most severe ones and completely ignoring the small stuff.

"We've got incoming. One flying humanoid and a massive beast," Ilea said. "Know anything about them?"

She finished healing Maria, who was now breathing much lighter, and moved on to Edwin. Surprising her, the man stood up on his own, his wounds mostly mended as she touched him and finished healing the cracked bones in his chest.

"Where's Arthur… Felicia, I told you to—" Edwin started.

"He's gone. Dead. You started it, and we finished it," Felicia said with a firm, defiant gaze.

Edwin's jaw clicked shut, and he fell silent.

"The two you mentioned are Kyle and Tiana. Hunters in Arthur's employ. They won't like it when they find his corpse," Maria said, cracking her neck as she turned visible. "He must've had a way to call for them in an emergency."

"He's dead," Edwin murmured. He looked at Felicia with wide eyes, then shook his head. "We have to take those two down, here and now, or they'll know who's responsible. All of you, I'll pay you everything I have left if you help in this fight. With everyone here, I doubt they'll stand a chance."

Ilea glanced at Trian. They could find information here on both the Golden Lily and where Kyrian might've been teleported to. She didn't want to flee and risk losing that chance.

"I'd like to search this place myself. If they're trouble, I'll help."

Trian just nodded, perhaps following Ilea's lead.

"That's why I came back," Maurice said with a grin. "I'll always help those in need… if they have deep enough pockets."

"I like helping," Popi chimed in.

"We should get out of this hall," Edwin said and pointed to the partially collapsed stairwell leading up to the battlements. "Kyle is a powerful necromancer who can turn into the monster you saw. We wouldn't want to face him in even this semi-enclosed space. Tiana will be with him. She's an ice and silver mage, far more resilient than she may seem.

"I suggest we split up. Me, Maria, Trian, and Aliana will face Kyle. It will take a lot of damage to take him down, and you don't want to get close to him. The rest of you, go for Tiana."

Ilea glanced at Felicia. The two of them locked eyes for a short moment before Ilea smiled and gave her a nod. "Let's finish this."

"Up," Edwin said as he hurried to the stairwell. They came out into the open air on top of the crumbling walls towering around the spacious courtyard of the ancient castle.

"Start heating up the area," Edwin said, and Popi spread his arms, the temperature rising drastically.

"I claim her silver things if what you say is true," Maurice said as he shrouded himself in a dark mist and ravens, eagles and monster-like birds of prey appeared out of nowhere around him.

Ilea summoned her ash in turn, condensing as much of it as she could into small spheres to be expanded or used at a later time. Maria was already out of sight, and Edwin's blades burned with a red flame as he walked to the front of the group. Felicia and Trian hovered in the air behind them and Aliana positioned herself behind some half-demolished walls that would give her a little cover.

"Don't let them escape," Edwin said when something heavy impacted the ruined walls.

A moment later, a creature of blood and claws slowly climbed over the ramparts, growling at the group with its wide mouth open, dark red eyes glaring at them. Its body was all fur and corded muscle, its head a weird fusion of wolf and stag. The organs and flesh under the skin seemed to pulse and bulge as if moving.

Tiana flew up behind the beast a moment later, her appearance still that of a finely dressed librarian. Her mouth was turned down in displeasure. A gust of cold wind swept over them upon her arrival, mingling with the heat from Popi. Her eyes opened wide as she looked at the group.

"Go," Ilea said and flew up, teleporting as close to Tiana as she could, speeding up with her wings as a sphere of ash spread out before her, covering both of them in a cloud. Ilea smirked as the woman vanished. *Of course,* she thought as a freezing cold spread through her, making her blink away as well and orienting herself to find her enemy again.

Tiana was floating a little bit away, raining a shower of ice spikes onto the battlements below, though most were stopped by the swirling gusts of wind Felicia had summoned. Edwin, Trian, and Aliana were engaged with the beast already, which was none of Ilea's concern for now as she rushed at the ice mage once more.

A group of birds bombarded Tiana as well, blades of wind and flashes of heat appearing around the mage as she retreated in the air and past the ruin's walls, taking the hunt above the ocean. Popi couldn't fly, it seemed, and he turned to focus his attention on Kyle instead.

Ilea found it hard to catch Tiana without risking being damaged by one of her ice spells. She left behind a cloud of icy air in the shape of a rose whenever she vanished, spreading freezing cold from where she left and reappeared. After a few quick teleports, the enemy mage was fully on the defensive, trying to catch any of her pursuers in one of her traps as she cooled the air around her.

It will only be a matter of time until she runs out of mana.

The thought kept Ilea at a distance, so she summoned her bow and continuously formed ashen projectiles and shot them toward the woman, not letting her use any meditation skill.

She pulled back the large string of her artillery bow, aimed, and sent out an explosive arrow. Though it was blocked by an expanding sheet of silver, the exploding projectile blasted the woman off balance before two blades of air cut into her chest.

Tiana turned in the air, trying to gain control again as a swarm of crows smashed into her, forcing her to use her magic. A sphere of ice formed around her, trapping herself and the birds within before it fell down toward the water.

The three hunters followed, hovering around the sphere as it hit the water. It froze on contact, keeping the sphere on the surface, but the woman inside was unable to move away.

"She can recover her mana this way," Felicia said, sending a couple of blades of wind into the icy sphere. Cuts formed but quickly froze over again.

"Pull me out if I get stuck," Ilea said as she landed next to the sphere. Her ash spread out around herself and the sphere of ice before she activated Embered Body Heat, heating up both her blood and the ash around her. Then she smashed her fist into the ice, destructive mana flowing into the sphere, combating the mana that in turn tried to freeze her arm.

Ilea's healing and Ice Resistance pushed against the icicles forming on her arm with every punch, the ash around her helping against the biting cold that threatened to freeze her in place with every moment she continued to stand there.

Cracks formed with every hit, reforming but unable to completely alleviate the damage. Their mana wrestled against each other, chunks of ice flung away as Ilea unleashed punch after punch, floating motes of liquid silver splashing out at her.

The element hissed and burnt itself into her ash, past even her armor, but she kept on attacking, Destruction and Wave of Ember continuing to damage the silver mage's defenses as birds pecked away at the remaining ice, many of them freezing in place. Blades of wind continued to slash into the sphere around them as well.

Finally, the ice sphere cracked and shattered, falling away. Ilea's fist hit Tiana's silver armor and was immediately swallowed up by the metal, her whole arm now stuck. A burning pain shot through her, her arm freezing up while her flesh melted from the molten silver.

She pushed her recovery to the max while pumping destructive mana into her enemy, who was still having to deal with Felicia's and Maurice's attacks, which were now only being blocked by shields of silver that expanded and contracted around her.

Ilea focused on the ash around her, pushing it toward the woman's eyes and throat while using her legs to kick at Tiana's armored shins. Finally, she got a good kick in, knocking her off balance, which let Ilea get her free left arm around the silver trap.

Grabbing the woman's arm, she crushed it with all her enhanced strength, standing firm on the ice and pulling the mage around before she slammed her onto the floor of ice she'd created.

The silver encasing her right arm dripped off, and her healing continued to fight the ice crystals forming inside her body, her enemy's magic somewhat slowed by Ilea's near-boiling blood. Ilea summoned more ash and sent it down at Tiana. Wind blades and birds that turned into dark streaks of magic crashed down in turn, silver and ice shields appearing to block them.

Ilea's left arm was still firmly holding her enemy hostage, likely disabling her ability to simply teleport away. Her right arm was half melted, her healing unable to fully push back against the silver and ice. The position didn't allow Ilea to get in a kick or even knee the woman, but her head was close enough.

She smashed her forehead against the silver that expanded out of the woman's hair ornament, slamming down again and again. Destruction and Wave of Ember whittled down Tiana's defenses as her healing fought the spreading cold in her body and the silver flowing through the cracks of her armor, melting her skin and muscle below.

The look in Tiana's eyes turned from determined to fearful as Ilea didn't relent. Maurice appeared in a smoke of feathers, blades flashing in the sunlight as silver expanded to deflect the attack. His second blade became stuck in the ice as it expanded to trap his arm as well.

As soon as it reached his flesh, he winced, the cold spreading fast, reaching his shoulder in but a moment. He clenched his teeth as Ilea continued to bash her bleeding skull against the silver shield, the flesh on her forehead having come off long ago.

Suddenly a massive gust of wind crashed into them, sending the three flying and destabilizing Tiana's silver magic. Maurice was sent to the side, gasping for air as he struggled to fly away from the woman, his right side frozen solid. He landed in the water a moment later.

Ilea was still holding on to Tiana with her left hand. Her right arm was still mostly destroyed, reversed healing spreading through her foe's body continuously.

Then they hit the water. Ice spread around them immediately, encasing both of them in a prison of frozen water. She was unable to move, unable to get any momentum to punch or kick her way out. The mana-infused ice also prevented her from teleporting.

Still, she held on, channeling her mana into Tiana, whose magic seemed to weaken with every passing moment.

Ilea saw the desperate look in Tiana's eyes, silver forming in the tight space between the ice and her body before it cut through her own arm right below her shoulder, separating Ilea's direct connection to her body. Unlike Ilea, who was being slowly eaten away by the ice magic that now encased her, Tiana didn't seem to need a physical link for her magic to work.

Ilea persevered, holding her breath and focusing on her Veil, Ice Resistance, healing, and the ash spreading in the minuscule space between her body and the freezing cold ice, heating everything up as much as she could with Embered Body Heat.

The spikes of ice that formed and stabbed at her were mostly stopped by her Veil, and the rest were stopped by her armor. It seemed her enemy was panicked enough not to be able to focus on her weak spots, such as her eyes and the small spaces connecting her armor pieces.

We're sinking…

Into the ocean.

The thought reached Ilea's mind as she realized her Sphere was unable to perceive anything but water anymore. And she pushed that thought as far away as she could. She had to get out. She let go of the separated arm her ash was heating up, trying to counteract the ice magic. To no avail. She was caught in the ice, unable to move enough to punch or kick properly. And she was out of air, only her healing managed to make that less of a problem than she would've expected.

Summoning an explosive arrow into her hand, she activated the rune right before the thing was frozen solid. The explosion ripped through her and the ice. She heard the dull sound of her armor withstanding the explosion and saw small cracks forming in the ice. She tasted blood in her mouth, but Ilea was more than used to Claire's explosion magic.

She grinned and summoned all the explosive arrows she had left. And then she activated all of them at the same time, lighting up the small sphere of ice far below the surface of the ocean. The ice splintered and water flowed in.

Ilea was free – but only for a moment as the ice reformed again just a second later. But it was enough time for her to blink out. Out and upward, again and again, before she spread her wings above the water, continuing to heal the damage she'd sustained from both Tiana and her own attempts to free herself. She coughed out the water in her lungs, trying to focus on the fight instead of her need for air.

"Are you alright?" Felicia shouted, looking down at the water before a barrage of ice lashed out from below, the spikes deflected by a whirlwind of air around Felicia. Ilea simply held up her arms to block the attack. No ice spread after the impact, leading her to believe that Tiana was running out of mana.

She finally breathed in.

"Don't worry about me! She's lost an arm. Don't let her get away!" Ilea shouted and looked around, blinking twice before she grabbed Maurice out of the water. The cold had spread through nearly his whole right side before her mana started healing the damage, counteracting the terrifying power devouring the man.

"Shouldn't have got close," she said, her wings flapping as they got higher, watching Felicia in the distance as Tiana emerged from below, the water around her freezing, her severed arm now replaced by a silver one mixed with blood. Her eyes were unfocused and bloodied, and she screamed before ice spikes shot out toward them.

Ilea moved her body in front of Maurice, continuing to heal him as the magical attack glanced off the Veil and the ash wall she formed behind her. Tiana instead focused on Felicia, who deflected as well as she could.

Maurice stopped Ilea with a gesture, his birds appearing again from above and diving at Tiana. "I'm fine now," he said.

Ilea nodded and let go of him before she vanished and charged at Tiana again.

She wouldn't get trapped below the water this time. The silver mage looked to be running on fumes, the pain of her lost arm visibly getting to her, and her health was surely now at the point where her concentration would likely be inhibited as well.

Felicia fired off smaller blades of wind, slowing Tiana as she gained the upper hand in their ranged battle. Tiana's ice attacks were now being deflected without even touching Felicia.

Ilea appeared next to Tiana, swinging her fist, then moving slightly to avoid the silver arm that was raised to block the attack, ducking and using her left hand instead. The hit wasn't deflected, and Ilea felt bones crack when her fist collided with the woman's ribcage.

Tiana spat blood before grabbing at Ilea with her silver arm. But she had already blinked away, a flurry of wind blades slashing at the beaten-down silver mage. Blood spurted from new wounds that formed as her armor was pierced by the wind projectiles.

Then she vanished, reappearing closer to the mainland before she vanished again. The three followed, some of Maurice's birds keeping pace with Tiana. Still, Ilea didn't want to go in recklessly, knowing that the silver mage was on her last legs.

Maurice didn't have to worry about that, and an eagle-like creature crashed into the woman right after she had used her teleportation ability, causing the two to tumble downward as the bird pecked and clawed at her in a battle to the death.

Blood and bits of flesh and cloth were ripped from Tiana as the bird slowly froze. Then the two of them spiraled to the ground, the impact sending the silver mage tumbling as the bird of prey shattered into black and red pieces.

Tiana struggled to rise as a group of crows started pecking at her, freezing solid moments later. Maurice's onslaught didn't stop before a blast of wind sent the birds spiraling through the air and the silver mage to her knees. A second blast forced her arms to open wide, and Tiana was no longer able to respond when a thin line of wind magic sliced through her neck.

The ding that rang in Ilea's mind let her know the fight had ended even before Tiana's head unceremoniously fell to the ground.

"One down," Ilea said, blinking over to Maurice, who had collapsed to his knees and was coughing up blood. He shivered and sighed when she started healing him.

"Damn cunt nearly got me," he said, looking over at the corpse.

"Recover your mana, we're going back to help the others," Felicia said as she walked over.

Ilea nodded and finished up healing Maurice, which took longer than expected. The damage to his organs and tissue had been extensive.

If anybody other than me had gotten caught in that ice sphere…

The thought lingered only for a moment. It had to have been her. Checking through her messages, she found her Ice Resistance had increased again but she'd review all that after the fight had ended.

I need something other than a bunch of arrows to counter a situation like that.

"You're good, come on," Ilea told Maurice as she walked over to Tiana's corpse, storing the head and body in her necklace before she ascended, the three of them rushing back toward the castle ruin.

* * *

Bestial roars could be heard from several hundred meters away. The courtyard was in ruins, the top of the castle resembling a mere pile of rocks at this point. The beast was still alive, though just barely. It was burnt to the bone in some parts and was missing one of its arms and eyes.

Their own group didn't look much better though. Popi was eating a pastry and sporting a massive gash in his chest that sent a cascade of blood down his armor. He was leaning on the ramparts off to the side, no longer in the fight.

Edwin had lost an arm, but the wound looked nasty. Black and festering. Maria looked ready to drop at any second. Blood soaked her face as her void magic blocked the beast from advancing on them.

Aliana and Trian were standing before her and Edwin, small but high-pressured streams of water forming and lashing at the monster, burning its mantle of flesh and muscle before lightning crackled through it, eliciting more roars.

Yet the beast still advanced.

Ilea landed next to Popi, as did Maurice.

"You alright there, big guy?" she asked, touching Popi on his shoulder as she examined him, healing mana flooding into the man while she activated her meditation skill.

"Popi… is tired," he said after a moment and closed his eyes.

"Go help the others," Ilea said to Maurice.

The massive monster was an impressive sight and reeked of death and blood. Ilea wondered if she could've won alone against either Tiana or Kyle.

One of them, maybe. Both at the same time? Doubtful.

Ilea gulped.

The Birmingales, Trian's family, now Arthur Redleaf and his fighters. A coordinated attack of enough high-level fighters is all it takes. I'll have to remember that.

Popi's wounds slowly closed as Ilea watched the creature protect itself from the wind blades and birds attacking its side with swipes of its hide-armored arms.

The beast looked terrifying. Or it would've to her former self. Now she was more impressed by its speed and endurance. By a man being able to turn himself into that.

And despite the heavy injuries and magic from an entire group of dangerous attackers raining down on him, he remained standing. He kept them at a distance, slashing at his foes with his one arm as he circled them, using fallen stones and ruined walls as defensive measures while wind, water, lightning, and void magic were hurled his way.

And he didn't even try to get away. Commendable but stupid. Ilea would've been out of there as soon as she spotted more than two enemies at her own level.

Tiana tried to run and failed though. Got to remember that.

The wound on Popi's chest finally closed up.

Now, let's finish that beast.

Ilea appeared next to the monster, punching at its already heavily injured, armless side. Her offensive skills pushed mana into it and it roared in pain, wind cutting into it too while a murder of crows finally managed to latch onto it, pecking and clawing at the burnt wounds and exposed skin. Then a burst of lightning seared its face.

The beast howled in pain and anger, flinging its body at Ilea with all its strength. Ilea disappeared and reappeared just outside its range before she darted in and punched again. The monster turned and rushed toward the group of mages.

Ilea was right behind it when Edwin's remaining sword burst into bright red flame. The remaining clawed arm of Kyle's monster form descended toward Edwin before the warrior vanished and appeared just a meter ahead of it. His blade swung upward and cleaved through the beast before its massive form slammed down on him.

Edwin was crushed, his sword clanging onto the stone floor. Maria touched the injured beast and closed her eyes, a surge of mana leaving her body before she collapsed to one knee. A ding filled Ilea's mind as the monster's head deflated. Ilea blinked and looked at Maria, who was sitting down now, breathing hard.

I wonder if she could rip out my brain that easily. Humans are dangerous. Another one for the list.

Ilea moved to the beast's front and checked on Edwin. He looked close to death, his eyes barely focusing on her.

"You look like shit," she said, pulling the monster's chest up with one arm. She touched Edwin with her boot and checked his extensive injuries.

"I don't need your..." the man said before a coughing fit briefly consumed him, "...help," he finished.

"You do," Ilea said and started healing.

Felicia rushed to him and touched his brow.

"That was close," Maria said through strained breaths.

Yeah, Ilea thought.

"Do we know anything about the teleportation gate that was used on me, Kyrian, and Zoy?" Ilea asked. Neither of them being in Iz with her, at least at that particular exit point, gave her some hope that they weren't there at all.

"No," Maria said. "There are still people in the castle. Perhaps they'll be of use in answering that question."

"I'd like to talk to any of Arthur's staff who survived once we're done here. Edwin should be fine in a minute or two. You should recover your mana," Ilea said to Maria as Edwin's missing arm regrew before them. It was quite a sight to see, apparently, as all of them except Popi watched the process with emotions ranging from disgust to fascination.

"I don't think so. Edwin and I will take care of them."

"No, you won't. Arthur Redleaf is dead. Your goal is fulfilled. Kyrian vanished, and I want to know where," Ilea said without looking at the woman.

"I will go with you," Felicia said.

"As will I. If we can find him," Aliana said, "we should try."

"Fuck it, I'll come too. I know the place and can show you around. Plenty of Arthur's stuff to plunder as well," Maurice chimed in and chuckled.

"Don't interfere, mercenary," Maria said, but she didn't say anything else as she stood there and watched Edwin heal. He looked better now, despite his armor being in tatters.

"He seems to be exhausted. Perhaps you should take care of him for a while," Felicia said. "We also have to retrieve Arthur's corpse and get rid of it." She pointed toward the coastline. "You'll find the battlefield that way."

Maria looked at her for a long moment, then shook her head. "Thank you. For the help," she said, glancing at Ilea, Trian, and Maurice in turn before kneeling next to Edwin. "All of you."

"I'll take my payment in gold, thanks. I'll be waiting right there," Maurice said, pointing to an entrance deeper into the castle.

"You will get your gold, mercenary," Maria said as she helped Edwin up.

Maurice smiled and grabbed a torch as soon as they went inside.

"A tour, then, for the new lords and ladies of the castle."

TWENTY-TWO

Discovery Channel

"Who are you anyway? You said Shadow's Hand before, but your name was Lilith then too," Maurice said as they walked through the dark, dilapidated hallways that led deeper into the castle.

"I'm Ilea. And I am with the Hand, but I'm not here on related business. We were just here to kill Arthur," she said.

Maurice snorted and kicked open a heavy wooden door. "That was his workspace. What's the angle? Wealth? Research?"

"Family affair," Felicia said as they entered the simply decorated room. Ilea noticed the Taleen furniture immediately. This wasn't a castle built or made for humans.

Maurice grabbed an expensive-looking letter opener and pocketed it. "Ah, nobles. Lucky I grew up in the shit slums of Heruch."

"I didn't know the dwarves built outside of mountains," Ilea said, walking around the table to look at the letters and notes.

"You're from Baralia?" Aliana asked.

"Yeah, that an issue?" Maurice said.

"They have besieged Virilya," Felicia said. "Alyris has ordered an evacuation of the entire city."

Maurice whistled. "Now that is news. Might go there after this gig is over. Never been too patriotic, though, if that's your concern."

Felicia glanced at him and then looked at the letters. Ilea opened what looked to be a diary and read one of the entries from a few weeks back.

The motivations behind the Taleen's actions have yet to make sense to me. All of this technology at their disposal, but then again, this island is devoid of the creators and teems with their left-behind machines. Piles of dust that my botanists say were bones at one point, but who knows if it really was them? Did they vanish? Did they die out? Or did they leave, perhaps for a completely different realm altogether? Perhaps this gate will lead us to new answers. I fear more questions are all that I will find…

Ilea skimmed through the later pages, learning about the conquest of the Taleen dungeon, going deeper than Arthur had anticipated.

Another three of my strongest guards were vanquished today. Zoy has proven vital to this operation again. It is a miracle that I found such a willing soldier for this mission. Were it not for our aligning goals, I wouldn't even dare talk to her. The magic she wields is dangerous to any mage. To any man. To see her heal from fatal wounds on her own in mere hours, even regrowing lost limbs without a healer, is extraordinary. Her lack of sight is just a front. I will have to dispose of her before long, though, or she too will grow arrogant and betray me. No trust can be given to mercenaries.

"Did you and Zoy work together for long, Maurice?" she asked.

"Zoy? No, first time I've seen the woman. Seems a bit unhinged, but who isn't in this game? Couldn't identify her either, but she opened up to Popi a little. Hates the Taleen machines, I think. Probably something that happened to her at one point or another."

"The Taleen machines don't come out of their dungeons though," Felicia said, looking up from the documents on the table.

"Beats me. Maybe her family fell into one and got butchered," Maurice shrugged. "Can we move on? There's nothing else here."

Ilea nodded as she and Aliana collected the books and documents into their storage items. She continued reading the diary while Maurice led them further through the castle.

The teleportation unit in this dungeon is intact but likely unstable. One of my enchanters tells me its targeting runes are unbalanced. We will begin testing in the morning.

Ilea ground her teeth. The entry she'd just read was from four days prior. *Unbalanced targeting runes? Does that mean we were sent to random platforms?* she wondered before reading more.

The gate can be activated, but it looks like the destination cannot be chosen, not anymore. A defensive mechanism mistakenly activated by my most trusted rune mage. He paid with his life for that mistake. A loss I will not recover from for some time, but I cannot leave mistakes unpunished. To think we were this close and to fail nonetheless. Another expedition north wasted, the only two survivors telling of unsightly beasts and arcane storms. Incapable, all of them.

Ilea closed the notebook for a moment and watched the flickering flame of Maurice's torch. She thought back to what they'd found in Eve's hideout and sighed.

The next target, the next dungeon.

Maurice slowly opened another wooden door, this one leading into a somewhat large hall. Ilea saw the people inside moving into a formation as soon as they heard the door opening.

"They're scared," she said, feeling their distress through Hunter's Sight.

"Yeah, they're the caretakers of the plants. I'd be shitting my pants by now as well," Maurice said, pushing the door fully open with a grin on his face.

"Fellas!" he bellowed. Some of the people inside murmured with relief when they saw him, only for despair to spread immediately when the others walked into the room. One of the group, a nervous woman, flicked her wrist, a barbed root moving out of her robes toward them. Ilea stepped forward and caught the root, using her free hand to make a calming gesture.

"We're not here to kill you. Arthur Redleaf is dead. Choose wisely how you act now," she said, looking at the woman, ignoring the root that was trying to burrow past her Veil and into her armor, entirely ineffectively.

Felicia stepped forward. "I'm Felicia Redleaf. If you served my father, then I ask you to do the same for me."

The group seemed to calm at her words, the root going for Ilea withering away.

"What are all these plants?" Aliana asked as she paced around the room.

The room was filled with hundreds of varieties of plants – none like anything Ilea had seen above ground. Though they reminded her somewhat of ones she'd seen beneath it. Twisting vines and strangely colored flowers, among many others, filled the space.

"Father was always obsessed with them. That's why he kept an entourage of vegetation mages around. Mages who could be used to feed thousands instead kept for his own hobby," Felicia said as she touched one of the plants. Two of the mages instantly winced, while another moved his hand toward her.

"You mustn't!" the man exclaimed.

"He's dead. You no longer have to worry," Felicia said, removing her hand from the plant.

"Ravenhall could use them," Ilea said off-handedly before she looked at the group. "Do you know about the teleportation platform?" she asked, but no one replied. "He said there was more than a single enchanter."

"I... I am an enchanter under Lord Redleaf," one of the mages said, stepping forward. He looked like an accountant. "Please spare my life and those of the others."

The man knelt before Ilea, the gesture making her a little uncomfortable. She grabbed him by his robe and gently raised him up.

"No need to worry," Ilea said. "Come with me, I need to have a chat with you."

She walked back into the hallway they'd come from, closing the door behind the man as Felicia started talking to some of the other mages. The man seemed terrified, his eyes avoiding her own.

"Look, I'm not going to hurt you, okay? And if you want something out of this situation, then maybe I can help you with it. If you help me first," Ilea said. She let him think about it for a moment. "Now, the gate you found here. It was activated and sent me and a friend away."

The statement made him look up for the first time.

"You were sent away? When? How did you get back? Did you find another dungeon?" he asked, murmuring to himself as he straightened up, looking ready to take notes.

"You sent people away, didn't you?"

"None of them returned. The runes… I was sure the destinations were random, the gate perhaps even completely shut down."

"I was sent to another Taleen dungeon. A place called Iz. My friend wasn't there. Is it possible he was sent to the same dungeon?"

"Iz… Iz… Are you sure that was the name? That's unprecedented… one syllable…" the man said, his tone more excited now.

"My friend?" Ilea prompted.

"Yes… I mean, no. The chances of him appearing in the same dungeon… given we assume there are hundreds if not more in Elos… no, statistically speaking, I don't think he'd have been in the same dungeon. But are you sure it was Iz?"

"I'm sure. Why is it relevant?" Ilea asked. "And can you help me find him?"

"It is relevant, very relevant. The dungeon below us is called Iztacalis. We've found references to a major city, a stronghold with the name Iztaca. If our theories are right, then you might have found something akin to the core… the very center of the Taleen civilization…" He was speaking quickly now, and Ilea calmed him down again.

"Even if that's true, I want to know about my friend, not Iz. So tell me everything you've learned."

"Yes, of course. Yes." The man rubbed his chin. "Well, he was sent somewhere else. To another Taleen teleportation gate. It is possible that the gate isn't able to send him back. The destinations and activations are often erratic, random, it seems. Some people return through the same gate, others are lost, or their gate suddenly leads to another destination. The platform here is one of the more erratic ones."

"Can you find out where he was sent?"

"I'm afraid it's not that simple. I'm sorry." He paused, slumping down a little as he raised his hands as if to ward off a blow. A long moment passed before he looked at her in relief and continued. "I… I mean… more study of the runes is necessary, but my knowledge is limited, and my ability is inhibited by my comparatively low level. Arthur might have been able to tell you more, but…" he trailed off.

"Yeah," Ilea murmured.

"I won't be able to determine where your friend went, but perhaps with more understanding, with more time… I could find a way. It's not… I mean…"

"What were you working on anyway? What was Arthur's goal?"

"To replicate the Taleen teleportation technology. That's why I signed up initially and why I never tried to run… At least, that's what I tell myself," he added more quietly. "The man, Arthur… I won't waste another thought on him, but the *goal*… Imagine it! A network of teleportation gates between human cities. Weeks or months of travel through the wilderness," he said and snapped his fingers, "in mere instants."

Ilea nodded slowly.

"The possibilities for travel, for trade… It would change how we live, how large our settlements could grow, how we fight and expand," he said before his smile faded slightly. "It would also impact the way we wage war. Anyone who holds this technology would dominate any engagement. Fighters healing and resting in a stronghold could be sent to a distant battlefield in a mere moment. Of course, it would have adverse impacts as well, but I still believe that the positive possibilities far outweigh the potential dangers."

"You're pretty convinced of the idea," Ilea observed. She saw his points as well. Ilea supposed that with Classes and magic, the importance of logistics wasn't quite as dominant as on Earth, but it would still make an enormous difference.

She imagined different militaries appearing in Dawntree or Salia the instant an elf was sighted. Then there was the demon summoning in Ravenhall. Thousands could've been evacuated, fighters from other places transported there to help.

"The Taleen had this technology, didn't they?"

"They did, but we don't know why they vanished," he said.

"Could it be something to do with the ancient and powerful teleportation network they built and used?"

The man smiled. "Yes, that is possible. Which is why testing and safety is of utmost importance."

"What's your name?" Ilea asked.

"Christopher Volaris," the man said and bowed deeply.

"I'm Ilea, a Shadow from Ravenhall. The friend I mentioned before, Kyrian, he was teleported away by Arthur when he activated the gate here. I see your points in regard to the technology at play here, but I'm not personally interested beyond finding him and bringing him back. Still, maybe we can make a deal?"

He crossed his arms, his back straightening slightly. "I'm listening."

"Ravenhall was decimated by the recent demon summoning. I have friends in high places with the Hand. Places that could provide resources if you make your case. I'm sure Claire would be interested in this project of yours, she's one of said friends in high places, and I can think of at least one talented young enchantress who might want to join this research. Do you need to be here to conduct it?"

"Not with what we've recently documented. The inscriptions, mana pathways, everything is written down. While we theorized earlier that the materials themselves were primarily important, we recently dismissed that theory. I cannot be definitive, and I may very well have to travel to more Taleen ruins to examine more gates, but for the time being, there is plenty to study without direct access."

"Good. Then would you like to work under my employ? Or Claire's, I suppose. She'll draft any relevant contracts. To continue your research, to find out where Kyrian was teleported to, to find a way for me to reach him, and, I suppose, to find a way to replicate the teleportation gates used by the Taleen dwarves."

She could tell Christopher was trying to hide his excitement, the corners of his mouth twitching upward ever so slightly.

"I will need access to Lord Redleaf's documentation and the notes of the other enchanters," he said, his voice tense.

"I'm sure I can arrange that. We'll talk about the details in Ravenhall. It's probably best if we don't advertise this deal to the others," Ilea said.

She'd inform Felicia because it concerned Arthur's work and the documents they'd taken, but she knew the woman would agree, if only for Kyrian's sake.

* * *

"Welcome back. I see you've found a new guide," Maurice said and glowered at Christopher, who suddenly appeared very interested in the stone floor.

"There doesn't seem to be anybody else in the castle as far as they know," Felicia said, walking up to Ilea. "You mentioned Ravenhall being in need of vegetation mages?"

"I mean Ravenhall is basically empty right now, so they're in need of most mages," Ilea answered, looking at Christopher. "And the people who fled Virilya will need to find a place to stay."

"And they'll need to be fed as well," Felicia smiled. "Half of them don't wish to be employed by the Redleafs again. It wouldn't be too difficult for them to find a new employer, but I thought I'd ask."

"I'm sure Claire can draft some enticing contracts for them. If they're interested in that, we can take them with us." She could tell the mages were more afraid than anything else at the moment, so she addressed them as a group. "I'll protect you on the way to Ravenhall, and I can promise more than fair employment."

A few of them glanced at her now.

"I'll have a chat with them," Christopher said and winked at her.

Quick to adjust, that one, Ilea thought. She watched him go to the others and talk in excited whispers before she found a table and sat down at a long wooden bench.

"Ale," Maurice said, setting down a mug as he joined her with a smile on his face. "Important to have a drink after a battle to the death."

Ilea looked at him. An absurd thought, she supposed, but she found that she agreed. She grunted in agreement and grabbed the mug, drinking deep before she set it down again, finally checking the numerous messages still lingering in the back of her mind.

'ding' Your group has killed [Inheritor of the Storm – lvl 250 / Child of Blood – lvl 241] – For killing an enemy twenty or more levels above your own, bonus experience is granted.

So, the others taking down Arthur still gave me experience?

'ding' Your group has killed [Rose of Everlasting Winter – lvl 224 / Champion of Silver – lvl 220]

'ding' Your group has killed [Necromantic Enhancer – lvl 248 / Blood Monster – lvl 240] – For killing an enemy twenty or more levels above your own, bonus experience is granted.

Both near two fifty, yet they'd still lost against their group of barely two twenties. The fights hadn't even seemed close – not against the blood monster, at least.

Note to self, don't get mobbed.

'ding' Azarinth First Hunter has reached lvl 228 – 5 stat points awarded

'ding' Azarinth First Hunter has reached lvl 229 – 5 stat points awarded

'ding' Inheritor of Eternal Ash has reached lvl 224 – 5 stat points awarded

'ding' Azarinth Reversal reaches 2nd lvl 18

'ding' Wave of Ember reaches 2nd lvl 14

'ding' Wave of Ember reaches 2nd lvl 15

'ding' Embered Body Heat reaches 2nd lvl 2

...

'ding' Embered Body Heat reaches 2nd lvl 4

'ding' Ashen Wings reaches 2nd lvl 16

'ding' Body of Ash reaches 2nd lvl 18

'ding' Ashen Warrior reaches 2nd lvl 18

'ding' Ashen Warrior reaches 2nd lvl 19

So damn close, she thought, biting her lip. Another Ashen Warrior level and she'd be able to advance another skill to the third tier.

There were still more messages remaining.

'ding' Ice Resistance reaches lvl 8

...

'ding' Ice Resistance reaches lvl 15

'ding' You have learned the General Skill Silver Magic Resistance – lvl 1
A rare magic, to be sure, and just as deadly. Not quite corrosion or poison, silver magic can be devious, its effects complex. You have survived and are one of few who have been exposed to it and lived.

'ding' You have learned the General Skill Harmony of the Drowned – lvl 1
You have been submerged in liquid for longer than most can survive. You crave to become a creature of the deep and have proven that you will go to any lengths to achieve that. While your biology doesn't strictly allow for gills, magic has its ways. You can stay submerged in liquid for much longer.

Another one for the defensive arsenal. And what is that drowning spell? I wasn't down there for that long, was I?

She supposed that without her healing, and possibly some other body enhancement spells, she would've been out. The thought was sobering.

At least she now had another skill that would help.

They had found and fought the Birmingales and had found and killed Arthur. Ilea thought of Eve and took a deep breath. Perhaps she'd find out more about the Golden Lily from everything they'd found, but it wasn't a priority now.

Eve was dead. Kyrian was not, and he was out there somewhere, perhaps able to get away and come back, perhaps stuck in some extensive underground dungeon. But just as she had helped Trian, just as she would've found a way to support Eve, she would find him too, and she would bring him back.

Ilea opened her eyes and stood up. There was still plenty of castle to be searched through, plenty of documents to be read. It would be a long day, but she was glad to have found Christopher. It felt like a step in the right direction.

TWENTY-THREE

Pancakes? Pancakes.

Ilea sat back in her chair, her boots on the table as she dropped the letter back on the pile. Aliana was sleeping wrapped in a blanket in the corner of the room.

Why did she get the comfortable armchair?

Ilea scratched her head and heard Edwin knock on the door. Felicia went to open it, rubbing her eyes in the process.

"We found more supplies if you need any food or drink," he said. "Not sure how long that will last with those two mercenaries down there. And, well, Maria."

He looked at the documents on the table. "Are you sure you want to go through all that, Felicia?" he asked. He sounded worried but mostly just tired.

"I'm sure, Edwin," Felicia said. "Anything else?"

"I'm the male heir. I'm supposed to..." Edwin said and faltered. He glanced at Ilea, then back to Felicia. "We could leave, you know. Now that..."

"Who cares what we're supposed to do? We did what we came to do, and I don't intend to throw away our family's legacy."

"Arthur's legacy," Edwin said and stepped closer, his eyes narrowing slightly.

Felicia didn't relent, glaring at him. "Our mother's legacy. You never wanted it, did you?"

Edwin broke eye contact, sighing.

"Did you even plan anything beyond killing Father?"

"I don't need you to berate me," Edwin hissed back.

Felicia calmly went back to her chair and sat down, taking the next document.

"I'll go check on… those supplies," Ilea said, rubbing her eyes. Standing up, she grabbed Edwin's arm and dragged him out. "You come too."

"Ilea, I appreciate your help, but this is none of your business," Edwin said as soon as she closed the door.

"I care about Felicia," Ilea said. "And frankly, I don't exactly care where you're going from here on out or what you'll do. What I know is that Felicia seems more driven than ever, and I don't think either of us should get in the way of that. Can you leave her alone for a bit and think about your situation?"

The man didn't respond, pausing and closing his eyes for a moment.

"Why are you still dressed in your fucked up gear anyway? And where's the supply room? Come on, maybe we'll find something new for you," Ilea added, tapping his shoulder as she walked past. She turned back a moment later and saw him just standing there.

Did he really not plan for anything that happened after? Ilea asked herself. She was quite sure he had, but maybe he just hadn't believed that succeeding was on the cards. Not really.

The always confident Edwin Redleaf.

She supposed he just needed some time to process everything.

Edwin did eventually lead her downstairs and through another large hall, raucous noise already coming from the room at the far end. The mages they'd found were sitting in the hall awkwardly, looking around with anxious glances.

"A maaaan for only he could satisfy my neeeeeds!"

The singing voice belonged to none other than Maria, who was perched on a table inside the spacious storage room, empty bottles of wine and ale scattered on the ground around her.

"Ohhh, Lady Ilea, what a pleasur…" Maurice said as he staggered into view, bowing slightly before he nearly fell, staggering until he met the wall of the room.

Popi had claimed his own table, carefully mixing ingredients together in a metal bowl.

"Does literally everyone have a storage item at this point?" Edwin asked when they entered the room to see Popi summoning flour and eggs out of thin air. Ilea just looked at him with a smile.

"This looks fun. A break from work," she said and joined them, grabbing a bottle of ale before she sat on the table beside Maria.

"Cheers," she said, opening the bottle. Maria smiled at her, then downed the rest of her wine.

"Aaaah, what a sight," Maurice said as he stumbled toward them.

To be young and lacking a high-level Poison Resistance.

Ilea smiled at the man, who was barely able to stand. Still, the number of already empty bottles was impressive. Enough to leave most normal people passed out at the very least.

"I think you've had enough, Maria," Edwin said as he grabbed her shoulders.

"Ed... you're so mean. Always so mean," she said and closed her eyes as she fell onto his chest, hugging him close. "So nice," she murmured as he walked out of the room with her.

"There goesch half the party..." Maurice said, taking Maria's place next to Ilea. "Hi there ssschugar." He looked at her with a drunken smile.

Ilea sighed and watched Popi work while she enjoyed the good ale, thinking of Eve and Kyrian and remembering the rare moments they'd shared together in the bars of Viscera and Ravenhall.

Then she easily broke Maurice's hand as it fumbled with her armor. The man whined but then laughed. "Ah you're a cold one, eh..."

Popi turned around at the noise. "Please don't kill him, he means no harm." He smiled and handed Maurice a cupcake that the mercenary took with a grin and ate.

"Don't worry, Popi," Ilea said and got up, grabbing a crate full of ale and walking outside, putting it onto the long table in front of the mages in the next room.

"Want a drink? Would be a waste if we left it here," she said, knowing they could easily take it all back to wherever they went. Storage items gave them that luxury.

Nonetheless, Ilea went back and grabbed each crate before putting them on the table. Christopher was the first of the mages to join her, grabbing a bottle of ale and lifting it in her direction.

"To the demise of Lord Redleaf," he said and smiled. Ilea mirrored the gesture and went to look for Trian. She found him in the first hall they'd fought in, staring at one of the corpses.

"Trian," she said, walking over. "We're having a drink. Might be better than looking at corpses?"

He looked at her and sighed, then nodded. "Sorry, I just..."

She touched his shoulder. "We're alive. And Kyrian is out there. Let's take it one step at a time. Remember?"

He breathed in deep, then gave a weak smile. "Right."

She brought him downstairs, watching his expression through her Sphere.

Suppose we all need time.

Ilea cracked her neck. If she was honest, the main thing she was looking forward to was finally fighting another monster. Not the monstrous humans they'd hunted down but beasts and machines hidden in some fucked up dungeon deep underground. The thought distracted her from memories of Eve and Kyrian.

One step at a time.

Maurice had already joined the mages, telling stories of adventures and grandeur. Of faraway kingdoms and exotic beasts and women. Ilea noticed one of the mages was looking at him with a little too much interest as she grabbed another bottle of ale from the crate and cracked it open, handing it to Trian before she got one for herself.

"To team thirty-four," she whispered, raising her bottle.

* * *

"These documents all have mentions of 'the Order'," Felicia said. "I would assume it's the Golden Lily, but none mention any names, cities, or anything else really. Just goods transferred and money exchanged. Information about decisions either accepted or refused, all in a code. I'm afraid you'll find it difficult getting to them through any of this."

A few hours had passed and Ilea had gone to check on her. Most of the mages were passed out or sleeping by now. Maurice had retired with one of them, and Popi had provided a massive chocolate cake for everybody.

"I'll still take them if you don't mind," Ilea said, putting all the documents into her necklace. "And the research on the Taleen gates."

Felicia looked at her for a moment, then smiled. "Kyrian. Of course. I'll set it aside."

"Thank you."

They stood there for a moment, both silent.

"You could work with me, if you want to, in the capital," Felicia said.

"It's under siege."

"For now." Felicia smiled. "I'm sorry. I shouldn't have suggested it."

"It's alright. I appreciate it, Felicia. I just don't think I'm made for the kind of work you're offering."

"Politics, intrigue, assassinations, budget calculations? None of that sounds interesting to you?"

Ilea snorted. "Yeah, absolute dream."

"What do you plan to do instead?"

Ilea shrugged. "I'll take the mages and Trian back to Ravenhall. Then? I'm not sure."

She sat down on a chair and crossed her arms and legs.

Eve is dead.

She sighed.

Kyrian has been teleported to some random dungeon.

She took a long breath and looked at the ceiling.

I helped Trian fight and murder the nobility of Lys. And he's not been the same since.

Finally, she chuckled.

At least Claire's in her element.

"Way too many close calls," she murmured.

Any of their fights could've gone the other way if a few things had been different. If Maurice and Popi had faced them, if Zoy hadn't vanished, if Tiana and Kyle had already been on the isle, if Ronan and Bale had been ready to face them...

"But you're here," Felicia said. "Alive."

Ilea nodded. "Yeah."

"If you don't want to join me, I won't be able to protect you directly. It's not certain yet how Lys will react to the deaths of the Birmingales and Arthur Redleaf. I suggest you lay low for some time."

"I don't plan to dabble with politics and wars again anytime soon, if that's what you mean," Ilea said. "There's a whole world of magical things out there."

Felicia grinned. "Do visit when you get back. And promise me not to be too reckless. I would hate to lose a friend."

"You know me. Always well prepared and overly cautious. And anyway, it would take death to kill me."

"Then let's hope there's a resistance for that as well."

Ilea's smile faded. "You be careful too, alright?"

"War brings a lot of opportunities for children of an ancient noble House whose Lord is suddenly gone."

Ilea rolled her eyes and left, ready for some sleep herself.

I imagine she'll rise fast.

But I won't be outdone.

* * *

I want some pancakes...

The thought was the first thing that entered her mind as rays of sunshine slowly invaded her personal space the next morning. The room looked utterly medieval and barren. She sent healing magic through her body, activating meditation at the same time. The two had been more than a blessing for potential hangovers.

I need to wash my armor again, she thought, blinking twice to get outside. Her helmet vanished, the rough ocean air brushing against her skin as her wings spread. She flew downward, spotting a rocky shoreline where she could stand. Just in case a massive sea monster suddenly appeared.

Popi might be able to make pancakes...

Her feet planted firmly on a rock, she summoned her helmet and held it under the ocean water, filling and dumping it out a couple of times before she shook it off. Ash came into existence around her before it moved into her helmet, clinging to the sides and swiftly cleaning the salt and other filth out.

Putting the helmet on afterward, Ilea started doing the same with the rest of her armor. Looking at her chest piece, her fingers brushed across the broad fissure where Petra Birmingale had cut through it with her blade.

Far too risky.

The poison had damn near killed her. And yet she found herself smiling at the memory.

The process didn't take long but she sat down for a moment afterward, enjoying the view of the morning suns hanging low over the horizon, shining onto the endless ocean that spread before her. She wondered what lay beyond the endless depths. There was no world map available, no satellites giving a clear picture of the land masses in Elos. At least, none she knew about.

With all that had happened, including her realm traveling, even seeing Earth when they'd used that teleportation device in the demon realm, Ilea still wasn't sure what this all was. Perhaps just a different dimension, or maybe she was still in the same universe, just on a planet far away. Even so, that didn't explain the magic, statuses, and skills she had acquired on the way.

Ilea stood up and looked at the suns, rolling her shoulders. "Let's get those pancakes," she said, spreading her wings before she flew up the rocky cliff toward the castle standing atop it.

* * *

"Milk, sugar, egg, flour, molten butter... that should be mostly it. The dough should be thick but liquidy. Don't heat it up for too long, you want it fluffy," Ilea explained as well as she could remember.

"Very simple. Done similar things before," Popi said with a smile and got to mixing the batter.

"Breakfast?" Maurice asked, entering the ruined dining hall with one hand rubbing his forehead. Most of the windows were broken in or had at least lost most of their once magnificent color. Green, probably, as it was likely built by the Taleen.

"Breakfast, yes," Popi answered as Maurice sat next to him. "Her recipe."

"Her recipe? Hmm... do you have a recipe for a headache cure too?" Maurice asked.

"Of course, I have healing magic. You'll have to come over to me though," Ilea smiled. She was wearing her armor, her helmet placed on the big table as she lounged in her fancy chair.

"I know you can teleport," Maurice murmured as he got up and shuffled all the way around the table.

"And I know you can fly," Ilea said, rolling her eyes at his complaints.

"Moving up hurts my head," he said, flinging a silver coin her way. She touched his armored stomach and poured healing magic toward his head.

"Oh, by the gods…" he said, sitting down on the chair next to her. "You did that in ten seconds?" His spirits had lifted considerably based on his awestruck facial expression.

"I did. You're welcome," Ilea said and watched Popi heat up the first pancake on his little heating plate, his magic pulsing below the metal.

"Thanks, Ilea. You're really useful. Want to join our little crew?" Maurice said, theatrically smelling the browning pancake.

"Nope," Ilea said, her stomach rumbling.

She remembered the advances she'd received from other adventurers whenever she showed up at the guilds, a big fat healer tag identifying her as the most useful asset to anybody's party. But she supposed those days were over.

"Popi is certainly a damn good reason to consider it," she added, then looked at Maurice. "You, on the other hand, that's more than a couple minus points."

"We could travel around the lands, get easy jobs, kill a bunch of people, and get rich. Piece of cake with the war going on," Maurice said, leaning back in his chair.

"What lands?"

"The Empire, Baralia, Kroll, the Nipha Empire, wherever you want to go. Even the Northern Plains. You'd like them, I'm sure."

"Is that the North I've heard about before?"

"The North? No. No no. These are the Northern Plains, the northernmost lands of the Human Plains."

"Why would I like them?"

"Barbarians. Constantly fighting each other and raiding the northern towns of more civilized countries. You're not from there?"

"I shouldn't have healed you," Ilea said, narrowing her eyes theatrically.

Maurice laughed.

Popi slid a plate with the first pancake her way. He hesitated, frowned, then summoned some berries and syrup, nodding to himself.

"It will pair well," he said.

"I know," Ilea answered. She smiled and thanked him before she started eating.

She soon saw Trian enter the hall as well. He sat down at the table without saying a word.

"What about you? Care to join our little crew?" Maurice called over to him.

Trian looked at him and shook his head.

"Boring shits," Maurice said. "More for us."

"I'm done fighting humans. At least for a while," Ilea said.

"Won't be able to avoid that anywhere," Maurice said as he received a plate from Popi.

"I will. If I go to places most humans don't dare to explore."

Maurice snorted. "You're not the first to think that way. And you won't be the last to die out there."

"She won't die," Popi said with a smile. "I'm sure of it."

"Thanks for the confidence," Ilea said.

"Where would you want to go?" Trian asked her.

"I'm not sure yet. North, maybe, the real north. Beyond the mountain range overlooking the Navali Forest. Or west, through the forest of the elves, to see what lies beyond. Or south, into the desert and beyond."

"I thought you wanted to find your friend?" Maurice said.

"I do. But with how I am now, I can't even destroy a Taleen Praetorian. If I do get to him at some point, and he hasn't managed to get out of whatever situation he's found himself in, I'll need to be a lot stronger than I am now."

Plus, Christopher needs time to figure out a way for me to follow or find out where Kyrian was actually sent to…

"A Shadow, eh?" Maurice murmured as he ate. "Well, I won't stop you from dying."

Ilea didn't think herself unkillable or immune to danger, but she had a bunch of tools that would help her survive, like others had. Adam Strand had traveled to the demon realm, and for all she knew, he was still alive. Albert, who had found Cless, had some sort of long-range teleportation, and she was sure he had been to places no other humans dared go.

And then there was Verena, another Elder of the Shadow's Hand, who had charged that massive demon with her fire axes. She'd probably seen more than the Plains. Ilea was certain they all had, and if there were a few of them, there were surely more out there.

And if others could explore the most dangerous places this world had to offer, without dying, why couldn't she do the same?

TWENTY-FOUR

Farewells

All the remaining people on the Isle of Garath were gathered in the destroyed courtyard of the castle ruin. They had built a pyre and set all of the bodies onto it.

The winds were strong, and it looked like a storm would soon be upon them. Ilea smelled the salt of the ocean, wild waves breaking on the cliffs below.

The heat of rising flames made her focus on the pyre. Popi's magic had set the wood ablaze from all sides, and the whole thing was turning into a raging inferno.

"He was a horrible father," Felicia said as the fires burned.

"To you. Silver mage nearly got me. Tough one, her," Maurice said.

She was. Ilea thought. *And it didn't help her in the end.*

"May they find their rest," Trian said.

Ilea looked at him for a moment, then looked up at the sky. A light rain had started to fall. She walked over to Trian and touched his back, holding her hand there as the fires burned.

"Did you find anything in the dungeon?" Trian asked after everything had burnt and Felicia had dispersed the ash out over the ocean with her wind magic.

"Only bones and broken machines," Ilea answered. Compared to the other Taleen dungeons she had seen, the one below the Isle of Garath was tiny.

Trian didn't reply.

Christopher and the vegetation mages who wanted to go to Ravenhall had gathered already, ready to leave with their bags and equipment. Everybody else was prepared to leave as well.

Ilea went to Maurice, shaking his hand before she hugged Popi.

"Don't be too stupid out there. If you ever want to open a store, I'm sure we can arrange something in Ravenhall," she said as she let go.

"It was nice meeting you, Ilea," Popi smiled. "I made this for you," he added, summoning a cheesecake. "It's my favorite. I hope you like it."

Ilea received the gift with reverence. "Thank you, Popi," she said, making the cake vanish into her necklace.

"Damn shame you're not joining. We could use a healer out there," Maurice said.

"I'm sure two level two hundred adventurers will be fine without me."

"Yeah, but we'd be finer with you," Maurice answered.

Edwin and Maria were standing a little to the side, and Ilea waved to Christopher and the mages coming with them as she walked over to the blood mage.

"Ilea. Trian," Edwin said, nodding to each of them.

"Edwin. Maria," Ilea said.

The man smiled. A tired expression. "Thank you both."

"And thank you," Trian said.

Ilea glanced at Maria, who met her eyes. She nodded her way, and Ilea mirrored the gesture. She was glad their partnership had come to an end.

"Good luck out there," Ilea said.

Edwin gave her a nod.

Ilea smiled and turned, joining the mages when Felicia and Aliana walked over.

"Ilea," Felicia said, closing the distance and hugging her. "Thank you. For everything."

Ilea glanced at Aliana as Felicia let go and hugged Trian as well.

"If you ever need anything, you'll find me in the capital," Felicia said.

"I'll make sure to visit," Ilea said.

Aliana stepped up. "If you find any news in regard to Kyrian..."

"I'll let you know," Ilea said. "Make sure not to overextend."

Felicia smiled. "Right back at you."

"Good fortune," Aliana said. "And travel safely."

The rain started to pick up as Ilea turned toward the pile of gear the mages had gathered.

"I'll take that," she said, putting all of their luggage and equipment into her necklace. "Just grab onto me and Trian."

"What are you planning to do?" Christopher asked.

"We're flying, of course."

She waited until the mages were ready, each one holding on to either her or Trian, then glanced back at the others and smiled.

"Safe journeys to you all," Ilea said, specifically smiling at Felicia, Aliana, and Popi before her wings spread out and she ascended, slightly weighed down by the people hanging off her.

Kyrian, you dunce. Leaving me and Trian to do this ourselves.

They flew higher and higher, some of the group below waving at them before Ilea sped up and headed south. Toward Ravenhall.

* * *

The flight back took significantly longer than Ilea's rushed arrival. She didn't particularly mind though. They paused in a small forest clearing near the cliffs when she could tell the mages were barely able to hold on anymore. The trees were small and scrawny but still provided some shelter against the ocean winds and potential monsters on the hunt for prey.

Her wings crumbled away, the ash vanishing as she touched the earth, the four people hanging off her letting go, stumbling on the ground, and breathing hard. One of them, a big-bellied man in his thirties, fell on his back, his chest heaving up and down as he struggled to keep his lungs working.

The red-haired woman next to Ilea recovered the quickest, rubbing her arms before she cracked her knuckles and neck. "You used healing magic, didn't you?"

"I did. I don't think you'd have lasted for this long otherwise." Ilea looked around, checking the area through her Sphere and Hunter's Sight. It seemed safe enough. Monsters had good instincts, which were currently likely screaming at them not to approach her.

"Trian, a fire?" Ilea said as she walked toward one of the trees, looking up at the top of it before she stabilized the trunk with both hands. One powerful kick and a crack of wood later, all that was holding up the small tree were her arms.

"Gods," the red-haired woman said, staring at the scene. Christopher and the last mage they had taken with them, a young boy in his teens, looked on in shock as well.

Ilea was a little confused but concentrated on turning the trunk sideways, dropping it on the ground before she summoned one of her remaining Taleen greatswords. The long blade, reflecting the afternoon suns in its greenish metal, came crashing down, sending splinters to the sides, Ilea's enhanced strength cleaving the frail tree in two with three strikes.

"Instead of staring at me, you could gather some stones and small sticks to start a fire," Ilea said, glancing back at the group, who quickly sprang into action.

Ilea continued her work wordlessly for another ten minutes, some of the strikes missing and digging into the ground or glancing off the trunk. As soon as it came to making actual logs, she stored the greatsword again and used her hands instead, ripping the chunks of wood apart to make sizable pieces.

A scream rang through the clearing, making Ilea blink toward the sound immediately. A second blink and she saw the scene in her Sphere. The big man had caught the attention of something that looked like a mutated boar.

The thing was damn near as tall as she was, and it looked pissed. Ilea appeared before the bald man and casually looked at the beast.

[Fanged Boar – lvl 59]

"Shouldn't you be able to handle that?" she asked, looking at the man, who was at level one hundred and nine. Blood was streaming down his leg from an injured thigh. Ilea crouched down and checked on him, stopping the bleeding with her healing magic. The boar stood defiantly, one of its tusks coated in blood.

"Why are you not running away?" Ilea asked as she got up again. She didn't see any young nearby, and the beast was quite obviously male.

"Th.... They don't leave..." the man behind her said through gritted teeth, the pain from the wound quite obviously discomforting, "...once they draw blood."

"Well, there's our meal then," Ilea said, blinking next to the boar and smashing in its head with a single precise strike, crushing its skull and brain. Its body twitched as it fell to the ground.

'ding' You have killed [Fanged Boar – lvl 59]

Ilea stored the beast in her necklace and walked back to the man, who was staring at her with a combination of awe and terror.

"Come on," she said, healing his injury and helping him up as he carefully tried putting weight on his previously mangled leg.

"You're a healer too..." he said, shaking his head. "I'm so... sorry," he added, looking for anything else to say.

"Don't worry about it."

Trian had already started with the fire. He glanced over at Ilea as she walked back to her pile of wood.

"Everything alright?"

"Yeah. Just a boar. Dinner came and found us," Ilea said and summoned the monster, then looked around the group. "Any of you know how to treat a boar corpse?"

"I do. Got a knife?" the red-haired woman asked. Ilea looked at her for a moment, noticing the scar on her cheek for the first time, then summoned a Taleen dagger and sword, handing both of them to the woman, hilts forward.

"Cheers," she said. She placed the sword on the ground carefully and started to cut into the thick boar hide with the dagger.

The smell of blood joined the scent of the trees and ocean soon after. She occasionally glanced at the boar's crushed head, then looked at Ilea in turn. She didn't know Ilea saw all this through her Sphere but decided not to react.

They continued after eating a meal of freshly roasted boar and grabbing a few hours of rest. Ilea stored the remaining meat in her necklace. It would even stay warm.

Storage items are awesome.

The weather took a turn for the worse after that, and it began raining quite heavily. Her healing supported the group throughout the flight and would likely prevent them from catching a cold.

Another quick break came and went before they continued once more. This time, they flew through most of the night and the next day, with only short breaks in between.

On the third day, they arrived at the top of the snow-covered mountain and saw Ravenhall in the distant valley stretching before them. The forest, the one following the shoreline on their side of the lake, was still partially destroyed from the demon whale. Ilea smiled as she looked at the walls of the city, rebuilt already. Higher this time.

She breathed in the cool air and looked at Trian, then the rest of the group. Most of them were exhausted from the long journey. They were faring better than on their first stop at least. Trian always looked tired these days. But she hoped he'd improve once he saw his sister again.

"We're nearly there. Come on guys, time to fly. You'll be in a real bed in an hour's time," Ilea said, clapping her hands together. The groaning from the assembled individuals made her sigh.

No appreciation for the gift of flight.

* * *

"They've certainly been busy," Ilea murmured as they approached. The noise coming from the city, combined with the winds, nearly drowned out her voice.

Hundreds of people, carts, mercenaries, and soldiers were on the road leading to Ravenhall, craters still visible on the massive field of battle that had decided the city's fate.

Ilea felt some pride in knowing that she'd taken part in that battle and that, because of it, these people would have shelter again. She couldn't help but smile when she saw the black flags of the Shadow's Hand fluttering in the wind above the city gates. The wall had also been repaired, and it even looked higher than before.

It was the Hand that had brought ruin to Ravenhall in the first place – at least, it had been one of its members – but the people around them didn't seem to care. Ilea and her companions joined the refugees, adventurers, and merchants coming from all over and watched their relief at finishing a long and perilous journey. To finally be home.

It took a while for Ilea and the others to reach the gates, but considering what they'd done in the capital and on the Isle of Garath, Ilea planned to follow Felicia's advice and lay low. As well as they could, though she produced her Shadow badge when they reached the guards at the gates.

"Shadows," the guard said, nodding with respect. "No toll for you."

Ilea waved the others past, giving the guard a nod in return. She saw he was wearing black instead of the gray and red of the Empire, but his level was below even one fifty.

Though many traveled toward it, the city seemed nearly deserted inside. Compared to the previously bustling streets and shops, Ilea found many a storefront still destroyed and empty. Merchants had put up their stalls in the streets themselves, while all sorts of architects, builders, and mages walked around, discussing improvements and repairs.

She led the others through the streets, finding a second massive wall farther in, also guarded, and a third one surrounding the centermost part of the fortress city with its large guild halls and government structures. She reached the four-story stone mansion where Claire had taken up residence, not missing the black banners hanging on the facade.

A guard clad in black armor nodded at Ilea. The man was at level one-eighty. Not quite high enough to be a member of the Hand himself.

Provided they haven't changed the rules yet.

"Your badge?"

Ilea summoned it and handed it over.

"Thank you. Go on," the guard said, not asking anything of the others.

Enough trust to let me in with company.

Ilea led the others up to the top floor. She found she couldn't see into many of the rooms through her Sphere, her perception cut off by enchantments on the walls and floors. When she knocked on the heavy wooden door of Claire's office, she heard Claire's muffled voice from within and entered.

Claire's eyes grew wide when she saw Ilea, and she got up from her chair and walked over to her. She glanced at the group of people waiting and gave Ilea a look.

"Hey, Claire," Ilea said. She felt a sob bubbling up from within and had to pause for a moment to collect herself.

After everything that had happened, she felt as if the walls she'd put up had just come crumbling down. Everything had happened so quickly, one thing after the next. Trian, his family, Eve, Edwin, the Birmingales, the attack on Virilya, Arthur, Kyrian. She heard ringing in her ears and closed her eyes, sending healing magic into her mind.

"Do you want to sit down?" Claire asked in a calm and quiet voice.

"I..." Ilea began haltingly. "No, it's okay. These people are mages who wish to be employed. We escorted them here."

"Mages?" Claire asked, looking at the group again. "Nature mages and an enchanter… Yes, I would very much like to talk to you. I'm Claire. I'm with the Shadow's Hand and a member of the government of Ravenhall. It's good to meet you all. However, these two have been traveling for a while. Is it alright if we discuss your request once I've spoken to them?"

Christopher stepped forward. "Christopher Volaris. I understand, of course. Is there a place where we could wait?"

"There's a lounge down the hall. I'll be with you as soon as I can. And don't run off. I'll beat any other offer you'll get in the city or anywhere nearby," Claire said. She gave Christopher a pointed look and nodded to the others. "There's food and water in the lounge. Feel free to help yourselves. And welcome to Ravenhall."

After the group thanked her and left, Claire ushered Trian and Ilea toward her, neither of them speaking.

"What happened? Where's Kyrian?" Claire asked.

Ilea breathed in deeply and sighed. The healing flowing through her mind helped. She touched Trian's shoulder and helped him over to the armchairs before she looked at Claire again.

"We…" She bit her lip. "Eve. She's dead," she said, a sob escaping her.

"Oh dear," Claire said, walking over and grabbing Ilea in a hug. "You found her?"

Ilea nodded into her shoulder. "She'd been… hunting people. Killing people. Important people, by the looks of it. But we don't know who killed her. She didn't ask for help, you know?" Ilea looked up and into her eyes. "We could've helped her."

Claire nodded and squeezed her tighter.

"And then we… we found Edwin and his group. I don't remember if I told you about him. We struck a deal, found evidence, the Birmingales, and we went in. We fought those people, the ones who'd m—"

Ilea stopped herself, looking over at Trian. He was just sitting there, staring at the floor.

"We killed them, Claire," Ilea said, moving away and toward the window. She shook her head. "Then the capital was attacked by Baralia. Trian managed to get evidence of his family's murder to someone important in the central district before we left. But we'd agreed to help Edwin. Edwin Redleaf, son of Arthur Redleaf. In return for his help with the Birmingales, we helped him settle the scores with his father."

Claire rubbed her temple. "You killed Arthur Redleaf?"

"Felicia did. And Aliana. Don't share that with people, I don't think they'd want anyone to know," Ilea said. "Sorry, I just… A lot's happened."

"I can see," Claire said and leaned against her desk. She was surprisingly composed.

"The nature mages and Christopher, they'd been employed by Arthur," Ilea continued. "That's where we found them, and with the war and all that, we thought it would be good to bring them here." Ilea paused. "Then there's Kyrian."

Claire's grip on the desk tightened slightly as she prepared for the news.

Ilea shook her head. "No, not that. He's alive. Should be. I'm sure he is," Ilea said. "Can I have a drink?"

"Go for it,"

Ilea kept talking as she checked the different bottles on the cabinet by the armchairs before pouring herself something that smelled palatable. She told Claire everything. Claire nodded to herself absentmindedly throughout before she looked up.

"Pour me one of those too."

Ilea did and proceeded to answer every question that Claire had. Aki occasionally joined in with details that Ilea had failed to mention, his tone curt. He'd been quiet throughout all this, she noted. She'd have to have a chat with him too. About everything.

"The Golden Lily," Claire murmured. "That was her target. And Kyrian has been sent off to some Taleen dungeon who knows where." She drank.

"I thought Christopher could help us with that. He's been studying those gates for a while, and he's the only enchanter left from Arthur's team," Ilea said.

But Kyrian has already been gone for several days. Might he have found a way out? She didn't want to assume her friend was dead.

Focus on what you can do. Kyrian is strong.

"I will talk to him."

"There's also Iana. Iana Birch. Has Balduur arrived?"

"The smith, yes. Quite a presence. I did notice his daughter. A powerful enchantress."

"She could help. I know she wants to work on her own things, and she seems like she'd like a challenge. She might be able to learn something from Christopher as well. Maybe you could employ them directly?"

"Of course, Ilea. I'll talk to them both."

There was a pause then. For a long moment. Finally, Claire spoke again.

"I'm sorry. About Eve."

Ilea glanced at her, then turned to the window and looked out onto the square. "Me too."

"Kyrian is a Shadow. And until we find him, I won't accept that he's gone." Claire walked over to Trian and touched his shoulder. "With all that, I think it's best if you two stay here, hidden until we see how the situation in the capital changes. Even with evidence, this may cause some issues. Especially with Arthur Redleaf dead."

"I don't plan to stay," Ilea said. "Fuck that."

The idea of continuing to be surrounded by a city full of people and all the baggage and complications that came with it made her feel nauseous.

She needed a break. She needed to hit something. Something that when she killed it, wouldn't keep her up at night.

Claire frowned. "There may be assassins coming for you two, perhaps even me, in the coming months."

Ilea finished her drink, walked to the cabinet, and poured herself another. Only then did she look at Claire. "I'm done with this shit. The murder, the war, the politics."

Claire bristled. "You're involved in this, no matter how you look at it, and now we have to make the best of the situation. You need to lay low until we know how things change. Ravenhall is where we have connections and power. Anywhere else in the Plains, you'd be on your own."

"I don't plan to stay in the Plains."

"What?" Claire asked, nearly spilling her drink.

"You know what we talked about after we cleared Ravenhall," Ilea said. She'd thought about it plenty, and now she'd made a decision. It was the only thing that made sense right now. "I'll go north. Beyond the Naraza mountain range. Think anyone would be crazy enough to follow me there?"

"You're the crazy one to even consider that," Claire said. Then the corners of her mouth quirked upward for the first time since they'd arrived. "But I'm not particularly surprised." She paused. "You'd be facing uncharted territory. Creatures that no bestiary could prepare you for. No support, no cities, no settlements."

Ilea smiled. "Exactly."

Freedom.

Claire sighed. "There's no changing your decision, is there?"

Ilea shook her head. "I have my third-tier Blink. It brought me back from that Taleen dungeon and, arguably, from the Great Salt. Even if I get lost, I'll find my way back."

"How long do you intend to stay away?"

Ilea shrugged. "I haven't thought about specifics."

"That's still just a basic consideration," Claire sighed. "Well, you do have your healing, and you've survived thus far. Somehow. At least make some preparations in regard to food, water, and emergency tools. You have that necklace of yours, after all."

Ilea gasped. "Food, yes!"

The idea of going without her usual meals made Ilea shudder.

"I need Keyla. She was the cook at the Golden Drake. A restaurant that Eve showed me and Kyrian. She's insanely good. If you find her, and if you can somehow get hold of that restaurant, the place, I mean, make her the manager. You won't regret it," Ilea rambled.

Claire took a few notes, then summoned a book and flipped a few pages.

"You have a storage item now too?" Ilea asked.

"Moving up in the world," Claire said off-handedly. "The restaurant, yes. It was previously owned by Wallace Urn, Elder of the Shadow's Hand.

Repossessed by the Hand. I'm sure I'll get a fair price if I talk to Sulivhaan about it. I'll see what I can do, Ilea.

"Now, Trian, we've found a place in the Haven for Aurelia, Samuel, and Orthan. It would be safe for you to join them there. Safer than most other places would be. Should I call for them to meet you here, or...?"

"We can go to the Haven," Trian said. "Claire, I..."

Claire waved it away as Trian's voice trailed off. "No need to explain things. We'll take you to them right away. I'll briefly talk with the mages you've brought and then have one of my assistants handle the rest. I'll be back in ten minutes or so. Is that okay?"

Trian nodded.

Ilea took a long sip from her glass. She gave Claire a grateful look before her friend left, closing the office door behind her.

"Thanks for the help with the retelling. I would've missed some of those details," she said, unsheathing the dagger on her belt. "And sorry for not including you more often. I know you've been there too. Through everything."

"I understood that making myself known would have caused potential issues. It's okay. Silent observation is rather natural for me. And I'm sorry too, for all that has happened. I think it's a good idea, you know, your plan."

"Going north?" Ilea asked. "Do you want to join in on that adventure?"

There was a long silence.

"I think... not. You mentioned Iana, that she's here in the city, and might be employed by Claire soon. I can't help but feel that I've not been of much help during all this. The intricacies of human interaction still somewhat elude me. I'm not the best friend one could wish for, being a dagger and all that." Aki paused. "Don't give me that look. I just think... it would be good to learn more about myself and to find potential ways in which I could do more. If that is at all possible. I doubt I'd discover anything by hanging from your belt, as interesting as your travels may be."

His voice was resolute. Ilea got the feeling he may even have practiced the speech. If that was even possible. Maybe when she was asleep?

"You want to stay with Iana?" Ilea asked. "And ditch me just like that?" She waggled an accusatory finger theatrically.

"An easy decision, really," Aki shot back, though his words lacked bite. Then his tone turned serious again. "But if you want me to be there, I'll stay."

Ilea chuckled. "Don't worry about me. I'm sure I'll meet a lot more cursed dagger people or something similar out in the wilderness. Might even have been able to befriend that Beastwolf if the others hadn't been around."

The dagger laughed in return. "Oh yeah, that's *totally* possible. And thanks. For getting me out of that dungeon, and for showing me so much of the world."

"Sure, happy to hang out. And I'll be happy to share stories once I get back."

"Do that, and try not to die out there."

"I'll do my best."

Ilea rejoined Trian after that, sitting beside him and holding his hand after a few moments of silence. She didn't let go until Claire returned.

"Done?" Ilea asked. "New magical employees?"

Claire nodded. "For now, yes. We'll work out the details in the coming days. They'll make a massive difference." She looked between them. "Ready to go to the Haven? Ilea, do you want to join?"

"Sure," Ilea said, getting up. "A massive difference, you say? Just their small group?"

Claire opened the door and led the way. "Experienced nature mages aren't easy to find. And they often live out on their farms or travel entire regions to support the locals. We recently started a project in the Haven to try and feed the city's population without external suppliers."

"And a few mages will help with that?" Ilea asked.

"You underestimate how effective a single nature mage can be. And with the limited space we'll use in the Haven, we need a lot. But the results are already promising. And one nature mage will be able to support thousands. That's already the case in a lot of cities, but none have anything like the Haven."

"And the Hand agreed? I thought only members were allowed down there?"

"Yes, but it's about time we used the space more efficiently. Verena Quil hasn't returned, Wallace Urn is dead, and Adam Strand has been stripped of his position. And neither Pierce nor Lucas has been in Ravenhall since long before the demon summoning. But Sulivhaan is sure they would agree."

"So Sulivhaan and Dagon are the de facto leaders of the Hand?" Ilea asked as they walked out onto the square.

Claire looked around and smiled. "Essentially. I'll tell you more on that subject once we're in Viscera."

"Intriguing," Ilea said in a deadpan voice.

Had Claire implied that she was now part of the Hand's leadership herself? In such a short time? Though it wouldn't surprise Ilea. She knew the mercenaries of the Hand weren't generally interested in administrative or leadership roles. The ones she knew were more interested in fighting, adventuring, and entertainment.

"What's with the new walls?" Ilea asked when they reached the centermost set.

"I managed to push through that idea. Like this, we can brace against attacks from both outside and inside. Takes more guards to man, of course, but considering recent events, the pushback was minimal. Even without guards, it could've saved thousands – if not the whole city.

"And this is the time to prepare the city and make vast changes," she continued. "Merchants have been coming since the day we cleared the demons, and with what you've shared from Virilya, I believe Ravenhall will be at least as populated as it was before the demons by the end of the year."

"And you're trying to prepare it for that?" Ilea said.

"Yes. And with the renown of the Hand, many mages, builders, and merchants will be interested in setting up shop as the city grows quickly," Claire said as they exited the city's central district.

"Even after what Strand did?"

"The public doesn't know the details, and while some may blame the Shadow's Hand, they've also heard of the heroic retaking of Ravenhall. If anything, the Hand's renown has risen."

They talked about some more of the changes happening in the city, and Claire told Ilea about other surviving members and citizens who'd managed to escape the demon attack. Many had returned, as had survivors from Morhill and villages in the mountain ranges.

* * *

Viscera was walled off as well now, their access to the main quarters granted only after a guard had confirmed Claire's identity and activated a nearby enchantment to open the heavy metal gates.

"To keep enemies both in and out," Claire said, nodding to the guard, who was also clad in black armor.

"Requirements lowered?" Ilea asked, seeing that this guard wasn't close to level two hundred either.

"Not for the actual members. They're the Shadowguard. I know the name isn't the best. We're still working on it. They're a supplemental force added to the city guard, employed, trained, and selected by the Shadow's Hand. Possible jobs and later membership are enough for many to join. I imagine the war with Baralia will sway more than one to join us instead of the Empire," Claire explained, leading them through the halls.

Viscera was cleaner than Ilea had ever seen it. It was impressive anyway, as were all of the improvements made to Ravenhall, but knowing how it had looked just about a month ago made it damn near unbelievable.

"Isn't Ravenhall part of the Empire?" Ilea asked.

Claire smiled. "It's complicated. Our talks with Lys have been... interesting. With the war now the Empress' main focus, we have far more wiggle room. Shadows are more coveted than ever, and while our rules don't allow Shadow missions to be directly involved in wars between humans, many still choose to take jobs without going through us.

"And with the recent demonstration of the retaking of the city, I think what kind of power a united Shadow's Hand holds has become clear. The major players in the Plains will want to be on good terms with us, and Lys is leading those discussions. It will be interesting to see where we're headed."

"You seem pretty involved," Ilea said. "What kind of job did Sulivhaan and Dagon get you exactly?"

Claire smiled again. "A city on the rise harbors a lot of opportunities, Ilea. And I don't plan to squander any of them."

* * *

The Haven didn't look as Ilea remembered. Several hundred meters of former meadows and forests had already been turned into farmland, a stone wall protecting the mages and workers from the monsters that still roamed the area. Far in the distance, she could see another wall, this one built around the lake where more demons had come from the Great Salt.

"Are there still demons coming through?"

"There are, and the guard positions on the walls are incredibly popular. It's a somewhat safe environment to fight level two hundred monsters, and demons provide far more of a challenge than any of the local beasts. The Haven won't only be used for food production and training exercises for the fully-fledged members of the Hand but also to train the Shadowguard. With demons regularly appearing, we don't have to be as conservative with training exercises in the Haven anymore either."

"Still dangerous to keep that thing down here," Ilea said.

Claire shrugged. "We haven't found a way to get rid of it, so we might as well use it. The enchanted gates added to Viscera should allow us to evacuate both the Haven and Ravenhall in case more dangerous beasts come through. But several investigations by a varied assortment of scholars and mages suggest the connection the pool provides to the Great Salt is simply not strong enough to let higher-level beasts pass. Unlike what we saw from Strand's runes.

"No Mind Weavers have come through yet either, but anti-mind magic enchantments are in place, plus permanent postings of several people with high-level resistances. I would've liked Weavy to be here to train people, but too many people would've disagreed, and as you said, he wouldn't have been safe."

"Not as optimized as you'd like it," Ilea smiled.

"No, but it's efficient, and I like that. And I consider it safe enough to have Leia live down here as well."

"Your mom?"

"Yes. The nature here seems to help. She's been... calmer, I think. And she enjoys having Cless around, too. The girl has been exploring the city and coming down here non-stop. Though she's a strange one. I suspect she's either got an incredibly vivid imagination or that she's a realm traveler."

"I see," Ilea said. She glanced at Trian, who'd been walking with them without saying a word. "I know she's a realm traveler."

Claire turned to look at her. "You know? How so?"

Ilea scratched the back of her head. "I think she's from the same place I'm from."

"Oh," Claire exclaimed. She stumbled slightly but quickly regained her composure, continuing in a whisper. "That explains some things. You both have an interesting outlook in certain respects. You didn't travel here on purpose, did you?"

"No. Just appeared here one day. I'll tell you more about it, but let's get Trian to his sister first."

"Of course."

They left the fortified farmland section of the Haven and walked for a while until they reached an area of the wall where Claire touched a section of rock. A rune glowed, and a previously invisible door opened.

"Once we know more about how things develop," Claire said, looking at Trian, "I'm sure we can situate both you and the others in Ravenhall, but I think it's safer for you to stay hidden for now. With you being past level two hundred, the Haven is probably no danger."

"That's fine. I just want them to be safe," Trian said and walked in without another word.

Ilea glanced at Claire, then followed them both in, magical lights illuminating once the door closed behind them. The place reminded Ilea of the Vultures' den. As far as underground hideouts went, this place seemed rather nice. The rooms were better furnished than the Vultures', and everyone had their own rooms.

They emerged in a living room with a magical hearth, shelves stacked with books, an alchemy set or something that looked like it, paintings hanging from the walls, and an adjacent room with a kitchen. Aurelia looked up from the book she was reading and jumped up with a squeak.

"Trian!"

She rushed over and hugged her brother. He stood there for a moment, then hugged her.

"It's good to see you, little one," he whispered. "Sorry it took so long."

Orthan walked out of the kitchen, wearing an apron. "Is it done?"

"It is," Trian said. "I just… they're still gone."

"They are," Orthan said. "You'll have to tell me about what happened, but it's good to know the people who did this to us are no longer out there." He walked over and touched Trian's shoulder as Samuel came out of the kitchen as well.

Orthan sighed. "There is little justice to be found in all this, Trian. But I know your father and mother would be proud. And now, here, you'll have time to grieve. We all do, and we're here together, House Alymie."

Trian nodded, a few sobs wracking him as he held Aurelia closer. "I'm sorry," he said and cried. "I'm sorry for what happened."

"It's not your fault," Aurelia said, and she started crying too. "I'm here. We're here, and you're back, Trian."

"Thank you for your help in all this," Orthan said, looking at Ilea and Claire. "I know the outcome would've been different without you. A team of Shadows who fought for House Alymie. Is Kyrian…?"

"He's been teleported away into some Taleen dungeon," Ilea said. "And I intend to find him, if he doesn't find his way back before I get to him."

"I'm sorry," Orthan said, his face falling.

Ilea nodded. "It's good to see you all together again." She walked over to Trian and touched his shoulder. "Take your time with all this."

He wiped his eyes and looked at her. Exhausted but present, no longer the shell he'd seemed the past few days.

"Thanks, Ilea. I will, and I'm sorry for how everything turned out. With Eve, with Kyrian. Part of me wants to come with you, but I don't think I can manage, not right now."

"Don't worry about me," she winked and ruffled his hair, enjoying the sudden irritated look he gave her. She laughed. "And don't worry about Kyrian. It's good to know you have a place to stay, with family and friends around you."

"Enjoy yourself out there," Trian said. "I suppose I should say you shouldn't get too ahead of me, but knowing you, that would just motivate you more."

"I'll crush you the next time we fight," Ilea said solemnly.

He smiled. "I'll look forward to it."

Ilea went in and hugged him.

He hugged her back.

"I'll see you around when I get back," Ilea said, then pointed to Aurelia and Samuel. "And you two better train up as well. You're in the Haven of the Shadow's Hand."

"Yes, ma'am," Aurelia said as Orthan chuckled.

"Good fortune on your journey, Ilea," Trian said.

She nodded, and she and Claire left House Alymie to regroup. The two of them walked back to the farmland, but before they left the Haven, a young girl stepped in their way.

Cless glared at Ilea with her arms crossed. "You're back."

"I am, and I'll be leaving again soon," Ilea said.

"Where's Kyrian?"

"He's been teleported away by some Taleen device. But I'm sure he'll get back soon. And if he doesn't, I'll find him. I'm sure he's okay." She believed it too. After everything that had happened, she found that she had to.

Cless smiled. "I know he is, silly. He's a strong Shadow."

"Exactly," Ilea said and grabbed the squealing girl in a hug.

She ran off right after, calling to one of the farmers excitedly.

Ilea looked at her for a moment and smiled, then left the Haven with Claire, who led them back to her office.

"So, about that realm traveler thing?" Claire said once they were safely inside.

Ilea nodded and explained her circumstances and what had happened. Claire had a lot of questions and, ultimately, frustrations with Ilea's lack of engineering and science knowledge that could've been helpful for Ravenhall and Elos.

The conversation trailed off after a while, and Ilea handed Aki over to Claire after telling her about his wishes. She was glad that Claire now knew about her past. All of her team did now, and she trusted them all. She didn't feel like they treated her differently either. If anything, she felt more comfortable.

They discussed the war and Ravenhall's future prospects a little more, but too many things were still uncertain, according to Claire. No matter what, Ilea knew that going north and getting stronger would only benefit the people she cared about, and hopefully she could learn some things about the Taleen as well.

From a more selfish perspective, she was also just glad to go back out on an adventure, to explore this magical world she'd found herself in, instead of taking part in human conflicts and wars.

She gulped, thinking back to the Birmingales, then to Tiana and Kyle, the close calls they'd had. Sufficiently powerful people could kill her. And hiding here in the Haven would change absolutely nothing about that. It would just be her and whatever monsters and secrets were out there to be discovered and to be fought.

"If there's nothing else, I'll go and prepare to leave," Ilea said after a while.

"Should I write you a list of necessities?" Claire asked, then shook her head. "Forget I asked. I don't need a reply."

Aki chuckled.

Ilea smiled. "I'm thinking food and…" She thought for a while. "Water?"

Claire sighed dramatically and looked at Ilea. "When do you plan to leave exactly? This week?"

"Later today," Ilea said and stretched. "It was good seeing you, though, and I hope everything works out. For you as well, Aki."

"Go get your food," Aki replied.

"Just don't come running back to me with complaints if you figure out you should've prepared far better for such an insane and perilous journey," Claire said.

"I feel like my list is pretty good," Ilea said and nodded to herself. "I'll see you when I get back."

Claire walked over and hugged Ilea. "Stay safe."

"You know I won't, and you're not my mother," Ilea said as they separated, waving to Claire and Aki before she put up her hood and vanished onto the streets of Ravenhall.

Now.

Food stalls.

She grinned, knowing that her storage necklace would keep things exactly as fresh or hot as when they'd been stored. She also still had plenty of Keyla's food stockpiled from when she'd hired her initially. *But If I plan for months away, I'd better stock up, or I'll be eating burnt monster meat a few weeks in.*

She whistled to herself and started down a random alley, following her gut and nose. Of course, she'd have to test the produce to see if the items were good enough before she ordered in bulk.

A lot of people would be cooking for her today.

* * *

Ilea was sitting on a random roof with a view of the lake before Ravenhall. Several empty bowls sat stacked next to her, and she was eating the last skewer she'd had before she stored the entire pile in her necklace. A necklace now stuffed to the brim with meals and various drinks. She supposed that if she were back on Earth, she'd have at least considered getting better shoes, rope, maybe a flashlight and matches, but here?

Here, she had magic

Ilea stood up and jumped off the roof, landing without issue before she ran toward the outermost city walls. Red runes glowed briefly as she sacrificed some health and jumped up and over the obstacle in her way, ignoring the guard shouting something about using the city gate instead. She teleported a few times and soon found herself in the partially devastated forest outside the city. Then, she spread her wings of ash and took flight.

Part II

TWENTY-FIVE

Journey through the Night

The suns were going down as Ilea sped through the mountain range in the southernmost part of the Empire, soon passing the last peaks before the terrain grew more even. What was supposed to be human-controlled land didn't show any sign of their presence or dominion.

Ilea couldn't spot a single town as far as she could see, nor any light or travelers. The wild lands, although mapped and mostly known, were avoided at night except by adventurers and the truly desperate.

Her wings moved in the winds, her destination northwest. Passing over the Plains, she could make out dark patches of forest in the distance below the stormy clouds passing above. Lowering her altitude, she flew just above the forest until she heard a roar that made her veer a little, interested in what kind of beast it was.

Another cry met her ears as she zeroed in on the location, hovering over a clearing where the massive form of what looked like a grizzly bear was trying to fight off multiple creatures clawing into its back and sides. Demons.

It mauled a spiky humanoid demon and threw it aside, several corpses already showing the path the beast had taken.

Ilea felt at least some responsibility to shred through any demonic remains she came across prowling the lands of Elos, so she blinked downward and put herself next to the creature, her fists slamming into the demons that threatened to kill the beast. She grabbed one by its throat, the claws of the rabid monster fruitlessly scrabbling against her Veil of Ash as she stared into its soulless eyes.

Her fist smashed into its face. Then she punched it a second time, then a third, before the demon's skull cracked. A ding resounded in her mind as she threw away the lifeless body. The monsters all turned toward her at once, rushing at their newfound prey. Ilea faced them and identified the large beast.

[Grenoth – lvl 122]

"Not a bear then," Ilea said as the beast, several meters long and high, roared at her and the demons.

She charged back into the chaos. Appearing above a bulky bone-armored spawn, she grappled it and drove it down into the earth and mud, the two skidding to a halt as she sent her destructive mana into its body. Claws lashed out at her before she silenced the creature by stomping on its chest.

She blinked and took three quick steps before she tackled another demon, sending them both into, and through, a tree. She heard several bones break. She lashed out with her hand and ripped out its throat, blood spurting onto her ashen shroud. A hard kick to its center of mass sent the half-dead monster flying into another tree, its body bending unnaturally before a familiar noise rang in her head.

One to go.

The Grenoth was slashing at the remaining demon, a muscular thing with a tiny head, no neck, and tree trunk-sized limbs. The not-bear was only able to keep it at a distance as it tried to move on its injured legs, bleeding from several spots on its back. The wounds were only visible to Ilea thanks to her Sphere, lost in the brown fur of the massive beast.

To think something like that could be taken down by a few low-level demons.

The demon was just about to slash into the Grenoth's snout when it jerked backward as Ilea grabbed it by the neck and threw it ten meters away into the dirt. The bear-like creature moved its clawed paw toward her, but Ilea simply flew toward the demon, avoiding the strike of the injured and scared animal.

"Spawn," she said as she identified the demon to be at level eighty-four. Not from the Great Salt then, it seemed.

The monster screeched toward her and started running again, unrelenting in its wish for blood and death. It lacked any coordination, pure instinct and blood lust whipping it toward her. It was met by a fully powered and perfectly aimed punch that splattered its brain into the clearing so fast that its legs continued moving for another three steps before its already dead body fell onto the grass.

The Grenoth roared behind her, but Ilea blinked next to it before she touched it carefully. A clawed paw smashed into her defenses with enough force to cut through a tree trunk, but her feet dug into the ground as the kinetic force went through her body, its paw stopped by her form, shaking slightly.

Healing mana started circling through the animal as she focused on the worst injuries first. The demons were vicious creatures, but she doubted the bear would have had difficulties against a couple of them. An entire group, however, and even this large beast would be brought down.

Ilea looked into the distance, the bear roaring into her ear. "Calm down, teddy," Ilea said, her ash blocking another wild attack so completely that it nearly tore out one of the animal's claws. It healed quickly as her mana flowed through it, the Grenoth calming down a little as its pain lessened.

"See? All better."

Once she'd finished taking care of the worst, she patted the monster on its head, dodging two wild strikes as she danced backward and laughed.

"You're welcome."

She sped off, running in the direction where the demons had likely come from, her Hunter's Sight helping her focus on the trail the fighting monsters had left in their wake.

Could've found this even without any skills.

Even so, Ilea doubted she'd have tried to follow the destructive path and massive paw prints on the wet ground if she didn't have her magic.

She was soon proved right when she found three demon corpses, one still breathing but so deformed it could hardly move. A stomp put it out of its misery as she looked around to see if she could find any more of them. There were none.

Might as well move through the area and see if there are more around.

She sprinted through the forest, vaguely to the northwest, scrutinizing any trails she could find. It had rained earlier, making it rather easy to spot all the indicators of animals or monsters living and hunting – or fleeing – in the forest.

A while later, Ilea came out into a patch of open space, wildflowers and tall grass growing in the field. Her ashen wings formed behind her before she flew over it, noting the hares that ran for safety at her approach. Another patch of forest followed, and the huntress was back on her feet and on the lookout for demons and other dangers that might lurk in the shadows.

Hours passed as she hunted, finding only a pack of wolves that had killed a deer-like creature. The animals ran for their lives when she came rushing in, the smell of blood in her nose before she took in the scene. Still, her search was fruitless even when she decided to continue through the air, unable to spot any demons in the vicinity.

She flew on for a while before the familiar smell of burning wood stopped her. Ilea followed the trail until she saw the light in the distance. A small campfire, it seemed. Cooked meat and the scent of blood mixed in as she landed and walked closer. She noticed a woman, concealed nearby, in her Sphere but still advanced on the fire.

"Who goes in the dark?" a male voice shouted, his face visible in the light of the fire, sweat gleaming on his brow as glowing red magic formed in his hand.

Ilea saw another two people nearby, a young woman staring at her with wide eyes as she clutched a staff with shaking hands and a man clad in several blankets, sweating and shivering with closed eyes.

Looks like arcane magic, Ilea thought as she tried to identify the man, whose eyes focused on her as his magic swirled in his hand. The concealed woman was now behind her, a bow in hand and ready to shoot. She'd be the first one Ilea would target, should the situation demand it. However, she wasn't in the business of killing random travelers.

"A lone Shadow," she said.

"You are welcome at our fire, Shadow," he said, relaxing slightly and watching her as she slowly made her way toward the fire, hands at her side.

Ilea was wearing the set of armor Balduur had made for her and the others. She wasn't wearing a pack, which was definitely suspicious, but identifying herself as a Shadow would eliminate a lot of questions.

[Mage – lvl 75]

"Is he alright?" she asked, nodding toward the shivering man.

"He is... injured. A monster attacked us on the road before nightfall," the man replied as he stopped channeling mana into his spell, though the rogue still hidden behind Ilea didn't reveal herself just yet.

Smart move.

She walked over to the injured man and touched his brow, checking his body with her healing magic. "What kind of monster?"

The man seemed about to object, but the question made him pause.

Claws. The deep wounds on his chest and belly would kill him if he was moved. Her mana flowed through him, and his breathing eased immediately.

"Demons," the man spat. "I heard what happened in the Empire, but there were few stories of them coming so far west into Kroll."

So I'm already in the Kingdom of Kroll.

"Where were they?"

"Half an hour north, Shadow. We took down the two that attacked us, but..." he glanced at the forest behind her for a split second, "...I think there were more."

Ilea stood up and looked at the man.

"He's going to survive. You should travel with a healer if you can. Now tell me what you know." She turned and looked directly at the woman hiding in the darkness. "You too, if you have anything to add."

The rogue tensed, and the man beside Ilea sighed.

"Come out. We didn't mean any offense, Shadow. You're alone, and we don't know your intentions," he said, though she could see he was slightly more defensive than before.

"Just tell me how many you saw and where they were, and I'll be off," Ilea said,

The rogue stepped out of the dark, half her face hidden in cloth, a cloak hiding the rest.

"I will lead you," she said, getting a sharp glance from the man in return. "It's okay."

Ilea looked at her and nodded. "I'll get her out if it gets messy."

The previously injured man started coughing and croaked out a plea for water. The rogue nodded to Ilea before she started moving into the forest, jumping into a tree with Ilea following on the ground below.

* * *

Hog, you damn idiot, Althra thought as she led the Shadow toward the demons they had encountered on the road westward. Travis was as good as dead, and he'd nearly fucked it up with that monster. She felt on edge, her instincts tugging at her mind as the woman silently followed on the ground behind her. *You're making a lot of damn noise, woman.*

They'd had no other choice but to rest and start a fire, hoping that none of the demons or anything else would show up to slaughter them in the dark. To think that smuggling escaped slaves out of Baralia would be interrupted by demons of all things. And now they had the luck to have a lone Shadow walk in on them. She didn't know what the woman had done to Travis, but she hadn't missed the magic. His skin had already looked better when they'd left.

Maybe he could move now? Maybe I could be a distraction while the others flee… Althra thought as she led the woman to her doom. *Or mine.*

"What did you do to the injured man?" she couldn't help but ask in a whisper.

Expecting no answer or a lie, she continued silently through the night.

"I healed his wounds. I told the mage you should get a healer."

But she's a warrior?

Althra was starting to doubt her decisions. Maybe she was a battle-healer who'd lost her team somewhere in the wild, or maybe she wasn't a Shadow at all. Thinking of blowing it off and hoping that Travis could walk or even run again, she turned to the woman and stopped.

"I th—"

The Shadow held up a hand and sniffed the air. "Found you…" she whispered into the dark before she started walking.

What is she—?

Althra followed the woman through the trees and soon heard wet ripping noises coming from the road ahead. Althra's eyes widened when she saw a group of horrific creatures in the distance. Nearby, a wagon had rolled off the side of the road.

"I think it's time for you to leave, huntress," the Shadow said from below, a gray mist forming around her.

And then she vanished. Althra's eyes frantically scanned the dark before she found her again, much closer to the road and the monsters. But again, she vanished, Althra instinctively following from her elevated position in the trees until she could see the road illuminated by the moonlight.

The Shadow was among the demons now, grabbing them with her bare hands before she smashed her fists into them, appearing throughout the circle of confused and raging monsters, the gray mist cutting into the creatures with ease.

Althra gulped, watching limbs get ripped out and thrown away, the sound of breaking bones and crushed flesh interspersed with screeches before everything was silent. The woman was standing among a pile of corpses.

Althra wanted to run. She took a deep breath. *Get a fucking grip.* She focused and approached the Shadow, the smell and sight nauseating but not the worst she'd seen.

"How often are they still seen in these parts? I thought the Empire took care of most of them."

Althra froze again, nearly falling from the tree she was on when the woman spoke to her from only a couple of meters away.

"I... I don't know. Sometimes, the Empire loses interest as soon as they cross the borders."

"Any cities destroyed?"

"Not that I know of. This is one of the biggest groups I've heard about," she replied as quickly as she could.

"Good. Well, be careful out there. They turn people they kill into demons."

I know, she thought as she jumped down from the tree, checking the wagon for any survivors.

"They're dead. There's some food in there though. Good luck," the Shadow said, then vanished. Althra looked around but couldn't find her again. Only dead eyes stared at her from the ground.

A rustling behind her nearly made her jump. It was just an owl.

Get the fuck out of here. Move, she told herself, and she jumped up again, her stealth skills activating as she sped back to her group.

* * *

Ilea followed the long trail of demons, most of them leading down the country road she had come across. The clouds above her hid the moonlight, turning the road pitch black. *Why were they traveling at this bloody time?* she asked herself before deciding that it wasn't her problem.

None of the demons had been above level one hundred. Stragglers escaping from the Empire. If more originally summoned beasts or even Mind Weavers had made it this far west, the situation would certainly be different. Even random adventurers could deal with one or two of them at this level. With great difficulty.

She checked her messages and found that while her Classes hadn't leveled, her skills had.

'ding' Body of Ash reaches 2nd lvl 19

'ding' Ashen Warrior reaches 2nd lvl 20

There it is…

The thought made her focus on her ashen Class' third tier advancements. A broad grin spread on her face as she looked at the possibilities.

3rd-tier skill points available [Azarinth First Hunter]: 0
Skills available for 3rd-tier advancement in [Azarinth First Hunter]:
None available

3rd-tier skill points available [Inheritor of Eternal Ash]: 1
Skills available for 3rd-tier advancement in [Inheritor of Eternal Ash]:
- Ash Creation
- Ash and Ember Manipulation

She rubbed her cheek and thought about it. She liked her ash and she knew from her previous experiences that there was a wealth of power on this path. Both options were a gamble as no further information was available.

Creation or Manipulation. I can barely damage any monsters with my ash, but I can already create it. Suppose I'll go with this one…

'ding' Ash and Ember Manipulation advances to the 3rd tier
Passive: Ash and Ember Manipulation – 3rd lvl 1:
Your control over Ash and Ember increases dramatically. Bend it to your wishes and shroud the path before you.
2nd stage: Ash and Ember have become your allies. Your control increases greatly.
3rd stage: You have proven to be a master of ash and ember. The elements themselves become an extension of your body, an extension of your will, for as long as they stay in physical contact with you.
Category: Ashen magic

She breathed in deep and smiled, her eyes closed as she felt the change within her. She opened her eyes and summoned ash around her.

An extension of my body, of my will.

She teleported, her smile widening when she found the ash around her had come with her, moved by the teleportation skill as if it was part of her very self. She started spreading the ash out and moved it around herself.

There was a noticeable difference between the ash connected to her and the ash floating freely, disconnected from her. She found the ash connected to her both easier to control and more substantial, though she didn't know exactly what that meant. Next she willed the cloud around her into three tendrils of ash, more condensed and substantial than any ash she had formed before. It felt a little strange with the ash connected directly to her Veil.

She moved the ashen arms to begin at her spine and extend over her arms, shoulders and hips. The change made it feel a little more natural. As if she was a spider or something, just with ashen arms instead of real ones.

Weird…

Ilea watched with wide eyes, holding her breath as the tips of the ashen tendrils turned sharp. A moment later, she willed them down, the tendrils moving faster than her ash ever had before, cutting into the ground like swords. After digging deep furrows in the earth, she willed them up again, using only her mind.

Holy shit.

Ilea read the skill description again before she slashed down with her tendrils and activated Wave of Ember, the spell activating through her ash, destructive mana burning into the ground.

She tried with Destruction as well but found the skill didn't activate, its description more limiting than Wave of Ember.

I should be able to heal with it as well… it's my body after all.

She laughed, spreading her arms wide as she moved her ashen limbs through the air, slow and serene at first before she lashed out, the air whistling as the ashen tendrils slashed through it.

Wait… reverse healing should work too! I can't fucking wait to try this.

Ilea quickly looked through her skills before her eyes widened. Embered Body Heat also mentioned her body.

The second stage mentions my ash singeing, but maybe…

She willed heat to form through her ash and into the tendrils she had created and controlled. Fueling them with heat and moving them around didn't require a lot of mana or focus. All of it felt so natural, so easy, as if it was the very purpose of the element.

She could feel the temperature rising, could see small glowing lines and bits of embers as her ash heated up far more than she had ever been able to push it before.

It would take time and practice for her to use all of this effectively in battle, but just seeing the cuts left in the ground and feeling the heat in the ash, she knew it no longer was just a part of her toolkit meant to obscure and defend herself but something she could use in a far more offensive manner. She wouldn't use them to move, simply to attack and defend.

"Hold up a minute," she said before moving her ashen limbs down to the ground, her mind making them push down as she tried to lift her body up.

To her surprise, it actually worked. Not terribly well, but she could lift herself up. With her wings and strong body, there was little this would add to her mobility, but she could already think of some applications. To change direction rapidly in a forest, for example, or to allow movement when all her real limbs had been cut off. Not that such a scenario was desirable.

Let's be honest, it'll happen soon enough. I should train to move with this.

Wait, if it's my body… I should be able to test my healing after all.

Ilea cut some of the ash from one of the arms and used her healing skill to fix the 'wound'. It made sense in theory, but she still found herself a little surprised to find it actually worked. With it being a part of her body, her Hunter Recovery recognized it as such and managed to heal it.

The mana expenditure for healing or creating the ash anew with her Ash Creation was similar, healing being a little more exhaustive. Still, a combination of both would allow for faster rebuilding, not only for her tendrils but also for her Veil or anything else she made with her ash, as long as it was connected to her physically.

Touching the ash, she could immediately feel the mana flow into it, letting her know about its properties and how the element could be healed.

Weird concept, healing ash that I created from mana alone.

She tried to use her ashen arms to move herself over the ground while considering the possibilities, finding it easier and easier with every passing minute. She had formed entire models of cities with her ash before, so moving them in a spider-like manner wasn't exactly the hardest task to do. At least if she concentrated on it.

She couldn't help but be impressed with the third tier of her manipulation skill, even compared to her other abilities. Then she looked at her State of Azarinth and Form of Ash and Ember skills. Both were body enhancement spells that increased several of her attributes and her overall power.

She didn't know if her ash benefited from everything in the same manner, but the ash connected to her definitely felt more powerful, easier to move, and far more resilient. She would have to consider the placement of her ash more going forward. Perhaps the eight arms out of her back would be sufficient and could be expanded whenever necessary, but shields formed around her real arms would be better.

Or I could just have a ton of ash floating around me at all times.

She chuckled, thinking about people's reactions when they thought her to be some kind of ash elemental.

Am I not that already? In some fucked up way…?

Time would tell how her ash would most efficiently be deployed, but for now, the eight arms on her back felt most natural. Eight was a number she could manage. Perhaps she would increase it with time and as she increased her skill in the element.

Third-tier Ash Creation, here I come.

The thought made her smile, and with the changes this had already brought, it would definitely be the first one she'd advance next time she got a skill point.

She walked over to one of the nearby trees and crossed her arms. Her real ones.

Azarinth Fighting and Ashen Warrior increased the damage dealt with her body. One of her ashen arms lashed out at the tree trunk, smashing into the wood with ease before it retracted back to her. She hadn't tried a similar move before, but her projectiles definitely had a little more difficulty destroying a tree.

Is the increased damage dealt only toward other living beings' health? Or to objects not categorized with a health bar as well?

Ilea wasn't sure, but the effect against the tree and ground was clear. Her ash hit hard.

Do trees even have health bars?

She identified the trunk but found nothing else than a simple ***[Tree]***.

No level or health bar. I bet there's some kind of sorcery to animate them. There has to be. She smiled. *Like a tree necromancer or something.*

She tried but couldn't use Destruction through her ash as the skill specified that a 'punch' or 'kick' needed to be used. Perhaps if she formed her ash into a fist, it might work. She did exactly that and formed a small fist at the end of one of her ashen limbs before assaulting the tree again. Sadly, the skill didn't activate.

Leaves me with a reason still to engage with my own two hands though.

It would've been annoying to change her whole approach because she'd gotten a new skill. Then again, the range of her ashen limbs was somewhat limited anyway. Extending their length beyond a few meters made it far more difficult to control them.

Using Wave of Ember with the same limb she had just used to test Destruction, the mana left her and a fiery spark entered the tree trunk, igniting it before the heat slowly fizzled away. The application was beneficial, but then Ilea thought of something else. She tested it quickly and smiled as a dozen glowing cuts appeared in the tree.

Before, she was limited to how quickly she could punch, and while she was now much faster at using her own body, she now had eight more arms with which to send out Wave of Ember, at least doubling if not tripling her damage output.

Plus, human opponents usually couldn't block ten arms at the same time. Maybe one or two, but the reach she now had allowed her to get behind an opponent's shield or get them in a blind spot. Combined with her ability to just explode the ash into their face or spread it around them, she'd be even nastier to fight against now.

She grinned at that but then thought about how she'd measure up to someone like the demon she'd fought in Ravenhall, the one that had nearly killed her. Perhaps she'd be able to take two or three of his punches now before her bones were shattered... but it wouldn't be enough. Not even close. *Same with a Praetorian.*

Ilea cracked her neck and smiled. *Only one thing to do then,* she thought and continued through the night.

* * *

A glint of light reflected in the distance as she ran. Deciding to see what it was, Ilea soon found a group of soldiers in armor and colors she hadn't seen before. They turned at her approach and shouted for her to stop. Ilea followed their orders and raised her hands as she identified them. *Barely one above a hundred.*

"What is your business in the Kingdom of Kroll?" one of them asked, his armor looking a little higher in quality compared to the others.

"Shadow passing through, officer. If you're looking for the demons, they're ten minutes down the road." Some of the soldiers looked at each other at that, and Ilea noticed two of them grip their weapons more tightly. "They're already dead."

The man locked eyes with her. "And why would a Shadow care to kill demons on the road?"

"That, officer, is my own business. Let me know if you have the location of any other groups of them. I'll be happy to clean up the mess," she suggested with a smile.

The man gulped, then waved for his group to continue. "That won't be necessary, Shadow. Good luck on your hunt."

"The same to you," Ilea replied and watched them leave. She followed the thinning trail for another twenty minutes, finding the burnt remains of at least three demons in the forest a couple of minutes off the road.

She definitely liked the lack of scrutiny even soldiers showed her now that she was above level two hundred and simply stated that she was a Shadow.

Who would travel in the wilds alone at night, claiming to have killed demons with complete confidence when standing against a group of ten soldiers aiming their magic at them? Who else but a Shadow? Or someone just as dangerous?

Giving up on her search for more demons, she decided to follow the road until she knew where she was again. The visibility was too bad for her to see anything farther than a couple of dozen meters.

Several hours passed without her encountering anybody as she sped over the road leading westward through the night. Only a single pause was necessary to regain her stamina and mana when it started to reach less than a fifth of her total, her constant use of her ashen limbs adding to the exertion.

Ilea stopped another hour or so later near a worn stone bridge. Wooden signs with fading writing confirmed she was going west. Most of the towns listed were indecipherable, but she could make out the word 'Karth' in the midst of them, the mountain apparently dominant enough to deserve a mention even on signs in the middle of bumfuck nowhere.

TWENTY-SIX

Back to the Roots

Ilea sped up as the light of day finally greeted her, the form of the massive mountain of Karth barely visible far in the distance.

Several hours of flying at her top speed brought her close enough to see the town of Riverwatch, her wings dissolving after she landed on the road leading toward the city. Ilea started walking, greeting a group of adventurers who were talking gleefully in the back of a horse-pulled wagon, a massive dead beast Ilea couldn't quite place lying between them.

Frog mutant or something?

Their enthusiastic mood took a hit upon seeing the Shadow. With apprehension clearly visible on their faces, Ilea decided against trying to join them for the ride and instead kept walking until they were barely visible to her on the dusty road. She came upon the bridge she'd crossed many times before and stopped, looking at the faraway walls of the city before she smiled, then crossed the river and ran into the familiar forest.

Seems like the drakes have repopulated.

She spotted a massive lizard, but it stopped and quickly rushed away when it saw her. "That's right, bitch!" she laughed and continued her run, her armored boots hitting the creeks and leaving deep marks in the soft earth wherever she passed.

The temple looked exactly the same as it had before, rundown and fucking old. *My first home in this realm,* Ilea thought as she walked through the stone halls, opening a door and looking at the skeleton still inside.

"Hey, buddy. Been a while." She waved and closed the door again so as not to further disturb the permanent resident.

"Lucky I found this instead of the city first. I might've become another ice or fire mage, thinking it to be the coolest option," she said, brushing her hands against the stone as she looked through the ground with her Sphere, blinking into the small hall she'd found after her arrival.

Touching the wall, there was still no Bluemoon Grass, but she felt the power within. It would grow again, in time. She felt a little bad about eating probably dozens if not hundreds of years' worth of the elixir in just a couple of months. Then again, the supposed death rate was far too high to have even considered sharing it.

"Oh hey, look, it's drake scales." She took one of the remaining pieces. To think she'd lugged tons of the stuff around after spending so much time cutting it off the monsters she'd killed.

Maybe I'll do that with dragon scales soon enough. The thought made her smile.

Walking into the library, her hands grazed the cracks and missing stone on the wall where she had trained her Destruction skill. Walking back, she checked the fountain.

[Fountain of Clarity]

"Still sounds as stupid as it did back then," she smirked. Drinking a little of the water, she felt its very faint magical power. Summoning a cup, she found the effects quickly faded as soon as it left the beautifully crafted spring.

Ilea checked the stone around it and found several enchantments on its side and within. Runes were carved into the well, still active. She couldn't tell exactly what it ran on. It had managed to keep her alive back before she'd even had a Class, but with her current health pool, its effects were barely noticeable.

And it's fading quickly. So no easy health potions.

She found the effects faded even within her necklace.

She felt almost nostalgic, being back in these familiar halls that were now clad in complete darkness. She now found it as natural to see through her Sphere as her eyes. Considering the enchantments and runes she'd seen before, the Azarinth Order certainly weren't novices.

The training golems were impressive, even now, though she didn't fight them again, knowing they would be destroyed near instantly. The healing fountain wouldn't be incredibly helpful to most people, even someone below level fifty, but it could be a great asset to a city.

Ilea didn't know anything about the limitations of building one, or of having it powered. Perhaps it required a spell or sacrifice to activate initially. Maybe it was linked to the Bluemoon Grass or the source of the plant. Or perhaps existing healing orders knew of similar enchantments but found that just using healing magic was more effective.

She wasn't about to jot down every single rune on the well, but maybe a journey to the temple with Iana, Christopher, and perhaps even Weavy would shed some light on the magical fountain.

She blinked down into the large hall where she'd fought against some kind of guardian golem. Parts of the thing still remained on the dusty floor, magical lights illuminating the eerie hall. Ilea walked toward the treasure room, where she felt something weird in her Sphere.

Really. Another hidden passage?

Ilea smiled and followed the wall, the perfectly ordinary-looking stone bricks damn near screaming at her in her Sphere. Blinking around brought her nowhere new. Either an enchantment had been placed to prevent overeager initiates finding it or there really was nothing.

Her fists and ash started digging into the stone, Ilea's weapons damaging the hard surface as if it were drywall, ripping out big chunks with each hit. She waved the dust away, her ash clearing the shattered stone.

Right when she started feeling silly for going berserk against a cellar wall, her fist broke through. Ripping at it, a huge crack formed that let her see through. Her Sphere was still unable to see, but her eyes told her there was something in the darkness beyond.

Ilea continued clearing out stone until she could fit through the opening. Her Sphere immediately expanded when she passed the invisible threshold. No dungeon notification popped up as she had hoped, but she found a rune on a nearby wall connected to a magical light. That much she understood, and she pushed her mana into the rune, causing a dim blue light to illuminate a perfectly intact stairwell.

Using her Sphere, she could make out a single room below. She checked for traps as she carefully went down the stairs. More lights were activated when she touched a rune at the bottom, the big room coming to life before her eyes.

In it was a round table, mostly covered with a large, yellowed map, as well as several chairs, dust and cobwebs clinging to everything they could. The dust made the air heavy, the smell of leather permeating her nose and Sphere.

Hidden meeting room?

Nobody had used it in their last days, it seemed, neither skeleton nor undead prowling the room. Ilea stepped up to the table, then breathed deep and blew the dust away from the map. When the dust settled, she found it looked much like her own, just with a lot more cities, empires, and kingdoms, many of the names illegible.

Figures reminding Ilea of chess pieces stood in various places on the map. Getting out her notebook, she compared the few legible names and found most of them differed from what she knew. Riverwatch and all the cities west of it weren't even on the map. She couldn't find Lys but saw a country called the Lyrian Empire in the same area, though it was much smaller. She did find Ravenhall, for the lone city in the mountains had retained its name through the centuries.

Ilea felt a little pride at that but shook her head at the absurdity of the fact. The Shadow's Hand was no glorious order making the world a better place. They were mercenaries. She grinned. *Oldest bloody mercenaries though, and the baddest of badass.*

"Wish I had my cellphone to take a picture," she complained, sitting down on one of the chairs and finding it somewhat comfortable despite the cobwebs and the cloud of dust that immediately clung to her armor.

Taking one of the wooden pieces from the map, she twirled it in her fingers before her eyes fell on the symbol painted on the piece's chest. One of her gauntlets vanished before she sacrificed a couple of hundred health to activate her third-tier State of Azarinth.

One of the runes, the one on the back of her hand, looked eerily similar to the one painted in blue on the little figure. Standing up again, she studied the placement of the figures but couldn't figure out what it meant. Some were grouped up near Karth, others were in formations in the forest. Single pieces stood alone near the northern mountain range or in the forest, their rich, dark color quite a contrast to the dull brown of all the other figures.

Ilea didn't recognize any of the other symbols – even her State of Azarinth rune wasn't exactly the same – but she couldn't help but be convinced it represented the Azarinth Order. Checking them for similarities, she put nine figures into her necklace. Perhaps one of the librarians she had met would know about their significance. The dark figures had no discernible shape or symbols, so she took one and looked at it intently.

"Can you see me? Dark god of death?"

Nothing happened.

"I swear, one of these days it's going to happen. I'm just going to doom all of life because of some stupid joke," Ilea mused, replacing the black figure.

Looking at the map more closely, she saw it ended not far beyond Karth in the western direction, but the south and north gave her pause. She touched the ancient, frayed fabric. Both the south, where she had hunted the Swordfish creature with her team in the Isanna Desert, and the uncharted wastelands of the north, her current destination, looked to have been ripped off.

Why would they rip them off instead of just leaving them out in the first place?

The room had little else that held Ilea's interest. She wrote down the positions of all the figures in her notebook, just in case it became relevant, before she stored the map itself. She was sure Dagon would be interested.

Ilea looked through the room once more, but there weren't even any books. Still, she was happy the map had survived, considering the state the library in her training hall had been in. Going back up the stairs, she returned to the hall with the guardian and blinked back up. Another blink and she was on top of the temple.

The trees around the temple had grown close, taking back what had been theirs in the past. Leaves rustled when the wind blew through them. Ilea looked around as a drake's call sounded in the distance before she looked down at the stone roof.

"Still here?"

The question answered itself when she crouched down a little and cleaned away the leaves and dirt that covered her etchings of a compass rose and the small mountain to the southwest. She smiled and straightened up, not adding anything to the map today.

Ilea closed her eyes and breathed in deeply, enjoying the quiet, the nature. She had been little more than drake food when she'd arrived in Elos.

"Seen a lot, haven't I?" she said, glancing down at the compass rose. She cracked her neck and smiled.

Still alive and kicking.

She narrowed her eyes and turned northward. Toward the mountain range she couldn't see in the distance but knew to be there. Quickly glancing toward the lone mountain in the south, she waved at it and spread her wings. The ashen protrusions moved in the wind before her legs left the roof, ascending toward the sky.

Ilea sped north, her mind focused and brimming with excitement. Kyrian, Trian, Felicia, Claire, Keyla, Balduur, Dale, Walter. People she cared about here in Elos. She wanted to make sure they were safe, wanted to make sure they could trust in her strength. And for that, she needed to find more monsters, more magic, more power.

She kept flying low, only a couple of meters above the canopy, avoiding some of the higher trees sticking out of the forest like overgrown buildings. Regularly checking the western sky for any signs of movement other than leaves and small birds, she advanced on her destination. Ilea had her Sphere and some other skills active at all times now, making her prepared for an ambush. Combined with her healing and high speed, she hoped it was enough to survive alone in the north.

The mountains grew closer, but visibility was good today, meaning she was likely still a while away from her destination. It took her what felt like an hour to get close to the mountain range, close enough to see them reach up into the clouds and beyond. Accelerating, she flew in an upward curve to pass the mountain tops, ignoring the routes any expeditions would have planned to use. Claire had mentioned before that the expeditions had all failed.

Maybe they didn't fail and simply found a nice place to stay and decided to become independent.

The thought vanished when she crossed over the lowest mountain before her. The vast, endless landscape stretching behind it was littered with massive cracks and crevices running deep into the stone, steep mountains and deep valleys flowing into each other for as far as she could see. She strained her eyes, seeing dark storms far away and snow covering the higher parts of some mountains.

She slowed down and hovered, gulping while trying to think about where to go. Looking east, she couldn't see the ocean, the mountainous environment continuing farther than she'd thought possible. Except for the south, she couldn't find an end to it in any direction.

Purple lightning flashed in one of the dark storms, making her head turn. She saw more lightning flashing, bright and powerful, followed by dull booms of distant thunder. Ilea felt the hair on her neck standing up. *Not thunder… impacts.*

It's getting harder to breathe.

Ilea noticed it, but it wasn't an issue. She knew about higher altitudes having lower levels of oxygen, but strangely, it felt like the air was thicker, almost *heavier*.

Shaking her head, she broke herself out of her reverie and flew downward to a nearby valley with deep cracks at the bottom. Her eyes widened when one of the high mountains overlooking her destination seemed to turn black, enveloped by dark clouds that moved toward her.

She slowed down and watched as the mountain was swallowed, and though her instincts were telling her to run, her mind was unable to pry itself from the view. The massive clouds moved through the air like a beast prowling the skies.

Move.

Ilea started rushing downward. Her whole body screamed at her that something about that storm was dangerous. Trusting her instincts, she quickly reached the ground, looking for somewhere to take shelter.

There were small cracks in the rock, but other than protrusions sticking out and providing shade against the sun, there was nothing she felt was safe enough to actually hide behind.

The crevice.

Enhancing her speed with the third tier of her aura, adding blinks to cover even more distance, she rushed toward her new target.

Ilea blinked past large rocks, seeing not a single living being on the surface as the sky darkened and a purple flash cut through stone a couple of hundred meters to her left. The shock wave sent her tumbling through the air, all her power and body fighting against the natural force. Her healing spell told her something was wrong with her left side, but she couldn't figure out what, simply pushing mana toward it and feeling the damage subside, albeit slowly.

Let's not get hit.

The storm was now right above her, the light of the suns a forgotten memory, unable to pierce whatever it was that formed the massive storm front. No rain fell from the dark clouds looming over her, and Ilea's breathing and heartbeat accelerated as she enhanced her body to the fullest.

The only sounds she could hear were her own wings, her frantic breathing, and her heartbeat. Even the strong winds that had accompanied her previously had been scared off or pushed away by whatever was happening. A distant purple impact sent a wave of air into her back, and Ilea was happy to find her speed picking up as a result.

The valley wasn't visible anymore, hidden behind high hills and sharp stones sticking out of the ground all around her. Another bolt of lightning hit the stone, this time only a hundred meters to her right, the explosion of rock sending shrapnel, some as large as boulders, flying in all directions.

Her body was hurled backward from the wave of pure power. She tried to stabilize herself, pieces of rock impacting against her Veil and the ashen mist she started forming around herself. She blinked out of the way of another flying rock as big as a car, now stable enough to fly again.

What the hell is this bullshit…?

She continued forward, using the terrain around her to ignore the flying automobile-sized chunks still crashing to the ground around her. One of them forced another blink as it hurtled down at her from a steep angle.

The booming sound of stone on stone, sending debris and air outward, made her reduce her hearing capabilities so as not to take damage there as well. Crossing over another large hill, the crevice at the bottom of the valley was visible again, still a distance away. Her eyes focused on what she assumed to be shelter.

Her awareness suddenly peaked, the terrain that had rushed by her a moment earlier slowing down to a crawl, the flying debris pushing through the air like a stone through water. And then she saw it. Above her, the sky turned purple, tendrils of energy zapping at the clouds before they moved down toward the ground, trying to find ways to go as they snaked through the air with moderate speed.

Ilea blinked backward, knowing she had two seconds to prepare herself. The ash around her moved forward, forming several walls, as her arms shielded her body, her legs moved up to her stomach, and her wings cut forward through the air to cocoon her small form. She sacrificed five hundred points of health to increase her State of Azarinth for a moment, her healing already kicking in to recover the health while she formed more ash to protect her.

Ilea felt herself fall as the purple bolts of lightning moved through the air like cracks in the sky, invisible to her a moment later as they passed her ashen defenses. Ilea prepared to blink again when the lightning impacted around forty meters in front of her. The shock wave came a moment later, her ash vanishing like sand washed away by the tides. Her Veil resisted for a moment before the force pushed through.

Ilea's muscles and bones were pushed backward, her vision nearly going dark when her skull cracked in her helmet. The force nearly shattered her bones, some of them snapping and tearing out of her skin as they slashed through her organs and tissue from within, only stopped by the armor on her back as she was flung through the air like a rag doll.

Fighting with all her will to stay conscious, her healing skill took over. Trying to stop the internal bleeding, Ilea focused on her heart and brain. Then her body, flying at high speed, was slammed into a rock. The bones still sticking out of her skin cut through even more of her flesh as she was flung sideways, finally landing on the ground where her body tumbled for twenty more meters before coming to a stop.

Blood seeped out of the thin openings rent in Ilea's armor, her head lolling toward the sky. One of her eyes had miraculously survived, the bloodied thing barely registering the dark clouds above while Ilea tried with all her power to stabilize her dying body.

A purple tendril of energy slashed through the sky above, the lightning striking somewhere far off, the resulting wave of air nearly sweeping her body up again. Ilea willed her hands to dig into the stone with whatever strength they had left. One of them still responded, and a swift jab brought her some stability at the cost of even more of her body rupturing.

Her vision went dark for a moment before she came back to consciousness, breathing hard. Flying debris rained down on the ground next to her, small pebbles dinging off her surprisingly intact armor. The bleeding was under control now, but half of her organs were still mush, her heart and brain damaged and on the brink of failure.

Ilea's instincts took over as her hand gripped the ground, a massive rock crashing to earth a couple of dozen meters from her, her body lifted up slightly by the resulting shock wave. She landed again with a groan, blinking her prone body away when a stone the size and weight of a tank crashed into the ground where she'd once been. The movement made her cough up blood.

Some of her organs had recovered but got injured again as a result. Not as badly as from the initial impact, at least. Her brain and heart recovered and bones snapped back into place, Ilea using the existing bones instead of building new ones to save time but also because nothing had been completely pulverized.

As soon as the bleeding was taken care of and most of her organs were functioning at least somewhat, she spread her wings, one good eye focused on a crevice that looked to be close now.

Lightning struck again, making her turn her head, wincing at the damage the movement did to her spine. Luckily unable to feel the pain, she found the lightning had struck behind a large hill several hundred meters away. Focusing forward again, Ilea continued to heal her body, which was going quicker now that she wasn't leaking blood and no more of her bones were trying to damage her. She was back.

Energy lashed the ground behind her. She increased her speed as she rushed through the desolate landscape, veering left before she entered the crevice. Yet her speed was too high, her body too badly injured for her to navigate through the quickly thinning tear in the land properly. She hit the wall before stabilizing, grazing the other side of the crevice before landing hard on the ground some hundred meters further down.

Finally, her body came to a halt. A scar had been scraped into the stone from her fall, and the ground had cracked from her landing. The impact of more lightning sounded above, but she felt none of the resulting shock wave. She'd made it.

'ding' Arcane Magic Resistance reaches lvl 7

Fuck yeah.

Breathing out, Ilea started laughing, wincing at the pain when she reactivated its perception. Half her body was still mush, but she was recovering quickly now, stable again and soon to be back at peak condition. It was good to feel the pain. To know that she'd survived. She couldn't feel her legs, but that was a minor concern.

A hiss made her tense up. Her one eye frantically searched for the source of the noise as her second one started rebuilding. A moment later, she was staring at a huge eagle that clung to the side of the crevice, a snake as broad as herself and longer than she thought possible struggling against the eagle's claw that had dug deeply into its body as it hissed and tried to bite at the unmoving bird.

It's looking at me.

The creature was immense, the size of a small aircraft, each talon nearly as large as Ilea herself. Its very being radiated power, though it was too far away for Ilea to identify. Ilea focused on healing up, not moving a single muscle as her sight in her second eye returned.

Is it hiding or hunting?

The storm was still above them, but her crevice was a dark, quiet place, the only noise coming from the lightning impacts above and the occasional stone that fell. Ilea blinked closer to the stone wall and took shelter under a rocky protrusion, building ash again just in case a bolt of lightning managed to somehow find its way down the narrow crack.

The eagle was still watching her, but it already had a meal in its talons. If it was a wild animal, she'd likely be safe.

Maybe it's apprehensive of me as well?

Somehow, the idea didn't fit with the majestic monster that casually held onto the side of the crevice, its wings retracted, but they waited together for some fifteen minutes until light returned above. Now that the danger of the storm had moved past, Ilea noticed the grass and plants growing at the bottom of the crevice for the first time.

She watched the eagle raise its head and look back down at her before it jumped off, the wingspan too broad to fly straight in the crevasse as it ascended quickly, both using its wings and digging into the stone with its one free clawed foot. And then it was gone, along with the snake that had been less lucky than Ilea.

Ilea sighed with relief and found the air easier to breathe down here. Moving out of her hiding spot, she grinned. Excitement flowed through her, the adrenaline from her tense arrival in the north slowly fading as she activated her meditation skill and focused on controlling her quickening heartbeat.

She hadn't seen the levels of the beasts, but her instincts had sounded an alarm. Both the snake and the eagle would likely be formidable opponents should she stand in their way. They were hunters of prey themselves, and they survived here where strange purple lightning strong enough to kill her struck the earth who knew how often.

Maybe I'll follow the crevice? Ilea thought, remembering that the expeditions planned to use tunnels and similar cracks in the land to go into the northern territory. Given the lack of animals above, it seemed like the more sensible bet. Especially with how quickly that storm had moved around her.

Deciding to move further north and see what she could find, Ilea carefully walked along the bottom of the crevasse, looking at the flowers growing out of the dry stone, greeting the new visitor. *Life finds a way, hmm?*

The crevice soon opened up. Not by much, but enough to have allowed stones to fall into it more easily, some stacking several dozen meters high, their structural integrity questionable at best. A small clear stream flowed lazily through the fissure, ending in a small cave not far away. More plants were growing here, their green splendor reflecting the sunlight from above alongside the sparkling creek.

Movement caught Ilea's eye, a foxlike creature with scales instead of fur peeking out of a hole before it moved to the creek. Its red-brown form hid among the stones before it started lapping at the water. Ilea moved past with as little noise as she could, but the fox rushed away when she got closer.

Not as stealthy as the little guy.

Looking around, she blinked up onto a group of massive stones, the suns not reaching this part of the creek because of the steep angle. She jumped up, her wings spreading, before ascending to the top of the crevice and looking out over the terrain.

Hills and large chunks of rock inhibited her view, but she could see the dark clouds in the distance, purple flashes continuously hurtling to the ground. Even from so far away, she could hear the impacts and feel the tiny tremors.

Seeing a group of birds flying by, she jumped down again, grabbing the edge of the cliff to hide her body from the predators. The hairs on the back of her neck were standing as she watched the leathery wings of the vicious-looking birds flap in the wind. She smiled wide.

Welcome to the fabled north. It's been 0 days since your last near-death experience.

TWENTY-SEVEN

The Northern Night

Traveling through the cracks in the land proved rather simple for Ilea, seeing as she was gifted with flight, high durability, endurance, and, most importantly, teleportation. The creek she'd found previously was the only source of water she'd seen so far, and the shadows were already stretching far to the west, almost no light finding the bottom of the crevice she was currently moving through.

The howling winds could be heard above, but the lip of the crevice protected the creatures seeking shelter within. She could hear them before she passed over a set of boulders, her Sphere informing her about the size and form of what creatures lay beyond. One of them looked up, its scaled head turning her way before it hissed, causing the other two bipedal bird-like animals to turn her way as well.

[Burrow Dragoon – lvl 205]

She identified the closest one as the three fanned out to surround their prey.

"So, you want to play?" Ilea asked, ashen tendrils forming on her back.

Two of them advanced quickly. They were a little shorter than Ilea, but the claws on their feet were nearly as long as her hand. Yellow eyes focused on her as the last one of them jumped up and twirled before it crashed and dug into the earth.

Ilea's eyes widened as she jumped backward, seeing the dragoon advance through the stone with her Sphere. It reached her before the running ones did, punching up through the stone and its jaw snapping at the air before it landed again, digging back into the ground.

They had neither arms nor wings. Instead, most of their weight was probably distributed between claws and teeth. At least, that was what Ilea thought when she blinked next to one of the murder chickens, the monster just jumping up to burrow as its pal had done.

Ilea's fist along with five limbs of ash crashed into its side, and six servings of Wave of Ember with a side of Destruction rushed into the beast, the impact sending it skidding for several meters before it cried out in pain, hissing at her.

Heavier than I thought.

Stepping to her left, Ilea avoided the emerging dragoon, its clawed foot shooting out to dig into her ash. Crouching to avoid its attack, Ilea grabbed onto one of its legs and twirled around, throwing it at the other hissing monster.

The third beast emerged next, its maw closing around her foot before she'd let go of the second one, preventing her blink from activating. Its teeth ground through her Veil and fought hard against her armor before eight tendrils of ash smashed into the beast. Ilea pulled it up and out of the ground with her leg before she smashed her fist into its hard skull. Again and again she punched until one of its eyes closed with a crunch.

Ilea saw the other two approaching from below and spread her wings, ascending with all the power she had, dragging the dragoon out of the stone while she continued her assault. Her armor groaned under the stress, but the beast didn't manage to get through.

Its limbs stopped moving another three punches later, and Ilea put her hands inside its maw and pulled them apart. Sweat dripped from her brow as she groaned, finally breaking the beast's jaws open and dropping its lifeless body toward the hissing monsters below.

Blinking behind one of them, she grabbed its tail and whirled it around, bludgeoning the second one while her ash delivered Wave of Ember and her touch pushed in reversed healing. Breathing hard, she watched the monster get up and burrow as she held on to the other beast that was desperately trying to get away.

Jumping up, her wings helping in the process, she twirled and smashed the emerging beast with its brethren, smiling when it bit down into the other monster's back. Jaw locked in place, Ilea let go of them before landing on top of the now intertwined beasts, one groaning in pain as teeth, fists and destructive mana rained into its scaled head.

She broke through its skull and neck a moment later, focusing fully on the second one before they crashed down, her ash digging into its side until it stopped moving. The bloodied yellow-golden scales glittered a little in the fading sunshine that would soon leave the crevice behind.

'ding' You have defeated [Burrow Dragoon – lvl 205]

'ding' You have defeated [Burrow Dragoon – lvl 217]

'ding' You have defeated [Burrow Dragoon – lvl 222]

'ding' Wave of Ember reaches 2nd lvl 16

And here I thought the north was going to be good to raise my Class levels.

Ilea bumped her fists together and breathed out. There were scratches on her armor but no serious damage. Compared to the lightning bolt from before, where the force had been distributed amongst her whole armor, the dragoon had attacked a specific part, its teeth and jaw strength apparently enough to damage it.

Best not to end up with my head inside those jaws.

Leaving the corpses behind, she moved on as the land became darker and darker. The crevice became thinner and thinner until she could barely move through it at its lowest point. Instead, she had to jump up a bit higher to fit through.

Emerging on the other side of the narrow fissure, she found herself looking into a deep crevice. She could hardly make out the ground below as she jumped down. At the bottom, she found a small creek flowing slowly in her direction and vegetation growing out of the slits and cracks beneath her feet.

As the night progressed, Ilea could see sparkling stars shining down from the heavens, their light reflected in the water of the creek as a thin mist rolled into the crack from above like a cascade of water.

Ilea slowed when the area around her turned eerily calm and she couldn't make out the sound of the running water she knew to be just a couple of meters away. Her breathing quickened as she prepared for *something*. She just didn't know for what.

Seeing the mist pour in from all directions around her, Ilea thought it best to fly up and observe the area, but her body froze when she heard a noise. A humming, switching between high and low pitch in an eerily unnatural rhythm. Her body screamed at her to get the hell out of there, but she couldn't move an inch.

'ding' You have heard the song of a mighty creature – Your body is paralyzed for three seconds.

Time passed slowly as she watched something twist in the mist, four limbs moving toward her with frightening speed – a ghostly floating form dancing as if pushed by an unearthly wind before six white eyes opened and stared at her, black feline pupils staring into hers.

Unblinking and unwavering, the barely visible creature moved toward her in twirling motions, its eyes focused on her at all times. Then, finally, she could move again.

[Miststalker – lvl ??]

Ilea's wings spread as she felt her mana and health drain, the familiar sensation not surprising her. The creature's four limbs ending in what looked like blades reached out to her while she ascended, the soundless weapons slashing through the mist. The humming continued but left her unaffected.

Ilea was debating if she should engage the creepy monster when her body locked up again, causing her form to fall back down toward the mists.

'ding' You have heard the song of a mighty creature – Your body is paralyzed for three seconds.

'ding' Veteran reaches lvl 4

'ding' Health Drain Resistance reaches lvl 18

'ding' Mana Drain Resistance reaches lvl 19

The seconds passed before she blinked up, her wings forming just before she dropped again.

'ding' You have heard the song of a mighty creature – Your body is paralyzed for two seconds.

As she fell, her heart sank. There were dozens of the creatures moving through the mists, their songs intertwining into a terrifying concerto of death. All of them moved toward her.

Her health and mana started draining faster as more of the creatures advanced on her. She found she was only able to move again for a mere moment before another one froze her in place. She blinked up and away when she could, but not far enough to get out of the deathtrap.

'ding' You have heard the song of a mighty creature – Your body is paralyzed for two seconds.

As one of the monsters slashed a bladed scythe-like arm at her, Ilea's mind flashed back to her first encounter with a Taleen Guardian. The mist-like blade dissipated when it hit her armor, but she felt the magic flow into her, an odd cold feeling. Not a curse, but something else she'd not felt before.

With it came a stronger drain on her health and mana. If she didn't get out of here soon, she'd be left hollow and dead before the night ended. Blinking up, she rammed her hands and ashen limbs into the stone before the next message swam into her mind.

'ding' You have heard the song of a mighty creature – Your body is paralyzed for two seconds.

'ding' Veteran reaches lvl 5

'ding' Health Drain Resistance reaches lvl 19

'ding' Mana Drain Resistance reaches lvl 20

Her plan had worked, and she hung limply to the side of the cliff, halfway to the top. The ghostly monsters were unable to fly up to her but grouped in the mists below, sucking at her health and mana even from the bottom of the crevice.

Even so, whatever part of their magic was paralyzing her didn't overlap perfectly, leaving her with split seconds of movement in between. She knew she could blink out at that point, and part of her wanted to get away, but she stopped herself.

You'll have to face a lot more than a bunch of mist creatures if you want to face down another Praetorian, if you want to find Kyrian and get him out of whatever Taleen hellhole he's found himself in.

Instead, she stayed there, healing herself against the various drains the creatures used against her. Slowing her breathing, she pushed away the fear and held on.

Let's see if this works.

Ilea used the next split second of available movement to dig herself even deeper into the wall. She grinned to herself. *You're actually stuck here with me, mist monsters. I'm not your prey, you'll see.*

She hung there for a while, using all of her recovery to fight the powerful magic of the monsters below, none apparently able to fly up to pluck her from the wall.

'ding' You have heard the song of a mighty creature – Your body is paralyzed for one second.

Already down to a single second? Ilea checked her mana and found it getting low. *A break might be in order,* she thought, blinking up again and digging into the stone once more just before another message popped up.

'ding' You have heard the song of a mighty creature – Your body is paralyzed for one second.

She used the opening after the effect had passed to blink again. The mana and health drain started to wane at that point, the distance too great for the monsters' magic to affect her. Mist continued to pour down when she reached the top of the crevice and clambered over.

'ding' You have heard the song of a mighty creature – Your body is paralyzed for one second.

'ding' Veteran reaches lvl 6

Looking down, Ilea found dozens of white eyes staring at her, unblinking, before they started moving away, swirling and dissipating in the mist.

"Yeah, that's right," she said, then fell backward and onto the ground, lying there as the mist continued pouring into the crack. It seemed to come from the air, like the wind was carrying a white sheet before it released it over the landscape.

Ilea saw some sets of six eyes moving around in the distance up here, but none of them had noticed her so far, and it looked like the mists pooled in deeper areas like the crevices.

Below, the humming continued. The fact that it didn't *sound* like there were dozens of them there made it even creepier to her. She shuffled a couple of steps back, then breathed out, still sitting.

A couple fewer levels in Veteran at the start and that could've been it. Days since the last near-death experience… still zero.

She shivered and stood up, letting healing mana flow through her, meditation quickly returning her lost mana.

"Terrifying little buggers," she muttered, cracking her neck.

Suppose that's the only way to get stronger. I'll have to find anything I can just barely face and survive.

Ilea looked out toward a pair of them twirling in their own sea of mist but decided to observe more before she landed herself in another fight. Who knew if they could multiply or something? They could have any number of abilities.

Looking down into the crevice, she found that it had turned completely white. She couldn't make out a single one of the creatures. The flow of the mist had nearly stopped as well.

I should find another place to hide. The storms are too dangerous to—

Ilea's thought process was interrupted as she looked out over the lands. Dark mountains loomed all around her, cracks and crevices visible even from far away, some reflecting the starlight on the white sheet of mist that coated them. Not a single purple light was visible. Not a single black cloud either.

Ilea spread her wings and flew up a couple of dozen meters to get a better view. Other than seeing a little farther, though, it was the exact same result. She saw a couple of clouds, but they looked either gray or white. Not that that was an indicator of their safety.

Still, there was no purple lightning. It was quiet. Seas of mist had congregated in various areas where the land seemed to form into valleys. Ilea assumed most if not all crevices were filled with the stuff and likely the creatures that inhabited it.

Miststalkers, was it?

She couldn't identify a single one. Flying closer to a small mountain, she landed on its peak, standing on black stone. A thin sheet of ice glimmered in the moonlight, crunching and splintering when she stepped on it. There were lakes of mist and cloudy mountain tops wherever she turned.

'ding' Arcane Magic Resistance reaches lvl 8

"Erm, what?"

She blinked her eyes, watching black furry creatures scurry in the dark before they vanished again.

"Hello. Yes, what please?"

Looking up toward the sky, neither god nor demon replied to her question.

Does that mean there's magic in the air here? Or maybe just more magic than in the Plains?

Figuring she'd learn about what the hell just happened in time, she tried spotting the running creatures again. Four legs and a tail. They only seemed visible because of the absence of light where they ran.

Spreading her wings, she jumped off the mountain and glided over the lake of mist where she could see at least a dozen of the mist creatures, though they were too far below to affect her with their magic. Landing on a hill overlooking the lake, some of the creatures nearby quickly advanced on her, their eerie melody not affecting her anymore.

"What are you going to do now, you mist… shits?"

The answer, of course, was to drain her health and mana. They stood far inside the mist, too far away for her to try and engage. They might just be trying to lure her in there – where many more of them might be lying in wait. Training her resistances against the spells was certainly a possibility, but she didn't feel safe enough to run around with half of her mana and health missing.

Flying up instead, she continued her observations from the sky, though not too high as she saw things moving through the clouds. More of the leathery birds that moved in large flocks.

That doesn't look safe.

She wanted to fight one of them alone before rushing into a whole group of the creatures. At least it seemed they either didn't see her or didn't care about her presence.

Landing on an elevated position devoid of mist, she spotted a massive skeleton with a lizard-like head and four limbs. The tail was missing, but she found its skeleton lying on the stone a couple of dozen meters away.

The bone wasn't completely dry, a little blood and tissue still sticking to it, indicating a more recent death than she'd initially assumed. Identifying the bone gave her the name of the creature.

[Kalamon Bone – High Quality]

Ilea grabbed one of the ribs and pulled hard. It cracked after a while, making Ilea stumble back a little. Putting it below her foot, she stomped down and cracked it with her first stamp, breaking it with the second.

Not better than my stuff.

Moving on through the dark, Ilea glimpsed more mist creatures and deadly-looking birds, but other than that, nothing moved. Nothing visible to her, at least. She spent the night rushing from mountaintop to mountaintop, hiding from swarms of birds from time to time.

A loud hissing sound made her jump into a crack, and she could feel the tremors of something moving, but looking over the edge, she couldn't see anything. Nor had there been a paralyzing effect, but Ilea didn't really know what that meant. It was possible her Veteran level was now high enough to counter the effects, or maybe only certain strong monsters had the ability.

Ilea couldn't tell the mountains from each other as she moved constantly between their high peaks and the valleys beyond, the cracks in the earth leading down even deeper. With the mists, it seemed unwise to travel through them by night, but there were certainly enough hunters around above ground as well.

Birds and flying drake-like creatures occasionally dove down, but she could never see what they hunted or killed. It made her more wary of the skies, making sure to stay as invisible as possible to them. Her veil, which barely reflected light, and her small form, compared to the beasts she'd encountered so far, helped her in that regard. Or it might have been pure luck that none of the animals dove to kill her.

By the time the suns were rising on the horizon, the cracked and mountainous terrain expanded farther than her eyes could see in all directions. A smile formed on her face as she stretched and summoned a meal, sitting down on a stone atop a mountain peak. Her legs dangled, bumping the stone from time to time as she enjoyed Keyla's cooking in silence.

I'm lost as fuck.

TWENTY-EIGHT

Chicken Nuggets

With the emergence of the suns, Ilea watched closely to see what happened to the lakes of mist when the light reached their borders. Eating the last of her meal, she scanned the surroundings to find the closest crack in the land before jumping off the mountain and gliding down its steep side.

The sunlight was still partially hidden behind the mountain, but as it slowly came up on the crevice, Ilea saw how the mist was already dissipating. Miststalkers danced around before they too vanished, particles of mist floating up in the air, the last evidence of their existence shimmering in the light that finally rose over the mountains.

As quickly as the mist had vanished, black clouds formed and purple lightning started impacting faraway hills and mountains. Ilea watched a cloud form only a couple of hundred meters away and decided it was safer to traverse the chasms again. Jumping into the nearest one, she felt the air from the first lightning strike of the newly formed death cloud rush by.

Are the mist creatures in there? Do they turn into lightning stalkers by day?

A little apprehensive, Ilea scanned her surroundings. She couldn't see any mist. Which meant traveling was somewhat safe on the surface during the night and in the cracks by day. Not counting any creatures that may or may not be out on the hunt.

Ilea saw the first animals and small insects move out of their hiding spaces among the rocks and cracks, eager to find food and water now that the mists were gone.

Not exactly an abundance of resources around here.

She watched the animals and started walking northward. So far, she'd only found the dragoons that she could definitely kill, but they were below her level, meaning it wasn't exactly effective leveling-wise.

They were interesting opponents, but without an ability to seriously hurt her, combined with the low level, she wasn't particularly interested in hunting them. Nor did they seem to be around in high numbers.

There was a rustling sound behind her, but she couldn't see anything when she turned around. Checking for anything in hiding as if she was looking for a rogue, she found nothing. Smiling a little, she imagined Eve trying to sneak up on her here in the north. She looked down the crevice, then shook her head. She breathed in deep and walked on.

The Miststalkers were interesting, but as long as they attacked in such high numbers, she wasn't sure if she should approach them for the time being. Her resistances against their drains weren't insignificant and she could gain more levels, but seeing how fast they drained her, she wasn't about to jump into a group of them.

That was if they even reappeared the next night. Ilea had only seen one day and night in the north so far, and while the purple lightning had returned, she didn't know if the mist would. The leathery gray birds freaked her out, but although she hadn't fought against them yet, she thought they might be the best way for her to level up here.

Coming into another section of the crevice, Ilea sniffed the air and activated all her buffs, blinking behind a rock she could see through her Sphere. Looking around, listening and waiting for a minute, she couldn't make out anything. However, the smell of a recent fire was unmistakable.

Running through the crack, she found it. A crudely prepped fireplace, only cold ash remaining. The bones of an animal lay to its side, free of any meat. Checking her surroundings again, Ilea activated her Hunter's Sight, looking for any clues regarding the maker of this fire.

There was, of course, the question of whether she really *wanted* to look for whoever had prepared it, but the potential benefits of getting to know someone who knew their way around the north were obvious.

Might even be worth the risk.

Looking around further, she found half-faded tracks in the sand.

Boots…

'ding' Hunter's Sight reaches 2nd lvl 9

However, following the trail proved difficult, either because it was older or because the mists and stalkers had danced over it for a whole night or three. The trail continued into a small cave opening, darkness staring back at her when she entered.

Using her Sphere, Ilea walked through the narrow corridor before she heard a stream flowing nearby. The water flowed down into the unknown, farther than her Sphere could see. The space wasn't big enough for her to glide down with her wings, so she climbed down through the small gap between the water and the rock face. After a couple of meters, she could see the bottom.

Coming out as quietly as she could, she found the following cave to be a little brighter. She couldn't make out the light source as of yet. Trying to stay quiet, she walked through the cave, finding a large fissure in the stone at the other end. The water flowed down a small creek that had formed over the years.

Just another crevice?

There was grass growing outside the fissure, soft light breaking in from cracks above. It definitely looked like something Ilea wouldn't have found if she'd simply continued down through the outer gorge. The way led farther down, even opening up below, while the top looked narrower, only opening in certain parts to allow sunlight inside.

I wonder if the mists come down here too...

Ilea walked deeper into the unknown, following the small stream of water flowing down next to her, occasionally reflecting the sun when she passed a crack above her. The terrain led farther down before opening up into a moderately spacious cave with abundant vegetation. The stream ended here in a small pond hidden behind ferns. The trail, though, was still there, actually growing more pronounced and easier to follow.

Ilea heard a chirping sound before a blinding headache nearly brought her to her knees, the pain spreading through her before she shut it off, healing against the damage done to her mind and body.

She'd never experienced such a pure force of mind magic before. The attack felt like a combination of Weavy's and Eve's abilities, fine control shattering her mind with the force of a sledgehammer. Carefully surveying the damage done, Ilea healed it, focusing on her mind as she started meditating.

Her second stage Mental Resistance deflected part of the spell back at whoever was doing this, and she hoped it would provoke some sort of response. Her healing was now stable, and combined with her recovery of both mana and health, she could simply sit there and take it for a while. So she did. The attack didn't subside.

'ding' Mental Resistance reaches 2nd lvl 11

Might as well stay until it's at level twenty. With such a ridiculously powerful attack, that's gonna take less than a day.

The plan didn't work out though, the mind magic subsiding some two minutes later. She could still hear the chirping and decided to find out what it was.

In the grass nearby, just outside her Sphere's previous radius, she found a small yellow chick, chirping happily as it wiggled a worm out of the ground. Slurping it down, it looked at her and chirped again, flapping its small wings.

"You're fucking cute."

Carefully moving her hand forward, she petted the tiny chicken and identified it.

[Mind Shredder – lvl ??]

Ilea continued smiling and lifted the animal up. "Sorry, little guy, I don't have any bread with me." Looking into the bird's eyes, it chirped again before lying down in her hand. The thing was asleep in mere moments. "Aren't you the cutest murder mage. Mind Shredder... are you kidding me?"

She considered an illusion spell or something related to mind magic to change its appearance, but she didn't feel any magic coming from the chick anymore. Maybe her identify skill was wrong or influenced by something that had actually attacked her. Then again, why wouldn't a tiny chicken have an affinity for mind magic?

If there were hundreds of them, maybe she'd consider making chicken nuggets, simply for the levels, but just one was just too cute to harm.

But I'd get fried if even five attacked me at the same time.

Reminded of the Miststalkers, she wondered if there were more here. She couldn't find any with her Sphere, though there were some worms and insects, all dead for as far as she could see.

Using nukes to kill worms.

It was a mystery how such a small, cute animal that only needed worms and water to live had acquired such an insane ability with mind magic. She placed it down on the grass again and let it sleep, the bird likely exhausted from the magic it had exerted before.

Next thing I know, a worm is going to use earth magic to encase and eat me.

The thought didn't actually seem too strange, though of all the beasts she'd seen so far, the bird was the most surprising, simply because of its small size. With the severe lack of Mental Resistance most people had, it wasn't too far-fetched to think a single one of those chicks could've wiped out an entire expedition.

Or a single blast of that lightning.

The open area continued for a while, the vegetation slowly dwindling as the water source was left behind. With a final twist, the cave led into a wide-open space.

Ilea whistled softly when she looked out into the vast cavern, illuminated by light breaking in from a big opening in the roof, beaming down like a golden cascade over parts of the massive structures beneath. The tops of temples, towers, and aqueducts were all visible, their lower reaches vanishing in the darkness below where no light reached.

There was no notification, so this wasn't a dungeon. *A city? Under the mountain? Have I finally found some dwarves?* Something felt off about the place though. A dark and sinister feeling that made her apprehensive. This place was dead, long gone and rotting.

Spreading her ashen wings, she floated over a vast chasm to reach the settlement's highest tower. Looking down and seeing an unending void staring back at her made her shiver. She had no idea what lurked beyond that abyss. Part of her was scared, but she *wanted* to go down and find out what was hiding there, wanted to see what kind of monsters there were and how they would fight.

She smiled, feeling her magic flow through her, the power she had gotten.

Their attack on the Birmingales, on Arthur, some of it had felt exhilarating. She wouldn't deny that. At the same time, though, it had all been too complicated, too much to consider. Repercussions, politics, feelings of justice and revenge – it was all so overwhelming. No matter what, in the end, nobody had really won.

Here, out in the wilderness, it felt different. It felt as if she could let loose, could explore what her magic could do. There were no ethical questions here. Just the next fight.

She flew down and landed on the rooftop of a cathedral, its red clay faded and in disrepair. Moving past one of the merlons, she jumped down onto the square below, not quite angled right but solid enough to remain standing.

At the end of the terrace lay a broad gate leading into the cathedral's upper floor. The intricate design of its architecture reminded her a little of Salia, with towers with pointed tops and several distinct sections reaching up toward the sunlight above.

Railings, some damaged and bent, held onto the edges of the terrace, metal weaved into the shape of roses to create a mesh. Walking to the edge of the terrace, she found silver thorns had been placed on the outside of the railings.

Flaunting their wealth. Didn't work out in the end, now did it? She was quite aware of her own pompous house, but at least she hadn't added roses to her balcony railings. *Maybe I should…*

The door leading inside the cathedral was hanging by a single hinge, its heavy wooden frame a shade of its assumed former self. The color it had once had was long gone, and the wood was rotting, the interwoven metal lines the only indication of its ancient splendor.

Ilea moved inside and found herself on the balcony overlooking the massive nave. Its windows were now all missing their glass, the weak sunlight falling into the building through the empty metal frames, its brilliance reflecting on the silver woven into the construction.

Ilea walked beside the gallery's wooden railing, taking in the incredible architectural wonder, now forgotten and rotting away. Tables as well as chairs and benches lined the floor of the hall, metal cutlery and plates still remaining on them.

A dining hall? What happened to this place?

There were no skeletons, no signs of a fight, nor zombies or demons walking around.

Did they just abandon it?

Her reverie turned into apprehension when she reached the end of the gallery and saw the massive double doors leading out of the cathedral into the ancient town. The doors were cast in metal, inlaid lines of silver depicting an intricate rose.

It wasn't the door that had piqued her caution, though, but what sat before it – a tall figure in a wooden chair, one of its legs resting on the other and a book in hand. Their back was toward Ilea, and a hood prevented her from seeing any of the figure's features.

Ilea had tried to be quiet, but she didn't have any stealth skills, so she was surprised that the being hadn't seen her yet.

Or it's chosen not to react. Wait, is this guy still alive?

Her options were sneaking up and attacking, identifying them from closer up and going from there, or speaking up from a greater distance. Identifying them would serve nothing as her approach likely wouldn't change, and she wouldn't attack them without knowing more, so the last option seemed the sanest one and would allow for the highest chance of getting away, should it become necessary.

Ilea spread her wings and flew over the wooden railing, down toward the stone floor, where she landed with almost no noise. Checking for openings in the walls and orienting herself so she knew where the exits were in the cave outside, she stepped forward.

"Greetings, traveler."

TWENTY-NINE

Roses

She saw its head move back a little. At least she knew it wasn't dead.

"How unexpected. A tracker of some sort, I surmise?" a deep voice said. The man touched his book and turned the page.

Ilea wanted to get closer, but something told her the man was dangerous. Instead, she kept her distance.

"Found a fire, followed the trail." She paused. "Beautiful place. Is it yours?"

A hearty chuckle reverberated through the hall. "No. I do not claim possession of this ruin."

"What are you here for then?" Ilea asked, seeing a strand of red hair when he turned a little more toward her.

The man got up, dusted off his insanely intricate robe, then patted the book. "Just the attendance list…" he murmured, then shook his head. "I'm a historian," he said and turned, dark gray eyes finding hers.

Ilea took an instinctive step back when she saw his sharp, pointed teeth, the book held by hands ending in delicate clawed fingers, carefully resting on the leather bindings, and a pale face with red hair falling on each side.

Not a man at all.

She thought about how to proceed, but as long as he didn't attack, she would wait and see.

"You are afraid? Naturally. I am as surprised at finding a human here as you are at finding an elf," he said, the book vanishing in his hand. "Perhaps… perhaps we may find an arrangement that would benefit the both of us before you run off or uselessly die in a misguided attempt at killing me."

Ilea relaxed a little. The elf was odd, that at least she was sure of. He looked older than the ones she'd fought, and he talked instead of spouting nonsense and attacking... though that actually made her more apprehensive.

"Been a while since I met one of your kind. None of them were particularly pleasant."

The elf smiled, his mouth opening partially to show his teeth. He hissed, the sound long. Ilea wasn't sure if he was trying to intimidate her or if his jaw simply didn't allow otherwise. Ash formed behind her back, condensing into small pearls to allow for a quick fight, should one come to pass.

"Your species tends to spread. Too much. Too quickly. It is good for the young to experience warfare in a safe environment."

Ilea just looked at him. "Not so safe, given we killed them."

A challenge, perhaps, but his insult wasn't lost on her. The elf's expression didn't change, however, as he waved off her comment.

"Then you are a warrior. One capable of slaying elves. Where is your group? Don't humans normally move in bigger numbers?" the elf asked as he turned and looked at the massive double door.

She didn't reply for a while, thinking back to the elf below Riverwatch. He'd refused to follow them into the dungeon. Or hadn't been able to.

"It's a dungeon, isn't it? An elf claiming to be a historian, standing before closed doors that lead to an ancient city, full of libraries. Knowledge long lost in time." Ilea smiled and stepped closer, interested in his Class and level. "I'm a warrior, and as fate would have it, I've come here, at least in part, to explore dungeons."

He turned to her again and smiled, his teeth turning the gesture into something more vicious.

"Indeed? I thought you foolish for a human, but there seems to be something up there in that skull at least. Bring me what is hidden in this dungeon, and I will reward you. A task similar to those your guilds and kingdoms assign, is it not?"

"What kind of reward can you offer, elf?" Ilea asked, her head turning to the side.

He summoned a piece of gold. Not a coin, but a literal piece of unrefined gold.

"This is what you use as currency, is it not? To trade amongst each other."

The elf moved it from side to side, but Ilea's eyes stayed focused on his.

Am I supposed to dance or something?

"What do you use for trading then? Amongst each other, I mean," Ilea asked, crossing her arms before her.

The elf raised an eyebrow, "Do you suggest elves trade shiny metals as the basis of our economy?" Ilea shrugged, making him continue. "We trade knowledge, favors, and..."

He stopped, his smile waning. Ilea clapped her hands together.

"Good, let's do that then. Plus, I get all the shiny rocks and gear in there. Not really interesting for a historian."

The elf contemplated before he answered, "As long as you show them to me. Enchantments and metals can say a lot about a culture. You seek knowledge then? Or favors?"

Ilea was seeking strength, monsters to slay, and preferably dungeons. Getting anything in addition from an actual real-life elf would only add to her gains. Plus, Dagon and pretty much anyone else seeking knowledge would rip her a new one if they knew she'd botched this opportunity. She was also curious herself, if she was honest. The elves had been an enigma. An angry enigma killing thousands. She, however, wasn't about to judge a whole species by the actions of a few warriors.

"Sure, I'll show you the stuff. Does the dungeon start right beyond that door?" she asked, pointing at the rose.

"Indeed. However, I would prefer not to waste my time on this. Even if you claim to have slain one of our kind, I need to see your abilities for myself. I won't be left waiting here for a long-dead human who was foolish enough to fight through a dungeon above her capabilities."

Thought you'd never ask.

Ashen limbs expanded from the pellets Ilea had created, her spells activating as she breathed out, a grin plastered on her face as she moved into an offensive stance.

"The other humans in hiding may join as well. I'm well aware of the strategic benefits," the elf said, pulling back his hood to reveal pale skin and lightly curled red hair falling to his shoulders. Magic thrummed around him as he prepared.

"It's only me," Ilea said, rushing at him with a burst of speed. Her fist shot toward him before it collided with an invisible barrier. The force was distributed against it, part of it vibrating back through her arm before she moved away.

Her ashen limbs smashed into the barrier a moment later, and she pushed a total of eight spells of Wave of Ember into it. The elf raised a single eyebrow but didn't react in any other way, the barrier still standing strong.

[Mage – lvl ??]

Two question marks, could be just beyond my range or vastly more powerful.

Continuing the assault, she grew bolder and simply stacked her attacks again and again, her destructive mana slowly eating into the barrier before cracks formed and it shattered into glittering shards, at which point the elf vanished and reappeared in the middle of the hall.

Ilea blinked after him in an instant, her fist swinging at his face with all her speed. The elf's eyes widened before an unseen force stopped her arm.

Another moment passed and a thin barrier formed near her elbow and sliced into her flesh between the connecting pieces of armor.

He held her with his magic and formed a second cutting edge when she formed ash within his barrier, her arm still stuck but her ash now reaching out to him. Vanishing again, she watched him appear farther back as she healed her wound. The cuts were deep, ripping through tissue easily but not quite getting through her enhanced bones.

The elf simply watched her, gray mist swirling in his eyes, before she closed her fist again – ready to fight. A dome appeared around her suddenly and cut off all sound, runes starting to glow in a dark light below her. A cold feeling immediately spread through her and nearly made her vomit before she realized what it was.

Curses?

She had to hand it to the elf, his magic was quite a bit more impressive than Kyrian's. Her health started draining, but not at an alarming rate thanks to her own healing magic. Trying to blink out of the dome didn't work, and she could tell through her Sphere that digging under it wouldn't be an option either.

Instead, she spread out her ash, heating up as much as she could. Adding more and more to it, she covered the whole inside of the dome. Concentrating on her manipulation skill, she focused all eight of her ashen arms on a specific point.

Then, with an explosion of mana, she hit the barrier with all of them, repeated Wave of Ember spells ripping out a chunk of her resources. The barrier cracked and allowed her to teleport out, reappearing before the elf in the blink of an eye as her fist hit a barrier once again. He smiled, showing his teeth, and raised one of his hands.

"That is enough, human. I will await your return. Books and relics are your priority, as well as biological remains, should there be any."

Ilea activated her meditation, though the damage from his curse was already fading quickly with her high-level healing and resistance to his spell.

"I want to know something first."

He snarled and hissed at her, making her blink her eyes in a confused manner. "That was not part of our agreement," he spat.

Ilea chuckled and sat down on a nearby wooden chair. "Calm down, man. No reason to get all pissy. I know you lot don't like dungeons but I need to know why."

The elf looked at her and sat down slowly, claws digging into his chair before he replied calmly, "It is... forbidden."

Ilea sat forward, her elbows resting on her knees. "Really? Look, if that's the kind of information you'll give me in return for my services, I won't bother recovering even a single book."

He hissed and opened his mouth wide before he calmed down again, looking up at the ceiling. "Why would I bother? To play this game with a horrid creature like you…?"

"Traps in there, maybe your abilities are badly suited for the monsters inside. Maybe it's a sacrifice thing and the first one in dies. Or you're just bored, this is actually your dungeon, and you're a dragon trying to have fun with my little old human self," Ilea suggested and sat back. The elf stared at her in silence.

"Amusing," he said eventually, tapping one of his claws against the armrest of his chair. "I suppose it wouldn't hurt. It is forbidden. To enter dungeons. By those we serve. To add to that our biology is… sensitive to the mana density found within most dungeons. Just sniffing that door makes me want to puke."

Ilea nodded. "Interesting. Who is it, then, that you serve?"

He sighed. "I am tired. Of this, of your presence. You have my offer, and I will remain in this hall for seven cycles of the light. Do as you will."

The elf stood up and walked to the other end of the cathedral, taking a chair and summoning his book again.

"Seven cycles of the light? Who talks like that?" Ilea said, shaking her head.

The elf might know more about the Taleen, about my magic, or other dungeons. Worth bringing stuff back to ask him more. Not like I have much use for any stuff that belongs in a museum.

She stood before the door and turned her attention to the silver rose, the metal showing spots of rust.

If the lightning didn't kill me, this won't either.

She reached out for the handle and pulled, though only a little. She checked to see if the elf had moved, but he had remained in his chair.

The metal made a creaking sound, but her strength was enough to pull open the huge double doors with relative ease. She only opened one of them, peering through. Stairs led downward, and what greeted her beyond was a small field of green grass with silver roses growing in it, reflecting the light of the sun.

Stepping outside, Ilea took a deep breath, but she couldn't feel anything different. He had talked about mana density, but why did it affect elves and not humans? As Ilea closed the door behind her and walked on, a sound chimed through her mind.

'ding' You have entered the Tremor dungeon

The space was open and could've been reached by flying in from above, but it had felt right to her to use the large cathedral doors. As if she were truly entering the dungeon. She smiled when she spotted an armored knight standing with his back to her a couple of dozen meters ahead of her in the meadow.

Another talkative fellow, perhaps?

Ilea plucked one of the silver roses and smelled it. Metal was the only thing she could make out.

[Silver Rose]

Storing it in her necklace, she wondered how much something like this was worth in the human kingdoms. Somehow, she felt like her lack of affinity for plants would kill them quite quickly if she tried to grow them. Checking again to see if anything near the knight had changed, which it hadn't, she stepped forward.

"Greetings," she said cheerily, but the knight didn't respond.

His armor looked similar to the roses in color but was covered in even more rust than the decoration on the heavy doors. The sword in his right hand looked mostly intact, its handle beautifully crafted with a guard that looked like rose petals. Its blade was long, more suited to being a two-handed weapon, but the weight didn't seem to matter to the knight. A shield hung from his left arm, much more worn from age than the sword. Full plate armor finished the picture of a deadly knight.

He looked more impressive to Ilea than most of the adventurers she'd seen trying to emulate such a look. The knight turned when she took another step, metal lightly creaking as it moved. A closed helmet with two thorn-like protrusions reaching toward the sky hid any facial features that the man, elf, or dwarf had. All Ilea could see were white eyes staring back at her from the thin slits within.

"Hello, nice to meet you, Mr. Knight. Can you speak?" she asked, head cocked to the side, ashen limbs floating behind her. She waited. "I suppose not."

The knight didn't say a word. Ilea took another step, but that seemed too offensive for the being as it started walking toward her, raising its shield and pointing its sword at her.

"I guess your intentions are clear then."

Waiting for the knight to reach her, Ilea identified it.

[Knight of the Rose – lvl ??]

The sword lashed out toward her with a quick jab. Not enough to surprise her though. Ilea dodged backward to make space. Her ash moved out, three of the limbs impacting the shield the knight raised in response. He stepped sideways quickly and jumped to avoid the rest of her ashen attack.

Ilea's eyebrows rose before moving in, getting closer while her ash whipped out. The knight stepped backward while swinging, avoiding the ash with quick movements before he dashed first sideways and then toward her, thrusting his sword at her. Ilea had to blink to avoid the piercing strike but found the knight had already turned toward her.

Maybe don't blink into him...

Roses were crushed as he ran after her, his speed increasing with each step before swinging his blade at her. Ilea ducked down under the sword as her ash smashed into his side, destructive mana coursing into him. She felt some of her magic dissipate. *Intrusion prevention enchantment?* She didn't have time to contemplate it, his shield slamming down at her, forcing her to blink again.

Looking at the knight, she patted the side of her helmet. "You're a quick one, aren't you?" Her words had barely left her mouth before the thing was upon her again, launching a flurry of four fluidly executed strikes that she dodged with backward steps, most of her tendrils cut apart or blocked by his shield.

Evading his last blow, the sword swinging high above her, Ilea stepped forward, her fist impacting the shield he held before him as the force of her entire magical might crashed into it. Both held true, and a small wave of air pushed outward, rippling through the grass and roses next to the two warriors.

A brief moment passed before the knight stepped backward, sword coming down again to make space between them. Holding his weapon close to his shield, the knight was silent and careful, as if contemplating Ilea's every move.

She held out her hand before she formed more ash, a big cloud of it. The knight didn't move as she draped it all over him. Darting into the cloud from the side, she could see him respond exactly as if the ash didn't exist at all. His sword flicked out, and Ilea swerved away before she landed a punch into his side, his elbow jerking back to hit her.

The impact sent her stumbling back, followed by a sword strike that cut through her defenses, slowed down by her ash before stopping dead on her armor with a dull clang. Blinking back, Ilea felt an injury to her shoulder, and there was a small dent on her armor.

White eyes stared implacably at her before the knight charged again, his blade moving quickly and surely, leaving her few openings even with all her experience and high-level fighting skills. Her ash hanging on to him, she used reversed healing but again found a lot of the mana simply dissipating without effect.

A slash of his sword cut through the ash before he resumed his unrelenting attacks. Letting the sword glide through her Veil, she felt it scratch her helmet before her fist again met his shield. This time he pushed back, and Ilea's arm glanced off it before she blinked behind him.

Rotating, she drove a kick into his knee to little effect, the knight turning as he swung his sword. A step into a patch of dirt sent her tumbling and avoiding the blade, gaining enough time to blink away from him as the sword flashed toward her again.

Ilea's wings spread and she flew up, watching the knight below, who just stared at her. She summoned her bow and nocked an arrow. She was about to fire when she saw him draw a bow as well, far faster than herself. She saw the arrow coming and dodged sideways.

Of course. Where did he even get that from? I'm the only one allowed to pull bows out of my ass!

Trusting in her skills, Ilea returned to the ground and faced the knight again. Ashen limbs moved in from the side to hit it wherever possible while she simply stayed in his reach, dodging and weaving through the strikes. She could let some glance off and scrape against her defenses while others had to be dodged using her Blink.

Moving under the shield or to the side of it was followed by a hit with the sword's pommel or the knight's armored knee. Ilea was used to sword wielders struggling as soon as she had moved past their preferred reach. Not this one. Strike followed strike, and the once beautiful garden turned to trampled roses and churned earth as the two powerful warriors traded blows of ash and steel.

Sweat rolled down her brow, sticking to the inside of her helmet. Several dents in her armor marked every mistake, every step she'd miscalculated, and every time she'd misjudged his range. The knight stood there like a devil with two horns, shield raised and sword pointing at her.

His slow reaction whenever she blinked further away at least allowed her to use meditation frequently between exchanging blows. Still, she'd run out soon if she kept fucking up. She refocused and raised her arms, breathing out as she watched the knight come for her once more.

Sword slashing toward her, she moved backward, judging the distances correctly, and felt the air rush by her helmet, the sword passing through thin air as she stepped forward and to the left. Her right arm moved upward, punching his sword arm, mana dissipating from her skills, some into his body, some into the air. He stepped to her right and used his shield to slash at her. Ilea ducked and twirled to her left, her leg impacting his before the knight jumped back.

Jumping up, she watched the sword dig into the ground where she'd just been, her right leg kicking out before colliding with the shield, which he'd thrown at her. Landing several meters further back, Ilea crouched and panted, meditation flowing through her for two seconds while the knight rushed toward her, faster with every step.

No mistakes.

The moment passed, and his sword jabbed toward her with a piercing thrust, Ilea's body turning sideways as the blade rushed by. Grabbing onto his arm, she pushed mana into him while her limbs of ash hit his shoulder, three managing to swing around his shield before impacting his back.

Hearing the sizzle of her embers made her smile, but she couldn't let her concentration drop. The increasing effect of Form of Ash and Ember helped her get in more hits by the minute, but the effect had been maxed out for a while now.

I'll take you down... even if it takes a week to do so.

THIRTY

Tunnel Vision

Ilea lost track of time and space, all her focus on the knight before her. The knight that had ignored her ash flying into his eyes and helmet, had taken hits with her heavy gauntlets to his knees. Whose shield blocked all of her attacks with ease. Whose sword cut through her ashen limbs and left deep gouges and dents in her armor.

The dull light of the suns had long passed, the two warriors facing each other in complete darkness, neither seemingly inhibited by the circumstances nor the passing of time. Their only purpose was the destruction of the other as they danced through the once delicate field of silver roses, now churned to barren earth. Glints of silver shone briefly when Ilea's enhanced fist smashed into the knight's side, the impact of ash and metal against his heavy armor creating sparks that dissipated quickly in the air.

A spectacle of balance and endurance, the two skilled warriors battering each other continuously without either knowing the limits of the other. Ilea refused to believe her enemy was a sentient being at this point. It was either cursed, controlled, undead, or just a monster.

No grunts nor signs of exhaustion showed after all this time. Ilea was nearly spent, her brief respites in meditation not quite enough to keep her completely stacked. She moved through another of his openings, sacrificing a hundred points of health to enhance her strike that she moved past his shield and into his shoulder. A blink followed to avoid his retaliation.

She was one with the knight, his movements, his sword and shield extensions of his limbs, their strength and range more and more familiar to her as they slashed and danced around her in their endless desire to take her life.

Her mistakes had become fewer and her footwork had gotten better with what felt like every hour they'd fought. Every mistake punished with a strike that bruised her body and battered her armor or a shield bash blinding her with its sheer force.

And still, she was fighting, a broad grin on her face. This was exactly what she'd wanted, what she'd been waiting for.

After what felt like months of fighting humans, of dealing with all the complex, exhausting emotions that came with it, this fight felt freeing. Her opponent likely possessed no ulterior motives, no family, no shadowy organization pulling the strings. It was simple. Kill or be killed.

Ilea had wondered how a pure warrior with all their stats in Vitality, Endurance, and Strength would hold up against her accrued skills, and she increasingly believed this knight represented something of an answer. No magical powers, no sudden teleportation, no trick weapons, nor anything else. Just an armored man with a sword and shield.

Ilea doubted she'd have a chance without her ashen limbs, for his reach and control of the space around him, coupled with near-perfect and consistent footwork, made the difference between a sword and a fist clear.

Still, with time, she was learning how to exploit every weakness, how to move her body to bring his slightly taller frame into awkward positions. Long enough to get a hit in, though never more than one. Most of the time, she was forced to blink away right after to avoid his swift response, but if she'd learned anything in this world, it was that she should use every trick and ability she could to exploit an enemy's weakness.

A heavy step digging into the dirt, the knight closed the distance between them. His sword moved, its point aimed at her chest. A small step forward made his attack even quicker, just a bit more deadly, his shield already poised to counter any ability she might use against him.

Ilea sidestepped the blade as she had many times before, waiting for the very last moment to avoid a feint that had nearly cost her an arm earlier. Neither his leg nor shield moved, which still left four possible movements open as far as she remembered, but she stayed focused, her Sphere informing her about even the slightest twitch of her foe.

Pushing her right foot into the ground, she moved her body to the left, feeling his arm pass over her. She swiftly thrust a fist up, deflecting his arm a little, forcefully pushing destructive mana into it before blinking away, not waiting for his knee to strike her back.

Appearing far down the meadow, Ilea's meditation kicked in, her breathing heavy. Preparing for the next attack, she instinctively tensed up. Weirdly, no attack came. Breathing out, she took a moment to adjust. Listening while poised for another strike, all she could hear was the winds sighing through the last remaining blades of grass.

She stood and waited for a whole minute, refusing to check the notifications in her mind. One blink of an eye could be enough for him to get in a deadly strike.

My armor has suffered enough.

Still, if he was recovering, she had to stop it. Taking one step forward and then another, she carefully closed in on her previous position before finally seeing the knight in her Sphere. He was no longer standing. The man had fallen and lay there unmoving, his sword and shield beside him. Ilea checked her latest messages and smiled before she too found herself falling.

That was fun.

Her consciousness fading, she activated meditation and her healing, the soothing magic flowing through her as her mind focused. Power rushed through her blood again as she opened her eyes, but only darkness stared back at her.

I can't rest here.

She forced her body to move. The rush from the fight was fading, but her rational mind told her to check for dangers, not to sleep so close to enemy territory.

What about the elf?

Spreading her wings, she willed them to move her closer to the cathedral entrance at the top of the steps. Neither there nor behind the doors could she see the elf. He had either left or was still sitting in his chair. She sighed and leaned against the wall, sliding down it and closing her eyes.

* * *

Ilea woke up when the first sunlight reached down into the deep caverns, bringing with it the memory of her battle. Jumping up, she checked behind her, healing and meditation flowing through her body as well as all her enhancing abilities. Her stamina and mana had been dangerously close to zero when she'd finally beaten her opponent.

The knight…

He was still there, lifeless and eerie. His rusty armor, now even more damaged than before, fitted well into the scene Ilea surveyed before her.

Behind him spread a city, down into the dark. Splendid architecture flowed into the abyss before it vanished, the sunlight reaching no farther than a couple of hundred meters past the field of silver roses, which was more of a field of dirt and silver shreds now. Some roses were still standing near the edges of the meadow, unbent and uncaring of the events that had transpired.

Ilea couldn't help but start laughing. The clear sound rushed down the slope and into the city below, but she didn't care if anybody heard. This one was for her alone.

'ding' You have defeated [Knight of the Rose – lvl 289] – For defeating an enemy fifty levels or more above your own, additional experience is granted.

'ding' Azarinth First Hunter has reached lvl 230 – 5 stat points awarded

'ding' Inheritor of Eternal Ash has reached lvl 225 – 5 stat points awarded

'ding' Azarinth Reversal reaches 2nd lvl 19

'ding' Embered Body Heat reaches 2nd lvl 5

'ding' Wave of Ember reaches 2nd lvl 17

Calming down a little as she read through the messages, a smile blossomed on her face. *The first step.* She thought back to the first drake she'd killed, the first levels she'd gained from killing something that she'd fought alone. The rush of adrenaline and her joy for battle. It had been so easy, blinking around the drake as she'd delivered strike after strike, right before it shattered her bones.

Good times.

And now she'd taken her first step toward what she would become next. Her body tingled with excitement. Not primarily for more levels, eventual Class evolutions, third-tier skills, or better gear, but for the next knight that she would face. For the next battle that would take everything from her, from her skills, mind, and body. The next time she would dance at the tip of an unseen blade with an opponent worth fighting.

All of the politics, the revenge, all of the death that she'd experienced in and near Virilya had been a heaviness on her shoulders. She'd missed the feeling of a fight not weighed down by all of that. The rush, the danger of being alone in the unknown. Being truly and utterly free.

Savoring the excitement, she let the moment pass, thinking of an invisible Eve looking on with an annoyed frown. Of Kyrian giving her a thumbs-up and smiling. Wherever he was, he was likely stuck in a similar situation.

She sighed and closed her eyes. She knew she wasn't yet close to matching a Praetorian, the noble Houses threatening her friends, or even the Golden Lily, but it didn't matter. Because she'd just got one step closer.

She walked to the downed knight and checked on him. He was indeed dead. The helmet came off with a little more force than she'd expected, flying off into the distant chasm after she finally pulled it free.

There goes a cool-looking helmet…

It had been rusty anyway but would've still fetched a good price. Since she had her necklace, there was no reason not to store everything she could sell within it.

Claire will get herself some more work when I'm back. Just need a couple more lost civilizations added to the Ilea town building fund.

The face below the helmet looked dead. Deader than it should've looked. By now, she had seen her fair share of corpses, and this one was old. Some of his skin was coming off in places, yellow and cracked teeth showing through one of his cheeks.

"Undead fellow, hmm?"

There was no response.

I know terribly little about the undead despite having necromancer friends. Maybe I should care a little more about their hobbies.

She sighed and put her ten stat points into Intelligence as she checked her sheet. It seemed her Arcane Resistance had leveled again just from being in the north.

Nice.

Name: Ilea Spears
Unspent stat points: 0
Unspent 3rd-tier skill points [Azarinth First Hunter]: 0
Unspent 3rd-tier skill points [Inheritor of Eternal Ash]: 0

Class 1: Azarinth First Hunter – lvl 230
- Active: Destruction – 2nd lvl 20
- Active: Hunter Recovery – 2nd lvl 20
- Active: State of Azarinth – 3rd lvl 3
- Active: Blink – 3rd lvl 5
- Active: Azarinth Hunter Sphere – 2nd lvl 20
- Passive: Body of the First Hunter – 2nd lvl 20
- Passive: Azarinth Fighting – 2nd lvl 20
- Passive: Hunter's Sight – 2nd lvl 9
- Passive: Azarinth Perception – 2nd lvl 20
- Passive: Azarinth Reversal – 2nd lvl 19

Class 2: Inheritor of Eternal Ash – lvl 225
- Active: Veil of Ash – 3rd lvl 1
- Active: Form of Ash and Ember – 2nd lvl 20
- Active: Ash Creation – 2nd lvl 20
- Active: Embered Body Heat – 2nd lvl 5
- Active: Wave of Ember – 2nd lvl 17
- Passive: Ash and Ember Manipulation – 3rd lvl 1
- Passive: Ashen Wings – 2nd lvl 16
- Passive: Eyes of Ash – 2nd lvl 20
- Passive: Body of Ash – 2nd lvl 19
- Passive: Ashen Warrior – 2nd lvl 20

General Skills:
- Elos Standard language – lvl 6
- Harmony of the Drowned – lvl 1
- Heavy Archery – lvl 4

- Identify – lvl 7
- Meditation – 2nd lvl 17
- Veteran – lvl 6
- Arcane Magic Resistance – lvl 9
- Blast Resistance – lvl 12
- Blood Magic Resistance – lvl 8
- Corrosion Resistance – lvl 3
- Crystal Resistance – lvl 6
- Curse Resistance – 2nd lvl 2
- Dark Magic Resistance – lvl 1
- Earth Magic Resistance – lvl 5
- Fear Resistance – lvl 5
- Health Drain Resistance – lvl 19
- Heat Resistance – 2nd lvl 4
- Ice Resistance – lvl 15
- Light Magic Resistance – lvl 2
- Lightning Resistance – 2nd lvl 5
- Mana Drain Resistance – lvl 20
- Mental Resistance – 2nd lvl 11
- Mist Magic Resistance – lvl 1
- Pain Tolerance – 2nd lvl 4
- Poison Resistance – lvl 20
- Silver Magic Resistance – lvl 1
- Void Magic Resistance – lvl 7
- Water Resistance – 2nd lvl 1
- Wind Resistance – 2nd lvl 1

Status:
Vitality: 650
Endurance: 233
Strength: 182
Dexterity: 193
Intelligence: 621
Wisdom: 614

Health: 6500/6500
Stamina: 2298/2330
Mana: 5354/6140

Sighing, she could only imagine the battle if her Strength and Vitality had matched the knight's.

Someday, perhaps.

Grabbing him by the rim of his chest plate, she dragged the heavy corpse toward the double doors and pushed them open. She grinned when she saw the elf sitting in his chair.

"Hey, elfling, not a book but maybe still interesting."

He didn't react.

Is he asleep? Do elves sleep?

Dragging the corpse toward the other side of the cathedral, she chucked him right next to the sitting elf, metal clanking as it hit the stone floor. His eyes opened before he looked toward the corpse and then her, then sighed theatrically.

"Do I need to explain to you what a book looks like?"

"This isn't one?" Ilea asked, trying to look as confused as she could.

He just shook his head and summoned the one he'd been reading when she'd found him the day before.

"They are leather-bound, usually, but other materials can be used. Inside are pages made of paper, usually containing letters or sketches, even paintings," he explained without a hint of sarcasm, opening the book to show her. "Do you know these words? This is a letter, here."

Ilea stared at the book and blinked. "Aaaah, a book. But you can't eat that. You can eat that thing." She pointed to the corpse.

The elf blinked, then his eyes narrowed before he hissed. "Sarcasm. Of course. You are most bothersome. Right, normally I would agree, but the meat of an undead... a thousand years... maybe even older... won't be very tasty. Human warriors usually aren't." He looked at the corpse and then at her. "That was sarcasm as well. I forgot that you don't eat your kind. A peculiar thing, but not the weirdest I've seen."

"Took me a while to kill that one. You know its age? The gear is enchanted, I'm pretty sure." Ilea commented, sliding a nearby chair behind her and sitting down.

He stared at her and put his book away again, crouching down near the corpse before he touched it. "Your armor is damaged already. I surmise this exploration will take some time," he added in a murmur. "It is old, but the rust makes that much obvious. Similar to modern enchantments I've seen. It does, however, look suspiciously dwarven. With mana intrusion defenses, as most warriors would use. It is finely connected, but the helmet is missing."

"It just flew off, no idea how that happened," Ilea said with a straight face while shaking her head sadly.

He looked at her, sighed, and touched the knight's armor again. "This is something, at least. As per our agreement, I will answer a single question of yours."

Ilea had kind of forgotten about that part, simply proud to have slain this foe, so she asked the first question she had ready.

"Do you eat each other as well? Like other elves, I mean."

That's a stupid question, Ilea, she thought, but her mood hadn't diminished in the slightest.

The elf walked toward the altar near the end of the cathedral, raising the undead knight and moving it through the air on a shimmering barrier.

"Of course we do. Hunting and not eating the kill is a waste." His mouth remained open for a split second, but he didn't continue. "Does that answer your question, human?"

"I guess."

Gonna have to think of some more interesting things for later. I could've guessed that myself.

She left him to his devices, heading back through the double doors and closing them behind her. As much as he hadn't betrayed her yet, the thing was still an elf. Their reputation was questionable at best.

Now, where's my next fight?

* * *

Passing the former rose meadow, she soon stepped on a stone road that led downward into the darkness. Nothing moved in the distance, and no more knights could immediately be spotted, despite Ilea carefully surveying the area. She hoped there were more.

After a couple of dozen meters, the first line of mansions towered before her, the city and abyss beyond hidden by the warm-colored stone of the massive houses. It had a red tinge to it, perhaps a type of sandstone. If any paint had ever graced the structures, it wasn't visible anymore.

Everything looked abandoned, forsaken, and old. It was obvious that the buildings were crumbling, but there was no indication that a fight had happened here.

As if the people had been wiped away in an instant.

The knight was indication enough that at least unlife was still around. Ilea couldn't help but compare this place to the Taleen dungeon she'd been in before. The green lights, machines hiding behind every corner, and utilitarian architecture had made it feel eerie, like an outpost of some alien race abandoned to the machines when the air ran out.

This felt more serene. Like a place where an important mine had once provided jobs and a flourishing market but was now abandoned, the mine dry. Blinking into the upper floor of the mansion before her, she found herself in a dust-covered room. Metal frames remained on the wall, anything that had ever been inside them now a mystery.

The wooden floorboards groaned when she took a step, nearly breaking under her weight. Furniture remained, all of it barely holding together. Ilea was scared it would fall apart under her touch. It didn't – not quite yet, anyway.

It didn't look like the room was fully furnished. It looked like the people who had lived here left in a hurry and took what was important with them. Despite checking through drawers and cabinets, under beds, and in every chest, there was nothing of note remaining.

All she found were rusty knives and a sword whose handle broke when she raised it, the once likely beautiful blade clattering back into the chest she'd found it in. Staying quiet for a while, Ilea listened for any noise. Any movement that would indicate she'd attracted not quite unwanted attention.

Everything was quiet. Wind came in between the metal frames where windows had once adorned the large apartment. The second and ground floor brought similar results – old and broken items. The height of the doorways, the size of the objects, and the general culture made her think of humans.

The undead she'd killed had been human, but there was no reason to assume he'd been an original inhabitant. It was possible he was a guard placed by someone powerful exploring the dungeon as well, in which case she had all the more reason to be apprehensive.

The other two houses closest to the rose garden had similar interiors, just as dilapidated and useless as the first one. Ilea sketched down a small cathedral in her notebook, as well as the garden and three big squares. A small skull was added to the square on the left.

Still enough to explore. Guess I'll be focusing on the sunlit part for now.

She searched another mansion before she blinked up to the roof, looking over the area. Spreading her wings, she jumped from house to house before she found a large square, several hundred meters long. In the middle was what looked like a fountain, though the water that had once added to its splendor was long gone.

Ilea squinted and saw a lone figure enter the space from one of the side streets. His armor didn't glint, not anymore. Still, it was unmistakably a knight. The man looked like a mirror image of the one she'd fought the day before.

Jumping down from the house, she checked to see if any more were around but found the area otherwise as deserted as every part of the city she'd explored so far.

Guess we'll be fighting for a couple hours again. A smile formed as she casually strolled toward the knight. *Glad I've got my helmet, I'd seem fucking nuts if anyone saw me smile at doom all the time.*

After Ilea had walked into and through the fountain pond, the knight finally spotted her. His shield and sword rose in the same exact manner as her previous foe before he started jogging, then full-out charging. Heavy steps rang on the old cobbled stone.

Ilea focused, her skills circulating power through her body, as he rushed at her with his chipped and rusted sword. The weapon was a ghost of its former self, but in the hands of its wielder, it remained just as deadly.

Her dance began once more.

* * *

Hours passed, with Ilea trying different things, overextending from time to time, and paying the price with more damage to her armor and bruised tissue that healed but cost her time and mana. She was used to the weight of his weapon, the speed of his movements, and the perfect, near machine-like accuracy of his counters, thrusts, and slashes.

She was aware a single misstep could cost her life, but the fact actually calmed her. She was in control. This was something she knew, every muscle burning, ash covering the ground, her arms and armor.

She'd nearly gotten the knight too, his health surely low, until more were drawn by the noise, their combined attacks forcing her to retreat.

"Fuck! You damn fucking asshats. I nearly had him down!"

Her shout provoked another volley of arrows, all three knights now aiming at her flying form as she flew and blinked into and through various buildings to lose them.

When she couldn't hear or see the knights anymore, she blinked up to the roof of the building she'd found herself in and looked around. A plaza spread before her, starting after the neighboring row of houses and spreading for several hundred meters.

Old dry trees lined a road leading toward a massive building that had enough towers and detail to be a city of its own. She counted eight massive towers sprouting from different sections, each not as high as the centermost part of the massive structure. She immediately flew closer.

Ilea landed and peeked out from behind a tree, the towers glowering down at her, spaced around the complicated central construction, each looming over their own little buildings connected to the core structure, as if each were a fungal growth spreading outward. It still managed to look linear, symmetric, and certainly impressive. A shame that it lay lost and forgotten somewhere underground in the far north.

Ilea watched over the courtyard and started walking along the trees. The lack of life gave the imposing structure a near-divine feel. If anything had survived in this ancient graveyard, it was in there. Nothing intercepted her as she snuck up on the building.

The side entrance was closed, the big metal double doors worn, the silver symbols hanging loosely out of the dark steel. She could see the hallway behind the door with her Sphere, and a blink confirmed there were no enchantments preventing her from entering. Just to be sure, Ilea blinked out again and nodded. If some kind of dormant runes didn't suddenly come to life again, she should be fine.

Inside, the halls were dark, only glimmers of sunlight making it through the windows. The floor looked like marble to her, but its sheen was long gone. Checking the doors leading toward the closest part of the facility with a big tower, Ilea found them closed.

Again, she used her blink to take her inside. It was a big dome-like room in complete darkness, its shape only apparent thanks to her Sphere. Standing quietly in the dark for half a minute, she made sure nothing else was in there with her.

Blinking back into the hall, she held her breath when she reappeared. Two knights had just walked by, their heads focused forward. Their arms and armor looked less worn than the ones she'd seen outside.

One was carrying two short swords in his hands, each straight with a broad blade. Guards protected his hands, the steel nearly untouched by time. Sunlight gleamed off the weapons and handles when he moved past a window. The second knight carried a halberd cast entirely in steel. His weapon didn't look as clean and unused as the other knight's.

Ilea held her breath as she watched, her instincts telling her to run and hide.

[Kingsguard - ???]

Shit. Three question marks.

She closed her eyes for a short moment and flowed healing through her mind, then steeled herself. It wasn't just the level that shook her but the way they walked and moved their weapons as well. These weren't enemies she wanted to fight the way she was right now, and most certainly not two at the same time.

The knights passed, and she blinked to the next spot, deciding only to teleport for now as it was the most silent form of movement she could muster. Especially with her battered steel armor that creaked with every step she took.

Things are getting exciting now, she grinned.

THIRTY-ONE

Palace Guards

Kingsguards, eh? Meaning I'm in the palace?

Ilea blinked again, not moving too far so as to see any potential enemies before they noticed her. She'd explore a little more until one of them actually saw her.

I've gotten away from Praetorians, I'll get away from these guys.

They were much smaller to boot, only reaching close to two meters in height. Shorter and fewer legs meant a likely slower running speed. The three question marks worried her a little, of course. It was the next barrier and could mean anything between level five or six hundred and a thousand, if not more.

A couple of minutes later, she came up on a big opening toward the center of the complex. Cracked white stairs led upward. She blinked, avoiding another set of knights coming around the corner. Waiting between two pillars, she watched them move past before they continued on in the circular hallway around the center.

Blinking closer to the entrance around thirty meters further in, there were two Kingsguards standing motionless. Both were equipped with sword and shield. There were no more pillars between her and the knights, and while she was close enough to blink into the room behind them, she wasn't close enough for her to see what was inside.

The doors were massive, dwarfing the two undead in front of it, and were made of dark steel with silver engravings, just like the side entrance she'd used to get in. The ceiling above her was solid, and she couldn't see anything below her either.

Probably the throne room.

Ilea smiled and blinked inside, appearing in a crouch and looking at the two knights behind her through her Sphere, still guarding the gate she had just passed. They didn't move.

It *was* the throne room. Empty and massive. Two large thrones stood on a platform in the distance and withered flags hung on either side of the hall, some having fallen to the ground after all these years. Other than a few shimmering lines of silver, they had lost their color.

One of the thrones looked a little more pompous, and both, of course, were made of or at least coated in silver. A big flag of a rose hung on the wall behind them. Massive pillars stood in rows on either side of the hall, and Ilea immediately blinked behind one of them.

Kingsguards and a throne room. She checked every corner to make sure nothing was waiting to ambush her. *If there are Kingsguards, there might be a King. An undead King who could be even more powerful than all these knights.*

Part of her was screaming at her to get out, that she was getting closer to the center of this place, and she knew she wasn't ready to face whatever beings might be waiting for her. Still, she'd gotten so far, why not take another few steps? She had her blink and Sphere, after all.

And if anything, the potential danger just made this whole thing feel far more exciting.

As she blinked closer and closer to the thrones, nothing suddenly screamed or rushed at her. She stood before the bigger of the two, sitting down as gracefully as she could. Ilea smiled.

"Welcome, citizens. Your queen will now declare the newest laws," she whispered with a smirk, resting her head on one of her arms as she lazily lounged on the throne.

Sadly, the thing was fixed to the ground, otherwise she would've considered taking it with her. The noise of ripping it out would likely alarm the knights outside.

Or the one walking in from behind.

She blinked behind the throne, crouching just out of sight from the knight walking into the hall, thanking her armor for not making a noise.

Close one.

Blinking again, she reappeared a couple of meters behind the knight. It was another Kingsguard, carrying a single long sword. Identify showed three question marks.

Ilea fought down the urge to engage him, knowing that the noise would at the very least alert the knights standing guard just a hundred meters away, outside the main doors. If this knight didn't cut her to pieces before anything else even noticed.

Instead, she held her breath and blinked back through the doorway leading behind the throne room. She quickly scanned her surroundings, but other than stairs leading down, there was nothing.

I'm probably going to trap myself down there.

Of course, she still went, blinking down the spiral staircase that led deep under the city. Finally coming out after three blinks, she wondered if the Kingsguards patrolled all the way down here. At least she'd notice when he came back down.

The walls, floor, and ceiling were marble down here. Definitely too spacious to be just a storage room or the royal cleaning chamber.

What kind of fucked up experiments will I find here, I wonder?

Following the hallway, she arrived in another spacious hall. There was furniture here, benches, many doors leading somewhere to the side, different pots with growing shrubbery, and two knights in the distance, guarding a single corridor going farther in.

Ilea quickly blinked and crouched behind a marble pot that had some kind of red plant growing out of it. Checking the knights through her Sphere, she found ample cover on either side of them, some of the pots overgrowing with shrubs.

The hall was wide, and there were several doors on each side, though no guards were visible here. Looking up, she studied the red plant, perfectly fine and growing even though not a single bit of sunlight reached this place. Magic lamps on the ceiling shone down and illuminated nearly the entire hall, though some were broken. Listening carefully, Ilea could hear water falling in a fountain farther down the hall.

There's still power here.

This hall was powered, with plants growing under its lights. Either this was part of the dungeon and the higher mana density that the elf had mentioned somehow powered it all, or a massive power source was hidden away somewhere.

A mana crystal that works for a couple thousand years or something?

Ilea checked the two closest doors with careful blinks but found them locked. She couldn't blink inside either, which suggested some sort of enchantment.

Ilea tried all the doors and found an open one on the right. Opening it carefully and very slowly with her ash, she moved it just enough to allow her Sphere to see inside. The enchantments had to be connected to work – she'd learned as much from Claire's office in Ravenhall.

It was a good thing that she checked, as a knight stood motionless a couple of meters behind the door, shield and sword in hand. Ilea summoned some of the Dragcal meat she still had from a previous mission and ripped off a little piece.

Moving it with her ash, she put it between the door and its frame. Testing the stability, she pushed at the door with her ash but found it unable to close. None of the guards had been alarmed.

She blinked inside and found another hallway, blinking again just when she saw a sword enter her Sphere. *Patrolling.* She waited until the knight was close and blinked again. It hadn't reacted. She glanced back at it.

[Kingsguard – lvl ???]

How many of those are there down here?

The hallway had several doors, but only two were open. Both had a bed and some furniture inside. Checking through all of it as quietly as she could, Ilea found a book bound in leather and a smaller notebook in the same table drawer.

She blinked back out into the hall with her treasure. The books were in perfect condition, as were the furniture and the beds. Something was definitely keeping this area of the dungeon fresh. The knight she'd spotted from behind wore a set of armor that, although dust-covered, was still perfectly fine. *And a sword as deadly as when it was made.*

Blinking behind a counter, she found some bottles that looked like spirits as well as a bunch of kitchen utensils, ice in a metal crate, and a runed metal plate next to a sink likely there for water. She took the bottles with her and blinked into the hallway again.

There were five more doors she hadn't checked, but they were too close to the knights and offered nothing for her to hide behind. They looked like Kingsguards too.

Could almost be statues, given how still they're standing.

Blinking as close as she could without being seen, she was finally able to make out the knights through her Sphere.

Which means…

Ilea blinked into the corridor behind them, grinning below her helmet. Checking out the corridor, her perception ended in a small room that she blinked into as soon as she could. The knights hadn't heard her.

This room also contained a closed door, albeit a bigger one than the ones out in the hall. It too was warded with runes to prevent her from damaging it or entering. Ilea doubted it would hold up to a full-on assault, but that would most definitely alert the two guys protecting this place.

Ilea considered if she could use their power to break down the door, but where would she go afterward? Plus, she had no idea what one of them might be like in combat, let alone two. For now, it was more reasonable to look for another way in. A key, maybe, or someone who could crack the enchantment inside the lock. It felt frustrating, and she kind of wanted to just use force, but patience won out in the end.

At least I have a more specific goal now, she thought with a smile.

And she'd already found two books for the elf. She blinked toward the knights again and out into the hall, hiding behind cover.

Fighting two of them at the same time was unreasonable, and with active enchantments, she didn't know if there could be something to trap her down here.

I'll go see what they can do, and then I'll talk to Elfie.

Blinking back through the hallway, she came to a stop near the last bench, sitting on the ground to hide from the guards. Her Sphere barely reached the stairwell, but she blinked inside nonetheless.

Her question of whether the knight would patrol all the way down here was answered when she saw him a couple of meters farther up through her sphere. Blinking past him and up again, she was back in the throne room, humming the theme tune to a famous spy movie franchise.

Ilea realized that she found the thrill of hiding from powerful monsters quite fun. But probably less fun than facing them in a battle to the death.

"The day is still young," she said to herself as she watched the gates to the throne room open, blinking behind a pillar. As two knights rushed in and scanned the room, Ilea blinked past them and out of the doors.

They hear better than me, damn.

Moving around the palace, she found the enchantments from underground didn't affect anything up here. Everything was rotten, unusable, or just empty. Looking down from one of the towers closest to the main gate, she saw a single guard at the front entry that was situated towards the darkness. The light was already fading when Ilea looked down from one of the towers closest to the main gate.

The guard had a single long sword, bigger and heavier-looking than the one wielded by the knights she'd fought earlier. Jumping down, she landed in the plaza before the palace and waved at the guard, who slowly pointed his sword at her, lifting the thing as if it were a mere toothpick.

"Come on, let's see what you can do," Ilea said as her ash spread out and the Kingsguard slowly stepped toward her. He stopped ten meters shy of her and raised his blade, slashing sideways. Ilea noticed a thin line moving through the air thanks to her Sphere and crouched under it.

Neither her ears nor her eyes would've known anything had happened, but she trusted her Sphere, probably more than her other senses. Another strike, this time a slash from above, confirmed it. A thin cut formed on the stone below when his weapon came down.

Ilea blinked closer and was met with a thrust toward her heart. Dodging sideways, she was hit by the knight's fist crashing into her chest. Her armor held, but she was bruised, her rib cage damaged but holding.

At least he didn't break every single one of my bones with one attack.

"I'm going to kill every single last one of you," Ilea said when the knight slashed twice, making her blink right into a third attack he'd started when she activated her spell. The invisible blade cut into her armor at the thigh, going through her ash, her Veil, and the metal.

Ilea jumped backward but found herself losing balance. Probably because the leg that had previously been attached to her hip was now falling to the ground before her as the knight swung his sword again.

Blinking back, thankful that her pain perception was off, she spread her wings and flew upward. Seeing the line of air move through her Sphere, she twirled but couldn't avoid one of her wings being cut through.

Shit.

Falling toward the ground, she focused on stopping the bleeding on her leg as another blade sliced through the air. Ilea blinked again, trying to get around the palace to hide behind the building, her heart pounding in her chest. She was still falling as her second wing reformed, stabilizing before she sped up, blood pouring from the stump of her leg.

Okay! Not ready for those!

Flying over the palace, she continued on before blinking into one of the nearby buildings. Teleporting four more times, she came to rest in an abandoned apartment. The bleeding had stopped by now as she hopped over to the ancient bed and sat down.

Looking down at her missing leg, she gulped. Both her leg and the armor had been cut through cleanly, as if an industrial laser had been taken to it.

What exactly was that? Wind magic? Neither her armor, leg, nor bone had offered much resistance, it seemed. Still, her other leg had a cut only going about halfway into her armor. *So, I did stop it eventually.*

She breathed in deep, trying to get her heartbeat down again before she summoned a set of leather armor and took the left boot. It would take another couple of minutes for her leg to regrow and a ton of mana, but at least she wouldn't have to run away barefoot. She smiled to herself as the adrenaline faded.

A successful infiltration, and I'm not dead.

Putting her boot on over her newly regrown leg, she stood up and checked her surroundings. The sunlight had faded somewhat, but she saw a darker section of the city up ahead. It made her curious.

Ilea blinked out and soon found a wall separating this part of the city from another one. Parts of it were broken down, and she was now definitely in an area where no sunlight reached during the day. Her Sphere was the only sight she had.

She tensed up when she heard scraping. Metal against stone, uneven and close by. It got louder and louder until she saw a hunched-over knight missing an arm and half his head stumbling into the reach of her Sphere.

His breathing was heavy, the chipped and dented massive sword scratching into the stone before he looked up, as if sniffing the air. He turned away and growled right before rushing off with uneven movements, sword smashing into walls and other obstacles along the way.

Ilea considered for a moment, then sighed and turned to make her way back up to the cathedral.

Lost enough legs for one day.

THIRTY-TWO

Questions

The way back was quiet, Ilea avoiding any knights she saw moving through her Sphere. Few even noticed her blink by, and none pursued very far. Soon, she found herself in the rose field again, exiting the dungeon into the cathedral at the very top of it.

Ilea found the elf cutting into the corpse of the knight, all the armor lying carefully distributed on the ground.

To think this is the safe haven instead of the boss encounter, Ilea thought as she watched the cloaked elven barrier curse mage experiment with a human corpse in a massive, desolate gothic cathedral.

"Hey, I'm back. Found some things that might interest you," she said, sitting down on one of the benches near him.

The elf held up a finger, continuing to cut before he stuffed his hand into the corpse. Three seconds later, he ripped something out and showed her a shriveled heart, smiling through the blood on his face.

Ilea smiled back from under her helmet. "Congratulations on dinner."

The elf threw the heart her way and sneered. "Dinner. Look at it, corrupted. It's not human anymore."

"What does that mean?" Ilea asked, looking the heart over in her hand. It looked just like what she imagined a several-hundred-or-thousand-year-old heart from a corpse would look like.

He shook his head. "It means it is corrupted and no longer human. What is there not to understand, human?"

Ilea gave up and summoned the two books. "I found these, although I can't read them."

He hissed. The blade he'd been using on the corpse dropped onto the ground without care as he held out his hands, moving closer to her.

Ilea tutted. "Dude, you've got blood on your fingers."

He blinked, as if woken from a trance. "Oh yes. I was just..." he said, summoning a piece of cloth to clean himself. "How is it in there?"

"Old. Most of it is dust. There are knights in there called Knights of the Rose, and the dungeon itself is called Tremor—" Ilea started, but he interrupted her, summoning a small book and a writing implement.

"Slow down. And remember to enunciate."

* * *

Ilea told him about all she'd found, which wasn't a lot, but he seemed more than happy. He hissed a few times as he wrote everything down with a creepy smile.

"Is that all you have found so far?"

"Pretty much."

"For the price of a leg, I suppose?" he asked, accepting the two books and starting to look them over.

Ilea eyed him but didn't comment on the leg. "Can you read the language?"

He opened the books and nodded. "This city was a part of the Rhyvor Kingdom. There are plenty of relics and dungeons in the area, but I believe this was the capital. I have spent years learning this language."

"Why?"

"Why? I believe it is the capital because, well, these are the most extensive ruins I've found so far. And you speak of a palace-like cathedral. As to why it has taken me years to learn this language, it's rare to have books survive this long. A good thing humans tend to store things with runes against decay in place. A peculiar notion."

"How so? Isn't it understandable that one stores things in a safe place?"

The elf carefully closed the book. "Because your race expires so easily and quickly," he said with a smile.

"So wouldn't it make more sense to store knowledge in books for the next generation?"

He hissed, but the sound was different than before. "You're right," he said, looking at her with interest. "It does." He paused, then hissed again. "You have honored the trade."

"Good. Then why do you attack and kill humans? Half a year ago, your kind slaughtered thousands by invading cities in the west," Ilea said, taking out a pen and her notebook, opening it at a page with *'Elves'* written at the top.

He thought for a moment. "The west? I suppose that would be the easternmost parts of the Navali Forest. Perhaps the elves who attacked were bored?"

Ilea thought of the destruction in Salia, shaking her head slightly. "Bored? Thousands died…"

The elf raised his brows in confusion. "Are you not here, fighting these undead creatures? It is natural to hunt, even for some of your kind. You should be one who understands."

"Challenging foes, yes. I wouldn't go around killing civilians for sport."

"I understand, though it is difficult for me to feel the way you seem to feel. The ones killed, did they not have free will? Did they not have the will to fight?"

"They didn't have a chance."

"Then they were weak," he shrugged.

"You're frustrating," Ilea said. "Would you kill one of your young, just like that?"

"If they provoked me. Your way of thinking is peculiar, human. I cannot tell you why your cities were attacked, only that I, perhaps, would have chosen differently. It is not for me to know nor to decide."

"For whom is it then? Who do you serve? Another race? Some god, or just a more powerful elf? What kind of government do you have?"

He looked at her and closed his notebook.

"I might answer more of your questions, depending on the contents of these books. For now, I consider my duty fulfilled."

"Are you not afraid this knowledge might help humanity fight you?" Ilea asked as a way of provoking him.

"I am sure most of our kind would welcome a good hunt, and if it is elves who perish, then they will have fought well," he said, standing up. "At least, for once, it would be an enemy of flesh and blood."

An enemy of flesh and blood? Ilea wondered what that meant, though she had her suspicions. *Is that how all of them think? Some of those I fought sounded far more arrogant. He just considers those unable to fight back weak. A very cold and pragmatic way to look at the world, I suppose. Do they not care about their own, at least?*

"What's the book about?" Ilea asked.

"I have merely started with the first paragraph. Would you like a translation to Elos Standard?" the elf asked, not looking up from the book.

She raised her brows. "You would do that for me?"

He hissed. "I would."

"Thanks, but no," Ilea said. The elf looked at her for a moment, then turned away as if confused.

She supposed he had his work cut out for him, and Ilea was already thinking about how to tackle the dungeon instead. She could fight a single sword and shield knight, but not a Kingsguard.

The problem was that she couldn't just fight the knights where they stood because more were often patrolling nearby or could hear the noise.

Find single ones then. Lure them far away from any others and fight them alone.

She was already walking back toward the dungeon entrance. The night had just started, but that wasn't a detriment for her. She knew the rose field would be safe, at least most of the time, if the knights didn't change their patrolling patterns.

And if whatever that hunched-over thing was stays behind that wall farther down in the city.

Quickly moving through the houses, Ilea returned to a roof overlooking the first big square she'd found. Her enhanced sight pierced the darkness, but she found it hard to see the whole square. It was one thing to see when the moons were hidden behind clouds, but it was completely different to see in a dark cavern that seemed to swallow light.

Movement caught her eye – a single knight, as far as she could tell. Forming an ashen projectile, she aimed and sent it off. Hearing it impact something, she blinked down into the house below. She heard the knight's footsteps a second later, running over the square toward her before he jumped on top of the house.

Casually jumps ten meters high.

Checking him with her Sphere, she found it wasn't the same knight she'd fought before. This one held two blades. Still, he was alone. Blinking to the roof of the house opposite, she took a step. The noise immediately made the knight turn toward her.

Ilea jumped backward to the next house, and the knight followed in hot pursuit. The warrior's speed made Ilea blink a couple of times to get away, ultimately stopping in the rose meadow. Her own little dirt patch she had claimed for her murdering.

Not exactly murder, she told herself. They were undead after all.

His swords rushed at her, and Ilea noticed this one was much more aggressive in his movements and attacks than the shield-wielding knights. Dodging and weaving past his blades, her ashen limbs thudded into his armor. Some were cut through by his swords, others dodged by quick side-steps and twirls, but two of her attacks landed.

His abilities and weapons weren't meant to defend – they were meant to overwhelm and kill. At the end of the day, he wasn't much faster than the other knight had been, the only real difference being the lighter weapons and absence of a shield. A difference Ilea adjusted to in the first couple of minutes of the fight.

This time, she was much more defensive, not going for openings and instead letting her ash do the job while she concentrated fully on deflecting and moving away from the dangerous blades. While the speed and maneuverability of his two short broad swords were higher, they paid for that with their more limited reach.

After a while, Ilea tried exploiting the rare openings he gave her. Dodging to the left, she avoided a slash of his right-hand blade. She twirled, his second blade cutting through her Veil and scraping against the back of her armor before her left fist hit the small of his back with full force and all her offensive potential. He turned, one blade slashing at her before his second weapon moved in, forcing her to blink back as far as she could.

Meditation and healing flowing through her, she simply stood there, waiting for him to engage again. It was a battle of attrition, and with her healing, she excelled at that.

His flurry of attacks would continue for ten to fifteen slashes without giving her even the slightest potential for an opening. Were it not for her ashen limbs that had more reach than her arms, this fight would have taken days, if not longer. The swings he wasted on destroying her ash instead of attacking her body certainly helped with dodging.

Ilea's movements were getting more refined as she immersed herself in the fight again, and while the shield-bearer had inflicted several damaging cuts, this one was much easier for her to handle.

The fight ended as abruptly and anticlimactically as the first one had after what felt like a couple of hours. The knight fell, his rusted swords falling to the ground, followed by his body. Ilea fell to her knees as well, her helmet vanishing.

"That wasn't as hard, huh?" she asked into the void with heavy breaths and a smile on her face.

'ding' You have defeated [Knight of the Rose – lvl 294] – For defeating an enemy sixty or more levels above your own, bonus experience is granted.

After a couple of seconds, Ilea frowned.

"Where are my levels?"

There were none, and her questioning didn't change that.

I'd have gotten two back in the Taleen dungeon for killing something sixty levels above my own. And he was at an even higher level than the last one.

Unfortunately, her status didn't offer the exact numbers needed to progress.

Ilea walked over to the knight, stored his weapons in her necklace, and started removing his armor piece by piece and stored it all. Only the man himself remained.

Scratching her head, she thought about what to do. If she burned him, the light might alert more of them, but she didn't feel like burying an undead. What if he rose again?

Picking the corpse up and stepping out of the dungeon, she dropped it on the ground in the cathedral.

"Hey, can they leave the dungeon?"

The elf stood up and came close to the corpse.

"You have killed another one. Impressive. Monsters can leave their dungeons, yes. Although I have yet to see one of these knights do so," he explained as he went to touch the body.

"I think you experimented with the last one enough. I'd like to burn them going forward."

He looked at her with questioning eyes, hissing, "You would waste them like that? Why?"

"A farewell of sorts. Do you have nothing like it in your culture?"

The elf considered. "Not the same, but I suppose I can understand the sentiment. Why give that courtesy to your enemy? I am curious."

Ilea looked at the undead, his face half-rotten. "They are long dead. Once, they may have been renowned warriors protecting this place. At least, I'd like to think so. It's the least I can do to burn them. Maybe that way, they can't be used as puppets again."

The elf looked at her, the gray mist in his eyes moving as if sentient.

"Interesting."

"Can you help me burn them?" Ilea asked. "I don't have any wood with me. And I don't want to burn them outside this cathedral. The light may attract more."

The elf looked at her, then turned to the body. "A farewell?" he hissed after a long moment, then walked to the elevated platform where the first dead knight lay. He summoned piles of wood to build a pyre before levitating both the knights with barriers.

They were carefully placed onto the wood. Then he summoned a small metal cube that started glowing before a small stream of fire formed in front of him. The wood was set alight in moments, Ilea stepping closer as smoke started rising and the smell of burnt flesh reached her nose.

He stepped next to her and remained silent as the fire engulfed the two corpses.

"*Ner cerithial,*" the elf whispered after a while.

Ilea smiled. "*Ner cerithial,*" she repeated, getting the impression that it was something meant to wish them well. A send-off, perhaps.

The elf glanced at her, then hissed, the sound strangely affirming.

"How much wood do you have? I think there's going to be plenty more," Ilea said.

"You wish to burn every single undead in there? How many are there?"

"No idea. But yes, I do. Guess I'll be collecting wood from now on."

He hissed, this one sounding like one of resignation.

"I believe that will be necessary."

THIRTY-THREE

Of the World

"It is an interesting taste, I will admit that. But ingesting poison on purpose?" the elf asked.

"It's old," Ilea said, looking at the bottle in her hands, one of the spirits she'd found in the palace. "I don't know how it actually works with Poison Resistance and higher Vitality. I suppose you'd need stronger beverages to get the desired effects."

"And what would those be?"

Ilea considered the question. "Hard to describe. A light buzz. It helps you relax, also makes you more talkative, though also less receptive to threats, generally speaking. Reaction time is slowed as well. And if you drink too much you get dizzy, can't walk well anymore, and you might even lose your memory of the evening."

"It sounds undesirable for battle and detrimental to survival."

Ilea raised a finger. "But also, fun!"

He shook his head, hissing in confusion.

"You said your people are split into different domains," Ilea probed. "Is that a political decision, or something else? Is each just a family?"

"Neither. It is more to do with magic."

"Magic? Explain."

"You first. You mentioned you're not from this realm? Expand on that."

Ilea locked eyes with him and smiled. She'd offered the information to keep him talking, and it seemed to have worked. Still, she wasn't about to go into specific names or descriptions, lest the elves find some way to invade Earth.

"I'm not from Elos. I woke up one day in this realm suddenly and without warning. I didn't have a Class or any weapons."

"Peculiar. I understand that realm travel is exceptionally difficult. I doubt many of my domain have tried, let alone succeeded. Summoning is a different thing, but the demon realm is not the same."

"What do you mean, 'not the same'? I've been there before, actually."

He hissed. "You've been there? How?"

"A powerful human summoned a bunch of them and managed to open a rift to their lands. The Great Salt," Ilea explained.

"A name I have heard spoken by one of the Mind Weavers… A human. How did you return? Were you summoned again?"

"There was technology there… far more advanced than anything I've ever seen. It… I won't share how exactly I got back. Not with what you've told me so far."

The elf frowned and hissed, but his smile returned. He looked at the glass and took another sip of the ancient spirit.

"The Great Salt is different in that it can reach us more easily, at least with summoning magic. I hear the same is true for realm travel, but I am not certain of this. Our kind is rarely interested in matters of the fabric."

"The fabric?" Ilea asked.

He hissed. "Yes. That which connects all."

"All realms?"

"All, as far as I know, but this is not knowledge I deeply understand."

Ilea smiled to herself. "To think I'd be sharing a drink with an elf somewhere in the north and I don't even want to kill him."

"We have an agreement."

"Sure," Ilea said.

Too scared to admit you feel the same. She looked at him for a long moment, then considered. *Might be worth a shot.*

"Do you know of the Taleen dwarves and their machines?"

She saw his smile wane.

"I do," he said, the tone of his voice entirely different.

"A friend of mine… he was teleported away with one of their platforms. I—"

"He is lost," the elf interrupted. "Dead."

Ilea shook her head. "You can't be sure."

"I am sure," he said, then sighed. "Their machines… no, let us not speak of this."

Ilea sat back. He knew things, things that could potentially help her, but at the same time, she didn't want to push him too much or he wouldn't share anything else with her.

"Your domains, do you fight amongst each other?" she asked to change the subject.

He hissed, then was silent for a minute before he spoke.

"Elves… we… yes, we fight, though not for political gain or power as you said your kind does. Merely as a sport, sometimes revenge or because of law. But mostly... just because they want to."

"They... you don't? Want to fight other elves, I mean?"

He didn't reply, staring into space.

"Why do you think they want to?" Ilea asked after a while.

The elf looked away. "It is in our nature."

Ilea stood up and stretched. "I'd be hiding behind a wall somewhere far away if human nature was so one-dimensional. But here we are, an elf calling himself a historian and a human exploring dungeons that could easily take her life. I suppose we can be more than our nature. Or maybe this just *is* my nature."

She tapped her cheek, thinking about it for a moment. He didn't reply and turned his attention back to one of the books she'd brought back.

Ilea cracked her neck, ready to go back in and fight. Somehow it felt comfortable to talk to the elf, to someone who wasn't part of her species altogether. As if she was on vacation in a distant place where nobody knew her.

"What's it about?" she asked, nodding at the book.

He looked at her and hissed. "*The Wines of Rhyvor*. It is a guide for the vineyards of the future."

Ilea shook her head and started laughing, turning around and going toward the double doors.

"Speaking of which," she said, placing the rest of the bottles she'd found on a nearby bench, "maybe you'll be able to sort these by quality."

* * *

Ilea spent the next few days luring single knights back toward the meadow. Their range and skills were ingrained into her mind after fighting them for hours upon hours. Most of the ones close to the entrance wielded swords and shields, some rare ones dual-wielded blades. So far, she hadn't found one with a halberd or large sword and no shield like those she'd seen in the palace.

By now, it was night again, and she was rather exhausted. None of the fights had taken as much of a toll on her as the first one – a combination of meditation and healing had kept her going. She assumed her Reconstruction was helping with the strain this entire endeavor put on her mind.

Stripping the last knight of his armor and putting it into her necklace, she allowed herself to relax. *You need some sleep.*

The clattering of armor falling to the ground made her turn and look around, her skills burning with the little mana she had left after the fight.

"What?"

Ilea looked down at the armor on the ground and raised her eyebrows.

She soon found the problem, scratching her head after taking off her dented helmet. She was unable to store it in her necklace.

[Legate Guardian Necklace – Ancient Quality] [Storage capacity at 250/250]

Well, that sucks. I'm full. At least all the corpses had been stored. *Sixty-four storage units for eight armor sets? That's insane.*

Of course, it wasn't necessary to keep them all, but even with all her attacks, it was hard to damage them even slightly. She could make very light dents and sometimes rip a connecting piece, but otherwise the knights fell dead because her intrusive mana had killed them. At least, that was what she assumed.

Well, it is what it is. Maybe the elf has an idea of what to do with them?

Ilea lay down near the stairs to the cathedral for a breather. She was covered in both sweat and blood – not a condition in which she'd summon and sleep in her bed. She didn't really want to get out of her armor for now either, even with the damage it had sustained. Still, checking all her messages made her smile.

'ding' You have defeated [Knight of the Rose – lvl 263] – For defeating an enemy thirty or more levels above your own, bonus experience is granted.

...

'ding' You have defeated [Knight of the Rose – lvl 291] – For defeating an enemy sixty or more levels above your own, bonus experience is granted.

There were eight of them in total, and this time she did level up.

'ding' Azarinth First Hunter has reached lvl 231 – 5 stat points awarded

'ding' Azarinth First Hunter has reached lvl 232 – 5 stat points awarded

'ding' Inheritor of Eternal Ash has reached lvl 226 – 5 stat points awarded

Twice in Azarinth.

'ding' State of Azarinth reaches 3rd lvl 4

'ding' Hunter's Sight reaches 2nd lvl 10

'ding' Azarinth Reversal reaches 2nd lvl 20

With the level ups, only Hunter's Sight remained below its maximum current level in the second stage.

I'll have to focus on stalking them for a while.

Even so, Ilea doubted leveling it up would be quick as the actual fights didn't incorporate the skill's usage at all.

'ding' Veil of Ash reaches 3rd lvl 2

'ding' Embered Body Heat reaches 2nd lvl 6

'ding' Body of Ash reaches 2nd lvl 20

Considerable level ups. Finally! After such a long time chasing other goals…

She grinned to herself.

Don't you dare die out there, Kyrian. I'll outlevel you so massively that you won't even recognize me anymore, and then I'll get you back.

I wonder how Claire will react if I get to two fifty, or three hundred even? Probably ask for more money…

She giggled, wondering how strong she'd need to get to face the other knight variants in the dungeon.

Oh, and there are the Miststalkers too, and probably tons of other dungeons and things out here…

Ilea wondered about potential creatures waiting somewhere in the north, soon falling asleep. She dreamt of dodging a knight's attacks as he threatened to reap her life. That was the one thing she was focusing on right now, after all. The rest would come later.

* * *

It was still night when she woke up, rested and prepared for fighting. Her skills, which had flared up initially, were deactivated again, her battles having continued in her dreams.

"God, fuck," she murmured, rubbing her eyes.

Another set of rose knight armor was still lying on the ground next to her as she scratched her head.

A yawn left her as she stretched. "What shall we do today?"

Summoning a meal, some sort of chicken soup with vegetables and a fresh lime-like taste from a Ravenhall street vendor, she sat back and ate. The suns started shining into the dark cave when she was nearly done, illuminating the houses in the distance. She could make out the palace if she squinted, or at least the towers reaching above the rooftops.

Ilea stood up when she was done, putting the box away into her necklace. *How can this many meals equal five storage points and a single set of armor is eight?* She knew it had to do with volume and individual pieces. There was definitely some way to stack things, but either it didn't apply to armor or the pieces were simply not similar enough.

They did, however, look the same to her. Then again, her own armor took up considerable space whenever she stored it. Connecting the armor pieces on the ground together with the appropriate hooks and strings, she dragged them all toward the cathedral. Inside, the elf was still reading, writing notes or a translation into a second book he'd conjured out of nowhere.

Does he have space issues too? Maybe he doesn't lug around entire sets of armor.

Ilea left the armor in a corner of the room and went toward the remaining ash on top of the platform at the far end. Setting up some of the wood she had gotten from inside the dungeon, she carefully put the corpses of each slain knight onto the pyre.

"Elfie, got fire?"

The elf absentmindedly summoned the cube and threw it toward her. Ilea caught it and looked it over. It was entirely smooth, just a small cube around eight centimeters on each side. She pushed some mana into it and was met by fire rushing toward her face and into the openings of her helmet.

The elf put down his book and looked at her in disbelief, but she simply continued pushing mana into the cube and turned it around, the flames not even singeing her skin with her high resistance. It was enough to set wood aflame, but compared to a fire mage's spells, it wasn't worth a mention.

Jumping down from the pyre, she threw the cube back to the elf. He inspected it before it vanished.

"I see your success is accelerating. Eight this time. Congratulations on the two levels," he said, then continued working. Ilea walked closer and looked at his second book.

Wines of Rhyvor. He's translating it.

"What about the second book? Is it of more use?"

He hissed and wrote another line. "Perhaps. It is encoded, however, and I've yet to crack it. Translating this one helps me calm down. It is... irritating. Why make it harder for knowledge to be accessed?"

"For spies, maybe?" Ilea suggested, but he just hissed, a gesture she was used to by now. She wasn't sure yet if it was like a sigh or a groan. Then again, he did those too sometimes, which didn't help.

"I am aware of its uses. I am simply vexed by their existence, human."

Ilea nodded, walking back to the armor and dragging it toward the elf. The first set he had studied was neatly stacked on a bench.

"Can you forge something out of this? Mine is breaking apart."

He scratched something on the page with his pen and looked at her. "Do I look like I can forge armor?"

Ilea smiled. "You elves are just so amazing that I thought I'd ask. Any idea where I might find one? Need to sell some of the knight sets too." She considered if that would bother him. Old armor was history too, after all.

"Elves have two classes as well. You should know that if you've killed any of us. Yet we are in the north, not the Great Salt. There are still people about, albeit only a few. I'm sure a smith or two is among them," he said, his tone just as dry as hers.

Ilea stored the armor in her necklace, bringing it back to capacity. All the corpses she'd stored amounted to the same units a single set of armor needed.

Should just leave them on the bodies... or maybe a box?

Remembering how she'd stored all the things in Salia and how little space it occupied made it a reasonable idea. There were, of course, plenty of things in her necklace that she could sort out, but throwing away five perfectly good cakes or two kilos of Dragcal meat just wasn't on the cards.

The fire burned through the knights and their old bones, everything quickly turning to ash. It had taken all her strength to bring them down, and now a simple fire took care of everything.

Damn necromancers.

"You don't have the location of a city where people live that I could go to?"

"There is no city in the north. Not anymore, as far as I know. I have locations of other dungeons and am willing to give them to you on the same conditions we agreed upon before. Some are far away. Do you have a way of traveling quickly?" he asked, carefully turning the page of the old book.

Ilea nodded. "Depends on what you'd consider quickly. I can fly, at least."

"Flying? Foolish human..." He sighed and stopped working. "The Famine Crows will tear you apart if they catch you flying in their territory. There's worse up there as well."

Ilea squinted at him. "Well, I've flown by night. I know the storms are happening by day. Nearly killed me before. Famine Crows? Are those the ones with leathery wings? I never got close enough to identify them."

He summoned a notebook and flipped through the pages before showing her a sketch of the leathery birds she'd seen before.

"Famine Crows. I have seen them travel in groups of up to forty. Their levels, I would guess, are above three hundred fifty, but not above five hundred."

Meaning he's able to identify up to three fifty but they don't have three question marks? Ilea speculated.

"I have also seen them rip apart anything they touch. The only thing they don't attack is the mist."

"You mean the Miststalkers?" Ilea asked.

He turned in his notebook again and showed her one of the six-eyed monsters. "They are a part of the mist. I have my theories about them, but as I have said, not even the crows attack them."

Ilea smiled. "Well, there's little meat on them."

"I suggest you travel by day and only through the crevices and cracks of the terrain. Yet... you have faced these knights, in a dungeon, alone. I doubt you will wish to travel safely."

"Finally, you understand something. Got a map I can copy?"

She was debating if she should stay until her armor was completely done for. It definitely had a couple more fights in it, but maybe it would be better to survey the area and find some better armor. Going back to Ravenhall was an option as well, but she doubted she'd find this dungeon again if she left now with her long-range blink.

He hissed in response, looking at her with pursed lips. "That is information I have collected over many years. What will you pay in return?"

Ilea rolled her eyes and spread her wings. "Never mind. I guess I'll just find them myself. Sadly, that means it'll take me longer to find any more books for you." Glancing at him, she smiled. "A tragedy, really. All that forgotten knowledge. Old runes, maybe even poetry..."

The elf hissed again. "Alright, stop. Yet how do I know you will not simply vanish with this knowledge?"

Ilea shrugged. "You don't. I don't mind lugging a bunch of books with me though, especially if you can translate them. I'm mostly looking for dungeons and monsters to fight. Learning a thing or two about them in the process might be beneficial too."

She also wanted to learn more about the Taleen and their technology from him, but he'd been more than a little evasive whenever she'd asked anything related to them in the past few days.

"Look, I'm working with an elf, isn't the fact that I'm not attacking you or running away screaming enough proof that I'll honor the deal?"

He considered her words and eventually nodded, putting his notebook away and summoning a big tube. Inside was a map, which he rolled out and flattened with his magic as she stepped next to him. It covered nearly the whole table he was sitting at.

Ilea's eyes bulged when she took it all in. This wasn't just a simple map with some dungeon locations. Every crack and narrow corridor he'd found was carefully marked. Considerations, mentions of monsters and their locations, as well as places where the mist pooled were all noted. Hiding spots for the night and deeper layers, caves as well as water sources. High peaks, dangerous zones, and what she was looking for most keenly: dungeons. There was a whole bunch of them. Each named.

Has he really not stepped inside?

"Where are we now?"

He pointed at one of the northernmost dungeons: *'Rhyvor Capital – Tremor'*. The name she had given him.

Ilea nodded. "I think the closest ones are enough for now. Not that I don't have enough with this one already. Did you find any adventurers near any of them? Maybe some have lower-leveled monsters or are half empty or close to the surface?"

He looked over the map before putting his finger on one: *'Root Vault'*.

The dungeon was located west of their current location, but Ilea had no idea exactly how far it was. There were no reference points that she recognized on the map. However, there were many landmarks both outside and in the crevices that would lead her to the right destination. And they would let her find her way back to Tremor. She was already sketching into her own notebook, only focusing on the area leading from Tremor to the Root Vault.

"Anything you can tell me about it?"

"I could not enter, but there were signs of intelligent life. Fireplaces and hidden sleeping pockets in the stone walls leading up to the dungeon. It is possible these belong to the denizens of the dungeon itself, but it is rare for monsters to show such intellect. Especially ones from what you call dungeons. The entrance does not lie deep underground, but there are strong roots growing even beyond the point where I felt the mana grow denser. Perhaps you will find a trail there."

Ilea nodded and copied some of the notes next to the dungeon marker. Two other places were labeled that were even closer than the Root Vault: *'City – Rhyvor?'* and a place he had simply named *'Cliffs'*.

"Anything you can tell me about those two?" she asked, finishing her crude copy as she added the crevices, water sources, big mountains, and other notable features he had chosen to include.

"Other than that, they are *nar el ceroth*, dungeons. I would suggest you don't go to the Cliffs yet. I heard repeated powerful screeches from within, ones that would likely paralyze you before you could even enter."

Ilea closed her notebook. "What's your Veteran level at?"

The elf frowned. "I won't tell you the specific level."

"Right," she said, used to his reserved answers by now. She didn't know exactly how the skill worked yet, only that really powerful creatures could produce sounds or spells to paralyze her completely. "I'll keep it in mind. Any other tips before I go out? I've not been in the north for very long."

He didn't look at her as he rolled up the map again.

"Come on, you wouldn't want your only cooperative and capable dungeon diver to die in an invisible volcano or something," she joked.

The elf sighed and shook his head. "There are wolf-like creatures that appear at night." He turned to a page of his book where he'd drawn a simple but completely black wolf. "I haven't managed to identify them, but I have seen them disappear and appear at random."

He paused and closed his book again. "I've seen many species here. Many resemble what I have seen in the south, simply stronger and faster versions thereof. Do I have to tell you to avoid the ones as large as mountains?"

Ilea waved her hand in response. "I'll try not to enter their mouths."

"That might actually be the best option, if you can avoid the teeth. Other than the arcane storms you have mentioned, there are occasionally blizzards near the mountain tops as well as strong winds if you fly too high. Both are at least as dangerous as the arcane lightning," the elf explained, Ilea taking some notes in the process.

Natural winds as strong as Arthur's magic? she asked herself, remembering her cracked bones. If it was anything like as dangerous as the lightning, she'd try to stay low.

"Thanks. I'll be back in a couple days, maybe more, depending on what I find."

"I may not be here anymore. But I will return in time, to see if you have survived."

"If we miss each other, I'll leave a message here in the cathedral, along with any books I may find."

He hissed at that and put his map away, summoning the book on wines again in order to continue his translation. Ilea looked at him for a few moments before she turned away. She was glad she'd found Elfie here.

Elfie, I think I like that.

Elfie was someone who'd explored the north for a long time already – and an elf, for that matter. Dungeon locations were just one thing she could learn from him. She had a feeling he had a lot more to offer, and perhaps she could help him out in turn.

She decided to fly to the opening where the suns shone inside instead of up through the small crevice she had entered from. Looking outside, she found herself on the side of a mountain between rocks covering up most of the area.

Climbing out, she squeezed through a small crack, her armor scraping against the rock, and emerged on a steep downward slope. Arcane storms raged in the distance as she searched for the closest crack in the lands below.

Checking her notes, to the east of the Tremor dungeon was a long range of mountains, which she could see from her elevated position. *And there's another big one there, with a massive valley and a fissure at the bottom.* Ilea found it a moment later. According to the map, there were several smaller cracks leading to that valley.

Listening for storms, she activated all her buffs in preparation. With her destination in sight, she pushed off and accelerated in a steep dive with all of her speed. The clouds moved quickly and unpredictably, sometimes turning as if they were beasts themselves.

Ilea made it. Lightning cracked a couple of hundred meters behind her when she blinked the last stretch into the thin crack, smashing into the wall before she could stabilize herself. Pieces of rock fell downward as she ricocheted off the wall, jumping down and landing on the somewhat flat terrain below, now in the shade.

A trickle of water flowed through the ravine, ending somewhere between a bunch of boulders. Checking her map again, she would have to follow the crevice until she entered the valley, then head westward in a curve until she reached the Root Vault.

I wonder what it's actually called. And why did he call it a vault, of all things?

Ilea flew low and at moderate speed to be able to react to anything that jumped her, thinking about the Tremor dungeon and her talks with Elfie. For what it was worth, he actually seemed kind of nice – a little weird at times, but not unpleasant.

Like two strangers meeting on vacation?

The comparison made her smile. Of course, she was here for more than sight-seeing, and she had an inkling that the same was true for him, but she didn't consider her road one quickly traveled. Each step would take time until she could face more Taleen dungeons and find out more about their gates. Until she could take down a Praetorian.

She gulped, hoping that her decision to leave the Plains wouldn't come back to bite her in the ass. If Baralia pushed past Lys, Ravenhall could become a target, and she wanted to be there to help her friends and the city she'd come to call home if the need arose.

Ilea shook her head, trying to get rid of her worries and focusing on the here and now. Every fight against monsters up here in the north would leave her stronger, more capable. There would be many Taleen dungeons in her future if she wanted to find Kyrian – not to mention the far-off goal of revenge against the Lily. She should focus on that.

A loud roar cut through the air, but it was too far away to be meant for her. *And the way that thing sounded, it's far too big to be interested in such small prey.* The sound had come from ahead, so Ilea picked up some speed, finding herself more interested in seeing what it was than her self-preservation.

Coming around a bend in the crack, where it started to open up more and more, she saw the end of a massive scaled tail slither through toward the next section of the ravine, sunlight glistening on parts of its green skin. At the end of this section, she could see two ways forward. She was pretty sure one went west and the other northward.

With the tail going west and her destination lying in the same direction, her next step was cut out for her. A smile blossomed on her face as she watched the dark clouds above move past, quickly finding cover as arcane lightning smashed into the overhanging walls of stone.

THIRTY-FOUR

Hallowfort

Coming out into a wider valley, Ilea ducked behind a big boulder. An arcane storm was passing by above, and the valley was simply too open to provide ample cover.

The tail she had seen belonged to a snake, glistening green as the lightning cascaded over its scales. The next hiss that followed was enough to freeze her in place.

'ding' You have heard a mighty beast's roar. You are paralyzed for 15 seconds.

That's a long fucking time.

She didn't know if the size and strength of an animal would influence the paralysis duration. Maybe it had to do with the volume of the sound they could produce alone. Or perhaps it was a separate skill they used for hunting.

By the time the paralysis wore off and Ilea risked another peek beyond her boulder shelter, the snake had moved on.

It just tanked the lightning... Could I eventually do that too?

The thought excited her.

Another goal to add to the list. If I could shrug off something like that, I could definitely pull Kyrian out of whatever robot hell he ended up in. And I could just stand there and have that lightning hit me. Now that would be an entrance.

Would need a ton of setup to actually use it as an entrance though...

Checking for storms, she kept to the side of the valley and rushed through as quickly as possible, right until she could see the crevasse in the middle. Ilea quickly blinked toward it and flew down, landing on her feet a moment later.

The area here seemed deserted, likely because of the huge snake that had just passed through. Flying onward, she kept her Hunter's Sight activated to find any trail she might otherwise have missed.

The map Elfie had shown her helped tremendously with navigating the terrain. She could see dead ends and knew when there was cover nearby, so she became bolder when traveling the surface. Storms could appear and move quickly, but when her next destination lay just fifteen seconds of flying away, she'd risk it.

For a while, she traveled through the cracks, only finding small critters that fled immediately when they heard or saw her. The Root Vault couldn't be far off, Ilea figured, as she came into the crevice that, according to her map, led right to the dungeon.

Flying over a small hill, she saw the first roots that gave the vault its name. They snaked through the area like vines, creating wooden veins on the stony walls of the crevasse and burrowing through the dirt like worms. The area darkened as the crack in the land turned into a cave that led further beneath the ground.

The wooden roots spread out from the cave mouth like an infection, and Ilea traveled right into its center, leaving the crevasse and sunlight behind. More and more roots obstructed her view as she continued. Some were now as large as herself, breaking through the stone on all sides of the cave.

Wood magic?

The way forward sloped downward at a steep angle, and as the darkness grew, the roots changed. Thorns big enough to impale a human now grew out of the wood, illuminated by glowing flowers. Ilea gulped. This wasn't some oasis in the wasteland that was the north, it felt like a deathtrap. Turning her head, she spotted something in her Sphere.

Fresh blood.

She crouched down and touched a red stain on a nearby rock. Someone or something had gotten injured. Recently. Her sense of smell coupled with Hunter's Sight and her Sphere quickly led her to a small side tunnel. It was dark when she blinked into the tunnel. Water was dripping from the ceiling somewhere, and she could smell blood.

After several jumps further down, nearly no light found its way into the dark cave anymore. Her eyes could still make out the silhouettes of rocks and boulders, but Ilea was mostly trusting her Sphere at this point.

Soon, she could hear voices and saw light flickering on the walls beyond. Ilea slowed down as she got closer. A deep, gruff voice was talking quietly.

"It will be alright, Scales."

"Something is coming," a second voice said, ethereal, as if wisps had followed the sound to Ilea's ears.

Ilea stepped closer and now saw the trio in her Sphere. There was a lizardman grasping a nasty cut in his belly, a hooded and masked figure looking her way, and something that looked like a robot. Perhaps a slimmed-down version of those giant mechs Ilea had seen in cartoons back on Earth. Except this one was only a little larger than a human and nowhere near as bulky.

This one had thick, circular legs and arms connected to a broad oval-shaped torso. The limbs and main body appeared to be attached by cables and metal panels. Tubes extended from both its limbs and its central core before plugging into the thing's back. A set of pipes came out of its shoulders, ending in what appeared to be exhaust valves, and a nearly square head was set into the top of the torso. The robot was holding its hand against the wound as the lizardman coughed.

The hooded figure suddenly appeared before Ilea, a sword, clad in black lightning, leveled at her. Ilea instinctively moved to the right, hitting the figure's hand with her left wrist and punching at his side with her right fist. The man hit the wall of the cave hard, something breaking in the process.

[Rogue – lvl 172]

"I'm not your enemy," Ilea said. "But if you attack again, I will slap you again."

She walked on toward the other two after checking the rogue's vitals with a tendril of ash. He was fine. The robot turned to her when she approached, saws extending out of his arms. The lizardman's breath was coming in pained grunts, and his yellow reptile eyes stared at her in the dark.

"Calm down, I'm a healer," she said, continuing toward the lizardman, the robot not moving as he watched her. She knelt before the injured lizardman, her back to the robot. "What happened to him? His health is draining quickly."

Poison, she thought as she pushed healing mana into the creature. He groaned in pain, making the robot tense up a little behind her, two spear-like objects slowly extending out of its chest.

"Stop... Stonebreaker..." the ethereal voice said, the one Ilea now knew belonged to the rogue. "She is... healing him," the hooded man added as he rejoined the group, breathing heavily.

"What did you do?" the robot asked, rushing to the masked figure's side. His was undoubtedly the deep, gruff voice Ilea had heard earlier.

Ilea stabilized the lizardman, his eyes closing as the poison she sensed coursed through his body.

"The rogue? I broke something near his shoulder, nothing more. He has several cuts on his legs as well. Those worry me more, but they didn't come from me."

"Damn fool," the robot said and tried to rip away the mantle covering the rogue's legs.

The hooded figure stopped him. "I will be fine. No poison," the ethereal voice said. Ilea could see wisps of smoke coming from behind the black mask under the hood, its smooth surface turning her way.

Ilea continued healing and said, "I'll take care of him afterward."

The robot glanced in her direction, though it had no eyes in its headpiece. "You asked what happened to him? One of the monsters in the nearby dungeon happened. He was poisoned. His health is draining."

Whatever poison it was, Ilea acknowledged, it was strong.

"The one with the roots?" she asked.

The robot walked over to her and crouched down next to the lizardman. "Yes. We knew there were monsters with venom, but they're more cunning than we anticipated."

His voice isn't coming from the head, Ilea noticed. Were her own body poisoned, she'd be healed already, but the different biology of the lizardman made it harder than healing another human. Still, she fully trusted her skill, not helping guide the mana or focusing overly on specific parts of his body.

"No antidote? Do you have whatever caused the poison? Maybe that will give me some info."

The robot nodded, checking one of the packs lying next to the lizardman before he took out a box.

"No antidote yet. The alchemist has given up on it. Their poison varies in properties and even changes completely from time to time." He took out a monster's claw about as large as her hand that looked more like a thorn, gray and ending in a sharp slightly glistening tip. "Careful, human."

She just looked at him and grabbed the thing. Rolling down the pant leg where her armor had been sliced off, she turned the thorn and pushed it into her leg. It pierced her skin with a little application of force.

The robot stiffened. "What… what are you doing?"

"Testing," Ilea said with a smile.

'ding' You have been poisoned by Drop Saurian venom, -25 Health per second for five minutes.

Enough to kill me, without healing, and that's from a single scratch of this thing. She looked at the lizardman and frowned. Luckily, he was over it already. *Good thing I found them.* The lizardman was at level one forty and the robot man at one eighty, both identifying as mages.

"Why would you poison yourself? Do you have a way to produce an antidote that way?" the robot asked, obviously confused.

Then the lizardman opened his eyes and gasped for air. Ilea let go of him and simply let healing mana flow through herself instead, the pain a dull pulsing in her leg as she walked over to the rogue.

He tensed up when she touched him but relaxed when she took care of his shoulder and then the cuts on his leg. Something about his anatomy was strange but fascinating nonetheless. Ambiguous in a way that she couldn't quite figure out.

Ilea continued looking at him through her healing skill even after his cuts had been healed. "What are you?" she asked, looking at his mask.

He pushed her away a little and got up, Ilea not resisting.

"No wonder you can't get poisoned," she said, turning to the others.

The rogue didn't reply, but she didn't press him any further. Perhaps revealing such information was offensive to whatever species he was.

'ding' Poison Resistance reaches 2nd lvl 1
You are a target of assassins or not very good at distinguishing berries. Surviving either of those, you have developed a general resistance to poisons. 2nd stage: Either you need better guards or you need to stop eating everything you see. Experience has granted you the ability to sense poison. Additionally, its spread throughout your body is slower, reducing its effects.

That's why I poison myself, Ilea thought with a smile.

The rogue walked over to the others as Ilea watched them help up the lizardman, who was still weakened from his exertions and near-death experience.

"We have to go. A trail of blood was left behind that could lead them to us," the robot said, turning to Ilea. "What do you seek as payment, warrior healer?"

Ilea scratched her chin. "I need a place to sell my things and, more importantly, a smith. You've got a lot of metal on you. Know anyone around that fits that description?"

The robot moved in a way that approximated a nod. "I do. Come with us," he said and started walking into the dark. Then he paused. "He's not a pleasant one, but perhaps you won't be too bothered by his presence." He laughed, the sound echoing in the cramped and dark cavern. "If the poison doesn't kill you before we get back, that is."

A click echoed in the enclosed space as a small part of his helmet opened up, something akin to an eye flashing, an enchantment activating, before light flooded into the dark cave.

"Quiet now, or we'll attract unwanted attention," he added before they climbed down through a tight opening.

"You were the one laughing out loud," Ilea pointed out.

"True. I should shut up too then," he chuckled.

Ten minutes of silent climbing later, they came into a tunnel that seemed unnatural, its walls straight rather than rough and twisting. Now that he stood upright, Ilea noticed for the first time how tall the robot was. He was easily two and a half meters, even taller than the lizardman. The rogue was the only one similar in size to Ilea.

"Where are we going?" she asked after a couple of minutes of walking down the corridor.

The light of the robot's headlight flashed over at her before it shifted forward again. "Hallowfort. Our home."

Ilea looked at the others, but they ignored her, lost in their own thoughts. "That doesn't really tell me anything, robot man."

He laughed at that, deep and loud, before he checked behind them.

"We should be safe now. You'll see, adventurer. Given your worn armor, I think you'll fit right in. I will show you to the smith, and put in a good word for you, as soon as we're there. Though I doubt that mess you're wearing is fixable," he added. "Shame. Looks like it might've once been a good piece."

"It was," Ilea said, absentmindedly touching the gap in her chest piece where the Birmingale girl had punched her sword clean through it.

Feels like so long ago.

"We're here," the robot said. They stood in front of a section of the wall that looked to Ilea's eyes like any other. Though still smooth and looking more man-made than earlier tunnels, there were no distinguishing marks or features. Her Sphere told a different story, though. This piece of wall was actually a thick stone plate, covering an entrance.

Pushing the plate aside, the robot gestured for them all to go into the newly revealed passage. Following them inside, he pulled the massive stone gate back into place with a handle that was attached to the other side.

Moving past the others, he touched a runed plate embedded in the wall at the other end of the short tunnel. A section of the ground opened up immediately. Fresh air rolled out, and Ilea only realized now how stale it had gotten the deeper they went.

"Careful, it's a bit of a drop."

Ilea waited until they were all through before she looked down, jumping and landing two seconds later, glancing at the waiting trio. They stood at the edge of a massive cliff, crystals growing on the stone behind and around them, stretching for kilometers into the underground cavern, illuminating everything in a pale light.

Ilea stepped toward the edge and looked down. Several hundred meters of air ended in what looked like a massive lake. Natural stone pillars grew from the lake up toward the ceiling, everything covered by patches of white crystals.

A bridge lay a hundred meters to her right and led over a chasm to a massive plateau. Warm torchlight flickered in the distance, interspersed with magical lamps. Houses of all sizes and styles dotted the plateau, which was actually the top of a massive statue depicting a humanoid figure, though its head was missing. The stone monument stood on the natural rock below before all was swallowed by the distant lake.

"Alright," Ilea smiled. "I'm impressed."

She finished taking in the view and glanced over at the robot. His metal body was rusted in parts, dark gray and black as well as patches of red showing.

"Welcome to Hallowfort."

"No monsters here?"

"Rarely. They reside down in the lake or in the Descent. We're safe here from the storms as well as most wild beasts. Come now, a warrior able to heal will be a most welcome visitor," he said, making for the bridge.

Ilea nodded and went to follow but stopped as the lizardman fell to one knee before her.

"I owe you my life, warrior," he said.

Ilea grinned and flicked his lizard-like head. "You owe me a drink."

The lizard looked confused when the robot started roaring with laughter.

"You heard the girl. Come on, before you get yourself into more debt than you can carry," he said, helping him up.

A three-meter-tall guard wearing dark full plate armor and carrying a hammer as big as Ilea grunted when they came over the bridge and entered Hallowfort.

The town wasn't big, nothing compared to any of the cities in the Plains. Perhaps a village, or even just a large camp, but what it lacked in numbers and size, it won back in diversity. To Ilea, it felt just as alive as any bigger city she'd been to. Half the species running around, trading and shouting, she had never seen before.

Is that a dwarf?

The man was as tall as a kid but with sturdy arms and legs, no hair on his head, and a scar on his scalp.

The smells of unknown foods mixed with body odors that were entirely alien to her as they walked through the village. She grinned to herself.

Now this is a proper adventure.

The robot stopped when they arrived at a small house. "I'll see you later, let me know how it goes," he said to the rogue.

The man didn't reply, nodding slightly at Ilea before he vanished. The lizard bowed deeply before he too said his goodbyes, at least for now.

"Come on in," the robot said, opening the door. He stepped into a contraption near the wall before his chest opened. Steam blasted from both the pipes on his back as well as the chamber itself before a man about one meter forty in height jumped out. He had a black bushy beard, and one mechanical eye looked at her from under a mop of greasy black hair as he stretched out his hand.

"Terok Stonebreaker, very happy to make your acquaintance."

Ilea smiled and shook his hand. "Ilea Spears. The same. You were moving that machine?"

"Never seen a dwarf and his rig?" He laughed and walked over to it. "It's smaller than most, but trust me, this thing can take a punch. The runes and gears allow for the finest movements when coupled with my metal magic. Not the most beautiful thing, but it does the job. Don't ever insult it or I'll pummel you." He laughed again before punching the exoskeleton.

"Fascinating. You think I could get one of them too?"

He frowned. "Well, you could try, but it's hard without metal magic. The fine control, I mean. You need specific metal too, and a lot of metalwork and enchanting experience, though I suppose you could simply pay someone to build you one. Still wouldn't exactly recommend it, seeing as you've trained to fight without one. War machines take a while to learn to control, and far longer to master."

Ilea smiled. "Maybe something for the future then, I've got plenty to work on as it is." She looked at the machine and then back at Terok. "You mentioned knowing a smith. Is it you?"

The dwarf grinned. "Oh yeah, the smith. Not me, but I have someone in mind," he said and opened the door again, beckoning her to follow.

"Scales was good as dead, so I'm glad you appeared," Terok said as he led her through the village. "What brings you here anyway?"

"Looking to fight monsters," Ilea said. "And maybe find some Taleen ruins."

He laughed. "Monsters, we got plenty. Taleen ruins might be more difficult to find. Deathtraps of the worst kind, those. Recommend you get a bit stronger first before you try and delve anywhere like that."

"That's the plan. You know much about them? Being a dwarf and all?"

Terok squinted at her. "Cause I'm a dwarf I should know about the Taleen? I feel insulted. But no. Ancient civilization, that one, same as plenty of others you'll find here in the far north. Most dwarves I know aren't particularly fond of what the Taleen left behind. Building machines to fight *for* them, it's not our way. Not my way."

"You like things more hands-on then?"

"In the thick of it, yes," he grinned.

"I get it."

"I can tell you do."

Ilea spotted smoke coming out of a large building across the road and heard the sounds of a hammer hitting metal.

"What about that one?" she asked as Terok led her further into the village, away from the forge.

"She's not bad, but I'll introduce you to someone better. He's just… a little peculiar, and being close to him is dangerous… but I have an inkling that you'll be fine."

THIRTY-FIVE

Floating Wisdom

Terok led her down a stairwell into the stone itself. Everything here was carved into the inside of the statue that the settlement was built upon, many side halls leading to living quarters or rooms with other purposes.

This place is bigger than I thought.

The space was full of adventurers of all shapes and sizes. Some looked to be comprised of floating energy, others wore heavy armor, fur sticking out from between the pieces or horns adorning their heads. Some had leathery wings, and still others had green tails.

Their weapons too looked to be chosen with their respective sizes and forms in mind. A large stone-skinned being with a round belly and three eyes bore a sword twice the size of Ilea. Many didn't look to be armed, but Ilea assumed they used magic of some kind, or perhaps they weren't combatants in the first place.

Some of the beings looked at her when she passed, but nobody seemed to care much. A refreshing reception compared to most humans, who immediately started whispering about her being a Shadow.

After another few minutes, Terok stopped and motioned down a hallway. A ruddy red glow came from the far end.

"Hey, master smith!" Terok shouted down the hall. "This warrior here has saved a friend, a citizen of Hallowfort. Thought you could offer her your services in return!"

They waited for about a minute, but no response came. Ilea looked at the dwarf, who seemed increasingly unsure about his life choices.

"Why can't we just go in?" Ilea asked.

He gestured at the ground and walls. "There are runes in place to prevent entry, curses and dark magic. He normally only works with those who can cross them unharmed."

Ilea's grin must have been rather terrifying.

"Oh. Why didn't you just say that?" Ilea started walking down the hallway. "I'll see you around, Terok. Thanks for showing me the way."

He watched on, jaw hanging slightly open, before he chuckled and shook his head.

Ilea could feel a light feeling of nausea spreading in her stomach, but it was nothing major. Nor was the health drain that started a couple of meters farther in. Her healing easily canceled it out. She heard Terok laugh, so she glanced back at him.

"Good luck, then," he called.

Ilea gave him a thumbs-up as she moved toward the smithy. A couple more steps, and the sounds from behind her were cut off entirely, replaced by the sound of a hammer hitting metal coming from farther down the stone hallway.

The hallway soon opened up, with stairs leading down into a large space where a being made of dark mist hovered near an anvil. It… he? had two arms that looked solid, while the rest was more fluid and cloud-like, similar to her ash.

[Smith – lvl 212]

Higher level than even Balduur.

She decided to wait until he was done with whatever he was working on. There was a plethora of machines in the room, tools and metal structures she'd never seen, nor did she have any idea what purpose they served.

Sitting down on a workbench a little to the side, she continued healing herself. Neither the curse nor the health drain had lessened since she'd entered. The thing that the smith was working on, which was shaped like just the handle of a weapon, looked awfully small in her Sphere.

Isn't the blade done first and then the handle added?

Summoning her notebook, she wrote down the name of the poison and the monster that had attacked the lizardman. Another thing she could hunt and kill, hopefully at a similar level range to the rose knights – or even higher.

Terok mentioned something else as well… the Descent. She smiled to herself. *I've got an elf ready to trade information, and now I have an entire settlement to explore and ask questions.*

Her thoughts were interrupted when a whisper echoed through the whole room.

"A new traveler seeking the work of Goliath," the smith said, turning around, two golden eyes looking out of the dark mist as it held up the finished product.

"A door handle?" Ilea asked, looking at the thing. She blinked. "I'm Ilea, it's good to meet you."

"A job for one of my dear friends. Payment for a joke well told," he explained and hovered a little closer. "You… you are here for that armor, are you not? Or have you lost your weapons too?" he asked, the whisper coming from several directions at once, confusing Ilea quite a bit.

"Just the armor, my weapons are fine," she said and stood up, walking around the room to discern how he did the thing with his voice.

"I am not interested in working with mundane steel. Have you found any interesting metals on your journey?"

Ilea considered, then summoned her elven set of armor, now mostly destroyed, that she'd found in the Taleen dungeon.

The smith hovered after her and stopped next to the workbench she'd put the armor on. "Niameer steel. Rare to see it these days. The elves of old used to favor it, did they not?"

Ilea cocked her head to the side and turned around. "Why do I hear you like a surround sound system?"

The smith made a weird noise, his eyes squinting a little and bobbing up and down. A laugh, perhaps.

"It is what I am. The magics of the dark are not favorable for those of the living flesh. You must have felt it when you entered? The curse, my unending hunger for life and its source."

"You mean that's you? You didn't put up runes to make people not come here?"

He shook what passed for his head. "No runes. Simply my nature. It can get lonely as a result. Sadly, most cannot stomach being close to me. Your kind… what are you then? An elf? A dwarf? No… you would not like the mana here, and you are too tall for a dwarf. An Awakened, then, but one of life?" he asked inquisitively.

"I'm human."

His eyes moved up a little before he spoke. "Human? What a rare visitor. It has been long since your kind walked these lands. Those of weak blood now find it hard to travel here. To even stand where you do is an achievement not gained without strife. I salute you," he said and bowed a little. "The Awakened often find conversation tiring, yet it leaves my forge silent. Were it not for my work, one might question why I even rose to consciousness."

The smith was either old and wise, a being of great power, or perhaps just a madman who had gone crazy here in his forge.

The elves don't like the mana here? Because of the density? Awakened? Since our kind walked these lands?

"It's nice to meet you. I salute your dedication to the forge. You are the first smith of such a level I've met."

The smith made his weird sound again. "Amusing. Humans are a curious race. A long time it has been. Truly. For this alone, I shall grant your request."

Nice.

The being leaned forward. "A set of armor, then, for the young warrior." He inspected the mangled Juggernaut armor she had offered him. "That damage, were you caught by surprise? Or is this due to how you fight?"

Ilea smiled. "I like a very direct approach."

He shook his head, the black mist swirling and obscuring the two golden eyes set within before it all stabilized again.

"How did you survive this kind of damage? Though I suppose a battle-healer might be able to recover, even if their armor is broken. Very broken."

Ilea crossed her arms in front of her. "I'm trying my best, okay?"

"Do not feel offended, human. It is a good metal, all the more so for its rarity. It is strange, however. It usually excels in hiding sound and light, not in its durability. As a precious ore, it can certainly hold up to other, baser metals, but with time, its shape will dent, its glimmer will fade," the smith explained as he lifted some of the pieces up, looking them over carefully.

Ilea summoned one of the rose knight sets onto the workbench instead. "What about these then? The ones who fought me recently used that." She placed a sword beside it, just in case it was a different metal.

Grabbing the chest plate, the smith contemplated, turning it over and over again. "I am uncertain with all this grime and age. Do you have more?"

"Sure," Ilea said with a grin. "I've got plenty."

His eyes moved up, the change almost making him look happy. "Good. I cannot determine its properties without working it. Hold on."

He took the breastplate, put it on the anvil, and started to hammer. He hit harder with each strike and paused as if considering before each swing, tapping it from time to time before he came down hard again. Finally, he grunted and chucked it into the biggest forge in the room, sets of runes in the room and inside the forge lighting up before the heat in the air went up by at least fifty degrees.

No wonder nobody comes in here, Ilea thought, noticing the flare, but her Heat Resistance and healing kept her healthy. Even so, it didn't stop getting hotter. Soon, her clothes started catching fire, the room not cooling down for a long while.

Ilea covered herself in ash, then stored her armor when the steel started glowing and burning her skin. She summoned a set of leather armor when it started to cool down again.

'ding' Heat Resistance reaches 2nd lvl 5

She looked at the goop of glowing liquid that remained of the rose knight's chest plate, then at Goliath spreading his arms as bits and pieces of impurities floated away.

"Stonehammer steel… the armor you have brought is ancient. It has become brittle. But that is to be expected as it held up for a long time. For rust to form on such a sturdy material… A ruin, perhaps, turned into a place of creation? I would be interested to see more of this metal. Not ore, but the ancient kind you have here," the smith said in his ethereal whispers.

"Of course, half for you, half for me, alright? Make me as many full sets of armor as you can, and try to model it after the Niameer set. How does that sound?"

Goliath glanced over at the set and picked up the helmet. "With the horns as well?"

"With the horns," Ilea said, a broad smile on her face.

She watched the smith's eyes light up when she dumped all the armor and weapons she'd gotten from her battles in Tremor so far.

"Marvelous. To think such quantities have remained in use throughout the centuries."

Ilea clapped her hands. "Cool. Can you make it black?"

* * *

The smith started working immediately, talking about coating the set with another lesser metal that wouldn't weaken the structure but would change its silver color to a darker, matte black.

It wouldn't be quite as dark as the Niameer steel, but Ilea didn't mind. As long as she wasn't a shining beacon of silver walking around and reflecting the sunlight, she'd be more than happy.

She sat back and watched him work, meditating to recover the mana she was constantly using to keep her healing up. Her Heat Resistance leveled a few more times as well. Fortunately, since a lot of the work involved waiting for the forge to melt the metal, it left ample time for conversation.

"You spoke of Awakened… what are they?"

"The Awakened are those not born from consciousness, those not of the womb of a mother but of mana itself. Gifted sight and understanding by time, long past. By the nurturing touch of life and death itself. I am such, myself."

He's speaking in riddles, Ilea smiled. She was taking a liking to this smith.

"Were you once monsters? Roaming the wild on instinct alone?"

"Precisely. Or so I believe. I have felt it. I have… memories… from before," he said, "Powerful, one must be, to attain choice. We gather in places dense in the energy of the world. Magic itself."

Ilea slid a little farther back on the bench and rested her back against the wall. "So any monster can become sapient, thinking?"

"In theory, though most do not attain thought, clad in instinct. They remain warm in simplicity. I have thought much on the value of conscious thought itself."

"Come to any conclusions?"

"Not yet."

Maybe this is what happened to that demon spawn I fought in Ravenhall? Gained enough Intelligence or awakened somehow to thought?

"How old exactly are you?" she asked, genuinely interested.

He looked at her, his eyes sparkling with golden light. "I do not know the answer you seek."

Ilea nodded as he floated over to the forge, taking the container now filled to the brim with fluid metal. She could feel the heat on her again, but it quickly vanished when Goliath poured the metal, his entire form radiating magic as he shaped it.

Waiting for a few minutes without moving, he placed several big tools that looked like metal versions of vacuum cleaners around the glowing shape of metal.

"Three minutes," he said and activated the devices, an icy cold enveloping the Stonehammer steel, cooling it down in such a drastic manner that the whole room filled with mist. Finally, he grabbed the steaming piece and dumped it into a container filled with fluid.

"That is one piece done. Let it cool completely before you touch the metal. With half of what you have given me, I will create four more complete sets of armor, if that is what you request. The coating I will do as the last step."

Ilea nodded and smiled. "That's perfect. How much gold will it cost, by the way?"

"Gold? No, you misunderstand, human. Gold has little use for me. Bring me worthwhile work and materials. That is sufficient as a trade."

"Well, if you say so. You could probably buy interesting metals with gold as well though, just saying."

"A human desperate to separate with her wealth. Truly as rare as one so far in the north. Well, it is no wonder, with us hiding deep underground." He produced another weird guttural sound. "Gold, I have found, is a fickle mistress, one not as convincing as true skill. I may miss working on the most prized ore simply because the owner was incapable of paying for my services."

Ilea still thought it would be beneficial, but then again, who was she to question the business model of a thousand-year-old floating smith spirit?

"Fair enough. Mind if I stay here while you work? Your magic is helping with my resistances."

He grunted and continued, the heat soon rising again. "Not at all. It is rare enough to have a guest. If my cursed presence is not upsetting your stomach."

Ilea chuckled. "I've met people with better curses than yours."

"Better… that is an amusing perspective."

"You mentioned elves not liking this area before. Why do you think that is?"

The smith turned and grabbed one of the swords Ilea had placed on the workbench. "Few I have met. And they are often secretive. They have shared with me that places brimming with energy such as this, such as the north after it... changed, are not places that elves seek to reside in. Though I did not pry. I am merely retelling rumors of old."

"What change are you talking about? And why do you believe they came north then? if they disliked it so much?" Ilea asked, sitting up.

Goliath looked at her for a while before answering.

"Long ago, a change befell these lands. This place... it became... so terribly more pleasant. I do not know why, yet the energies of the world condensed and twisted, as if bringing out the color and vibrancy of life and death itself. Fewer travelers have visited since then, and no humans reside in these parts anymore. You are the first one I have seen in a while." He paused. "As to why an elf would visit this place, I lack the answers you seek. Why, perhaps, you might ask, would a human come this far?"

Ilea summoned her notebook and wrote some of the info down. It seemed interesting. Maybe whatever had happened was the reason Tremor had been forgotten and since taken over by mindless undead.

As opposed to being a city bustling with... wine merchants.

"I've come here for a few reasons. One of them is just to explore and see what kind of interesting creatures there are," Ilea said. "You mentioned a place of creation, what did you mean?"

"Hmm, yes. I believe your kind call them dungeons. Places so vibrant with the force of life that new beings are born from it. They are pleasant, and beautiful."

"But we're not in a dungeon now. Why don't you stay in one?"

Goliath's eyes bobbed lightly. "It is dangerous, as you might know. Powerful beings are not only born there but are also attracted to places dense with the force of life." He chucked another few pieces into the liquid, steam rising from the metal. "Human, might I ask of you a favor?"

THIRTY-SIX

Metal Gear

"What is it?" Ilea asked, jumping up.

The smith walked over to the devices that looked like vacuum cleaners and checked something on them.

"The water is being used up. The air is too dry, and the forge too hot. It is rare I need to cool with ice, yet your metal requires it. Would you be so kind as to get me some more water from the lake?"

She looked at the massive containers, twice as big as herself and easily as broad as she was tall.

"You mean the lake below?"

"Might this undertaking be impossible for you? Perhaps I might be able to contact my helper, but I believe she is on guard duty for another week."

Week-long guard duty. Sounds horrible. The giant near the bridge, perhaps?

Ilea shook her head. "No need, I'll get you some water. Any other way out than the door? That thing won't fit through that corridor, and I doubt my storage item will hold such a massive thing."

"There is another way out," Goliath said in his usual whisper and moved over to the water tank.

He lifted his arm and aimed at the stone wall next to it before energy gathered in a dark orb, shooting out a second later. The blast completely obliterated the wall. Then a rune glowed near the wall, and the fresh air was cut off immediately, likely because the airflow was not to be disturbed.

Ilea didn't question the occurrence. There needed to be an exit, now there was one. She nodded and spread her wings, looking down into the abyss. They were situated somewhere near the waist of the massive stone statue on whose shoulders and decapitated neck the town of Hallowfort had been built. It was still a couple of hundred meters down to the water.

Two of her ashen limbs moved over to the container and lifted it from the metal hook it hung from. Goliath's golden eyes were focused on her during the whole process. Ilea just looked back and winked at the smith before she flew out, dragging the container behind her with the ash's strength alone.

Letting herself fall, she took in the crystal light that illuminated the world below the wasteland. It was mostly stone and water with little vegetation, likely because the suns didn't reach down here at all. The water extended farther than her eyes could see, more an underground sea than a lake.

The crystals were reflected on the water's surface when she reached it, glistening in their unending brilliance. Holding onto the massive bucket with all her ashen limbs, she flew sideways and dunked it into the water, slowly lowering it afterward. As it filled up, Ilea noticed some dark shapes in the water deep below.

Fishies coming to play?

But the bucket was full, and she didn't want to damage Goliath's tools just because of her curiosity. *Later, much later.* Underwater combat wasn't something she looked forward to, even though she knew that at some point it would likely happen.

Using all the strength in her ash and wings, she pulled the container out of the water and flew up. Looking up, she saw the statue reaching high toward the ceiling of the cavern, hands held together as if praying or meditating.

Heaving the huge bucket back inside, she carefully hung it back where she'd taken it from, noticing the change in temperature immediately upon entering. Some of the water already started to steam.

"It's already going. Shouldn't I hang it outside where it's cooler?"

The smith turned, again focused on her. He didn't speak for a long moment.

"I must ask, young human. Are you a child of ash?"

She was a little confused, especially because more of the water was already evaporating. "I'm an ash creator, if that's what you mean. Um, your water?"

"Do not mind the water. I thank you for bringing it." He straightened and faced her. "Truly, one touched by ash. It is an honor." He bowed a little.

Ilea raised an eyebrow. "Thanks?"

"The runes do not use liquid water alone, simply the element nearby. Be it in the air or in the tank. Once there are insufficient resources, the ice machines will stop working."

"I see," Ilea said, looking at the water tank before she turned back to him. "Why do you think it's worth a mention, by the way? Ash creation, I mean."

The smith moved to cool her second new set of armor, activating the ice runes exactly three minutes later to rapidly cool it down again.

"Ash..." he started, putting each piece into new containers with the liquid from before. Not water but something that looked more sluggish. "It is connected with death. Unattainable for those not close to it. Those who have suffered and prevailed. It is said that they are the ones chosen by ash. Or the ones with an understanding of the natural element, depending on the philosophy and theory applied. You will find that many like myself will come to acknowledge your connection. It is natural to show respect in the face of a child of ash."

Ilea remembered some of the requirements that had initially let her Class evolve into Ash Wielder.

Come to think of it, there must be religions based around certain elements or schools of magic as well. The healing orders are one thing, but maybe the magic domains Elfie mentioned too? Maybe there's an ash thing with Awakened like Goliath? Or other beings? Did I accidentally join a death cult or something?

Fishing out the pieces that had been finished first, the smith put them on a workbench and dried off the strange liquid with a towel. Taking a massive two-handed hammer, the smith swung down, magic dancing around the hammer head before it impacted hard on the chest plate.

A ring resounded, and the hammer was rebuffed a little, the force traveling through the smith as he held the hammer, more weapon than tool, steady in his two massive arms.

"Serviceable."

Goliath gestured for her to see. Ilea nodded before she took the breastplate and put it on the ground.

"Damaging the floor okay?" she asked, looking up at the smith.

"Please do," he replied, eyes glinting in the darkness of his mist-like form.

Ilea smiled and crouched down to deliver a punch, her skills flaring up and five hundred health vanishing to activate her state's third tier. She struck it with her fist, a small shock wave whipping the air outward in all directions, forcing the steel armor into the stone below. Neither her arm nor the armor showed any damage, the stone floor losing out as the weakest link.

"Seems usable. Wonderful work," Ilea said, grabbing the piece and ripping it out of the ground. She quickly identified the pieces.

[Rose Hunter Armor Helm – Rare Quality]

[Rose Hunter Armor Chest Piece – Rare Quality]

[Rose Hunter Armor Bracers – Rare Quality]

[Rose Hunter Armor Gauntlets – Rare Quality]

[Rose Hunter Armor Legs – Rare Quality]

[Rose Hunter Armor Boots – Rare Quality]

"Very nice. Any idea about enchantments? My previous stuff had weight reduction and durability on it."

Checking one of the pieces, the smith made a noise.

"Rare. Perhaps with better metal, I might be able to forge you a set of ancient quality. There is no enchanter here worthy of mention. That dwarf who brought you here might be able to help, but I suggest you look for someone more dedicated to the craft."

Ilea nodded. "I doubt these sets will hold up for very long, so maybe quick and dirty is enough right now. Do you know if he's a bad enchanter, or is there any particular reason that you wouldn't recommend his work?"

The smith put the third set into the forge. "I do not know if he has any talent at all. Dwarves like to use their war machines, ergo enchanting is always necessary. Yet those actually using their machines are rarely the ones best at enchanting. Many different talents are required to create a war machine."

She thought about it. "I'll go ask him then. Maybe he can recommend someone."

"Do that, young one. I will be done in three hours," he said before continuing his work.

Ilea smiled. "I'll be back then. Thank you."

She kept her leather armor on for now and blinked out of the room, back into the corridor. As she appeared, a feline-looking humanoid with a tail nearly ran into her but then vanished before her eyes.

Awesome, Ilea thought as she walked back up to find Terok's house again. Seeing the dwarf inside, tinkering on his machine, Ilea knocked on the door and waited.

"Who is it?"

"Your new friend," Ilea said, smiling under her hood when he opened the door.

Terok motioned her to sit on a worn chair in what looked like his kitchen. She had to duck a little when she went inside. Only the hallway was high enough for what was essentially his mech suit.

"I'll be with you in a minute," he grunted, putting a goggle on his non-mechanical eye before sparks shot outward. "Fucking shit. Dreaded cursed limp son of a bitch," he grumbled before chucking his tool at the opposite wall.

Ilea crossed her legs and pulled back her hood. "Anything amiss?"

"Oh, not particularly," he said and walked over to a box, taking out a bottle. She could tell there was a cooling rune on the crate. "Want one too? I don't have anything fancier than the ale from down the street. Not the worst I've had."

"Gladly."

"A woman of taste." He laughed and threw her a bottle. "Back so soon? Did the old mystery mist work with you?"

The question made her smile as she looked at the label on her bottle, which was peeling off already. *'Bleaker's ale'*. She removed the cork and took a sip.

"He did. He's making me a few sets of new armor."

"A few?" he asked, raising a brow.

"I use them. Problem is, the old smith isn't exactly an enchanter. Heard you lot do that with your machines. Any experience in the trade?"

The dwarf nodded and sat down, taking a swig from his bottle of ale.

"Some. I would suggest someone better, but there's hardly anybody here. Enchanters aren't usually the best fighters, and you need to be good or sneaky to survive here. I tend toward the latter." He winked, then pointed at her. "The smith is an exception. Fucker's been here for longer than the very statue you're standing on, I'd wager."

"Yourself? Been here long? I don't suppose you were born here?"

He looked at her for a long moment, then took a sip from his ale. "No. Bunch of outcasts and scavengers here. Everyone's welcome. Bit of advice, though. Some don't take kindly to people who ask about their past. Been a few… incidents."

Ilea nodded. "Right, apologies. Just making conversation."

"That's what they all say," he said, then he laughed. "No worries. Born in the south, dwarven town. Don't want to share the name. Few issues with loans and a local, let's say, cunt. Lo and behold, left that place and now I'm here."

"Sorry to hear it."

He waved her off. "Life is good. Far more treasure here than I could've ever imagined. Yourself?"

She didn't miss the slightly bitter tone but chose not to pry. "I'm a Shadow from the south, the Plains."

"I know the Plains, but what's a Shadow?"

Ilea smiled. Part of her was happy that he didn't know the Hand. "Mercenary order of humans far away. Was involved in some… murders, and the disappearance of a friend. Lo and behold, I left, and now I'm here."

He laughed. "Right you are. And what's the goal?"

"For now? Just exploring, fighting monsters, getting stronger. The disappearance has to do with a Taleen ruin and one of their gates."

There's also a war going on. She looked at the label on the ale. *And now I'm in the north, while my friends are all back there. Am I just running away? Using all of this 'getting stronger' as an excuse?*

She sighed and drank.

Even if she was, and she wasn't sure, she'd still get stronger. If she was honest, she just didn't know what to do. She'd felt overwhelmed by Trian's situation, and just as much by Felicia's. Hunting other people, killing them for revenge. It still felt absurd, even after they'd planned and executed everything.

Maybe she was grasping at straws with her reasoning, maybe she should've gone with Felicia, maybe she should've stayed with Trian and tried to help him figure things out, or maybe she should've just been a Shadow, helping people during yet another crisis.

But she didn't want that.

She wanted to be here. She didn't want to see people dying. She didn't want to kill other people. She just wanted to fight. She loved it, loved finding new monsters, figuring out their powers, figuring out how she could face them. She loved the feeling of power when she used her magic. It felt the same way as when she'd gotten her wings for the first time. It felt exciting. Compared to everything else she'd felt in the past months.

She supposed it was easier, in a way. The thought made her feel a little guilty. And still, with how this world worked, with how levels worked, wasn't she being rational? Every level brought her a little closer to actually being able to survive whatever dungeon Kyrian was stuck in, and every dungeon meant the possibility of more gold to fund Christopher's research. Even if all that failed, getting stronger also meant she could explore more dangerous Taleen dungeons and other places.

She finished her bottle, trying to focus on the now.

Terok nodded. "Yeah, tricky one with the Taleen gate. You seem like a tough one, and you're fighting alone. Suppose the healing helps, but be careful out there. Seen plenty of risk-takers. Many don't come back."

Ilea smiled as he chucked her another bottle. *And the ones who do are far more powerful than before.*

She thought about Goliath's words in relation to her ash. *And they're close to death as well.*

They were silent for a while, Ilea thinking on what she wanted to do, on what she *could* do.

When she'd appeared in Elos, it had felt like a new start, like all her obligations, all her connections to other people, all the responsibilities and expectations that she'd felt had all been cut. It had felt freeing to be here, to explore this new world.

Things didn't quite feel as simple anymore. Still, she could make her own choices. And for now, at least, exploring this region was what she *wanted* to do.

"About the enchantments, can you do weight reduction and durability or something similar?" she asked eventually.

Setting down his bottle, he looked at her, "Aye. Neither above level two, but it's better than nothing."

"Do you take gold for your work?"

"I do. Would rather have some good metal, though, if you have any to spare. Maybe you can get some from the smith. My machine is breathing its last breaths," he sighed.

Ilea thought about it for a moment. "How does Niameer steel sound? Supposed to be good for the 'sneaky' bit you mentioned earlier."

The dwarf nearly choked, then he laughed. "I'd enchant whatever you like for a lifetime at a chance of Niameer."

"Is it really that good? Got pretty fucked up from the monsters I've fought."

The dwarf nodded with a smile. "It's exceptionally durable for the flexibility it provides. You've seen my rig, it's not a simple breastplate. There's a lot of moving parts, small enchantments and runes placed all over. Niameer is great for that. Elven gold we called it in the P—" He cut himself off, then resumed. "Don't think the elves use it much anymore. Not flashy enough, I suppose."

"How much would you need for your machine?" Ilea asked, looking over at the thing.

The dwarf held up a finger, going over to his rig. He took some measurements with a tool, his mechanical eye sounding like a lens zooming in before he jotted down some numbers on a notepad hanging from the wall right next to the rig.

"Two standard ingots would cover all the smaller parts, gears, and the important enchantments I'd have to put on. Even if it would be better than my current rig, I wouldn't waste Niameer on plating."

Ilea chuckled. "I didn't even know it was such a special metal. Not sure it made me much sneakier either. Just that it took more abuse than anything else I'd had before."

The dwarf visibly winced at that and shook his head. "Humans. You lot..." It sounded like he was trying to bite down curses, but she wouldn't have minded.

"Two standard ingots. If you give me the plans, I can ask the smith to make the parts for you while I'm there. Then I get lifelong enchantments from you, any information you can provide that I might need, connections here, and beyond if necessary, and you show me the new rig when it's done. Deal?"

He shook her hand faster than she could blink, a big smile on his face.

"You are... a blessing. First you save the rookie, and now this." He laughed loudly before finishing his ale. "I'll get the plans for the new parts. Wait a moment." He walked to one of the back rooms, murmuring to himself.

Local smith, check. Local enchanter, half check. Dwarf, elf, Awakened? Check, check, check.

When Terok came back, his beard and hair looked even more disheveled than before, a big grin on his face as he thrust a stack of papers down.

"Those detail what I need. Measurements and proportions are noted as well as everything else a smith would require. If Goliath doesn't want to make it, I'll take the steel as ingots. Oh, and if you need a machine or something designed, I can help with that too, of course. I'm more an engineer than an enchanter, but I've picked up quite a few things in my years."

Ilea took the papers and made them vanish. "I'll see what I can do," she said, getting up. "Thanks for the ale. It was... alright."

Walter would be appalled, she thought. Still, it was impressive that they had a brewery down here at all. With time, whoever produced it might get better at it.

"Good to have met you," Terok said and grabbed her hand with a hard grip. "Come back whenever you need anything."

"And you, Terok," Ilea said.

She made her way back to the smith and found he'd finished another set and was working on the fourth.

"Ah, you have returned, human. Have you found an enchanter?"

Ilea nodded, checking the pieces of her old armor. "I have. The dwarf. He also confirmed there are few better at it here, but I don't need the best at the moment. 'Best I can get' is enough. He agreed to do as many enchantments as I need, forever, if I give him some of the Niameer steel."

"Oho... a deal in his favor to be sure. Yet I suppose he does not know the number of sets of armor you will want him to enchant." His eyes danced with joy.

"Two standard ingots, he said, but I offered to ask you to forge what he needs directly," Ilea said and summoned the plans, handing them to the smith. He floated a little away from the forge so as not to set the paper on fire accidentally.

Looking through them, he answered, "The Stonehammer steel deal I consider repaid with the forging and coating of your armors. I am willing to melt down your Niameer to ingots, but... this..."

Goliath stopped talking, turning to the next page before he held two of them up against the light of the forge. Ilea saw some bits overlapping but didn't understand the designs.

"He is a dwarf, is he not?"

Ilea didn't understand. "I mean, short stature, big beard, uses a big machine suit to fight. Looks like the other dwarves I've seen around here."

"This might look like what a dwarf would make, but the detail is... astounding. In my age, only those calling themselves Taleen have reached such boldness. Such... ingenuity. Marvelous. I will forge his pieces."

Ilea smiled at that. "Make the rest into ingots, I'll hold on to them for now. May I ask what you know of the Taleen?"

The smith carefully pinned the papers to a wall and activated a rune, a thin shimmer coming to life before them. Protection of some sort, Ilea assumed.

"Once, they chose to find and destroy me. Perhaps envious of my work or simply annoyed at the competition. Even though I did not charge gold for my work and chose to serve every and all kinds of beings."

"That's exactly why someone in a similar line of work *would* want you dead," Ilea said, and she couldn't help but chuckle.

The smith looked at her, confusion somehow apparent in those two golden eyes. "Is that so? It is saddening." He shook his head, then looked at her. "Is it not our moral duty to create?"

"Not everyone creates, I suppose. I would consider much of what I've done here destruction. As much as I'd like to share your philosophy."

He stared at the ceiling for several moments. He summoned a hammer and looked at it, then reached out and tapped the chest piece of her leather armor.

"It is the nature of the world, is it not? My words, they are merely the musings of an old spirit. Even in the forge, to create you must strike, bend, and destroy. For steel to be reborn. The same is true for all beings, all creation. A fact I cannot change. Now come. Let us finish your armor."

THIRTY-SEVEN

Real Steel

Ilea smiled brightly at the finished product. The armor had the exact same form as her old set that got shredded by demons, though a little less dark. Still black, but Niameer steel had a midnight-like property to it that the coating to her Rose Hunter sets just couldn't replicate.

A good thing that she found a smith as insanely capable as Goliath. Mere hours to make entire sets of armor, and it fitted perfectly too. It was heavier, certainly, but her power had increased continuously since she'd found the first set down in the Taleen dungeon.

Plus, I'm getting enchantments done as well.

Goliath's eyes danced happily as he watched her move around in the armor.

"It looks great," Ilea said, summoning her Veil and ashen tendrils onto the set to see it all together. She felt almost childish with how cool she felt in this freshly forged set of heavy armor. The horns were perfect too, reaching out from the side of the helm and angling down and forward.

The set was something between half and full-plate. Her joints were somewhat exposed, but this would allow for far more flexibility than something that covered everything. And like this, it could get dented and destroyed without impairing her mobility.

"I love it."

Goliath bowed in the air. "It is meaningful to be of service, ashen huntress. I thank you."

"Why huntress?" Ilea asked, curious. She identified as a warrior, as far as she knew.

The smith started melting down an ingot of Niameer, another ten of which had been put in a crate and stored in her necklace, including those reserved for the dwarf.

"The armor was made for you. It has chosen the name Rose Hunter. You remind me more of a huntress than a rose, but I know little of flowers."

Ilea laughed. "I'll take that as a compliment." She summoned the silver rose from the Tremor dungeon. "I think this is why it chose the name. This comes from the same ruin."

Goliath looked joyous and carefully took the rose. "Marvelous. You see, my curse withers most plants, especially delicate things like flowers. They are of life, after all."

As he attempted to hand it back to her, she held up her hand. "Keep it. I can get more of them."

"A gift I shall treasure, Ilea, huntress of ash," he whispered and bowed.

"You said the Taleen came for you. Do you mean their machines or the dwarves themselves?"

Goliath didn't reply, carefully forming a small piece of glowing Niameer with two pliers before finally putting it into liquid, a sizzling sound coming from the bucket.

"They came with their guardian machines. Neither of the two dwarves that died that day were fighters of any capability. Creators they were, their machines putting up a formidable resistance."

I mean, it's a floating level two hundred creature with a hammer with a head as big as my chest. I wonder how it'd do against a Praetorian, knowing so much about metal.

"And their machines were so different than other ones you've seen?"

"Oh yes. Quite astounding. An internal mana source, capable of harnessing a part of the ambient mana around them. Truly groundbreaking. I was unable to replicate it."

"And you think Terok is making something like that?"

The smith poured another form before he answered. "Not at all. Whoever is responsible for a mana source like the ones found in a Taleen machine is far beyond even my capabilities. A true master. Most exoskeletons I have seen were brutes, massive and specialized in destruction alone. No such machine would require such precise and small pieces of Niameer. The Taleen Guardians, I believe they were called, had no such steel but a more common metal found in the south. To think they formed it into what became such quick and agile opponents… It is… impressive."

Ilea summoned a Taleen sword and showed it to the smith. "That the metal?"

"Indeed." He took the blade and inspected it. "It's perfect. As much as one can make out of that steel."

Ilea summoned a second one, then decided to dump all of her remaining Taleen weapons bar one dagger and one sword. The weapons appeared on a workbench – spears, maces, warhammers, and swords.

"You can have all that. Not sure if it will be any use to me."

Goliath inspected the weapons, dismissing most of them quickly before holding two of the swords and looking at them. He turned the blades and moved them around.

"Impressive."

"What is it?"

The smith turned toward her and showed her the blades. "They are identical to my eye."

Ilea nodded. "Well, the Guardians look the same as well. Must have used some kind of mechanical production."

Did the dwarves have their own little industrial revolution?

"Blades forged by machines… of this quality? I will study them more. If you find a production facility, machine, runes, or enchantments, please do show them to me," Goliath added before motioning to her armor sets. "They are done."

Ilea smiled brightly and stored all of it in her necklace. Four full sets of Rose Hunter armor, plus another one that she was wearing. Each set took up ten units of storage space in her necklace, taking its total to one ninety-two.

"Thanks, Goliath, you really saved my ass here."

"Do not speak of it. You have brought me ample compensation. This is the last piece for your dwarf as well. Let him know I will want to see the finished product," the smith said with excited eyes. Ilea was getting better at gauging his emotions, at judging the small movements and changes in the golden light or their form.

Twirling once, she came to a stop in a stance. "Will you remain here? I might come again in a couple weeks… for reforging, and with new metal," she said, moving back into a casual position.

"Of course. Perhaps I will be able to improve your armor while I learn more about Stonehammer steel."

Holding out her hand, she smiled when the smith shook it. "I look forward to that. Have fun."

"Good luck on your hunt, ashen warrior."

* * *

Terok's eye nearly popped out of his head when Ilea returned.

"Five whole sets? Wow… you know I… ah, fuck it. Yeah, lay them out. Did Goliath agree to form ingots at least?" he asked, checking the first piece of the empty armor, nodding at its quality.

Ilea just summoned one of the Niameer steel pieces he'd ordered and twirled it through her fingers, smiling at the dwarf.

Terok made a half-strangled sound of joy and surprise. "You damned miracle. You sure I won't be cursed or murdered for accepting your help?" he laughed.

Ilea stored the piece again and motioned to the sets of armor. "Only if you don't finish the job. I'd like to leave today, if possible."

The dwarf cracked his knuckles, a big smile on his face as he started working. "Unreasonable requests are my specialty."

* * *

Ilea decided to stay and play around with her ash a little while he worked. She felt out the limits of her ash manipulation and came to the conclusion that eight semi-sturdy limbs were the ideal number.

Semi-sturdy was the best because it allowed them to still be easily movable. Highly dexterous with steel-like tips dense and sharp enough to penetrate the hide or armor of weak opponents. Of course, she preferred to use them with Wave of Ember against enemies like the rose knights who she couldn't hurt with the ash's purely physical properties.

Switching between different levels of density in different parts of the limbs let her optimize a little while Terok finished her last set. Finally, he exclaimed happily, "It's done!"

When Ilea blinked next to him, Terok nearly jumped into the wall face-first.

"Don't do that again," he said after he'd calmed down.

Ilea just looked at her armor.

[Rose Hunter Armor Helm – Rare Quality] Enchantments [Weight Reduction 2 / Durability 2]

[Rose Hunter Armor Chest Piece – Rare Quality] Enchantments [Weight Reduction 2 / Durability 2]

[Rose Hunter Armor Bracers – Rare Quality] Enchantments [Weight Reduction 2 / Durability 2]

[Rose Hunter Armor Gauntlets – Rare Quality] Enchantments [Weight Reduction 2 / Durability 2]

[Rose Hunter Armor Legs – Rare Quality] Enchantments [Weight Reduction 2 / Durability 2]

[Rose Hunter Armor Boots – Rare Quality] Enchantments [Weight Reduction 2 / Durability 2]

Not quite as good as Iana's, but that was to be expected. It certainly made a difference, however, and the weight reduction enchantments would give her movements more speed.

"Perfect, here you go," Ilea said, dumping all the Niameer steel pieces, screws, and springs that Goliath had forged onto Terok's workbench. The dwarf frantically looked through all of it, peering at each bit and bob in turn.

He grunted after a while and smiled brightly. "All there... this is going to be a long week."

"Do enjoy yourself. I might return at some point for more enchantments. Don't die on me."

The dwarf chuckled. "Same to you, same to you." He was already lost in his work as he started distributing the pieces into separate piles.

"Goliath said he wants to see the end result. I think he can hear you if you go down a bit and shout," Ilea added before she quietly left, leaving Terok to his passion. She had remained here long enough, not a single point of experience gained as she'd waited for her gear to be finished.

Still, now I have a smith and an adequate enchanter nearby. Huzzah.

There was more to find in Hallowfort, she was sure, but at the same time, she was itching to use her new armor against something that tried to kill her.

Spreading her wings, she flew directly toward the exit she'd dropped in through. Testing it out, she found she could blink through it. Whatever enchantment was on the door prevented neither her Sphere nor her blink. That meant finding the way in and out would be simple enough.

She wove her way through dark tunnels and caves until she finally breathed fresh air again. It was dark in the main tunnels, but the shattering impacts coming from above told her that the suns were still up outside. The roots to the root vault dungeon lay exposed, the entrance like the gaping mouth of a carnivorous plant.

A big fucking plant.

She knew the knights in her dungeon were capable foes, ones she could use to level both her skills and levels, but perhaps the beasts in here were even more suitable.

Stepping into the big opening, she jumped down onto one of the roots that led farther in. She jogged a little until she passed her previous excursion point and continued deeper. The roots became gnarled and coated in thick, armor-like bark.

'ding' You have entered the Penumra dungeon

Writing the name down in her notebook, she took in her surroundings. Stone with roots growing through it. She just hoped they didn't come alive suddenly – the size of the things would easily be enough to crush her.

Jumping down another couple of roots, the space below her opened up. Like a network of webs spun by tree spiders, illuminated by reddish moss growing on the walls as well as what looked like fireflies, their golden light contrasting with the red. Jumping to the side of the massive cave, she touched the moss and grabbed a little.

[Penumra Moss – Poisonous]

Is that the second-tier effect of Poison Resistance? Ilea asked herself before she heard movement a little below her. Looking down, she glimpsed something red before it vanished under the roots. Her Sphere wasn't quite close enough to give her a view of what her eyes had missed.

Grabbing more of the moss and putting it in her necklace, she focused her senses around her. The fact that the moss was poisonous wasn't particularly helpful. Useful enough to level her resistance, perhaps, but it likely wasn't anything special like the Bluemoon Grass had been.

Considering it nearly killed me, maybe it was poisonous in a way as well... or cursed.

Ilea glanced behind her, the thought distraction enough for something to have sneaked up on her. She turned just as a claw slashed at her. It broke through her Veil and scraped against her armor, though not managing to dig into it significantly.

She answered with her fist, striking the head of the beast that looked like a starving dragon, with two long arms and legs, covered in red hide. The thing didn't react, its head lacking any discernible eyes, as it clawed at her again, this time in a frenzy.

Ilea blinked behind it but found the beast turned quickly, continuing its assault as her ashen limbs smashed into it, not managing to break through the hide.

[Drop Saurian – ??]

At least it wasn't at three question marks, but Ilea had to blink again, flying upward this time to avoid its relentless attacks. It moved frantically, too quickly for her to reasonably dodge, using its teeth as well as all four legs to attack when it got close enough.

Ilea looked at the shallow scratches in her armor, the silver metal shining through the dark coating, and frowned. The beast jumped around the roots quickly, landing upside down above her before it shot toward her. Ilea blinked again but found three more of the beasts crawling up the sides of the cavern. Ilea smiled, forming big swaths of ash around her as she tested blinding them in some way, heating up the ash as well.

The beasts moved quickly, jumping toward the root she was on before they attacked, their aim still focused on her body as she blinked upward again to avoid them. Two of the Saurians crashed into each other before they jumped again. The third one was nowhere to be seen until it shot downward from above, Ilea only able to blink away because she saw it through her Sphere.

Four thorn-like claws suddenly shot toward her, stopped by her Veil. She looked for their origin to see another two monsters crawling over the cave wall, weird growths swelling on their backs.

Some sort of mushroom?

Ilea watched thorns emerge out of the growths before they shot toward her. Blinking up twice more, she was back at the entrance. The beasts didn't follow, already out of sight. She didn't hear them either.

The Drop Saurians were stealthier than she would've expected, given their reasonable size. Comparable to a tiger, perhaps. They had teeth and claws long enough to penetrate clean through her skull and then some, as well as a thin tail. It seemed they traveled in packs and were able to find her wherever she went. Neither flying, ash, nor heat could deter their tracking.

Magic perception, perhaps?

The fact that more of them had shown up at the entrance made this a difficult dungeon to approach. She would have to be able to kill them quickly and efficiently, or at least be able to separate them somehow. The ranged ones made for a further annoyance.

Ilea sighed and cracked her knuckles. *Knights it is,* she thought, then rushed back through the valley she'd initially come from. No storms looked to be close by, letting her push her speed as she ignored the small critters that sometimes showed up.

Maybe I can hunt something out here as well... The birds Elfie mentioned don't seem viable, but maybe I can try some things with the Miststalkers again.

If she could somehow outlast one of them, she could likely gain experience without too much trouble.

Ilea quickly reached the area again where she had first entered the crack in the land, the mountain with its entrance to the Tremor dungeon visible in the distance as she carefully checked for storms.

After she'd waited for a couple of minutes, a dark cloud started moving over the very mountain she was heading for, ominously moving through the sky before purple lightning shot down and shattered the stone below. The shock wave made Ilea duck back down into the crevice until the storm had passed a few minutes later.

Checking around her again, she rushed forward, her wings pushing her to her highest speed before she blinked, finding herself in the small cavern that led down toward the dungeon. Breathing out, she blinked down and hovered in the air, overlooking parts of the Tremor dungeon and the cathedral at its top.

Making her way down, she entered the cathedral through the empty window frames and landed quietly. The elf, still working on the book, looked up to meet her eyes.

"Returned in one piece. Found your smith?"

Ilea released her Veil and smiled under her helmet. "Indeed. Learned something about wine?"

He hissed at her. "Let me know if you learned anything interesting. Is the smith someone who could tell me some stories about history?"

"I'll share what I learned if you promise to not kill anyone there."

"Why must my kind be so hated?"

"Because you go around killing people?"

"No more than anybody else," he murmured.

Ilea walked past him with a smile. "I'll ask if they mind visiting elves next time I'm there. Or maybe you could put on a mask or something..."

He hissed and went back to his book.

THIRTY-EIGHT

The Slowing Grind

Ilea looked for and quickly found a knight to fight, luring him toward the destroyed field in front of the cathedral before she began the battle.

The fight took hours. When it was over, many scratches on her armor revealed the shinier metal below as she dragged the dead woman out toward the cathedral.

Opening the door, she carefully removed the armor and dumped it in the corner of the hall before storing the corpse in her necklace. There was plenty of space both here and in her storage item, but she planned to stay here and fight for a while.

"You can work with the armors if you want to, but I'll need the metal. Let me know if you want any of it permanently," she said to the elf as she walked back to the dungeon entrance. Elfie just hissed at her, as per usual.

Back inside, she summoned the Penumra moss and ate a bit of it. Her healing skill was active and checking for any changes.

'ding' You have been poisoned by Curse of Penumra, -40 Health per second, -40 Mana per second for one minute.

Just a poison then. Nothing to worry about.

She waited out the minute as she meditated and canceled out the health drain. She didn't know how much her resistance had reduced the effects, but checking her health drain with no healing confirmed that the message had already been adjusted to her defenses.

Ilea didn't get a level in Poison Resistance, and the knight kill hadn't gotten her any levels or skill levels either. There were plenty more of both the moss and of the knights, though the latter would be the main focus for now.

Let's get to work.

* * *

Ilea left the dungeon later that night when the dungeon was cast in darkness and the mists had settled outside.

Squeezing through the rock, she looked over the terrain, a sea of mist visible in the valley below. Some smaller specks were visible as well, but there was nothing with less than at least a couple of the stalkers inside.

Can at least try... she thought, flying down while checking for dangers both in the air as well as on the ground.

When she landed near the smallest pool of mist she'd seen, the first stalker noticed her. Her health and mana started draining immediately, her meditation and healing kicking in as well.

Ilea waited for a while until the Miststalker was at the edge of the thin fog. It twirled a couple of times but couldn't actually exit. Its blade-like arms, ending in scythe-like appendages, slashed through the air but couldn't quite reach her.

As soon as the thing realized it couldn't attack her, it started twirling in place, the drain effects increasing drastically. Enough that her health was now gradually declining, even with her healing active.

Yeah, that's not going to work.

A second and third Miststalker noticed her and soon joined in, but Ilea had already changed her goal from potentially fighting them to training her resistances. She tried reaching out with an ashen tendril to use her reversed healing but couldn't reach the creatures.

Might as well chill for a while, she thought with a smile as she blinked backward.

Ilea meditated through the damage, her pain turned off, as she watched her health and mana. Repeating the two-step program, she made sure no other creatures in the vicinity were creeping up on her. Her black armor coating helped keep her hidden, she supposed.

The training showed results quickly, with the first resistance levels coming in after a short while.

This might change things. More difficult to drain both resources, and I can damage them passively.

She continued but quickly noticed that while the drain speed slowed considerably, the damage didn't seem to bother the monsters. At least, she couldn't determine any difference in their behavior.

A numbing feeling spread inside her before her health dipped under fifty percent, making her blink backward twice to get out of their range. As she meditated and healed herself back up, she wondered how long it would take to kill the Miststalkers. She doubted the passive effect alone would be enough, considering they were literally draining health from her.

I need to add my ashen limbs to deal direct damage on top of the resistance ability damage.

To strike the things with Wave of Ember effectively, she would have to get close enough for their rather long-ranged scythe-like arms to hit her.

Maybe this was good. To have a change of pace after focusing so much on taking down a knight. Her resistances would grow, and in time, she might be able to fight the Miststalkers too. Getting back up after her mana was full, she walked back to the edge of the mist to find the monsters had lost interest already.

"Hey, ghosties!" she shouted to the closest one, which turned at the sound. Six eyes looked at her before it slowly twirled toward her.

It would be a long night, but Ilea was smiling all the same.

* * *

Around two weeks passed… or maybe it was three? Ilea wasn't sure.

Either way, she spent the days luring and fighting single knights in the Tremor dungeon and the nights resistance training against the Miststalkers. Occasionally she had to run and hide when other beasts or birds hunted her near the small pool of mist she'd chosen as her training ground. But it was good to be kept on her guard and to not forget where she was.

The only reason the mist beings didn't kill her was the borders of their prison. One of her sets of armor was a little dented by now but still wearable, the silver metal far more durable than the set Balduur had made for her or the Niameer steel she'd had before.

Ilea walked out of the dungeon and into the cathedral, dropping the latest set of armor on the pile. *Number fifteen…* she thought before checking her messages again.

'ding' You have defeated [Knight of the Rose – lvl 310] – For defeating an enemy seventy or more levels above your own, bonus experience is granted.

…

'ding' You have defeated [Knight of the Rose – lvl 278] – For defeating an enemy forty or more levels above your own, bonus experience is granted.

Checking through all fifteen messages, she found that only two of them had been above level three hundred. Weirdly, she hadn't noticed much of a difference in those fights, only realizing after the fact that they'd been at a higher level.

She'd assumed Class evolutions might happen at that level, but monsters were different. Perhaps they didn't evolve, or perhaps it just didn't make a big difference. They were mostly thoughtless undead, after all. The main thing that they retained from life, it seemed, was their capacity to fight.

Undead. Defending their old city from any intruder that might attack.

And now they were providing ample experience for her, she was most certainly glad they had remained.

'ding' Azarinth First Hunter has reached lvl 233 – Five stat points awarded

…

'ding' Azarinth First Hunter has reached lvl 236 – Five stat points awarded

'ding' Inheritor of Eternal Ash has reached lvl 227 – Five stat points awarded

…

'ding' Inheritor of Eternal Ash has reached lvl 229 – Five stat points awarded

'ding' State of Azarinth reaches 3rd lvl 5

'ding' Blink reaches 3rd lvl 6

'ding' Hunter's Sight reaches 2nd lvl 11

'ding' Veil of Ash reaches 3rd lvl 3

'ding' Embered Body Heat reaches 2nd lvl 7

'ding' Wave of Ember reaches 2nd lvl 18

'ding' Ash and Ember Manipulation reaches 3rd lvl 2

'ding' Meditation reaches 2nd lvl 18

'ding' Health Drain Resistance reaches lvl 19

…

'ding' Health Drain Resistance reaches 2nd lvl 1
Some creatures have the ability to drain your health. You have been subjected to such a spell and have endured. This skill will help you endure more easily and turn the tables on your enemies.

2nd stage: Your health is yours; with each point lost, it will become more difficult to steal from you what is yours alone.

'ding' Mana Drain Resistance reaches lvl 20

'ding' Mana Drain Resistance reaches 2nd lvl 1
Rare foes have the ability to drain your mana, either for their own use or simply to weaken you. Having encountered one such being, you have learned of its destructive effect. This skill will help you reduce the effect any mana-draining abilities have on you.
2nd stage: Your mana is bound to you, making it harder for anybody to drain it from you. In addition, the mana removed from you damages the enemy, should they desire to use it for themselves. This effect increases with every point of mana lost.

Her progress was slowing considerably, despite the fact that she'd been fighting for her life for weeks. Being more familiar now with the knights and their fighting style likely impacted how much experience she received from them, but they were still at such a high level compared to hers that it was worth it.

The second-tier additions to her resistances weren't quite enough yet to shift the balance with the Miststalkers, but as soon as she was able to face them, she'd have even more creatures to fight. Enough to never run out, really.

Not that she'd found an end to the knights in the dungeon so far. The first couple of streets and the large square she had initially fought in were empty now though since none of the knights farther inside the ancient city had taken up the patrolling duties of the fallen.

Ilea had continuously invested her stat points into Intelligence and Wisdom. She wanted at least as much Intelligence and Wisdom as she had Vitality. The amount of mana she had was directly correlated to how long and effectively she could fight and survive.

Intelligence would also add to her offensive potential, considering that the knights didn't much care about physical attacks. She was pretty sure that her mana intrusion and reversed healing were the main reasons she could kill them. And still, it took ages to kill a single knight only forty levels above her own. She needed more.

Elfie hissed in an excited manner when she returned this time. It seemed his initial plans to leave had changed once she'd brought back the books. They hadn't talked much in the past weeks, both of them focused on their respective passions.

Today, however, he beckoned her toward him and smiled.

"It is done."

A book lay before him, the smaller of the two she'd brought him, and the elf had written its contents in a fresh notebook to the side.

"Cracked the code?" Ilea asked as she stepped next to him. The second notebook had writing she could at least recognize – it was the same script as in the book on wines.

He nodded and pointed at the first paragraph. "Service record, Guard Captain Reyker. Sixth day of Sol, 358. The king has ordered more festivities to take place next week, despite the rumors and tensions regarding the southern border. Queen Invalar has approved the dispatch of the suggested scouting troops, as well as the reinforcements to be sent to the border."

He traced the lines until he hit the last bit of what he'd deciphered so far, then looked up at her. She didn't really know what to do so just smiled at him.

"Good job. So, you know how to decipher it, and now it's just a matter of writing it down?"

The elf sighed and sat back. "It's rather difficult. Although yes, I've cracked it, it's a brilliant code that does not allow for quick translation. I needed a full two days and nights just for that passage. Though to think it is a service record... Already we know the name of the guard captain. Political tensions, perhaps? And we know the name of the queen of this country."

We? Well, I guess I got him the books.

Ilea stepped back. "A good find, then. More useful than a book on wines."

"You should still read it. There is plenty of history in that one alone. Some of the vintages were not made with nature magic; instead, the winemakers simply let the grapes grow with... well, nature alone. They believed the taste would be improved."

"I might check it out when I get bored," Ilea said, heading back toward the dungeon, ready to sleep for a few hours until the suns were back up. "I'll take fighting knights over reading a marketing brochure on ancient wine any day of the week. Enjoy translating the rest."

"I will," he said and hissed with an excited tone.

THIRTY-NINE

Knights Knights Knights

Elfie offered to answer another question when Ilea came back to the cathedral later to rest after another few fights.

She sat down in one of the chairs and poured herself a drink from one of the ancient spirit bottles. She could still taste the botanicals. Despite its age, the drink was quite refreshing.

"Well, I always wondered about dragons. They're mystical beings where I'm from, only existing in legend, but are usually depicted as insanely powerful beings of some kind. Think it would be cool to ride one into battle. Heard of them?"

The elf looked at her. He blinked repeatedly, as if his brain had short-circuited, before he started laughing. He nearly choked as he tried to stop himself.

"What? People kind of avoid naming the beasts, so I thought it'd be a valid question," she said, sulking a little in her chair.

It took him another minute to calm down, and he summoned some kind of blue drink and took a sip before he said anything.

"Dragonriders… ridiculous. Ludicrous. Thoroughly laughable. I have not heard of anybody avoiding the name, but I suppose they wish to avoid bringing the terror down on themselves. None of those I have known to proudly proclaim they would hunt the legendary being have ever returned. Not even the Monarch himself proclaims such an absurd victory. My only advice is to run… run and hide if you should ever come across such a monster. Those wishing to challenge or even worship such beings are fools. The only records I have seen in my travels, the only tales possibly holding a kernel of truth, speak of despair."

"Alright, I get it."

'Despair', Ilea wrote in her notebook, taking his words seriously. *First Dragonrider Ilea – The legendary warrior healer returns from her journeys.* She could already hear the proclamations of the newspaper boys and girls. If newspapers had become a thing by the time she reached the apparently ludicrous goal.

"Your little human body will combust even getting close to one of those creatures. The forces at play are entirely beyond your imagination."

"I said, *I get it,*" Ilea repeated, not letting the elf destroy her dream so easily. If her levels weren't somehow capped at some point or her body vaporized, she didn't see how it could be written off as unachievable. She fought monsters, she got levels. It was that simple.

I guess it kind of rules out the idea that the elves are as powerful as dragons, or serve them…

"You just lack imagination," Ilea said, still sulking a little.

"You will learn. In time."

Ilea smiled. "I won't take advice from someone too scared to even enter a dungeon."

He hissed her way.

"A joke," Ilea said. "But if the mana in there is a problem, and if you want to, you've got a healer here who can help."

Elfie looked at her for a moment and then hissed again, though it sounded far less aggressive. He shook his head.

"Suit yourself," Ilea said.

A bit of pain and discomfort wouldn't stop someone on a real mission. At least I can take my time to clear out the whole place on my own without an annoying second person stealing my kills and experience.

She sighed and stretched. "Where's my next opponent?"

* * *

Tenth day of Nul, 358

The Soul Rippers have proven to be most dangerous, even to experienced veterans in the ranks of mercenaries as well as adventurers. Queen Invalar has ordered the dungeon entrance to be shut to avoid further nocturnal incursions from the beasts.

Ilea read through the translated log book written by the guard captain. *Likely a Kingsguard captain… can't imagine how powerful that one was…*

Around half of the log book was now translated. Just over a month after he'd cracked the code, the elf had transcribed a lot of the book. He was still frantically deciphering, telling Ilea about each new discovery he made.

The book told of a looming war with an unknown nation, a previously rather unproblematic dungeon suddenly taken over by beasts described as Soul Rippers, and the daily business of the guards. Assassins and spies apprehended, questioned, and likely tortured.

All this was overseen by a man called Reyker, the author of the logbook. There was an underlying dislike for the king in his words, but he never missed an opportunity to praise a decision by the queen. Invalar was the surname of the two rulers. Ilea had a feeling it was more than just loyalty the man felt toward the queen.

She left the book and checked her armor again. She was on her fourth set already, and it was time to switch again. Dents and cuts lined both her arms as well as her torso, since the knights usually didn't try to hit her legs or head. Ilea changed into a fresh set and chucked the barely usable one onto the massive pile of armor in the corner of the cathedral, most of it not hers.

The elf hissed at the noise. "The metal. It bothers me. Are you even trying to find anything new in there?"

Ilea rolled her eyes and summoned her notebook, flipping to the page with her map of the dungeon, which was growing by the day.

"Look... all the buildings with nothing in them are marked. The Kingsguards are still too strong for me, so I'm not bothering with the palace yet."

She closed the book after he'd taken an annoyed look and hissed. Still, she didn't take it personally. She knew he was just struggling with deciphering the book. Apparently, the captain had changed the algorithms every month, giving Elfie a new riddle every fifty pages or so. That was how many days the months in Rhyvor had.

Be happy it isn't any fewer.

Elfie left the cathedral from time to time, but then again, Ilea sometimes stayed in the dungeon for over a week at a time, only going out to get rid of the armor. She'd killed another twenty-four knights, but the only reason she knew the exact number was because of the corpses stored in her necklace. She tried not to think about that too much.

Now down to her last usable set of armor, she was inclined to visit Goliath again. Fighting through the Tremor dungeon had proved to be a longer-term project than she'd initially thought. While she was getting more used to the knights, she was a long way to fighting two or even more at the same time. Still, she'd gotten a couple levels and perhaps a new step to further power with the last month's fighting.

'ding' Azarinth First Hunter has reached lvl 237 – Five stat points awarded

...

'ding' Azarinth First Hunter has reached lvl 240 – Five stat points awarded, one 3rd-tier skill point awarded

'ding' Inheritor of Eternal Ash has reached lvl 230 – Five stat points awarded

…

'ding' Inheritor of Eternal Ash has reached lvl 233 – Five stat points awarded

'ding' Hunter's Sight reaches 2nd lvl 12

'ding' Hunter's Sight reaches 2nd lvl 13

'ding' Embered Body Heat reaches 2nd lvl 8

'ding' Embered Body Heat reaches 2nd lvl 9

'ding' Wave of Ember reaches 2nd lvl 19

'ding' Ashen Wings 2nd lvl 17

'ding' Health Drain Resistance reaches 2nd lvl 2

…

'ding' Health Drain Resistance reaches 2nd lvl 4

'ding' Mana Drain Resistance reaches 2nd lvl 2

'ding' Mana Drain Resistance reaches 2nd lvl 3

While her levels were steadily rising and the knights were still providing good experience, growing her resistances against the Miststalkers was taking a long time. Considering how long she'd trained with Trian, Eve, and Kyrian, she was certainly prepared for the time-consuming resistance training.

Still, on some nights, Meditation was all that prevented her from just going back into the dungeon and fighting more knights instead of sitting near the sea of mist. She kept telling herself that in the long term, it would be worth it.

She had finally received another skill point to advance one of her Azarinth First Hunter skills to the third tier. With how big of a change the third tier of Ash and Ember Manipulation had brought, she hoped for something good.

3rd-tier skill points available [Azarinth First Hunter]: 1
Skills available for 3rd-tier advancement in [Azarinth First Hunter]:
- Destruction
- Hunter Recovery

- Azarinth Perception
- Azarinth Fighting

I said I'd take Recovery first, Ilea remembered, sitting down on a chair and thinking about it. She had enough knights in there to last her a while. Probably enough to reach two sixty at a reasonable pace. Increasing her healing capabilities didn't seem like it would help that goal for now. Perhaps it would help with the Miststalkers, but her mana drained as well while fighting against them.

Fuck it… Fighting or Destruction.

Summoning a coin, she flipped it in the air.

Heads for Fighting. Tails for Destruction.

She caught it and opened her palm.

Destruction it is.

Anything that would increase her damage somewhat would hasten the next third-tier skill. Depending on how many knights were left, she might even choose Azarinth Fighting the next time instead of her healing skill.

'ding' Destruction advances to 3rd tier
Active: Destruction – 3rd lvl 1:
Send a destructive pulse of mana into your enemy with every punch or kick. Your Intelligence stat enhances the damage potential.
2nd stage: The amount of mana used per strike can be regulated with a maximum of 20 mana per strike.
3rd stage: Because this spell is derived from healing, it partially ignores protection against Mana intrusion.
Category: Healing

Ilea read through the newly added third tier before a big grin spread on her face.

Fucking worth it.

She didn't know exactly how much this would change her damage output, but she was sure it would be significant against the knights. A big chunk of the magic from both Wave of Ember and Destruction simply fizzled away whenever she struck their enchanted armor.

Before she continued though, she had thirty-nine sets of rose knight armor to deliver to Goliath, as well as plenty of sets to be repaired or completely remade. Still, it was hard for her not to go back in immediately and test out how long she'd need for a single knight with her third-tier upgrade.

The elf was looking at her.

"What?" she asked, and he hissed again.

"Perhaps you could check one of the other dungeons on your map. Find some new things there. The book on wines is translated and it is... difficult to keep working on deciphering this one."

A plea? Really?

"You're bored."

"If you want to call it that."

Ilea smiled under her helmet and walked to the damaged sets of armor. "I'll see what I can do. I'll ask Goliath if you can visit too."

It would take her a couple of trips to get all the armor to Goliath, but night would fall soon and she'd be able to travel through the terrain more quickly, ignoring the valleys and flying down toward Hallowfort in a more direct manner.

Stepping toward the platform at the end of the cathedral, she said, "Your fire cube thing?"

The elf summoned the item and threw it her way. Ilea looked it over before pushing some mana into the ten-centimeter cube. A swath of flame burned into her helmet, singeing her eyebrows.

The elf just looked at her and shook his head. "You're doing that on purpose. Even an animal would've learned how to use it by now."

Ilea smiled and summoned a bunch of wood, spacing it out to create enough room for all the dead knights. It took her a while, but eventually, she had a pyre going with all of the corpses she'd collected over the past month.

She waited until the fire had consumed them all.

FORTY

Wingwoman

Ilea brought all of her sets of armor to Goliath to have them reforged and asked him about Elfie as well. Apparently, as long as he wore a mask, he wouldn't disturb anyone. Some of the Awakened might react with hostility to seeing an elf in these parts, but most likely wouldn't care, even if they didn't try to hide at all.

Next, Ilea decided to check in with Terok. When she arrived at his home, the dwarf invited her in immediately to look at the modified war machine. The tubes looked sleeker, and there were a few additions to the arms and legs that she was pretty sure hadn't been there before.

"The steel you got me is incredible. She handles like a dream now," he said and raised his bottle toward her. "Your hunt going well?"

"It's going. A slow grind, to be honest, but I do enjoy immersing myself in battle."

He laughed. "We're not the same, you and I. If shit hits the fan, me and whatever team I'm with have already fucked up."

"What do you do then?" Ilea asked. "Dig for metals?"

"Explore ruins and dungeons. But not quite in the same way as you. Lots of riches out there, just always comes with a lot of risks as well. Usually, there's one or two people dedicated to illusions, light magic, or shadow magic present to hide the team from monsters. Then there's people for protection and support, various spells to help us get out if the dungeon denizens become a little too much to handle or if they find us in the first place."

"And you?"

He grinned. "I'm the one punching through the vault door at the end. Or picking the lock, messing with the protection enchantments, what have you – I'm a man of many talents."

Ilea looked at him for a long moment. *Might have something for you there, Terok,* she thought, but she decided not to bring it up quite yet.

"The dungeon here in Hallowfort – what can you tell me about it?" she asked instead. "You said it was called the Descent?"

He smiled brightly. "The Descent, yeah. Peculiar one that one, compared to most other dungeons I've seen in the region. Plenty of routes lead down, each more treacherous than the last. It's a city, or the ruin of one, built around a dungeon that leads farther down into the earth than anything I've seen before. Scavengers have mapped entire sections of the Descent, but every other month, someone still finds a new path or a way farther down."

"The city is part of the dungeon?"

"It is... perhaps one day long past it wasn't, but monsters prowl the streets and tunnels now. A lot of it's submerged as the lake leaks into the upper levels of the dungeon. Groups of scavengers regularly secure some of the better routes, but they often get destroyed or taken over by wild beasts. The walls are brittle. A single crack can lead to whole sections being flooded in a matter of days.

"The city is just the way there though. Most of it has been picked clean by the residents of this town or the ones who came before. It is said that the true treasure lies deeper. Some of the murals, statues, and rare surviving documents written in Standard apparently talk of the Descent as an endless dungeon leading deep into the earth, littered with valuable metals, machines, and beasts beyond your wildest imaginations."

"You've been down there?"

Terok nodded. "Some of the higher levels. There are trees there... green and lush, as well as wild animals – completely docile. A lot of the meat you can get here comes from there. I don't think we'd be able to sustain Hallowfort if we didn't have that dungeon. I only explored parts of the first three layers. Each had a distinct climate and creatures not found in any other dungeon in the region, at least, not that I've seen. The monsters are dangerous too, too dangerous for me or any of the teams I've accompanied."

"Not scared of powerful creatures coming up from there to attack the town?"

"Sure. Sometimes some find their way into the labyrinth below, but it's a rare occurrence, and they generally leave again without intervention. Powerful creatures tend to dislike the lower mana density closer to the surface. It's much denser down there, more so the farther you go. You're human, right? Didn't you notice anything different when coming north? I hear your kind sometimes even has difficulties breathing."

"I noticed it once when standing atop a mountain. Neither in the dungeons nor in here though."

"Interesting. Well, you are above two hundred. And you might have a resistance skill already. But yeah, monsters rarely roam too far from where they feel comfortable, or so go the theories that come from far better-read people than me. Never wondered why the beasts here in the north never came to destroy your Plains? Or our cities in the mountains?"

Ilea took a sip of ale. "I just thought it was too far away. Animals don't like it in certain parts of the world. They need food and a climate suitable to their preferences… Suppose the mana is just another part of that," she added, understanding it now.

Perhaps that was also why elves didn't like to enter dungeons. The higher density was something they disliked. Monsters were just the opposite, she supposed, disliking the less dense mana.

Though Elfie said something about it being forbidden as well.

"You plan to go down there then?"

"I'll check it out sooner or later. It does sound intriguing. Probably want to finish my current location first though."

"Any chance of sharing that one with me?" Terok asked with a hopeful grin.

"Soon, maybe," Ilea said. "I want to have it for myself a little longer."

He smiled. "I understand. Rare for you fighting kind to find good hunting grounds."

"You showed the machine to Goliath yet?" Ilea asked, changing the subject. The smith had wanted to see the finished product.

"From the hallway. Can't exactly go in," Terok said. "I shouted for him a few days ago, but he just told me to enter. He didn't disable the magic."

"I'm not sure he can. Tell you what…" she started, thinking.

Terok leaned forward.

"I think I'll need your help at some point in the not-too-distant future."

"Another deal?"

Ilea nodded. "The rest of my Niameer steel. You can use it for plating, maybe."

He crossed his arms. "What kind of help are we talking about?"

Ilea considered how much to share. She didn't want to lie to him.

"Help me sneak past some dangerous-looking three-mark beings. And get me past an enchanted door, with some of said three marks in earshot."

"Tough one that. But for Niameer… I'll try. You'll get my best, but Ilea, it's possible I won't be able to help." His brow was furrowed, his expression more serious and sincere than was typical for the dwarf.

"I'll take your best," she said.

He nodded, though he seemed slightly apprehensive. "I'd normally suggest we scout first before agreeing to such a deal, but it'll take time for me to get used to more Niameer in my war machine. Let's say, if I fail miserably, I'll owe you one, or three, considering the value of the metal."

"Fair enough," Ilea said. She had no other use for the steel anyway, and she did want to find out what was hidden below the palace. "Shall we go visit Goliath then?"

He nodded and climbed into his machine, the thing closing with a hiss before its eyes started glowing lightly. It started moving a moment later with much more grace than before.

Ilea grunted in surprise. "The metal really made that much of a difference?"

Terok laughed. "You have no idea. It's like night and day."

She grunted again and opened the door, the dwarf following before they walked down to Goliath's forge.

Checking if she could heal the dwarf through his machine, she found it possible, though a little inhibited. "Do you have anti-mana intrusion enchantments?"

"Yes, but healing should get through mostly unhindered."

Would you listen to that? A potential test subject.

"Let's try something then."

He was a little apprehensive as she led him into the corridor toward Goliath's forge.

"I'll heal you, you'll get better in time," Ilea said.

Terok sighed but followed. The curse and health drain soon took effect before the exoskeleton opened up and Terok puked onto the ground while she healed him.

"Ready to go on?"

Terok nodded. He looked sick and pale, but through her healing magic, Ilea could tell he was fine. His health wasn't falling, and the curse would soon fade as well. Getting a resistance skill wasn't that difficult with a healer, after all.

"You should feel better in half an hour or so."

"Half an hour... oh fucking gods," he cursed, but he didn't object further, either because he'd get a skill out of it or because he really did want to meet the smith.

* * *

"Truly impressive work. I will finish the plating as the ash hunter has requested. It would be a shame to leave such ingenuity trapped in unsafe casing," Goliath said.

Ilea was still holding on to Terok as she healed the damage done to him. Without a Health Drain Resistance and apparently less health than what six hundred Vitality provided, she definitely needed to be there.

Terok had demonstrated some of the smaller tools, weapons, and intricate movements he could now accomplish with his new rig, but she didn't really understand the difference between what a conventional war machine could do compared to his. She hadn't seen another one, after all.

"It's an honor to have your work be part of my rig," Terok said with an appreciative nod as the smith got to work.

Ilea accompanied him back to his house when they were done, dropping the four new finished sets of armor Goliath had made near Terok's workbench before she walked to the door.

"I'll come back and get everything tomorrow. Think you'll be done enchanting by then?"

He laughed and cracked open another bottle of ale. "For you, I'll be done in the morning."

Ilea smiled under her helmet and nodded once, blinking outside before she rushed off the side of the massive statue, spreading her wings to avoid walking through half the town. She had a new third-tier ability to test that, hopefully, would increase the speed at which she could kill the knights a little.

The dungeon below Hallowfort sounded very interesting, but as long as she could still reasonably grow in Tremor, she would focus on that. At least for a while. The knights were around level two sixty to three twenty, though mostly below three hundred.

Rushing back through the night, she kept an eye out for flying monsters, but none came close enough for her to be concerned. A few Famine Crows sped toward her on the last stretch, but they were far enough away to pose no danger.

She'd found that, for some reason, the beasts didn't like going down into the cracks and crevices. The Miststalkers' humming didn't paralyze her anymore, allowing Ilea to use the upper parts of the cracks as hiding spots whenever she traveled through the night or trained with the beings in the first place.

Time to go see Elfie.

FORTY-ONE

Ilea Spears

Ilea's black wings slowly dissolved as she landed in the cathedral.

"Hey, guess whose favorite human is back?"

The elf looked at her for a whole three seconds before focusing on his book again.

"Your favorite human," she said, pointing at herself. She hissed when he didn't react, trying to imitate him.

Elfie glanced at her and hissed as well. "What are you doing?"

"Getting your attention," Ilea said and cleared her throat. "I asked some people in Hallowfort, and apparently it's fine for you to visit, though you might want to wear a mask to obscure your features." She saw his eyes widen as he listened. "There's an ancient smith there called Goliath who's a good source of history, but there are probably others there. I haven't explored the town much as the foods generally don't smell super enticing to me." She looked at her hands. "Might just be because I'm human."

"A settlement, then?"

"Yeah, can you show me your map? You'll find it near the entrance to the Penumra dungeon. The Root Vault, I mean. That's the actual name."

He got up and summoned the tube, rolling the map out onto an invisible barrier a moment later. Ilea walked up to it, then glanced at the elf.

"Can you promise me not to murder anyone there? I need the smith and enchanter to continue my fighting here."

She expected him to be offended, but he simply nodded.

"I swear it on my name, Niivalyr Olanis, and on my magic. If I am not attacked first, I will not attack or kill any denizens of Hallowfort."

"Cool, I'm Ilea," she said, holding out her hand. "Nice to meet you, Niivalyr."

He looked at her hand with a confused expression. She took his hand and put it into hers, then shook it.

"I'll probably still call you Elfie though. Just feels right."

"And I will call you human, Ilea. But we met some time ago. It is confusing to me why you insist on this strange gesture."

"You can let go now," Ilea said. "We do that when we learn someone's name. Before, we were just strangers who happened to be in the same place."

"And what are we now?"

"Acquaintances? Coworkers? I wouldn't mind calling you friend, but I guess I'm still a bit apprehensive of your kind considering what I've experienced."

"Many of my brethren would consider you a lesser creature. I suppose I can agree to call you an acquaintance, human."

"My good friend Elfie," Ilea said with a grin, enjoying his annoyed hiss as she summoned her notebook and pointed at his map before she started explaining how he could get to Hallowfort.

She really hoped this wouldn't be the worst decision she'd made in a while, but if she wanted to consider him a friend, she needed to trust him at least a little. Plus, while he was strong, she doubted he could slaughter the entire town. Some of those guards looked menacing as fuck, and most were into the two hundreds. Plus, there were the experienced scavengers and adventurers who lived there. Looking at him, she smiled.

I think he'll fit right in.

"Good luck," she said when he rolled his map back up.

"I will return soon. Human?"

She looked at him.

He hissed. "Thank... you?"

"Are you not sure about thanking me?"

He hissed again. "Is it not what your kind does?"

"You don't thank each other?"

"We give and we take. Thanking... most would think it weakness," he said and looked away.

"I appreciate the gesture then," Ilea said. "Don't really see why it would be weak, but hey, you be you."

She walked to the dungeon entrance, checking her notebook as her ashen limbs pushed open the heavy double doors. They closed behind her as she flipped to the map she had started.

Plenty of buildings were on it already, though few held anything more interesting than dust and old furniture. The sheer volume of rotting and dusty items left behind indicated the number of people who had fled the city.

She still hoped to find a few more *interesting* things, especially since she theorized the top part of the city had been the wealthier one. Seeing how the log book spoke of a king and queen, she assumed the dilapidated mansions had been owned by the aristocracy.

Several sections of the district were already marked as cleared. From time to time, she encountered a knight patrolling through what she considered safe territory, but it was rare. Soon, she had cleared everything all the way up to the palace.

Today, she would take care of the last knight she'd marked near one of the bigger cathedrals. She'd made it a habit to search areas only once no enemies remained so she could fully focus her skills on searching instead of constantly expecting an ambush.

The allocation of undead knight patrols was unclear to her. Some areas held groups of up to four, others lacked even single knights. Either way, her tactics didn't change. Lure a single knight with ashen projectiles or tendrils until she could fight them on the big square in the noble district. There was ample space there, nothing to annoy them, and the sunlight remained there far longer than farther in.

Jogging through the buildings, she soon reached a roof from which she could see the cathedral in question. Definitely the building that stood out the most in the area. Looking left, she saw the palace in the distance. She planned to avoid it for now.

Checking her map one last time, she closed the notebook and stored it, then jumped down from the roof and walked toward the big building. She knew only a single knight remained inside. The two previously patrolling around the building had already been taken care of.

Ilea pushed the door open with a creak and waved at the knight, who noticed her immediately. Her casual demeanor didn't seem to intimidate or irritate the warrior as he brandished his sword, shield at the ready. She waited in the doorway as he started to run, then quickly chose a side street and sprinted off.

Upon reaching the square, she checked that a stray knight hadn't somehow made its way there, but it was empty. The early sunlight seeped through the small opening high above as Ilea turned and skidded to a stop.

She was met a single second later by a sword rushing past her dodging form. The air howled as it was pushed apart by the strong and true strike. Ilea took a step past the knight's arm and shield before hitting it with her left fist. She activated destruction, and her mana seeped into the undead knight with no mana visibly being deflected.

Oh hell yeah.

A big smile on her face, Ilea blinked away and prepared for the next attack, meditation already active. Her mana perception was incredibly limited considering her lack of a related skill, but she'd previously felt how the knights' armor blocked her intrusion. This time, it had felt like she was hitting a plain old drake.

The third-tier description didn't say it ignored mana intrusion measures completely, so she assumed at least part of the attack had been deflected, but it had definitely made a difference. Now it was simply a matter of following the steps of a dance she had damn near perfected weeks ago.

A battle of attrition followed, the warriors matched in skill as they focused solely on destroying one another with sword scraping against steel and fists hitting armor, each movement flowing into the next. Ilea, the warrior in black, would blink thirty meters away, only to be quickly followed by the running swordsman, sunlight reflecting off his silver shell.

The hunt continued for hours, ending in neither spectacle nor grand finale. As sweat dripped from Ilea's brow, rolling past her eyes and down her cheek, she prepared for the next attack that didn't come, recovering her lost resources as the knight collapsed. Steel clattered to the stone floor, sword and shield falling to his side, before silence returned to the square.

Ilea sank to one knee, dispelling her Veil from around her armor and storing her helmet in her necklace. The light from above reflected on the new scratches and cuts she had sustained on her armor, revealing the lighter metal beneath. Most had simply been caused by her deflecting the knight's blade or shield, to allow for openings. Three of the cuts were a little deeper, feints she had failed to predict.

'ding' You have defeated [Knight of the Rose – lvl 318] – For defeating an enemy seventy or more levels above your own, bonus experience is granted.

Three eighteen...

He'd been just a little faster than most of them, a little more cunning. Even with them being undead and unfeeling, they still retained some individuality. It was what kept her on her toes, in addition to the fact that a single true strike could seriously injure her. She guessed that the fight had taken close to three hours – a massive improvement compared to previous encounters.

'ding' Inheritor of Eternal Ash has reached lvl 234 – 5 stat points awarded

That surprised her. The last two knights hadn't given her a level, and she hadn't expected one from this one. She assumed it was because he was over three hundred.

She cracked her neck before she started unhooking his armor, storing each piece in her necklace before only the corpse lay before her wearing an old, rotting garb, any symbols, stitching, or colors faded with time.

The knight's eyes were black, as was his hair. She closed his eyelids before storing the corpse in her necklace to be burned at a later time. For what it was worth, she would make sure nobody used the knights' bodies again. Even if they didn't care anymore.

To Ilea, they each held potential for her to grow, to level up, and to get more experienced with her skills. Each was a challenge to overcome, a worthy opponent to face and defeat. Worthy at least of being burnt after their death.

She continued her search of the now empty area. The cathedral held little but dust, other than a whole library of ruined books once holding more knowledge than a human could learn in a lifetime. None of the enchantments had held through the ages, and all she found were empty mana crystals on the likely once expensive shelves. It made her even more curious about what was going on in the chambers below the palace throne room.

Ilea faced two more knights before night fell, when her training continued out in the wild lands of the north. Once again, she looked for the smallest pool of mist she could find, and the stalkers twirling in its midst quickly focused on her and started draining both her life and mana.

Ilea meditated with her eyes open, taking in the movements in the sky and on the land far away, seeing rare predators in this barren place, interspersed by the dancing forms of an uncountable army of Miststalkers.

* * *

Ilea slept every third day for a couple of hours at most. She'd chosen one of the houses overlooking her fighting square as her new home, placing her bed inside as well as a shelf from the cathedral that still looked somewhat serviceable.

Since it was made of stone, it had mostly weathered the ages, and it now held books she'd got back in Salia and the selection she had taken from her home. The lack of windows didn't bother her, and the climate was cool and mostly dry. Nothing that disturbed her resistant body. Even the cold winds near Ravenhall no longer affected her.

She sat on the roof to eat a meal every other day. Keyla's cooking was always a highlight. It was almost like her creations embraced her very soul. She did ration it though, sometimes eating the still tasty but not so high-quality street food she'd procured in Ravenhall before leaving.

She had a smith and an enchanter nearby. And she had the monsters she'd sought in the north, monsters who would help her grow in power. All she had to do was fight and kill them. Though there were creatures she didn't dare face yet even in Tremor.

Nor had she tried to cross into the section of the dungeon where the sun didn't reach. Exploring past the half broken-down wall remained a line that felt like a goal to achieve, something specific to work toward. It felt good, she found, more attainable perhaps than fighting the Kingsguards. Life was good. Or as good as it could be in the circumstances.

She occasionally thought of her team in Ravenhall, and wondered how they were doing. She hoped Claire's influence and the Shadow's Hand could keep them safe from potential retaliation.

And she thought of Kyrian. By now, she hoped he'd found a way to escape whatever place he'd been teleported to, or to at least survive and get stronger. Part of her had hoped that she'd find out more about the Taleen and their teleportation, but even if Christopher had learned anything in the south, she didn't yet feel confident enough to face anything powerful enough to keep Kyrian trapped. So, she focused on what she could do right here, and that was to fight and get more levels and abilities.

Kyrian was a Shadow just like her, and while he might not have a way to teleport out of a dangerous dungeon like she had, he was an expert in foraging and hunting. He was also used to hiding and taking advantage of his long-range abilities and damage over time from his curses. He would find a way back to Ravenhall. And if the dungeon he'd found himself in was too much for him to escape from, Kyrian would be smart, lay low, and wait, remaining patient and slowly getting stronger.

At least, that was what Ilea told herself.

Days turned into weeks. It was a life Ilea had never thought possible or sustainable, let alone enjoyable. Yet here she was, living a life of battle and meditation, only interspersed with visits to Hallowfort or the occasional conversation with Elfie. Each passing week made her feel more grounded, more confident in her abilities, every step taken with more and more deliberation.

* * *

Sitting atop her roof, Ilea looked over the drab and forgotten city that now felt familiar to her. Familiar and comfortable. While it had been an unknown and dangerous dungeon when she'd entered it for the first time, she now found the quiet of its streets calming, the meager sunlight coming in through the cracks above giving the forgotten city a serene atmosphere.

It felt like she was standing in a monument of history, the ancient buildings and streets like a reminder that all things come to an end, even if some undead might still roam around here and there. In a way, it put into perspective what she'd experienced in the Taleen dungeon, what she'd seen in Salia, and what she'd done in Virilya and the Isle of Garath.

All of it felt less present now, less overwhelming. Perhaps what she'd really needed was a long vacation, and she found that clearing an ancient dungeon of its undead infestation was exactly the kind of holiday adventure she enjoyed.

It felt as if the stones making up the once-occupied buildings, each and every one having a purpose in a bustling society, were now reduced to something more natural. As if the city itself was as much a part of the environment as the mists and storms above and the dark abyss lurking below.

The only place she knew still held life was the palace piercing high into the distant horizon. Secrets were buried underneath it, hidden behind locked doors and guarded by powerful warriors she didn't want to face quite yet.

Her map had grown, though the space around the palace was still empty, but she'd gone deeper into some areas, and most of the city that was at a higher altitude than the palace had now been cleaned out and marked as safe.

She raised her notebook with ash, the element swirling around it. A thought – not even that – was all it took now. It was as if the ash was alive. Only her will was needed to make it appear. The black mist didn't feel like it was created or controlled by her but rather like a steady companion by her side.

By now, Ilea had reached level two forty in her second class and spent the third-tier skill point on Ash Creation. Her efficiency in fighting the knights had remained similar since Wave of Ember was still unable to send most of its destructive mana into the protected enemies. Yet her application of the skill had changed.

She had become more confident, the limbs of ash moving around shields and avoiding strikes of swords like sand running through fingers trying to grasp it. More of her attacks hit, and fewer of the enemy strikes landed, deflecting them with her Veil or quickly forming ash dense enough to soften the glancing blows just enough to protect her armor from heavier damage.

Checking through the notifications before preparing to leave, she quickly scanned the undead knights she'd defeated.

'ding' You have defeated [Knight of the Rose – lvl 264]

'ding' You have defeated [Knight of the Rose – lvl 281]

...

'ding' You have defeated [Knight of the Rose – lvl 259]

She'd bested over a hundred. Each and every single one a long-fought battle, the memories of them blurring together into a sea of blades and punches.

'ding' Azarinth First Hunter has reached lvl 241 – 5 stat points awarded

...

'ding' Azarinth First Hunter has reached lvl 255 – 5 stat points awarded

'ding' Inheritor of Eternal Ash has reached lvl 235 – 5 stat points awarded

...

'ding' Inheritor of Eternal Ash has reached lvl 248 – 5 stat points awarded

'ding' Destruction reaches 3rd lvl 2

'ding' Hunter's Sight reaches 2nd lvl 14

'ding' Hunter's Sight reaches 2nd lvl 15

'ding' Embered Body Heat reaches 2nd lvl 10

...

'ding' Embered Body Heat reaches 2nd lvl 13

'ding' Wave of Ember reaches 2nd lvl 20

'ding' Ashen Wings reaches 2nd lvl 18

'ding' Ash Creation reaches 3rd lvl 1
Active: Ash Creation – 3rd lvl 1
Create ash in a certain radius around you. It can be used as a surge to blind or as a shroud to hide.
2nd stage: You can control the density of the ash to an extent.
3rd stage: You have proven your dedication. Ash swirls to aid and destroy at your whim.
Category: Ashen Magic

Training with the Miststalkers had progressed, but not to the extent Ilea had hoped. It would remain a strict resistance and meditation training for now, though the latter skill hadn't managed to level even once since the last time she'd checked her stats.

Still, Ilea noted that her Arcane Resistance had gone up a few more levels. The passive benefits of being in the north seemingly continued even underground.

'ding' Health Drain Resistance reaches 2nd lvl 5

...

'ding' Health Drain Resistance reaches 2nd lvl 14

'ding' Mana Drain Resistance reaches 2nd lvl 4

...

'ding' Mana Drain Resistance reaches 2nd lvl 12

It wasn't that the training wasn't effective – her skills were improving, after all – but Ilea still couldn't engage them in direct combat. Even with her new third-tier Ash Creation. Of course, she could damage some of the spirit-like beings with Wave of Ember and Reversed Reconstruction from a distance, but in the end, she still lost out in damage, even when there were only two or three of them.

Directly fighting inside the mist was even worse. The added dodging and possible hits from their incorporeal blades drained her resources even more, and while Destruction added damage, it wasn't enough to turn the tide.

Overall, Ilea had gained over a hundred stat points from her leveling. Given how her Miststalker endeavor was going, she decided to continue to buff her key stats of Wisdom, Intelligence, and Vitality.

Status:
Vitality: 705
Endurance: 233
Strength: 182
Dexterity: 193
Intelligence: 706
Wisdom: 714

Health: 7050/7050
Stamina: 1982/2330
Mana: 6698/7140

Jumping down from her position on the roof and pushing open the double doors, she found the cathedral utterly abandoned. Elfie's chair and table remained, as did some of his work, but he wasn't there.

Ilea shrugged, then flew up to the opening in the cavern's ceiling. After checking for arcane storms or any blizzards that might drift over the mountain top, she rushed off.

* * *

Hallowfort was the same as when she'd last visited. Lights from the crystals above and the magical torches in the city shimmered off the water below as Ilea dove past the city, heading directly toward Goliath's forge.

When she appeared inside, the smith looked like he was napping. He was sitting on top of the anvil with no light sparkling inside the black mist of a head.

Shit, did Elfie kill him?

"Hi," she said cautiously, hoping her fear wasn't about to become very real.

Golden eyes opened slowly and focused on her.

"Human. Welcome back. I was in meditation to pass the time, and here you come to provide entertainment. How have you been?"

Ilea smiled and dumped nine sets of damaged rose knight armor on a nearby workbench.

"Splendid. Mostly just been fighting, same as last time. It was... marvelous."

Goliath made a bubbling noise, his eyes dancing around happily. "A treasure, truly, to find joy in such a gruesome and instinctive pastime." He sounded sincere.

She laughed and motioned to the sets of armor. "It really is. And now you can forge again. Maybe we're not so different, you and I."

"Perhaps not. And I thank you, young child of ash, for sending another traveler my way. Niivalyr is a splendid conversationalist. An interesting perspective, though perhaps marred by his own history."

"Elfie? He visited then. Glad to hear that. What do you make of him?"

"Hmm. The young elf seeks answers and purpose in places, peoples, and books," Goliath said, his eyes dancing with amusement. "Yet he remains ignorant to the answers and purpose lurking within his very self. The path is there, but he must be the one to see and to choose it."

"I have no idea what you're talking about," Ilea said. "But it sounds like you like him, and that's nice."

Purpose lurking within him? I wonder what he means. Elfie's not exactly been open about how he feels and what his purpose here is, other than the vague history thing.

Goliath laughed before he glanced at the damaged steel. "New armor for the warrior?"

Ilea nodded with a smile. "New armor for the warrior."

FORTY-TWO

Undead Rose

Entering the dungeon, Ilea spread her wings and hovered down toward the first line of buildings. She opened her notebook and looked at the areas marked as safe. There was plenty to go before the thick black line that indicated the part of the dungeon where no sunlight ever reached.

She'd been curious before, but just looking past the broken-down wall made her feel on edge. It wasn't just the darkness. She was fine out in the mist-covered northern lands at night. This was something else. She felt like finally finding out what that 'something' was.

Tapping on the map, she chose the safest spot to quickly retreat to and put it back into her necklace. Her increased stats and third-tier Destruction and Ash Creation gave her a little more confidence, but she couldn't help but be a little apprehensive.

Not because she was scared of an unexplored section of dungeon or because a dangerous beast might lurk within. Simply because she'd trained in the city of Tremor for so long and the wall had constantly been a line she didn't cross. A mental barrier of sorts, reinforced by her behavior in the past months.

But today, she would cross it.

Reaching the wall wasn't a problem. A large section before it had already been cleared of enemies and the last stretch was devoid of patrols, so Ilea slipped through the houses in silence. She formed several clumps of ash around her, most densely near her back. Veil of Ash was moving around her armored body and her eyes were piercing the darkness before she blinked beyond the wall.

Immediately she noticed the smell, the higher humidity, and the visibly rotten state of all the buildings around her. The lack of any sun for who knew how many hundreds of years hadn't improved the charm of this part of the city by any means.

The farther down the slope she went, the more collapsed houses she saw. Her hopes of finding any useful information for Elfie dwindled with every passing minute. At least it was intriguing. The thrill of a new discovery was taking over her fear as she slowly stepped through the dark, her Sphere the only thing that let her see.

Pitch fucking black.

The thought was interrupted when she heard the sound of metal scraping against stone. A sound she'd heard in Tremor before. Quite a while ago, when she'd got close to the wall that separated what she assumed to be the noble district from the rest of the town. The creature appeared in her Sphere a moment later, each walking toward the other.

[Undead Rose Knight – lvl ???]

Her eyes opened wide at the three question marks and the knight's appearance. A chunk of his head was missing, and his left arm was entirely gone. The sword, the same size as a normal knight would use, was being dragged behind him, his one remaining hand holding it in a lazy manner. His armor was rust-covered and dented.

Cracking her neck and spreading more ash around herself, Ilea breathed in deeply and stepped out from her hiding spot.

The undead looked at her immediately, tensing up and screaming with a voice that sent shivers down her spine.

No paralyze effect. Nice.

The thought barely processed as the knight had already jumped forward and smashed his sword into the ground where Ilea had stood the blink of an eye earlier. Screaming again, it found her and followed.

Ilea stepped backward once more, the knight not hitting the ground this time but simply landing and following. His sword slashed sideways, Ilea dodging downward but not quite quick enough to get away.

A blink saved her, but the monster was catching up fast, moving with more force than anything she'd encountered in Tremor so far. Where the Kingsguards had been deliberate and deadly and the normal knights controlled, efficient, and precise, this undead was entirely wild and savage.

Ilea read as much in the three or four movements it had shown her already. She dodged another strike, this time without the use of blink, the sword crashing through the wall of the house next to them.

The blade hadn't been angled perfectly, but its sheer force still broke through the stone, the knight following the sword through the wall as if his body was dragged with it. A split second later, the wall exploded outward, but Ilea was already gone thanks to her Sphere and Blink abilities.

The knight followed.

She tried to analyze his movements, his turns and twists, but she found it all bizarre and unpredictable. Some strikes missed her completely, hitting houses, the floor, or even just air, the knight spinning with the heavy blade as he completely overextended. Other strikes were deliberate, feints or clever thrusts that anticipated her movements and dodges as if some of his former experience remained and shone through amid the frenzy in his mind.

A quick step brought the knight toward her, his sword creating sparks as it dragged on the ground behind him before it swung up at her. Ilea stepped to the right, her ash expanding on her left before his sword swiped past, shaving off some of the black floating mass as his blade moved up in an arc and crashed into the ground behind him.

The strong swing dug the sword deep into the stone. Ilea stepped forward, her fist hitting the knight's back with all her skills. He let go of his sword in a split second and slapped at her with the one hand he had. Her ash moved in and blocked some of the force, her Veil taking the rest before she was thrown backward.

She heard the knight's steps before he was upon her, thrusting his sword at her chest before she blinked behind him. Reappearing, Ilea's eyes opened wide and formed a thick layer of ash before her as the thrown sword rocketed into it all, cutting through sideways and slamming into her chest.

The world spun as she was flung backward, crashing through two walls and into another street entirely. Her armor was dented, and her chest was bruised and bleeding from within.

Nothing that would stop her.

She blinked to the side when the undead landed next to her, his sword crashing into the stone where she'd just been lying. She sacrificed a hundred health as she watched his movements, her chest healing up, and she let his next thrust scrape past.

Her fist slammed into his body, his forward momentum barely interrupted as her destructive mana flowed into him and her eight limbs of ash slashed around his body, trying to find gaps in his armor to deliver Wave of Ember. His highly damaged armor made that simple.

His movements grew wilder and more ferocious with every attack she managed to deliver, and the two of them crashed and brawled through an increasing number of houses before he managed to get through her defenses with a wild slash, after which he let go of his sword to deliver a kick.

Ilea's ashen limbs were still touching him, the connection disabling her ability to blink. Though his kick landed, a piece of his armor got caught between her chest and leg pieces. Ash accumulated above her when the force of the hit traveled through her, dragging the knight a little forward before his fist landed on her Veil.

He landed two hits as Ilea tried to disconnect the interlocking pieces of armor, preventing her from blinking. His third punch broke through her defenses, Ilea's helmet taking the brunt of the hit, before she finally managed to dislodge his leg armor and blink away.

The hit disoriented her for a second, but she was back again when she saw the sword flying at her, jumping over it with ease. While his sword skills were wild and, in a way, brilliant, his hand-to-hand ability was lacking. Lacking an arm, to be specific.

She stepped in the way of the running knight, who nearly stumbled. Ilea moved to the left with a spin and kicked low at his shin. A loud screech of metal on metal rang out before the heavy knight lost his balance and smashed into a house, the whole thing tumbling down as Ilea healed the bruise on her shin as well as the lightly cracked bone beneath.

Bricks were sent flying as the knight jumped out of the pile of rubble, sword in hand again. As he screamed, Ilea jerked her head to the left when a second knight came flying in, this one without a head but with both arms intact.

She knew two would be too much for her, but she wanted to try at least. With a grin on her face, she replaced her dented armor pieces with a fresh set and identified the second knight as she dodged his blade.

[Undead Rose Knight - ??]

Let's see how long I can go before it becomes impossible...

The two knights rushed at her with reckless abandon. They weren't outright attacking each other, but every uncontrolled strike hitting the other gave Ilea an opening to get in and deliver a couple of hard hits.

She was already angling herself so that her controlled retreat would go toward the upper city and not further down. Ilea was quite aware that killing the two of them wouldn't be possible, not while they fought against her together.

She dealt more damage than against the normal undead knights, but each movement, each swing of their blades, was unexpected. When one of the knights caught the thrown blade of the other and slashed at her with both at the same time, she laughed out loud.

Ilea moved backward over the pitch-black rooftops and saw that three of the knights were now following her. One of them was jumping toward her when a sword caught him in the side of his head, but it simply shifted his momentum a little, the flying blade ricocheting off him.

The third knight was already next to her, swinging his blade into her side, crushing her arm and digging into her chest piece. Ilea blinked away, landing on the second floor of a building, the walls giving in before she tumbled onto the street beyond. Her armor had been pierced, and blood streamed down as she closed the wound. Several ribs had been broken, but the damage wasn't as bad as she'd expected.

Before she could stand up, she turned her head toward the sound of movement from her right and saw yet another undead knight. No sooner had Ilea jumped up and spread her wings than the knight landed with a loud boom where she'd just been lying.

She vanished in a blink when a knight's blade slashed through the air. Ilea ascended as fast as she could, and as more blades were thrown her way, the third one impacted her back and sent her tumbling.

She coughed up blood and could no longer move her legs, but her wings stabilized her a moment later, healing flooding her entire form as she pushed to reach the sunlit section of the dungeon.

Well, I wanted to find out what was down here. Now I know.

Her heart pounded in her chest. Ilea dodged another blade before she emerged into the sunlight, blinking into a nearby house and then into the next one. She stopped two dozen blinks later inside an empty and dust-covered attic, her ash punching a hole through the ceiling to let in some fresh air.

Falling down on her side, Ilea could feel her shattered spine reforming, but she found the process slow.

The armor.

The back was dented in and stuck, so she stored it, glad for her necklace. She lay there and healed, her breathing soon returning to normal.

Another close one.

A grin crossed her face. It scared her to know that those undead knights were down in the deeper sections of Tremor, but the rush she'd felt, coupled with her excitement at facing them again, overwhelmed the fear and the instinctual terror of losing her life.

The vacation I needed, she thought, sitting up and stretching to check if her broken back was fine again before she went back out to fight something.

FORTY-THREE

Mist and Death

Standing over a dead knight in her usual battle square, this time Ilea didn't have a scratch on her. Her ash had moved in to help deflect the blows before her Veil took the brunt of the attacks, which helped tremendously. Plus, the knight had been a sword and shield variant, already lacking in offensive potential compared to the dual-sword sort.

Storing the corpse and armor, she headed back to the cathedral. The fight had taken around two hours, the knight finally falling after she had whittled away at its health with Destruction and Wave of Ember.

'ding' You have defeated [Knight of the Rose – lvl 281] – For defeating an enemy twenty or more levels above your own, bonus experience is granted.

Another knight down.

Ilea wondered how many remained. She could still level for a while, but another dungeon would become necessary at some point. While the feral undead knights were interesting, she doubted she could fight them efficiently. Not yet. It was the same with Penumra. The beasts grouping up, like the Miststalkers, made them difficult to farm.

Maybe I should ask Terok to help with the enchanted vault below the palace.

She couldn't fight the Kingsguards yet, but it felt wrong to leave that secret undiscovered.

So many options. Annoying that I'm too weak to fight half of them. She smiled. *Maybe I'll finally check out that Descent dungeon below Hallowfort.*

* * *

Ilea followed Terok's tracks from his home to a small building near the shoulders of the statue with Hunter's Sight. She wore her traveling clothes and a hood that covered much of her face.

She couldn't read the sign out front, but the sounds and smells coming from within clearly marked it for what it was – a dive bar. The place was built from stone and wood. Inside, beings of all kinds lounged on chairs or barstools, some glancing her way before quickly losing interest.

The lighting was strange. Turquoise colors came from above, but Ilea wasn't sure if they were some kind of luminescent plant, mushroom, or magical tech. A six-armed being with no discernible head played a strange curved wooden string instrument, the sounds reminding her a bit of some jazz she'd heard before, though there was an almost sinister tone to this version.

All in all, a small establishment, but seemingly well-visited. She found Terok sitting at a table in the back corner. He wasn't alone.

"Someone looking for you, dwarf," a masked humanoid with a lithe, cloak-covered form said in a strange, whispering tone.

Ilea looked at Terok's companions. One was a wisp-like being of dark energies, not humanoid in the slightest, small tendrils of energy moving toward a cup filled with something that glowed softly. The other was a humanoid with dark red chitin covering his body and four eyes, entirely devoid of pupils, directed at her. All three were close to the two hundreds in level, though only the four-eyed creature exceeded it at two ten.

Terok turned and glanced at her with a smile. "The lone huntress. Come to play a round of cards?"

"Some other time, maybe," Ilea said. Whatever they were playing, she didn't recognize it.

"Business, then. More enchantments?"

She shook her head. "Quick talk outside?"

Terok nodded, downed the drink sitting before him, and excused himself.

"What can I do for you?" he asked when the two of them stepped into a small alley behind the pub, the bright crystal above visible.

"You know the dungeon I'm clearing," Ilea started.

He nodded.

"The job I mentioned earlier. I think it's time. Full disclosure: there's a vault down there."

Ilea let the implications of that speak for themselves.

Terok grunted. Unsurprised. He glanced at her while tugging on his beard. "Just me?" he asked. "You mentioned three marks before... could use an illusionist at least."

Ilea shook her head. "I'd prefer just you. I know the layout already, and I know the enemies. You should be fine if you can sneak around. Can you teleport?"

"Teleportation alone won't get you past everything, but yes, it's part of my skill set. And no offense, Ilea, but if you could sneak past them, I'll be fine."

She smiled. "So, we sneak to the vault and you get me in. Are you still in? Can always find another favor to trade for the rest of that Niameer I gave you."

"I'm in," Terok said without hesitation.

"No further questions?" she asked, narrowing her eyes.

He scratched the back of his head. "Well. I might've bet a little too much in a few of those games. For... a while, in fact."

"How much?" Ilea asked. "I'd help you out, but I don't have a ton of gold left."

"I can handle my own debts. Those sets of armor you bring to me. The metal they're made of... I could sell that," he said. "I think a few dozen ingots of that stuff and I'll be fine. I assume there's plenty more where it came from, yeah? So, the Niameer plating for the job, then a cut of any other metal we find because you insist on going in without a proper team. You get me to that vault, protect me on the way, and get me out if shit goes wrong. I'll have a look and we see what we can do. Sound like a deal?"

"That easy? Where's the Terok I know?" Ilea asked with a smile.

He sighed. "Bit of a rough patch the past few weeks, I'll be honest. Lots of duds, lost a young illusion mage too. The losses add up."

"Sorry to hear that."

He nodded. "Doesn't really get easier. But yeah, with your healing and your survival so far, I'm keen on working with you. Plus, you have no clue how much that metal is worth. I can easily rip you off." He winked, and she wasn't sure if he was joking. Not that she cared. Gold wasn't particularly interesting to her.

"As long as I get whatever's in that palace," Ilea said.

Terok whistled. "A palace, eh? Interesting. But yeah, you got it. I come with you and crack open what you need cracked open, or I'll find you someone who can if my abilities and rig aren't suited for the job, though I doubt that. But a palace... You sure you want to open it up in the first place? Might unleash something better left alone."

"Like a cursed vault?" Ilea asked. She thought back to the throne room in the Taleen dungeon.

"It's locked up for a reason, though I suppose a palace sounds better than a tomb. I'm done with opening tombs, I tell you."

He shook his head as if trying to dislodge a memory.

"There's a story there."

"A few, yeah," he replied. "I assume you want to go there immediately?"

"If you have time in your oh-so-busy schedule," Ilea grinned.

Terok chuckled. "I'm playing cards. Badly. So yes, I have time. Let me get my rig ready and I'll be with you."

* * *

Ilea waited for Terok near his home, glad to have found the dwarf. Without him, she would've likely never even found Hallowfort in the first place.

No Goliath then, and no armor. Would've had to find another place to fight less dangerous monsters.

She hoped Terok was as good at his job as he claimed to be, but she was already confident, mainly because he'd mentioned finding someone else if his equipment and skills weren't up to the task.

Humility could be seen as insecurity and a sign of inexperience, but with a dwarf close to level two hundred, wearing a Niameer steel-enhanced and mostly self-built and maintained war machine that impressed even Goliath, she assumed his humility just meant he was experienced enough to truly understand his field and his limits.

He joined her mere minutes later. He was wearing his rig, which made him taller than her, but not by too much. She could tell it wasn't built for strength alone.

"Ready to go. You lead, I follow," Terok said. "No monster encounters, if possible. I won't be very helpful in a fight."

"I'll keep that in mind," Ilea said with a smile.

* * *

Ilea sighed and fell on her ass when the knight was finally defeated. A dual-wielding variant she had lured to her fighting square.

"Is it dead?" she heard Terok ask from some distance away. She saw him in her Sphere but hadn't heard him approach at all.

"It is," she said. "Your rig is quite sneaky. More so than I expected," she added as he appeared next to her, his teleportation ability as efficient and quick as her own. Another surprise.

He knelt down and touched the damaged armor. "Yeah," he murmured, standing up again. "How many of these have you killed?" His voice had an edge to it.

Ilea shrugged. "A lot."

"What do you do with the corpses?" Terok's jaw was tight, and he was speaking faster than usual.

"Burn them."

He nodded and expelled a long breath, releasing the tension.

"Good. This isn't a normal undead. Well, kind of. It's strange. It's not quite the same as what I've seen necromancers command, but there's a magical connection here."

"What do you mean, 'connection'?"

"A connection to someone or something, that's all. As far as I've seen, necromancers who command their undead, spirits, or whatever kind of creature they enslave or control always have some form of magical connection. Like a very slight tether, barely noticeable. This one is weaker than anything I've seen before, but it's there. Compared to undead you might find, let's say, in a tomb, hypothetically..."

"Hypothetically," Ilea said and nodded with a smile.

"When they rise on their own, there's no such connection, but they may be stronger due to the high mana density required for something like that to occur naturally. I'm not a death mage or necromancer so I couldn't tell you the details, but generally, natural undead are more powerful than their controlled counterparts. It does seem strange though... This knight you killed, it was ridiculously resilient. Didn't hit you though."

"I've been training with them for a long time. They do hit pretty hard."

Terok chuckled. "Yeah. I believe you," he said. "This is a dungeon, and it does feel like they're empowered by this environment, but the connection is confusing. Maybe an artifact or something?"

"In the palace?" Ilea suggested.

"Possibly, but I can't determine the direction. However, this is good. They might be powerful fighters, but it seems like the connection might prevent them from acting in more erratic patterns. May be helpful when we sneak past them. How different are the three-mark versions?"

"Just stronger, as far as I know. Their gear is less dilapidated, and the one I faced used some kind of ability to cut me up at a distance. Might've been wind magic, but it felt like a long-range razor."

"Right. We keep to the plan of not alerting them then. Can you agree to that?"

"Sure. But it sounds like you're already doubting my answer," Ilea said, raising an eyebrow.

He sighed. "Yeah. Well, you did tell me what you were doing, but it's different to *see* it. You fought that thing for nearly two hours."

Ilea grinned. "I'm getting faster."

"Yeah," he said drily. "That's why I'm questioning your dedication to the plan. People like you... I generally try to stay as far away as I can. Most do."

"People like me?"

Not this again.

"You do realize you just fought an undead capable of killing you for close to two hours without a break, without a team, and your reaction to me pointing that out is joy because you're getting faster?"

"Yeah," Ilea shrugged. "I like fighting, what can I say?"

Terok grunted. "The love of fighting, power, wealth. There's always something," Terok said, though seemingly not to her. He was quiet for a moment. "Just stay safe, alright?"

Ilea was about to tell him about her healing, her resistances, her blink, and all that... but she didn't. She could see that this wasn't really about her.

And she could see that even with all of her explanations, she couldn't fool him. Not that she really wanted to.

She hadn't wanted to fool her teammates or anybody else she'd met in the past. It was just that most people didn't really get how exciting all of this was to her. They didn't really get that while yes, she was working toward certain goals and trying to better protect and help her friends, when it came down to it, what she really wanted to do was just fight.

The drakes had been a matter of survival, mostly. Same as the Stalker-hounds. But her extended stay in the Taleen dungeon? Her choice to join the Hand? Her venture to the north? No, there was something else. Something more. Even now, she could feel that these normal undead knights were no longer scratching that itch. They weren't dangerous enough, not anymore.

When she fought with a monster, one that she knew could kill her, the feeling was intoxicating. As if her entire being lit up, her mind, her spirit, her soul. If there was anything like that. There was no other way for her to describe the feeling.

She felt alive, more so than she'd ever felt. All of her magic, the healing, the Classes, the levels, they were just tools that enabled her to face the next monster, to find the next challenge. And she'd used it all to try and reassure her friends that she was at least considering her safety. But Terok it seemed, understood.

"I don't plan to die," Ilea said finally. It was the only thing she found that she could say.

She knew what Terok meant when he said he tried to stay away from people like her. She did feel an itch to go and fight the three-mark knights, the Kingsguards, the undead in the dark section of the dungeon. Just to see how far she could go, how long she could last.

And yet she didn't. Because there were people she cared about. Kyrian, who she wanted to get back, and everyone else she wanted to protect and help out. She didn't want any of her friends to experience anything like what Trian had gone through. She didn't want any of them to find her like she'd found Eve.

For all that, at least, she would try to restrain herself. *The next target. The next dungeon. The next drake.* She could see it, the potential to get lost in it all, to get obsessed, to take risks that were too much, even for her. *Maybe that's why I clicked with Eve.* If anything, she owed it to her, to err on the edge of caution. Or to try.

Terok looked at her and nodded. "I don't think any of them did. But who knows? Maybe you're different."

Ilea smiled. "Great. Then let me show you the palace."

* * *

Ilea and Terok watched the patrolling knights for a while, Terok noting down what he found as they watched the palace from different angles for the better part of the afternoon.

"Alright. I'll go and have a look inside," he said.

Ilea glanced his way. "Just like that? You know they're three marks. If they—"

"I'll try not to alert them."

"You won't have a healer with you."

"I'll take no healer over an inexperienced scavenger, no offense. You might be good at fighting, but this is different work."

Ilea looked at him, then sat down on top of the flat roof they'd chosen for their last surveillance location.

"Alright. I trust you, Terok. Don't try to clean everything out and run away."

He chuckled. "I might've if I hadn't seen you fight one of those knights. I'll either benefit from your fast growth or I'll loot your corpse when you die. Same result as clearing out the palace right now." He gave her a thumbs-up. "I'll make sure to burn your corpse. Might even shed a tear or two."

"That's reassuring."

"I know, right? I'll be back in less than twenty minutes. If not, come looking for me."

* * *

Terok was back before fifteen minutes had passed.

"Not too extensive," he said, obviously tense.

"Take a breath first, then talk," Ilea said, summoning a bottle of ale from her necklace and handing it to him.

He blinked at her, then exhaled deeply, his previous tension fading somewhat. "Thanks. Sorry, the knights in there are… terrifying, really. Something about them not being ravenous monsters but silent and disciplined. Freaks me out." He somehow shuddered with his entire machine body. "Helps us though, obviously. They're predictable."

"Did you find the door?"

"Not just one door. Plenty of enchanted ones. And they're something else. Barely ever seen anything as intricate."

"You can't get in?" Ilea asked, but he waved her off as he took a swig from his ale.

"It wouldn't be an issue normally. A week, maybe two, but the problem is they're directly powered by the same source that seems to control the knights."

"Why is that a problem?"

"With a direct source as powerful as whatever's hidden within the central door of the palace cellars, we can't just blow through and overcharge it. I'll have to actually crack the enchantments or the locks, which takes more time. Normally I don't have that time, but in this scenario, I can just go in and work on it for however long I want to. The knights can't hear me, and they didn't even react to me putting up noise-canceling enchantments either."

"So now you're sure? There's something in there that is controlling the knights?"

"Definitely."

"And if it's some undead necromancer ready to kill us as soon as we open that vault?"

"Then we run," Terok said and laughed. "With whatever we can hold under our arms."

FORTY-FOUR

Guard Captain Reyker

Ilea and Terok found Elfie in the cathedral when they returned.

He looked up from his book and glanced at the two.

"Elfie, this is Terok. Terok, Elfie," Ilea said.

"That is not my name," Elfie said.

"An elf? Here in the north?" Terok said. He took a deep breath. "I'm not one to judge. This isn't a place where the wars and history of the south matter."

"Niivalyr is my *actual* name. Something the human knows, despite her casual insolence. I will assume you are here to help Ilea access the palace vault?"

"Vaults. Though, yes, one is more prominent than the others," Terok said. "May I ask what the relationship between the two of you is?"

"Business. She goes into the dungeon and retrieves information and artifacts on my behalf. I'm a historian."

Terok laughed, the elf hissing in turn. "An elven historian. Now that's something," he said. He shrugged when Elfie waited for him to continue. "That's all. Something. Didn't mean any offense. All kinds of strange beings find their way into this region."

Elfie glanced at Ilea. "I'm glad you're getting closer to the secrets of this dungeon. I've not been idle either." He summoned a book and held it toward them. "The deciphered and translated recordings of Guard Captain Reyker, servant of King Invalar of Tremor, capital city of Rhyvor. Should I read it to you, or will your dull mind be able to handle the letters? There are many."

Terok laughed. "Alright. Yeah, I see how you two haven't killed each other yet."

Ilea smiled. "Nice, Elfie," she said, taking the book out of his hands and flipping it open. "I'll have you know that my mind can withstand even powerful magic. I doubt some letters will knock me out."

"I'll need to get some things from my home now that I've seen what we are up against. I'll be back soon to start," Terok said. "I'll let you know when I make any progress."

"Thanks," Ilea said, then started reading.

... Tremor is not the only place affected. Cities all over the kingdom report changes in their dungeons, more powerful monsters with unprecedented abilities and levels. Void magic seems to be more prevalent than anything else. The queen has ordered us to keep this information quiet for now. A panic is possible, depending on the nature of the beasts...

Ilea read through the reports, though most were simply daily activity reports about one kingdom or another, places she had never heard of. Comparing the names with her notes from back in the Azarinth temple, she found no matches.

Different times? The part of the map that would've shown the north was ripped off, so maybe the Azarinth Order just didn't reach that far?

... The king insists on elven perpetrators, but I have my doubts. He listened to me, at least, agreeing not to instigate more aggression based on mere assumptions. I have to find evidence, but the dungeons are impenetrable. My own strength is not enough to break through – the Soul Rippers are too many, too powerful. Even with the entirety of the Kingsguard, I wonder if it would be possible. They don't wander out of the dark, but if we want answers, we have to seek them in the depths.

Ilea kept reading. Rhyvor had been at war with another human kingdom. Both of them had been located here in the north. Their cities had gotten more and more destabilized by the high-level monsters appearing and taking over the dungeons that had initially brought so many people, as well as wealth and power, to their kingdom. Adventurers drifted off to other places that were safer and more prosperous. Mercenaries fought for better-paying employers, and the army was stretched increasingly thin to protect the citizens and walls.

... Tremor is all that is left. The flames of war have taken all but the capital. The king has lost his mind, the news of his son's passing summoning a wrath I have never seen in him. His Majesty has barricaded himself in his laboratory, and the queen is nowhere to be found. I will bring an end to this. We will scourge the beasts that brought this terror upon our lands, both human and monster. Should the chroniclers find and decipher this, then they shall know the name of Rhyvor. In glory we fight!

The pages were blank after that. Ilea sat back and tapped the closed book. It had been hours since she had started reading.

"Human kingdoms... in this region," she murmured. Of course, the knights, the undead, the writing, the architecture – it all suggested human handiwork, but with the storms, the mists, and all the powerful monsters around, she hadn't really considered it feasible.

And there's no mention of any of the north's weather phenomena in the book. What the fuck happened here? Soul Rippers, void magic monsters, dungeons changing? She glanced over at Elfie. *Is that why you came here? To find answers to those questions?*

She shook her head.

Either way, it looks like Captain Reyker failed and the city fell. Maybe the king in his laboratory was responsible for the undead? Or some artifact or spell he cast back then?

"Elfie, do you know anything about the Soul Rippers? They're mentioned several times."

The elf looked at her but shook his head. "The beast is unknown to me."

"Just seems like something we should be on the lookout for. Supposedly stronger than whatever else was in the dungeons around the city before and enough to make the captain think the whole Kingsguard wouldn't be able to handle it... They're above level five hundred, each of them, based on the triple mark."

"That may not have been the case when this city was still standing. Dungeons change the beings within," Elfie supplied but didn't elaborate.

"I see," Ilea murmured, closing the book. "Thanks for the translation."

"I will wait for more to work on. I hope the dwarf proves to be resourceful."

"I'm sure he will be," Ilea said with a wink.

* * *

When she woke up, Ilea found neither Elfie nor Terok in the cathedral. She had just decided to meditate and train a little with the Miststalkers when she heard something land nearby.

"Sleeping in a dungeon is dangerous. Nobody teach you that?" Terok asked, standing up from his crouched landing.

"Sneaking up on me is dangerous too, nobody teach you that?"

"Nice bed," he said with a chuckle.

Ilea stored it away and stretched. "It's only been a few hours, you already got something?"

Something clicked out from the left arm of Terok's war machine. He approached her and let it fall into her hand.

"A key? To the closed-off chambers?"

She could practically smell the grin beneath his beard.

"Maybe. It's a work in progress, but someone has to try and use it. Might fuck shit up, might work. I thought you should have the honor."

"Didn't you say it'd take weeks to do this?" Ilea asked, looking at the small shiny key.

"What can I say? Under-promise, over-deliver. But more seriously, I found a flaw in the main vault door. It's not present on any of the other doors I checked. Either it wasn't set up correctly, or someone has already fucked with it. I'm leaning toward the latter."

"Someone fucked with it? Meaning there are others who know about this dungeon?"

"Potentially. But this place is ancient. It could've been decades or even centuries ago. We won't know until we're in there. Just don't be disappointed if it turns out the vaults are already emptied. Happened to me a few times before. You don't have any loot until it's safely stored away in your home."

"Right. So how does it work?"

"The key should in theory disconnect the enchantments imbued in the lock from the source of mana that keeps them running," Terok explained, heading outside. "I'm not actually targeting the enchantments themselves, which would be far trickier."

"I can try it, sure. You can hide behind the plants down there," Ilea said, following Terok out into the dungeon. *Let's see if you're just an extraordinary sales dwarf or if your products actually live up to expectations.*

Terok started hovering, moving as naturally as he would on the ground. "Trust me, I'm as interested as you are to find that out."

Ilea smiled and started flying toward the distant form of the palace, pale moonlight illuminating the underground city. Terok caught up with her, and the two flew a couple of meters above the buildings below them.

"Ready?" she asked. "Worst that could happen is us being trapped with a level one thousand necromancer and his ten most loyal guards, all triple marks rushing to dissect us."

"You forgot about the doors closing behind us with enchantments preventing us from teleporting out," he said drily.

"Now you're just making me more excited," Ilea shot back with a grin.

If she was honest, she did feel a little anxious. Just the fact that they weren't killing the Kingsguards but sneaking past them worried her. Still, she did want to find out what was in there.

Having stayed in Tremor for this long already, she didn't want to wait any longer now that there was potentially a way down into those vaults. Maybe there was knowledge they could use or a way to stop whatever kept the undead moving. Not that she wanted to do that, really. She wanted to fight them all, head-on.

"If we get stuck, you distract them and I'll find a way out," Terok said when they reached the courtyard, not a single knight in sight.

Ilea nodded. The plan was as simple as it got. Putting a finger to her mouth, Ilea checked the palace. Stepping inside, she made sure to stay hidden in the long hallway. Knowing where the throne room was and where the knights patrolled made it easy to reach the main hall.

The two waited next to the thrones for the patrolling knight that would soon come up the stairs. Ilea looked at Terok, tapping her armored leg while waiting for the Kingsguard. Finally, the knight showed up, walking through the throne room in his beautifully crafted armor, his sword sharp and deadly.

Ilea itched to engage, but she knew it would end in disaster. Probably. There was a chance that—

A tug on her arm brought her back to the present. Terok was motioning toward the stairwell. Teleporting down, the two of them found themselves in the underground hall a couple of seconds later. It looked virtually unchanged from the last time Ilea had been there.

Blinking thrice, Ilea appeared behind the two knights guarding the central path that led to the massive closed door. The gate was silver in color and, of course, had a rose embedded in it. Looking back, she could barely see a glimpse of Terok hiding behind the plant she'd just been standing by.

Alright. Treasure and weapons, not high-level monsters or curses unleashed upon the world.

She breathed in deep and summoned the key, then went and checked the door. She found a single small opening, magic visible as it washed over the length of the metal. The entrance was seamlessly set into the white marble wall. The key looked simple in comparison, likely made from some of Terok's spare metal.

Ash formed around her, creating several walls facing both toward the two knights and the hallway as well as toward the door. Buffs already active, Ilea sacrificed five hundred points of health to activate her third-tier State of Azarinth as she slid the key into the small opening. A dull humming noise thrummed in her ears when the key was fully inside, fitting perfectly.

Metal magic must be a nightmare for locksmiths.

Checking the knights, Ilea found them unmoving, just as before. Ilea grinned and turned the key. She heard a dull click before the key was pushed outward. A handle slowly extended from the smooth metal door.

Hey, that's something.

Ilea waited for a moment, then used her ash to grab it. Nothing happened, so she opened the door a fraction to let her Sphere pass through.

She checked for movements and waited to see if any misshapen experiment lunged toward her. It didn't. She turned back toward Terok and let her ash float aside. Bowing a little, she gestured for him to enter.

The dwarf appeared next to her a couple of seconds later, floating to avoid making any noise. Ilea put the key back into her necklace while Terok set up some enchanted plates of metal in the hallway. There was a sizzling snap as the magic was set in place, and Terok landed on his metal feet.

"There you go. Sound canceling activated. Vision should be blurry enough for the one patrolling not to see us. He doesn't walk far into the hall." He paused and chuckled. "It actually worked."

"Yeah, almost too easy," Ilea said.

"Hey, we're staying vigilant, right? Let's see what we've got," he said, pushing the door open a little more.

Ilea summoned one of her heavy gauntlets and set it down behind the door, adding her ash to wedge it in a way that even a fast-closing door would likely get stuck. She was just aiming to prevent the enchantments from reactivating so that they could teleport out if they needed to.

"Let's make sure we don't get trapped in there. Your enchantments will stay active for a while I assume?"

"Couple days at least. I'll check on them periodically," Terok reassured her, stepping inside with his floodlights turned on, illuminating a variety of odd machines. The room turned out to be a long hall with several doors leading into smaller rooms.

Ilea stepped farther inside and Terok followed closely behind, his light giving color to the things Ilea saw through her Sphere. The ground and walls were marble, the same as in the hall outside. Metal boxes, bags, books, notes, and many other things littered the many workbenches interspersed with machinery that looked like something out of an eighties science fiction movie.

Several glass tubes lined the opposite wall. As soon as she was in range, Ilea stopped dead. She motioned for Terok to stop too.

"There's a person in one of those tubes. I think she's alive."

"Great. I was hoping nothing would be alive down here," he muttered.

Ilea looked at the woman-shaped figure through her Sphere. The liquid in the tube somehow stopped her Sphere from giving more detail, but the outline suggested it was an older woman with long, flowing hair and slender features.

There was a ruined silver dress near the tube, covered in long-dried blood. She could hear a quiet humming from farther down the hall and saw a dome-like machine at the end with several broad cords extending into the walls. A glass casing protected something inside, but Ilea couldn't see through it with her Sphere.

"One of the cords on the walls is missing," Terok said, his light illuminating an empty socket. His light followed the thick cables leading out of the metal dome before he found one of them connecting to the machine incorporating the glass tubes. "Found the culprit."

Terok's light flashed into the tube and revealed a female human who looked to be in her fifties, with long, gray hair and a body marred by three scars across her stomach and chest. They looked nasty enough to have killed most. She was thin and malnourished.

Ilea knew her heart was beating.

"Should we wake her up?"

"Are you nuts?" Terok said quickly. "Just identify her... Let's explore the whole place first before we tinker with anything."

[Mage – lvl 262]

"She's level two sixty-two. A mage," Ilea shared, tapping the glass. The woman didn't respond in any way, either sleeping or frozen. Some kind of brackish liquid swirled in the tube, and Ilea was sure it wasn't water.

Terok walked off and checked out the dome. "Found our energy source. We should probably get out of here."

Ilea turned to him and found the dwarf looking into the glass cover of the dome-like machine. Stepping beside him, she looked inside and saw a man in his thirties, with broad shoulders and a long silver beard and hair. His eyes were closed and his arms were folded over his naked chest. Scars marked his body too, but he seemed in a much healthier condition than the woman.

"His mana's flowing away. Somehow, the machine is gathering it all up and distributing it through the tubes—" Terok began, but Ilea stopped him.

She turned around. "Something's happened. Prepare to fight."

Her range of perception near the glass tubes had changed. Something was trying to go unnoticed. Terok's light flashed through the hall, revealing mist in the air.

"Quite perceptive, girl," a female voice rang out.

Ilea looked through the mist and spotted a portion that seemed ever so slightly different. She would never have noticed it without her training with Eve. Looking right at the spot, she replied, "Remove your mist and we'll talk. We're not here to kill anything but unthinking undead."

Her own ash started to spread into the room, limbs forming behind her back. Terok took a step away from her, toward the dome-like machine.

"You are adventurers, are you not? Are you enemies of Rhyvor?" the voice asked, ignoring Ilea's request.

Ilea stepped forward, ignoring the burning mist that made its way into her armor. Her healing and resistance took care of it.

Someone to level my Mist Magic Resistance.

Grinning at the find, she stepped a little deeper into the mist, feeling her health drain.

"Rhyvor is long gone. Tremor is a dungeon now. The only people remaining are undead Knights of the Rose. Now stop it with the mist magic."

"No..." gasped the woman from within the mist. It was a pained sound.

Ilea heard a sob, then braced herself as the mist grew denser and more chaotic. She raised her ash into a wall before her but found no attack forthcoming.

"It cannot be. Everything we… everything I sacrificed. You're lying. You came here to kill us, didn't you? Just another set of assassins, sent here to… to…"

"I'm just standing here, really. But I'm happy to have a little bout," Ilea said with a smile. "So, what will it be, mist woman?"

Nearby, Ilea heard Terok mutter something that sounded suspiciously like 'crazy human'.

A few seconds of silence passed. Then the mist washed to the side of the room, evaporating slowly. The woman who had resided in the glass tank stood before them, silver eyes staring back at Ilea intensely. She raised a hand to wipe at her eyes, then shivered. Her naked body was veiled in mist.

"It can't be. Rhyvor…"

She breathed in deep and closed her eyes for just a moment, then focused, the pain and worry in her face gone. The frail-looking woman stood straighter and stared resolutely back at Ilea. The simple shift made her seem older and far more dangerous.

"I feared as much…" she said, none of the worry remaining in her voice. "Do you have proof of your words?"

"You want proof? Look around the city. The knights are covered in rust, and all of it is buried inside a mountain," Terok said. He sounded nervous to Ilea but managed to hide it relatively well.

Then it all clicked into place for Ilea.

"Your injuries. You have no way of getting past the Kingsguards, do you?" She didn't see a reaction. "You can't leave this place."

How long has she been trapped down here? Ilea wondered, the woman still staring unwaveringly into her eyes.

"Who are you?" Ilea asked.

The woman looked at her and raised her chin, her expression strained. "I am Elana Invalar, Queen and Regent of the revered Kingdom of Rhyvor." She paused and considered both Ilea and Terok, then narrowed her eyes ever so slightly. "You have managed to enter these chambers, so perhaps we can come to an agreement."

Ilea smiled, recognizing the name from Reyker's diary.

"What do you have to offer, Queen of Rhyvor?"

FORTY-FIVE

Royals

"Adventurers," the queen murmured, her lips a thin line. She sighed. "You will be rewarded accordingly." Her tone suggested there was no discussion to be had, despite the circumstances.

Ilea and Terok glanced at each other.

The queen pointed at the dome-like machine. "The necromancer you see in that machine, he's powering all of this. All the knights attacking you outside. I need a healer to wake him up safely, and I need an army to destroy the knights still binding him to this place."

"That's a lot," Ilea said. "Maybe we can start with an explanation of what all this actually is and why it's here?"

The queen was silent for a while before she responded.

"He is Maro Invalar, King of Rhyvor, and my betrothed. The purpose of that machine is to protect Tremor from its enemies. I wished to be with him..." She made to continue, then paused, collecting herself. "...When I heard about our son. Perhaps it was a mistake. The runes and enchantments placed on this chamber were the most intricate, most expensive we could get. They had to be locked for his cursed machine to work. And he needed someone here to look after him."

Ilea didn't fail to notice that the queen avoided her eyes when she said the last sentence. Was it true? The man looked far healthier than she did. If anyone needed to be taken care of, it looked to be the queen herself.

"Why didn't you leave? Get help?"

"These were not choices made easily," Elana said. "I waited, and when I tried to go out there once more, hoping that his undead had wiped out our enemies, the Kingsguards, who should've been under his control, attacked me. They would not enter this chamber, but they no longer recognized me."

"We're sure all of this isn't made up?" Terok asked.

The queen gave him a glare. "I stand before you, naked! Years upon years in deep meditation, centuries have come and gone with me *locked in here*!" she shouted, the mist flaring up around her. After a moment, she inhaled deeply. "My dignity is no more. I just wish for this nightmare to end. You will be rewarded, handsomely. Just... get us out of here."

"Reyker's diary talked of Soul Rippers in the nearby dungeons, and war," Ilea said. "I think it matches well enough with her story."

"Your call. I vote not to wake up the ancient necromancer in his machine," Terok said.

"I've had pretty good experiences with necromancers so far. Maybe this one's nice too." She turned to look at the queen. "I'm not sure we can help with most of what you've asked, at least not yet, but what I can offer is a healer."

Her face lit up at the mention, silver eyes glinting with hope. "Can you bring them here?"

"Sure," Ilea said, then pointed at herself. "I'm here."

Terok grunted something about her being an idiot, but she ignored it. Instead, Ilea smiled and walked over to the machine containing the king.

"So, you've been down here for how many millennia?"

"I wouldn't know," Elana said as she joined her at her side.

"Sounds rough," Ilea said, then summoned a set of clothes, handing them to the woman. "Might be a bit loose fitting."

Elana looked at the clothes for a long moment, then took them and put them on with a sigh.

"Terok, can you check the machine and see if we can wake him up safely?"

"Already on it," he said, his metal head opening up to reveal colorful lenses.

"You haven't eaten in a while, I assume?"

Ilea summoned a meal and handed it to the woman, who had sat down on a nearby chair.

Her guard is down. Ilea thought, her Sphere revealing the small, rapid movements of Elana's chest. She was repressing sobs.

"I've never met a queen before," Ilea said, motioning to the meal again.

Elana nodded and took the food. She waited, eating slowly at first before she wolfed it all down in a distinctly un-queenly manner.

She's so close to my own level. So, I could be a queen? Hell yeah.

But Ilea hated the idea after thinking on it for two more seconds. The responsibilities would be ridiculous, and there would be no time to fight monsters or explore, let alone have long brunches. No, Ilea was much happier being on adventures.

Ilea summoned another plate of food and handed it to Elana. She glanced at a faded painting of a pair of humans clad in royal attire hung on the wall.

"Do you have lights in here?"

Elana wordlessly touched the wall, where a small metal plate lit up. Warm magical light flooded the room. Ilea immediately recognized her as the woman in the painting, though she was older now, without the smile or the beautiful blonde hair that reached far below her shoulders. A sparkling queen with a charming king. His silver hair was shorter, and he was clean-shaven with a hard jawline. He was taller than her in the painting, his green eyes almost piercing the canvas.

"He hated it." Ilea turned to the woman, who was looking at the painting as well. "Hated the formal clothing, the speeches and appearances. Rhyvor would have fallen decades earlier if it weren't for me."

"Does it matter now?" Ilea asked.

Elana looked at her and then back to the picture. "I suppose it doesn't. Thank you for the meal."

"Tell me about yourself, about the king and this kingdom."

Ilea wanted to make sure she wouldn't wake up a necromantic death god of old. Getting some more backstory might help her with a decision.

The king, Maro Invalar, was apparently the most charming man Elana had ever met. The stupidest as well. They, with their group of adventurers, had ventured into the unknown, only to find several undiscovered dungeons. Building a camp between them, on a mountain that reached high above the surrounding lands, was the beginning of their long journey. A journey that led to the foundation of Tremor and the kingdom of Rhyvor.

The wealth and power from the dungeons as well as resources found in the area quickly made them influential. Elana and some of her teammates soon showed they were good at other things than fighting and adventuring, becoming the ministers of trade and housing as well as owners of the local adventurer's guild and inns.

Everybody loved King Maro. People from far away flocked to the newly formed kingdom and swore fealty on the basis of his name alone. Yet early assassination attempts, power struggles with the nearest human and dwarven kingdoms, and internal conflicts cause a political storm to flare up.

The two of them decided to marry. The king apparently had little interest in ruling and the inherent responsibility, but Elana was born for it, born for the cutthroats, the schemers. He was the benevolent king, the one who loved his people, many of them quite literally.

Elana, meanwhile, lived a life of duality, acting as the disinterested queen who could be easily influenced by external powers on the one hand and being the iron ruler on the other. It was, of course, her tale she told, and Ilea had no way of getting proof for most of it.

There were some things she could verify, however, like the Soul Rippers being one of the beasts in the dungeons nearby, the name and nature of the captain of the guard, and many of the events Elfie had translated in the log book. Elana even knew about the wines and their history, as recorded in the second book Ilea had found.

The queen smiled as she studied Ilea. "It's nice," she said. "To talk with someone after all this time. I had nearly forgotten. Thank you, Ilea."

Ilea sat back. "Do you regret it? Being the queen of this land?"

Elana smirked. "I would have had you flogged for that question back in the day."

"I'd like to see you try," Ilea said, leaning forward and cupping her head.

"You are not quite as untested as I thought. You are young, aren't you? Peculiar... the way you talk, behave. Perhaps the times have really changed. Not as I had predicted. Or perhaps you are not from here at all." She smiled inquisitively. Ilea might have been intimidated if the woman weren't so frail-looking. "I do not regret anything. I question my decisions, I question and revise, only to be better the next time. Now, perhaps, there simply is no next time."

Ilea had enjoyed talking to her. Her emotion, her body language, her stories and the way she told them. She believed her. If it really was all made up to manipulate her, Ilea would be impressed.

She's royalty with decades of experience, she reminded herself.

"I'm not from this world," Ilea conceded. Nobody knew her in the north, and at this point, even an elf hadn't reacted in any particularly weird way to hearing it.

Elana nodded once. "Rare. I might have thought as much if your level was higher. Realm travelers are the rarest breed. Perhaps you did not intend to come here?"

Ilea leaned forward a bit more. "What do you know about people not intending to travel through realms?"

She seemed too eager, she knew it as soon as she said it. Elana smiled like a shark scenting blood in the water.

"I could sell you this information for your help... but I think gaining your trust is better. I apologize if this offends you, Ilea. It is a way of thinking I have cultivated for many, many years. I think we could have been friends, perhaps, long ago. When I wasn't shouldering the responsibility of a kingdom and its people."

"You're not anymore," Ilea pointed out.

Elana's eyes grew distant. "This city remains... my husband remains. And the creatures are still bound to this place. Perhaps after all is taken care of, I might be free."

She paused, looking at the painting for a while before she answered Ilea's questions.

"Scipio, a mage from our original party, had always been interested in the phenomenon of realm travel. He even aspired to learn it someday." She shook her head and chuckled. "The man invaded a dwarven city just to talk to a captive of theirs who claimed to be from a different world."

"Was he?"

"Perhaps. He was still a dwarf, however. Scipio returned with economic ideas unheard of as well as agricultural suggestions that led to Rhyvor's fame for wine. Perhaps the dwarf was simply extraordinarily smart, a pioneer of his time. Or perhaps he really was from another world.

"Scipio had collected records on similar people in the past, but they were few and rare, most discredited as madmen and women. He wanted to explore the elven lands to the south, claiming they would be the ones to have realm travelers amongst them. Of course, he only assumed as much because of their secrecy and their ability to appear and vanish as they pleased."

Ilea was certainly interested now. "What happened to him? Did he find what he was searching for?"

"Who is to know? Scipio never returned. We met someone who claimed to be from another realm around twenty years later, or was it thirty? Sadly, he came from a desert realm of survivors. Not much to be gained for a kingdom of the likes of Rhyvor."

"Did you believe him?"

Elana shrugged. "A level three hundred sand creator is not someone easily dismissed."

Ilea laughed. "And he couldn't have helped you out with your city's problems?"

"The man had long been gone. He talked about finding a desert and founding a library of sorts. I don't know if he ever succeeded. I did not hear about it in my lifetime, at least."

"You're not quite dead yet," Ilea smirked.

FORTY-SIX

Awaken

Terok stepped away from the machine after a while and sighed.

"Seems like the machine is using his mana and health to keep the nearby enchantments going, and it amplifies the death magic that keeps the undead going. It's just… It's a bit strange."

"He's no longer in control," Elana said.

"Yeah. The city is a dungeon now, so he's lost control."

"What does all that mean?" Ilea asked. "If he's not in control, why are the knights still patrolling?"

"They're still using his health and mana," Terok said. "They're part of the dungeon. Him? May or may not be part of it too."

"So, he might turn on us if we wake him up?"

"He will not," Elana said. "Maro is not the smartest man alive, nor the most cunning, but he knew his magic. He took a risk to use this device, that is certain, but any second-rate death mage or summoner would restrict their connection to any being they controlled enough to not be influenced by them should another mage overwhelm their spell."

Terok grunted. "I tend to agree. If this guy built this machine and is the one who controlled all of those knights, he's certainly a powerful necromancer."

"Or an exceptionally stupid one who overestimated his abilities," Ilea said. "He's stuck here, after all."

"Any clue about his level?" Terok asked. "I can't identify him."

Ilea checked.

[Mage – lvl ??]

"Too far above me to see, but he's not a three mark," she said. "Probably rules out the idea that he's in control of the three-mark Kingsguards."

"Likely. But even if we wake him up, he'd still be stuck in there until the knights are dead and burnt."

"So, worst case scenario, he comes to and sends the creatures after us?"

"Probably. Well, and whatever magic he can cast against us directly."

"Sounds survivable," Ilea said and turned to the queen. "You still want to wake him up?"

"I do," she said. "Maybe he can shed light on how we can stop the undead, but knowing him..." She shook her head. "Why did I ever follow you in here?" She glared at the glass pane, her eyes softening for a split second before she refocused.

Ilea wondered what enemy had pushed these two to activate this machine, to get stuck down here for millennia. All of it was ancient history, just like the dust and rusted knights above. It wasn't a vault full of treasure, but Ilea was intrigued by this find either way.

And part of her hoped the necromancer would attack.

"So, how does one wake up an ancient necromancer?" Ilea asked.

Elana stood up and unplugged one of the tubes, then moved a lever next to the machine. "I think he just needs to be at higher health, then a push of healing mana should do the trick. At least that's my theory. You're the healer, you'll be able to tell," Elana explained as the glass cover opened up, steam rising as it fell away. The thing stopped after it opened halfway. Elana cursed, then grabbed on and pulled.

Ilea gave her a hand. With a bit of wiggling, it went down the rest of the way, the liquid inside seeping into containers below.

The necromancer was raised up slowly, his arms and legs connected with tubes to the dome-like machine. No curse or anything had been released yet. Ilea sighed and extended a limb of ash, checking his vitals through her Hunter Recovery, arms poised and ash at the ready for any surprises. She kept an eye on the exit through her Sphere.

There were no injuries that she could detect, though his health was low. It went neither up nor down.

"Giving his life for his kingdom," Ilea murmured.

Elana sighed. "He's always had a flair for the dramatic."

Ilea heard her conflicted tone. *A bit annoyed? And a bit proud? Let's see if his brain is still functioning.*

She healed the King of Rhyvor. It took her a couple of minutes to get him back to a reasonable level of health.

After reaching half of his maximum, she started pushing healing mana toward his mind at intervals of ten seconds. At first, he didn't react, but after another minute, his head jerked to the side.

Elana gasped, and Terok took a step back.

The next pulse made his eyes shoot open.

Maro coughed and hacked up some of the not-water before he looked around, his intense green eyes taking in the three people before him. He blinked, then smiled and laughed. This was interrupted by another fit of coughing before he laughed again, though it was more of a cackle really.

"You fools! You have freed me! Now you are *doomed*!"

Terok went into a defensive stance, but Ilea just looked at Elana, who rolled her eyes so hard they nearly left her head.

"I mean, it was a little funny," Ilea said.

The queen just shook her head, her lips drawn into a thin line. But her eyes sparkled, and soon she had a smile on her face. The tears running down her cheeks suggested it wasn't because of her husband's joke.

"Maro, you fool..."

Ilea was about ninety percent sure it had been a joke. If only because she would have wanted to make a similar one.

The necromancer looked at Elana with a kind smile before he turned to Ilea. "Finally, someone with a sense of humor."

He tried getting out of the machine, then frowned when he found himself unable to move. His muscles didn't seem to have degraded as a normal human's would have after all this time. A result of his level, perhaps, or the machine itself.

"I don't suppose we won the war?" Maro said in a tired voice, glancing down at his gray beard. Emotion flashed in his eyes as he looked at Elana. "Oh no... how long have you been looking over me?"

She just shook her head again. "It doesn't matter. You're back now. And you can get us out of here."

He nodded. "I'm sorry. For everything,"

Elana didn't speak, her jaw clenched as she looked at him.

"You're stuck," Ilea said after a while.

"I am indeed," he said in a joking manner, though his smile was gone a moment later. "Tremor is a dungeon, then. I have lost control. The knights are above my own level now. I can feel it."

"You built this machine knowing this could happen?" Terok asked.

The necromancer looked at him and nodded. "Interesting design on that war machine. I'd like to see you fight in that—" His eyes turned to Ilea. "Is that... Stonehammer steel? Never mind. Yes, I knew this could happen. Though I felt I had no choice. To think, I didn't succeed, nor were the knights destroyed." He shook his head. "They had breached the walls. What happened to our city?"

"Your knights were fighting back, but there was chaos," Elana said.

His eyes went wide. "They fled." He paused. "They left us here... to die." He started laughing. "Ruthless. I would've expected more from Reyker."

"He went to fight the Soul Rippers," Ilea said. "According to the journal he kept."

"I should've been out there, fighting," Elana said.

"You would've been slain," Maro whispered.

"I would've died fighting for Rhyvor. And instead..." She sighed. "It's gone now. Ashes."

"Our kingdom does not remain?" the king asked, looking at Ilea.

"I don't think so," Ilea said. "No humans inhabit these lands anymore. Tremor is mostly underground, and from what I've heard of Rhyvor, all that remains are ruins. I'm sorry."

"Don't be. It was not you who failed. And now I'm stuck here. But we are alive, both Elana and I. Are the other rooms in the vault outside still locked?"

"They are," Ilea said.

"Then I will open them once I'm out to reward you for your help, but we need more help than what you've already provided."

"The knights," Ilea said.

He nodded.

"They're three marks, the Kingsguards at least," Terok said.

"Until they are laid to rest, I will not be able to leave. I don't suppose..."

Maro glanced between them and smiled.

"You want us to fight three-mark undead? Former Kingsguards equipped with Stonehammer armor?" Terok asked. "I don't think you understand what kind of situation you've found yourself in."

"I planned to fight them eventually," Ilea said.

Terok glanced at her. "You did? Really?"

"Yeah. I mean, they're interesting. And powerful. I'm sure the levels will be good. Now I have a reason beyond that... Why not? Though to be fair, I was hoping for some kind of treasure or something down here."

Maro laughed, a full belly laugh, his eyes shining. After a few seconds, he quieted. "A kindred spirit, I see! Well, for one, you've now found me, King Maro Invalar, treasure of the Tremor vaults, ancient necromancer full of magical secrets and enormous power," he said, winking.

Ilea found the gesture strangely attractive. It really shouldn't have been, but his absolute confidence and self-awareness coupled with his current situation and the sly grin on his face despite everything made her smile in turn.

"And who might you be, adventurers?" he added, the tone of his voice shifting to something with more authority, the look in his eyes suggesting that maybe the magical secrets and enormous power he mentioned before weren't just some sort of joke.

"Terok," the dwarf said, his war machine giving a small wave. "And if she wants to fight those knights, then that's her fight. They're beyond anything I could or would ever want to face in battle."

"Ilea," Ilea said with a grin. "I will expect at *least* a banquet once we get you out."

Maro's eyes sparkled. "Ilea and Terok. It is good to formally meet you. The banquet, well, I'm not currently informed about the state of our pantry, but I think it's safe to say I'll have to make some acquisitions before I can host a banquet in your honor. Once I'm freed, you'll receive whatever is left in the vaults of Tremor. I'm sure there's some gold, storage items, armor, weapons, and the like still left." He paused for a moment. "And I offer to travel and fight by your side for a time, to give advice and share what wisdom I've acquired in my own years of adventuring."

Ilea crossed her arms. "Why do I get the feeling that isn't a reward and you just want an excuse to travel around with us?"

"Well, I have been stuck here for quite some time," Maro smiled, then closed his eyes for a moment. When he looked at her again, his smile was gone and he looked tired. "I'm sorry. I tend to joke around even when the situation doesn't merit it. It's..."

He paused again, glancing at Elana, their eyes meeting. It felt to Ilea like a lot was communicated in that short look before Maro turned back to her and Elana looked away.

"It's a lot to take in. It feels as if I was asleep and the world ended while I was gone. My world, that is. Know that I'll do what is in my power to help you, Ilea, and you, Terok, if you get me and my wife out of this vault."

Ilea nodded. "Sounds like a deal, but I'll have to think about the traveling together thing. It's been fun to explore the north alone. I'm not sure I'd want to add an ancient necromancer king to my traveling party."

It did sound fun, she had to admit. She wanted to see how he fought, how powerful he really was. And now she had another resource to ask questions and potentially someone who could help with her Taleen conundrum. And while she wasn't incredibly interested in mundane treasures like gold, armor, and weapons, she could still take all that to Claire.

"The queen isn't stuck, but we'd have to sneak her past the Kingsguards," Terok said.

"Not unless you can somehow teleport or shroud me," Elana said.

"Can't we just tunnel out of here?" Ilea suggested.

"It'd take a while to get through those enchantments," Terok said. "But maybe I can figure something out. It'll take some time though. And I'd want at least a part of that treasure, even though fighting those monsters is far more dangerous than this kind of work."

"Are you asking me?" Ilea said.

"I am."

"Sure, we can figure out how to split things after the fact."

"Yeah, depending on how long we each need for our tasks, risk calculations and all. Just don't want to waste my time here. Though cracking this vault is rather intriguing professionally. Certainly a more interesting job than most of my recent endeavors. Let's hope it pays better too..."

"Time is what we have," Elana said. "And we have some catching up to do as well."

Maro looked at her. "We do."

"So ancient necromancer king, any secret tips to getting strong enough to fight those Kingsguards?" Ilea asked.

He looked at her, the grin back on his face. "You find dangerous monsters, then you fight them, preferably alone. And, well, the main thing to keep in mind is that you should try to not die."

"That's crazy. You really are wise and old and all that. I never would've thought of that."

"These two are lost," Terok said. "Queen Invalar, you knew how to handle the machine, are you familiar with the enchantments of the vault too?"

"I can show you the basics, but Maro will know more," Elana said. "Come."

Maro looked at her as she and Terok stepped away for a long moment, his expression more serious again before he glanced back at Ilea.

"How did you find her?" he asked, his tone sober, quiet.

"In one of those tubes," Ilea said.

He sighed. "Good. At least she had a way to pass the time with less strain. And she's likely had time to process things."

"You do seem pretty casual about everything, now that you mention it."

"I don't know you, Ilea, not really, and you don't know me. While I haven't enjoyed the role of king, I did always have a knack for people – persuading nobles, calming tensions, preventing potential civil wars, all that. That was what I was good at until things got… out of hand, I suppose.

"With all that, know that I will find time to process all that has happened, but that time is not now. Right now, I need to convince an insane adventurer to fight undead monsters twice her level to free me from this place. And I need to make sure she doesn't die trying."

"You're saying you're good at manipulating people?"

"Yes. And to answer your next question for you, it's the blunt truth. Because you seem like you'd be interested in fighting powerful creatures one way or the other. And you give me the impression that you'd be very displeased with attempts at deception. So here we are. I don't know how the lands have changed with time, but I have extensive knowledge of the local dungeons, the creatures within, and various magic schools, and if you show me how you fight, I'm sure I can give some pointers, even to someone already past the two hundreds."

"The dungeon knowledge would be nice to have. But these lands aren't quite as you remember them. This is considered no man's land. Human expeditions have apparently failed time and time again in trying to get here. Tremor is below one of the many mountains in the area, and Terok is from a scavenger town hidden in the cracks of these lands, living off the ruins of old."

Maro looked at her with a considering gaze. "That's impossible. Tremor is the only remarkable mountain for miles. There are no cracks in the land." He paused, then his eyes widened. "Perhaps the changes in the dungeons were more widespread than expected. A monumental environmental shift. Perhaps a magical catastrophe or something very powerful meddling with nature."

"Dragons?" Ilea suggested, which made Maro laugh.

"Here? You're crazy. Well, maybe if the changes were that drastic. Even then, why would any of them do such a thing? They hadn't cared for our kingdoms for thousands of years."

"It's hard to say how much time has passed since then."

They spent a few minutes comparing Terok's and Maro's knowledge of local dungeons, and there was almost no overlap. Except for the Descent. Maro at least knew of its existence, though his info didn't match what Terok knew.

"So even that has changed," Ilea said. "So you can't really help me get to a higher level faster."

"A higher level? What is the goal, exactly?"

"I need to face a bunch of high-level monsters – more specifically, machines. From the Taleen, if you're familiar. A friend of mine is stranded somewhere in one of their dungeons. At least, that's the working assumption."

"And you want to get them out. I have heard of the Taleen. Elusive dwarves from the south. To think that such a small faction remains while Rhyvor has fallen," Maro murmured.

"Small faction?" Ilea asked. "What I've seen of their cities is dungeons now too, ruins. But they had pretty insane technology. Some sort of teleportation gates and machines that still fight to this day."

"Teleportation gates? I see. That would... change things. Perhaps they fooled others into thinking they were inconsequential after all. Interesting, but alas, my knowledge is outdated, and space magic is not a specialty I'm familiar with anyway. If Scipio was still around, he'd probably be able to give at least some insight."

"Elana mentioned him already. He was looking for realm travelers and apparently never returned."

Maro looked at her for a long moment. "Ah, that makes sense. As to your conundrum, do you know the power of the machines residing in these dungeons?"

"Three marks, no specifics."

"Show me your magic," Maro said, again with perfect confidence.

Ilea summoned her ash, formed a few limbs, then decided to show her wings as well, and she flowed a bit of healing into him as well.

"Teleportation?"

Ilea blinked.

"What kind of attacks? You can heal, so strike me. I can take it."

Ilea smiled and did just that. Using all of her abilities, she threw a single light punch to his arm, her magic sizzling into and through him. She saw him wince, but the look in his eyes changed almost instantly to one of curiosity. She healed him and stepped back.

"Now now, that is quite something," Maro murmured. "Ash creation, teleportation, flight, mana intrusion, and, most curiously, arcane healing. There was a small order in the south that I'd heard was boasting about this kind of healing. To see it now… Part of your intrusion was based on this healing too, if I felt that correctly."

"It is," Ilea confirmed. "You knew the order?"

"No. Which also means you didn't know it. A relic, then, found or given. Either way, you wield a dangerous combination of magics. And it seems you understand your strengths already – your creation and your healing. And you're an instinctual fighter. You trust your abilities, I can see that. When was your last evolution, if I may ask?"

"At level two hundred."

"Then your next will likely happen at three hundred. You're not close yet, but I'm sure the change will be substantial if you manage to survive. Enough, perhaps, to face down three-mark monsters."

"You think so?" Ilea asked. Three hundred didn't feel super far away, but she was surprised to hear he thought she could face level five hundred beings.

"With what you have already, yes. Yes, I think it's possible. And you'd likely be a stronger fighter than me."

"What's your level, anyway?"

"Past three hundred, but not far," Maro said. "You'll know soon enough if you keep fighting. And if you have any specific questions, I'll be happy to answer them."

"I'm more interested in fighting you, to be honest," Ilea said.

The king laughed. "Sure. Once I'm out, I'll have to kill you anyway for the whole 'necromancer taking over the world' plan."

"Ah yes, the 'necromancer taking over the world' plan. I'm familiar with it," Ilea said. "I'm the hero who will face you and lose, but then rise up from the ashes while you're on a rampage, then I have a training arc and return to face you again, and you'll be like—"

"You fool, I have faced you before, you are nothing to me! You will die here!" Maro interjected.

"Oh, but I'm not the same as I was last time, necromancer," Ilea said, ash spreading behind her.

Maro made a shocked expression, perfectly acted. "You… what is this… power I feel?! You will never win!" he roared, the sound descending into laughter at the end.

"Can you two shut the fuck up for one minute?" Terok added with a shout of his own.

"She's saving the world!" Maro informed him, then turned back to Ilea. "Some people don't get it."

Ilea shrugged.

"Now, on finding your friend. I think you're on a good path. I suggest focusing on level three hundred for now, if you don't have anything else to go on. The Kingsguards might help with that. Try to get as many resistances as you can as well. Fighting more diverse monsters would be preferable, as much as that may slow things down. You can heal your injuries yourself. You should also look into Pain Tolerance. The second tier is difficult to achieve, but it would be invaluable for a warrior or a battle-healer like yourself."

Ilea smiled.

"Oh. Of course," Maro laughed. "Once you hit your evolutions, more options will open up, I'm sure of it. The resources left in the vaults here and potentially my direct help, if you're interested, should both help as well. As long as you don't die prematurely."

Essentially what I've been doing already. But I suppose it's good to have a more specific goal. Level three hundred. That'll take a lot of monsters. But if the jump is as big as my last evolutions, I'm inclined to believe him.

Ilea looked down at her fists and smiled. She didn't know exactly what she'd expected to find down here in this vault. An ancient set of rulers was certainly not it. But if anything, this confirmed that there wasn't a shortcut. She needed to go into Taleen dungeons, fight the strongest machines they could throw at her, uncover whatever secrets were hidden, and gather resources, allies, gold, and gear to help Christopher with his research.

And all that, she knew, would help both Claire and Trian too. And herself, because her magic would get cooler, and she could fight more dangerous monsters.

She thought of the masked person she'd seen flying above Virilya, the power that they'd wielded. She thought of the basilisk, a four-mark beast, and the elves that had attacked Dawntree and Salia. There were a lot of dangers out there in the world, and she felt as if she couldn't stand still. She had to face the next danger not only to survive but to then face the next challenge. And if there was nothing in her way, she would go out there and find it herself.

Ilea smiled to herself, thinking of the Azarinth temple, of the wolves that had attacked her on her first day here. While she had long eclipsed them, she knew there was always another creature out there more dangerous than the last, a monster that would get her blood pumping, something worthy to fight, to defeat.

Always another drake.

FORTY-SEVEN

Underground Paradise

Ilea left soon after, though Terok stayed to discuss potential ways to at least get Elana out in a more reasonable time frame.

When she walked into the cathedral, closing the double doors with the ash floating behind her, she found that Elfie had returned.

"Hey there, historian."

The elf rolled his eyes before he looked back to the book he was reading.

"Did the dwarf die?" he asked a moment later while Ilea checked her armor for damage.

The undead knights had barely scratched her, courtesy of her ash creation's third tier. If she could somehow make it more durable, the stuff could replace her armor permanently.

I'd never have to worry about steel again. That would be nice.

"He should be fine if he doesn't drunkenly stumble past his runes."

The elf sat up and looked at her. "Did the key work?"

"Question for a question. Why did I find elven armor in a Taleen dungeon? I thought you lot didn't go down there?"

Ilea sat down with one arm resting on the chair, her head cocked to the side. The elf stared at her with his gray eyes.

"Either someone brought it there, or a cursed one died in the dungeon."

"Cursed one?" Ilea asked. "So there are elves who enter dungeons?"

When he didn't answer, she smiled.

"The key worked."

"That's all?" he asked with a grin on his face, hissing a moment later. An amused sound, Ilea thought.

Ilea shrugged. "Questions and answers, Elfie. Isn't that the bargain you suggested? You're being a dick, so I'm being a dick."

His claws dug into his chair, but his smile remained, a spark of either joy or madness reaching his eyes. Ilea couldn't quite tell. He considered for a moment, then hissed again, as if he had come to a decision.

"There are some who choose to enter dungeons. They are forever marked as cursed ones. I believe they call themselves the Cerithil Hunters. A preposterous name."

"You don't seem so sure about that. What does it mean?"

He made to speak, then chose not to.

"Why do they go into dungeons if they're then marked as cursed? I thought you couldn't even enter?"

"They seek to destroy the Taleen creations. I understand they seek to find their source and bring an end to them."

Ilea listened. She could tell something was different. He seemed almost... emotional.

A connection to the Taleen. Elves who delve into their dungeons... to find their source? Where they're created?

She was sure she could learn more from him, but the topic felt delicate, not something easily shared, so she didn't want to pry further just yet.

"We found two survivors of Rhyvor. King Maro Invalar and his wife, Elana. He activated a spell or machine to defend the city against its attackers. That was long ago, and it seems the attackers were repelled and the undead remained, but nobody was left or willing to rescue the rulers. I woke him up, but to get him out of there, we'll have to kill all the knights still connected to him."

The elf stood up and started pacing. "Alive... after all this time... to speak to the rulers... and you believe them? You think them the true royals?"

Ilea shrugged. "Probably. Might be a fake story, but the undead he controls are called Kingsguards. He might be a prisoner too, but it doesn't make sense. The captain of the Kingsguards... all of that would be fake otherwise. And why leave them in control of the knights if they aren't who they say they are? I don't know, Elfie. I don't dislike them, personally. And I don't really care if they're king and queen of this forgotten kingdom."

Elfie began to spread a curse around him. "I do. Is there no way to get them out?"

"Not for now. He's stuck, as I said. Can't leave without the knights being dead. Maybe you can go in and help take care of them? Now I know elves go into dungeons, can it really be that bad? Cursed ones... You already use curses – it'd be a fitting name for you."

He hissed and hurled a powerful barrier at her, but Ilea simply blinked through it, ignoring the growing curse around her.

"You're right, actually. With that weak-ass magic, you'd be useless in a fight against the knights," Ilea snickered, dodging another barrier. "What's your level anyway?"

The elf calmed down, his magic subsiding before he sat down again. "You can't tell yet? Your Identify skill is execrable. Did you arrive in this realm without one?"

Ilea stayed quiet.

"I'm two eighty. Meaning your Identify skill is below the level of a human child. Impressive." He clapped.

She smiled, ignoring his provocation. "Why do they want to destroy the Taleen machines?" she asked instead.

The elf tapped his chair with a nail and hissed. He glared at her and then blinked his eyes. "Because, human, the dwarves – all dead and gone by now – left behind more than ruins to explore for you and your squabbling little species. The machines are spreading throughout the lands of the Domains like an infection, searching the vast forests and mountains, to find and kill every one of my kind, every warrior that stands in their way. Like a curse placed on us by a dead people."

Ilea looked at him. This was certainly something new, something nobody had ever talked about.

"The Taleen send out machines to hunt down elves?"

"They do. Tens of thousands of them. My people welcome them as a challenge, as a rite of passage to reach maturity."

He spat on the ground, his expression turning to one of horror immediately after. Ilea watched in amazement as he dropped to his knees and cleaned up the spit with frantic movements.

"We fight them, destroy them by the droves," he continued. "And the cursed ones go into their dungeons and destroy what they can find, but it doesn't change anything. The machines still come, unstoppable, in greater numbers with every passing year."

Ilea leaned forward as he sat down again, his face not revealing any sentiment in regard to what had just happened. "How long has this been going on?"

The elf ignored her question. "Can you get the queen out if the king is stuck?"

"Maybe. She lacks a teleportation ability to get past the Kingsguards. There might be a way for Terok to get her out, and he's working on that right now. I'll be hunting down monsters to get stronger. I'm not quite ready to face the Kingsguards yet." She smiled. "But I will be."

He hissed, a contemplative sound.

"Is that why you're a historian? You're trying to figure out why the Taleen are coming after you?"

The elf looked at her. "I am over six hundred years old, human, and even I was only deemed mature after facing down a sea of Guardians, killing my first Taleen Centurion."

Ilea chuckled. "Guess I'd be classed as mature too, then."

He hissed.

"Why not join those Cerithil Hunters? Bring an end to the machines?"

"You tread dangerous ground, human. Now begone. Leave. I am tired of your presence."

Ilea grabbed one of the bottles they'd found in the king's chambers and poured herself a glass. Looking at the elf as she set the bottle down, she took a sip.

"No, I don't think I'll do that."

His curse flared up again, but she just sat there, ash swirling around her as she stared into his eyes and took another sip. Healing mana flowed through her, taking care of the damage as it was caused. His attack was nuanced, dangerous, and lethal, but she'd faced worse before, and either way, he lacked the punch to finish the job.

He really might be at two eighty.

The elf stopped his magic after a minute, simply turning away to continue reading. At least Ilea wasn't annoying him with further questions.

So the Taleen army I've seen wasn't made just to defend whatever Iz was. They built robots to hunt down elves. But why?

She didn't know. They mustn't target humans, otherwise either more people would know about this or they'd all be dead and unable to tell the tale.

Probably good news. Kyrian might still be alive if the machines don't actively hunt him down. As long as he can escape whatever place he got sent to.

Cerithil Hunters… She wrote the name in her notebook and smiled. *Has a good ring to it.*

* * *

Night had fallen when Terok joined Ilea in the cathedral. She'd decided to wait for his update before she left for an extended period of time. And she wanted his advice. With Maro's knowledge being so outdated, a scavenger from Hallowfort could surely provide some more up-to-date knowledge on local dungeons and dangerous beasts to hunt.

She poured each of them some of the ancient beverages they'd found earlier, the two of them sitting in the warm magical light provided by Terok's machine.

"You sure this stuff is safe to drink?" he asked.

Ilea smiled. "No. But an ancient king just confirmed that resistance training is important."

"You're using that as an excuse," he chuckled.

"Don't worry. I can heal you if it fucks you up."

He sighed and took a sip. "Hmm. Not too bad actually. They left behind good enchantments."

"Think you can get her out?"

"With time. And potentially some help. I'll keep working on it, if only to get into their good graces. Whatever they do after they're out of that vault, I'm sure it will have an impact."

"Planning ahead, eh?" Ilea smiled.

"We're not all sustained by fighting monsters day in, day out."

"Speaking of which, I need a local guide. I'll have to fight a ton of stuff to get to three hundred, and I think I'd enjoy some variety."

Terok nodded. "You're really planning to go through with it."

"Thought I was kidding?"

"I'd hoped you were, but no," Terok said. "So, what have you found and fought in the region already?"

She relayed what she'd encountered so far, and Terok nodded along, his eyes occasionally widening in between deep draughts from his glass. Eventually, the two moved on to specifics, the first topic being how to tackle the Penumra residents called Drop Saurians. Ilea currently found them too dangerous, mostly due to her inability to fight one at a time.

"Can you blind them, maybe? Obscure whatever it is they sense with?" she asked.

"We've already tried smoke, freezing, fire, dark magic. They seem to rush into whatever magic they can find. You've seen how big they are, haven't you? Once they notice anything intruding on the dungeon, they group up, more and more appearing every second. Your high Poison Resistance might be enough to battle them, but combined with the ranged monsters, I doubt you'd be very effective. I don't believe they can heal themselves, at least."

Ilea put a question mark next to the hastily sketched Drop Saurian inhabiting the Penumra dungeon in her notebook. It would've been the closest dungeon to Hallowfort – next to the Descent, of course.

"Levels unknown?" Ilea asked, and she saw him nod through her Sphere. "I could try again, but it might not be the best start. If they catch me and prevent me from blinking, I'd be toast... probably." Their damage potential was hard to gauge, but it likely wasn't below the knights of Tremor.

"The city ruins leading to the Descent," she said, turning the page in her notebook. "You said those are dangerous?"

"Yes. People aren't as nice as they are in town, so you have to look out for any random person down there, Awakened or otherwise. It's all very old. Different monsters from farther down sometimes make their way up and walls break, flooding entire sections. The tunnels that run along the coast bring the most dangerous creatures, other than the Miststalkers that sometimes wander in at night.

"They're called Blue Reapers. They use mind magic, supposedly, and lightning. They're pretty small, but anybody who encounters them drops dead damn near immediately. Foaming at the mouth and paralyzed. Even groups can't take them down. And they can switch to area attacks that are just as powerful. The only saving grace is that they don't seem interested in protecting the place – most likely, they wander in from another dungeon. They don't attack if not provoked."

"Might be a stupid idea to do so then," Ilea said, "I do have resistances for both those types of magic though, so depending on just how hard they hit, they might be perfect for leveling."

Terok laughed at that, waving her off. "Most everyone in Hallowfort would love to see the little fuckers taken care of. We don't have guilds here, but there are prices for their tiny heads. An easy way to make some gold as well, if you're looking for that."

Ilea tapped the notebook and wrote down 'Blue Reaper'.

"What about farther down? You said there were different layers to the dungeon."

Terok gestured for the pen, and Ilea handed both her pen and the notebook to the dwarf, who added a couple of sections to the page.

"The first layer is mostly harmless. To a human, it might even be nicer than Hallowfort. Why, some of the more nature-inclined species would rather reside there. The second layer is a big cave with traps and mostly earth magic insects of varying levels. After that comes a massive layer filled with water. I never ventured there but came close several times.

"Farther below lies Heroes' Descent, probably a place built by the former inhabitants of the city above and those who made the statue that Hallowfort sits on. My information gets unreliable here, but those who venture there or farther either come out rich or die trying. Mostly the latter."

He added some information on each of the layers, though it wasn't much. If there had once been a town in the fourth layer called Heroes' Descent, it probably meant that was the starting point for the ancient citizens.

"You think it goes much farther down?"

"The language of the city is Standard, and they liked their statues, murals, and inscriptions. It is said that Heroes' Descent is where the strongest are tested, where they are trained and sent to recover artifacts, magic and technology of the deep. That dungeon was like a religion to them. There's information on more layers there, but it's apparently neither accurate nor plentiful," he explained, moving a hand through his black greasy hair. "Guess you'll find out when you go there."

"I suppose I will," she said and nodded. "What about the monsters in the lake below Hallowfort? I saw some shapes but decided not to engage back when I was there."

"Nothing worth the trouble. Most creatures are below two hundred, except the whales. Black creatures lined with bone, if the stories are to be believed. Some say they feast on Miststalkers at night. I suggest you wait on finding out more about them until you can survive and kill entire groups of stalkers."

Ilea grunted, but if there was a reason not to fight underwater, she definitely welcomed it.

"Any other places or monsters? Maybe not underground?"

Terok scratched his beard but looked skeptical. "None of the beasts up there are any easier to deal with than what's down here. The few you might be able to kill without getting overwhelmed are either below your level or too elusive to catch, even for specialized trackers. You could go look for Awakened farther north or hunt Feynor, but you don't strike me as someone who would want to hunt and kill intelligent creatures."

Ilea remembered the vacant look on the face of Petra Birmingale. She'd killed plenty of that kind of foe, but he was right. She didn't want to hunt and kill them. Not for her own power alone. Revenge, self-defense, or someone whose humor was based entirely on puns would qualify, but purely for her own gains? That was a line she didn't want to cross. Perhaps for the greater good or to stop some overwhelming force threatening all that she held dear. Even then, it would be a hard choice. One she hoped she'd never have to face.

"Never heard of Feynor. Another kind of awakened beast?"

"No. They reside as close to the highest mountains in the north as they can. Sentient and apparently related to dragons. They apparently look more like lizardmen, but I've never met any. Everyone who has reports that they attack on sight. A tough people, and in recent years they've come closer and closer to Hallowfort."

Terok finished his drink. "You asked about the Taleen before, and that friend of yours who was teleported away. Took the liberty of asking around. Didn't get too much, but got something. There's a dungeon a couple hours flight northwest. But I doubt that Guardians would do much for your experience, and according to my source, it's a dangerous one, even in terms of the Taleen. Lots of Centurions, at the very least. Probably worse machines there too. Few have even tried to get in very far."

"I appreciate it, Terok."

A way to find out more about the Taleen.

But if it's as dangerous as Terok suggests, I should make sure I'm ready. Before I rush in and find another set of Praetorians and no trace of Kyrian.

She gulped.

Am I scared? No. No I just need to get a little stronger first. That's all.

She breathed in slowly. *Scared or not. I'll get there. In time. Another thing to look forward to.*

"I'm not sure how smart it would be to explore another one. At least not until I'm more confident that I could face Praetorians. Maybe once I get to three hundred like Maro suggested."

"Do let me know when you do. Their tech is impressive, and I'd love to see the inner workings of their production facilities. But they're always riddled with traps and machines trying to kill you. Everyone who ever showed an interest in their tech has either given up or not returned."

"You think you could replicate anything?" Ilea asked.

Terok laughed, his voice reverberating in the big hall. "You think nobody has tried? No, I go my own way. I hear the best dwarven engineers have cursed the designs as impossible to copy, and I'm not going to pretend that I'm better than them. Inspiration is what I seek. I'm a metal mage and engineer, not a machine designer. They can try to figure out the autonomous designs of the Taleen for as long as they want to. I doubt they made them easy enough to simply replicate. Not with how many traps and defensive measures their towns are lined with."

Perhaps copying a teleportation gate might not be on the cards after all...

Christopher and Iana would continue to try, of course, and both Ilea and Claire would likely fund them anyway. Just for the chance to bring the technology to humanity and the Shadow's Hand.

For now, though, the Descent seemed a much more promising path.

FORTY-EIGHT

Alien Town

Mists covered the land and crows flew in the distance, moonlight reflecting off their leathery wings as ash shrouded Ilea in darkness. Quickly, she moved over the desolate terrain, ignoring any moving creatures as she made her way toward the Penumra dungeon. The place that would lead to Hallowfort and the Descent. Her goal was to find enemies of a similar or higher level to the knights, though preferably less durable against her attacks.

Might be able to advance some of my resistances as well.

Diving into the crevice in the mountainous terrain, she soon found herself in front of the gaping cavern entrance leading down into Penumra. Terok had confirmed her instincts with what he'd told her about the Drop Saurians. An enemy she might want to face at a later time.

That list is getting longer…

Ignoring the dungeon for now, she made her way down the caves and toward Hallowfort. Moving through the darkness, Ilea finally blinked out into the open, where the light shining from the crystals reflected off her ash and armor.

As Ilea landed, her wings dissolved. The Awakened standing on the other side of the bridge looked at her but didn't move as she walked toward him. Stepping onto the massive statue on the other side of the bridge, she looked up at the three-meter-tall warrior.

[Warrior – lvl 228]

The Awakened was clad in heavy black full-plate armor, two big horns jutting upward from their helmet. Ornaments of varying detail and design decorated each piece of their armor. The helmet was closed off entirely, with neither eyes nor face visible, if such things were even part of the being standing before her.

"Greetings," Ilea said, bowing her head slightly. "I'm told the elevator leading to the Descent is located in town. I've visited before but haven't seen any obvious entrance."

The massive form bowed in return, an ethereal voice speaking to her a moment later.

"Greetings, friend of ash. You speak truth. Find the stairwell leading down from within the establishment called the Abyss. I would lead you there, but I am not to leave my post."

Ilea smiled, her smaller form and the forward-curving horns on her helmet making her look a little like the Awakened's younger sister.

"I'll find it. Thank you, dark-plated warrior," she said, a little unsure of the form of address, but it felt right. Goliath had used random descriptions of her in their conversations, and she liked the gesture, which was apparently quite common in Hallowfort.

"You honor me, ashen one," the being said and bowed again.

For a guard, this one was definitely the strongest, most stylish, and friendliest Ilea had ever met.

The Abyss...

Ilea read the signs and descriptions of the various different shops and houses as she walked through town. Now that she wasn't just passing through, she noticed more of the architecture. Most of the houses were built from stone or metal, with varying degrees of craftsmanship. Either they had very different ideas about how and what to build, or it was relatively normal to build your own house, however basic it looked in the end.

Ilea stopped in front of what looked like a big bird's nest, closed off at the top, where a hatch had been placed within the dense mesh of steel thread.

Perhaps some kind of metal magic bird lives in this one?

Other buildings looked like what an advanced bug would build – mud and stone somehow hardened and formed into dome-shaped houses that looked to be melting. There were many she couldn't penetrate with her Sphere. The quality of the enchantments suggested the designs of the buildings were very much intended. The places she could look into were empty for the most part. Some even gave her the impression of being completely abandoned.

Suppose being a scavenger isn't the safest job out there.

There were people on the street, but it definitely wasn't busy compared to some of the human settlements she had been to. Dwarves, Awakened, cat and lizard beings, and more exotic creatures floating or crawling about – Ilea identified them all, though none acknowledged her. Most were below two hundred but definitely close to it, just like Terok.

A certain strength was required to survive in the north, but apparently it was less than she'd initially expected. Surviving was, of course, different to thriving. She doubted many had seen a level-up message in months, years, or even decades.

They were veterans, every single one of them. While she had come here to fight the monsters lurking in the north, the people living here instead seemed to survive amongst them. They had to make a living somehow, collect things to sell, or grow food themselves. Hallowfort gave her the impression of a safe haven at the center of a particularly stormy region of islands, a place to rest and prepare. For creatures of all kinds.

Ilea wondered how many of them had actually been born here, how many knew no different life than one surrounded by vicious beasts, arcane storms, and dungeons. Nature that wanted to kill you just as much as the monsters looking for food. How many of them cared? Terok seemed content enough with his scavenging lifestyle, and while Goliath was probably hundreds or even thousands of years old, he was content with forging and staying in his domain.

I'd probably go mad after all that time...

Then again, she'd never really considered getting to that age in the first place. How one of her kind would react and change after all that time was unknown, especially considering skills like Meditation, Hunter Recovery or Mental Resistance. Goliath didn't seem to strive for power or domination. He was only focused on creation and metal. She could definitely see someone like Balduur following a similar path.

For her, it was different. She had fought for months on end, but there was the constant danger of death, the progression in both her skills and levels, the results of enemies being killed and removed from dungeons.

To think she could now fight for hours at a time without even getting a headache was definitely scary, particularly when thinking about the possible heights a human or any other species could get to when the systems governing skills and Classes were involved. The reliance on killing to level up wasn't lost on her. The saving grace for the world's morality was that wild beasts were still worse and more powerful than any sapient beings she'd met, be they elves, Awakened, or humans.

Taking a random stairwell leading down into the statue, she soon found a sign that read *'Abyss'*. Most of Hallowfort seemed to be located within the statue, not atop it. Ilea figured many of the species living here were likely not reliant on light, perhaps even being averse to it.

Living quarters were much more chaotic here – Ilea could only really identify the doors and windows. Even then, some of the openings looked too small, the furniture too alien for her to grasp their purpose. In a way, though, she was happy to find herself in a place so distant from a human settlement. She was the stranger here in connections, species, and culture.

A single magical lamp placed in what looked like a worn steel lantern lit up the underground street lined with closed doors of stone, wood, or steel.

It flickered from time to time as she made her way up the slightly damp street, holes and loose rocks as well as mushrooms decorating the tunnel, toward the torchlight illuminating white lettering on a sign spelling out the word 'Abyss' in Standard. The sign was attached to a building cast into the stone wall, simply cut into the inside of the once impressive monument to whatever civilization had once resided here.

Warm golden light fought hard to penetrate the murky glass windows. The name definitely fitted the surroundings. Nobody checked patrons on entry, so she simply opened the heavy wooden door, which was painted black, and walked inside.

Descending a stairwell leading down, she arrived in a broad hall. Magic lights lined the walls. Most of them were warm, but some had a reddish or even blue tone. Ilea noted that parts of the bar were completely dark as well, as if the light was sucked into a void. The whole left side was taken up by a counter with bottles, trinkets, and apparatuses lining the shelves and wall behind. Their colors and shapes reminded her of a medieval alchemist's shop.

Some of the patrons looked at her as she made her way toward the bar. A tune played in the background, but she didn't notice until she was standing at the bar that there was a group of floating creatures summoning and moving black swirls to create the sounds.

Magic band.

The whooshing sounds and high-pitched noises in between reminded her more of an alternative meditation session than background music in a pub. She was the stranger here, that was for sure.

"What can I get you?" asked the cat person behind the bar. The male voice was almost a purr, and his black fur, piercing yellow eyes, and ears atop his head finished the look. It made her smile. If cats became more humanoid, this one definitely kept the smoothness she associated with the animals.

Do they keep cats as pets as well?

"Ale, if you have any," she replied, looking at his casual pants and lack of a shirt. His black shorts seemed to be there more for the pockets and belt lined with tools, daggers, and cleaning rags than fashion.

The cat person purred and looked into her eyes for a moment before stepping aside smoothly. She noted that he made no noise as he did so.

[Mage – lvl 211]

He could compete with Walter. Though Ilea doubted his ale was anywhere near as good, especially after what Terok had given her previously. Perhaps she had to get the old barkeeper to visit and teach some of the brewers in the region a thing or two. *Now that would be a journey.*

An open bottle was placed before her a moment later. "Five copper," the cat person said, Ilea summoning the amount and putting it on the counter.

"I'm looking for the elevator leading to the Descent," she said as the cat cleaned a glass with one of the rags.

He pointed toward the opposite corner of the room, where an opening in the wall revealed steps leading downward.

"I suggest waiting. A Blue Reaper was sighted yesterday. Sorry lad who went down made it out half dead only thanks to a healer being close by."

"A friend of mine mentioned a bounty on them. How much?" Ilea asked, noticing a nearby lizardman looking her way with interest.

"The usual price. Ninety silvers for the corpse. Maybe one gold coin."

"Where do I bring it?"

"Big building up top, has a dragoon skull hanging outside."

Ilea tipped him a piece of silver for the information. The cat's eyes narrowed, but he nodded and took the money.

As he did so, Ilea noticed someone approach. A creature clad in a long black coat, a white mask resembling a vicious predator adorning its face. It looked like black mist was all that resided beneath its garb.

"Warrior in flesh. Human. I greet thee. Thou art no Awakened, but I beseech thee to heed the call of the Dark Protector. The one to unite all and bring peace..."

Ilea grabbed the bottle and took a sip before she stood up.

"Sure, I'll buy them a bottle of ale if I see them."

Interesting taste, this ale... Think I prefer Walter's, but it's refreshing. Probably put different kinds of shit that only grows up here in it.

Walking toward the elevator with her bottle, she noted that the closer she got, the more people looked her way. Some spoke in strange sounds to each other before what she assumed was laughter came from wherever their voices were produced. Insect-like beings, possibly Awakened.

"Meet me here, Sato, the Revered One, if you will fight in the great war. Treasures and fame wait for thy human soul." The ethereal voice somehow carried across the room to her ears, but Ilea had no interest in another war. Human or not.

The band kept on playing as she passed through the opening and made her way down the stairs, coming out in a large stone cellar. A level two hundred warrior stood guard. They looked similar to the one near the bridge, though smaller. Smaller even than her, but the sword on their back looked vicious nonetheless.

"Blue Reaper down there somewhere. Here to kill it?"

Ilea didn't reply at first as ash formed around her, swirling lazily as some of it condensed into spheres behind her back, limbs forming at the same time.

"Yeah," she said, her buffs activating before she walked off the edge of the open elevator shaft. Chains led downward on each side, but no platform was visible.

Her wings spread behind her as she fell. There wasn't quite enough space for them to expand fully, but they still slowed her down. The descent was longer than she'd expected, and Ilea floated for at least a minute before she hit the ground with a dull impact.

There was no source of light around her, and more and more ash came to life as she took in the surroundings through her sphere. A tunnel, though seemingly a not natural one. Somehow, from the way the bricks were laid into the stone walls, the way the ground was cobbled, she thought it more familiar than the town up above. Terok had said it had been a city at some point, one that had revered the Descent, the dungeon above which it had been built.

Or in which it had been built.

'ding' You have entered The Descent dungeon

She couldn't detect any movement, any noise. There were three separate directions she could choose, hallways leading into the dark. The ground was worn, many travelers, scavengers, and adventurers having walked here before.

Activating her Hunter's Sight, she focused on what she knew about the Blue Reapers. They had mind magic and electricity, as well as more than two legs.

Let's see what I can find, she thought as she walked into the darkness with a smile on her face.

FORTY-NINE

The Blue Reaper

Ilea walked down one of the tunnels at random. A couple of minutes later, she noticed blood on the floor. It was dry, but her Sphere picked it up even in the pitch-black darkness. No corpse, but that could mean anything.

The bartender did say the guy who was attacked had escaped.

There was no trail leading anywhere, so she kept walking onward. A clicking noise met her ears as she continued. Stopping near the opening at the end of the hallway, she was pretty sure whatever was causing the clicking would be inside the room or hall beyond.

Alright, Reaper thing…

Her wings took her upward, and she floated into the next chamber just as a hard push of mind magic smashed against her mental defenses. A blinding headache made her stumble before her healing repaired the damage. Another wave washed over her, bringing her to one knee as she breathed hard, blood flowing from her nose as she heard a shrieking noise coming from ahead.

Taking a stumbling step, her healing mana flowed through her brain. The next step was steadier, and now the creature was within range of her Sphere. She saw six legs ending in sharp bone, two legs angled up toward her and a sparkling ball forming between them. Its head looked a little like a mantis, with two antennae growing upward.

Blue lightning illuminated the creature like an ominous predator in the dark, its bony carapace exuding a blue glow before a flash of lightning zapped toward her. Ilea dodged to the side, quick enough to avoid the scorching beam.

Her mind heated up again as she saw the creature recoil, screeching in pain as it scuttled backward. As it formed another ball of lightning, Ilea thought it would certainly have made for a dangerous look were it not for the fact that it was barely as big as a dachshund.

[Blue Reaper - ??]

As lightning zapped her way, she formed a wall of ash before her, but it managed to penetrate both the wall and her Veil. The magic burnt through her skin and organs. Healing the wounds, she decided to dodge the blasts. They weren't enough to incapacitate her, but a series of attacks would be dangerous.

That small little fucker is more powerful than Trian… but I can survive the magic and stay alive.

She ticked off the mental note as she blinked next to the creature. Landing on it, she spread ash around, her limbs crashing into it with Wave of Ember as she held it down with her hands and body. Lightning coursed through her as her mind was rattled by the panicking beast's powerful magic.

Her fist landed on the monster's head, damaging one of its antennae, and it screeched, trying to get out of her grasp. It had a surprising amount of mana stored in that small body, Ilea's healing barely keeping up with the ridiculous lightning and mind magic damage it dealt every second.

Her second strike with her fist, which hit one of its legs, broke both the bone and the stone floor. The creature's mental attacks subsided somewhat, but the lightning continued. Ilea repeated the attack on another of its legs. The creature was still trying to get away from her, clawing at the ash with its sharp arms.

Another crack echoed through the chamber, then another, the monster screeching as a massive mental attack blinded Ilea's senses for a moment. Her body locked up, and the creature crawled out from her grasp. Even though three of its eight legs were broken, it still moved rather quickly.

Ilea heard it and saw it in her Sphere as soon as her healing brought her back from her stunned state. She saw one of its eyes had been blown out, likely from the feedback of the mental attack it had just used. A blink brought her right back next to the beast, her ashen limbs smashing into it, and Ilea stomped down as hard as she could.

Lightning flashed in the dark, the smell of burnt skin reaching her nose as she stomped again. The monster's exoskeleton was tough but nothing compared to the knights in Tremor. A third kick broke another leg before Ilea knelt down and punched at the creature as it used the rest of its mana to send out waves of lightning and mind magic. Ilea resisted and healed them all.

A final punch caused a resounding crack, breaking the back of the creature and killing it instantly. Ilea coughed and rolled to the side, breathing hard as she noticed the pain in her throat and eyes. Blood had run down her face, and several of her organs had been damaged by the lightning.

Resistance my ass.

'ding' You have defeated [Blue Reaper – lvl 363] – For defeating an enemy ninety or more levels above your own, bonus experience is granted.

'ding' Azarinth First Hunter has reached lvl 256 – Five stat points awarded

Ilea coughed again, reconstructing her eyes in the bloody sockets left behind after the energy had popped them. Slowly, she felt her breathing return to normal. She'd gained another level. What the Blue Reapers lacked in defense, they certainly made up for in magical power.

But the difference was that she could kill these enemies in a couple of minutes while knights, even those at her own level, took hours to take down. Problems would occur when there were groups of them. She was fairly sure she could handle two. The mind magic was manageable, and the lightning had only started to hurt her when she'd touched it.

Calming down from the short but intense battle, she checked her health and found it topped off again, her mana recovering quickly thanks to Meditation. No pain remained, and her resistances – coupled with her defensive skills and healing – had prevailed.

Blue Reapers were on the menu.

Grinning at her success, Ilea stood up and lifted the small corpse. Trying to smash its head had proved difficult. The skull, while tiny, had insane resistance – so much so that the stone below had cracked before the bone had. Its leg joints were the weak spots, and Ilea carefully checked where they were and which ways they could bend. Smashing them might actually be less effective than just bending them backward with enough force.

After a couple of minutes of testing, she found that holding them at a certain angle and then punching down was the easiest way to crack them. As soon as the creature couldn't move as quickly, it would be a sitting duck. If it overwhelmed her, she could simply leave and heal up before coming back to finish the job. She considered even several could be manageable using such tactics. It had a way of seeing her, both in her ash as well as in a dark hallway, but she'd expected that much.

"Now to find your nest, little bugs."

Storing the broken and bleeding corpse inside her necklace, she walked on. Another positive of fighting the reaper was that her armor hadn't been damaged. The coating had heated up a little, small marks showing where the lightning had surged the strongest, but otherwise the latest Rose Hunter set was perfectly fine.

Though she saw more cave openings and tunnels as well as cracks leading to lower floors, some time passed before she heard another clicking noise, the grin on her face returning as she prepared for battle. This time, she slowly floated toward the noise, her magic adding more and more ash to the swirling mass that surrounded her.

A pulse of magic punched into her mind, and her wings wavered as she lost control. She caught herself a split second later as her ash surrounded the reaper. Limbs of ash extended and smashed into it, Wave of Ember coursing through the monster while its destructive power flowed through her mind. Ilea found that with meditation and her healing, the damage was just about controllable.

The lightning attacks it sent out were blocked by her ash and Veil, and the damage that got through was healed. Ilea built up more ash than she could reasonably control, but it made it harder for the enemy's magic to get to her. Focusing on her eight limbs, she kept on attacking, dodging the lightning strikes whenever possible.

Jumping closer right after it had missed an attack, she grabbed one of its legs and broke it just the way she'd done with the corpse's. Other than the lightning nearly locking up her muscles in the process and frying a good portion of her right side, she encountered no problems. The leg cracked at the joint and Ilea moved back again, healing and meditating as the beast screeched.

Its magic continued to blast into her, but she simply out-healed whatever got through her defenses, a thick mist of ash clouding the whole area up to the ceiling. The reaper's mantis-like head kept its eyes on her, dragging its broken limb uselessly at its side as it sent destructive waves of magic at her mind and body.

Again, Ilea blinked next to it and broke another leg at the expense of her own health. With two of its legs broken and more damage coming in from her ashen limbs, it finally decided to try and flee.

Checking her health, Ilea found it well above half and blinked next to the running creature, grabbing on before she started smashing her fist into the carapace around its small frame. The dull sounds of bone hitting rock bounced through the dark halls, only the thrumming of lightning occasionally adding to the noise. Ten hits later, something cracked, then silence returned.

'ding' You have defeated [Blue Reaper – lvl 329] – For defeating an enemy seventy or more levels above your own, bonus experience is granted.

'ding' Inheritor of Eternal Ash has reached lvl 249 – Five stat points awarded

Ilea smiled, much less damaged from this encounter than the last. Not overextending at first certainly helped. Blinking before the lightning hit her was preferable, but having the whole area full of ash had made it hard to get away from the moving critter. If the ash touched her and the enemy, she couldn't blink.

Next time I'll do better.

Still, it was much simpler than facing the knights.

Storing the corpse, she continued onward. Next to experience, she'd be gaining silver for killing the Blue Reapers as well. That wasn't why she was there, but it was a welcome addition.

When the hallway ended, Ilea saw a big chunk in the wall was missing, revealing a small tunnel beyond. The marks and cuts on the walls as well as the size of the opening indicated that the reapers had carved it out.

How long did that take to do?

This was likely the route that one or many had used to come into the Descent. Ilea crouched and moved into it, finding the opening just high enough for her to crawl through. Were this a tunnel of Rhyvor, filled with Rose Knights crawling around, she'd turn back and seal it with whatever she could find. Though hyper-aggressive on her part, she thought this might work.

Ilea followed the tunnel, crawling through as she listened for a clicking noise. Around ten minutes later, she heard it. The tunnel wasn't completely straight, allowing her to blink to safety, at least against lightning blasts coming her way. Either the reapers hadn't anticipated a foe would do something like this, or this was literally the stupidest way to engage them for anybody but her.

She found the critter behind a bend, her mind immediately blasted with magic as soon as it heard her. The thing didn't even need line of sight.

Just like me.

Listening carefully while she healed her mind, Ilea was pretty sure there was only one of them. Blinking behind the reaper, she wrestled it and resisted the lightning that immediately spread through her body. There was one crack and then another before she let go and blinked back to her safe spot.

The smell of burnt skin came to her nose as her tissue reformed and healed. Watching the beast writhe in pain from its broken bones made her focus on her own recovery for a minute before she blinked in again, all her offensive skills working in tandem.

Ilea broke another two of its limbs, its central shell showing a crack, before blinking back again. The tunnel was actually an even better place to fight them than the hallways.

'ding' Mental Resistance reaches 2nd lvl 12

Smiling at the notification, she appeared above the creature and smashed her fists onto the carapace as well as the small space allowed. With her mana intrusion dealing most of the damage, it was less of a detriment than she'd initially anticipated. After another four hits and several sections of her body being burnt and damaged, the reaper fell.

'ding' You have defeated [Blue Reaper – lvl 341] – For defeating an enemy eighty or more levels above your own, bonus experience is granted.

Storing the corpse, she crawled on to find more. Meditation and Hunter Recovery worked hard to restore her to full health in the process. Her crawling speed wasn't exactly spectacular, but it allowed her to meditate during her search.

Ilea slowly grew frustrated after crawling for what felt like hours and not finding a single additional enemy. The tunnels weaved through the stone, opening more and more places to explore or get lost in.

She tried to sketch her route in her notebook but made sure to leave little crosses to mark where she'd been before with arrows to show where she'd come from. The markings were perfectly visible to her Sphere in the dark tunnels.

Ilea had expected the claustrophobic and dark space to be at least something of an issue, but instead, she felt like a crazed miner certain of finding a new vein in a gold rush. The only problem she foresaw was if the reapers repaired the tunnels and perhaps removed her markings, but she had no way of knowing if they'd do that.

At least the critters weren't that fast, and she'd likely be able to outpace them with her blink to heal and meditate.

For a while, at least.

FIFTY

Wormholes

Ilea stopped in her tracks. She'd already been in the dark tunnels for hours without finding a single reaper. Now, straining her ears, she finally heard the clicking. Quicker, alert, and still quite a distance away. There were at least two of them. A challenge she wasn't sure she was ready for.

Still, she wanted to test herself. After such a long search, she wouldn't just turn around and crawl back. Ilea trusted her defenses and her recovery. Blinking away was always an option.

Just have to stay conscious.

Crawling around the bend, the clicking intensified, and two reapers quickly crawled toward her before their magic assailed her mind. Ilea stayed conscious. Counting the seconds as she watched the monsters form balls of lightning, she blinked back around the bend and saw the bolts flash into the walls. Her health was draining, and her head pounded in a way she hadn't felt before.

The headache was so strong she had to turn off her pain perception, most of her focus going toward it. She heard the sound of dripping, then realized it was her own blood coming out of her nose and ears. The damage was still manageable though, her healing working hard against the enemy attacks as they kept on coming. At least they came in waves, not as a constant stream. She filled the tunnel with ash and heated it up before seeing the critters move through it and toward her.

When one of them had rounded the bend, she blinked behind the one behind. Grabbing its hind leg, she cracked it while its lightning coursed through her. The mantis-like head of the reaper ahead turned, lightning flashing toward her.

Ilea lifted up the monster she was still holding onto as a shield, the magic running through it, through her, and then into the ground. The dazed state and movements of the electrocuted beast before her made her grin, despite her draining health and heavily injured body. Ilea broke another leg and then blinked away.

Four seconds, she thought, the mind magic having gotten weaker. The injured reaper wasn't quite as proficient anymore with two broken legs and a slightly burnt body. At least the lightning could injure them as well.

She coughed, several spots in her throat bleeding and burnt. Ilea focused on healing her organs, bringing them back to working order before she blinked again, creating more distance between the healthy reaper and herself. It was dangerous as she was moving into unknown territory, but so far, she hadn't heard more clicking.

After another bout of healing, she noticed that the injured bug was falling behind. Coughing again, she blinked beside the healthy one and then again to the injured one. Grabbing it, she broke another leg before she started punching its central shell.

Each hit sent sparks and embers into the dark tunnel, gouts of lightning surging around them before cutting into the stone and scorching both Ilea and the wall. Finally, there was a crack, and the beast died. Ilea blinked away immediately – just before a flash of magic burned into the wall.

Again and again, she blinked, trying to put as much distance as possible between her and the uninjured Blue Reaper, the marks on the walls visible in her Sphere like a lifeline guiding her to safety. Stopping when the mind magic didn't reach her anymore, she started healing.

Her body was in a rough shape, but she'd been through worse. Perhaps not *much* worse, but definitely worse. The dangerous part was that one of the monsters was still alive and looking for her.

Ignoring the message about the first reaper for now, she simply focused on healing as much as she could. When she felt comfortable to face the remaining foe, she blinked toward it. Ash spread out and heated up, and her limbs smashed into it with Wave of Ember before she grabbed and broke one of its limbs.

She blinked back immediately as more lightning coursed through her body, destroying what it could before it burnt into the stone. Taking a moment to heal herself, she continued her now tried and proven tactic against the Blue Reapers. A few more moments of battle, and the beast was dead.

'ding' You have defeated [Blue Reaper – lvl 380] – For defeating an enemy one hundred and twenty or more levels above your own, bonus experience is granted.

'ding' You have defeated [Blue Reaper – lvl 333] – For defeating an enemy seventy or more levels above your own, bonus experience is granted.

'ding' Azarinth First Hunter has reached lvl 257 – Five stat points awarded

'ding' Inheritor of Eternal Ash has reached lvl 250 – Five stat points awarded

'ding' Destruction reaches 3rd lvl 3

'ding' Ash Creation reaches 3rd lvl 2

'ding' Embered Body Heat reaches 2nd lvl 14

'ding' Lightning Resistance reaches 2nd lvl 6

Ilea was lying on her back in the dark tunnel, coughing and healing. Her sense of pain was entirely shut off, but her recovery skill certainly painted a bleak picture of her body's state. Soon it would be fine again, but fighting two reapers at the same time was definitely a stretch. She would survive it if she didn't make a bad mistake – and as long as a third one didn't show up – but their damage potential was ridiculous.

And I was worried about a knight cutting off my leg.

Ilea had gained ten stat points, but she wasn't sure where to invest them. Vitality seemed like a good idea as she lay there, blood leaking through every opening in her armor, her body writhing as its tissue reformed.

She thanked whatever cruel system or magic governed this world that she could shut off her perception of pain. A blanket of warm ash had formed around her at some point, trying to comfort or protect her. A sigh went through her a couple minutes later, her body fully recovered.

Three of them is a no-go right now.

In an emergency, she'd try, but if she could avoid it, she would.

Ilea lay there in the tunnel, no noise or light anywhere close as she healed herself. Smelling the blood on her, Ilea decided to go and wash her armor in Hallowfort as soon as she got back.

Collecting the reaper corpses, she continued her search, ash heating up around her while her Hunter's Sight worked to find any clues pointing her toward more enemy monsters.

* * *

After a well-deserved bath with some added heat from her Embered Body Heat, Ilea's bug extermination continued. Being close to Hallowfort proved to be a blessing as she could visit Goliath and Terok when she needed a break from the slaughter. Combing the tunnels was grueling work, and after a while, the reapers seemed to actively avoid her.

Days passed, though Ilea couldn't be sure how many. It was hard to tell below ground. All Ilea knew was that the experience was good. Knowing the bugs' weak spots and exactly what they were capable of made the one-on-one fights a simple matter of extermination.

While fewer in number, they were much higher in level compared to the knights. At least most of them. Checking her messages and her skills, she was quite content with her decision to look for the critters. Her new stat points had mostly gone toward Vitality. Mainly because she didn't want to die.

'ding' You have defeated [Blue Reaper – lvl 352] – For defeating an enemy ninety or more levels above your own, bonus experience is granted.

...

'ding' You have defeated [Blue Reaper – lvl 361] – For defeating an enemy one hundred or more levels above your own, bonus experience is granted.

'ding' Azarinth First Hunter has reached lvl 258 – Five stat points awarded

'ding' Inheritor of Eternal Ash has reached lvl 251 – Five stat points awarded

'ding' State of Azarinth reaches 3rd lvl 6

'ding' Blink reaches 3rd lvl 7

'ding' Hunter's Sight reaches 2nd lvl 16

'ding' Embered Body Heat reaches 2nd lvl 15

Returning to the corridors of the Descent, Ilea felt the small tunnels were quite a bit more dangerous than whatever this underground city could throw at her. At least the upper levels starting right below Hallowfort. Finally stretching her body and moving her arms and legs in the free space, she sighed in relief.

Her thoughts were focused on getting a bottle of ale in the Abyss and maybe renting a room suitable for humans.

"You sure it's this way?"

A squeaky voice cut through the corridors as Ilea floated toward the exit with her wings and heated ash. She saw the group of adventurers a moment later in her Sphere, completely oblivious to her approach as she was still hidden behind a bend in the tunnel.

"Wait, something's there," another voice hissed, making them all stop.

Torchlight illuminated the hallway as Ilea's wings dissolved, the ash around her cooling. Landing on her feet, she rounded the corner and stood before a group of warriors and mages.

There were five in total, each armed, armored, and ready for whatever was to come. One was definitely a dwarf in his or her war machine, this one larger and far bulkier than the one Terok used. Two wore full plate armor, tall but otherwise impossible for Ilea to describe. The last two were mages based on clothing stereotypes. Armored robes, metal reflecting the torch-light. Quickly identifying everyone, she found all except for one below two hundred.

Scavengers, then?

"Greetings," she said to the group, who appeared apprehensive.

"Warrior... greetings. Is this the way down?" one of the big armored beings asked.

Ilea cocked her head before replying. "There were some stairs and holes leading down, but I didn't go there."

"What did you do then?" the squeaky voice asked – one of the mages. Two of the others looked at him, one even hissing. They weren't sure what to make of her, that much was clear. Nor was Ilea looking for conflict. She wanted to sleep.

Summoning one of the Blue Reaper corpses, she held it up and dumped it between her and the group, the closest warrior taking an instinctive step back. Light flashed from one of the mages, but he canceled the spell as soon as he understood what had happened. They stared at her with wide eyes and slack jaws.

"Is that a reaper?" one of the mages whispered, seemingly unable to raise his voice even in the presence of a mere corpse.

"How the hell...?" muttered one of the warriors before his words became a series of impressive curse words.

"I was hunting these. I'd suggest not going that way, there's a tunnel system they use, ending in one of the hallways. Good luck on your hunt."

Ilea picked up the corpse before walking through the group, who parted at her approach, dark blood dripping from the dead reaper onto the floor.

FIFTY-ONE

Cake

Ilea flew back up through the elevator shaft after realizing there really was no platform to be used. Coming out at the top, her wings dissolved, the guard nodding as they let go of the sword on their back. It was the same warrior she'd met when she'd gone down earlier.

Music was being played in the bar, this time less alien than what she'd heard before. The instruments looked more like intricate guitars, and the sounds made her feel serene. The masked priest person was still around, talking to two patrons sitting at a table, trying to convince them to join the great war, whatever that was.

Ilea reached the counter and nodded to the cat waiter. He sniffed at her and frowned.

"Exactly. Room and a bath?" she said, grinning as he put down a silver key.

"Thank you for taking care of more reapers. The room is on the house, as usual. For three days. Water runes for a bath are inside. Last one on the first floor," he explained.

Ilea took the key with a smile, glad to be out of those tunnels and back in a civilized place.

"Thanks," she said and put down five coppers, prompting the cat person to slide a bottle of ale her way.

* * *

The key slid into the lock and clicked when she turned it. Entering, she locked it again and pushed mana into the runes near the door, knowing them to be intrusion barriers against sound and teleportation.

Thanks, Claire. For your unrelenting lessons.

Blinking out and back in revealed them to be not quite enough to stop someone like her, but it was still more impressive than all the inns she'd been to in the Plains. The furniture was dark blue and black, leather mostly.

A blueish light shone from an intricate metal sphere with rings and floating pieces surrounding the magical bulb in the middle of the room, forming a mesmerizing pattern on the stone walls around her.

There was also a bathroom with a tub, big enough to accommodate most creatures she'd seen in the bar below. Runes would gather the water before filling the carved stone bath. Ilea wondered how the runes gathered enough to fill the whole thing, but she'd seen similar designs in human inns. Even Earl had a bath with runes like that.

Touching the intricate patterns on the metal plates, water soon started flowing as Ilea dumped her armor on the ground next to the tub. Putting a couple of her ashen limbs into it, she quickly heated it up to a boiling temperature before stepping in.

She let out a sigh, continuously heating up the water as steam filled the bathroom. Ilea took her time with rubbing all the dried blood as well as pieces of muck off her. Sighing again, she went under, the boiling water bubbling around her. A cheap bubble bath. Luckily she was exceptionally heat resistant. It was certainly enjoyable.

She chucked in her armor pieces when she was clean herself, the boiling water taking care of whatever dirt and blood was left on them. She noted that the cracks on the coating caused by the lightning remained, burned deeply into the metal.

Ilea found she liked the look of the cracked armor, now that she saw it with her own eyes and not through her Sphere. Putting the set into her inventory, she put it onto her body before heating herself up to dry it off.

The main room had several sleeping options, catering for different forms and sizes. Ilea turned her head a little when she looked at the cocoon-like blankets hanging in one corner of the room. She wondered if those would be comfortable, but she felt too tired to try them out.

The bed creaked a little when she sat on it, and it wasn't quite as soft and comfortable as she liked. Standing up again, she summoned her own. There was enough space for it, though barely.

Lying down, Ilea thought of magical lightning sizzling in the dark. She was asleep in mere moments, meditation and healing flowing through her mind as she calmed down.

* * *

Putting the key on the counter, Ilea waited for the cat person to approach her. "I don't know how long I'll be gone."

He nodded and took the key, his ears twitching once.

"I'm Ilea. And thanks for the room," she added, realizing she hadn't introduced herself to him yet.

"Haiden. Fortune on your hunt." He bowed his head a little as he said it, eyes closed.

Ilea didn't plan to go back down into the tunnels right away, instead wanting to sell all the dead Blue Reapers she'd acquired.

I really have to clean out my necklace…

Perhaps she could sell some other things she had with her while she was at it.

Leaving the Abyss, she made her way up to the top of Hallowfort. A group of cloaked warriors and mages walked past, all below level two hundred – scavengers, most likely. One glanced at her with what looked like human eyes – the first human she'd seen in the north, if it really had been a human. Neither of them initiated a conversation.

Maybe a survivor from one expedition or another, she thought, walking up the stairs to the highest level of the small town. The small square was at the center of the statue. Ilea spotted the building with the dragoon skull immediately.

It was a squat structure constructed of large stone boulders rather than bricks, but it still managed to look immensely solid and structurally sound. The roof overhung the walls as if the building was wearing a massive wizard's hat. Moss grew from the top, in parts reaching down to the walls. Ivy too. The picture was completed by dozens of pots with different herbs and plants, some hanging from the edge of the hat-like roof. It was situated close enough to the edge of the statue to overlook the crystal sea below. The door was thick and wooden, a dark brown that nestled into the gray of the stone around it.

Ilea read the sign hanging a little crookedly from the roof right next to the door, a small lantern next to it, its light brightening the dark letters: *'Hunter's Den'*. Few people were in the square, but it was definitely one of the busier places in Hallowfort. Her Sphere only detected a single occupant inside, and Ilea entered quickly, curious about the person's form.

A jingle sounded when she entered, a cluster of blue crystals beside the door tinkling when it opened. There were even more pots with plants here, small glass cages with what looked like full ecosystems trapped inside. At the back of the store, broad shelves were stuffed with monster parts, books, and trinkets of all kinds.

Above them, weapons covered the walls. Boxes with more stuff sat all over the floor with no discernible system or structure in place to categorize their contents. A counter was placed in the middle of everything, a small bell the only thing placed on it.

Behind it was a workbench, judging from how wide and sturdy it was. Made of pale wood, its surface was covered in mortars, bowls, glass jars, tubes, knives, cutting boards, and an assortment of plants, herbs, and meat.

Ilea wasn't quite sure if it was a meal or some alchemical tincture that was being prepared. The fox dozing in the middle of it all didn't seem to know either, head resting on its front paws as it calmly dreamed, not having woken from the entrance jingle.

Walking up to the counter, Ilea tapped the bell once, a clear ring filling the air. Her Sphere revealed no other being than the fox inside, but she'd been deceived before.

The fox opened its eyes slowly, a yawn escaping its maw as it stretched its paws, reminding Ilea more of a cat.

"Yesh… yes, yes. Welcome," the fox said. Its voice was not of a very high pitch, slightly gravelly, and definitely female.

Ilea smiled, her helmet vanishing into her necklace, and the fox sat up quickly, orange-red eyes opening wide.

"A human… and at such a high level? Remarkable. Welcome to the Hunter's Den. I'm Catelyn, owner of this store, and it is my joy to meet you, bearer of ash," she said, bowing her small head a little.

"Greetings, Catelyn, blessed by fire. I'm Ilea. I was told I can sell monster corpses here."

The fox stood up on all four legs. She wasn't taller than a normal fox from Earth, but her presence felt different, a glint of fire dancing in her small vulpine eyes.

[Mage - ??]

She was above her in level too, but Ilea had no idea by how much.

"You flatter me. To think a human honors the customs of the Awakened. It's rare to see one of your kind here. You may buy and sell with gold and silver, as well as other… interesting valuables."

Ilea summoned one of the Blue Reapers and held it up.

"A reaper… so you were the one to silence it. Bring it here, before it grows entirely cold. I assume your storage device keeps them fresh. Hold onto the others for now if you have more."

Ilea nodded and walked around the counter, avoiding any rogue boxes and containers on the ground before she put the reaper down. Catelyn had made space on the workbench with her two tails, expertly moving everything out of the way as if they were arms. Ilea could've sworn she'd only had a single tail a moment before.

"Don't mind it," Catelyn said, noticing Ilea's glance. "I can grow more than just two. Without thumbs, one must find other ways to handle a knife."

Carefully opening the reaper's broken shell, Catelyn filled an empty vial with the blood of the creature before stoppering it with a cork. She lifted a knife a moment later, cutting through some of the creature's throat before ripping the mantis head clean off. Ilea was impressed at the strength and quality of the blade.

She made a mental note not to fuck with the fox as Catelyn cupped the head in her paws before slurping out the eyes. She gave a long sigh, Ilea just standing there and waiting until the fox consumed the second eye as well.

"Excuse me. They're just so fucking *delicious*. One gold coin per corpse. Just pile them up, Ilea."

Ilea looked at the next reaper she summoned, its dead eyes staring back at her. She squinted and moved the creature's head closer to her mouth. Then she slurped.

She immediately noticed a prickling, burning sensation going down her throat, her healing informing her of literal burns, though she quickly recovered. The taste was more neutral than she'd expected but the consistency reminded her of gelatin. She coughed and retched a few times but ultimately swallowed the eye.

"Gross," she said and summoned a bottle of ale to chase down the disgusting lightning-infused monster part.

Catelyn stared at her for a long moment and then laughed. "Why would you... you're human!"

"Why wouldn't I? You made it seem delicious," Ilea said, a little offended at the deception. She put the other ten dead reapers down.

Catelyn chuckled and opened one of the table's drawers before rummaging around and handing over eleven pieces of gold. One of the coins slipped from her grasp, but Ilea's ash extended to catch it. All of it vanished into her necklace a moment later.

"Full price for the last one too because that was funny," Catelyn purred before the corpses vanished. "You're not injured?"

"Healed already."

Catelyn nodded, fire dancing in her eyes as she smiled. "Anything else you're willing to part with?"

"You're an alchemist?" Ilea asked as she went through her necklace.

"Among other things, yes. Are you interested in trying some of my tinctures? I've always wanted to test them on humans. Few agree," Catelyn said, resting her furry head on her front paws as she lay down on the table. "Isn't it weird for you to see a talking fox?"

Ilea was caught a little off guard by the question. "I'm in the north, aren't I?"

"That you are. Just... normally it takes a bit longer for humans to adjust, the few that manage to get here, that is."

"Do lots of humans come through?"

"Come through? No. Are many rescued from their failed expeditions? A few. Some stay, some leave."

Ilea nodded along, looking through her possessions.

"I don't suppose you're interested in moss from the Penumra dungeon?"

she asked, but the ensuing groan from the fox was answer enough. "I still have some cakes… for some reason, they take up a lot of space."

"What are cakes?" Catelyn asked, sitting up and cocking her head.

Ilea summoned one, a plate appearing on the table with its heavy strawberry and cream goodness. Her five cakes used up as much space as over a hundred meals from Keyla did. Ilea tried not to question the logic of it all and was simply glad she could carry so much food.

Catelyn sniffed the cake and walked around it with delicate steps, then glanced up at Ilea with a questioning look.

"It's food, take a bite. Decide what you want to pay for it after," she said with a grin, hoping that sugar was as addictive to foxes as it was to humans.

She's never even heard of cakes.

Catelyn was a little suspicious but still raised her knife. A quick blazing flame enveloped the metal and vanished again before she cut off a piece.

"You first," the fox said after bringing the piece closer to her mouth.

Ilea shrugged and used an ashen limb to cut off a piece for herself. It had been a while since she'd eaten dessert, and she couldn't help but smile at the overload of sugar and the heavy cream.

As fresh as if it was made today… I do wonder what Popi and Maurice are up to. She hoped they were still alive.

Catelyn watched her and then took a bite herself, her eyes opening wide before red flame surrounded her. Heavy mana pushed against Ilea as she wrapped her Veil around herself, ash flowing out to defend against the powerful magic. Catelyn's eyes glowed a deep red, her teeth growing more vicious and longer as they smashed into the piece of cake again and again until not a single crumb was left.

The fire settled again quickly, and the embarrassed-looking fox avoided Ilea's eyes as she licked the sides of her snout. Some of the herbs on the table were singed or completely burnt, but Ilea noted that the table itself was unharmed.

"What kind of wood is that?" Ilea couldn't help but ask.

"That's a secret. Maybe I'll tell you… for another cake."

Catelyn's orange eyes met her own. For a moment, they were both silent.

"I'll take the money," Ilea finally said, putting the other four cakes down. Catelyn put them in whatever storage item she had and put down twenty-five gold coins, carefully stacked with fluid motions.

Ilea put them away without another word. She understood that this wasn't to be mentioned ever again and that she'd just received an urgent yet unofficial request for more cakes to be delivered.

FIFTY-TWO

Exterminator

Summoning the last of her Dragcal meat, Ilea freed another two units of space in her necklace. Cutting out a piece, sizzling it, and eating the thing, Catelyn put a big coin on the table, worth ten silvers.

Popi could make a killing here.

"The rest is mostly weapons, armor, and clothing," Ilea said, summoning a few pieces to show the fox.

Catelyn didn't seem interested.

"You mentioned something about potions? What do you have? I'd be willing to try things out as well." Ilea was pretty confident in her healing as well as her Poison Resistance.

A glass vial filled with yellow liquid suddenly materialized before the fox. Her orange fluffy tail caught it and thrust it toward Ilea.

"It's supposed to make you heavier, but I've experienced... side effects."

Ilea stared at her inquisitively.

Catelyn coughed. "Mostly throwing up and diarrhea."

Ilea took the vial, removed the cork, and smelled it. Her Poison Resistance didn't inform her about anything, so she downed it. The potion took effect after half a minute, Ilea's healing monitoring the whole thing as the surprised fox quickly moved everything away from near Ilea's head and ass.

"I am a little heavier. Interesting feeling. Nothing more than what a minor weight reduction enchantment would have on a set of armor. Opposite effect, of course," Ilea said.

And then it started, her stomach suddenly contracting before her healing calmed the muscles down. It was soon gone again.

"Something happened to my stomach about fifty seconds in. Can't say exactly what went wrong, but you definitely have to work on that."

Catelyn grumbled and handed her another potion. "I hoped it worked on red-blooded individuals at least… This one is a health potion. Paralyzation as a side effect. As well as… vomiting. Again."

Ilea took it and twirled it around before opening the vial. This time, her Poison Resistance warned her about a low-level poison.

"Am I getting something for this testing?"

"Of course… of course. I'll pay you with shiny coins."

Ilea grunted and sacrificed five hundred points of health, red runes lighting up below her armor. Catelyn looked on with interest as Ilea drank the liquid. She recovered fifty points of health almost instantly.

'ding' You have been poisoned by Red Beetle juice – You resist the poison

Interesting… complete resistance?

Ilea put the vial down and had to stop her stomach from convulsing again.

"Poisoned, but I resisted the effects. The stomach thing again. Catelyn, are you sure you're an alchemist?"

The fox turned around herself on the table, avoiding Ilea's eyes again. "Of course I am. The best in town."

"Do you burn and eat the others?" Ilea smiled.

"Now, don't challenge me, young huntress," Catelyn replied, showing her teeth playfully.

"Calm down, fire-fox. I was wondering if you knew more about the Blue Reapers. I discovered a cave system that looked to be dug by them. Is there a dungeon somewhere with the beasts inside?"

"They dig wherever they go. The ones you faced are hunters and explorers looking for food sources for their nest. I'd assume there's a dungeon somewhere, but even I don't face them. Your resistances and healing must be impressive. I hear bigger ones have been sighted as well, so be careful where you go."

"I'll be back with more corpses. You buy everything from the Descent?"

"Pretty much. Though I don't have infinite gold, so don't think about bringing hundreds of dead reapers to me," Catelyn said, resting her head again. "Those… cakes, however…"

She licked her snout again.

"Right," Ilea said, walking toward the exit and waving her hand. "I'll stop by when I have more interesting things for you."

Maybe she'd browse all Catelyn's trinkets and tools at some point, but for now, she was glad to have a place where she could sell the stuff she found, especially corpses.

Wouldn't want undead Blue Reapers, if that's a thing. Maybe next time I'll ask if I can pet her…

The thought surprised her.

Kind of creepy, Ilea. She's a person. But I mean, at the same time, she's a fox. And she looks so fluffy.

Ilea whistled a tune to herself, thinking on the strange conundrum she'd found herself in. She soon came to the conclusion that at the end of the day, consent was the deciding factor, and if she wanted to pet the fox, she would just have to ask.

* * *

Grabbing a bottle of ale from Haiden, she made her way back down into the Descent. She had gotten enough gold from her sales to get equipment made by Balduur. Not that she necessarily needed something from him now that she had Goliath.

My cakes made twice as much money than several days' worth of fighting…

It was a bizarre thought, but it made sense. They didn't have any animals here to get eggs and milk – at least, she hadn't seen any. Sugar would have to be brought in, as would strawberries and any other ingredients. Being a traveling merchant with high survivability and stealth skills would definitely be a good way to get rich in Elos.

Finding the right buyers would be key, of course, but she had the notion that smiths all over the Plains would pay quite handsomely for Stonehammer steel, given how Balduur had fawned over her inferior Niameer armor.

Going back the same way she'd taken days prior, she soon found the tunnel entrance to the Blue Reaper cave system. Ash was constantly moving around her, ready to intercept an enemy attack in the darkness of the underground maze.

Before she headed in, Ilea checked her stats.

'ding' You have defeated [Blue Reaper – lvl 372] – For defeating an enemy one hundred and ten levels or more above your own, bonus experience is granted.

…

'ding' You have defeated [Blue Reaper – lvl 312] – For defeating an enemy fifty levels or more above your own, bonus experience is granted.

'ding' Azarinth First Hunter has reached lvl 259 – Five stat points awarded

'ding' Inheritor of Eternal Ash has reached lvl 252 – Five stat points awarded

'ding' Veil of Ash reaches 3rd lvl 4

'ding' Mental Resistance reaches 2nd lvl 13

She smiled. Another day in the tunnels, another level in each of her Classes. Part of her wanted things to go faster, for her progress to be more explosive, but she reminded herself that every little bit mattered.

* * *

Ilea focused and blinked again, putting more distance between her and the large group of reapers farther into the cave. She had found more pockets of them, more or less confident now about where their nest would be located. Yet her exploration was slow. Few of the critters closer to what she assumed to be their nest walked around alone.

There were over a dozen in the cavern before her, and she heard them clicking as she fled yet again, knowing she'd drop dead in mere seconds if they all engaged her. It was frustrating, knowing the monsters were there but being unable to fight them.

She'd killed enough of them to get her Azarinth Class to two hundred fifty-nine, which made her feel even more antsy. She was so close to two sixty and another third-tier skill point.

Come on, just a few more stragglers or duos, she thought, grunting as she crawled through yet another tunnel.

"Tunnels, tunnels, tunnels," she repeated as she healed her mind against the mental strain of the hunting activity. The constant dripping of water didn't help. She was close to the underground sea, she knew it.

"Plip, plop, drip, drip," she murmured, imitating the water.

Then she slipped on the wet ground, falling with a decidedly unceremonious thud. She cursed, then screamed in frustration. The shout echoed down the tunnel as she whined.

Ilea rolled onto her back, then slapped her face.

One more level. Come on.

* * *

Ilea's eyes opened wide as she perceived the enemies in her Hunter Sphere.

Three…

Previously, she'd avoided more than two, but her battles had improved and she knew that even five of them couldn't easily knock her out now. A little bit more Vitality and Wisdom would make a small difference, as would the skill levels she'd gained.

The three Reapers were clawing at the walls as Ilea sent out an ashen spike, hitting the one closest to her. Its mantis-like head was knocked forward, and all three of them turned toward her, their six legs clacking as lightning gathered around them.

Ilea moved back to the last bend, her healing already fighting the mind magic flung her way. Trying to create ashen walls between two of the critters and the third proved ineffective, their lightning crackling as soon as it touched the barrier, burning through in an instant.

Blinking to the one farthest back, she wrestled it down and grabbed onto one of its hind legs before she heard a snap before quickly blinking away four times. With blood streaming down her face, healing magic flowed through her as she breathed raggedly. Eyes closed, she trusted in her Sphere and focused her healing on her brain and mind instead.

She focused and waited. She'd learned that mind magic cast by the Blue Reapers generally had an effective range of around forty meters, perhaps a little more depending on their level. The hind legs, she'd found, had the highest impact on their speed. The injured bug would fall behind.

Moving too far away would make them flee if they were too badly injured, so she waited nearby, healing as much as she could until she saw them enter her Sphere once again. She took a breath and sacrificed health to boost her body enhancement magic.

A blink brought her close to the two healthy critters, smashing the head of the one closest to her with her fist, then crouching low to use its small frame as a shield against the second one's lightning. The reaper tried to get away but wasn't quick enough to escape her grasp.

Her wings closed around her, and she formed several walls of ash to intercept the lightning bolt that nonetheless broke through, damaging both the beast and herself. She broke another leg before she let go of the monster, blinking this time to the critter lagging behind. She clung to the creature and punched down with wild strikes until its carapace cracked.

The creature screeched as Ilea smashed it into the wall, another two hits finally breaking through and killing it. Ilea made some distance, her health low now as she coughed up blood and healed. But there was no level up from the kill.

Shit.

She healed for a little longer and then blinked back in. Once again, she went for the creature she'd already injured, gritting her teeth against its lightning and mind magic as she broke a second leg and then a third before the other reaper reached her again. Ilea didn't stop, smashing downward once, then twice, before finally cracking the shell.

Ignoring the damage her body had sustained, she blinked to the last monster, grabbing it by one leg and smashing it into the wall. She lashed out with her fists, delivering whatever destructive magic she could into the insect. Ashen limbs moved behind her, all eight of them bashing into the armored carapace as her health slowly drained, her body burning up from the surging lightning.

Meditation and her healing were the only things keeping her conscious, standing, and attacking. At some point, Ilea realized she was kneeling on the ground, her arms limp at her sides. She felt no part of them. A bit of her brain must've fried up. Her healing was still active though, reporting the disastrous condition her body was in.

Her senses didn't tell her much anymore, her Sphere the only thing that gave her a picture of her surroundings. Ashen limbs swung out from her back, smashing into the creature that still struggled against her attacks. She knew she could blink away. Away to safety. Some part of her mind wanted to get away, wanted to get out, to find sunlight, to rest, to sleep. It was reasonable.

And yet, she didn't. She was here, facing the last reaper, and while she couldn't move, her body, her ash was still there.

With what little thought she had left, she willed her magic to destroy, barely conscious as she felt her ash cut and burn the injured monster before her, flashes of heat flaring up whenever Wave of Ember was released.

With a final crunch, her ash broke through, and the reaper stopped struggling. Ilea noticed several notifications popping up in what felt like a daze. Blinded and half dead, Ilea remained kneeling, ash whirling around her as it formed a protective cocoon.

She could barely focus on breathing, and while her perception of pain had been deactivated long ago, she could hardly feel anything at all now. Yet she still felt the familiar feeling of her healing magic, no longer battling the constant enemy spells. She breathed in and shuddered, feeling the warmth flooding into her mind and brain.

Her ash floated lazily around her, Ilea's last wish fulfilled, and being without an enemy to destroy now, it instead sought to protect. She could feel it, trusted it. A minute passed and then two, clarity coming back to her as her healing moved on from her mind to her organs and then the rest of her body. Soon her health started to rise, all the bleeding and burns not preventing it from doing so any longer.

A cackling filled the dark tunnel, followed by wild coughing, the clang of Ilea's helmet being taken off and cast aside, and the wet sound of blood hitting the floor. The dull light of Ilea's Form of Ash and Ember lit up her immediate surroundings. Perhaps it wasn't wise to start laughing so close to the reapers' nest, but Ilea didn't care. She had survived. And it felt good.

Not just good. It felt intoxicating.

When the feeling passed, she gulped, feeling guilty. Guilty and embarrassed. The risks she'd just taken had been unnecessary. Stupid. And yet she'd choose the same again every single time. Against twelve reapers, sure, she would flee. But this was different.

Dancing on the very edge, she smiled to herself, her breathing slower now as she looked at her ash. *'Close to death,' Goliath said. I guess I can't really deny it.*

And it made sense to her too. If she failed against something minor like a few Blue Reapers, how could she ever face a Praetorian, a Kingsguard, or even an undead knight? To gain the kind of power that allowed her to face those monsters, she had to take risks, had to push herself, more and more. Because she knew her body could take it, knew her mind could take it.

Just enough of a challenge to push me ahead but not enough to overwhelm me entirely.

It was difficult to gauge, and she knew if she went too far, she'd end up dead. And while a more rational part of her urged her to be more cautious, to find a team again to fight with, to slow down, to prepare, to take weeks and months to get to the next level, it just sounded so very boring, so very safe. Now that she knew how it felt to push herself just enough to come out on top, how could she go back?

'ding' You have defeated [Blue Reaper – lvl 321] – For defeating an enemy sixty or more levels above your own, bonus experience is granted.

'ding' You have defeated [Blue Reaper – lvl 392] – For defeating an enemy one hundred and thirty or more levels above your own, bonus experience is granted.

'ding' You have defeated [Blue Reaper – lvl 330] – For defeating an enemy ninety or more levels above your own, bonus experience is granted.

'ding' Azarinth First Hunter has reached lvl 260 – Five stat points awarded, one 3rd-tier skill point awarded

'ding' Inheritor of Eternal Ash has reached lvl 253 – Five stat points awarded

'ding' Ash Creation reaches 3rd lvl 3

'ding' Ash and Ember Manipulation reaches 3rd lvl 3

'ding' Ashen Wings reaches 2nd lvl 19

Checking out the third-tier list, Ilea didn't have to think very long to make a decision.

3rd-tier skill points available [Azarinth First Hunter]: 1
Skills available for 3rd-tier advancement in [Azarinth First Hunter]:
- Hunter Recovery
- Azarinth Hunter Sphere
- Azarinth Fighting
- Azarinth Perception
- Azarinth Reversal

At least a bunch of her skills were now available to be upgraded, but one in particular had just saved her life – again. More offensive potential would definitely be a good thing though, and she didn't doubt the third tier of Destruction had played a vital role in her fights with both the knights and the Blue Reapers.

Still, seeing her body ripped through and burnt, her brain barely functioning, she selected her only recovery spell. The reason she had come so far, the reason she could survive even when she'd been beaten to a literal pulp.

'ding' Hunter Recovery advances to the 3rd tier
Active: Hunter Recovery – 3rd lvl 1:
Send a healing pulse of mana into yourself or your ally with a touch. This skill can be channeled. The effects on your own body are vastly improved.
2nd stage: Your control is increased greatly. You can now focus your healing on specific parts of the body. As long as mana and health remain, your Hunter Recovery will restore your body. Lose your head and see for yourself!
3rd stage: You have healed your body time and time again and know every cell and where it belongs. Sacrifice a large amount of mana to boost your healing to unprecedented speeds. A lack of knowledge about your body may result in heavy damage.
Category: Healing

Reading through the notification, Ilea sighed and closed it again. She'd have to test it later, but it sounded good. Really good. Exactly what she'd needed against the enemies in her last battle.

Her mana had never dipped very low, the fights being short and brutal. It wouldn't help much against the knights either, given how long the fights took, but perhaps the skill would allow her at least to approach the more dangerous foes in Tremor.

Only one way to find out, Ilea thought as she started on her way back to Hallowfort, whistling a tune to herself in the dark and claustrophobic tunnels.

FIFTY-THREE

History

Now that she had her healing and Destruction in the third tier, Ilea considered her next target. She wanted a change of pace and decided on the undead knights in the dark zone of the Tremor dungeon. They were higher level so would benefit her more in terms of skills and levels, even if they took a bit longer to kill.

She wondered if she could lure one of them out individually. Despite their high level, she felt like they were safer to engage than the Kingsguards around the palace.

Just a matter of not getting hit. Can't be worse than mind magic blasting my brains out.

Ilea landed on a rooftop in what she had marked on her map as the dark zone. When she'd come here previously, it hadn't taken long to find one of the undead knights, but their ensuing fight had taken them through dozens of streets, and more had only shown up near the end. The Rose Knights had definitely populated the sunlit part of the city more densely.

Hovering down to the street, she was shrouded in ash. It took her a while of silently walking through the dark city to find something until, finally, she saw a leg in her Sphere – but it wasn't that of an undead knight.

Carefully moving a little farther without making any noise, she saw the creature hanging off the wall of a building. It had two legs and arms, both long and thin, with five-fingered hands that ended in claws as long as her forearm. It was at least four meters long, its torso thin and elongated just like its arms and legs.

A shiver went down her spine. There was something alien about the creature that Ilea couldn't place. Something wrong. Its head looked a little like a blooming flower, tentacle-like extensions writhing within.

Other than the tentacles, the creature hung entirely motionless and silent. Waiting, preparing. Something deep within her told Ilea to run, to hide, and to never come back to this place. It was a terror she hadn't felt in quite some time. Not something logical, either born from the beast's magic or something instinctual within her.

Curious, she thought as she observed the feeling.

She decided not to listen to her instincts. Instead, she created a projectile of ash and sent it at the wall opposite the beast, interested in how it would react. She couldn't quite identify it from her position, but she was prepared to blink away at any moment, should it attack her directly.

When the ashen spike slammed against the stone wall, Ilea barely noticed the motion as the beast jumped off its perch and landed, hands grabbing at the spot where the projectile had impacted.

It was now standing on the ground, its slender form slowly standing up on its thin legs as its hands again grasped at nothing, her ash already dissolved. A moment later, it went back on all fours, returning to the waiting position it had been in before.

[Soul Ripper – lvl ???]

Sounds about right, she gulped, unable to take her attention off its elongated body, off the smooth leathery skin that covered it. *Nope.*

With that single word in her mind, Ilea blinked back toward the higher sections of the city. She knew exactly what Guard Captain Reyker had meant when he'd talked about them. Ilea would definitely face the creature eventually, but she needed a moment to process what she'd seen.

Even after magical insects, undead knights, and talking foxes, its sheer presence was *wrong*. The way it moved was silent and deadly. It unnerved her, more so than anything she'd seen before. The demons in the Great Salt felt like puppies in comparison. Maybe it was the triple mark. The simple display of its power and the danger that it posed.

First, undead knight.

Ilea calmed herself down, slowing her breathing. She felt a little upset at how easily the thing's mere presence had made her freak out.

You need to get a grip. That's hardly the worst you'll ever face, she told herself.

At least she knew the knights weren't the only beings in the dungeon. It also confirmed that the captain had likely failed his last quest. Also, the Soul Ripper didn't have the ability to sense her, meaning she could hide from it.

Focusing on her search, Ilea found what she was looking for some minutes later. The roaming form of an undead knight. His eyes were white, just like those of the other knights, one of them looking at her through the cracked helmet. His armor showed more rust than the knights above, his sword dull and really more of a bludgeoning weapon. Even better, this one had only two question marks.

Perfect, she thought as she watched it through her Sphere.

It still had an intact head and both its arms, dragging a rusty sword on the stone floor. Ilea wondered if the king controlled this undead as well. Given how erratically they moved and fought, somehow she doubted it.

Checking for an escape path to the higher areas of the dungeon, Ilea shot an ashen projectile at the being. The knight hunched down and screeched at her before its powerful legs propelled it off the ground.

A series of dodges and quick movements followed where Ilea tried to avoid her pursuer's attacks without using her blink, jumping and flying instead. She knew they could easily sense her and sometimes threw their weapons to intercept her form when it vanished. Against them, blinking was only for dodging when all else failed, not to reposition or to run away. At least, not when there was no cover between her destination and the monsters.

Many a house was destroyed along the way, the knight ignoring the walls, fences, and heaps of rubble that stood between itself and Ilea's fast-moving form. Despite stumbling, sometimes falling down completely, the undead managed to keep up.

Ilea would be able to get away if she moved at full speed, but the undead was far more tenacious than its unliving brethren in the sunlit part of the ancient city. Crashing through solid stone walls as well as smashing face-first into the ground didn't seem to dissuade or damage the creature in the slightest, which did give Ilea a little bit of pause.

At least a second knight didn't appear, despite the noise her hunter continuously produced. Ilea had chosen the same route she'd taken to come down into Tremor's lower section, hoping that none of the knights would stroll into her escape path on the way back.

Reaching the half-collapsed wall, she rushed over it and turned in the air before she slowed to a halt, waiting for her enemy to come charging toward her. A couple of seconds later, she knew the knight had given up.

Well, fuck. That doesn't work.

Running back in, she found him walking back to the lower parts of the dungeon, so she hit him with a projectile of ash. Again, he screamed at her and engaged. This time, she dodged more narrowly, taking small steps and jumps back toward the wall as the undead pursued.

As soon as she reached the wall, the knight turned and rushed off again, running at a full sprint. Ilea reached his side a couple of seconds later and body checked his heavy form, sending him into a nearby building, the impact running through her very bones.

"Alright," she said. "Your turf then."

The knight's response was a flying sword, the massive dull piece of metal sailing over her as she crouched under it, the knight's form following behind. She deflected its fist and used his momentum to smash the heavy undead into the ground. The move dragged her back a couple of meters along with her tossed foe, Ilea letting go of him before he could grab her.

Stepping back, she watched in amazement as his sword flew out of the wall it had been stuck in and returned to the knight's hand. He crouched low and growled as he took a couple of steps, circling her. His armor was dented now, a piece of his side missing entirely, ribs and rotting flesh showing below.

Four quick steps brought the two-meter-tall figure right in front of her. Ilea braced for a quick attack, but he simply studied her, waiting for a reaction before his hand shot out. Ilea stepped out of his reach before the sword slashed at her in three quick attacks, two of which she deflected and one she dodged entirely as she continuously stepped back.

As her Veil reformed where she had deflected the attacks with it, Ilea felt a dull ache from where the blows had struck. The sections of destroyed ash quickly gathered around her again to form a defensive mist.

There came another screech, and this time, it was answered. A second knight stood on top of a nearby building before it jumped down, landing with an eerie grace, sword at its side, held by the one arm it still had.

Ilea decided the test was a failure then and there. Maybe she'd try some more if she had any ranged attacks that could deal reasonable damage, but as it stood, she had to rip off the knights' limbs or incapacitate them before their kin arrived. As much as the knights above seemed more trained and aware, the ones down here had retained some level of cunning.

Ilea gave it up and rushed back to the wall, both knights leaving her alone as soon as she reached it, returning back into the darkness. Sighing, she sat down on a nearby roof, legs dangling down as she summoned one of Keyla's meals. A proven alchemical formula against frustration and failure.

Temporary failure, she reminded herself.

She made a mental note to add the Soul Ripper to her list of potential targets, then focused on her food.

* * *

The suns were setting when Ilea made her way back to Hallowfort, and signs of mist were starting to appear when she reached the entrance to the Penumra dungeon. She knew there had to be another way or even several to reach the scavenger town, but she liked to see the dungeon from time to time, to be reminded of another goal, another possible frontier to explore. A place to test and strengthen herself once she was ready to battle the beasts within.

It was an untapped resource. A place that likely hid secrets – and power. She was fast realizing that the north was full of such resources. All she needed was the strength to tap into them. Seeing the gnarled roots and murky depths beyond gave her a buzz of energy. *Soon,* she thought with a smile.

Making her way through the dark tunnels, she quickly reached the town. Ilea went for the Abyss immediately, walking straight through the bar that looked the same both day and night. The guard was someone else this time around, but the burly warrior ignored her all the same.

Finding herself in the dark hallways of the old city below Hallowfort, Ilea decided she wasn't hunting for Blue Reapers today. She wanted something new, and after her failed test with the undead knights of Tremor, she felt a little frustrated. The north was full of powerful creatures, but so many were just beyond her reach. For now. Perhaps the Descent had something in store for her that was both easy to kill and a little less ridiculously dangerous.

She teleported and squeezed through the tunnels of the ancient city below Hallowfort until she saw light shining up through a small opening in the floor. Terok had talked a little about the different layers, but when Ilea finally found a crack leading farther down, and to a source of light, she was still surprised to hear the chirping of birds coming from below.

A blink brought her into a vast open space, her eyes adjusting to the crystal light glowing from pillars reaching down from above. She spread her ashen wings to stop her free fall as she looked around. A lush forest of dark green pine trees spread a couple of hundred meters below her. Rivers ran through the landscape like veins, ending in a lake that reflected the pale light from the crystals above.

Looking around her, she realized the rivers flowed away from the lake before pouring into wild waterfalls, disappearing into the darkness. The lake itself was formed by streams flowing down from the distant cliff-like walls that looked like mountains stretching high into the air before connecting with the ceiling.

Ilea refused to call it a mere cave. It was more of an underground territory. The light, flora, and the lake painted a picture she could only compare to the Haven under Ravenhall. The entirely too-even ceiling she was now hovering under reinforced the unnatural feeling she got from the place. A shiver ran down her spine.

This thing has layers, she remembered, and she had to focus not to forget that she was inside a dungeon in the north, of all places. There was no village near the lake, no houses, and no boats to use to fish or enjoy the crystal light.

Ilea took in the sights and enjoyed the serene atmosphere. Compared to the endless lake above, stretching below the statue holding Hallowfort, this place felt almost removed, the dangers of the north near forgotten.

After flying for a while, she spotted what she'd been looking for, landing and looking around at the dense and wild forest. Taking in her surroundings, listening and smelling for anything that might be a threat, Ilea jumped up and held herself near the top of a pine tree. A couple of hundred meters nearer the wall, wooden buildings sprouted from the cliffs like mold clinging to each and every corner of an abandoned house.

Terok had mentioned a camp of sorts for those who sought to venture deeper into the dungeon. Even the highest level held danger enough to force such a construction. As far as the dwarf was concerned, the hallways above held more danger than this uppermost layer, but Ilea would judge it on her own. Visiting the little collection of houses would likely be beneficial. Maybe they sold maps of the areas already explored or, at the very least, information about the creatures living here and farther down.

She felt a thrill just looking at the small community. People who had decided to build their lives around the dangers of a dungeon. A few of them were likely quite powerful. Perhaps more powerful than her. She grinned at the thought.

Someone appeared in her Sphere, making Ilea prepare for a fight as her buffs surged.

"A lone hunter. What do you seek in the Descent?" a male voice asked. It came from a creature wreathed in shadows that twisted and turned around him.

He had four arms, two by his side, two crossed over his chest. She noted the four short swords, two sheathed on his back and two at his sides. His face was hidden behind a black metal mask with no eyes. Two small horns sprouted from his cheeks, a single line of red paint in between. A black hood covered his head, and billowy black clothes covered by a cloak hid the form below.

Ilea jumped down from her tree, noting the figure's slight increase in tension.

"I seek to hunt monsters."

[Warrior – lvl 252]

He peered at her for a few loaded moments. Ilea wasn't quite sure what to make of it, but at least he seemed to be alone.

"And what is your purpose here, warrior of shadow?" she asked.

Relaxing a little, he said, "I am the protector of the scavenger camp you see hanging from the cliffs. You are not one I wish to fight, but know that should you murder and destroy without reason, I will be forced to do so. Tell me now if you seek the death of one among us, and we might find a way to prevent unnecessary bloodshed."

"Relax, shadow guardian. I'm really just here to kill monsters."

"Good fortune to you then, warrior of ash," he said and gave her a nod.

Ilea watched him turn away before she called after him. "Wait a second." The guardian turned his head. "Do you wield shadow magic?"

He turned to her fully now and cocked his head. "You seek to learn? Or simply to test your strength?"

Ilea smiled under her helmet. He hadn't dismissed her immediately. "I seek to test your strength. On my body."

Two of his arms shot up as if to ward her off. "I have neither the desire nor the physical ability to engage in sexual activities with your kind."

Ilea shook her head. "Not sexual fun, fighting fun. She winked. "I want a resistance against shadow magic. And it might benefit you to face someone close to your level once in a while."

The guardian considered, then shook his head. "No. I have my duties, warrior of ash. I will await the tales of your exploits."

With that, he vanished into the nearby shadows, leaving Ilea alone again.

* * *

Ilea soared up, quickly covering the distance to the camp clinging to the side of the cliff. Sturdy wood had been used in the construction of the foundations, placed deep into the stone. Either there were no dangerous birds or other fliers on the first level or the residents simply didn't care about the lack of defenses.

Square and circular platforms were accessed via wooden stairs and small elevators operated with chains that reached through the platforms. She noted that one of the biggest elevators had chains long enough to reach the ground floor. Likely the way anybody without a flying ability accessed the camp.

The houses in the camp reminded her more of tree houses built on Earth. They had a magical touch added to them, of course, some hovering with dangerously little to support them. Not enough, it seemed, to keep up with gravity, but runes and enchantments likely tipped the balance in the structure's favor. Ilea didn't spot more than twenty buildings, but tunnels leading into the stone cliff suggested more residential space.

Other than the guardian she'd already encountered, nobody seemed to care much about her. Still, she got some looks, and a couple of merchants were already beckoning her toward them, their wares in boxes around them or distributed on spread pieces of cloth.

She walked up to one of the vendors, a dwarf with gray hair, leather goggles, and a feathered hat that would make Robin Hood proud. His skin was wrinkled, and she saw some of his teeth were missing as he smiled at the new customer.

"Welcome. Now, what will ye be lookin' for? Me gots trinkets, potions, poisons, maps, camp gear..."

Ilea grabbed one of the maps. It read, *'Descent – 1st layer'*.

The dwarf's gap-filled grin flashed again. "Maps it be. More detail and more perfect scaling than anybody else's!"

"Is there anything on this layer above level two hundred?" she asked the vendor.

The dwarf shook his head. "Only the odd scavenger... farther down you'll have to go. The map shows the points of descent, ladders and elevators to lead you down into the second. I'll make you a deal, layer one and layer two, both maps for ten gold only!"

Ilea just walked away. Ten gold for two maps of a place she would likely travel to death? She felt like the deal wasn't great, but more to the point, she wondered if it wouldn't just be more fun to explore this place on her own.

She smiled. *Who doesn't like surprises?*

FIFTY-FOUR

Scouting the Unknown

"Alright! Six gold!" the merchant called from behind her, trying to get out from behind his wares and chase her, but Ilea wasn't in the mood to haggle.

The next merchant she talked to was a little more accommodating. The claws on his long hands, as well as the teeth growing out past his leathery lips, made the reptile-like vendor stand out from the others. A dirty cloth covered his eyes. Ilea had no idea what species he was, but she assumed he was an Awakened of sorts.

"Greetings, traveler. May I interest you in any of my wares?"

Ilea looked at the wooden boxes, some of which were closed, including the one the merchant was sitting on.

"At what layer are there monsters above level two hundred?"

"Ah, a newcomer then. For ten silvers, I'll tell you what I know about the monsters and their levels, though I must warn you – even after all this time, new things keep creeping up. You might get this information in the tavern from listening alone, but I offer it now, if you are in a hurry."

He got me.

Ilea summoned the money into her fist and opened it above his palm. The merchant caught the money and continued.

"On this layer, you will find few even reaching the lower two hundreds. Food and water are plentiful, however."

He saw her bored expression and hurriedly continued.

"In the second layer, made up mostly of treacherous tunnels filled with traps and nasty insects, you will find most monsters near the two-hundred mark. Other than what their corpses might bring you, there is little of value there.

"The third layer is mostly filled with water. You will find valuables there if you can swim and hold your breath for long enough. The beasts, I hear, are less hostile but similarly dangerous to the ones in the second layer."

Ilea nodded for him to continue.

"The fourth layer is the one most high-levelers want to get to. The Heroes' Descent, the ruins of a city believed to have been built by the same people who built the one above. Dangerous to be sure, and if you're looking for beasts to kill, there are plenty there at levels most avoid."

Ilea waited, but it seemed the merchant was done. "What about the deeper layers?"

He shook his head. "Few dare travel there, and none would share their findings with the likes of me. Rumors about a silent, dark forest in the fifth and strong winds in the sixth are all I can share, but the reports are not reliable."

How long have you guys been down here… and that's all you know?

Ilea was nearly regretting her decision to come to the camp at all. She was now in territory few humans ever traveled, ever could travel, according to everyone she'd met so far. Just because other species were around didn't mean they could stroll into level two hundred and higher dungeons with ease.

It was a surprise to find a camp with scavengers and people, but Ilea had expected them at least to be able to fight whatever was around here. She'd hoped more of them would be like her, or at least enough of them that there would be more information by now. Did they just hide in the city avoiding monsters while life carried on around them?

I guess that's what people in most human cities do. Not sure why I expected non-humans to be any different…

Still, if no one knew what was down there – it meant she could be the first.

Maybe I can even name one of the layers if I'm the first to get there? The Bored Drake Layer? No… The Ash Layer… no, that sucks… The Layer of Lilith? Ugh.

She shook off the musings and refocused on the merchant.

"Do I really need a map going down or can I just orient myself… well, downward?"

The merchant chuckled. "That will work eventually, yes. I suggest that any new delvers stock up on food and water, rope, and healing potions and hire an actual healer for the team. Antidotes to common poisons as well as maps providing guidance to the well-established and safest routes are recommended. You, however, don't strike me as a new delver, even though you might not have visited this specific dungeon."

Ilea nodded, all of that completely unnecessary for her. "Thanks." She tossed another big piece of silver into his hand, giving his wares a last look. Nothing struck her fancy.

Instead, Ilea just let herself fall off the side of the platform. She heard a yelp from someone who saw her maneuver, a blink close to the bottom bringing her safely into the woods and onto stable ground.

So, it's just a matter of going down, she thought, spreading her wings and ash around her. She intended to work on the last couple of skills yet to reach the pinnacle of the second tier.

Quickly finding one of the rivers, Ilea followed it until she arrived at a waterfall cascading into darkness. Stepping into the river, she could perceive cracks below it through her Sphere, one of them big enough for her to fit through.

Jumping down, she blinked through it and found herself in a small cave. Some of the water from the river above pooled in a small basin before it ran along the tunnel, slowly eating into the rock. Ilea wasn't sure if this was already the second layer or if it was merely a cave belonging to the first one.

Reaching the end of the tunnel, she found her answer. The smooth surface of the next level could be distinguished even in the dim light, its color a lighter shade than the one of the cave itself. Ilea saw water seep into a thin crack, likely formed over centuries. Below was a layer of stone and then what Ilea assumed to be earth. Worms made their way through it, unaware of the warrior blinking into the damp tunnel below them.

Ilea immediately reduced her sensitivity to smell. *Disgusting.* She hoped the information regarding the monsters here was true and they held little value for her. Looking down, she found her boots sinking into the moisture that had collected, brown water dripping down from above. Choosing a direction at random, she started walking.

It didn't take her long to find the first trap. Loose earth with sharpened wooden sticks hidden beneath. *Nasty.* Ilea reached an ashen limb down into the earth and ripped out one of the sticks. The thing was flimsy but sharp enough to penetrate through cloth, maybe thin leather.

Her Poison Resistance informed her that there was something amiss with the substance on the tip. A low danger level, apparently. Storing the armored pieces of her left leg, Ilea smashed the stick into her skin. The thing broke on impact, only managing to scratch her a little.

'ding' You have been poisoned by Dung Broth, -10 health per second for one minute

"Wow, really?" she exclaimed before grabbing one spike after another until the trap was effectively dismantled.

After a couple of minutes, Ilea had a bunch of scratches on her leg, her health continuing to drain. The poisons didn't stack when it came to damage, but the time went up with each additional wound. She assumed it was because more of the delicious broth made its way into her blood stream.

This would be enough to kill any human on Earth.

Deciding to test out her third-tier healing for the first time, Ilea waited until her health had lowered considerably. Activating the skill with the intent to heal to full health, she gasped as a huge chunk of mana was suddenly transformed into healing power surging through her whole being. It took a moment, but when she checked again, her health was full again.

Fucking damn.

Her mana, on the other hand, had gone down drastically, but it was a better conversion than she'd expected. Her normal healing magic gradually drained her mana, albeit at a much slower pace, while healing her rather rapidly – but this would allow her to heal up even massive wounds almost instantly.

She was sure that facing three Blue Reapers at the same time wouldn't be as much of an issue now. Four or five, she still doubted. But the high cost would make it incredibly risky.

Wait a minute.

A grin spread on her face as she sacrificed a thousand points of health to activate her third-tier State of Azarinth. Red runes glowed as she invested a chunk of mana to heal it back immediately. A couple of seconds later, her third tier faded, but with this, she could get a pretty good increase in power without the drawbacks of her third-tier State. At least as long as she had mana.

Another reason to invest in Wisdom.

She sighed and started meditating, down over two thousand points of mana. The fact that her mana recovery was a percentage instead of a fixed number made the whole thing feasible.

If only I could get Meditation to the third tier… maybe I could use it while fighting.

A hopeful thought, but one she put to the back of her mind again immediately. With this, Ilea could sacrifice more health without much worry. In a battle of attrition, it wasn't worth using – but against something like a Blue Reaper, it would certainly be effective.

Leaving the now useless trap and the broken pieces of wood behind, Ilea walked on through the completely dark tunnel. Thinking about the reapers, Ilea decided against facing more for now. Most of the groups she'd avoided had been much larger than four or five, making her third-tier healing simply another buffer before she burned up. Let alone the mind magic that would likely knock her unconscious long before her mana was used up. Burst healing her brain wouldn't help either when the damage came in near instantly.

Hmm, but maybe if I get another upgrade in some of my skills, I could go and try. I wonder if I could survive the lightning now? And then there's Penumra still waiting for me… So much to kill, so little time.

Ilea found a crude pressure plate and stepped onto it after checking out the enchantments. Her chest plate vanished into her necklace as a barbed arrow pierced her chest. She winced when she looked down but felt little of the pain, even without deactivating her perception of it. The arrow had penetrated about five centimeters deep, and the poison was now starting to take effect.

"Dung broth again… who the fuck is laying these traps?" she asked, wincing as she ripped out the arrow. Blood dripped onto the ground before she quickly closed the wound and resummoned her armor.

Maybe I should check the next arrow before I just let it skewer my chest. This is how I'm going to die one day, right after defeating some insane monster. Ancient trap testing fatality.

Ilea dismantled the following traps and checked them before poisoning herself. Not long after, she was pretty sure she was lost. Digging down wasn't really an option with her ash alone, but she hadn't encountered a single monster yet. Perhaps not buying those maps was a bad decision after all. She rolled her eyes at her own stubbornness and continued onward.

Hours passed. The smell of the place was starting to bother her, even with her senses reduced. It was dark, wet, cold, and full of crawling insects that weren't even worth squashing.

Ilea was just starting to consider going back to town when a filthy head popped up in her Sphere.

[Mud Goblin – lvl 152]

The little creature ran away right after it saw her, Ilea blinking to intercept it. The thing screeched before clawing at her with its hands.

Are they the ones building the traps? she wondered.

Checking around the tunnel with her Sphere, she found a half-dug hole in the middle of it.

"You are, aren't you?"

And you don't care to talk. You're just laying traps to kill scavengers and other creatures.

She watched the small goblin as it continued to try and claw past her ash, then sent a spiked ashen limb through its head. Ilea ignored the notification popping up, the thing too weak to give her much experience.

A couple of minutes later, she came upon another creature. This one literally looked like a monster roach, complete with chitinous plates and wiggling antennae.

Monster-sized roaches. Sure. I wonder what they're called here.

[Monster Roach – lvl 192]

"Really?" she asked, looking up toward where the sky would be, somewhere beyond the thousands of meters of ground. The monster roach rushed at her, its mouth clicking as it opened and closed, dozens of sharp teeth showing within.

Ilea closed her eyes and held up her arms before she sacrificed five hundred points of health, her right foot coming down in a stomp that splattered the half-a-meter-long creature's guts across the tunnel walls.

"God, fuck, that's disgusting..."

Ilea was hyper-aware of any traps after that, hoping she wouldn't somehow fall into the bugs' den. No number of levels would be worth swimming in a couple of hundred giant black bugs.

She used her ash to clean all the muck off her armor before she continued. The same tunnel continued on for hundreds of meters, but at least it was descending somewhat, the third level of the Descent getting ever so slightly closer with each step she took.

A while later, a distant light appeared. She blinked her eyes. *The end of the tunnel?* The thought was proved wrong when the light source came closer, identifying itself as a rapidly moving torch held by a running person.

Running for their life, Ilea realized, noting the frantic movements. The screams coming from the two people behind the first runner confirmed her assumption. As did the clicking noise of hundreds of roaches crawling on all four sides of the tunnel like a tidal wave of teeth and ruin. Ilea sighed and started forming ash around her.

"Run for your life!" a male shouted before he rushed past her, completely ignoring the possible danger in his flight. His brown coat rushed past, flapping as he held his cowboy-like hat. His face was distinctly human. Ilea was pretty sure he blinked at her before he was past.

A dwarven rig limped past her right after, though the only noise she heard was hard breathing coming from within. The last member of the group was a cat person in leather armor and a coat, who stumbled when she saw Ilea standing in the tunnel. Ilea watched her hit the ground, the harmonica she'd held to her mouth crashing against her teeth.

Wincing at the impact, Ilea slowly walked toward the fallen cat, more and more ash forming around her as it filled the whole tunnel. A wall of it solidified right in front of her, the rest of the ash floating loosely farther down the tunnel.

As soon as the first roaches reached it, Ilea pushed reversed healing into their bodies. She kept on adding ash to her wall as the beasts bit and struggled against the solid black barrier she had put up.

The dwarf fell against the tunnel wall, taking long heaving breaths as he tried to recover. Ilea slowly walked back toward him as the approaching bug wave tore away at her ash.

The first roaches started dying shortly after that, notifications popping up as Ilea pushed more and more mana into her reversed recovery, Meditation working hard to regain her resources.

Trying something she hadn't thought about before, Ilea attempted to shove a higher amount of mana into one of the roaches. Her third-tier recovery. Sadly, nothing happened, her mana staying with her and the roach dying half a minute later against her normal form of attack.

So reversed burst healing is a no.

Reaching the downed cat person, Ilea lifted her up with one of her ashen limbs, storing her harmonica at the same time. Checking on her, she found her unconscious but otherwise fine. She carried the girl a couple of meters farther back toward the dwarf, who was now looking at her, unmoving.

"Get her farther back. I don't see an end to the roaches yet," Ilea said simply.

The dwarf sprang into action at that, lifting the cat and matching Ilea's steps as he retreated.

"You're a lifesaver. I knew we shouldn't have trusted that idiot," he said in a weird accent Ilea couldn't place. "He'll run right into the next trap if he keeps going…"

Ilea saw the flickering light of the man's torch still moving away in the distance. She chuckled. "Well, worry not, your deus ex machina has arrived."

Ilea identified the cat first.

[Healer – lvl 181]

At least they have a healer with them. What about the dwarf?

[Warrior – lvl 203]

The dwarf was surprisingly not a mage. His suit looked savage in comparison to Terok's. A literal mass of steel, dented and scratched. She was surprised the three-meter-tall thing could even move, let alone as quickly as it did. It had a thick head without a neck, a single big floodlight burning from its center, the glass cracked across the surface.

"There's hundreds of the buggers… Should I start running, or are you as confident as you look?" he asked, holding the healer in one hand like a mere kitten.

Ilea was casually walking a little behind him, her back to the roaches, ash floating and connected to her as if growing from her spine.

"I'll be fine for quite some time. I'll let you know when we need to start to run," she replied with a smile. "Scavengers?"

The dwarf grunted. "I guess we are. On the way to the fourth layer. 'Mr. Know-it-all' has a treasure map of sorts."

"And you tell that so easily to the person currently keeping you alive," Ilea said, shaking her head.

The dwarf didn't seem to care much, his voice calm and steady. "I'm not one to ignore my debts, not like a certain human. Telling you about it is the least I can do for you saving my life."

"You sound like an Awakened. Are you not a dwarf?"

He laughed at that. "Sometimes I feel like one too. I was, however, born and raised in the mountains of the south. Proud to call myself a dwarf."

Ilea nodded, not quite knowing how to react. Behind her, the clicking noises didn't stop. She smiled and soon started whistling a tune to offset the horrible cacophony of dying roaches.

I do like this Descent thing, she thought, wondering what she'd find next.

FIFTY-FIVE

Treasure Hunters

The dwarf shook the healer one more time before she suddenly gasped and opened her eyes.

"Baron..." she said weakly. "The crawlers... I fell... what happened?"

"The stranger intervened. We'd be dead if not for her," Baron said, turning to flash his light at Ilea.

Ilea smiled as she looked into the yellow feline eyes, full of wonder. *How young is that one?* she wondered.

The roaches were now thinning out behind her, heated up and killed by Embered Body Heat and her reversed recovery, the latter of course dealing the majority of the damage.

Ilea could do this for at least another ten minutes before she'd want to get some distance between them. She wasn't about to run out of mana with a bunch of strangers standing next to her. The dwarf seemed sincere enough, but she wouldn't trust them blindly.

"My harmonica..." the cat person said with a sniff.

Ilea summoned the thing and threw it toward her. She caught it with a swift movement and immediately started to play a melody. Ilea felt her body relax a little, her mana recovering just a bit more quickly.

A bard? She cocked her head and looked at the cat, who held her stare. *Bard and healer.*

They continued through the tunnel, casually walking while the roaches died behind them. With the melody ringing through the cavern, Ilea almost wondered if the bard wasn't luring the insects to an ashen death.

Soon after, Ilea stopped. She recovered some more of her mana while the last dozen roaches worked their way through the wall of ash.

"Want to get some of the action too? The experience might be worth it for you guys."

Smashing his massive two metal fists together, the dwarf changed into a more aggressive stance. "It would be my pleasure."

His massive form stepped past Ilea, the head nearly reaching the ceiling of the large tunnel. Walking to the healer, Ilea swiftly wreathed her form in ash, expecting more than a little gore to come their way.

The wall crumbled when Ilea severed the thin connection she'd maintained, and around ten roaches, more or less injured, rushed toward them. Most of them focused on the massive form of the metal machine, teeth grinding against the heavy plating.

One heavy arm came down, and the first roach splattered against the walls while the others crawled onto the armor, looking for weak spots or ways to enter. The dwarf fell backward while trying to pummel another of them, squashing two others in the process.

Three of the beasts suddenly turned and came at Ilea and the healer, the cat immediately moving behind her. Ilea's ashen limbs shot out, piercing all three of the beasts. Blood dripped down as the corpses slid off, landing with a wet sound. The healer stumbled a step further back.

Ilea noticed the light in the distance had stopped moving.

"Are you alright?" she asked, the dwarf screaming and shouting as his huge mech suit churned in the mud, blood, and guts. He slipped but still managed to hit one of the roaches, injuring its jaw in the process.

Two of them were still alive, but another frantic movement from the dwarf squashed one against the wall. The last one was stomped to death by a massive steel foot. He stomped again and again, blood and bits of chitin covering a large part of his armored suit. He turned toward them, the floodlight turning warmer.

"What?"

Ilea couldn't help but laugh. Her Sphere let her see the healer's grin behind her. When the dwarf took a step and slipped, barely managing to keep standing, neither of them could hold it in any longer. They exploded with laughter at the floundering mech.

"You dumb fucks! I swear... once I get to you!" the dwarf shouted, but the laughter that followed was indication enough that he wasn't serious.

A second later, he found his footing and charged forward, the healer stumbling back and falling on her ass. Ilea just stood there, the massive form of the war machine stopping a few inches before the dwarf reached her.

"Didn't think so," she said with a grin, a little disappointed that he hadn't at least tried to slam her away.

The dwarf laughed. "No offense intended, stranger."

Ilea moved her ash to clean away the guts that had landed on her from his charge. "A little offended by your lack of trust in my resilience," she said, covering him in ash to clean off the blood and guts. He didn't move throughout, either trying not to anger her or understanding what she was doing. "Your friend stopped or dropped his torch."

"Not friend, more… dreadful acquaintance," he said after she was done. "Thanks for the cleanup. Not necessary."

Ilea snorted. "It stinks. Do you guys know how to get to the fourth layer? Might as well help me out after I saved your sorry asses."

"Aye… we know. At least if his map is to be believed. So far, it's led us into that." The dwarf pointed to the gore-filled tunnel, some parts still twitching. "Friends call me Baron. I'd be glad to help you get to the fourth layer. If his map is junk, I know some more conventional ways, but I think you'd want some of the treasure as well."

Ilea watched the cat glance at him and then her, squinting just a little. Ilea wouldn't have noticed without her Sphere and heightened senses.

"Nice to meet you, Baron. I'm Ilea. Depends on the treasure really, but I'd be happy to join you for a while."

The healer bowed. "Seath. Thank you for saving our lives," she said. Ilea wasn't sure if her fur was brown or if she really needed a shower. Seath was a little smaller than her and definitely thinner. The coat she wore was ripped in parts but still holding up.

Ilea checked her notifications while they slowly walked toward the torch. It seemed like nobody was particularly concerned about the man, who soon started shouting for help.

'ding' You have defeated [Monster Roach – lvl 184]

…

'ding' You have defeated [Monster Roach – lvl 194]

The messages turned to team notifications soon after. Ilea assumed it was considered a team effort once Seath had started her music. She thought about it for a while but came to the conclusion that it was only fair. To decide to become a bard and healer, likely without much direct combat potential, was already a dangerous decision.

'ding' Your group has defeated [Monster Roach – lvl 178]

…

'ding' Your group has defeated [Monster Roach – lvl 183]

'ding' Embered Body Heat reaches 2nd lvl 16

'ding' Embered Body Heat reaches 2nd lvl 17

Ilea smiled at the level ups. The bugs had been much too weak to give her Classes a substantial boost, but it had been a perfect opportunity for leveling Embered Body Heat. Some of the kills might even have come from the burning hot ash.

"Oh, thank God you survived," the man in the cowboy hat said when they reached him. He was stuck in one of the small trenches, his left shin pierced by one of the poop sticks.

"You left us to die," Baron said.

The man smiled. "Nah, I knew the stranger could handle it. Hello, by the way. Austin's the name, best ranger in town. Your armor looks fierce. Shadow's Hand, perhaps, or an Awakened?"

Ilea was at least impressed by how little the man seemed to care about his injury, blood continuously seeping into the pit. She moved two of her ashen limbs under his shoulders and gave him a lift.

"Wait, wait, don't move me so suddenly, the..."

He yelped and cursed when his leg came free of the trap, the wound opening wider in the process. Ilea set him down next to Seath, who quickly gathered mana in her hand before his wound started closing. Opening her eyes again, Seath sighed.

Austin leaned back, his head resting on the ground. "Fuck. Thanks, Seath. Glad I brought you along."

The cat person tensed a little at his words, though again not noticeable to the eye alone.

"And you, fierce warrior," he said, jumping to his feet, dusting off his brown coat, and grabbing his very inappropriate hat. "Thank you for helping out. We'll move along now, back to camp to recover."

He was obviously lying. Even Ilea knew it.

"I'm not exactly a fashion guru, but why the hat?" she inquired.

The man just grinned and walked past her, trying to tap her shoulder. An ashen limb intercepted him, then again when he tried a second time.

"I'm coming with you. You'll lead me to the fourth layer."

Austin groaned, holding his hands up in the air. "Baron, you fucking idiot," he grumbled. Then he shook himself and smiled. "Oh well. One more then. Yeah, alright. Alright. On the condition that you help us fight."

Ilea shrugged, not having a problem with that. Identifying the man, she was surprised to find him the highest-leveled member of the group.

[Ranger – lvl 210]

"You're human," Ilea stated after they'd walked in silence for a while, the three of them glancing at the dozens of roach corpses on the ground.

Austin looked her way, checking something on his crossbow once he'd picked it up from where it had been discarded farther down the tunnel.

"Yeah, red blood and a single heart pumping in my chest. You're one as well?"

"Human through and through. You're the survivor of an expedition?"

He nodded. "Got slaughtered a week in. Feynor. Probably on an expedition to explore the south. We killed a ton of them, but they had the numbers. The blood attracted one of those massive snakes, and that was that. I loosed a couple of shots and then advanced through the north until I came here."

Baron snorted but didn't comment further. Ilea had an idea about what might have actually happened based on Austin's display in this very tunnel, but she had no desire to press the matter.

"Where are you from?"

"Virilya, born and raised," he said and grinned. "Lovely, the Empire."

Ilea laughed, not quite believing anything coming out of his mouth. His green eyes were sparkling, similar to the king's. His jawline was smooth, and his grin not unattractive. Still, there was something sleazy about him. The way he spoke and looked at the others.

"It can be," she replied. "So, what's that treasure you have on your map?"

The man nearly stumbled upon the mention, flashing a glare at the dwarf and then at the healer. "Alternative way into the warded section of the fourth layer. Nobody's been able to crack it from the outside, so now we're going in from the other side," Austin said with a grin.

Ilea was pretty sure the dungeon had been there for at least a couple of decades. To think there was a section that hadn't yet been broken into...

"Are you sure nobody's been in there before?"

This time it was the dwarf who spoke. "Enchantments of the Red Church aren't simple. They're not just made to block off others. They're also dangerous to tamper with. Traps and monsters don't help."

Ilea wondered how long Terok would need to crack it. "Red Church?"

"It's the only name we have for whoever ran this city and the Heroes' Descent. Obsessed with the relics found within the deeper levels. You'll find enough writing and leftover books and records if you're interested. Most scavengers don't care."

Would at least get me a bunch of history to trade with the elf.

Austin held up a hand. "Trap ahead."

Ilea couldn't see it yet through her Sphere so she simply kept going, the other three looking at her with confused expressions.

"Hey, I'm a ranger, I can take care of it in a minute," Austin said.

Spotting the enchanted plate, Ilea checked for the connection and found a spear waiting to be shot out of a dug-out section in the wall. She activated the trap, catching the spear, which soared toward her a moment later, in midair.

"You know you don't really have to catch them," Baron said. "Most bounce off armor."

Ilea saw the thing wasn't even coated in poison. It was a simple wooden shaft tipped with a sharpened stone. "Were the goblins always here?"

"Yeah, bloody plague. No money to be gained in hunting them down either. Especially with how extensively they booby trap their dens," Austin explained.

Ilea just nodded. She wasn't interested either if the one she'd met was indicative of their general strength. *May the roaches and goblins kill each other in this world of dirt.*

Reaching the end of the tunnel, Baron looked at Austin. A dead end. Ilea knew there was something waiting behind the wall, but she waited before saying anything.

"Now, wait a minute before you smash me to a pulp, Baron. I told you I'd pay you back. Show some trust," Austin said with a grin, checking his crossbow before he selected a bolt from his quiver. "Should do the trick," he said to nobody in particular.

Loading his weapon, he shot it, and a whirlwind of air smashed deep into the earth and mud. When the air cleared, a passage was revealed, and Austin bowed. Seath actually clapped at that, but Ilea wasn't sure if it was intended sarcastically or not.

She hoped it was sarcasm.

* * *

"And the map says to go down there?" Baron asked, looking up at Austin, who didn't seem quite as confident anymore.

Ilea stared down the stone shaft, the thing long enough for neither her eyes nor her Sphere to reveal anything about the bottom.

"Well, I didn't draw the damn thing. Just didn't seem as big of a deal on paper," the ranger said.

The shaft was barely broad enough for the dwarf in his massive armor to fit. Ilea looked at Seath. "You and me go down first."

The cat person looked around, but it seemed neither Baron nor Austin was about to offer any help.

"You can heal, come on, don't be a wuss. Third layer down there?" Ilea asked.

Austin got out the map from his pack. "Yeah... well, not really. It's supposed to pass through the third layer entirely. Only way to get where we need to go."

Ilea nodded, appearing next to him and grabbing the map. "I'll be taking this with me as collateral should this be a trap in some way."

Ripping it from his hands, she rolled it up and handed it to one of her ashen limbs. Austin went red in the face and began to splutter.

"You give that back right now! You're a stranger, and I'm sure you don't want this kind of trouble. Baron?" Austin glanced at the war machine but made no move to attack quite yet.

The dwarf looked at him and then back at Ilea. "I'd rather have her on my side, Austin, no offense."

"That's like the opposite of no offense," Austin said, most of the tension leaving him as he rolled his eyes. "Have it your way, ash warrior."

Ilea appeared next to Seath and grabbed her around the waist and torso with three ashen limbs. "Just follow in a minute or two," she said to the others before she jumped down before they could delay any further.

She wanted to get to the fourth layer, likely the place where monsters in her needed range resided. Whatever treasure they were looking for, she couldn't imagine a lot of things being particularly useful to her. At least here in the north. Though gold was always welcome, of course. Taking the map had really been just to irritate Austin.

Freefalling into the hole, Ilea was surprised Seath didn't so much as yelp at the dangerous maneuver. Her Sphere would inform her about anything long before she needed to react, but she couldn't blink due to the healer in her ashen arms.

They fell for quite a while, longer than she'd expected. *Should've thrown a pebble first.* The thought passed through her mind when the ground suddenly appeared below her, approaching at a very high speed. Ilea's wings spread out, magic surging as they came to an abrupt stop, hovering a meter or two above the stone floor, which she now saw had carvings etched into it.

Seath groaned, so Ilea sent some healing mana through her. The sudden stop had left some bruises, and she'd been about to puke before a combination of her own healing and Ilea's calmed her down.

"Know anything about those?"

"What do you mean?" Seath groaned, still held by Ilea's ashen limbs.

"The etchings on the ground. Might be enchantments of some sort."

Seath looked at her. "I can't see well in the dark. Austin will have to have a look."

I thought cats didn't have that issue...

They waited for a while, Ilea trying to make sense of the etchings. A couple of minutes later, the others were on their way to join them. The sound of Baron grinding down the chute was unmistakable. Austin was simply sitting on one of the dwarf's massive shoulders with an annoyed look on his face.

"Stop, guys!" Seath shouted as the grinding grew louder before they came to a stop right above them. "Don't want to get squashed," she said, looking at Ilea with an accusing look.

Ilea was somewhat confident she could've stopped them with a hand, but this worked as well.

"We've got etchings in the ground. Barrier enchantment or trap maybe," she said. "Looks like your passage is closed."

FIFTY-SIX

Bloody Mess

The 'barrier', it turned out, was just a layer of stone without any enchantments or further tricks or traps. Just something that separated the third layer they'd apparently crossed and the fourth that lay beneath. Whoever had built this had just felt the need to decorate an entryway in a dark tunnel.

"To think they had an escape route straight to the second layer," Austin commented while Baron prepared a massive drill head for one of his arms.

Compared to Terok, he needed quite a while to switch it out. At least he had a storage item of sorts to keep the massive thing in. The ranger had looked at him a little too long when he'd summoned the jagged extension.

"Why did you help us?" Seath suddenly asked Ilea, the two of them leaning on the wall to give the dwarf space.

Ilea looked her way and then back at the dwarf, who seemed to be having difficulties screwing on the tool, cursing roaches and incapable smiths. She shrugged, smiling when the dwarf started to smash the wall, trying to force the drill bit to connect.

"I guess I didn't want to see people eaten by roaches."

"We're more dangerous to you alive," Seath noted.

Finally getting the extension on, Baron laughed as it whirled to life. Ilea couldn't help but notice the thing wasn't exactly fitted evenly, but with its size and quickly increasing torque, it would hardly be an issue.

I've survived worse than you three,

Ilea thought the cat woman's comment a little bizarre. Was she underestimating them?

"Are you a danger to me?"

She gave a sly grin. "I doubt it. It's just rare, you know... to find someone willing to help out without anything promised in return."

A lack of sleepless nights over the memory of your screaming as you're eaten alive by huge insects is return enough, Ilea thought, not voicing it as the sound of the drill hitting stone started to reverberate around them. She reduced her hearing to the lowest it could go.

She wondered how long her search for a way down would have taken without the help of these three. Probably not much longer, but the third layer was supposedly full of water, so she was thankful for skipping that one.

As the stone cracked, pieces of debris flew off to the side. Ilea caught one chunk of rock before it could smash into the healer next to her. Forming a wall of ash, she heard Austin complain before he jumped on top of the dwarf's machine, blood dripping down his forehead where a pebble had struck it.

A loud rumble, after a couple minutes of drilling, made Ilea spread her wings. She latched her ashen limbs onto the healer before the ground collapsed entirely, the dwarf laughing maniacally before he smashed his arms into the walls. Austin grinned, holding onto the mech's head.

"Down we go," Ilea said, falling past the dwarf before stopping a couple of dozen meters farther down, where dim lights illuminated the hallways around them.

Baron landed on the stone beside them, cracks forming where his immense weight pushed into the floor. Austin hopped off and looked around expectantly.

Ilea threw him the map, which hit his shoulder and dropped to the ground. The man whirled around and fumbled for his crossbow. Ilea just shook her head with a smile as the man snatched the map, looking at Baron with flushed cheeks.

"This is the fourth layer. We should keep as quiet as possible," Seath said.

"Probably traps all around too," Baron said, cracking his metal knuckles. There was no crack, of course.

Maybe with another ten thousand points in Strength.

Ilea took in the surroundings. Compared to the natural look of the first layer, this hallway looked similar to the city below Hallowfort.

"Hey, do you guys think the city above the first layer was always a dungeon?" Ilea asked.

It was Austin who replied. "Who cares? City, dungeon, whatever. Treasure in both and monsters as well."

Ilea rolled her eyes.

"Why build a city inside a dungeon? I think it probably turned into one after it was abandoned or its people were wiped out," Baron suggested.

Just seems kind of similar to Tremor. City turned dungeon. Maybe I'll find another live king and queen here.

The light illuminating parts of the hallways was magical, cold and flickering in places. The walls and floor were simple stone, nothing extraordinary like the marble in the palace of Tremor or the white stone Taleen dungeons usually seemed to have. A worn, dark red carpet lay in the middle of one of the hallways. Ilea sharpened her senses in her Sphere, and a familiar scent hit her nose.

"Blood," she said.

Austin nodded absentmindedly as he studied the parchment.

"Of course there's blood," he murmured. "Fucking rookies, coming to the fourth layer and complaining about blood," the man muttered before he walked off.

Baron shrugged, then followed Austin, his flashlight searching the corridors. Seath checked as well, closing her eyes as she likely tried to hear if anything was nearby. Ilea walked next to her, all her senses checking their surroundings.

"What's in the fourth layer then?"

"A bunch of nasty things," Seath whispered. "Pure Blooded, disgusting creatures that look like deformed humans. They're pretty fast and venomous, usually around..."

Her voice froze. Ilea followed her gaze and saw Austin with a raised crossbow, waiting. Baron's light shone on a creature around fifty meters farther ahead. It was about as tall as Seath but hunched over, with a face that looked like it had melted and two arms propping it up, both ending in nasty spiked bone.

Ilea blinked a little behind Austin to avoid getting into his line of fire. The beast seemed uninterested so far. Now she was a little closer, Ilea could see that its skin was torn, only bits and pieces remaining. A human, or at least a creature with a similar anatomy. Blood dripped from its body, primarily comprised of muscle and bone.

Kinda looks like demon spawn, Ilea thought. She wondered if it was a coincidence or if someone summoned them here, maybe an experiment with demon magic or the runes Weavy liked to use.

Her thought process was interrupted when the beast suddenly opened whatever was left of its mouth, a gurgling noise emanating from within before it tensed up and rushed toward the four of them.

Before the beast could even take two steps, Austin fired a bolt that smashed into its waist, blue light flashing before the thing collapsed onto the ground. It tried getting up, but another pulse of lightning went through it, its limbs spasming before a simple steel arrow thudded into its shoulder, cutting deep into its body.

Austin held up three fingers, counting down. When his last finger came down, there was a dull thump, some shrapnel digging into the stone floor.

The man winced when one of the pieces cut into his leather coat. Ilea raised her eyebrows.

Not bad.

Austin sighed, loading another bolt and firing it into the creature's other shoulder. There was another dull thump. Austin gave a thumbs-up after that and continued onward.

"What was its level?" Ilea asked him.

He loaded another bolt. "Two eighty. They're powerful but fucking stupid," he added.

"Why don't you hunt them until you reach that level?" Ilea asked. She was also wondering why Austin was the one walking in front and not Baron, who was quite literally the closest thing to an actual tank she'd seen so far in Elos.

Austin smiled. "Because one, I'm not fucking stupid. And two, I just said they're powerful. Do you want to see what they can do once they reach you? I don't."

I kinda do, Ilea thought, interested in how their attacks differed from the demons. Spawn usually had clawed hands, and these seemed to have single-bladed arms.

"Maybe we'll find out soon," Ilea said, hearing more noise coming from farther down the hallway.

Austin seemed to notice a moment later and lost a bit of the color on his face.

"What the hell are they doing? They shouldn't react to any of that," he grumbled, turning around and pointing behind them. "We're leaving. Back to the shaft, wait them out."

Ilea wasn't about to leave without testing herself against them. If their level was around two eighty, she'd at least try.

"Are there ranged variants? Can they see without eyes? And what's their usual level range?" she asked succinctly, ash forming around her as the three others ran back toward the hall they had come from.

Ilea blinked next to the running form of Austin, who looked at her aghast. "Gods, lady. Usually no ranged, they see well enough, and they can smell well but mostly rely on sight. Range between two fifty and fuck knows. I suggest you come with us."

He stopped beneath the shaft, crossbow on his back, then jumped from one side of the shaft to the other. Ilea watched in amazement as Baron bent his knees before jumping up, his heavy arms smashing into both walls before he dragged himself upward.

Pretty strong, or his suit is.

She glanced at Seath, who looked back at her, eyes frantically darting to the hallway before she jumped up into the exit with the most graceful movements of the three.

Blinking back toward the monster's corpse, Ilea moved it a little with her ash, checking for possible weaknesses. The tips of its bone blades were venomous, according to her Poison Resistance. The creature looked strong, fast, and certainly dangerous. Perfect, really, after all of those tunnels, bugs, and traps.

Let's see how you fare.

The noises from ahead definitely came from more of the creatures, but after waiting for a minute, they seemed to have passed.

Are you kidding me?

Ilea blinked toward them, her Hunter's Sight immediately picking up the droplets of blood that marked their route. More corridors opened up as she followed, the noises growing louder again, before a blink brought them into her Sphere.

There were six of them, running as if death was chasing them. Their movements were certainly not refined, feral almost. Ilea blinked next to the one closest to her. Identifying all of the creatures, none had a triple mark. Some were even identifiable.

Using one fist, she sent destructive mana and physical force slamming into the creature and smashed it into the opposite wall, an explosion of ash dimming out the light coming from the magical lamps above. She'd have to move the ash around her whenever she blinked, but if it blinded them somewhat, Ilea preferred to use it.

The monsters screeched, smart enough at least to quickly notice the intruder among them. Ilea blinked to the opposite side of the group, ignoring the one she'd already injured, and pummeled her ashen limbs and a fist into another Pure Blooded.

It whirled around faster than she'd expected, grazing her Veil as she stepped back. *Panicked,* she thought, appearing again on the other side of the group, continuously adding ash to the cloud blinding their vision. A quick grab and twirl sent one of the creatures crashing into the wall, its weight quite high but manageable for Ilea's enhanced body. A series of screeches rang out as the beasts slashed at an invisible foe, Ilea simply blinking to the wall, ignoring their attacks.

Observing the two she'd struck, she found them back on their legs, not looking particularly injured. Appearing next to one of them, she kicked at one of its legs, her ashen limbs attacking the other. Both attacks got through, the joint giving out against the brutal force. *One down.* Grinning at the result, Ilea decided it was the easiest way to deal with them.

The next five minutes were spent breaking legs, the creatures entirely overwhelmed by the ash around them. Whatever hearing ability they had was confused by the screeches of their brethren. Ilea didn't even blink anymore, simply letting her ashen limbs cut into the downed monsters, delivering wave upon wave of her destructive mana.

Being in contact with the ash around her additionally allowed her to pump reversed recovery into her enemies. *If only I could use the third tier here, one quick flesh explosion.* She grinned when the first one of them fell to her assault, her magic entirely nullifying whatever danger they posed.

'ding' You have defeated [Pure Blooded – lvl 269]

...

'ding' You have defeated [Pure Blooded – lvl 311] ***– For defeating an enemy fifty levels or more above your own, bonus experience is granted.***

The last one had been the only one above three hundred. Ilea knew exactly which one it had been too. It had taken her considerably longer to finish it, but, in the end, it died all the same, its senses overwhelmed just like the others. It wasn't enough to level up, but if she could hunt these creatures for a while, she'd be golden.

Damage output that can't reach me, fucking blinded by ash, and a trillion times faster to kill than Rose Knights.

She was brought back to the present by a sloshing sound from behind her. Another of the creatures soon came into view, Ilea's ash reforming right after she identified it.

[Blood Carrier – lvl ??]

"Come for them?" she asked, taking in the creature through her Sphere. It was bigger than the others, its mass at least five to six times more. It stood over two meters tall, its arms hung in front of it like clubs, and its spine jutted out from its back like a weird shark fin. Instead of sharpened bones acting as arms, this one had thick tree trunk-like limbs, ending in big chunks of bone.

A massive amount of mana suddenly formed around it. Ilea could feel it in the air. She moved her ash a little, preparing to blink. The move was definitely smart as the creature's speed increased, propelling it forward and forcing her to teleport. Appearing behind where the creature had been, Ilea watched it come to a stop and turn around.

I have a feeling that getting hit by that wouldn't t—

Her thought was interrupted as she blinked again. The thing was slow to start but definitely one of the quickest monsters she'd ever encountered once it got moving.

With all that mass too.

Quickly thinking how to damage the Blood Carrier, Ilea blinked behind it before it could turn toward her again, smashing the sharp ends of her ashen limbs into its massive back. The cuts were shallow but enough to keep her stuck to its back as she punched it with all her buffs and offensive spells.

Ilea focused on the spine that jutted out, doubting the tree trunk-like legs would snap quite as easily as those of the weaker variants. A surge of mana came from the beast, the creature moving backward before it smacked into her. Unable to blink, the impact pushed out all the air in her lungs.

Her bones held, groaning as the force shuddered through her body. The impact sent her flying toward the wall, but Ilea was still unable to blink. The problem was the monster moved as quickly as she flew, faster even. Ash spread behind her as she braced for the impact.

This time her bones gave, shattering and squashing her whole chest and stomach. The wall behind her was crushed, her form stuck within, armor bent inward. It had withstood part of the force, but the hit had been direct, the wall too close for her to do anything about it.

The beast moved away a single meter, mana surging again as Ilea blinked as far away as she could. Storing her broken armor, she sacrificed a thousand points of mana for her third-tier recovery.

She yelped as her bones moved back into the right position, her organs reforming from mush, the muscles around her lungs healing before air reached them again. Spitting on the ground, she added to the sea of blood that was forming in the small hallway, a fresh set of armor appearing on her.

I'd just worn that armor in. Now it's personal.

Dispersing all the ash around them, she waited for the beast to move. The mana buildup was noticeable, even without a perception skill. Blinking was the only move she had that was quick enough to avoid it.

Ilea waited for the last possible moment, blinking just far enough to hit it once. She messed up the first two tries, too far away to reach it with her fists. On the third try, however, her fist landed with grueling force, further damaging the spine while her ashen limbs delivered their payload, further cutting into the Blood Carrier's already mangled back.

Blinking right after to avoid another battering ram experience, she put some distance between them. The beast quickly caught on, starting to delay its charges as well as charging closer or farther away.

In the end, it didn't catch her off guard, its charges too slow and noticeable for her to be fooled by any variation. A single mistake could cost her another thousand or more mana, or even her life if she was unlucky, but now that she knew what the beast could do, it had become just another thing to kill.

It took a long while to crack its spine, the number of her attacks that landed few and far between because of its changing behavior toward the second part of their fight. After that, the thing got slower, weaker, almost sluggish. It was a wonder the monster still stood and moved at all, but Ilea could say the same about herself after being squashed against the wall like a fly. With enough blows exchanged, she did eventually come out on top.

'ding' You have defeated [Blood Carrier – lvl 382] – For defeating an enemy

one hundred and twenty levels or more above your own, bonus experience is granted.

'ding' Azarinth First Hunter has reached lvl 261 – Five stat points awarded

'ding' Inheritor of Eternal Ash has reached lvl 254 – Five stat points awarded

She sank to her knees, panting hard as she removed her helmet. Laughter echoed through the hallway, interrupted only when Ilea spat another mouthful of blood onto the ground. She immediately put her ten stat points into Wisdom, and her Meditation picked up.

FIFTY-SEVEN

The Inner Circle

Making her way back to the others, Ilea still didn't know why the creatures had moved where they did. Perhaps they were trying to get away from the Carrier, or perhaps they were hunting something.

Maybe they were just patrolling. Who knows what the fuck is behind these creatures. Battle of the necromancers... Descent versus Tremor... Fight!

"Come buy tickets now," Ilea said, smiling to herself as she backtracked through the hallways to the exit. Her new party members were still there, a little higher up but still waiting.

"It's safe for now!" Ilea called up. "None of the fuckers around now."

Austin was the first to land next to her. "They didn't come this way?"

Seath landed beside him before they all moved a couple of steps away to allow Baron to jump down. Ilea looked at his massive form, wondering how he'd take a charge from the Carrier.

"Not exactly," she said, but she didn't elaborate. Nobody asked either, and Austin went back to looking at his map as they walked back past the first corpse he'd left behind.

Ilea had to give him props for telling her about the monsters and their weaknesses even while fleeing. She might not have had the confidence to go after them so quickly otherwise. Any delay could have brought the Carrier upon her during her battle with the Pure Blooded. A good thing it hadn't.

"Where are we headed anyway?" Ilea asked as they walked through the dimly lit corridors, taking a right where Ilea had taken a left earlier. They wouldn't find what she'd left behind. She didn't care either way.

Austin looked up and pointed forward. "This... this is the inner circle."

Ilea had no idea what that meant, but Baron was apparently taken aback.

"What? Austin, are you fucking crazy? We shouldn't be here. Nobody is supposed to be here."

The dwarf kept his voice down but took a step toward the human. Austin just put his hands up in a placating gesture.

"Look, you really thought this came without risks? I told you it'd be dangerous."

"This is suicide! There's not just Pure Blooded here, you know that. If any of them find us, we're history, even with her here," Baron said, pointing at Ilea.

She raised an eyebrow but didn't comment. *Are they talking about the Blood Carrier I literally just killed?*

"What are you talking about? I've never been here."

"The fourth layer, the Heroes' Descent, is a city," Seath explained while the others stared at each other. "Well, it was at some point. Now creatures like the one Austin killed earlier run around and make it a nightmare to navigate it safely. Compared to the higher layers, you'll find a lot of potentially valuable things here.

"The problem is, there's a lot of closed-off sections, with enchantments and traps still in place against anybody who might open them. But we know the layout of the city. There were plenty of maps, and the previous residents were somewhat open about their beliefs and what they were doing here."

Ilea knew some of this already. "They were still alive?"

"No. Well, if you don't count whatever these creatures are as alive. But plenty of statues, notice boards, and even books all written in Standard remained. The inner circle is the heart of the Red Church. Nobody has managed to get into it yet, even after all this time."

"Supposedly," Baron said. "There wouldn't be any rumors about the danger without anybody having entered, now would there?"

Ilea nodded, though the information had much less of an impact on her than on Baron. If the Carrier was one of the most dangerous creatures here, then it wasn't quite comparable to Tremor, where Kingsguards and Soul Rippers roamed. She wasn't about to share any of that though.

"Well, we're here now. Where's the treasure? And what is it?" Ilea asked.

Austin continued down one of the corridors, ignoring her questions.

He doesn't know, does he? The thought amused her. Rumors and legends, sought by the desperate and hopeful. She just wanted a good fight, and after the one she'd just had, she was in a wonderful mood. *More to come, hopefully.*

They passed a lot of hallways, Austin occasionally choosing one, but Ilea was soon lost in the maze. The place was pretty big. She'd have found her way out eventually if she'd come down by herself, but finding this group had at least saved her some time.

"That's not supposed to be here," Austin murmured when they stood before a closed gate. Ilea could tell there were enchantments in place, feeling the thrum of mana coming from the door. Metal set in stone, the color the same light gray as the rest of the complex.

"Can you crack it?" Baron asked.

"Probably, but I'll need a while," the ranger replied.

* * *

"Why are we walking so far away?" Baron asked. An hour had passed since they'd reached the closed gate.

Ilea saw Seath smirking as Austin took out a bolt and aimed at the distant door.

"Blast radius," he said and loosed the projectile. Ilea snorted before an explosion rocked the surroundings, after which the distant screeches of monsters were slightly audible. "We'll wait for an hour or two until they leave again."

Ilea ignored that plan and started walking toward the metal door, now entirely mangled. Fires were blazing all around, some of the carpets beyond lit up entirely. She simply walked through the flames, her Heat Resistance and Veil making the exposure trivial. She ignored the sounds of confusion from behind her. None of them actually shouted, likely scared of the monsters that might hear them.

'ding' Heat Resistance reaches 2nd lvl 8

The hall beyond the door had dozens of benches lined up and an altar at the center of the far end. On it was a statue of a grotesque monster that looked a little like a dog praying. The head, however, was pretty much unrecognizable, a combination of features Ilea couldn't quite place.

The room was high-ceilinged, at least ten meters, with no windows. Paintings on the walls depicted different scenes, mostly centered around fighting or killing. The benches were wooden and in a rather good state, likely neither touched nor seen in quite a long time. No magical lights illuminated the room, but burning wreckage from the gate had started setting some of the benches as well as some of the paintings aflame.

Hearing noises from behind her, she spread out ashen spheres around her and activated her buffs as she cracked her neck.

"Welcome," Ilea stated as she observed the creatures rushing through the flames, briefly shrieking as the fire flickered over their bleeding bodies. She identified them as Pure Blooded, engaging the first one as soon as it entered the hall. Her ash enveloped them, the fire an additional factor to disorient them.

Taking care of them in much the same way as the last group, she found it even easier because the hall gave her much more room to navigate. Of all the monsters above level two fifty she'd encountered, these were certainly the easiest to kill.

There were seven of them, but her ash did the same job as before, and the beasts weren't smart enough to get distance or even flee when gravely injured. Their bladed arms cut through the ash, but not a single one of them landed a blow on her.

'ding' You have defeated [Pure Blooded – lvl 261]

...

'ding' You have defeated [Pure Blooded – lvl 302] – For defeating an enemy forty or more levels above your own, bonus experience is granted.

Might want to stay here for a while. Easier levels, but I suppose the fights are more boring too. Decisions, decisions.

Ilea had fought within a sea of Taleen Guardians. While they'd been considerably slower and less powerful, so had she. Plus, they'd six blades each and ranged variants as well. Without a trick up their sleeves, the Pure Blooded wouldn't pose a massive threat. At least, not without a Carrier or something else fighting alongside them.

There was no level up as most of them had been considerably below level three hundred. Ilea condensed her ash again, moving it into spheres behind her back along the eight limbs constantly hovering there.

She lashed out with one of the limbs, the sharp tip cutting repeatedly into one of the corpses before she finally managed to get through the shoulder joint, severing one of the bladed arms. Taking it, she looked at the bone, blood still dripping from it, before she noticed its glistening, sharp end.

[Pure Blooded Venom – Medium Danger]

Ilea didn't know exactly what medium entailed, but it couldn't be too bad. Stashing away a part of her armor, Ilea thrust the blade into her thigh. It penetrated easily, her strength combined with the apparent quality of the bone enough to get through her thick skin.

'ding' You have been poisoned by Pure Blooded Venom, -50 health per second for thirty seconds

Reasonable...

Ilea started healing, and the effect quickly wore off. She made her way around the room, the wound in her leg already healed and covered again by armor. She cut off and collected all fourteen of the creatures' arms and stored them in her necklace for Poison Resistance training later.

Should go back and get the others, Ilea thought. Then again, the bones she had could likely be used several times, and this group would hardly be the last one she'd face. Flicking the statue of the dog-like creature with her index finger, she grinned and looked around.

There were some doors leading farther in, and she chose the one that didn't lead downward. Austin had the map, but she didn't really care about that. It had been somewhat vague, mentioning neither monsters nor enchantments, simply stating which corridors to take.

One of the rooms had stairs leading down in a spiral, further than Ilea's Sphere reached. The other was just a small room. The metal door was locked, but a kick removed it from its hinges, causing it to smash into the opposite wall.

Weak fucking hinges – and locks, Ilea noted as she walked in, happy to find the door hadn't damaged anything. Not that there was much other than an altar in the middle of the room, a metal slab with cuffs to hold a person or whatever the fuck these people put on it. The floor was clean but worn. Ilea had her theories about that, the most likely one involving a lot of scrubbing of blood.

"Crazy blood magic church?" she murmured to herself, checking out some of the saws, blades, and drill-like tools on the opposite wall.

Austin entered the room as she was playing with one of them. She met his eyes and turned the tool's handle, making the drill bit twirl.

"This was used on the male genitals," she said in her most serious voice.

The man gulped, shivering as he composed himself as well as he could and started checking out the room.

"I'm joking. No idea what the fuck this is," Ilea added, throwing it vaguely in his direction. "There are stairs leading down."

Ilea left Austin standing in what she assumed to be either a torture chamber or an experimentation room. In the main hall, Baron and Seath looked at her in a new light, gaping at the torn-apart Pure Blooded scattered around the room.

The fire had died down now, leaving behind scorched benches and ruined paintings. Ilea had had her ideas about them when she saw them running from the roaches, but even so, while they were past level two hundred, they didn't quite seem to be made of the same stuff as members of the Hand.

She remembered them fighting in the outskirts of Ravenhall, each and every one of them battling for hours, hardened and unwavering. The group here wasn't that. While they were at the same level, except for Seath, her impression was that they were scavengers, treasure hunters, and looters. Not fighters.

Austin returned from the torture room and motioned for them to follow. "It's the other way."

The others followed him in silence, their mood a little subdued after having seen the corpses. The mention of the inner circle must have had more of an impact than Ilea had initially thought. Or maybe it was the number of enemies. At least now they knew it would be hard to continue without her there.

The stairwell was long, winding down into the depths of the fourth layer. After a while, Ilea couldn't sense any other passages. When they finally emerged from the stairway, it was onto a viewing platform overlooking a pit around forty meters down. In the middle of it, prowling, was a Pure Blooded. Bigger than any Ilea had seen so far. It didn't seem to spot them, or maybe there was magic in place that prevented it.

"Displaying their creation," Baron commented.

The hall was around twenty meters wide, and there was an exit at the other end, around a hundred meters back. All of it was built from the same light gray stone as the rest of the hallways. Corpses littered the place, both obviously Pure Blooded and skeletons that looked human.

"Here lies the path to salvation. The will necessary to break into the depths beyond," Baron said, reading from a nearby plaque. Ilea rolled her eyes.

"So, we fight that thing and go on?" she asked, eager to give it a go.

All three of them stared at her blankly.

"No, we turn around and leave. That's an Old Blooded. It's not even comparable to the Pure Blooded, not that they don't pose any danger. Austin's map might have brought us to an interesting place, but it's simply too dangerous for us to continue," Baron said, his huge metal arms crossed.

Austin held up his hands. "Hey, let's wait a minute here. Ilea, was it? It shouldn't be above level four hundred. Maybe if we give you support from up here, you can fight it?"

Seath was about to intervene when Ilea shrugged. "I can check it out at least. With her music and your bolts, it might be fine, depending on what the thing can do."

Looking at the beast, it had the same two-bladed arms and two legs as the Pure Blooded but stood much higher at around three meters. No joints were discernible from this distance. Its head was just a mass of flesh and eyes.

Looks like someone fucked with shit they didn't understand. Or this monstrosity was made with intent. Either way, it's fucked up.

"Alright. I hope you know that if you try to kill me off here, I'll ignore that thing and rip you three apart," she said seriously, giving each of them a quick glance.

Seath gulped, and Austin didn't have his usual smirk either.

"We could try to bypass it," Ilea suggested. "Do you guys have teleportation magic?"

Austin shook his head, and both Seath and Baron answered in the negative as well. Ilea blinked her eyes twice.

Really?

She couldn't fault them – skills showed up pretty much at random, after all – but perhaps they should have left the exploration business to people who could circumvent obstacles like these. Trian and Eve would be in and out of this place without so much as alerting the thing. Terok and Elfie were likely the same.

"Intervene only when I say so. It doesn't seem to see you here. Seath, can you heal and buff at that distance?"

The cat shook her head, "I... I can't... only at twenty meters."

Ilea thought about asking her to come down with her, but if she had to worry about anybody else, it could be a problem.

"Then it's just Austin's crossbow bolts. Again, only when I ask for it, and don't try to join in when it looks like the beast is about to die. If it rips me apart completely, I'd appreciate you distracting it."

Before any questions could arise, Ilea jumped down and spread her wings, slowly advancing on the creature.

As soon as she was around thirty meters away, it jerked up and jumped off the ground. It was faster than the Pure Blooded, but not quite as quick as the Carrier. Twirling in the air and flying toward the ground, Ilea avoided its bone blades and landed on the stone floor. A bone cracked under her armored boot as she prepared to engage.

[Old Blooded – lvl ??]

Smiling at the lack of three question marks, Ilea's ash fanned out just when the creature entered her Sphere again. As her wings took her silently to the side, she noted the monster kept its focus on her, dodging a bladed arm that came at her much faster than a Rose Knight's sword.

The beast was wild, cutting into the ground when she dodged sideways, the second blade too quick for her to avoid as she blinked away. Ilea activated Meditation, anticipating this would be a long fight.

Another monstrous creature to fight. Ilea did wonder why most everyone seemed to think of the north as a dangerous wasteland that shouldn't be entered under any circumstances.

She liked it very much.

FIFTY-EIGHT

Two Monsters

The feint came too quickly, and Ilea's form was blown backward. The bone had dented her armor but hadn't managed to break through, slowed sufficiently by her Veil and the ash fanned out before her. Healing spread through her, the damaged tissue repairing itself quickly as she rolled away.

A kick sent her flying again, but Ilea twirled in the air before she landed on her feet, avoiding the next attack and punching hard into the beast's abdomen. Her ashen limbs targeted its left shoulder, cutting into it with abandon, delivering Wave of Ember whenever it made contact.

Its second arm hacked at her from above, and Ilea took a casual step to the right. The blade scraped past her Veil as she delivered another two punches to its chest. She blinked behind it when the creature tried to knee her.

A hard punch to its spine was all she managed before it pivoted, Ilea flipping backward to avoid a horizontal attack. The monster was upon her before she even landed, her wings forming and taking her a couple of meters farther back to avoid another slash before she moved in again, a broad smile on her face.

* * *

Austin looked on as the woman battled the nightmarish creature, his face blanching as he barely managed to hold onto the crossbow in his hands. She had helped them out, even saved them, without asking for anything in return but for them to lead her farther down into the Descent.

Now he knew she didn't need anything they could offer. Scavengers were usually the only ones occupying Hallowfort and the Descent, ready to explore and make money. True fighters were few and far between.

He wasn't exactly incapable, but fighting against another man or Awakened in a mock battle was one thing. Battling the monstrous creatures lurking down below was something else entirely. He hadn't lied to her – he hadn't dared.

The thing wasn't above level four hundred, as far as he knew, but even groups of Pure Blooded were too dangerous to face. She hadn't mentioned taking whatever treasure was at the end for herself, and the fact that she'd helped them out made him think she wouldn't just murder them.

Still, he was afraid. More than he had been in quite a while. Perhaps as much as when the expedition had been slaughtered by Feynor and his ass had been rescued by a group of Awakened hunting the dragon worshipers.

The north was scary, for sure, especially when you knew jack shit about it, but with a bit of ingenuity and proper preparation, you could delve to the fourth level of the Descent without too many issues. This one had been rushed, he knew as much, but he had few options remaining.

His hand shook a little when Ilea was thrown at the wall, the blow somehow not penetrating her armor. Austin was sure he'd be cut through cleanly if a single attack from the beast landed. Baron would be able to withstand for a while, but even as a group, the thing would most certainly overwhelm them.

He breathed out when Ilea disappeared from the cracked wall and punched at the monster's back. It was learning too, not as stupid as the smaller variants that would walk into the same traps over and over again.

Austin knew a couple of people who had gotten a bunch of levels just hunting them down. Some had died after encountering the beast in front of him. He firmly believed that the three hundreds were a threshold humans couldn't cross.

The Old Blooded was becoming more cautious, respecting Ilea as an enemy to be taken seriously even though she wasn't close to three hundred. While the beast was becoming more and more defensive, Ilea went on the offensive, the black limbs coming out of her back slashing at the thing. He was pretty sure they weren't penetrating very deeply, if at all, but she still continued. Perhaps it was just meant as a distraction to get her punches in more quickly.

Baron and Seath looked on from either side, neither making a noise, scared they could alert it to their presence. Austin wasn't quite sure which of the two was the real monster – the Old Blooded or the human warrior that disappeared and reappeared, matching the blood creature's movements as if she was a match for it.

He couldn't help but smirk a little. *Shadow*. The black armor was something that had faded from his memories in his years in the north, but he remembered avoiding the mercenaries whenever possible, always fearing they'd been hired to apprehend or kill him.

Austin had reached the necessary level to join the Hand while in the north, but that wasn't his path. Not when there was so much to be found and gained here. His way of fighting and thinking wasn't quite fitting either.

The pay is shit too.

He watched in awe as Ilea avoided a flurry of attacks in the dim light with sure steps, neither tripping nor inconvenienced by the corpses, bones, and rubble in the hall.

He had no idea how long they'd been fighting, but it was definitely too long for anyone to reasonably hold their concentration. Austin was pretty sure Ilea hadn't messed up a single time. Each hit she took was unavoidable and a result of the beast's sheer prowess and high level. They both learned in the fight, each step and attack calculated and executed with near perfection.

The only way he could follow was through his perception skills that enhanced his eyesight. His bolt was ready in case she needed it. At this point, it wasn't a question of betraying her or not, more one of not angering her. If she managed to take them to the treasure mentioned on the map and the records that he'd stolen from Krentin, then she truly was a blessing brought to him in the most desperate of times.

* * *

Ilea finally got through, her ashen limbs cutting enough tissue to damage the integrity of the monster's right arm. Now it was only a matter of time. The thing had grown more apprehensive, responding rather than initiating as the fight had gone on.

Now its right arm was sluggish, Ilea immediately focused on that side while the monster tried to keep her at its center. It was still moving a little faster than her, but avoiding its slowed attacks was now much easier. With each hit the arm took, the Old Blooded would slow down.

Ilea's ash cut through a joint connecting two bones and the arm came loose, clattering into the graveyard around the two fighters. Ilea breathed out and took a couple of steps back as the beast screeched, anger and irritation showing in some of its eyes.

Blood dripped to the ground as the monster moved, crushing bones below its massive deformed feet, now with only a single bladed arm to attack Ilea.

Stepping back and avoiding the next slash, Ilea focused her ashen limbs on the open wound on its shoulder, delivering more and more of her mana into it. Blinking away from a kick that came just a little too quickly, she breathed out and let meditation flow through her.

Cocking her head to the side, she watched the beast slowly turn and fall down. Blood continued to seep onto the floor from the massive wound. She waited for a minute and then two, mana continuously recovering before she finally heard the notification in her mind.

'ding' You have defeated [Old Blooded – lvl 362] – For defeating an enemy one hundred or more levels above your own, bonus experience is granted.

'ding' Azarinth First Hunter has reached lvl 262 – Five stat points awarded

'ding' Inheritor of Eternal Ash has reached lvl 255 – Five stat points awarded

'ding' Veil of Ash reaches 3rd lvl 5

Ilea put her points into Wisdom again.

The group of treasure hunters jumped down as Ilea walked to the arm she'd cut off. The beast hadn't managed to get through to her skin even once, mostly just bludgeoning her with its massive bone blades.

[Old Blooded Venom – High Danger]

She put it into her necklace and went back to the corpse. Her ashen limbs started to cut into it while she checked her armor. There were dents to be sure, but she didn't feel like replacing it already. Ilea was down to four usable sets of Rose Hunter armor, and this one still had a helmet that was fine, so she stuck with it for now.

"That was very impressive," Baron said as he stepped up and summoned a bladed extension for one of his arms. "May I?"

Ilea stepped away from the corpse and nodded, watching as the huge thing came down and cut into the arm. She grinned when he didn't manage to get through with a single hit, nor with a second or a third.

"You were ridiculous, do you need healing?" Seath asked, but Ilea waved her off.

"I'm alright. Thanks."

Baron cursed as he continued to smash his bladed arm into the corpse, blood spraying around as Ilea raised an ashen wall to stop it splattering her.

Austin rolled up his map and started wandering through the hall, looking at the bones and corpses.

"There's, like, fifty of them here," he commented, kicking one of the dead Pure Blooded.

Ilea turned to him after Baron had finally managed to cut through the arm. "Do they fight each other?"

"Who else would've taken all of these out? I always ran when I encountered any of the bigger ones. Some people say they fight each other, others say they don't. Never seen it myself."

Ilea nodded to Baron and made the second arm vanish into her necklace. It had the same *'High Danger'* warning as the other one, and she wasn't about to test the effects while the group was close by.

"Want the rest of the corpse too?" Baron asked.

Ilea thought about it for a moment. Maybe the necromancers or Elfie could use it. Then, looking at the assortment of eyes, she decided against it.

"I'd rather burn it all. Can you do that, Austin?"

The man snorted. "Nah. I can splatter it more if you like."

"Can we move on? The smell here is disgusting," Seath commented. "Let Baron handle it."

Austin motioned to the exit on the other side of the hall, a metal double door set in stone. Ilea let Baron take care of it, the dwarf smashing the thing open with a punch. His floodlight flickered on and illuminated the dark corridor beyond.

"Wait," Austin said, throwing a stone down the hall. The thing rolled a little before it was set aflame by a trap. The group watched the fire die out a moment later.

Ilea took a step into the hallway. "We can deactivate them one after another."

She smiled. She had good Heat Resistance, and poisons likely wouldn't finish the job either. Checking the mechanisms and plates connected to the walls, Ilea found they were all the same fire-breathing ones they'd set off with the stone.

There were darts and smooth spears set in the last couple meters of the hallway, beyond that, another set of doors. Stepping in, fire enveloped her, her Heat Resistance, armor, Veil and healing easily powering through the flames, which didn't even come close to the green ones she'd encountered in her first Taleen dungeon.

I'm much tougher as well now. Might want to try that again when I get the chance.

"Are you alright?" Baron shouted down the hallway.

Ilea turned slightly and gave a thumbs-up.

Why always fire? Ilea wondered as she walked through the flames, her mana rising thanks to her meditation, even while walking through the traps. She avoided the last set of spears and darts, smashing the walls with a couple of punches and removing the projectiles before checking them with her Poison Resistance.

[Blood Poison – High Danger]

Blood blood blood blood. What is it with this place?

The spears were simple steel without any poison. The mechanisms to fire them were somewhat complex, however, likely creating enough force to punch through quite a formidable defense.

Ilea didn't test them out and just smashed the walls instead. Some of the spears fired anyway, the traps seemingly constructed in a way to fire in the event of damage or tremors. The projectiles shot past her. One flew down the hallway, but the angle would prevent it from hitting anybody.

Ilea couldn't see through the doors at the end of the hallway with her Sphere so walked back toward the group again, destroying all the fire-creating traps in the process. Most of them were just steel tubes set in the walls with something that looked like small crystals at the end, likely powering the enchantment placed on a metal plate. Ilea remembered the Taleen traps had never had such an obvious power source.

Crafty. I wonder how the Guardians are powered. Maybe they're just some type of metal insect creature after all and not machines?

Destroying the last trap, she found the spear that had shot down the hallway stuck in the wall, just a meter away from the waiting Austin.

"Was that on purpose?" he asked, smiling at her.

Ilea snorted. "Doors have enchantments on them," she said, leading the group back down the corridor.

Through her Sphere, Ilea saw Seath looking at the walls, split by cracks or with whole sections broken in, gulping as she looked at Ilea's back.

Austin checked the door for a while before sighing. "Seems like a hardening enchantment, a perception barrier, and some triggers for something. No idea what."

"Can you disable individual ones? I can check behind it if you disable the perception barrier," Ilea suggested.

"Awesome. Sure, I can try. That will take a while though."

"How long?"

He held up five fingers.

"Five hours?"

"Minutes," he smiled.

Ilea looked at Baron, whose war machine nearly filled the entire width and height of the corridor. They were lucky the dwarf hadn't gotten stuck yet.

"There you go," Austin said after fiddling with the runes scratched into the door. Ilea felt something in the mana shift, and her Sphere suddenly revealed what was in the room beyond.

Nice work, she thought, seeing the packets below the door. "There's something below the door. I'd assume it's explosive. Or filled with chemicals or something."

Austin nodded. "Any way we can go around? I don't think I can disable the triggers without setting them off."

"The room's pretty wide. I can see cages with skeletons inside. Some have been violently broken open, so we might have company inside. We should be able to drill in... here," she said, pointing to the hallway's left wall. "My punches didn't set off the triggers, so I doubt some drilling will."

"Let's drill as far as we can then. You tell the big man when to stop," Austin said.

Baron was already applying the drill bit to his war machine. "On it, let's get that treasure."

Ilea grinned. "If there's actually anything else but more monsters trying to kill us in there."

One good necromancer means there's a bad one in here. Equivalent exchange, yin and yang, all that jazz.

The three of them waited a little to the side as the dwarf started to drill. Ilea made her helmet vanish, then summoned a meal of noodles with meatballs, covered in a dark creamy sauce with a note of wine. Seath looked at her imploringly with her big round eyes. Ilea sighed and summoned another portion. Neither of them had been prepared by Keyla.

"Care to share another one?" Austin asked as he sat down and smiled at her.

Ilea stared at him but didn't move. The man sighed and got something out of his small pack.

"What's your story? Joined an expedition as well?" he asked as he started eating.

Ilea chewed and swallowed. "I am the expedition."

FIFTY-NINE

Poison

"You're a Shadow, aren't you? Or is the black coating there for another reason?"

Austin was looking at Ilea with an expression she couldn't quite place. Parts of her armor had been damaged in the fight, revealing that her Rose Hunter set was coated in a layer of black steel.

"I'm a Shadow, yes. Or was, I guess. Not on a mission currently. Though the black was mostly just for stealth."

Their voices barely carried over the drilling. Baron was progressing well, already a meter into the wall, though he'd have to remove quite a bit of the stone because of his massive form.

"Ever been to Virilya? City still exist?"

Ilea stuffed a meatball into her mouth and started chewing, swallowing a moment later,

"Yeah. Baralia was at war with the Empire. Virilya was under siege a couple months ago when I left. No clue how things currently stand. I didn't want to get sucked into all of that."

No more than I already had.

The man made a hissing sound, drawing in air. "It's been years but that doesn't sound like a smart move for Baralia."

"Why not?"

He took another bite of his jerky. "The Empire is old, one of the oldest places in the human territories. I just don't think it'll fall. Call it a feeling."

"If it means Ravenhall will continue to do well and slavery stays out of that territory, then I'll call that a win."

Ilea didn't want to think about the thousands upon thousands who would suffer and die in the war itself. She shook her head, pushing the thought aside.

"A true Shadow, then," Austin said and laughed. "You think they'd let me join?"

Ilea took another bite, the drilling stopping for a moment as Baron retracted his arm to continue on another section.

"Of course, you're above two hundred. It's a few hundred gold, but maybe the payment has changed since the demon fiasco."

"Now that's a story I'd like to hear," Austin said, sitting up a little, a big smile on his face as he looked at her with anticipation.

Ilea waved him off with her fork. "Not that big of a deal. One of the elders summoned a couple thousand into the city and vanished into the demon realm. Nearly wiped out the population of Ravenhall and many surrounding cities. The Hand lost a lot of people too, but we managed to clean it up in the end, as well as we possibly could."

Austin sighed. "You're not one for storytelling, are you? Makes sense that Baralia attacked then if the Empire was dealing with runaway demons and the Hand were occupied with their own fuck up. Oh well, not that it matters here."

Ilea was fine with letting the topic drop there. She didn't feel responsible for either the demons or the war, but thinking about the chaos and all the dying people, the slaughter the demons had caused, and the ensuing war made her ill. Not to mention the murders of the Birmingales and Redleafs.

"Doesn't matter here," she agreed with a nod.

"How far in do I have to go?" Baron asked then, a couple of meters deep already.

"Around another three meters, big man," Ilea said, using her Sphere.

"Big dwarf, little lady," he grumbled before continuing his work.

It wasn't long before he spoke again.

"I think I'm done, guys," he said, his metal head poking out from the new section of hallway he'd dug out.

Ilea and Austin went to check the wall. They could break through now they were quite a distance away from the packets below the doors.

"You still have no idea what they are?" Ilea asked.

"No, could be anything from poison to fire," the man admitted.

Ilea knocked her knuckles against the stone wall. "They'll activate no matter what? How long to deactivate the enchantments?"

Austin frowned. "Not sure I could even do that. Honestly, I'd just throw in a couple bolts and let them explode in here."

"Then let's do that," Ilea confirmed, eager to continue into whatever hellhole this inner circle was.

The group stood outside the hallway in the room Ilea had fought the Old Blooded in previously.

"Three... two... one..." Austin called out.

A dull rumbling sound reverberated through the room. A hissing sound followed before a red gas filled the hallway and rushed toward them.

"Ah, fuck, retreat guys," Austin said, and he, Baron, and Seath rushed back and worked their way up the walls to reach the balcony above.

Ilea didn't follow, instead waiting as her ash spread to block out the gas and redirect it to the side. She let some of it through on purpose and identified it with her Poison Resistance.

[Blood Vapor – Medium Danger]

Medium.

Taking a step toward the gas, she breathed it in.

'ding' You have been poisoned by Blood Vapor, -30 health per second for two minutes. Paralysis resisted.

Ilea walked into the poison, but the only thing that changed was the notification refreshing. Moving her ash, she created a sphere around herself before heating it up as much as she could. After waiting for a couple of minutes, she breathed in again and found the poison notification didn't refresh.

She continued to walk around and burn the gas with her ash, or at least heat it up enough for it to become ineffective.

"Are you alright in there?" Baron shouted.

Ilea formed a thumbs-up with ash that she sent hovering a little over the red gas before it disintegrated.

Just to be cool.

'ding' Poison Resistance reaches 2nd lvl 2

Her cleanup continued for another five minutes. The poison had apparently spread toward them, and little of it had spread into the room beyond the still-closed door. She noted that the section Baron had created now contained a secondary entrance. The plan had worked.

Ilea returned to the main chamber. Motioning to the others that the poison had been dealt with, Baron jumped down pretty much immediately. Either he trusted her more or he had some confidence in his own survivability.

"Good job. You must have a high Poison Resistance. That was Blood Vapor, right?"

Ilea nodded. "Yeah. I just heated it up, seems like the poison's dealt with. Just don't stray too far from the center of the room."

They walked down the hallway and through the entryway created by the explosion, followed by Austin, ever cautious, and Seath.

Magic lights built into the ceiling around five meters above them lit up most of the place. Some of the circular glass casings were cracked and broken. Ilea wondered if someone had deliberately tried to destroy them.

Ilea immediately noted the cages scattered throughout the room. The steel was rusty in places. Some contained skeletons of monsters she couldn't place, others held what looked like humanoid people of various species.

"Stumbled upon a happy place here," she grumbled, swinging one of the cage doors, the hinges creaking from age and wear.

The room turned out to be a rather large hall filled with cages spaced out at regular intervals. Ilea listened but couldn't hear anything moving. The previous occupants of the open cages must have either died or found some way to escape. Some skeletons lay broken on the ground as well.

Austin looked around. "Something's still alive here. Be careful."

"Any idea what it could be?" Ilea asked, glancing at the ranger.

He checked the ground several times. Blood stains, as well as discolorations, littered the stone. Lifting a small piece of bone, he shook his head.

"No idea. I'm just sure something's been moving around here, disturbing the place in the past week."

They walked through the hall, the three scavengers staying close together while Ilea moved a little ahead.

Movement suddenly flashed in her Sphere, Ilea catching a thin leg moving through the corner of the room behind them.

"We've got company," she said, blinking toward where she'd seen the movement.

Her Sphere picked up something that looked like a spider. It definitely looked similar to the monsters they'd encountered in the inner circle so far, but something was dripping from its body, the legs were mere bones, and its body was disfigured.

The torse was formed of a chunk of amalgamated muscle, with eyes peeking out from random places and eight bony legs jutting out below. It was around a meter tall and long, more if the legs were outstretched.

Ilea rushed toward it as it turned to her.

[Blood Tainted – lvl 128]

Its low level was a little confusing, but as it jumped at her a moment later, Ilea's ashen limbs intercepted it. The ash pierced the creature's center mass and kept the thing suspended in the air as more and more blood dropped to the ground.

"Careful, explosion!" someone shouted, but Ilea just watched as the spider's fleshy core burst in a flash of red, blood and guts smacking against her Veil before a now familiar poison entered her system.

'ding' You have been poisoned by Blood Vapor, -30 health per second for two minutes. Paralysis resisted.

She started heating up the localized cloud. Her defenses had held, absorbing most of the blast.

"Does your map say anything about how long it is from here to whatever treasure there is?" Baron asked. "Otherwise, I'm out. This place is riddled with dangers."

"We have two healers. I doubt the blast would've taken any of you out, so they're alright. Unless there are hundreds of them waiting behind that door," Ilea said, pointing to the metal gate at the end of the hall.

Crossing the distance, Austin checked it. "No enchantments on this one." He tested the handle. "Locked."

Ilea motioned him aside and kicked the door. The metal bent inward, but it didn't open. A second kick broke the lock entirely, and Ilea yanked it open.

"Get the fuck out of here," she said, seeing the spiders move into her Sphere in the distance. The sound of dozens of them scuttling about it filled the air.

Austin was the first to react as he scrambled back, quickly followed by the other two as Ilea pushed the door closed. She formed thick walls of ash behind the metal door, some of it seeping in and pouring her destructive mana into the monsters that started to pile up on the other side.

I've become quite the exterminator…

The things died like flies, their poison, blocked by her ash, slowly filling the room beyond. There had been no light coming from within, but Ilea knew from her Sphere the room was filled only with machines, tubes, and crates.

They'll be sad to find this at the end of their treasure map.

The last of the spiders died, Ilea ignoring the dozens of kill notifications. Their low levels did little for her experience.

Stepping inside, the poison was reactivated. Spreading out ash, she waited on burning it all and checked out the room instead.

A big chair was situated in the center, with cuffs attached for feet and hands as well as a bunch of detachable additions that would allow for less humanoid or perhaps winged creatures to be fastened to it.

Most of the large vials hanging from one of the walls were broken, and the ones that weren't contained a red substance. Ilea assumed it was blood.

Checking the crates, she found mostly trash or strange instruments. There was a book she quickly stashed in her necklace before she continued. Her ashen limbs moved the spider corpses into the least cluttered corner as she started to clean out the poison gas, figuring there wasn't anything of real value down here.

Except, perhaps, for this key…

She'd spotted it next to a long-dead skeleton. The golden metal was somewhat tarnished but still impressive-looking.

Seems important. Even has a ruby or something in it.

"Hey, is it safe in there?" she heard Austin yell, the need for looting audible in his voice.

Putting the key into her necklace, she removed her helmet to get some light from her Form of Ash and Ember.

"Taking care of the poison now, couple minutes!" she called back offhandedly.

Next, she moved over to the red containers. She picked one up. Turning the vial in her hand, she identified it.

[Vial of Blood]

Useful.

Not finding anything else that might be of interest after looking through all the crates with her Sphere, she started fiddling with the chair. Tubes connected it to the big glass containers on the walls, most of them shattered and broken.

'ding' Poison Resistance reaches 2nd lvl 3

Baron's floodlight broke into the room at that point, most of the gas having been burnt up by her ash.

"Should be safe enough now," she said, clicking one of the cuffs shut and trying to open it again with strength alone.

Austin looked around as he entered, frowning as he took out a portable magic light. Ilea glanced his way and then at the light.

"Why didn't you use that instead of the torch till now?"

He didn't reply, instead looking around and focusing on the glass containers on the walls.

"Because monsters sometimes fear fire," Baron supplied, coming into the room in a crouched, sideways scuttle.

Austin unhooked some of the tubes and started unscrewing the containers from the walls.

"That's the treasure?" Ilea asked.

"This is blood they used in their experiments. The right buyer will pay quite a bit for it," the ranger explained.

"So, you're dooming all of life to become Pure Blooded? For gold?"

"I don't think you understand," Baron intervened. "This substance was and is still apparently found on lower levels. The Red Church simply brought it here and experimented with it. Drinking it on its own is a high-quality health potion, but it's a versatile substance. Allegedly."

"You've never seen it… None of you have…" Ilea said.

Austin carefully removed the tank and looked at her. "Who cares? It sells, and you get your share."

Ilea smiled. "And it was used to create the Pure Blooded and the other variants?"

Austin looked at her, then at Baron.

"That's a theory," the dwarf supplied.

Ilea tapped her thigh. "I'll get the thing then, and you'll get the equivalent of how much it would have sold for. As far as I'm concerned, the only thing you supplied was the map."

"You what?" Austin asked. She felt his heart rate accelerate. "I mean, yes, that's a great idea," he added quickly.

"How much would all the liquid in this room sell for?" Ilea asked as a voice shouted from outside.

"Austin, you sleazy fucking dimwit!" the unfamiliar voice shouted.

Ilea noted that Seath was nowhere to be seen.

Austin's eyes darted toward the voice. "Fuck."

Ilea rolled her eyes. "You stole the map, didn't you? Give me the stuff, I'll store it safely at least." He hesitated but ultimately handed it over. Grabbing the two tanks still hanging on the walls, Ilea ripped them off and stored them as well. "What are you looking at me for? This is your problem," she said to Austin.

Austin's trademark smirk was back on his face before he dusted his cloak down. "Baron, move out of the way, would you?"

The dwarf obliged, stepping out of the room before the others followed.

Ilea looked at the new group approaching. The one in the middle looked humanoid, other than the bug-like head on his shoulders. A lizard person was standing at his side, a massive sword dragging behind it on the ground, its tail twitching from time to time. Both were around two meters tall.

Next was a human, a woman Ilea thought she recognized. She was formed of a black mist, only recognizable as a person due to the two arms holding a long halberd. The last one in their group was a serious-looking Seath, the healer bard standing with arms crossed at the bug person's side.

"You owe me my map and whatever you already found," the bug person said, likely the leader of their group.

Ilea looked over at them, meeting the eyes of the lizard warrior, who grinned and flicked her snake-like tongue.

They seem fun.

SIXTY

Overconfidence is a Quick and Direct Killer

Austin stepped forward.

"Krentin, what a joy to find you here. You played me, Seath. Impressive. I'm sure we can find an arrangement, though." He smiled as if they were all good friends. "You can have the map back and whatever's in there. We didn't find anything useful. We did, however, clear out all the monsters on the way here."

He smiled and gestured for them to go and look in the small room.

"He didn't kill anything. The human in black armor did all of the work," Seath said. "And she has a storage item, so if there was anything in there, I assume it's already gone."

Krentin made a clicking noise, forming a fist with his armored hand before he removed the silver chain holding his hood.

"I don't want this to end bloody. Human, are you working for that man?"

Ilea carefully identified all of them. Krentin was the highest-leveled of them at two twenty-eight, and the mana coming from him felt powerful. The dark wisps licking at the air reminded her of Walter.

The lizard person she identified as a female warrior was at two twenty-one. She wore heavy plated armor, and her sword was curved and nearly as long as Ilea was tall, a red sheen visible near the blade. Her slitted, dark red eyes were staring at her with a fierce intensity. Ilea noted that she was breathing hard, either because of some injury or maybe because of excitement.

"I work for myself," she stated, eyeing the rest of the group.

The woman was a level two ten healer, but from the way she held herself and was geared, Ilea knew there was more to her. She wore a thin set of steel armor with a brown hooded cloak. A scarf prevented people from seeing anything but her blue eyes. The black shadow-like being that reminded her of Goliath was a mage at one eighty-five. Whether they were using the halberd for show or in combination with spells, Ilea wasn't sure.

Krentin scratched his head. "You're complicating things. Considerably."

Ilea didn't disagree. Evaluating the group, she was pretty sure the lizard person and perhaps the healer were the only real fighters of the group, purely based on how aware they were, how tense and prepared their body language seemed. They reminded her of Shadows. Austin seemed glad the attention had shifted to her instead of him.

"She's dangerous, Krentin," Seath said.

The bug person looked at her, considering.

Ilea thought about releasing some obscuring ash and just getting out of there, but she kind of wanted to fight the lizard woman. To see what she could do with that sword.

Let's wait a couple more minutes.

"Dangerous? I've invested too much to stop here," the mage said, turning to Ilea. "Are you willing to part with what you found in there? I'll pay you five gold for your trouble. Just leave it here and vanish, no repercussions."

Ilea grinned at that. *No repercussions... how very generous.*

"I don't have business with anybody here. I cleared the way, and I'll keep what I found. How does that sound?"

Krentin sighed. "Knock them out."

Ilea felt magic surge from the black wisp person. A moment later, a blast of mind magic ripped through her mind, both Baron and Austin staggering before they fell to the floor. Ilea simply stood there and looked at the mage, who wobbled a little in the air, one arm touching their head.

"That's your last chance. Do you really want to do this?" Ilea asked, her eyes locked with the lizard, whose sword was now poised and ready to fight.

"Boss... she's a tough one," the wisp said in an ethereal voice, respect evident.

"Are you fucking kidding me? We're five against one now. Move!" the mage said, dark magic forming between his hands. The group exploded into movement, fanning out and readying their attacks.

Ilea didn't give them time. They did have the numerical advantage, but they were in a somewhat small hall and knew only limited things about her abilities.

The difference between us...

Ilea appeared in their midst, a burst of ash darkening the room before projectiles shot out from within the cloud, destroying the five magic lights that were still working. The healer had already rushed past her, and the lizard had teleported to Ilea's old position, now peering around as the room fell into darkness. Ilea blinked next to Seath, who was playing her music, avoiding the dark magic burning into the stone floor and the cages where she had just stood.

...is that you feel pain.

Ilea grabbed Seath's arm and broke it with a swift motion. A kick to the struggling cat woman's leg snapped the bone, her defenses laughable against Ilea's empowered body. The bard screamed as she collapsed. Ilea blinked next to the other healer, who was disoriented in the dark but had closed her eyes.

Ilea's fist was blocked by an armored arm, but her ashen limbs cut into the healer's shoulders and back, making her wince as blood splattered on the ground. It wasn't armor, Ilea noted, but solid stone covering her arms. A hard kick sent the woman flying, crashing against one of the steel cages and bending the metal with her impact.

Crouching, Ilea heard the whoosh of a huge blade as it whistled over her head, followed by a kick that she avoided with a short roll. She got up to see red eyes staring at her in the dark. A red mist was visible around the lizard, who was advancing on her at high speed, her sword smashing the cages and the ground while Ilea dodged black lightning coming from their boss.

Deflecting one of the slashes, she pummeled the lizard's arm, denting the armor slightly. She poured destructive mana into her, but Ilea didn't stop there, stomping on the stumbling warrior's tail before her foe vanished. Ash formed around Ilea a split second before black lightning crashed against it, burning through layer after layer before reaching her Veil.

Ilea blinked next to the mage, who was floating at the other end of the room, his lightning burning into the ground where she'd just stood. Seath was still crying out in pain, and it seemed the mind mage wouldn't attack her anymore because of the feedback he'd got from her resistance. The human healer wasn't making a sound, likely taking care of her wounds for now.

Krentin turned toward her in the air, letting her get close. She whipped her ashen limbs against his armor, and while most glanced off the sleek metal, two found purchase, cutting into his shoulder and part of his face. Even as her fist landed, Ilea knew quite well he wanted her to touch him. She, however, was confident of outlasting a mage of his level.

I survived the Blue Reapers, she thought as dark magic in the form of black lightning coursed through her. She lashed out again and again, his armor denting and destruction continuously burning down his health in conjunction with her reversed healing.

He started blasting her with dark magic orbs that she couldn't dodge at close range. Instead, she simply delivered more damage as he started to retreat through the air. When his back reached the wall, all he could do was block with his arms as well as he could. He created a barrier, but she blasted through it with a combination of her fists and her ashen limbs.

The lizard appearing next to her made Ilea blink away again. Checking her resources, she found her health already down by a third. Sacrificing nearly a thousand mana, she healed herself back up in seconds. Her mana and stamina were also recovering as she stood there, meditation flowing through her.

Then she heard a cough coming from the direction where she'd just attacked Krentin,

"Stop… you can have what you found… just leave…"

Ilea looked his way and cocked her head. "That would be convenient, now wouldn't it?"

The lizard appeared a couple of meters in front of her, sword raised, her maw revealing a wicked grin. Blood stained the floor from where Ilea had injured her tail. The healer stepped up behind her, eyes still closed, stone now covering her whole body. Seath wasn't playing music, but she was standing to the side. The black wisp looked around but didn't make a move.

They're obviously much weaker.

"I didn't come to the north to kill people, and you're hardly worth the trouble. You could have played nice, but you chose to fuck around. Just get the hell out of here," Ilea said. Then she paused. "Lizard girl, you stay." She crossed her arms.

Krentin nodded in the dark as he began his retreat.

"We won't come after you in vengeance, I swear it on my name. You won't regret this decision."

Taking a step back, Krentin limped toward the exit. Seath hissed at the pain from her mangled leg, her healing ability not working quite as quickly as Ilea's third tier. She looked at the cat woman. Austin and Baron would make her life a nightmare if they survived.

"No worries about the vengeance. You're free to try, actually. I welcome a challenge."

She saw a smile fighting through Krentin's pained expression, blood still dripping from his wounds. The dark wisp looked her way, stopping for a moment before it joined Krentin at his side. The human healer circled around Ilea and made her way to the exit.

"Human. What's your name?" Ilea asked.

She stopped and turned slightly. "Jonna."

Ilea smiled. "Jonna. That's a good combination of Classes."

The woman's lips curved upward slightly before she nodded and left, the wounds on her back and shoulders healed completely.

Ilea walked over to Baron and checked him through his massive armor. *Breathing.* Sending a pulse of healing mana into his mind, he was startled awake. She did the same with Austin, who wasn't dead either.

Ilea barely knew them, but since Krentin hadn't ordered those who had stolen from him killed immediately, it made her think she'd made the right decision in letting them flee. The bug man was a little overconfident, perhaps, but having their corpses splattered here just because

Austin had stolen a map and they wanted their stuff back didn't feel reasonable.

If anything, she'd seen the fight more as a challenge. A way to test herself against a group of level two hundred fighters. She had improved, to say the least. Had they attacked someone she cared about, however, there wouldn't have been anyone left standing.

The lizard woman hissed. "Why keep me here?"

Ilea looked her way. "I want to see if I can take hits from your sword. I want to face you. No teleporting, no ash."

The lizard woman's expression changed immediately. She hissed with excitement and bowed a little. "I am Hana. It is an honor to face you, warrior of ash."

Ilea mirrored the gesture. "Hana, I'm Ilea. Let's move to the lit hall farther out."

"What the fuck happened? My head hurts... Ilea, what did you do? Where are the lights?" Austin grumbled, but she just ignored him.

Baron was looking around, his flashlight activating before he started following Ilea.

"Did you give them what they wanted?" he asked.

"Nah, I just broke some bones."

"You won...? Why didn't you kill them? You have no idea what angering Krentin will do. He won't stop until he has your head!" Austin yelled, following the pair now.

Ilea turned to him. "If he's so dangerous, why steal from him?"

He snorted. "He attacked you too, didn't he? You could've taken all they had!"

"And kill another five powerful sentient people. For what? Gold? Another storage item or some armor?"

"You did save us, Ilea," Baron said. "I commend your admittedly strange thinking."

Ilea smiled at him. "I guess you've grown on me."

"I mean it. Thank you," Baron said and bowed.

"No compliments for me?" Austin asked from the side.

"You?" Ilea asked, leaving the hall and joining Hana, who was already moving the corpses to a corner of the hall. "You should be glad to be alive."

Austin smiled. The man clearly knew exactly how well he'd come out of that situation. His stupidity hadn't been paid for with death – at least, not yet. If Krentin really was the way Austin had described, it would be a dangerous couple of months to come for the ranger.

"You still owe me four gold and twenty silver, Austin," Baron said. "And I can't see a treasure map anymore."

The man winced before quickly crushing one of his bolts, creating a big cloud of smoke. Through her Sphere, Ilea watched him scale the walls and sprint out of the hall. She just shook her head.

"I don't think you're getting your money back," Ilea commented. "You want me to go after him?"

Baron shrugged. "Nah. You know, after traveling with him for a couple of days, I'd already pretty much written it off." He hesitated, looking at Ilea and Hana. "I don't suppose you're looking for someone in your team?"

"Not really. Always happy to have a drinking partner when I visit the area though." Ilea winked. "See you around, Baron."

He chuckled. "I thought as much, and I'll take you up on that drink any time. Good luck on your reckless adventure. I remain in your debt."

Bowing to her again and nodding to Hana, he too slowly made his way up the wall, massive fists crashing into the stone before a powerful pull took him onto the balcony and out of sight.

Finally, some goddamned peace and quiet.

Ilea sighed and changed into more comfortable clothes. She cracked her neck and nodded at Hana.

The lizard woman prepared her sword, checking her armor before a thin red mist formed around her. "I might not be able to stop. Once we start."

"Don't worry, I've fought a berserker before," Ilea replied with a smile, ashen limbs at the ready.

This time, she didn't avoid Hana's strike, a quick overhead slash. The blade cut into her Veil, the force of the strike traveling through her, damaging parts of her forearms that she quickly healed.

Hana shouted as more red mist formed, and as the sword pushed down harder and harder, Ilea was forced to push it aside, the blade slicing down into the floor with ease. She lashed out with her fists, one hard punch landing on Hana's side before she let go of her sword and jumped away.

The lizard woman ignored the injury as she held out her hands in a battle stance. Ilea grabbed the sword and ripped it out of the stone, feeling a sudden pull that dragged it toward Hana as she did so.

"Interesting. An enchantment?"

The weapon suddenly jerked upward and out of her grip, then curved toward the lizard, who just smirked, revealing sharp teeth and a reptilian tongue. Her red eyes glowed as she caught the heavy weapon with ease, holding it to one side and going into a crouch.

"An enchantment, yeah. I like to throw it," she said as Ilea rushed at her.

This time, the blade moved much more quickly and with less force to allow for more strikes and better maneuverability. Ilea dodged most of the blows, deflecting the last one with three of her ashen limbs before she stepped into melee range.

Hana kicked at her, but Ilea simply caught her massive leg and held onto it, twirling before she smashed the lizard woman into the floor with a loud crash, forming cracks in the stone floor. Hana kicked off the ground and spun in the air, landing before she spat out some blood.

"You're quite strong... for a mage."

“Am I not a warrior?” Ilea asked, smirking at the lizard and slowly taking steps toward her.

Hana prepared her blade. “Of course, that’s what it says, but I saw what you did with your ash and those arms coming out of your back… That’s no way for a warrior to fight.”

Ilea smiled and rushed at her again. Mage or warrior. As long as she could fight, she didn’t really care what she was.

SIXTY-ONE

Regeneration

Ilea shared one of Keyla's meals with Hana, a true sign of respect. She'd thoroughly enjoyed the hours of battle against the lizard woman. Carefully opening one of the two barrels of ale she still had from Walter, she poured two cups and handed one to the lizard.

The lizard took the cup with her good arm, the other one still broken and bleeding. She had refused healing, her berserker skills having kept her injuries in check right until she ran out of mana.

They had paused a few times to meditate. Often, they didn't rush at each other immediately again and again, leaving ample time for recovery even during their bouts. Ilea had only used her strength and physical attacks, delivering neither Wave of Ember nor Destruction through her blows.

"So, you met Krentin a couple years ago?"

"Six or seven years ago. Something like that. He asked me to show him my power. So, I attacked him and we fought," Hana explained. "We were below two hundred then, both of us."

"I can't see him winning that fight."

"I didn't have a healing skill then, and trust me, he's stronger outside and at long range. You caught him at a disadvantage."

Ilea grinned, taking a sip of Walter's ale. She savored the taste for a moment before speaking. "You think I couldn't have won without the edge it gave?"

Hana took a sip as well and looked first at the cup and then at Ilea. "This is fantastic... Not from Hallowfort, that's for sure." She took another sip. "It'd be a fight to see, but with your healing and defenses... no, I think you'd win nine fights out of ten."

"That's not good enough," Ilea grumbled.

Hana didn't know about all of her abilities, but nor did Ilea know about all of Krentin's. At least she knew she outmatched the lizard warrior, mostly due to her versatile ash. Without her added limbs and mana intrusion abilities, it would be more even. She had forty levels on the lizard, but that meant little if she couldn't land any hits.

Hana chuckled, the sound having an added hiss. "You will stay here then? Train against the blood monsters?"

Ilea thought about it. She had plenty of poison to work with now and some people to train resistances. "While I'm here. But I don't think I'll stay for long. Do you think Krentin will stay true to his word?"

Hana finished her food and ale before she spoke. "He's crafty, smart, and can be deceptive. All reasons I decided to work for him. From the way he looked at you, I believe he has taken a liking to you. Perhaps you will find him trying to woo you instead of sending assassins or coming to kill you himself." She laughed.

Ilea smiled in response before donning her helmet again. "Well, the dungeon is dangerous enough. No need for fighting among the few sapiens in the region. Not with the intent to kill, at least."

Hana grabbed her massive curved sword, the blade reflecting some of the light coming from the magic lamps above. "I *have* been fighting with the intent to kill," she said with a smile.

"Oh, I know," Ilea answered with a smile of her own, closing the barrel and storing it in her necklace.

Hana stood up and twirled her sword. "Perhaps I should explore on my own too, otherwise I'll never be able to smack that smirk off your face."

"How did you know I was smirking?" Ilea asked, activating her buffs and preparing to fight.

Hana just shook her head. "And you can heal yourself too. Lucky find, your Class."

Ilea cracked her neck. "Excuses? From you?" she asked, but she didn't disagree.

* * *

Ilea relaxed for a while, waiting until Hana was likely quite a while away. She had shown obvious signs of injury, her movements slowing down as she favored her left leg more and more. Ilea didn't get why she refused her healing. *Misplaced pride, probably.* She was glad none of her teammates in the Hand had acted like that.

She sighed, thinking of her team back in the south, of Eve. It would've been nice to share what she'd found up here with her.

I wonder how they're all doing. Kyrian, you better not have died.

Claire and Trian would be in Ravenhall. She hoped Baralia hadn't advanced all the way to the south. If anything, she hoped the Empire had long since broken the siege and pushed the Kingdom back north.

Did Felicia get involved as well?

Ilea shook her head. It had been a while since she had thought about it all, too focused on her own advancements, her exploration of the north, and all the challenges it brought. This was what she'd wanted, after all. Avoiding wars and politics and humans fighting each other when there was a vast world and untold magics out there to discover.

Yet here there are Awakened squabbling over old blood containers.

She sighed and summoned one of the bones she'd gotten from the Old Blooded. Checking it again, she slammed it into her leg.

'ding' You have been poisoned by Blood Poison, -50 health per second for five minutes, light paralysis.

Fuck that's potent.

The five minutes passed before Ilea stabbed herself again. Her mana recovery, boosted by Meditation, easily kept up with what she used to heal herself. Her combat skills weren't draining her, after all. She was only using her Sphere, which was always on, as well as her main buffs, State of Azarinth, and Form of Ash and Ember, the former free of charge since she'd reached the third tier.

Thirty minutes and four additional uses later, the venom was gone from the arm. It was now all in her body and had been taken care of by her healing.

'ding' Poison Resistance reaches 2nd lvl 4

'ding' Poison Resistance reaches 2nd lvl 5

Two levels for a single arm.

She smiled and retrieved the other arm, continuing her solitary training. After half an hour had passed, she needed a break due to sheer boredom.

'ding' Poison Resistance reaches 2nd lvl 6

'ding' Hunter Recovery reaches 3rd lvl 2

Need to heal a ridiculous ton of damage just to get that up.

Thinking on it for a second, she thought of training by sacrificing her health and then healing it quickly with her third-tier recovery.

Hey, wait, that's illegal! the small voice of her conscience shouted, but it was worth a try. If she had ways to damage herself and heal again, why not?

If it doesn't work, I can just cut off my legs or something…

Perhaps a place that had proven to be able to kill her wasn't the best location for such an experiment, but Ilea wasn't overly concerned, sacrificing two thousand health to activate her third-tier State of Azarinth.

Now to look for that hidden secret in the treasure room nobody seemed to notice.

Her healing recovered the lost health without the use of the third tier, preserving some of her mana, as she meditated and walked back to the room filled with cages. It was dark now. The lights, previously protected by a layer of glass, had been shattered by her ash.

Back in the blood tank room, she searched through the boxes but found nothing else of value. Many of the metal tools looked cruel more than anything else. Torture devices, surely. Ilea took her time to search everything as she waited for her health to tick back up. As soon as she hit full health, she sacrificed another two thousand hit points.

She hadn't gotten a level up for either of the skills yet, but both were in the third tier and likely needed a shit ton more experience than previously. *Good way to work on both, though.* She wasn't quite sure how much being in danger would add to the equation, but it was probably a lot.

Waiting a couple of minutes for her mana to recover again, she turned to the wall that she'd gotten a weird feeling from earlier. It was either another trap or just a hidden wall. She could still sense stone behind it, but something was off.

Ilea searched for a hidden switch for a while but couldn't find anything. Instead, she ripped off the shelves clinging to the wall and started punching her way through the stone. She wasn't quite as efficient as Baron, but her fists were getting the job done nonetheless.

Ripping out a chunk of stone, her next punch hit something that caused a reaction. An explosion ripped through the room, most of it smashing into Ilea's Veil and flinging her at the opposite wall, metal denting and glass shattering as she hurtled through everything in the room. The trap had burnt through her Veil, her skin a little scorched below her armor, but she'd only lost around a fifth of her health.

"Damn," she murmured, healing herself as she peeled herself out of a pile of broken wood, metal, and stone before quickly walking back to the opening. She could now see the hallway beyond through her Sphere and blinked into it immediately.

It was dark inside, with no magic lights on the ceiling. Stepping carefully over the stone floor, Ilea surveyed everything. There were a couple more cages in here, smaller than the ones in the previous hall. They looked like ancient birdcages, all lined with a metallic mesh that glowed faintly.

There were notes sitting on a wooden table, a candle at half capacity sitting next to them. Grabbing what looked like an enchanted stick, she willed magic into it, and a small flame came out of the top.

Magic match.

Lighting the candle, she stored the match in her necklace and held up the small bowl-shaped candlestick holder.

Movement in one of the small cages made her look up. Her Sphere hadn't been able to penetrate the shimmering enchantment that moved through the thin mesh of metal.

Stepping closer with her candle, Ilea found a familiar creature staring back at her with white eyes. Smiling at it, she waved and crouched down.

"Well, look at you. How long have you been stuck down here?"

The creature was a little larger than her hand, its form vaguely humanoid, with short arms and legs without fingers or toes. Its large white eyes looked as if they led into an endless void of whiteness, and the four wings sprouting from its back shone with the same light.

Other than its eyes and wings, the rest of its form was made up of what Ilea could only describe as darkness. An absence of light. There was no surface she could see, no blemishes, nothing. Just darkness.

[Fae – lvl 71]

"I can get you out, you know," Ilea said calmly, remembering how defensive the Fae she'd previously met had been. Back then, she'd healed it after it let down its defenses, allowing her mana to pass. Feeling a prodding in her head, she just smiled. "I can't communicate with you that way," she said, touching an ashen tendril to the cage and letting healing mana flow toward it, not sure if the magic around it came from the Fae or something else.

Ilea recalled that not much was known about the Fae. It could be that they were just peaceful animals with some rudimentary intelligence. Still, from the way it looked at her, with its elongated and curved white eyes, Ilea felt like there was more to them.

The head of this one was somewhat dragon-like, with two black horns protruding from its skull. She couldn't discern if any part of it was actually solid matter or if it was all just some kind of floating shadow.

Ilea sat down and checked out the lock on the cage. It wasn't big, though certainly enchanted, but she doubted it was there to keep someone from opening it from the outside.

Taking it into her armored hand, she squeezed. A crack filled the silent room, then the magic around the cage vanished. She opened her fist to find a broken lock lying within.

The Fae twirled around, its magical wings keeping it in the air without much movement. Ilea spread her own ashen wings before sitting on the ground and smiling at the creature.

"I got wings too, see?"

SIXTY-TWO

Blood and Bones

Big white eyes looked at her as Ilea slowly flapped her wings. She extended a tendril of ash toward the Fae before it stopped, blocked by a barrier in the air. Sending healing mana through the ash, Ilea rested her head on one of her knees. Turning its head to the side, the little creature deactivated the barrier, allowing Ilea's ash to pass and the healing to begin.

Ilea was again startled by its physiognomy. It was as if its mana flowed out into the air, as if its physical body ended but its magical one didn't. When she healed and observed humans, it felt like their mana was inside their bodies, flowing similarly to blood. Ilea's ash, for example, expanded the flow because it was considered part of her body.

Is it an air creator or something?

The creature wasn't hurt, but Ilea still sent some of her mana into it. She knew it felt pleasant to humans. The Fae twirled in the air again, and Ilea stopped a moment later and smiled.

"You can go now if you like," she said and stood up, checking the rest of the room.

One of the cells held the skeleton of something that looked a little like a snake. *Could a necromancer raise that again?* She wasn't sure but stored it in her necklace anyway. She wouldn't take the blood monsters. Raising them again seemed like a bad idea.

The Fae was hovering behind her while she looked through the rest of the room's contents, not finding anything else of interest. Turning around, Ilea faced the curious creature.

"You don't want to go?"

It just looked at her, floating closer before it bumped into the ash of her

Veil, recoiling a little before it flapped its wings once. The white eyes didn't blink. They probably couldn't.

Extending one of her ashen limbs toward the creature, Ilea watched as it circled it. Finally, it landed, standing on the ash and looking down at it, the two black horns facing straight up.

"You want to stay with me then?" she asked. The little thing didn't give her the slightest hint of understanding. She didn't mind either way. It wasn't her task to take care of it, but nor would she refuse its company. "You're free to join."

Ilea checked the room once more before walking out. The Fae floated behind her, flitting about and bumping into her ashen limbs. When she reached the hall where she'd fought Hana, she sat down and examined the notes she'd found. Fortunately, the text was written in Standard.

Experiment 428

The goal was to combine the blood or 'life essence' of the being designated by the unknown as 'Fae' and the pure blood. Properties such as high affinities for mind and space magic were hoped to be found in the resulting specimen.

Mixture was applied with the layer four Tuner to human and dwarven specimens. Lizardman and Feynor specimen requests have been rejected.

Results include deformation, mutation, and spontaneous vanishing. All specimens perished or teleported to unknown locations within the span of two months.

Due to results not meeting expectations, funding has ceased. Specimen 'Fae' will be kept in hidden containment room, enchanted cage infused with space magic blockade III. Permission to connect cage to layer four Tuner has been granted. Potential buyers for specimen 'Fae' to be contacted.

The page was somewhat conclusive. *Didn't find a buyer, then.* Ilea put the page back into her necklace and read the next one.

Experiment 452

General goal: Combination of specimen 'Life Serpent' with various successful previous mixtures and pure blood. Healing and regeneration properties are expected in the resulting specimens.

Mixture was applied with layer four Tuner. Specimens subjected to substance include human, dwarven and Feynor heritage. Permission for rare specimens granted should results meet expectations.

Results were mixed, some rare specimens showing enhanced regeneration as well as added healing abilities. No extraordinary Classes or traits were discovered. Mixture will be applied to specimen V.

Ilea put the page back into her necklace and studied the last one she'd found. The Red Church or whoever had conducted these experiments hadn't seemed to care much about ethics while injecting humans and other sentient lifeforms with their blood cocktails. If Ilea's theory about the Pure Blooded was true, the end result wasn't pretty either.

Contrary to the first two pages, the last one held very little information, most of it scratched through by a knife.

Experiment 632

The goal was to combine————with————including pure blood mixed with Specimen VI——.

Mixture was applied with fourth level Tuner. Permission for lower-level Tuner granted regardless of success. Due to————, further testing is necessary.

The results part had been removed completely, leaving Ilea a little intrigued about what the fuck had been going on down here.

"What do you think, little Fae? You must've heard and seen lots of what was going on in these cursed halls..."

The little creature looked at her with big white eyes but gave her no answers.

"To be honest, as long as there's stuff to fight, I don't really care much. Seems like whatever shit they did, they fucked up badly. Or perhaps turning into frenzied blood creatures was the actual goal."

And now it seems like they're gone. Just infested ruins left to explore. Like Rhyvor. Maybe Maro knows something about this church or the city that was once here?

Ilea got up and put the last page away as well before continuing her recovery training. Jumping up to the balcony overlooking the hall, Ilea found the Fae suddenly appeared next to her.

"Teleporting around, hmm?" She looked at the Fae. "I'll be exploring a little more. If there are any monsters, you should stay back and let me handle them."

Ilea wasn't sure the Fae understood, but looking at its near-glowing white eyes, she got the impression that there was more to the creature than its cute form suggested.

* * *

Ilea continued through the corridors, working on her skills with the Pure Blooded venom. She only found and fought a single one of the creatures in what felt like half an hour.

'ding' Poison Resistance reaches 2nd lvl 7

...

'ding' Poison Resistance reaches 2nd lvl 9

'ding' Hunter Recovery reaches 3rd lvl 3

She checked various gates but found most of them unlocked or already broken, only dust waiting for her. When she did stumble upon a locked gate after hours of walking through the extensive underground settlement, she summoned the key that she'd found.

Might be worth a try...

She put it in the lock and, with a click, the ruby shone slightly before the door ceased to shimmer.

Hey, a problem solved by not hitting something really, really hard. I am an intelligent and civilized woman after all.

Her reward was to face another Old Blooded in its tomb, though this one lacked the intensity of the last one, more cautious in its approach to battle. It took a while, but she was getting used to their reach and style of fighting by now.

'ding' You have defeated [Old Blooded – lvl 371] – For defeating an enemy one hundred levels or more above your own, bonus experience is granted.

'ding' Azarinth First Hunter has reached lvl 263 – Five stat points awarded

'ding' Inheritor of Eternal Ash has reached lvl 256 – Five stat points awarded

'ding' State of Azarinth reaches 3rd lvl 7

'ding' Destruction reaches 3rd lvl 4

'ding' Veil of Ash reaches 3rd lvl 6

'ding' Meditation reaches 2nd lvl 19

Ilea took her time exploring the rooms beyond the enchanted door and found more of the same red liquid that Krentin and his crew had been interested in. Ilea was content that she had the substance rather than Krentin, the Shadow's Hand, or someone like the Golden Lily.

Worst thing I'd do with it is drink it and gain some weird resistance. Someone else? Who knows.

She considered it for a moment, looking at the sloshing liquid that had survived the test of time.

The Fae looked at her.

"You're right, I shouldn't," Ilea said, continuing her search.

She found about sixty gold in a chest too, which would've likely made most other adventurers' day, but she was more annoyed about the lack of dangerous enemies to fight. And sixty coins was really nothing to write home about, not after what she'd found in the Taleen ruin below Dawntree.

There was a metallic noise as the Fae bit down on one of the coins before it made it hover back into the chest, a small bite-sized piece missing.

Ilea laughed. "Gold isn't tasty, eh?"

The Fae's eyes suggested it was amused, but maybe Ilea was reading too much into it.

She found some ancient-looking armor as well, which seemingly wasn't enchanted, but it was made from a metal she hadn't seen before. It looked too old to be used in combat.

* * *

After another three hours of traveling and training in the depths of the inner circle, Ilea and the Fae came upon another enchanted door, again opened by the key she'd found. It was likely a general key handed out to people with a certain degree of power. The skeleton she'd found it on must have been someone rather influential.

Contrary to the previous doors, this one didn't lead to another hall or dark room. Instead, it was a rather small room holding a single thing. An elevator.

Closing the door behind her and locking it again, Ilea saw through her Sphere that it only went up. She was ready for a change after exploring so many similar halls without any fights. She thought about the different dungeons she could go to but first, she'd visit Goliath and ask him about the Fae as well as the metal she'd found.

Activating the rune in the elevator, the two of them shot up, the machine screeching as it slid through its metal cage. Ilea looked at the Fae on her shoulder, which looked entirely unconcerned with their current velocity. Ilea wasn't quite sure how far they went, but after stepping out of the elevator and opening another enchanted gate, they found themselves in another dark corridor.

She was pretty sure they were above the first layer, or maybe in a hidden part of the dungeon. She flipped through her notebook to the page on the city directly under Hallowfort. Marking a random spot, she started moving through the darkness as she had on the fourth layer.

An hour later, she found herself in a familiar location. The hole in the wall was too similar to the one she'd found upon going after the Blue Reapers to be anything else. She sketched down the areas she'd traveled through in her notebook before walking into the corridor leading to the Abyss.

"There's gonna be other people up there. I wouldn't trust them too far, little Fae," Ilea said, spreading her wings of ash and ascending through the darkness until she came out in the lit guard room.

She wasn't sure if the fully plated Awakened with wisps of darkness coming out of his armor was one she'd seen before, so she simply nodded slightly. Unlike her previous encounters, though, this one went to one knee and bowed his head.

"I greet you, Spirit of Old."

The greeting was directed almost certainly at the Fae, not Ilea, and he only lifted his head when they were ascending the stairs leading to the pub. He went back to his post a moment later.

Ilea walked through the pub and got more than a couple of looks, directed mostly at the Fae clinging to her shoulder. The creature didn't stray from her, looking around, but apparently nothing struck its fancy. Haiden, the barkeeper, stopped cleaning his glass and just stared at her, a smirk on his feline face.

Stepping outside, Ilea turned her head and smiled at the Fae. "You're quite the attention grabber, aren't you?"

Walking through Hallowfort, she soon headed down the stairs leading to the ancient smith. Maybe he'd know more about the creature.

"There's going to be a curse here, though I'm not sure if it'll affect you. I'll heal you if necessary," Ilea said when they reached the corridor, feeding healing mana into the creature as she continued, the nausea and health drain starting a couple of steps later.

She lifted her eyebrows when her influx of mana was cut off, a shimmering barrier of translucent white light instead forming around the Fae, which seemed unconcerned.

Shrugging it off mentally, Ilea walked on until they passed the sound barrier and heard loud snoring echoing through the room. The sound stopped immediately when she walked down the stairs, and the smith's golden eyes snapped open.

"Thought you couldn't sleep, old man?"

"Child of… what's this? A Spirit of Old… You are truly full of surprises, human… inheritor… no. Friend of ash, perhaps." The smith got up from the workbench and inclined his form a little to show respect, though Ilea wasn't sure whether it was to her or the creature. Maybe both.

"What is it with this little guy? Found it in a cage in the fourth layer." Ilea said, "You didn't answer my earlier question."

The smith clasped his black hands together, creating a coarse noise. "I cannot sleep biologically, though the thought of it… has been a romance of mine, human, for many hundreds of years. Coupled with Meditation, it is… pleasing… to lay down my body. Neither necessary nor logical but… a pleasurable feeling. Fleeting yet satisfying."

Goliath had a way of explaining things that resonated with Ilea. Though perhaps it was just the topic of appreciating sleep that spoke to her.

"As to the Spirit of Old sitting on your shoulder, I thank you. For saving it and bringing it into the light again. Farther and farther they stray. Many of them are stuck or worse in places not suitable for them, yet it would be against the will of magic to deny their nature."

"Can it understand me? Why the reverence? Some kind of religion for you Awakened?" Ilea asked, summoning a meal as she hopped onto a workbench.

The smith walked up to her, a hammer appearing in one of his hands before he smashed it into her chest, finding her Veil of Ash impenetrable.

"Religion? Hmm... perhaps there are similarities, yet I lack knowledge of the human ways to say for sure. It is a deep respect, gratitude, and perhaps even love. Remove your ash, the damage on your chest piece is substantial."

Ilea shrugged and did as he asked, and the hammer struck true, heating up the metal immediately and forcing it into shape again.

The smith needed all that preparation and heat treatment to make this armor and now it's repaired by a couple hammer strikes?

She wondered what exactly the Awakened's skills did. Perhaps repairing something it had created was simpler than making something anew.

SIXTY-THREE

Awakened

"Gratitude and love? Seems like an interesting story. Any chance you're willing to tell it to a human?" Ilea asked with a smile, storing her helmet and starting to eat. She offered some to the Fae, but it just looked at the food curiously, not willing to touch any of it.

Ilea made it a game to try and force-feed it, with several tendrils of ash holding small morsels of rice or vegetables. The Fae dodged and teleported around her body to avoid them, the morsels that got through hitting the barrier and lighting up in white flame. Ilea ate them before they disintegrated, the fire not an issue given her Heat Resistance. She did notice it did more than just burn her, but she couldn't quite place it.

The smith crossed his arms, done with repairing her chest piece. "The story is not something I would usually share with a human. It is not a story lightly shared. You, on the other hand, have proven a friend to me, to us. To the darkness, the depths of magic and the arcane itself."

Taking another bite, Ilea waited for Goliath to continue.

"Little is recorded, for lack of fingers, tools and ingenuity. Stories told with feelings, emotions transferred through thought, paintings, sound, or magic itself. Know that much is lost as I translate thoughts into words. In the time before, before me and most of those alive or dead in this age, it was sung that there were no Awakened at all and that the Spirits of Old were the first, the first to lead others lost to instinct into what you might call consciousness, into seeing the world and into understanding, into growth, possibility, unshackled, perhaps, from our ancestry, our fate.

"And through the ages, your kind, elves, and dwarves fought against the Awakened. It was only logical to respond to the unknown with fear and aggression. For many, it was thus. We deem the Fae, Spirits of Old, though some are likely not older than you, the oldest of our kind, some of the most powerful. Never did they actively intervene, yet shelter they provided to the injured, the broken, and the newly born of our kind, be they shadows, wisps, or beings of any shape and kind born to conscience through the arcane, guided by others or, as some claim, by the Fae themselves. They were fathers and mothers, protectors to many who would otherwise have been rid from this world."

Ilea flicked the magical shield of the Fae, who was now sitting on her shoulder again, eyes fixated on the smith.

"Nice job, little one."

The Fae looked at her and, once again, seemed amused.

"It's below level one hundred. Do they have abilities that would allow them to provide shelter against high-level elves, for example?" she asked, thinking of the most powerful species she could.

"Perhaps," Goliath said.

"Mysterious," Ilea said with a smile before nudging the little Fae. "What secrets do you hold, ancient one?"

The Fae flew closer and poked her cheek.

Ilea showed Goliath the armor she'd found as well, but he deemed it unusable for her, the metal suitable for something ceremonial at best.

"Thanks. I'll be on my way then. Anything else you need? Apart from rare metals and stories of my ludicrous adventures?" Ilea asked, motioning to the Fae, who latched onto her shoulder again.

"No, friend of ash. I wish you fortune on your journey."

Ilea smiled and waved. "Until we meet again, friend, wielder of flame and steel."

* * *

The stars were bright that night, lakes of mist appearing in the distance when Ilea emerged from the caves, flying past the Penumra entrance and up through the cracks in the stone. Landing on the ground, Ilea looked at the Miststalkers dancing a couple of dozen meters away.

"You're out. Do you want to return to your home now?" Ilea asked the little Fae.

She smiled at it when it released her shoulder, floating ahead and twirling in the air. A moment later, the creature flew back and bumped Ilea's helmet a little. The wind brushed against them, then Ilea found herself alone in the desolate land.

"Return safely," she murmured, happy to have shared some time with her silent companion. An uncomplicated being. Ilea hoped she'd meet it again someday, perhaps changed enough to communicate with it.

And find out they're racist supremacists... who knows.

Ilea smiled to herself as she imagined what kind of place the Fae would've gone to.

Now. Where do I go?

She had several options, and her main goal was still to hit level three hundred. The Descent didn't seem to have a lot of monsters so far, and she'd maxed out the usefulness of Rose Knights and Blue Reapers for the time being too. At least until she could face larger groups.

I could go to that Taleen dungeon that Terok mentioned.

She didn't expect to be able to clear it or face the higher-leveled machines, if there were any, but she could at least get an idea of the layout, of what kind of machines were around.

And maybe I can find out more about the dwarves.

She gulped.

Have I been avoiding this?

There had been so many places to explore in the north, but now the Taleen dungeon seemed like such an obvious choice, part of her didn't want to go. It did feel like more of a challenge than any other place she could visit and explore. But realizing that made her want to face that challenge.

Her first battle with the Praetorians was some time ago now. Still, she remembered the cold curse spreading through her stomach. She touched the area and slowed her breathing.

You've been to Iz. You survived another battle with them. There's no expedition here either. Even if I'm not strong enough, who's saying I can't use that dungeon and whatever machines are in there as a way to get to three hundred?

Yes, it made sense. She *had* put it off, and now she could feel her fear return, she wanted to face it and conquer it once and for all. She smashed her fists together and smiled.

Time to destroy some machines.

* * *

She made her way back to Tremor, hoping to find Terok. He could guide her to the dungeon or at least refer her to someone who could. But when she entered the cathedral, she only found Elfie.

He talked about the… Cerithil Hunters, was it? Perhaps they have knowledge of the Taleen?

"She returns. And with more levels," Elfie said. "If you are looking for the dwarf, he should return soon. He was talking with the royals."

"I am. I'm going to explore the Taleen dungeon nearby. Feel like joining?"

He looked at her with a considering gaze. It took him longer to respond than usual.

"And why would I want that? I wouldn't be going into the dungeon itself."

Ilea remembered what Goliath had talked about, what Elfie had shared about those cursed elven hunters who went into dungeons to fight the Taleen machines. But she hadn't questioned why he was out here, alone. Why he called himself a historian, what he was looking to find here. And she wouldn't. Those were his choices to make.

Why would he join her? Why would she want him to join?

Ilea shrugged. "To get some air? Destroy escaping machines I missed, maybe? Provide a safe retreat, should we be overwhelmed? You're familiar with them, have fought them. You can also provide translations as we go further in. You do know the language, I assume?"

If he'd spent decades learning the Rhyvor language, Ilea had no doubt in her mind that the elf could read whatever language the Taleen had been using.

Tapping his pen on the open book before him, the elf hissed slowly before he closed his eyes for a moment, then looked at her with a focused gaze.

"Alright, human. I will humor you. When do you intend to leave?"

Ilea smiled. Somehow, this felt like more than just one friend asking another to join in on a random adventure.

"I'll ask Terok when he shows up. He could guide us, and his skill set could prove useful too, if he feels like helping out. For a share of the loot, I suppose." Ilea glanced at the book Elfie held. "What's that book anyway?"

Elfie stood up, straightening his black mantle. "Questions for the King and Queen of Rhyvor. If we cannot talk face to face, there are other methods."

"In their language, I suppose?"

As she posed the question, Terok, clad in his black and red armor, flew in through one of the destroyed windows before landing smoothly.

"In their language, yes," Elfie said, making the book vanish. "It is a good way to build trust. We have made every effort to alienate other species in the past."

Terok snorted. "And present, if slaughtering and hunting down counts as alienating."

The elf hissed but didn't deny the dwarf's accusations.

"Terok, your timing is impeccable. Were you waiting for me to show up?" Ilea asked.

"I'm back here every hour or so. He's got a lot of questions, and the Invalars aren't exactly busy. Still working on the enchantments, but it'll take time. Better to keep everyone busy. Easier to work like that."

"Makes sense."

"You back for a reason?"

"Yes, actually. Need a guide, thought you might be interested," Ilea said. "But I don't want to interrupt your important work."

"No worries. Could use a break, to be honest. What were you thinking of?"

"You mentioned a Taleen dungeon?"

"Oh. It's time to go there then? Sure, sounds like there could be some loot involved. I'll just try and stay hidden. And far away. Elf coming too?"

Elfie hissed, an affirming sound that made Terok laugh.

"Let me just dip back inside and inform the royals in case we all meet a horrible end in the coming days," Terok said. "I'll be back with you soon."

* * *

The moons were shining down on the lakes of mist below them as the trio scanned the sky for dangers. A human, a dwarf and an elf on a mission to explore a dungeon filled with machines built by the Taleen. Hours passed, the three flying in silence.

When they finally reached an incline leading to a mountain towering over the surrounding hills and crevices, Terok slowed down. No mist was visible nearby, and the three descended before landing in a rather large crack that led upward.

"Should be near the mountain," Terok said. "It's not a popular one, this one."

Ilea was a little surprised to hear that. "Why not? Guardians are between one fifty and two hundred, aren't they? Should be right in the range of most scavengers I've seen in Hallowfort. Or are they higher-leveled here in the north?"

"It's pretty far from Hallowfort, and not everybody can fly. You'll find out inside why it's unpopular," Terok said, his floodlight illuminating rocks and a thin creek making its way down the mountainside.

As a strong wind buffeted her armor, Ilea noticed how Terok and Elfie had to fight against it more than she did. Her second-stage Wind Resistance was the likely culprit. Or the wind simply liked her.

"You have no idea what's in there, do you?"

The dwarf didn't reply, which was answer enough.

When they made their way up the mountain, Elfie moved a couple of meters behind the other two. Ilea assumed he didn't want to step into a dungeon accidentally.

Now that she knew elves could technically enter dungeons, the whole situation had changed. She thought back to the elf below Riverwatch, hissing at them right at the entrance to the Calys mines.

He could've come for us, could've slaughtered us. Why would they be cursed? Are they not allowed to enter? Is it just that? Or something more, something magical?

She found the situation here amusing, perhaps distracting herself from the fact that she too would now be entering an unknown Taleen dungeon.

What would Walter think if he saw me here, traveling with an elf? What would the group from Riverwatch think? What were their names… Eleonora, the bird mage, Oliver, who helped with my fire magic, Aaron the bard, and Geronimo, the annoying ranger.

She smiled at the memory, wondering where they were right now, what kind of adventures they'd had since then. She'd certainly have a few stories to tell if they ever met again.

It took them another twenty minutes to climb the crevice, crossing the last patch in darkness as the stone jutted out over them. Ilea saw an entrance crafted not by nature but something else in the distance, an angular opening carved into the rock.

"There it is," Terok exclaimed. "There's no mist here, nor arcane storms during the day," he explained to Elfie, who wouldn't be joining them in their exploration.

"If you're not going to join us, maybe build a fire or something?" she said to the elf, who was staring toward the entrance.

He glanced at her and hissed. "Try not to die, human."

She grinned and copied his hiss, noting that he didn't react with annoyance. He looked serious.

"And remember, the shorter the name of the dungeon, the larger it is," Elfie added.

She gave him a nod, wondering how he knew that. Either way, the tip was appreciated.

"Come on," she said to the dwarf as she walked to the entrance, preparing her skills.

She could feel it. She was scared, and that pushed her onward.

"Hmm," Terok muttered. "This isn't exactly a forgotten and unused path. Some of the rocks and sand suggest that travelers have come through in recent weeks at least. We might not be alone in there."

We'll find out once we're inside, Ilea thought, walking through the small opening.

No dungeon notification popped up immediately, meaning it was either further in or not here at all.

"Further in," Terok said, reading her mind. "This was dug out by someone. I doubt the Taleen would've used such an ugly entrance."

Ilea hadn't found the Taleen architecture to be particularly extravagant or beautiful, but she agreed that this entrance didn't seem similar. It was plain stone, with the barest minimum of carvings.

When they reached the actual dungeon a couple of minutes of climbing down later, the contrast was even clearer.

'ding' You have entered Izna dungeon

"There it is," Terok chuckled as the two found themselves in a dimly lit hallway, the familiar green light bringing up memories for Ilea – both good and bad.

A shorter name than the one below Dawntree, but longer than Iz. Thinking of which, Iz is a pretty short name.

"Which way, experienced scavenger?" Ilea asked, refocusing on the now.

Terok looked around. "The ivy is growing a little thicker that way, so I assume that's where the mana is thicker. Doesn't mean much in Taleen dungeons, but anywhere else, you'd find higher-leveled monsters there. Your call."

Ilea noted the familiar green ivy growing all over the walls, snaking along the stone just like it had in the other Taleen dungeons she'd visited.

"I think we should go toward the less dense area first," she said, starting to walk leftward. "Why all the ivy?"

"Something to do with the metal they use in their machines. I don't know if it's a byproduct of some kind, if has a purpose, or if it just showed up after the dungeons had been left alone for hundreds of years," Terok said, following her as he checked the walls and floors, his floodlight shining with subdued intensity. "Something moved through here. Recently. Not a machine either, as far as I can tell."

They soon came out into an open room, not exactly a hall but definitely bigger than anything she had in her house. Several stone tables were placed in the midst of it, torn tapestries adorning the walls. Ilea noted the skeletons and half-decayed bodies of various beings splattered against tables, lying on the ground, or slumped against the walls. She knew exactly what had happened to them when two green eyes turned toward her.

[Taleen Centurion – lvl ??]

Like all the ones she'd faced before, it had six spindly metal legs that would carry it toward her as quickly as she could perceive its movements and two hands, all made of the same greenish metal. A spear appeared in one hand. The same type of spear that had cut through her defenses and skin as if they were mere paper. That had broken her bones as if they were cardboard.

Ilea knew about her enemy, about the cold eyes that wouldn't stop until she'd ripped its body apart, about its core that would explode once sufficiently badly damaged. She knew it wouldn't stop until she'd burnt every circuit or enchantment that somehow forced the thing to live on, fighting and hunting.

Ilea didn't remember what level she'd been at the last time a Centurion stood in her way. This time, ash spread around her as eight limbs formed on her back, each swaying slightly, poised to attack at any moment.

"This is my fight, Terok. Wait in the hallway back there. Don't come back until you hear the explosion."

"Explosion?" he asked as he watched the Centurion stand up from its crouched position on one of the tables, its legs moving like a well-oiled imitation of an insect, its head predatory, sleek, and adorned with two vicious green eyes at its center.

Ilea didn't wait for the dwarf as her buffs flared up to their highest potential, three hundred health sacrificed for what she knew was to come. A moment later, the Centurion moved toward her, its spear thrown in a motion she was oh so familiar with.

Her senses enhanced, Ilea tensed her muscles, her eyes following the spear as it came for her. A quick move of her hand and it impacted her Veil, glancing off her armor below as she sent it to the side, the metal cutting into the stone floor before it came to a stop several meters away.

She shook her hand, having felt the heavy impact. Ilea grinned and vanished, reappearing right in front of the machine, her fist crashing into its metal chest, all eight limbs of ash striking it, and Wave of Ember releasing as her other fist struck the Centurion's next spear, already held in a defensive position.

The Centurion skidded back a couple of centimeters, and Ilea followed, her ash continuously smashing into its metal body as she dodged a spear thrust and got closer. Another punch raised the large machine slightly, two of her ashen limbs scraping the metal and nearly cutting into its torso.

She deflected the next strike of the spear with her arm, the metal ringing against her armor, her Veil not quite enough to block the powerful blows alone. But together with her armor, she was confident.

Focusing on her opponent, she felt thrown back to the Taleen dungeon below Dawntree. She remembered how it had felt to fight Guardians for hours, for days on end, the joy she'd felt, the advancements she'd made.

A lot had happened since then. The Praetorians in the very same dungeon, Salia, the Shadow's Hand, Trian, Edwin, Eve. And now she was here, facing the machine that felt the very same as the last one of them she'd fought.

But she wasn't the same anymore. She let the memories flow through her, the fear that she'd felt, the grief, the anger. She let it all come and pass.

Ilea breathed in deep and exhaled, raising her arms in a mixture of her Azarinth Fighting style and her kickboxing muscle memory. She watched the machine take its next step, then charged.

SIXTY-FOUR

Helping Out Strangers

Ilea fought the Centurion, getting back into the same flow she'd had with the Guardians and then the Knights of Tremor. She fought until she felt its mana gather and she knew the Centurion was about to detonate.

As it tried to grab her with its arms, she blinked behind it and continued her assault, spreading ash around the two of them and building wall upon wall of it. She focused each hit on the Centurion's center, where white light started to form. Blinking away at the last moment, she closed the dome of ash she'd formed and crossed her arms.

The blast ripped through her ash and into her Veil, scorching the floor and ceiling as bits of rock and metal flew past her, some into her Veil. Finally, she relaxed again. The last time she'd faced a Centurion, she'd been left closer to death than ever before. Granted, the explosion had happened a lot closer that time.

Moving her Veil, metal splinters and pieces of stone fell to the ground. Ilea noted shrapnel had dug into the ceiling and stone benches, one table nearly split by what looked like a part of the Centurion's arm.

The first one, she thought, wondering what kind of machines were lurking in this dungeon. If there were Praetorians, would she be able to face them? Would she have to train up first? Either way, she felt like the path was clear now. All she had to do was walk it.

'ding' You have defeated [Taleen Centurion – lvl 310] – For defeating an enemy forty or more levels above your own, bonus experience is granted.

'ding' Inheritor of Eternal Ash has reached lvl 257 – Five stat points awarded

"Big boom," Terok commented, appearing next to her. "Sounded intense. Taleen Centurion, eh? Heard of them, but aren't they rather uncommon?"

Ilea shrugged. "Good luck, maybe."

"Good luck?" Terok asked before he laughed.

She grunted, looking around the room.

"That one has the least ivy growth," Terok said, pointing toward one of the three doorways they could see.

"And how do you know that through closed doors?"

"Checked while you were contemplating life. Or basking in your *insurmountable* power," he said with a smirk.

Ilea chuckled, faking a serious tone. "You're living dangerously, dwarf."

This time, he outright laughed. "Your elven voice needs some work, lassie. I'll shut up when there are more enemies nearby, though. Don't want any additional party guests."

Terok picked the lock and opened the door before Ilea walked through without another word. Some banter was welcome, but Centurions were dangerous. She'd rather not find them and a scavenger party at once. Not that anybody would've missed the explosion for at least a couple of hundred meters, depending on how many doors and enchantments were in the way.

The two moved through the corridor, occasionally stumbling upon a skeleton in rotten gear, the dwarf commenting on how long he thought they had been down there and how little the things on them were worth.

Normally, Ilea would've just taken all of it with her, but Terok knew his metals. Not as well as Goliath, perhaps, but she could save some of her necklace space for actual valuables.

Another stash of gold would be nice. Can't go back to Claire empty-handed.

"We're nearing the surface..." Terok said after they'd been walking for a while and came upon a big stairwell leading upward with a smaller one on each side leading down. No torches, statues, or anything else adorned the area; there was only the green light shining down from above. Ilea felt it too, smelt the fresh air coming in.

Taking a step up, Ilea immediately blinked back, spears shooting out from the side walls before they buried themselves in the opposite walls. She just continued upward, this time more aware of the mechanical parts beneath the stone.

Most of the Taleen dungeon was lined with gears, pumps, and traps. It had been a while since she'd walked through one, and the traps were often disguised between other machines, whose purpose she didn't know. She saw the next trap, but not wanting to destroy half the stairwell, she simply activated it again.

"These weren't made for adventurers exploring a dungeon in the north," Terok commented, close behind her.

"You're not the one activating them," she shot back.

He shrugged. "Hey, if I don't *have* to risk scratches on my gear..."

Rolling her eyes, Ilea emerged at the top of the stairwell, and the breath caught in her lungs as she looked at the landscape before her. Up here, the winds were howling, Terok shielding himself from the force. They were on the other side of the mountain, where the dungeon abruptly stopped, as if a bite had been taken out of the structure.

A couple of hundred meters below, Ilea could make out what looked like a crater in the land. In it was a serpent-like animal with four arms, big enough to walk over the walls of Ravenhall. She thought it might be a salamander, but the head didn't fit. Instead, it had what looked like a chameleon's head.

"A Behemoth Kalamon," Terok observed, his tone not indicating any concern.

"That thing isn't dangerous?" Ilea asked.

"Well, if it moves close enough to you, you're paste. I don't think they eat living creatures, though. Live and let live. The fact that they don't hide like their smaller kin makes me think there are few out there even capable of hunting them."

As it just lay there, Ilea doubted she could even scratch the beast. Somehow, she was disappointed that it was apparently a peaceful animal. Its imposing form and its head's kind of goofy look made her feel like a small bug in a world of massive creatures.

"How can something like that even sustain itself? If it's not eating animals I mean."

"The storms, probably," Terok shrugged. "If anything is abundant in the north, it's mana."

"You think I could hunt one?" Ilea couldn't help but ask.

"Not sure why you'd want to. It's got a level and health like anything else. The size would make it awkward to fight, and I hear they have illusion magic just like the normal versions. Practically, you *could*. I'd suggest getting a couple more levels before you try though. There's a reason this one doesn't even try to hide. Once you can eliminate the sea of Miststalkers as well as the Famine Crows, you could try, I guess. Not that you'll listen to my advice anyway."

"What's that supposed to mean? You've been living here for decades. I'll at least consider your opinion."

The dwarf just laughed. Giving her a short nod, he grunted, "I'd just like to see you try and kill that thing."

She shook her head and looked out toward the rock and stone sprawling into the distance, mountains growing so high before they vanished into darkness so deep her eyes couldn't make out their peaks.

"Beautiful, isn't it?" Terok said as he sat down, his armored legs dangling from the ledge of the dungeon.

Ilea just looked at the endless sea of stars, the unknown spreading before her very eyes, filled with monsters to fight, abilities to learn, and secrets to discover. She breathed out and closed her eyes, smiling as she let the wind wash over her.

Her reverie was broken by the dull boom of an explosion from inside the dungeon. Her eyes opened again, the moonlight reflecting off distant stone formations with pale blue light.

"Come on, let's find out who we're sharing the dungeon with."

Blinking back into the stairwell, Ilea quickly moved down and took one of the two staircases leading farther down. Terok was falling behind when she came out on a balcony overlooking a big hall illuminated by green lights.

Down below, there were several Taleen machines, pieces of one burning in one part of the hall. Gears and tubes filled big chunks of the hall, many of which were dented, destroyed, or on fire. Steam was rushing out of several damaged tubes.

Ilea spread her wings, but Terok grabbed her before she could move. His grip was hard, urgent, metal fingers almost digging into her skin.

"What is it?" Ilea asked, watching what looked like three Centurions following three teleporting mages around.

"Careful, those are elves," Terok said.

One of the figures, a brown-haired elf with fine features, screamed as a Centurion's spear punched through his armor and was sent crashing against the nearby wall.

Ilea nodded. "Yeah, I can see that. Cursed ones."

A coincidence? Or did Elfie know they were here?

"They're getting fucked pretty badly."

Another elf, this one wearing a black helmet, got hit hard but managed to remain upright, skidding back a couple of meters.

"Just be careful if you go in there. Elfie is one of them, but these could be different."

Ilea just grunted. She'd her own experiences with elves, but knowing that these ones had entered a dungeon changed her apprehension to curiosity.

The third elf, who was holding no weapon and clad in matte golden armor, was doing rather well, reappearing around his Centurion time and time again, his claws dragging across the metal with head-splitting screeching sounds. Unfortunately for him, another machine was joining in, making it two versus one.

As a glancing blow made him stumble and retreat, Ilea made her decision and pried Terok's hand from her arm.

"Would be a shame for them to be slaughtered by mindless machines."

Terok blinked at her and smiled. "Your choice. You know the risks. They might jump you the moment you save them. Killing is what they *do*. Usually."

Terok took a breath to continue, but Ilea was already floating next to the balcony. Given how they were handling the Centurions, or rather, being handled by them, she wasn't too worried.

"Let them try. We can see if they're irredeemable idiots or just reckless hunters. Run away if you're scared."

With that, Ilea blinked toward the group, hearing Terok mutter a string of very colorful curses behind her.

Appearing next to the brown-haired elf, she extended an ashen limb to the groaning warrior, who was barely conscious, and pushed some healing mana toward the wound. Without it, the male would likely bleed out.

She heard him whisper a word that she didn't know, saw blue eyes peering out from a face distorted by pain. Marred with blood, his leather armor – not a very high-quality set, Ilea noted – was in tatters.

[Warrior – lvl 220]

Ilea didn't respond, instead watching the other two continue their fights. The golden elf, his long white hair flowing behind him as he vanished and reappeared time and time again, was slowly being pushed back by two Centurions that had started working together.

The last one now had cracks in his black helmet, revealing strands of red hair below. He was deflecting the spear attacks from a Centurion that was forcing him back toward the wall. He was either out of mana or gravely injured.

Ilea blinked in front of one of the machines, dodging the attack from the Centurion in the center of the hall before she vanished again, hoping she'd attracted its attention. The red-haired elf failed to completely deflect a blow and was sent sprawling before slamming back-first against the wall.

[Warrior – lvl 212]

Ilea reappeared before the red-haired elf as he struggled to get up and prepare for the Centurion's next attack, a spear throw. The next blow would likely be enough to cripple him further or even kill him.

Ilea moved her hand, deflecting the spear into the wall before she sped up, her ashen limbs smashing into the Taleen machine before her fists followed. Dodging its blows, she continued on the offensive until it summoned back the spear.

"Can you move?" Ilea called over to the elf slumped against the wall, deflecting two thrusts before side-stepping a third, ashen limbs continuing to pummel the machine. She smirked at the second machine that had approached and begun focusing on her instead of the golden elf too.

Now we're talking.

The red-haired elf seemed a little surprised by this sudden intervention but relaxed slightly. He nodded, wincing from some unseen injury, as Ilea deflected another three quick attacks, the second machine now attacking as well.

She was impressed by the immediate teamwork of the Centurions. Their silent cooperation and deadly attacks, paired with the lifeless green eyes glowing in their insectoid heads, painted the terrifying picture most people were so afraid of.

Ilea wasn't on the defensive yet, despite the two Centurions' coordination making it harder to get attacks in with her arms, as her ash gave her another avenue of attack, the machines dividing their attention between her body and the ashen limbs. Which was a fatal mistake.

Perhaps it would've been an actual fight if they'd just focused on her body with abandon, but their split attention created plenty of openings and room to breathe. Enough that she could resume her conversation.

"Fly to the balcony, or otherwise just get as far away as you can."

The red-haired elf grunted and moved to the other side of the hall, teleporting between metal limbs before helping his brown-haired teammate stand. Ilea spotted a burst of fiery wisps that was left behind whenever he disappeared.

"Goldie! Move your Centurion toward me!" she shouted, deflecting another three blows before she was forced to blink a couple of meters back. Two spears were thrown right after, but she was prepared. Ducking a little, she let one pass over her shoulder while the other glanced off her arm and slammed into the wall behind her.

The machines closed the distance, allowing her ash to continue dealing damage. Ilea was getting confident enough with deflecting their blows to forgo her blink and maintain thin connections with her foes to deliver her reversed Hunter Recovery. It would take a short moment for her to sever that connection, but she knew she could take a hit or two.

Goldie wasn't doing what she'd asked. Instead, he was trying to fight the remaining machine alone, continuing his teleporting in its range. *They learn to counter that,* she thought, glancing at him as she kept her attention primarily on the two machines. The obscuring ash she'd spread didn't seem to bother them in the slightest.

A moment later, the gold elf was hit by one of the Centurion's elbows, its momentum combined with the attack knocking him to the ground hard.

Ilea was about to blink, severing the connections, when a couple of hundred kilos of mechanized dwarf rammed into the gold elf's Centurion.

Ilea smiled wide.

The impact destabilized the Taleen machine enough for it to miss its next attack on Goldie. The elf pulled himself up, obviously injured as his white hair was now stained with splashes of dark red.

Terok got in a couple of hard hits before he was thrown off, but in the meantime, Ilea had kited the two Centurions toward the third one, intending to finish them together.

"Take that elf and get out of here!" she shouted, Terok spinning in the air before teleporting to avoid a spear thrown at him, appearing next to the confused elf.

"Come on, lad," she heard him say before grabbing Goldie and flying off.

Ilea smirked and spread more ash around her, three sets of green eyes focusing on her, spears at the ready as they circled her.

Now it's a party.

SIXTY-FIVE

Decisive Battle

Ilea crouched on all fours, spears rushing past her before her ashen limbs lashed out, each hit delivering Wave of Ember. Blinking, she appeared behind one of the Centurions, shifting her head a fraction to the side as it tried to backhand her with a quick blow.

She grabbed onto the offending arm, then kicked at its legs, getting in two clean hits before she had to jump away, her wings taking her over the spear that was thrown after her. There was a moment of silence as she hovered over the black mist of ash that now covered a big part of the hall, ready to move at her whim.

Blinking back into it, she closed in on the Centurion she deemed most heavily damaged. The ash around her formed walls to slow down the other two machines. Her arm deflected a gleaming spear blade that was thrust at her before she delivered another hard blow to the machine's torso.

She noted her mana had fallen to nearly half, her eight limbs taking a toll on her resources, especially when coupled with all her other buffs and attacks. She also had no time or breathing room left to use Meditation.

Knowing they likely had no way of regenerating, Ilea decided to stop using her ashen limbs and simply focused on Destruction to conserve mana. The physical damage from her blows only used up Endurance, of which she still had plenty to spare.

As the three machines learned to deal with her, they became increasingly defensive, going so far as to give her time to recover some mana. They were machines, but to what extent they could think or make decisions, Ilea didn't know. Were they prioritizing their own lives or the destruction of the enemy?

She knew that once they reached a certain level of health, they focused on offense only. She just had to get one of them to that level and perhaps the blast from its exploding core would damage the others enough to finish the fight.

A quick set of punches after she appeared behind the most damaged Centurion brought its health sufficiently low. Ilea added a dented leg to its injuries with a hard kick just as its core started to crack, white light escaping from within.

It's about to blow. Better make it count.

Stepping under its attempted grapple, she twirled to dodge an incoming spear throw and grabbed one of its legs. Ashen limbs swirled around her arm and onto the metal to give her even more stability.

The core was brighter now, and Ilea turned and gave a half-grunt, half-scream of exertion as she threw the body toward the two machines looking on from behind the ash barriers. Uncaring green light shone in their eyes as white light enveloped them.

The explosion happened outside her range of perception, and though her Veil was burnt through, her high Heat and Blast Resistances negated most of what managed to get to her Stonehammer armor. The coating at the front was burnt off, revealing the silver steel below.

Ilea grinned from ear to ear when she heard another explosion follow shortly after. One Centurion's health had been low enough, just as she'd hoped. The final Centurion staggered toward her – having been rocked by the twin explosions of its comrades, its own core was now starting to fracture, light spilling out.

Its green eyes focused on her. Then the thing crouched and jumped, hands outstretched before a blinding light enveloped it. Ilea blinked backward, ash forming in front of her as she crossed her arms. The blast ripped through her, sending her careening into the wall behind.

This time, though, her Veil held. Her back was a little injured from the impact, but otherwise she was fine. Pieces of the wall fell to the ground as she pried herself out of the hole a moment later. As Meditation and healing magic flowed through her, Terok appeared right next to her.

"Are you okay?"

She gave him a thumbs-up and looked around the room. "Check if more are coming. If so, warn me."

Then, looking at the elves, who were watching her from the balcony, she spread her wings and quickly closed the distance. Ignoring Goldie's hissing, she extended her ash to the brown- and red-haired elves to extend what counted as her body to the elves, neither of them stopping her. She gave the latter a quick look and pushed healing magic into him as well.

"Impressive that you're still conscious," she murmured.

"We didn't need your help," Goldie said through gritted teeth. He loomed closer and made as if to strike at her before a quick hit from Ilea's flat hand sent him stumbling into the railing, where he would've fallen were it not for his teleporting ability. He reappeared a few feet away on the balcony and hissed, now with more venom, his claws growing in size and thrumming with magic.

"I'm healing your friends," Ilea stated simply, not reacting further. "You should think very carefully about your next words, hunter."

She was honestly surprised when he actually listened to her. He yelled inarticulately in her direction before disappearing and reappearing in a corner of the room below, where he started clawing at the stone walls, screaming and cursing.

"We appreciate the help," the red-haired one said, sighing as he relaxed and closed his eyes. He stood upright, though only supported by the nearby wall. Ilea gave him another nod, quickly checking her messages as she meditated and pumped healing mana into them. Both had been close to dead, so it would take a while.

'ding' Your group has defeated [Taleen Centurion – lvl 312] – For defeating an enemy forty or more levels above your own, bonus experience is granted.

…

'ding' Your group has defeated [Taleen Centurion – lvl 305] – For defeating an enemy forty or more levels above your own, bonus experience is granted.

'ding' Azarinth First Hunter has reached lvl 264 – Five stat points awarded

'ding' State of Azarinth reaches 3rd lvl 8

'ding' Blink reaches 3rd lvl 8

'ding' Veil of Ash reaches 3rd lvl 7

'ding' Blast Resistance reaches lvl 13

Ilea glanced over when Terok landed on the balcony.

"Clear," he said with a wave. "I checked a couple dozen meters into the next hallway, but it was quiet. Other than the angry one down in the hall, we're good."

She nodded. "Thanks."

The brown-haired elf on the ground was slowly opening his eyes and coughed a little. He groaned and sat up, looking around. Goldie was still raging below.

At least he's channeling his anger issues into something productive. Like tearing down the Taleen dungeon's walls.

The red-haired one didn't so much as move, eyes trained on Ilea.

"Goldie deserved that and you know it. I won't attack you two if you don't do anything stupid," Ilea said.

To her surprise, it was the elf sitting on the ground who responded.

"I… thank you… for saving us, human. Unnecessary as it was." He said the word 'human' as if it left a strange taste in his mouth. The gratitude was clearly begrudging at best, but his tone seemed sincere. "Also, define 'stupid'."

His blue eyes gazed into her own, and Ilea now noticed how his long brown hair was braided and fell to his back. It was his voice only that outed him as a male, his features delicate and sleek.

You're staring, Ilea.

"Something like attacking your rescuers instead of the horribly mean dungeon walls."

Down below, Goldie had started to calm down.

"I… see," the elf replied. He looked at her with curious eyes.

"You're Cerithil Hunters, are you not?" Ilea asked. The elf's blue eyes looked into hers again.

God he's dreamy.

He coughed and looked away as certain thoughts crossed her mind. Perhaps they showed on her face, because Ilea noticed that the red-haired one was smirking, albeit damn near imperceptibly.

"We are Cerithil Hunters," the brown-haired elf said. "None of us expected to find so many Centurions here. The dungeon was rumored to be dangerous, even for the northern territory, but even so…"

Goldie appeared on the balcony again, brushing rubble and dust from his thin metal armor, which was dented in several places. "You saved his life, human. Good for you, shameful for him. Now leave. This dungeon is our burden, and we welcome no humans here."

Ilea just smiled at him.

Terok's laughter cut in before Ilea could hit the elf again. "You're living dangerously, elf. I'd shut up if I were you. Real quick too."

Ilea stepped closer to Goldie. "Your 'burden', eh? What if I claim it, then? Make it *my* burden? Let's have a bout. You against me. If you win, I'll leave you alone and you can go die against the next group of Taleen. If I win, I get the dungeon. Maybe I'll let you help out and you'll get one or two helpful pointers along the way."

She really just wanted to see how strong they were, but it made sense to offer the challenge. Goldie didn't seem too keen on reason, so maybe a fight would help settle things.

Ilea saw the red-haired one smirk at the suggestion.

"I accept human. To the death," Goldie said.

Ilea blinked at the elf.

To the death? Why?

"Not to the death. Didn't you listen to the terms? Do the others accept as well? I meant all three of you against me." Ilea looked at the other two in turn.

The red-haired one laughed. "I accept as well. To the death."

"Oh, fucking hell. Alright, to the death then," Ilea said in exasperation, glancing at Terok.

He shrugged. "Told you so."

"I don't think this will be necessary, human. We are grateful for your help. A simple battle to determine who holds claim to the dungeon will be sufficient," the brown-haired elf tried, but the red-haired one put a hand on his head.

More reasonable that one, Ilea thought, looking at the blue-eyed elf. She could tell that he was overwhelmed with the situation, frustrated too, compared to the casual manner in which the red-haired one handled it and the angry reaction from the gold one.

Jumping down into the hall, Ilea smiled when the elves followed. Magic came to life on the red-haired one's body, red lines forming on his skin, the color scheme fitting his hair perfectly.

"I am prepared," he said. "Heranuur, cursed hunter of Cerithil. Thrilled to face thee in battle."

It seemed like he was looking for the right words. Perhaps he'd tried to translate a phrase. He brandished his blades and bowed a little. Goldie rolled his eyes.

"Ilea, warrior of ash. Thrilled to face you in battle too, Heranuur," Ilea said.

Maybe it was a bit much to challenge all three of them at once, but she felt like finding out what they could do. Plus, she didn't like their attitude. Especially Goldie's. Given how much they'd struggled against the Centurions, she was pretty sure she could take them down.

Neither of the others introduced themselves.

Ilea vanished when the fight started, choosing Goldie as her first target. She went straight for his face and found that he didn't even try to dodge, instead choosing to attack her in turn. She smiled as both their attacks landed, her hit disorienting the elf. She landed three more punches before an explosion hit her back, burning away at her Veil before she turned and rushed Heranuur.

They're just charging in. Did they not watch me fight?

She ignored the blasts and slammed into the elf with all her speed, the brown-haired one trying to catch her. Heranuur kept using his explosion magic, but she just traded blows with him, healing what damage he managed to get in.

This is almost too easy, she thought, landing three more punches on Heranuur before he went down, coughing blood. She looked up at the ceiling and sighed, seeing Goldie and Heranuur staggering in her Sphere, while the brown-haired one seemed unsure. She could feel magic from around him that hadn't been there before, but he seemed conflicted.

"I think we're done here. Or do you want to be knocked out?" Ilea asked.

"You have proven to be the stronger one," the brown-haired one said, his magic fading. "We admit defeat and adhere to your terms."

Goldie hissed as he staggered up and fell again, holding his head. Heranuur coughed blood and stood up, then laughed. "You are a warrior indeed."

Seems like I have their approval. Maybe now *they won't do anything stupid.*

She was pretty surprised at their lack of coordination and teamwork. They had some power, sure, but it felt as if that was really all there was. No finesse, no judgment, no dodging, just stubborn fighting.

If she and Terok hadn't shown up, she was pretty sure they'd all be dead by now.

SIXTY-SIX

Factory

"You really didn't want to kill them?" Terok asked as he appeared next to her. "Well, I don't blame you, their gear sucks. I'll go collect whatever's left of the Centurions."

He patted her shoulder with a metal arm and walked off, leaving her with the decision of what to do with this group of young elves.

Are they actually young by elf standards? Do they develop slower?

Goldie had passed out in the meantime, either from too much screaming or the more likely culprit, blood loss.

The one called Heranuur was watching her intently, black eyes giving her a calculating look. His black plate armor was basically falling apart, and wavy red hair poked out from the cracks in his helmet.

Maybe he's from the same domain as Elfie, with his red hair?

"What should we do? The dungeon is yours now, human," he said. It was nearly a hiss, but not quite.

"For starters, you can call me Ilea," she said, choosing to ignore the fact that 'human' was likely a derogatory term. "As to what you will be allowed to do in my dungeon? I'll think about it. Maybe Elfie can help me out. I don't want to murder you idiots or get you killed. Why did you even go after the Centurions anyway? None of you seem capable of fighting one yourself."

Heranuur looked a little confused. "To destroy the Taleen, of course. They are the enemy of our people. There is honor in their death. Finding more than a single Centurion is great luck. Perhaps we would have won."

"You were losing. That one was dying already," Ilea said, pointing to the brown-haired elf, who was kneeling over Goldie's now unconscious form and presumably treating his wounds. He cringed a little as his failure was referenced.

Heranuur huffed. "Perhaps. Though you showed up, and we won. Even Seviir is still alive." He said it as if it perfectly explained their reasoning for attacking foes far beyond them.

So Goldie is Seviir?

"But that doesn't explain why you..." Ilea started, but she gave up. She looked at the fierce two-meter-tall warrior, the two jagged daggers he'd used back in their sheaths on his belt.

Does he not understand the danger here? Maybe all the muscle is using his brain power.

She smiled to herself. She'd taken a lot of risks as well, many of them simply because she enjoyed fighting things more powerful than her, but there had been at least some consideration of retreat and healing. At least, she liked to think so.

Maybe he thinks the same. But he doesn't have a healing Class, she thought, feeling very much validated in her reasoning.

"You over there, with the brown hair. What's your name?" Ilea demanded.

The elf scrambled up and stuttered, "My name is N... Neiphato."

He was the most timid of the three, but Ilea felt like there was something about him, like he was holding something back. She shook her head and focused.

"I'll ask again. Why fight the Centurions? You were losing."

He answered immediately. "A Cerithil Hunter does not stop. Our cause is to destroy the Taleen." The words sounded practiced, as if he was well used to answering the question. Or perhaps had repeated the phrase to himself more than once.

"So you wouldn't stop attacking a foe that would likely have killed at least some of you... to destroy the Taleen? But if you'd fled, you could have come back stronger. You'll kill more Taleen that way. If you die... well, you die."

Neiphato hissed in response, his blue eyes flashing. "You know nothing, human. To flee would be... *shameful*. Of course, by becoming cursed hunters, we are tainted already – but we bear that shame in order to defeat the enemy. It is... complicated."

His words were passionate, but there was doubt in there as well. A strange combination.

Ilea sighed. "Right. Well, I'm going to bring you to an elven friend. He can decide what to do with you three. I'll continue to explore the dungeon with Terok here." She pointed at the dwarf, who grunted and waved from the other side of the hall where he was still collecting shrapnel. "Taleen will be destroyed one way or the other. Sound alright?"

Neiphato hissed with an affirming tone. Heranuur simply shrugged and bent to pick up Goldie, who was still unconscious.

* * *

Ilea led the group out of the dungeon. The suns were still visible, peeking in through the main entrance a dozen yards or so away. The air was cool, and Ilea couldn't hear the sounds of arcane lightning nearby.

Elfie was sitting on a rock, reading and presumably enjoying what was likely considered fine weather for the north. Or at least less deadly. He looked up when they approached, his eyes growing wide when he spotted the three elves trailing behind Ilea like lost puppies. He hissed under his breath but composed himself quickly.

"You are a little early," he said dryly, putting his book away.

Ilea ignored the jibe. "Need some advice, Elfie. There's a lot of Centurions in there, and guess who we found trying to get themselves killed by said robots?"

The elf's expression was neutral, but Ilea could see his left eye twitching. He got up and took a couple of casual steps toward them, looking at each of the three elves in turn, frowning at the unconscious Goldie.

Ilea noted that only Heranuur met the older elf's eyes. Not that Goldie *could* meet anybody's eyes at the moment. But Neiphato was intently studying the ground in front of him. There was definitely a subtle tension in the air. Heranuur stood stiff-backed and defiant, while Neiphato was cringing under Elfie's gaze.

Elfie hissed, the sound tense, threatening. Ilea had never known him to take this long to speak. She decided that he was choosing his words very carefully. There was a look in his eyes she couldn't quite place.

"I believe you have found three rather inexperienced elven hunters. Would that be a correct assumption?"

Ilea smiled under her helmet. *Well said.* She noted his lack of mockery, disregarding his usual slightly condescending attitude, and the fact he'd avoided the term 'cursed ones'.

"That sounds about right. Now, I'm not too knowledgeable on elven customs. If they were humans who I'd just saved from near-death-by-robot, I might send them off to the nearest town to recover. Does that apply here?"

Elfie was quiet for a while. Eventually, he closed his eyes and sighed. "You won't persuade them to stand down, human."

There were two hisses of agreement. Neiphato's hands were clenched tight, while Heranuur eyed her cooly. Whatever their reasons, they seemed intensely committed to their current course of action. She could respect that.

Ilea nodded toward Goldie. "Won't persuade them, eh? Managed to convince that one."

That got a laugh from both Terok and Heranuur, who glanced at each other for a moment.

"Regardless, I beat them in combat, so apparently I can now decide who goes into the dungeon and who doesn't, when, and for how long," Ilea explained. "Do you think they'll honor the deal?"

"You made a deal? How could I say if they will hold to it? I don't know them," he said with disinterest.

So, no culture of being honor-bound by one's word? No sacred teachings binding them to an agreement decided by battle?

Heranuur ground his teeth. "We will abide by the terms, hum— Ilea," he said.

Ilea shrugged. "Just don't get in my way."

Heranuur hissed, but the sound died when Elfie hissed from behind. The sound was more threatening now, and his magic had started to spread out. He glanced at Heranuur, then said a few words in a language that Ilea didn't speak. He hissed again. This time, the sound seemed frustrated.

"I will... make sure they do not bother you, Ilea," Elfie said.

"Any plans?" Ilea asked. She could see the annoyance in his eyes before it made way for a conflicted expression.

"Just go. Please."

"Alright." She could tell there was more to this, and she wondered what he'd told the elves in what she assumed was elvish. "Will you stay here, at least?"

"We will."

She felt as if he was close to saying something like 'I tire of you, human'. Or 'Leave me be, human'. But he didn't.

Ilea nodded his way, glanced at the defeated Cerithil Hunters, and walked back toward the dungeon. Terok followed her after a moment.

She had done them a favor, had saved them from near-certain death. The bout had ended not in death but in a new chance at life. Perhaps she was too trusting, but she could wipe the floor with the lot of them if needed. Elfie included. Not that he'd enter the dungeon anyway.

She wondered what they'd do, but the responsibility was Elfie's now, and their new chance was their own to waste.

"Want me to scout ahead?" Terok asked.

Ilea shook her head. "We move together. Stay back if more machines show up. When I tell you to run, you run. Don't stop until you're out of the bloody dungeon."

She could think of more than one thing that would cause such a reaction.

Terok shrugged, giving her a thumbs-up. "I'll be the map guy then."

* * *

They ventured through several trapped hallways before more Centurions showed up. Ilea dispatched them, and while there were a couple of close calls, it was easier than most of her fights in Tremor.

Terok joined her again when she was done, two earth-shaking detonations having marked the Centurions' demise. Unfortunately, the confined space of the hall had led to Ilea's armor taking more than just a beating from the explosions – it was near-liquidated.

She switched it out for a fresh set of Rose Hunter armor, only three remaining in her necklace now. There were five sets back in Tremor, but the flight would take a couple of hours out of her fighting schedule.

"Do you even try to stop the explosions?" Terok groused.

"No idea how to," Ilea said, cracking her neck as she read through the notifications.

'ding' You have defeated [Taleen Centurion – lvl 305] – For defeating an enemy forty or more levels above your own, bonus experience is granted.

'ding' You have defeated [Taleen Centurion – lvl 307] – For defeating an enemy forty or more levels above your own, bonus experience is granted.

No level ups, but at least she had the satisfaction of destroying Centurions like they were mere foot soldiers in the mechanized dwarven army.

"Wait... you're a robot guy *and* you have mana sight. Is there anything you can tell me about them that might help? Are they connected to something like the knights in Tremor?"

Terok grabbed a scrap of metal from the dungeon floor, held it up to his bionic eye, then threw it over his shoulder.

"Trash. As to your question? No. They're operating independently as far as I can tell. At least magically speaking. But I believe they somehow gather ambient mana."

Ilea nodded. *Like solar energy?* The detonations definitely seemed more like a mini nuclear reactor, but mana was mana, and she was definitely no scientist of magic. But she knew at least that the 'ambient' technology was kind of a big deal. Otherwise, all the runes used in inns, or even in her house, would be powered by ambient mana, not someone pumping the stuff into it.

"The lamps work like that too?" she asked, pointing up at the dim green lights.

"Nope, mana crystals."

Ilea frowned. "And they held for a thousand years?"

Terok shrugged. "Maybe the machines change them. Perhaps you'll catch one doing it."

Ilea rolled her eyes. Then again, maintenance robots weren't that far-fetched, given that combat ones existed. She simply hadn't seen any of them yet.

Or all of them are just maintenance robots.

She laughed at the thought and walked toward the elevator at the end of the room. Terok followed her and started inspecting the small plate on the wall beside the contraption.

"Just one destination. I guess they liked their architecture simple."

Ilea snorted. "Rooms and hallways, yes. All the traps and machinery hidden behind it all? Fucking no. Let's not use it anyway, I don't want to make a ruckus."

Ilea blinked under the elevator and into the shaft below. Terok appeared in the air next to her, hovering perfectly still as he peered around, his headlight shining down into the darkness.

"Long way down."

She grunted. "Risky teleport there, or did you not tell me about some of your skills?"

Terok chuckled. "Part of the gig, lassie. Not everyone has it as easy as 'Miss Healer and Sphere Perception' over here."

Ignoring the jibe, Ilea spread her wings and let herself fall, accelerating until she reached terminal velocity. When the ground appeared in her Sphere, she spread her wings and blinked upward once before gliding to the stone floor.

She didn't wait for Terok, instead stepping out of the shaft and leaning against the rusty metal railing that followed a stone balcony overlooking a busy scene below.

Least I've found where all those Centurions are coming from.

Ilea was standing over an abyss several hundred meters deep. The whole thing was shaped like a triangle, with the other two sides coming together opposite her at least two hundred meters away.

Built into each side of the massive chasm were openings, almost like hanger bays, some of which glowed with a ruddy red light. Each opening led deeper into the white metal walls, creating its own space, like the floors of a massive underground carpark.

Every twenty or thirty meters down was another floor. The angles made it unclear how far each reached into the stone, but each was open to the main triangular chasm, either to make it easier to deliver things between them or for ventilation purposes.

The glowing light reminded Ilea of forges. Steam rose from some floors, others held tanks of molten metal, oil, or other unknown liquids with pipes that spiderwebbed up, down, and all around the facility. Some looked like storage levels stacked with metal sheets, screws, bolts, and green glass.

Looking further still, Ilea could see giant robotic arms moving continuously across immense assembly lines churning out pieces of metal in various shapes and sizes.

The ones that caught Ilea's attention, however, were the openings through which she saw those metal pieces being assembled into very familiar shapes. They had found the source, at least in this dungeon, of the Taleen robots.

"Piss off," Terok gasped, finally appearing next to her as he too looked into the production hell the Taleen had left behind.

Ilea looked over and smiled. "A lot of work to do."

"You're not joking. This is huge… bigger than anything I've ever seen. How the fuck did they even do that?" He leaned over the railing. "Machines assembling more machines…"

"That's exactly how they did it. What variants do you see?" Ilea asked, squinting but only making out Centurions on the first couple of floors. They didn't seem to take any notice of the two new onlookers.

Terok scanned the busy scene. "Centurions. Six legs and a spear… yeah, most of them look like that… There's hundreds of them, Ilea. I don't know if even you can handle all those. Oh wait, there's another one. Eighth floor… four arms, that one. No weapon I can see, but it looks black rather than green. Might be the lighting, but I'm pretty sure… no, wait, another one just walked by, definitely black metal. Tenth floor… six arms, each holding a weapon."

"Figured as much," Ilea commented. "I'd assume Guardians are the usual Taleen dungeon residents. Centurions aren't exactly normal machines."

Terok grunted his affirmation. "Makes sense. Lucky for you to stumble upon strong enemies to take out then, right?" He laughed, causing Ilea to look at him sharply because of the loud noise. "Don't shit your pants, girl." He pointed to a rune he'd placed on the railing. "If they have ears, they're not hearing anything."

Sneaky, didn't even notice it.

"Seems like a waste to destroy it all…"

Terok snorted. "Depends how you look at it."

The two remained quiet for a minute or two, the sounds of massive gears and machines at work all that was audible in the massive chamber. A gigantic factory making machines of war, if Elfie was to be believed, to hunt down the elves – and possibly others.

Ilea sighed. "What do you think their goal is? Why continue if the Taleen are gone?"

"Maybe they're not. Might be hiding somewhere. Who knows? The machines here alone are probably enough to swamp most of the dwarven cities. Personally, I'd sleep much sounder with all of it gone."

What if I find the control system? I could stop it all or make the machines clear out monsters, protect cities, or just help me fight. A bunch of Centurions to fight alongside me would be cool as fuck…

"You thinking of taking over?" Terok asked with a smile. "I'm thinking the same. We could clear out whole dungeons with those things. Easy money."

"Where's the fun in that?" Ilea asked, grinning. "Let's think about that when, and more importantly if, we find a way to control them. Feel confident about scouting a little?"

"I'd feel more confident with Class evolutions."

Ilea tapped her armor with one finger as she thought of a solution that didn't involve her time and energy. Terok apparently didn't like the look in her eyes because after a few moments, he took a couple of steps back.

She grinned. "Let's go back and talk to Elfie again. Might be we can smash four birds with one stone."

SIXTY-SEVEN

Legion of Centurions

It had been barely an hour when Ilea and Terok emerged from the dungeon once more. The air was slightly warmer now, and booms echoed in the distance.

Goldie was awake now, the veins on his head seemingly trying to burst from his skull as he paced. His perpetual glare locked onto Ilea as soon as she appeared.

He even has golden eyes.

She smiled. "Sleep well?"

He hissed and leaped at her, claws outstretched, but slammed face-first into a barrier. He sank to his knees, blood seeping out of his nose and mouth. He was still heavily wounded, yet the hatred in his eyes was palpable.

"What's going on out here?" Ilea asked Elfie, who was observing the scene with a scowl. The two other elves were standing nearby, weapons in hand but their poses relaxed.

"I did not expect you to return so early."

"We found something."

He raised a brow at her. "What?"

"Centurion production facility, we think," she said.

Elfie nodded, though he didn't seem particularly surprised. "So there is one here."

"Anything important you can tell me about it?"

"I assume it produces Centurions, if that is what you saw," Elfie said in a dry tone.

"Ah yes," Ilea said and instead eyed the armed elves. "What are you doing?"

Elfie sighed. "An evaluation of sorts. If they are dead set on fighting the Taleen, they might as well be prepared." He paused. "It is something to pass the time," he added casually.

Sure.

"Sounds good. Any specific plans?"

"I shall see if we can find some creatures they can fight and kill to level up, and in around two weeks, they will face a Centurion together. We shall see how it goes and go from there."

"If you're training them, maybe I can join?" Terok asked.

Ilea raised her brows. "You? Why? I thought you hated elves."

"Well, I've been close to two hundred for a while now. I think it's time. And given how they fought, I might be able to escape while they smash their heads and claws into whatever's trying to kill us. No offense, fellas."

Neiphato nodded slightly. Heranuur laughed, then waved Terok over. "Join us, dwarf. It will be interesting to see you fight and struggle."

"Oh boy," Terok commented, but surprisingly, he didn't complain.

Elfie hissed softly before he shrugged. "What's in there, and why would I care to train you as well?"

"I'll tell you all about it. And I'm happy to get things out for you if needed. Not that it matters. You owe me for Tremor anyway. That was one long-ass notebook full of questions I ferried back and forth."

Elfie glared at him but averted his eyes.

"An affirmation if I've ever seen one," Terok said.

"Why… did… you… not… kill us?"

The groaning voice came from the still-fuming Goldie, his claws digging into the barrier. Ilea wondered if he couldn't teleport out or if he wasn't willing to.

"Good energy," Ilea replied, glancing at him. "Maybe focus on staying alive for now."

"And what are your plans?" Terok asked her.

She noticed Elfie tensing up slightly. It seemed he was interested too. "Just destroying more machines. Still on that road to three hundred. Let's see who gets to the next evolution first, me or you," she grinned.

"I'm not sure I want to take that bet," Terok laughed. "But sure, might be fun. Good luck then, and call for me if you find anything that it seems smarter to examine rather than destroy."

"I might do that," Ilea said before she went back inside.

* * *

Ten minutes later, Ilea came into a small room with yet another elevator leading down. This one had neither Centurions nor anything else protecting it. As before, she let herself fall before spreading her wings.

This elevator shaft was considerably shorter. When she came out at the bottom, Ilea smiled broadly and crossed her arms.

"Well. That's something," she whispered and sighed. Not a sigh of another long workday in front of her but one full of anticipation.

She was standing in the middle of a square, around which were buildings that would have once been stores, guilds, inns, and shops with machinery and furniture still inside. If there had once been any color, it was long faded. Only the dark stone remained, ivy growing over it all. Some of the buildings were covered by it almost completely.

The square was lit by green light that came not from the ceiling but from lampposts placed around the square. More bathed the connected streets and alleys in a dim green light.

Did you arrive in a similar location, Kyrian?

She wondered if he was still in the ruin he'd been teleported to. Had she failed him? Taken too long?

No. He can take care of himself, I should trust him that far. Who knows, when I get back to Ravenhall, he might already be there.

She focused back on the now. Kyrian wasn't the only reason she was here.

The ruin, which had once had a scary atmosphere, was now full of possibilities. She had a feeling there would be Praetorians here, either in this city or the factory. After meeting so many weird and powerful monsters, it was interesting to think of challenging something that had previously filled her with dread. Something she hadn't been able to overcome.

Not a nest of mind magic-wielding beasts or knights devoid of consciousness but machines hellbent on ripping her apart. If she grew strong here, if there were enough Centurions to get her to the levels needed, she knew she could fight them again. She knew she could win.

A shiver went down her back, the thought somehow freeing. Had the loss back then really been so important? Did they represent something lurking in her subconscious? Ilea didn't know. But what she did know was that she wanted to face that fear, face that monster from her past. She would prepare, raise her levels, and use every advantage she could grab.

Level. Kill Praetorians. Save Kyrian.

A good plan.

As Ilea continued onward, she noticed the ceiling above wasn't visible. It seemed like the whole mountain had been carved out and the city placed within. The streets all ended in more squares or massive buildings. All except one. Ilea couldn't see the end of it, but green lights like fireflies formed a path for her to follow.

You could literally land a plane in here.

The thought made her chuckle, but thinking of the flying machines she'd seen in the Iz dungeon made her scan the skies. Or rather, the darkness hanging over the ancient city. But there was nothing there, no blinking lights or any floodlights looking for her.

Activating Hunter's Sight, she checked the area. Stepping through the square, she found several signs suggesting recent movement. The earth had been disturbed in places, and some of the ivy was damaged and loose.

Looking up, she saw what looked like a single Taleen Guardian walking toward the square, its head swiveling around, its green eyes scanning the overgrown houses, its six bladed arms at the ready.

'ding' Hunter's Sight reaches 2nd lvl 17

Ilea wasn't exactly concerned though and continued to look through the square.

Something definitely moved through here, and it wasn't a Taleen machine I've seen before.

When the Guardian entered the square, it spotted her immediately, fanning out its blades as a challenge.

Ilea quirked an eyebrow. "Really?"

Her answer was the machine rushing her, ready to strike.

Ilea's ashen limbs fanned out, and the six blades halted mid-attack, each crashing into an ashen arm. Ilea braced herself against the impact but found herself steady. The force exerted by the machine was easy, trivial even, to handle.

It tried wrenching its arms free, but Ilea's ash extended, swirling around its metal blades like snakes and holding them in place. She stepped toward the helpless machine and looked at it, its glowing green eyes staring at her impassively.

Maybe Terok can take a look at one while I hold it like this.

[Taleen Guardian – lvl 205]

To think she could handle a level two hundred creature so easily. With all her buffs deactivated and her ashen Veil down, it was likely still capable of injuring her, but against her full power, this one Guardian was like an ant trying to stand up to a human.

Her fist shot out, the sound of the impact reverberating with a dull clang. The machine tried to recoil but was held in place by her ash. She smashed another fist into it, Destruction and Wave of Ember flaring before the light in its eyes went out. Its legs gave out, and the whole thing clattered to the floor.

An idea grew in her mind as Ilea stepped over the machine, her wings spreading before she ascended. Flying over the nearby streets, she found a bunch of Guardians patrolling and some ranged variants sitting on roofs. Landing behind one of the ranged Guardians, she extended her ashen limbs.

[Taleen Guardian – lvl 150]

She formed a cocoon with her ash and pushed destructive mana into the Guardian, which struggled to move in the hardening black mist. A couple of seconds later, it was over, the machine falling inert and Ilea receiving yet another notification. Both of the kills were irrelevant to her current level.

Could hunt some of them for Embered Body Heat and Hunter's Sight...

Seeing that the surrounding streets and nearby squares only held Guardians, Ilea went back to the elevator. This wasn't her place to clear out. Flying up through the shaft, she blinked out, crossed the hallway, and flew down the longer elevator shaft, finally coming out on the platform overlooking the much busier production facility dug deep into the ground.

How many places like this are there? Ilea wondered. There had to be places where all the machines Elfie had talked about were coming from. This was certainly one of them.

Spreading her wings, Ilea jumped down and glided toward the first floor. The floor was metal, just like the support beams that held the weight of each floor, which stacked near infinitely. Ilea wondered if she would get credit for the kills were she to simply collapse the whole thing.

Quick way to level three hundred for a metal mage like Terok.

The ruckus would certainly gain a lot of attention. A Centurion might also survive the collapse, ending up stuck between the steel beams for eternity.

Cracking her knuckles, Ilea spread her ash and breathed in. The smell of fire, soot, and iron filled her nose. Unlike the city, this place was bathed in red light from the rivers of molten steel, forges, and sparks flying off the various tools in the vicinity.

It was warm, Ilea noted. Warm enough for her to sweat, which meant it was possibly too hot for someone below level two hundred to traverse. Her Heat Resistance was now at level ten of the second tier, but she'd find a way to bathe in some molten steel to raise it at some point.

Trying to cut into the large wires like extensions on the walls was apparently enough for one of the Centurions to come and check what was happening. The machine threw its spear immediately, uncaring of any possible damage to the environment.

Or trusting enough to know it would be irrelevant, Ilea thought, dodging the spear before she blinked into range, ashen limbs immediately crashing into the Centurion as she checked her surroundings for additional foes.

Spreading ash around, she made sure there was enough on the ground for a quick distraction in case she needed to escape. All the machines, forges, and massive robotic arms, as well as all the tanks and supplies, would make hiding rather simple.

She was pretty sure the Centurions weren't expert trackers, just warriors, made to be efficient killers. It was a riddle to her how they could be created at a level above three hundred, but she was pretty sure they were considered monsters by the system governing life in Elos. Maybe the Taleen had just been that amazing at magical robotics.

Ilea accelerated her blows, pushing hard to make sure the fight didn't last a second longer than needed. The Centurion wasn't comparable to the Guardian she'd fought previously though.

While both her speed and utility massively outclassed it, she didn't want to get hit directly. Nor did she want to fight more of them as it would force her to navigate and fight in the unknown steel forest. The big open hall from earlier was a much-preferred arena.

As she fought the Centurion, she wondered how the explosion would affect the surrounding factory. She didn't want to blow up the whole thing.

Worth testing if the explosions actually damage any of the support structures.

A couple of minutes later, Ilea's mana was down a thousand points, her offense draining it quickly with all her ashen limbs and excessive blinks as well as health sacrifices. Healing back to full, she finally managed to crack the core.

The Centurion threw its spear, but it skidded off her armor. The light shone through the cracks in its core, growing brighter while Ilea stood there, ash settling around her.

Then it turned and sprinted in the opposite direction. She stared at the fleeing machine in confusion, watching as it reached an opening on the platform and jumped off into the triangular abyss.

Ah... makes sense.

The explosion masked the noise of steam, metal hitting metal, and gears turning – but only for a second. Ilea was left standing between the production machines, nothing other than her ash covering parts of the surroundings indicating that anything had happened at all.

'ding' You have defeated [Taleen Centurion – lvl 310] – For defeating an enemy forty or more levels above your own, bonus experience is granted.

At least I still get the experience. So something's programmed into them that prevents them from damaging the surroundings. Meaning the explosion could actually damage all this.

Ilea was still thinking about the ramifications when she picked up the noise of metal legs on steel around her. Smiling, she let Meditation flow through her, breathing in deeply and closing her eyes. When three Centurions entered her Sphere, she opened her eyes.

The fight was longer, but she found her initial assessment of the surroundings to be wrong. It was actually even easier to face a group of them here because there was so much to hide behind. The Centurions had to navigate the maze with their large forms while she could just teleport and fly around.

With her superior mobility and their tendency to pop out of the metal maze at different intervals, the continued fighting always felt dynamic, and Ilea made it into a game of who could surprise whom first.

Hide and seek, just with a bunch of killer robots.

My kind of game.

SIXTY-EIGHT

Training Considerations

Her mana dropped to five hundred before she could take out another one of the machines. Ilea blinked out into the open and spread her wings, and another blink let her dodge a thrown spear before she was back up near the railings.

Exiting the production facility through the elevator shaft, she turned around and meditated, waiting to see if any of them pursued her. A minute passed and then two. Nothing followed, either because the machines had no way to fly or climb up or because they weren't supposed to do anything but defend their lair.

Ilea sighed and cracked her neck. She had a bunch of high-leveled enemies in there that didn't completely rip her apart in groups as well as a spot to recover her mana and health if necessary.

Elfie gave the others two weeks. Let's see how far I can get in that time.

* * *

The answer was mixed. It surprised her that nobody bothered her in the full two weeks, allowing her to focus fully on the task at hand.

After the first day, the machines only moved in groups of six, after the second, they started to keep the damaged machines at the center of their formations, and after the third, they actively prowled the first floor as soon as she destroyed her first Centurion. She couldn't fight for more than a couple of minutes before a second group showed up, making it ten to twelve Centurions versus her solitary self.

The number itself wouldn't have been an issue in the forest of metal and molten steel, were it not for their increasingly defensive tactics. As if they were a group of hunters trying to exhaust and corner a wild animal. The problem for them was that she wasn't exactly a wild animal. Her superior mobility was simply overwhelming, and the damage she put into them stacked up more and more.

The latest two kills had finally brought her ashen class over another threshold. Just in time before she went to check on Elfie, Terok, and the three young hunters. She hoped all of them were at least still alive. She trusted Elfie, and the mage could probably take care of the four of them, should they act out. And while he pretended not to be particularly invested, she could tell he wasn't here for no reason.

She sat down on one of the few benches that were still intact in the halls leading to the production facility and summoned one of Keyla's meals, taking off her helmet to eat as she mentally scrolled through all the messages from her extensive fighting.

'ding' You have defeated [Taleen Centurion – lvl 305] – For defeating an enemy forty or more levels above your own, bonus experience is granted.

...

'ding' You have defeated [Taleen Centurion – lvl 310] – For defeating an enemy forty or more levels above your own, bonus experience is granted.

'ding' Azarinth First Hunter has reached lvl 265 – Five stat points awarded

'ding' Azarinth First Hunter has reached lvl 266 – Five stat points awarded

'ding' Inheritor of Eternal Ash has reached lvl 258 – Five stat points awarded

...

'ding' Inheritor of Eternal Ash has reached lvl 260 – Five stat points awarded, one 3rd-tier skill point awarded

Ilea put some points into Vitality to ensure it was keeping pace with her Wisdom, and she buffed Intelligence as well to keep her damage output increasing.

Most of her damage was still coming from her ashen limbs that had the simple advantage of getting through the machines' defenses much more often. That was likely the main factor in her ashen class leveling once more than her Azarinth one.

Ilea took a mouthful of food and closed her eyes, savoring the flavor. It was an oily meat and vegetable soup with thin noodles. The spiciness reminded her of some cheap ramen noodles she would've eaten back on

Earth but elevated to another level with Keyla's expertise and fresh ingredients. She really had to go and hug the woman again for making her adventurer lifestyle not just bearable but outright luxurious.

Taking another slurp of soup, she checked the possible advancements for the third-tier skill point in her ashen class.

3rd-tier skill points available [Inheritor of Eternal Ash]: 1
Skills available for 3rd-tier advancement in [Inheritor of Eternal Ash]:
- Form of Ash and Ember
- Wave of Ember
- Body of Ash
- Ashen Warrior

Ilea was surprised to find such a choice. Previously, only her Veil and Ash Creation had been available for a third-tier level up, and afterward, her Ash and Ember Manipulation.

Going through the skills, she immediately decided against Wave of Ember as it was categorized as Ashen Magic. Body of Ash was a secondary priority too because its bonuses were inferior to Form of Ash and Ember as well as Ashen Warrior. Plus, it was both Body Enhancement and Ashen Magic. Ashen Warrior was purely Body Enhancement, while Form of Ash and Ember had the added Aura categorization.

Ilea read through the two skills again, even though she knew them by heart at this point.

Active: Form of Ash and Ember – 2nd lvl 20:
Ember glows within you, raising your resilience, speed, Strength, and Dexterity by 55% [275%].
2nd stage: The longer you fight while in the Form of Ash and Ember, the deeper roots it gains. Each minute of fighting adds 15% more power to the skill up to a maximum of 150%.
Category: Aura – Body Enhancement

The bonuses were absolutely insane compared to many of her other skills. Especially with both her classes enhancing Body Enhancements, each by two hundred percent. That was why she wanted to prevent herself from getting a purely Ashen Magic skill.

Passive: Ashen Warrior – 2nd lvl 20:
You are familiar with the fighting style of Ash. Damage inflicted with your own body and while shrouded in Ash is 70% [350%] higher.
2nd stage: Shroud your weapons in ash to produce various effects. Shrouded weapons deal additional damage. Affected by Ash and Ember Manipulation.
Category: Body Enhancement

The percentage bonus was higher for Ashen Warrior, and it was basically a direct damage buff. Ilea knew it affected her mana intrusion abilities too, which made it one of the best skills she had.

She thought about possible third-tier advancements that could be unlocked but finally decided on Form of Ash and Ember as her auras had been the staple of her power from early on. She would likely choose Ashen Warrior at two eighty, just to get another Body Enhancement ability up there, but if she got something similar to State of Azarinth's third tier, the two could stack.

Ilea hesitated, then shook her head. Both skills were really good, but she felt like the Aura was a safer bet for a good third tier.

'ding' Form of Ash and Ember reaches 3rd lvl 1
Active: Form of Ash and Ember – 3rd lvl 1:
Ember glows within you, raising your resilience, speed, Strength, and Dexterity by 55.5% [277.5%].
2nd stage: The longer you fight while in the Form of Ash and Ember, the deeper roots it gains. Each minute of fighting adds 15% more power to the skill, up to a maximum of 150%.
3rd stage: Familiarity with the skill removes its upkeep. When reaching the maximum second-tier bonus, you may reset it by amplifying your next attack with ash and ember.
Category: Aura – Body Enhancement

Ilea read through the new third tier and nodded. "Not bad."

The skill's upkeep would be by far the most mana-intensive skill she had up at all times. Now her recovery would be improved considerably, especially when not using Meditation. Her attack magic was what drained her during her battles, but it would help.

Even more sustain. She smiled at the thought. *Longest fighting and most durable warrior of all time?*

The second part of the third-tier ability, giving up the 150% of second-tier bonuses for a single empowered attack, was interesting. The second-tier bonuses weren't influenced by her Class bonuses, which would make it less of a dent to lose them during a battle. If it were amplified by her Classes, she'd never even consider using the new third-tier ability.

Either way, depends on how powerful the attack actually is. But I can't exactly test it without somebody to fight.

* * *

She heard the sounds of battle when she walked into the dug-out entrance leading into the dwarven ruin. Steel against steel rang out before an explosion drowned the sound. Stepping into the ruin, Ilea saw that the previously rocky environment had been mostly flattened, stones either moved away or pulverized by magic or sheer strength.

Goldie was either sleeping or knocked out, as was the brown-haired elf, Neiphato. Their bodies were sprawled on the hard ground, cuts and bruises visible, as were dents and damage on whatever armor they were wearing.

Ilea appeared next to Elfie, who had one hand on his chin and was staring hard at the two combatants, his eyes following every move.

"I see you've refrained from killing Terok," Ilea said by way of greeting. "Managed to keep the elves out of my hair *and* you're still actually training them? Color me impressed."

Terok disappeared to dodge a fiery explosion expanding from Heranuur's body, the tall, muscular elf laughing as his flame-clad blades deflected the metal spikes shooting out from Terok's armor, which looked scuffed but not dented.

Elfie didn't look at her. "I don't have any paint with me, human, nor would I waste it on you. You leveled again. Is the facility really full of Centurions?" he asked, his voice disinterested.

Ilea was pretty sure the elf cared more than he let on. "Yep, tons of them. It's going to take a long time to clear it out. I found something else last week. You guys didn't explore further?"

He scoffed. "The dwarf tried several times."

She nodded, impressed he'd managed to stop the dwarf. *Was he holding back against me?* She wasn't sure. Ilea knew her mana intrusion spells were very effective against barriers, maybe that was it. Coupled with her Curse Resistance and recovery, Elfie's abilities were quite ineffective against her.

"There's a Taleen city in there as well, Guardians and all. Reminded me of a dungeon I've explored before. I thought maybe they could explore and train a little in there, depending on how they do."

Elfie looked at her then, the silver in his eyes swirling before he looked back at the two fighters before him. They were breathing hard, eyeing each other. Ilea felt Elfie use a skill, causing Terok and Heranuur to groan before they continued their battle, neither very enthusiastically.

"Not a bad idea," Elfie said without taking his eyes off the fight. "They have been itching to kill for days now. I doubt Guardians will be a sufficient challenge for them, though."

"There's plenty in there. If it's anything like the first Taleen dungeon I explored, then there will be Centurions as well as traps. It won't be simple, and they don't have a healer."

Elfie chuckled. "You just want to have the Centurion facility for yourself, don't you?"

She grinned, looking at the two warriors, who had gone back to using more frantic and dangerous moves. "That doesn't change what I told you. They would be slaughtered in there."

He changed tack. "I would still like to talk to the Tremor royals. Face to face, that is."

"Just tell the elves to bring out documents and relics from Tremor." She gestured to the group. "When Terok reaches level two hundred, he might be able to get at least the queen out. Plus, shouldn't destroying this dungeon and the machines within have priority for you?"

Elfie was quiet for a while. "Do not presume to know what is and isn't a priority for me."

Ilea sat down on a nearby rock. She smiled. "Still so distrusting? Thought you were more comfortable around me by now."

Elfie hissed, then shook his head. "I..." He sighed. "I did not mean to offend you, Ilea. But you do not know me. And..."

He looked at her, then away.

"I'm human? Not an elf? Who cares? You're out here in no-elf's-land training a bunch of young elves and a dwarf wearing an armored machine. We're all out here, exploring, fighting. If you think I don't know you, then feel free to tell me more about yourself, whenever you feel like it. I'd be happy to know. You're the first elf that I've met who's been halfway decent."

He smiled this time. "That's all I am to you? An elf who is 'halfway decent'?"

"Thought I didn't know you?" Ilea winked.

He moved his attention back to the fighters. A quick teleport by Heranuur and a follow-up explosion sent Terok into the ground, the elf following before he hit an invisible barrier.

"That is enough," Elfie called out to them before looking at Ilea. "Can you heal them while you're here?"

Ilea nodded, extending her ashen limbs. "They should really get a healer. Maybe we can find one for hire in Hallowfort. I don't want to stop my own exploration to take care of them."

Elfie watched her as she healed up Heranuur, then Terok, and finally the other two elves. Each had what she considered severe injuries, making the fight she'd watched quite impressive.

Elfie hissed thoughtfully. "It will be good for them to learn and fight without a healer, at least for a while. If they cannot recover their own health, then they will have to deal with that."

"I see your point. But they'll need someone for resistance training."

"I have heard of Cerithil Hunters able to heal themselves. Perhaps something will reveal itself with time," he said as Ilea finished up. "They will face a Centurion today. Can you get one for them?"

"Send them to the room they fought me in previously. I'll drag one out for them to tackle," Ilea said. "You're free to join too, of course. Might be good to see them fight it."

Elfie just hissed at her.

SIXTY-NINE

A Test

Ilea watched the group fight their Centurion, ready to intervene if anyone got close to death. They started well, using some sort of formation that Elfie must've taught them, but as soon as they got a few hits in, the elves devolved back to just full-on attack, overconfidence and whatever else they felt taking over instead of a more measured and teamwork-oriented approach. It would work against normal Guardians, but one mistake against the Centurion meant they would get wounded, and unlike her, they couldn't recover very easily.

Their combined efforts did push the Centurion, but Ilea had to intervene when Goldie lost a leg and again when Heranuur just barely got away from having his head pierced, only losing an eye in the process. The Centurion eventually exploded, but the group would've had casualties without her.

They weren't ready.

* * *

"Teacher, eh?" Ilea said, appearing next to Elfie. "Let me guess, you always wanted to become one but instead were banished, and now you're looking to gather knowledge for the ages."

He scoffed, standing up as he looked the others over as they emerged from the dungeon. "How did they do?"

Ilea sat down on a big stone, watching the distant purple lightning. It was Terok who explained what had happened. When he was done, Elfie hissed.

"Until the Cerithil Hunters can destroy a Centurion alone or accept that working in a team is beneficial, they are not allowed in the facility. The city, however… I guess they can start exploring. Destroying Guardians could teach them something, I suppose."

Ilea heard a few hisses from the elves. She smiled at that. "If they don't die in there, that is."

* * *

Ilea spent the next few days fighting more Centurions, eventually getting a little frustrated with the constant green metal, the same noises, the same enemies. She decided to use the nights to spend some time with the Miststalkers, and her growing stats and skills allowed her more extended training, including some close-combat encounters when only a few of them were present.

They fought the same way as they danced, with serene motions that she could easily dodge, though she didn't, their direct attacks inflicting the same kind of feeling and damage as the mist used by Elana. At least it gave her more resistances to work on, and she did enjoy the nighttime northern scenery.

'ding' Mist Magic Resistance reaches lvl 2

…

'ding' Mist Magic Resistance reaches lvl 7

She managed to test her new third-tier skill a few times as well but found the main benefit to be the skill's upkeep removal. Giving up the 150% bonus to Form of Ash and Ember didn't feel worth it for one empowered use of the skill. Even if it hit for maybe twenty times the damage, she could get in the same amount of damage in just a few seconds with her ashen limbs.

Day in and day out, Ilea trained, fighting and destroying Centurions, which were becoming increasingly difficult to fight, while working on her mana and health drain as well as mist magic resistances at night. She didn't see Elfie or anybody else for the first five days.

On the night of the sixth day, she was sitting near a lake of mist when she noticed movement in the distance, a couple of hundred meters down the slope. The creature was completely black, as big as a horse and in the form of a wolf. It moved quickly, occasionally disappearing into the shadows, reappearing a couple of dozen meters away.

Ilea realized the movement she'd noticed wasn't from the wolf-like creature but the birds chasing it. Famine Crows. A whole pack of them. The wolf looked injured, slowing down before it entered a lake of mist.

The beast slowed down further as Miststalkers gathered around it, the birds rushing down from above, uncaring about the new circumstances. Ilea watched as the wolf entered the ground itself, vanishing as a whole flock of Famine Crows crashed down into the stone, surrounded by more and more Miststalkers.

The birds immediately started teleporting around, but contrary to what she'd expected, most of them crashed into the ground again or reappeared near it, the Miststalkers' scythes cutting into them as their health and mana were drained.

The first of them started to fall around ten seconds later. Some escaped, but at least half of the flock had vanished in the mist, absorbed into the spirits that completely surrounded them.

Smart wolf, she thought, blinking away from the lake. It was time to go back to the dungeon and see to the next group of Centurions.

* * *

Two weeks later, she had thinned them enough on the top layer of the facility to make it at least uncommon to find a second group while fighting a first one. Ilea had tested her theory about just throwing the Centurions down the massive abyss twice, both times unsuccessfully.

They were certainly durable, but Ilea suspected there was a lake or something at the bottom that prevented their demise. Either that or whatever governed the notifications in her mind didn't count their destruction as her work.

When the suns rose one morning, she returned to the entrance of the Taleen dungeon and found the campsite populated, unlike most days. She landed with a smile, greeting Elfie with a wave. He looked up and nodded. She noted he smelled of blood.

Summoning a meal, she placed it next to the papers he was reading through before summoning one for herself. Sitting down on a nearby rock, she put her helmet into her necklace.

"How was the hunt?"

The elf looked up and sighed, taking the meal. "You have a constant need for conversation do you not?"

She chuckled. "Haven't talked to anybody in days. You consider that constant? How often do you elves talk to each other?"

"I was only saying that to indicate my lack of interest in a conversation, not to indicate some difference between our species. My people can be just as annoying as yours."

"Sadly, you can't just eat them, right?" she said, pointing to the blood on his black coat, which flowed seamlessly into the red parts of the fabric.

He scoffed. "Few of your kind up here." Avoiding her stare, he started eating. "A wild animal," he added after a while.

"If you need a fight, I'm around," she said. "How's the exploration going? I want a full map by the end of next week."

Elfie laughed. "Then you will be disappointed. I have heard how big the dwarf thinks the production facility is. The city might be similarly expansive. Filled not just with Guardians but with Awakened too, as well as more dangerous Taleen machines and traps."

"Good. Then there's plenty of work to do. What kind of Awakened?"

"These Awakened call themselves Saurians. They would only agree to talk to the dwarf."

"I see. What are you reading anyway?"

"A surviving stone inscription of the Taleen that the dwarf copied."

Ilea stood up, putting her empty plate away and checking out the paper. "You can read their language?"

The elf snorted. "Of course I can. I know you think my level low for my age, but I invested in other things than just the power to destroy."

"Impressive," she said and meant it. "Maybe you can teach the Hunters. Might be beneficial to find out more about the Taleen's plans. I doubt any of those idiots would ever think about deciphering and learning an ancient language."

His face went through an array of different emotions before he finally settled on a sigh.

"Frustrated with them?" she asked.

Elfie took a mouthful of food before he swallowed. He glanced at Ilea, then looked up at the natural rock ceiling that sheltered them. "It is not them I am frustrated with."

"I wasn't really around a lot. Do I *really* annoy you that much?" Ilea asked and grinned at his exasperated expression. "I'm kidding."

"Why did you help them? In that first fight?"

"What do you mean?"

"I know you want to learn about the Taleen, about that friend of yours. Kyrian was his name, was it not? But you must have realized that these three Hunters are inexperienced, unable to share anything of use, so why did you help them?"

"Why are you taking the time to teach them?" Ilea asked in turn.

He hissed, the emotion behind it something she couldn't quite place. He didn't answer her for some time, so she thought about his question.

"They would've gotten slaughtered. Isn't that enough of a reason to help?"

"Is it? You didn't know them, you're not of their kind. And you've told me about what you know of elves. Your kind has many reasons not to trust ours."

"I've met both elves and humans who were monsters. What I found here weren't monsters, just a bunch of kids trying to do what they felt was right.

Or that's what it felt like when they talked about it. Why would I judge them for what others of their kind have done?"

He was quiet for a long moment. "Because that is what we do. Humans, elves, dwarves."

"Eh, some do that. But I'm special," Ilea said, adopting a fighting pose.

Elfie smiled. His gaze looked clearer, focused. "Maybe you are. Thank you for your insight."

"Sure. I gotta get back to fighting now. Levels don't level themselves after all," she said, proud of her continuing stroke of wisdom.

Maybe all those stat points are finally paying off.

* * *

After another week of fighting, Ilea checked her messages as she made her way toward the exit of the Taleen factory. She was ready to explore another place as well, so she checked everything from the past month.

'ding' You have defeated [Taleen Centurion – lvl 310] – For defeating an enemy forty levels or more above your own, bonus experience is granted.

…

'ding' You have defeated [Taleen Centurion – lvl 305] – For defeating an enemy thirty levels or more above your own, bonus experience is granted.

'ding' Azarinth First Hunter has reached lvl 267 – Five stat points awarded

…

'ding' Azarinth First Hunter has reached lvl 272 – Five stat points awarded

'ding' Inheritor of Eternal Ash has reached lvl 261 – Five stat points awarded

…

'ding' Inheritor of Eternal Ash has reached lvl 266 – Five stat points awarded

She split the sixty stat points between Vitality, Wisdom, and Intelligence.

'ding' Destruction reaches 3rd lvl 5

'ding' Hunter Recovery reaches 3rd lvl 4

...

'ding' Hunter Recovery reaches 3rd lvl 6

'ding' State of Azarinth reaches 3rd lvl 9

'ding' Hunter's Sight reaches 2nd lvl 18

'ding' Hunter's Sight reaches 2nd lvl 19

Her Hunter Recovery had leveled three times, the dedicated training proving its effectiveness. Hunter's Sight was close to its current maximum as well.

'ding' Form of Ash and Ember reaches 3rd lvl 2

'ding' Ash Creation reaches 3rd lvl 4

'ding' Embered Body Heat reaches 2nd lvl 18

'ding' Blast Resistance reaches lvl 14

...

'ding' Blast Resistance reaches lvl 18

'ding' Health Drain Resistance reaches 2nd lvl 15

'ding' Health Drain Resistance reaches 2nd lvl 16

'ding' Mana Drain Resistance reaches 2nd lvl 13

'ding' Mana Drain Resistance reaches 2nd lvl 14

'ding' Mist Magic Resistance reaches lvl 8

...

'ding' Mist Magic Resistance reaches lvl 17

Slow and steady. Ilea was growing, and she had enough sources to fuel her increases in power. She stretched and hummed a tune to herself. It was high time to explore something other than the construction of Centurions, for a while at least.

The royals must be thinking we're dead by now... she thought with a smile. They did have each other, but she didn't know if that was a curse or blessing.

* * *

When Ilea appeared outside the dungeon, she saw the others were still around. Two of the elves were sleeping on their bedrolls, the fabric more luxurious than any sleeping bags she had ever seen. Even on Earth. Each had chosen a dark color, either because of their status as Cerithil Hunters or to be a little camouflaged.

Terok and Neiphato were adding ingredients to a black metal pot hanging over a small fire. It smelled like food. Nothing particularly good, but she doubted any of them had an assortment of spices with them.

"Thought you guys just ate human meat," she said, walking toward them. Elfie wasn't around, but she assumed he was somewhat close by. Perhaps he was still exhausted from their recent conversation.

Neiphato looked at her, realizing she was talking to him and not the dwarf. He gulped.

"Some do like human flesh, yes. The lower-level ones with little muscle are considered a delicacy. We do eat other things as well, though. Plenty. Anything that moves, really. Though a few have even sworn off meat entirely."

"Any of them actually stick with that?" Ilea asked, crouching down over the pot and sniffing the broth.

"I believe so. The ones I knew countered their lust for meat with more hunting and killing. I do not think it makes sense."

She chuckled. "How's the map Terok?"

The dwarf hadn't spoken yet, but even in his armor, she thought he looked tired and worn. At least he'd risen to level one ninety-three. Not yet at two hundred, but close enough.

"Ilea... that city is bigger than you think. Mapping it is going to take, well... a long time."

Ilea nodded. "Too dangerous to rush things, I get it."

She looked up to find the brown-haired elf looking at her, blue eyes reflecting some of the light coming from the fire.

"Neiphato, right? I felt like you held back when we first fought. And I haven't seen you use any magic, but there was something there. Care to share at this point?"

He looked down at the ground.

"You're not going to tell me?" Ilea looked at him, but no answer seemed forthcoming. "Hidden talent? You can turn into a hideous tentacled monster? You get stronger when you eat people... A vampire, maybe?" She grinned, then sighed when she could tell he was getting stressed out. "Sorry. You don't have to talk about it if you don't want to."

"It is… a personal affair, human… Ilea, I mean."

"It's fine, sorry for prying. Care for some other questions?"

"I'm listening."

"I've been wondering why you were out here in the first place. Cerithil Hunter, cursed one… why cursed, by the way? Because you went into a dungeon? Is it forbidden by your government or religion?"

Neiphato checked to see if the two other elves were asleep or out of earshot. "Cursed because that is the status bestowed upon those who ignore the rules of the Oracles. One of their most ancient rules is to steer clear of places of creation, or dungeons, as you call them."

"So it's just a rule? But you can enter if you want? I mean, I've seen you in there."

"Not only a rule. The overwhelming mana density is dangerous and damaging. The first time I entered a dungeon was difficult. I was close to death while I adjusted. It was painful and prolonged. Perhaps it is punishment by the Oracles, or perhaps they wished to protect us. It matters not. I am here now, marked, cursed, a Cerithil Hunter."

Ilea nodded, trying not to show her surprise at all the information he was sharing. Perhaps she'd finally found an elf who actually liked to talk.

"Giving me this information… what would your Oracles say about that? Are you double-cursed for revealing their existence?"

Neiphato hissed with amusement, a grin revealing the sharp teeth in his mouth.

"Ilea… as much as it hurts to say it, I think they couldn't care less about me, you, or anything but their own affairs, whatever those might be. That is why I am here. You came here with Niivalyr, saved our lives, spared us when they were yours to take. When he sent us here, I thought us ready. But we needed more, a teacher. You showed us that too…"

He was quiet for a moment.

"You said someone sent you here? Another Cerithil Hunter?"

"No, we met Niivalyr in our search for a Taleen dungeon. He guided us here. Has he not…?" He hissed. "I should not have spoken."

Ilea raised her brows. *Elfie brought them here? He knew they were here?*

"That makes a lot of sense now," she murmured. "Don't worry, I don't hold it against him, and I won't tell him you shared this."

"I'm… please do not. He is a good teacher, but harsh. I do not wish to bring his ire upon me."

Terok chuckled darkly from where he stirred the contents of the pot. "Yeah, you don't want that."

"You mentioned your Oracles, that they have their own affairs. You don't know what those are?" Ilea asked.

"They are secretive. It is forbidden for someone of my status to even ask such questions, not that I haven't tried. It is their inaction that led us here, after all."

"Having leaders who don't care about their people – a tale as ooold as time," Terok murmured.

"And what do your leaders care about, dwarf?" Neiphato asked with a smile.

Terok pointed at the elf with a wooden ladle he'd produced from nowhere. Ilea wondered if he'd carved it himself.

"I am a scavenger of Hallowfort, a community where we actually care for each other, though I do wonder how much of that is due to our circumstances here. Other dwarves? Don't know. Metals? Gold?"

How terribly cliched, Ilea thought.

"Is gold not a metal?" Neiphato asked.

"It is. And not a very hard one. For those other than gold mages, it's difficult to guide mana through it. Now how would you compete in the ring with such a machine?"

Maybe not that cliched.

"So you're obsessed with forging because you're all into wrestling?" Ilea asked.

"Not wrestling, Ilea… such a mundane activity. A battle between two dwarves, each clad in steel armor, war machines, steam rising as the crowds cheer them on to destroy each other. A marvelous sight, one I could only dream of joining."

Ilea's eyebrows rose. "You wanted to become a boxer? I did kick-boxing once. A while ago now, though. Now I'm something else, I guess. Is the leader of the dwarves the champion of the biggest tournament or something?"

"Don't be ridiculous. Being a good warrior doesn't make one a good administrator or king. It helps, certainly, but only to get rid of competition." Terok chuckled. "I was more interested in tinkering with my machine than actually fighting in it. Not that I dislike it, but I lack a certain… vigor. You know what I mean."

Getting out of his metal suit, he tasted the soup and coughed.

"I know exactly what you mean," Ilea said with a smile, grabbing the ladle and trying a bit of the stew as well.

Fatty and too spicy. Surprised my Poison Resistance isn't reacting.

"May I ask a question too?" Neiphato said.

"Of course," Ilea said.

"You helped us. Why?"

That again? Ilea thought. "Is it really that surprising?"

Terok snorted. "You helped a bunch of elves that you didn't know. That's the kind of naivety I'd expect from a soft kid who grew up as a noble."

"I don't think it was either naïve or soft. Power allows for a certain freedom," Ilea countered.

"I still wouldn't save an angry child from a dangerous monster."

Yes you would.

Ilea just smiled at him. She would too. If the monster was weaker than her, why not give the child another chance at life? If the monster was stronger, that was reason enough to face it.

Terok looked away and huffed. "Don't look at me like that. An elf would probably kill the beast and eat both."

She couldn't help but laugh, especially after the elf didn't deny it.

"Don't eat kids," she said after a moment. "Or I'll murder you."

"Noted," Neiphato replied. "It is interesting. To learn about humans and dwarves."

"We're not exactly showpieces," Terok chuckled.

"Neither am I," Neiphato said, his voice soft.

"That food is rank, by the way," Ilea said to break the ensuing silence. "Are you trying to become a poison maker?"

Terok pointed at her. "Young lady, I will not have you talk to the cook that way."

He grinned, but something about the joke struck a chord in Ilea. She nodded and looked at the ground with a smile.

I am still young, aren't I? Feels like I've been here for a decade already.

"Why do you fight the Taleen machines?" Neiphato asked suddenly, steering the conversation back to the initial topic. "Your species has no stake in this battle... or is it the same reason why you saved me and the others?"

Ilea shook her head. "I intervene when something is happening in front of me, but no more than that. I don't think I'll go hunt down every single Taleen machine because they attack a bunch of elves far away. Elves that would attack me on sight."

"She likes the levels she's getting. Plus, they're a challenge. Her mind is simple like that," Terok whispered to the elf, quite purposely audible to Ilea.

"He's not entirely wrong," Ilea said. "I'm looking for a friend too."

Neiphato cocked his head inquisitively.

"He went missing, teleported away by one of the Taleen gates."

"I understand. Hunters use them to go into Taleen ruins. I hear that few make it back," he said, his eyes widening a moment later. "But I'm sure you will find your friend."

Ilea smiled. "No need for that. He's been missing for a while. But he's not stupid, and he's a resourceful fighter. I trust that he's alive. Do you know if there's a way to activate the gates? To use them to get to specific places? Or to find out where a gate has led?"

"I do not. I'm sorry."

"It's okay."

"You asked about my magic," Neiphato continued. "My domain... my clan. Some few are born with a gift." He paused, then waved his hand absently. "It does not matter. As soon as I reach the requirements, I will change my Class."

"What? No. What the fuck… what gift? Come on, Neiph, show me. Whatever it might be, I'll survive it… I'm pretty sure."

He was obviously uncomfortable, but she didn't let up. He'd be fighting to the death if he continued diving into Taleen dungeons after all, had been already, and his choice to go against the so-called Oracles wouldn't make for an easy life.

"I am a wood creator," he said finally.

"That's it?" she asked, confused at why he'd make that such a big deal. "I think I fought someone who had a Class like that. Pretty powerful. Why not keep it and train the Class? Your group could use a more ranged combatant."

Neiphato looked at her, then his eyes went to Terok, then back to her.

"It is about what… my clan… did. With all their powers, but specifically their wood magic. It is a cruel gift. Not one of life and creation but one of torture and death."

The way he squirmed when he said those words made Ilea think he hadn't just imagined or heard about it.

She shrugged. "That's what *they* did with it. I'm an ash creator. Do you think I just torture and kill with it?"

"You do kill a lot," Terok weighed in.

Ilea accepted that. "Fair enough. Well, the point stands. You're you, not your clan or anybody else. Do what the fuck you want, and if you have a good Class, you shouldn't give a fuck about what anyone else did with something similar. You could even do something better with it to show that you're not the same. Sorry, but in the end, it's your choice. And you should do what feels right to you."

Neiphato looked at her for a long moment before he winced at a nearby impact.

Terok held up the ladle. "Look who's back. You look fucked up. Fall into a Shredder?"

Ilea laughed at the frown that lined Elfie's face as he walked toward them. "No Shredders so far north. Haven't seen one at least," she said.

Ilea extended an ashen limb to check on him, but the elf had a barrier around himself to prevent any intrusions.

Suit yourself, old man. Old elf? Doesn't have the same ring, does it?

"What is this vile sludge you're cooking up, dwarf?" Elfie asked, stepping next to the pot and taking a sip from the ladle. Summoning different spices, he added more and more before finally producing what looked like a dead rabbit, already skinned and gutted.

Barriers appeared, slicing the rabbit into small pieces and lowering them into the stew. The smell changed immediately, still spicy and strong but interesting now instead of just overpowering.

"Cooking one of your hobbies too?" Ilea asked.

"I have dabbled with it, human. Not all elves are the same. Though I dislike the time it takes…"

He tasted the stew again before handing the ladle back to Terok.

And he never really commented on the food I gave him.

She remained with the group for dinner and then made to leave.

"Not heading back into the dungeon?" Terok asked when he saw her spread her wings.

"No," Ilea said. "Need a break and something else to fight."

"Do you plan to visit Hallowfort?"

"Maybe, not sure yet. Why?"

"I've been working on the enchantments to help free Elana, but I haven't gotten far," Terok said. "Documented the rune layers to work on it here, and I made copies too, gave them to a few people with a knack for enchantments and ancient magics. Few know these runes, but luckily Hallowfort has some pretty ancient beings, with interesting skills and knowledge to boot."

"You want me to check in on them? See if they found a solution?"

"Exactly, yeah."

"Who are we talking about? Do I know them?"

"Goliath you know. Not sure if you've met Catelyn yet. Owns a shop called the Hunter's Den."

Ilea smiled. "The cake fox. Yeah, I've met her."

"Cake fox?"

Ilea nodded mysteriously. "I'll check in with them. I'll let you know if anything came up when I return."

"Thanks, and good luck out there."

"To you as well, friend," Ilea said, then waved to the others. "And to all of you."

She hissed the most powerful hiss she could manage, eliciting hisses in return.

I do like them, she thought with a smile as she flew off toward Hallowfort.

SEVENTY

Inquisitive Fox

Ilea whistled a tune to herself as she landed near Penumra before she made her way toward Hallowfort. The town looked the same as always, except for the fact that there were two sentries standing at the end of the bridge instead of the usual one.

Ilea waved as she walked up to them, both clad in heavy plate armor. One had a massive curved blade on his back and the other a hammer whose head looked to be too heavy to lift.

Is there really anything like that in this world?

"Greetings, strong ones," she said and bowed lightly.

The guards turned toward her and bowed a little in response. "Warrior of ash."

"Hey, can I try to lift your hammer?" she asked, stepping a little closer.

The big guard looked at her for a solid ten seconds, then turned their head toward the other guard, who nodded. The hammer was handed over as if it were a mere plaything. Ilea had her auras active and was able to handle it with only a little exertion.

"Impressive," was all the Awakened said as she lifted it above her head.

Fuck, what's this made of?

She was sweating when she handed it back. "What metal is this?"

"Pure olvor. Several weight enchantments have been placed on it," the Awakened said, giving a guttural chuckle.

[Warrior – lvl 223]

"Impressive," she said with a smile. While she might be able to swing it, the weight definitely made it too unwieldy for her. *I'd like a hammer, though.*

Nodding to the two, she stepped past them when she saw the other guard's head sink in her Sphere. She turned around.

"Oh, may I check out your sword as well?"

She grinned as his mood immediately improved, handing over the big curved blade. *Fuck, these guys could be disarmed with a simple request to hold their weapons.* Then again, their arms could probably dish out some damage too.

The blade, which had a black sheen, was the lighter weapon by far and, as far as she could tell, well balanced. She tried swinging it in the air twice. Her Dexterity likely allowed for the swings to look impressive to an amateur swordsman, but the Awakened laughed when she handed it back.

"You should not use swords any time soon, ash wielder." It wasn't an insult, she was pretty sure about that.

"I don't plan to. It's a well-crafted weapon, Awakened swordsman."

"You honor me."

The Awakened bowed, and Ilea mirrored the gesture. She liked most of the Awakened she'd met so far, at least the bulky steel-obsessed ones like these guards and Goliath.

Maybe someday I'll end up just like them. Guarding some village I chose to retire in. But not for many years.

"Why are there more guards?" she asked them.

"Feynor on the move," the big guard replied.

She nodded and bowed again, leaving for the city.

And two guards instead of one would deter them? she wondered. Neither of them looked terribly fast, so a simple flight or teleportation spell would allow anybody to bypass them entirely.

She made her way to her first destination in Hallowfort, Catelyn's shop. Opening the door, she rang the bell. A minute passed before the fox appeared out of nowhere, standing on the big table situated in the center of the shop.

"Welcome to… oh, it's you! Hey, you leveled again! Still hunting knights?"

"Centurions this time," Ilea replied, still unable to identify the fox.

"I don't buy metal. Ask Goliath."

"Noted. By the way, I'll try to find some cake for you once I go back to humanland. At this point, though, that might take a long time."

Catelyn purred. "Worth waiting a thousand years for that."

"You know you could just go south and get all the cake you want," Ilea chuckled. "With all the gold you have."

"Your kind does not do well with ours, human. I'd be hunted down, this much is known."

Ilea snorted. It wasn't a real suggestion anyway. The fox seemed to be intertwined with this town too much. But she could certainly get her a place in Ravenhall or with the necromancers. Both they and Claire would probably agree to have the powerful Awakened amongst them.

"With your power, you could easily convince them otherwise. Even mine is probably enough."

"I believe your power will soon match my own. Do not underestimate the hate one species can hold for another, the hate one can hold for the unknown."

"I get it. Hey, I didn't come for a philosophical discussion. Terok told me he gave you a riddle to solve? Something with enchantments?"

Caetlyn's eyes sparkled. "Indeed. You two have spent time together."

"What's with that tone?" Ilea smiled.

"Well… perhaps an old fox has been curious as to what this ash-wielding human has been up to these past few months," Catelyn said. "Terok has tried to be vague, but he's not the best at being vague. And others have shared rumors."

Ilea arched an eyebrow.

"The Descent, a Spirit of Old, and Tremor. An interesting dungeon," Catelyn purred. "Have you found a survivor, perhaps? Of times long past?"

"Perhaps I did. Would that be interesting to an old fox?"

She purred again. "Very much. I care about things awakening near this town."

Walking around Ilea, Catelyn then appeared on the counter next to the bell, sitting up to be nearer Ilea's face.

"You are not a deceiver. If you have awoken someone from a time long past, I would like to meet them."

"To evaluate the danger?" Ilea asked, and the fox smirked.

"Yes. That as well. But first and foremost, to establish contact. If they are reasonable, they could join our community. Before the Dark Protector snatches up another potential ally for their conflict with the Feynor."

"I thought this was just a scavenger town? You're involved in this conflict then?"

Catelyn sighed. "When large factions clash, anyone in the vicinity will be dragged in regardless. We choose to be neutral, but this town could serve strategic value in a broader conflict. It could provide housing and protection, and it could potentially be viewed as a resource that another could exploit. Which, in turn, means that we have to be prepared to face what might come."

"Makes sense. I get how annoying it is to be dragged into things when all you want to do is explore ruins and fight monsters."

"I prefer managing my shop and working on my alchemy, but yes," Catelyn said. "The world outside does not stand still. It never has."

"It doesn't," Ilea agreed.

"Do you know if the being you awakened is from before the great change?"

Ilea crossed her arms. "What's the great change?"

"It is confusing… to think a people like yours, who keep records about all and everything, would not teach their children of this event. Well, your kind does not live long, I suppose.

"Thousands of years ago, the mana in the north changed. I speculate this occurred throughout the whole world. Some, coming from far away, have confirmed it, but others deny it. Many theories exist, to be sure. We Awakened profited greatly, finding many new places to dwell, and many more of us were born."

Goliath mentioned something similar, didn't he?

Ilea nodded. "The mana density changed. That's why the north is the way it is today. It was more like the Plains before this great change happened?"

"When light was no more. When the stars aligned differently," Catelyn added.

A lunar eclipse, maybe? Or a meteor or something, Ilea theorized, but it was an event from long ago. No librarian or scholar she'd talked to had ever mentioned it, but to the Awakened, it was apparently an important event.

"You were born before that?"

The fox shook her head. "No. Few who were there remain. Hence my question. Goliath is one of them... yet he dwelled in his smithy then as he does now." She chuckled. "What did you find, then, Ilea of ash? Kalin? Rhyvor? The Red Church? Or perhaps even the Old Ones?"

"I found the King and Queen of Rhyvor, Maro and Elana Invalar."

Catelyn literally burst into flames for a second before calming down again. "Rhyvor. Good. Not the worst. They are alive... Where are they? What are they doing?"

"Stuck in a dungeon until I clear out a bunch of triple-mark undead. Well, one of them is. The other one is just stuck in a room. The enchantment problem Terok gave you to solve is for her."

"Oh, so that's what it was about. Very well. I would like to meet them, see what I can do. You said triple marks?" She considered this for a moment, then shook her head. "I will not risk helping you. I hope you understand."

"I intended to kill them myself anyway."

"A dangerous challenge. But you have grown. Perhaps soon, you might be ready to face it. How can I meet them?"

"I can get you in. As long as you have a teleportation ability, but I think that's a given based on what I've seen."

"Accurate."

"So you solved the enchantment problem?"

The fox smirked, walking around her again. "Perhaps I have. Perhaps not. When would you like to leave?"

"Soon. I'd like to talk to Goliath as well, then I'll return, if that sounds alright?"

"It does. Now I'm excited for a small adventure! To meet the royal of a long-lost human kingdom. How, I wonder, did they survive? No. Do not answer. I wish to find out myself," Catelyn said and giggled.

Ilea smiled. "Anything else of note going on? Feynor are apparently on the move, whatever that means."

The fox made an irritated noise. "Ignorant creatures. Moving farther south and west with every passing month. I wish they would just stick to their territories."

"I keep hearing about these creatures. What are they, exactly, and why would they attack Hallowfort?" Ilea asked. In truth, other than Goliath, she had little reason to care about the town. Most of the inhabitants were competent fighters.

"Their physiognomy is similar to lizardmen, but with some important differences. The problem they pose is their almost fanatical belief in their own purity."

Ilea sighed. "They attack and kill anybody that isn't one of them?"

Catelyn nodded. "Basically. Usually, they stay farther north, keep to their… rituals and worship. I don't know what roused them, but in the past three years, they have been more and more active in these parts, as well as farther east and southward," the fox explained. "Well, they should not be an issue. This town is well defended."

"By you?" Ilea smirked, the fox doing the same.

"Precisely. But not just me, human. Hallowfort is old, and many of its inhabitants have lived here for hundreds of years, if not more. It is an oasis amidst the chaotic and dangerous lands of the north. Which is precisely why it could become a target. Both sides would lose people if they attacked. The dungeons take enough already."

Catelyn sighed and appeared on the table again, stretching and resting her head on her paws.

"Should you come across a war band, the town will pay you for information as well as your help in defending our territory. They will attack you one way or the other. Humans they hate most, next to dwarves and elves."

Of course they do.

"I'll keep my eyes open," Ilea said. "So the Dark Protector, Lord of Edge, is forming an army to fight them?"

"That is an interesting title. They do own a lot of sharp implements… Perhaps it is fitting," Catelyn replied. "But you are mistaken. The Dark Protector formed his army over a hundred years ago. The war against the Feynor, as well as his clearance of dungeons to make living space for us Awakened, has been going on for many decades. But recently they've been recruiting more aggressively."

"You think it's because of them that the Feynor are more active?"

"Perhaps. It is certainly part of the reason, but not all. There are many groups involved, influential beings both Awakened and friends of the

Feynor. Dwarves are supplying steel, and even humans, I suspect, are participating. A war among other species… It is a profitable endeavor."

"Any war is. Good to know I shouldn't get involved. What's your stake in all that?"

"My place is here. Hallowfort is one of the few places not torn apart by this conflict, and I intend to keep it that way. Let them have their war. As soon as it ends, there will be another. Perhaps the undead will rise and fight the Taleen. Or humans and elves will come from the south. Hallowfort will stand nonetheless."

"You're pretty confident of all this. The Taleen are focused on elven lands anyway, as far as I know," Ilea said, trying to get another angle on the story both Elfie and Neiphato had told her.

Catelyn nodded. "It is true. A gruesome battle. Yet I fear what would happen should one side prevail."

No further info, but at least she agrees.

"To speak of more mundane things, an expedition is forming," Catelyn continued. "Applications can be made in the Abyss. I believe you have been there before. To delve into the Descent, to the fifth layer and beyond. You might be interested. It is planned to be one of the most well-equipped and prepared expeditions in the last decade."

Ilea smiled. "Thanks for the tip, but I don't have a good track record with expeditions. I think I'll pass on this one."

"Your decision. I only hope more will return this time."

"How come there are still people around if so many die all the time?" Ilea asked with interest. Hallowfort was by no means deserted, but it was a rough environment.

"That is precisely what makes this town so unique. A sanctuary, if you will. For those sick of wars. Exiles, veterans, or simply beings such as yourself. Adventurers, I believe you call them. Explorers. Perhaps pioneers."

Ilea could feel the pride in her words. It reminded her of how Sulivhaan and Dagon talked about the Hand. They were the new elders now – at least until the lost ones showed up again. She didn't dislike the sentiment, nor Hallowfort itself.

Perhaps it was to the people of the north what Ravenhall was to the Plains. Sovereignty through power. The ultimate adventurer's hub, with just a little more freedom, and hopefully lack of prejudice, than most other places.

Ilea was sure Ravenhall wouldn't fall, not against Baralia, nor against Lys. She wasn't so certain of Hallowfort's future, but looking into the near-red eyes of the fox in front of her, she knew any battle for it would be vicious.

SEVENTY-ONE

Forges and Armor

Ilea juggled the two steel spheres she'd bought from Catelyn as she walked into Goliath's smithy. They were similar constructs to Elfie's fire cube. One was for water and the other for fire. Neither could really create the element, but they could siphon the necessary molecules to form them. At least, she thought it worked like that.

"The friend of ash returns. Welcome. Your power grows… I can feel it," Goliath commented, his yellow eyes sparkling with joy. "Oh, please, do refrain from using those in my smithy. The balance I cultivate is delicate." He actually sounded as worried as his ethereal whisper allowed him to be.

"Don't worry," Ilea said, putting away the spheres. "Thought I'd pop in. How are you doing?"

The smith physically recoiled, his eyes focusing on her as he mulled over her question. "How am I doing? Do you have no purpose here… other than to… care for me?"

Ilea smiled and wondered if hugging the smith would freak him into a coma. "I mean, I have some things to talk about, but isn't that what friends do sometimes?"

"I had not considered the possibility. Of being a… friend."

"How do you like it?" Ilea asked, genuinely curious.

The smith thought about it for a whole minute. As he did so, Ilea sat down on a workbench and started to eat one of Keyla's meals.

"I have not decided," Goliath said eventually, summoning a metal triangle into his hand and releasing a little bit of mist into the room.

"Sorry," she said, glancing at the food.

"Do not mind it, human. I know those of flesh cannot live without their sustenance."

Ilea smiled. "Still, I could have waited for later. Let me know if I should put it away. Another thing, by the way, are you male or female, or something else?"

"Peculiar. Humans do like to categorize, do they not? Sex is what you are describing? It holds no relevance to me. Think of me as you will."

Ilea swallowed a mouthful of food. A chili, or something close enough. Some of the veggies were unknown to her, but it tasted nice and hearty with just the right amount of spiciness.

"I found a Taleen manufacturing plant. They make Centurions there. Level three hundred, some even higher. The facility is massive… spans kilometers in each direction, and I have no idea how many floors it has. Thought you might be interested."

"That does sound intriguing. The dungeon to the northwest, I suspect. I believe Izna was the name. Too dangerous for me, I suppose. One Centurion I might face, but their numbers are higher there, are they not?"

"Yeah, hundreds. Thousands, probably. Already killed so many I've lost count. Well, I cleared the first level, and it doesn't seem like they come up there anymore, so you could check it out. The way there is dangerous too, of course. How fast can you fly? Any teleportation abilities?"

"That won't be necessary. I trust you, wielder of ash." He floated to the center of the room before a one-meter-high black obelisk appeared. "Perhaps this will finally have a use. Too long has it been."

She stood up and walked closer to it. "What is it?"

"It is a creation related to a skill of mine. A gateway, or a focus, perhaps. I may travel through it freely to any other obelisk of my creation."

"A long-range teleportation network? You know people would kill to have this ability."

"Little gain would it have for them. It is only usable by me. The range is limited too, but if my geographical memory does not deceive me, it should be possible. Should you wish for me to inspect this… facility, place this inside and I will find my way there."

Ilea nodded, but when she tried storing it in her necklace, she failed.

"I am afraid you will have to carry it."

Scratching her head, she nodded. "When I intend to go back, I'll come and grab it. Just leave it here for now, I guess. Gonna be a few days or so, alright?"

"Thank you. For such an opportunity. The Taleen manufacturing sites are well guarded, well hidden. I would cherish the chance to see one, feel it."

"I'll let you know when I've placed it inside."

"I would appreciate that."

"You can't just teleport back immediately once you've used them?"

The smith shook his head. "Once only per day."

Damn, that's much better than my skill. And I can't even place multiple anchors.

Well, I guess mine isn't restricted by distance. Otherwise, we might've been stuck in the demon realm for quite a bit longer.

"I wanted to ask something else," Ilea added. "Terok gave you a riddle of sorts? About enchantments?"

"Ah, so you *are* involved. I had thought it a possibility." A set of paper-like sheets appeared. "Here are my thoughts so far, documented to be learned from, as the dwarf requested."

"Thank you," Ilea said and took the pages. These she could store in her necklace.

Goliath held up a hand. "Oh… I forgot. Your armor. I have been working on a small gift with some of the metals you have provided."

"Oh?" Ilea grinned.

"Yes. Well, I have thought about it. Functionality is important, as are speed and practicality. Your other sets of armor, coupled with a strong metal, are the best you can get. Especially with the light weight they provide. At least for now. So, I thought instead of trying to improve on your armor, which you will inevitably destroy in a matter of months, I should make armor so cumbersome and limiting that the sheer task of wearing it will be a challenge worth completing."

Ilea wasn't sure where he was going with this when a massive two-and-a-half-meter colossus of steel appeared. Black in color and simple in design with two legs and two arms, it was all smooth and bulky. She couldn't discern any of the parts connecting to each other. Instead, it was one seamless piece of steel, with no holes for eyes and no fingers on the hands.

"Impressive… brick," she said, walking up to it and touching the thing. It towered over her as she stood there, taller even than the guardians protecting the bridge to Hallowfort. "How exactly am I supposed to use this without any connecting pieces? I won't be able to walk."

The smith's eyes glowed and sparkled. "I will let you discover the secrets this creation holds. On your own. Enjoyment like this, well, I haven't felt it for simple armor in many, many cycles."

He calls this armor…

She nodded and smiled, trusting Goliath and his experience. Somehow, she felt this armor was a more dangerous foe than the Centurions waiting for her back in the dungeon.

[Armament of Trials – Ancient Quality]

"Holy shit, it's ancient?" she said, putting it into her necklace. It actually vanished, taking up a solid ten storage points.

"Many days of labor, a high amount of quality steel, and all my expertise went into it. I will be interested in your progress," Goliath said, his dancing eyes conveying joy. Or sadistic malice. She wasn't sure.

"Thank you," she said. "I'll get the obelisk later."

* * *

On the way out, Ilea thought to check in on the expedition after she'd taken Catelyn to Maro and Elana. It was possible she could gain some rare resistances from them.

Walking through the tight alleys of Hallowfort, she quickly scanned through the levels she'd gained in the past month.

'ding' Azarinth First Hunter has reached lvl 273 – Five stat points awarded

…

'ding' Azarinth First Hunter has reached lvl 279 – Five stat points awarded

'ding' Inheritor of Eternal Ash has reached lvl 267 – Five stat points awarded

…

'ding' Inheritor of Eternal Ash has reached lvl 275 – Five stat points awarded

'ding' Destruction reaches 3rd lvl 6

'ding' Hunter Recovery reaches 3rd lvl 7

'ding' Hunter Recovery reaches 3rd lvl 8

'ding' Hunter's Sight reaches 2nd lvl 20

'ding' Veil of Ash reaches 3rd lvl 8

'ding' Ashen Wings reaches 2nd lvl 20

'ding' Embered Body Heat reaches 2nd lvl 19

'ding' Embered Body Heat reaches 2nd lvl 20

After a full month of fighting Centurions, the difficulty in leveling up third-tier skills really showed. Granted, they weren't the most difficult enemies for her to kill anymore.

'ding' Light Magic Resistance reaches lvl 3

…

'ding' Light Magic Resistance reaches lvl 16

'ding' Crystal Resistance reaches lvl 8

...

'ding' Crystal Resistance reaches lvl 15

'ding' Arcane Magic Resistance reaches lvl 17

'ding' Blast Resistance reaches lvl 19

...

'ding' Blast Resistance reaches 2nd lvl 1
Blast Resistance – 2nd lvl 1
Explosions can be an unpredictable and chaotic thing. You have survived quite an impressive one to get this skill. It will help you negate the damage ever so slightly the next time you choose to stand in one.
2nd stage: Despite common sense, you just keep on doing it. Either you should start reading safety manuals or embrace the fact you are a true explosion elemental. Your organs, bones, muscles, and skin have become partially shock-absorbent. Please stop.

...

'ding' Blast Resistance reaches 2nd lvl 4

'ding' Health Drain Resistance reaches 2nd lvl 17

'ding' Health Drain Resistance reaches 2nd lvl 18

'ding' Heat Resistance reaches 2nd lvl 11

'ding' Heat Resistance reaches 2nd lvl 12

'ding' Mana Drain Resistance reaches 2nd lvl 15

'ding' Mana Drain Resistance reaches 2nd lvl 16

'ding' Mana Drain Resistance reaches 2nd lvl 17

'ding' Mist Magic Resistance reaches lvl 18

'ding' Mist Magic Resistance reaches lvl 19

'ding' Mist Magic Resistance reaches lvl 20

'ding' Mist Magic Resistance reaches 2nd lvl 1
Mist Magic Resistance – 2nd lvl 1
Mist magic is a rare talent, found in students of the arcane adept in both wind and water magic. It is an elusive power, difficult to wield yet ultimately destructive and impossible to avoid. You have faced it and lived. This skill will help you do so again.
2nd stage: Through increasing exposure, you have learned to stop the elusive mist from passing through you.

Another resistance into the second tier. Arcane is nearly there too, it just keeps levelling. I love the north.

Of her eighty stat points, she put twenty into Wisdom and fifteen into each of Intelligence and Vitality. She also decided she wanted to keep Strength and Dexterity to at least a quarter of her main stats. So, she put fifteen points into each of those too.

Ilea smiled at her status as she entered Catelyn's shop.

Name: Ilea Spears
Unspent stat points: 0
Unspent 3rd-tier skill points [Azarinth First Hunter]: 0
Unspent 3rd-tier skill points [Inheritor of Eternal Ash]: 0

Class 1: Azarinth First Hunter – lvl 279
- Active: Destruction – 3rd lvl 6
- Active: Hunter Recovery – 3rd lvl 8
- Active: State of Azarinth – 3rd lvl 9
- Active: Blink – 3rd lvl 8
- Active: Azarinth Hunter Sphere – 2nd lvl 20
- Passive: Body of the First Hunter – 2nd lvl 20
- Passive: Azarinth Fighting – 2nd lvl 20
- Passive: Hunter's Sight – 2nd lvl 20
- Passive: Azarinth Perception – 2nd lvl 20
- Passive: Azarinth Reversal – 2nd lvl 20

Class 2: Inheritor of Eternal Ash – lvl 275
- Active: Veil of Ash – 3rd lvl 8
- Active: Form of Ash and Ember – 3rd lvl 2
- Active: Ash Creation – 3rd lvl 4
- Active: Embered Body Heat – 2nd lvl 20
- Active: Wave of Ember – 2nd lvl 20

- Passive: Ash and Ember Manipulation – 3rd lvl 3
- Passive: Ashen Wings – 2nd lvl 20
- Passive: Eyes of Ash – 2nd lvl 20
- Passive: Body of Ash – 2nd lvl 20
- Passive: Ashen Warrior – 2nd lvl 20

General Skills:
- Elos Standard language – lvl 6
- Harmony of the Drowned – lvl 1
- Heavy Archery – lvl 4
- Identify – lvl 7
- Meditation – 2nd lvl 19
- Veteran – lvl 6
- Arcane Magic Resistance – lvl 17
- Blast Resistance – 2nd lvl 4
- Blood Magic Resistance – lvl 8
- Corrosion Resistance – lvl 3
- Crystal Resistance – lvl 15
- Curse Resistance – 2nd lvl 2
- Dark Magic Resistance – lvl 1
- Earth Magic Resistance – lvl 5
- Fear Resistance – lvl 5
- Health Drain Resistance – 2nd lvl 18
- Heat Resistance – 2nd lvl 12
- Ice Resistance – lvl 15
- Light Magic Resistance – lvl 16
- Lightning Resistance – 2nd lvl 6
- Mana Drain Resistance – 2nd lvl 17
- Mental Resistance – 2nd lvl 13
- Mist Magic Resistance – 2nd lvl 1
- Pain Tolerance – 2nd lvl 4
- Poison Resistance – 2nd lvl 9
- Silver Magic Resistance – lvl 1
- Void Magic Resistance – lvl 7
- Water Resistance – 2nd lvl 1
- Wind Resistance – 2nd lvl 1

Status:
Vitality: 785
Endurance: 233
Strength:207
Dexterity:208
Intelligence:781
Wisdom:784

Health: 7754/7850
Stamina: 2314/2330
Mana: 7840/7840

"Ready to leave?" the fox asked.

"Yeah. Can you fly, or should I hold you?" Ilea asked.

The fox looked up at her and started floating. "I do not mind either way. Would *you* like to hold me, human?"

"I would," Ilea said and grabbed her, storing her armored gauntlets to feel the soft fur.

Glad it's not hard as steel or something, she thought with a smile before walking out of the shop and spreading her wings, taking the two of them toward Tremor.

* * *

Elana stared at Catelyn with cold eyes. "What did you bring this time?" The question was directed at Ilea.

She rolled her eyes. "Catelyn, store owner in Hallowfort." Gesturing to the queen, she added, "Elana Invalar, Queen of Rhyvor. Have fun, you two."

Walking over to Maro, she greeted him with a wave.

"I would wave back… but you know," the king said.

"Funny."

"Terribly. Hey, you brought an Awakened? Never seen a fox… and at level three twenty-eight. Not bad. Did he force you to bring him?"

"It's a female. And no, Terok asked her to help with the enchantments. Either she's going to suddenly attack and slaughter you or she'll actually provide some help. It's fifty-fifty."

Maro laughed. "Well, I hope she doesn't go crazy. Most Awakened I've met have been more reasonable than humans."

"Hey, I was wondering. Some of my General Skills are getting close to the end of the second tier—"

Maro interrupted her. "No idea. Mine have been at second and twenty for years and years. If you find anything out, do let me know. It's been driving me crazy. Even now at three hundred…"

"Ah, that sucks. I'll let you know, but if you're not there yet, I'll get you out before that anyway."

He laughed at that. "You have been leveling fast. Don't stumble on the last steps."

"You mean it would be a shame if you had to stay down here any longer than necessary," she suggested with a smirk.

"I mean, yes, that too. But now I have a fox to talk to. Hello there," he said, his gaze moving toward Catelyn, who had walked over to him with Elana in tow.

"Greetings, King of Rhyvor." The fox bowed. "Long has it been since your kingdom ruled in these lands. I am Catelyn, an Awakened, as you surely know. I am a long-standing member of the council of Hallowfort, a town founded long ago for scavengers and exiles seeking power and adventure in the north. Lands, I must add, which have changed greatly since you have walked them."

She looked at Elana and then Ilea before continuing. "While you have been down here all these years, have you been conscious of time and waiting to escape?"

Maro chuckled. "Greetings, Catelyn, one touched by fire. No. My wife was mostly lucid, but not me. It feels like a couple of months have passed, but not more. I must ask… does your fur feel as nice as it looks?"

Ilea gave him a thumbs-up while Catelyn sighed. "It does," the fox confirmed. "The lands you once governed are no more. If you want to build a new kingdom amongst humans, I suggest you travel south. You are welcome to join us in Hallowfort, but know that survival, even for one of your strength, is not guaranteed anymore in what once was called Rhyvor, later Kalin, and still later part of the Red Church's territory."

Maro looked at Elana, but her gaze was locked on the fox. "I did what I could for this kingdom. I am done with being a king, though many questions remain, including relating to the circumstances I find myself in. Perhaps you might be of help in that regard. My wife will have her own questions. Should you help destroy the Kingsguards and the knights keeping me bound to this place, I will be in your debt."

Catelyn shook her head. "I will not risk myself for you. I apologize. Though I believe you have found a capable warrior to help you along, charming one."

Charming one? What the fuck?

"Certainly. Then I will wait for her to grow in strength."

Elana spoke up then. "Terok informed you about the enchantments. You have come to solve this problem? I will help where I can in Hallowfort, should you cooperate with me."

"Now that I see the enchantments here, yes, I might be able to help with those, one shrouded in mist. I must know, however, will you challenge our sovereignty?"

"No. These lands are lost to me. I have been trapped in these halls for too long. I wish to learn what happened to our kingdom, our people. At least, what remains to be learned."

Her voice cracked a little at the mention of Rhyvor and its people, perhaps a glimpse at the real Elana hiding behind her mask. Or a calculated move. Ilea didn't know. Either way, she was pretty sure Catelyn knew what she was doing.

"I will aid you, Queen Invalar," the fox replied promptly, to Ilea's surprise.

SEVENTY-TWO

Resistance Dance

"Why do you think she agreed so easily?" Ilea asked Maro.

On the other side of the room was a bright red glow, where Catelyn was working on the runes, supported by Elana. There was an echoing crack, and the glow intensified a moment later. Ilea saw that the white stone of the wall was already starting to melt.

Are they going to melt a tunnel or something?

It did look like Elana would soon be free to explore and do what she wanted here in the north.

Maybe we are unleashing something dangerous after all.

Maro looked at the glow. "I don't think she was acting. You know, as cold as she got in the end, she cared. She really did. For Rhyvor... for everyone. Perhaps it resonated with the Awakened. She is a leader of a settlement too and likely came here to ensure we are no danger to her people. Though Elana would never admit as much, perhaps they're quite similar... her and the fox."

Ilea smiled. "Well, I'd better get going. Can't reach three hundred by talking to you."

"Wait," Maro said. "Something has been bothering me. I know you wouldn't want to run errands like this, but..." He grimaced, and Ilea saw real pain in the expression. She waited for the king to continue. "An ancient friend of mine, Gadrian, I... When Tremor was attacked, he would've been in Lisburg. I just... you know, I've been thinking about it and wanted to know... if anything remains."

"You think he's still alive?"

"I doubt it... and if he was, he wouldn't be there anymore. Just... it was a beautiful town, vineyards on hills as far as the eye could see. Charming buildings, and the most intricate, beautiful fountain you could ever imagine. A river flowing through it all."

He continued in a more subdued voice. "You know, Tremor was always bustling. People came together here – the government, the nobles, the parties, everything. It was all here. When I sought some quiet, I would go to Lisburg. I simply dared hope that... maybe a part of it remained."

The man paused before he spoke again. "You could take Terok. I also mentioned this to him, and he seemed interested."

"I'll check it out, Maro. Catelyn will know how to get there, or to whatever it has become," Ilea said.

It wasn't easy to see the usually confident and charming king in such a state. He'd lost everything, all his people and his kingdom. Thinking it all over in the last months alone with Elana couldn't have been easy. All the what ifs, the possibilities, the unknowns.

"I hope Lisburg is still around, in some way," she finally said.

"I hope so too."

* * *

Having established Lisburg's location, Ilea made her way back to Hallowfort. Catelyn didn't join her for the time being, wanting to finish the tunnel as quickly as possible.

Ilea didn't know why the fox prioritized getting the queen out, but she did. Perhaps the fox wanted to make a good impression or simply didn't want to get on the royals' bad side. She was probably powerful enough to deal with them individually, but a king and queen brought more to the table than just levels.

Back in Hallowfort, Ilea quickly checked the Abyss and found it more packed than the times she'd visited before. At least one patron was sitting at every table, some drinking, others playing cards. Still others were showing off their magic or weapons. There were Awakened, dwarves, machines she assumed had dwarves inside, as well as some rare humans. One human, in particular, let out a gasp when Ilea spotted her.

Jonna, isn't it? The battle-healer I fought.

Jonna couldn't get a word out before Ilea blinked beside their table.

"Hey," Ilea said with a smile under her helmet.

Krentin stayed calm, but Ilea could tell his muscles had tensed a little and his breathing was a little quicker.

"Warrior!"

Loud laughter came from the direction of the bar, and Ilea looked over to see Hana the lizard woman walking toward the table with four beverages.

"Joining the expedition?" Ilea asked.

"If you're looking for a team, we're not interested," Krentin said.

"Not exactly. I'm looking for people to train resistances with. How would you like to blast me with some of your magic?"

"Are you mocking us?" he asked, his features distorting into something Ilea couldn't even begin to guess at.

Hana sat down and started drinking her ale. "I don't think she is, Krentin. This is how she is."

"Why would you trust us, then? I could kill you at any moment, take back what's ours," Krentin said with narrowed eyes. The other two at the table were silent, tense.

Ilea shrugged. "I'm pretty sure I could escape if you tried anything. Plus, you'd get magic training against a real foe. The whole team could join in. Maybe this time you'd do better."

"We have an expedition to plan, human. Not interested," the mage said.

"Well, your loss. I'm sure I'll find some people to train with. Good luck on your expedition," she said and meant it, winking at Hana, who smiled at her. Ilea noted that the healer looked at the lizard woman and then at her with a frown on her face.

* * *

Returning to the bar, Ilea waited until Haiden showed up. The cat person nodded to her as he put some bottles away.

"Warrior of ash, you return. Stronger yet again, I presume?"

"A little. When's the expedition planned to leave?"

"Couple days, perhaps a week. It depends on the leaders. They would surely have you join if you're interested."

Ilea shook her head. "I'm engaged elsewhere at the moment. What I'm looking for are new resistances."

"I see. Well, I'm sure some would benefit from the opportunity. Let me inform them. I'm sure you'll have a queue by the end of the hour."

Haiden wasn't kidding. The news spread quickly, and Ilea soon found herself down in the city with a bunch of men and women at level two hundred, or close enough, ready to smash her.

It's not what it sounds like, she thought to herself, looking at the shady, geared, and armored figures before her.

"Just attack me," she said, replacing her armor with casual clothes.

* * *

Ilea spent the next three days training non-stop with the expedition team. More of them joined as time went on. In the end, even Krentin showed up to send some spells her way. It was a good change from hunting Centurions yet not so different from her Miststalker training.

On the third day, Ilea healed up and put on her Stonehammer steel armor again. Some of the adventurers lingered for a while before they joined up with the rest of the expedition back in the Abyss. Ilea joined them and got herself a bottle of ale from Haiden.

"Heard you've been at it for three days straight?" he said, arching an eyebrow.

She nodded, opening the bottle with her ash before taking a sip.

"Did they not ask you to join the expedition after all that?"

"No. I suppose my level intimidates them," she said, taking another sip.

Haiden chuckled. "Higher than the expedition leads… well, you certainly left an impression when you went and killed those Blue Reapers. Didn't think you'd advance so quickly. You're making a name for yourself in Hallowfort."

"Not sure how I feel about that," Ilea smiled, then turned to watch the expedition team. "Hey, they're actually leaving. I hope some of them survive."

She lifted her bottle to cheer them along. Some of them looked her way and nodded or gestured back in some way.

Haiden smiled. "These aren't similar to your human expeditions. They're well prepared, composed of veterans."

"Well prepared for what they know. Just like those human expeditions you mentioned. Well, I've stayed here long enough. See you around, Haiden."

"Good luck on your travels," she heard him murmur, his attention on the departing expedition. He probably knew many of them.

I do hope they make it back, she thought, thinking back to her first Taleen dungeon, the Praetorians in the throne room. She shook her head.

Making her way out of the Abyss and out of Hallowfort, she quickly checked the progress she had made in regard to her resistances.

'ding' Arcane Magic Resistance reaches lvl 18

…

'ding' Arcane Magic Resistance reaches 2nd lvl 1
Wielding the true arcane is a rare and powerful talent only accessible to a few. Raw energy tears not just at flesh and bone but at the magical structure and minds of whoever faces it. Its red glow turns purple the more refined it is. This skill shall help you counter masters of the arcane.
2nd stage: Your flow of mana has been ruptured many times by the raw form of magic, making it substantially more resistant to both adept mages and natural occurrences of the true arcane.

'ding' Blast Resistance reaches 2nd lvl 5

'ding' Blood Magic Resistance reaches lvl 9

...

'ding' Blood Magic Resistance reaches lvl 14

'ding' Corrosion Resistance reaches lvl 4

...

'ding' Corrosion Resistance reaches lvl 13

'ding' Crystal Resistance reaches lvl 16

...

'ding' Crystal Resistance reaches lvl 18

'ding' Dark Magic Resistance reaches lvl 2

...

'ding' Dark Magic Resistance reaches lvl 12

'ding' Earth Magic Resistance reaches lvl 6

...

'ding' Earth Magic Resistance reaches lvl 16

'ding' Ice Resistance reaches lvl 16

'ding' Ice Resistance reaches 2nd lvl 1
You have endured the biting cold of ice and lived to tell the tale. One of the deadliest climates and magics will now be less dangerous to you with this skill.
2nd stage: Freezing temperatures no longer affect your body. It is still not advised to jump in front of flying ice lances or to anger the spirits.

'ding' Ice Resistance reaches 2nd lvl 2

'ding' Light Magic Resistance reaches lvl 17

'ding' You have learned the General Skill Wood Magic Resistance – lvl 1

A connection made from a mage to nature has allowed this talent to take root. Facing the force of nature, you grow more accustomed to its effects, your body more resilient to the magic of the forest.

'ding' You have learned the General Skill Dust Magic Resistance – lvl 1 Dangerous and elusive magic that answers to those few who seek its complexity and understand its beauty. You have faced a mage of dust and lived, preparing you for the next confrontation, should it come to pass.

'ding' You have learned the General Skill Death Magic Resistance – lvl 1 Common in the deepest and most depraved parts of the world, the magic of death itself seeks nothing other than to destroy, to rot and kill. It is difficult to survive, but to someone like you, what is death but another challenge?

'ding' Death Magic Resistance reaches lvl 2

...

'ding' Death Magic Resistance reaches lvl 5

Contrary to expectations, the sensation of death magic was very similar to the feeling she got from Health Drain spells, except in this case, her health didn't go anywhere – it was simply destroyed. She noted it to be more potent, actively burning away her life force and body, but in a training scenario and against her healing, it was just another drop in the bucket.

She was already familiar with wood magic, and dust magic reminded her a lot of her own ash magic, though the mage who'd used it wasn't particularly creative, mainly just sending massive streams of dust her way.

* * *

Ilea flew back to the Centurion factory. While she wasn't particularly enthused about fighting them anymore, she was still getting experience, and there were simply more enemies there than elsewhere. She was also slowly clearing out the machines and would hopefully have something to show for it in the end. She set up Goliath's obelisk as well and informed him a day later.

Taking a break after a long fight, Ilea lazily looked over to the gathering energy near the black obelisk, dark smoke rising as she enjoyed a warm lava bath. A moment later, Goliath appeared next to the steel structure. He opened his eyes and looked around, the two golden pinpricks dancing with joy.

"Human of ash... you did not lie. A marvelous place, an outstanding smell... The mana is beautiful, deep and resonating."

She looked at him and smiled. "Well, knock yourself out. There are Centurions and probably worse below, though, so make sure to stay on this layer. Stray at your own risk. I'll try to have my fights reasonably far away from here."

"A generous gesture," he said and bowed, going on to touch one of the forges. "I will need time to study this... an incredible facility... truly, a wonder."

The smith completely ignored her afterward, floating to one machine and then another, dipping his hands into molten steel and adding mana to random enchantments.

Ilea remembered she hadn't tried out his armor yet blinking to a sufficiently large open space, then promptly summoning the humongous thing with her inside it. The first thing she noticed was that she couldn't really move. Not only the limbs of the armor but also her own arms and legs. The whole thing was a tight fit. She was impressed the smith knew her proportions so well after simply using a mold to create her sets of armor.

The next thing she noticed was her lack of sight. Her eyes were obviously unable to penetrate the thick steel, but her Sphere also seemed to be having difficulties getting through. She did have a vague idea about her surroundings, but it definitely felt muffled, subdued.

Her auras didn't help her in the slightest. Even with her enhanced strength, she was unable to move any part of the thing even an inch. Sacrificing five hundred health, she tried again but still found it impossible. There was no space to create any ash. Blinking, she found she reappeared outside the armor rather than it moving with her.

As if the skill knows I can't use it... or the fact that it's just a massive piece of steel.

Giving up on it for now, she put the armor back into her necklace and decided to try again once she'd gotten stronger or had anything else to try.

Wait, there is something...

Summoning the armor again, she used Embered Body Heat to make herself as hot as possible. This time, something did happen. Tiny runes lit up within the armor, adding to the light coming from her Form of Ash and Ember.

So heat can do something, at least.

Trying to add mana didn't do anything, the enchantments either rejecting it or simply ignoring her intention. Sighing, she gave up again, still unable to move at all or find out anything about the runes.

A little annoyed by the immovable hunk of steel, she continued with her daily business of destroying killer machines.

By now, the battles had blurred into each other. Days and weeks passed as she fought, slowly getting her skills and Classes closer to three hundred. With every level up, the fights became a little easier, ended a little faster. When she reached two eighty first in her Azarinth Class and then in her

Inheritor Class, she unlocked one more third-tier skill in each, further speeding up the process.

After a long while in the factory, she decided that the Centurions were simply not challenging enough to get her the rest of the way in any sort of reasonable time, or at all, with how little experience she seemed to be getting from them at this point. So, she checked her advancements, said a quick goodbye to the still-entranced Goliath, and made her way out of the dungeon.

As she headed out, she reviewed her progress. For her first third-tier skill at two eighty, she decided on Azarinth Fighting. It was purely Body Enhancement and provided her with one of the highest buffs she currently had. She couldn't really think of a reasonable third-tier skill, but the simple fact that it was such a good skill to begin with made her prefer it immediately.

Azarinth Perception enhanced, well, her perception. It too was purely Body Enhancement but didn't provide an immediate damage bonus. Azarinth Reversal was also interesting, but for the time being, she'd decided on Azarinth Fighting.

'ding' Azarinth Fighting reaches 3rd lvl 1
Passive: Azarinth Fighting – 3rd lvl 1:
You are familiar with the fighting style of Azarinth. Damage inflicted with your own body and related skills is 95.5% [477.5%] higher.
2nd stage: Getting used to fighting in close quarters, your reaction time is increased to accommodate your increasing speed and control.
3rd stage: Azarinth Fighting consists of more than offense alone. A true Azarinth Healer knows when to stand and let an enemy strike. You gain knowledge about sustained injuries and damage from incoming attacks as they happen.
Category: Body Enhancement

Ashen Warrior was the equivalent of her Azarinth Fighting, which ultimately had made her decide to get it to the third tier as well – as soon as her second Class reached two eighty.

'ding' Ashen Warrior reaches 3rd lvl 1
Passive: Ashen Warrior – 3rd lvl 1:
You are familiar with the fighting style of Ash. Damage inflicted with your own body and while shrouded in Ash is 70.5% [352.5%] higher.
2nd stage: Shroud your weapons in ash to produce various effects. Shrouded weapons deal additional damage. Affected by Ash and Ember Manipulation.
3rd stage: Your mastery of Ashen Warrior allows for more efficient movement. Reduces stamina consumption by a static 25%.
Category: Body Enhancement

'ding' Azarinth First Hunter has reached lvl 280 – Five stat points awarded

...

'ding' Azarinth First Hunter has reached lvl 290 – Five stat points awarded

'ding' Inheritor of Eternal Ash has reached lvl 276 – Five stat points awarded

...

'ding' Inheritor of Eternal Ash has reached lvl 288 – Five stat points awarded

'ding' Destruction reaches 3rd lvl 7

'ding' Destruction reaches 3rd lvl 8

'ding' Hunter Recovery reaches 3rd lvl 9

...

'ding' Hunter Recovery reaches 3rd lvl 12

'ding' State of Azarinth reaches 3rd lvl 10

'ding' Blink reaches 3rd lvl 9

'ding' Azarinth Fighting reaches 3rd lvl 2

'ding' Azarinth Fighting reaches 3rd lvl 3

'ding' Veil of Ash reaches 3rd lvl 9

'ding' Form of Ash and Ember reaches 3rd lvl 3

'ding' Form of Ash and Ember reaches 3rd lvl 4

'ding' Ash Creation reaches 3rd lvl 5

'ding' Ash and Ember Manipulation reaches 3rd lvl 4

'ding' Identify reaches lvl 8

'ding' Meditation reaches 2nd lvl 20

'ding' Health Drain Resistance reaches 2nd lvl 19

'ding' Health Drain Resistance reaches 2nd lvl 20

'ding' Mana Drain Resistance reaches 2nd lvl 18

'ding' Mana Drain Resistance reaches 2nd lvl 19

'ding' Mana Drain Resistance reaches 2nd lvl 20

'ding' Mist Magic Resistance reaches 2nd lvl 2

...

'ding' Mist Magic Resistance reaches 2nd lvl 5

At the dungeon exit, Ilea informed Terok and the elves of her intention to return to Tremor. They agreed to move to Tremor to train with the knights instead. With them growing in level too, the Guardians didn't provide enough experience anymore, the group running into the same problem as Ilea had with the Centurions, and were also unable to face larger groups of the higher-leveled machines.

SEVENTY-THREE

Azarinth First Hunter

"Alright. Let's see how this goes," Ilea said to herself as she stepped into the dark zone of the Tremor dungeon.

Compared to last time, she now had a way to gauge the damage the area's denizens would deal, a way to deal a powerful blow enhanced by her third-tier auras, and far more stats and resources to play with. She still didn't think it feasible to face two or three of the knights, though she'd give it a shot.

Summoning a little flask Terok had given her, she uncorked it and sniffed the yellow liquid inside. It was just paint. Something to mark the enemies she would fight. If they couldn't regenerate at all, she supposed damaging them sufficiently and fleeing was still a viable option, as long as she could find and fight the same enemy again.

The approach might have worked back when she'd first encountered the undead – she simply hadn't thought to try it. With her Azarinth Fighting in the third tier, the insane damage they dealt would hopefully be somewhat easier to deal with. Plus, with her third-tier recovery, it would merely be a minor inconvenience, even if she was literally cut in half. As long as she had mana to heal.

The alleys smelled terrible, the stone of both streets and houses more susceptible to the spread of rot and fungus. She was pretty far in already but had found no enemies to fight as of yet.

I wonder if the undead knights and Soul Rippers fight each other…

If they did, then they were either incredibly evenly matched or the monsters somehow replenished or repopulated. After such a long time, there had to be an explanation. The missing parts on most undead she'd encountered suggested they weren't on good terms with… well, something.

Did they each have their own territories and respect them? She doubted that, given that the undead knights were mindless, ravenous beasts.

They don't go into the higher parts of the city though.

Perhaps Maro had an explanation. Maybe they still followed some of the commands they had abided by in life, or maybe they disliked the necromantic energy coming from the palace.

A monster finally appeared a couple of minutes later, walking leisurely toward her down the open street. Part of its abdomen was missing, seemingly removed cleanly, with no sign of tearing, cuts, or ragged edges. Its armor was dented, bruised, rusted, or outright missing in parts, and it dragged its dulled sword along the ground.

The scraping noise was the only thing audible in the vicinity. As if announcing its presence. A challenge, of sorts, to anyone that would stand in its way. *Or perhaps a plea,* Ilea thought. Her auras flared to life, ash surrounding her as she waited for the monster to notice her.

[Undead Rose Knight – lvl ???]

Smiling at the information, Ilea uncorked the little bottle and doused her hand in the yellow liquid. *You're just what I want.*

The screech that came from the creature rattled through her very bones, yet it didn't paralyze her. Three quick, heavy steps brought the undead upon her, its sword clasped in both hands as its strike came down. Ilea felt the danger, felt that the hit would dent her helmet, crush her skull, incapacitate her.

She stepped aside, stone exploding as the blade came to an abrupt stop, buried in the ground. A kick from the undead followed, making her spin before her hand landed on the knight's shoulder. Ilea smirked as she left a yellow handprint behind – barely visible in her Sphere, but it was enough.

As the sword rushed at her again, Ilea blinked away, the attack too quick to dodge. When she reappeared, the knight had already leaped her way. A thrust, a feint, grazed against her arm, the real strike following right after. She dodged before driving a fist into the creature's vulnerable stomach.

Her mana intrusion rushed into him, ashen limbs extending behind her as the knight moved to deflect the blows. It gave her enough time to dodge his next attack, avoiding the strike that would have ripped off her legs, armor and all.

The knight was on her again, anticipating her dodge and smashing his elbow into her chest. Ilea, knowing the damage would be manageable, didn't blink, saving the skill for an emergency. The attack left her breathless, her chest plate denting inward as her bones groaned in protest.

Flying backward, she spread her wings to stop herself, twirling to the side when the knight's sword came flying toward her. He followed right after, landing next to her. Fists moved quickly, Ilea using her fighting skills and experience to deflect most of the blows, but her gauntlets were dented with each strike, her muscles below damaged and bones cracking.

She blinked as she saw the sword coming at her from behind, immediately healing her injuries. She watched the knight catch the blade casually, walking toward her with stumbling steps.

You can do this.

Strike after strike, Ilea weaved around the sword, taking hits where necessary as her ashen limbs delivered more and more damage, using every opening to get damage in herself with her fists. Knowing which attacks were feints made the fight possible, but the thing's sheer speed and power still occasionally overwhelmed her.

When the knight suddenly let go of his sword in the middle of a strike, his fist moved too fast for her even to blink. A faint feeling of danger washed through her brain before her head rocked back, nose broken and teeth ripped out.

Blinking into a nearby ruined homestead, Ilea switched out her helmet and used a chunk of mana to heal herself. The sword crashed through the wall behind her a mere second later, Ilea rolling out of the way before the knight landed next to her, a kick sending her through the opposite wall.

She managed to keep her arms in front of her, her arms breaking but protecting her core. Healing them slowly, she spread her wings in the air outside the house. The knight followed without pause, pouncing onto the top of the long-empty cottage. Sensing the attack coming, Ilea flew down, the blade rushing by like a projectile fired from a ballista.

No wonder they don't need a bow and arrow.

Ilea rushed down to engage when a second blade made her blink. *Here we go.* She used her momentum to land on the knight with a kick, pushing him backward as she sent destructive mana through him.

His arms moved quickly, grabbing onto her leg before she could get away. Ilea braced herself as the knight swung her, smashing her through a stone chimney as her leg strained from the force, nearly ripped clean from its socket.

A second knight landed on the roof. She saw the blades rushing back to their owners, frantically kicking with her free leg as ash spread around her. Ilea sacrificed a thousand health to enhance her power, kicking twice before finally wriggling free.

She blinked, avoiding the swords as she reappeared thirty meters away. Her eyes opened wide as she noticed the sword spinning her way. Her wings spread, but before they could even materialize, the blade sliced into her, cutting through her armor and flesh, stopping halfway through her spine.

As Ilea's wings flapped, her limbs started going numb as her blood and guts streamed out of the nasty wound. She still had her perception though, dodging the second blade that came her way as she sped toward the dungeon's higher section.

Can't properly heal with the blade in…

She twirled in the air, letting the second blade slam into a spire of crumbling stone. Ilea had disabled her pain, but when the first sword was ripped out of her to return to its owner, she couldn't help but yelp. Blood and innards filled the air, her wings the only thing still carrying her limp body onward.

Ilea's vision was getting blurry, but her Sphere was crystal clear. Storing her destroyed armor, she used eight hundred mana to heal herself, feeling returning to her arms and legs immediately as her spine reformed, her organs regenerated, and the two parts of her nearly separated body came together again. A fresh set of armor appeared right in time to deflect a new thrust.

Relentless bast—

She couldn't finish the thought, the second knight leaping from a rooftop next to her before she blinked away. She dove between two buildings to gain a second to breathe.

Don't get grabbed.

She blinked inside a house seconds before the monsters followed, quick and silent. The room was in near complete darkness, Ilea's fiery buff the only thing shining through the openings in her helmet and the thin joints of her armor.

Healing mana flowed through her as she sacrificed more health into her third-tier State of Azarinth. Moving toward the wall, Ilea tried getting the knights into an awkward position, their huge statures and weapons working in her favor in the cramped confines of the room.

Ilea's ashen limbs continued to deal damage, but she didn't know which one knight was marked, and there was no time to check. Their swords cut through the walls and crashed into the ceiling and floor.

Ilea jumped and rolled through their attacks, ashen limbs delivering damage as she spread her ash and used reversed reconstruction to add to their suffering. Thanks to her skill's second tier, she could keep her own healing up. As long as the knights were using their swords, she was semi-sure they wouldn't try to grab her.

Dodging one of their blades opened her up to the second enemy, its weapon crashing into her head before she could dispel her ash connection to it and blink. The sword cut through her helmet and lodged inside her head – then the monster *pulled*.

A cold realization spread through her as she felt the tendons in her neck separate, her spine holding for a moment before it too was torn asunder. Fear like nothing she had felt before surged through her soul before her head was ripped from her shoulders and tossed aside by the creature's blade.

Oh fuck.

A weird sensation spread through her, her Sphere and awareness splitting. She saw her body through her Sphere, saw it both as her center and away from her. The one eye that hadn't been crushed looked on as her body was kicked through the nearby wall.

Eye closing, she focused on her body and sacrificed a thousand points of mana to restore her head. Her awareness returned to normal as she blinked upward to avoid another strike.

No helmet. Fuck.

It was then that she decided to retreat.

Ilea made sure to avoid blinking as she flew toward the higher sections of the dungeon, keeping it available for an emergency as she dodged the thrown blades whenever they appeared behind her.

As she moved higher and higher, shivers wracked her body. She touched her face with shaking hands, checking her head with her Sphere as she sped up. She could hear her heart pounding in her chest.

All she could think of was the sound her neck had made when her head was ripped off.

* * *

The suns were shining through the crack in the cave. Ilea was angrily eating her food, conscious of every movement of her jaw, every gulp. Her movements suddenly stopped, the feeling of her split awareness flashing through her mind.

She shook her head, taking another bite and trying to focus on the taste. Ilea barely noticed the tears dripping down from her chin, noting instead the salty taste of the food.

You can do this, she reminded herself, Meditation flowing through her. *They can take your head, but they can't kill you. Never. Don't give in to fear.*

The memory of a scythe piercing through her stomach came up, but she pushed it away and slowed her breathing.

'ding' Fear Resistance reaches lvl 6

Are you fucking kidding me?

Ilea felt four different emotions at the same time. What came out was a soft chuckle.

Maybe I'm going mad.

The ridiculousness of it all was overwhelming. Healing back a lost arm was one thing, but she'd lost her head, her brain, her eyes, her nose.

And then the system, gods, or whatever the fuck it is mocks me with a fucking resistance skill...

As a shudder went through her, healing and meditation flowed through her body, calming her down. She was pretty sure that without them, even with all her experience, she'd be sobbing in a corner somewhere.

My perception skill didn't activate… so I had enough health?

A weird notion. Perhaps her ability to heal even fatal injuries made the skill less useful, only activating after sufficiently high health loss alone.

"Motherfuckers. I'll rip off your limbs and heads, then stuff those rusty swords up your asses."

The words came out hollow, but her gaze focused, the slight shaking in her hands fading with each passing minute.

There will always be another drake, she said to herself, over and over.

Finally, an unknown amount of time later, the suns having set and the city now clad in darkness, Ilea stood up. She stored the empty box of food in her necklace and put on a fresh helmet.

Retreat when a second one appears. I get it. And don't lose your head.

She didn't smile at her own joke, even though it was terrible.

Ilea clasped her neck with both hands and opened her mouth before letting a scream rip out of her, rippling across the silent ruins. She spread her wings before she jumped off the roof, her target the marked Rose Knight. Her eyes were focused, her body poised, her mouth a thin line.

Landing beyond the ruined wall that marked the beginning of the dark zone, Ilea started her search. She had the scent of the yellow paint, so her Hunter's Sight would lead her to the target. Noticing her perception focus on her own right hand time and time again, Ilea switched out the gauntlet before continuing her search.

I will find you.

It took an hour, but she picked up the scent, a grin blooming on her face.

I will kill you.

SEVENTY-FOUR

Helpful Advice

The blade cut through her Veil, scratching against her shoulder before it smashed into the floor. Ilea's fist lashed out into the stomach of the undead, and it replied in kind, sending Ilea spinning through the air as she healed her damaged rib cage.

The color was still there. The dents and scratches on his armor were still there. When she touched him, even if he resisted, she knew through her healing that the damage had remained.

They couldn't heal. At least not to a degree noticeable to Ilea. It wasn't unwinnable. As long as she didn't die and retreated once more of them joined, it was a matter of time.

She moved in again, ignoring a more defensive approach as her body slid past the blade, the dull weapon only cutting air. Ilea screamed as her fist smashed into the beast, her third-tier auras working together, five hundred health sacrificed. Her arm was wreathed in flame and ash, red runes and fiery lines glowing from the cracks and ripped-out pieces of her armor.

The strike landed with an ear-shattering crash, the knight flying through the wall behind him and into the warehouse beyond. In the meantime, Ilea healed the broken bones in her fingers and the light damage her arm had sustained.

Breathing out, she took the next seconds to meditate, to calm herself. Barely two seconds had passed when the undead came charging out from within the rubble again. Ilea jumped to the side, rolling before she turned and dodged its quick slashes, slowing him down with her ash as well as she could.

She tried to trip him, tried to send ash into his eyes, nose, and mouth, tried to rip the blade out of his grasp, but nothing worked. The undead was too powerful. Like a force of dark magic itself, it moved untiring, unrelenting.

And Ilea stood against it, cold eyes and a grin on her face as she deflected and dodged its attacks, getting in damage wherever she could, healing the wounds that every strike from the monster caused.

Ilea fought on, her whole being focused on the enemy. An opening showed itself, and she sent five hundred health into her third-tier aura, the ensuing punch sending the knight stumbling back. All eight ashen limbs drove into his neck, finally slicing through the rusted steel of its armor and rotten flesh.

The knight screeched, and Ilea screamed in turn. He lifted its sword, slashing from above with enough power in the blow to cut her in half. Ilea blinked, just half a meter to the left, and the blade passed by as her Azarinth aura once again came to life. She smashed her fist into the knight's head as her eight ashen limbs finished cutting through his neck.

Ilea blinked away and watched the undead sink to his knees, his neck sliced open and his head sitting at an unnatural angle. The knight fell to the ground with a clattering sound, movements ceasing as Ilea too sank to her knees. She was down to five hundred mana and a third of her health, though both were quickly recovering.

"I said I'd kill you."

Hearing noises nearby, Ilea spread her wings and ascended, flying away from another knight already entering the square. The notification was bright in her mind, the smile on her face vicious.

She had won.

She could kill them.

'ding' You have defeated [Undead Rose Knight – lvl 512] – For defeating an enemy two hundred twenty or more levels above your own, bonus experience is granted.

'ding' Azarinth First Hunter has reached lvl 291 – Five stat points awarded

'ding' Inheritor of Eternal Ash has reached lvl 289 – Five stat points awarded

'ding' Inheritor of Eternal Ash has reached lvl 290 – Five stat points awarded

Ilea immediately spent the points on Vitality, her beheading fresh on her mind.

'ding' Ash Creation reaches 3rd lvl 6

'ding' Ashen Warrior reaches 3rd lvl 2

* * *

Several days passed while Ilea focused on finding and fighting the undead Rose Knights scattered in the lower parts of the city. Marking them with colors turned out to be helpful but also showed how few of them there actually were. Knowing the distance from which they noticed battle made them even scarier.

Forcing herself to abide by her self-imposed rule to face one and only one undead at a time, Ilea slowly whittled them down. The damage to their armor as well as their lack of connection to Maro made such an approach possible. Still, Terok had informed her that if she waited too long, they might recover health as well. Just like any monster or human would. Simply at a rather slow pace.

Another one down, Ilea thought with satisfaction. It was the fifth one so far. She smiled brightly, breathing hard as her wounds closed, bones resetting while she waited and listened to the surroundings. It had been a short battle.

The undead was marked on her back, meaning Ilea had faced the same one the day before. Twice, in fact. She hadn't needed much to finish the job. Still, the knight had reduced her health by a third and broken most of her rib cage with the handle of her sword.

Fucking ridiculous.

'ding' You have defeated [Undead Rose Knight – lvl 520] – For defeating an enemy two hundred and twenty or more levels above your own, bonus experience is granted.

Highest level so far, Ilea mused, her health topping out again. She quickly checked through her messages from the past few days.

'ding' Azarinth First Hunter has reached lvl 292 – Five stat points awarded

...

'ding' Azarinth First Hunter has reached lvl 294 – Five stat points awarded

'ding' Inheritor of Eternal Ash has reached lvl 291 – Five stat points awarded

...

'ding' Inheritor of Eternal Ash has reached lvl 293 – Five stat points awarded

'ding' Destruction reaches 3rd lvl 9

'ding' Azarinth Fighting reaches 3rd lvl 4

'ding' Veil of Ash reaches 3rd lvl 10

'ding' Ashen Warrior reaches 3rd lvl 3

Back to levels getting more attention than skills again. Well, I won't complain. Both are helpful.

She put ten stat points into Vitality, bringing her health to eight thousand five hundred. The other twenty she put into Wisdom.

She saw the difference her Strength made, each hit crashing into her enemies with devastating force, Dexterity changed her ability to dodge, use openings to her advantage, and have her body keep up with her perception, while Intelligence boosted the damage from her spells. All three let her win against her enemies.

Vitality and Wisdom, on the other hand, let her survive. They let her get decapitated without her health reaching zero, let her recover her lost head without taking her out of the fight. Arguments could be made about her investments, but the experience was fresh in her mind. It felt right.

A sudden appearance in her Sphere made her turn her head, eyes widening as she slowly breathed out. A drop of sweat rolled down her neck as she looked toward a house on the other side of the street. Both the house she was in as well as the one she was looking at were mostly destroyed, with piles of rubble and an unmoving knight the only things nearby. Aside from the newcomer.

[Soul Ripper - ???]

It didn't move, simply looking her way, standing on all fours. No eyes adorned its head. It had no mouth to talk or screech. The beast looked the same as the last one she'd seen. At the end of its elongated legs and arms were slender fingers and claws, and its body was just as slim.

'ding' Fear Resistance reaches lvl 7

Way to go. Didn't realize I was shitting my pants.

Ilea didn't move a muscle and neither did the beast. The tentacles in its flower-like head started writhing a moment later, barely visible in the dim light provided by her buffs.

Ilea blinked her eyes.

It moved.

The monster lunged soundlessly with a speed surpassing even the undead knights. Perhaps it might have caught her, had it not been for her Sphere. She blinked up and behind the monster, smashing her fist and ashen limbs into its spine. She sacrificed a chunk of mana, destructive force coursing through the monster.

It didn't turn toward her when she landed, showing neither any injury nor interest in her attack. Instead, it lowered its head, right above the latest Rose Knight she'd killed. A sudden surge of mana nearly made her stumble, a force dragging her toward the beast for a mere split second.

When next she looked down, the undead's head was gone and, with it, a little of the floor. As well as the very air that had been near the monster's magic. She'd seen it before, Ilea realized. *Void magic.*

"What the hell are you?" she said quietly.

The beast turned quickly toward the noise. One of its hands lashed out, nearly grabbing Ilea before she blinked away. The beast held its hand near its head before it realized nothing was there.

"Not the brightest, are you?"

She had no way of telling if there was anything beyond instinct at work. It had fed on the undead or removed its head for some reason. Maria, the mage traveling with Edwin, had never mentioned if the voids she created put the removed tissue and blood anywhere.

Never thought about that. Something dragged me toward it, though. Gravity? Or space filling up rapidly?

At least Ilea knew not to get near its claws. That much was simple to deduce.

"I don't really feel like finding out what happens if you get me. But I won't fuck off without at least trying to kill you," she said defiantly.

I refuse to be afraid of this thing. Or anything. Fuck Praetorians.

'ding' Fear Resistance reaches lvl 8

Fucking damn it.

A grin filled her face as the beast jumped at her again. This time, she waited patiently, blinking and delivering the same blow as before. Her third-tier Azarinth Fighting didn't offer her an insight into the damage she'd sustain, so Ilea assumed the beast would simply grab her. The real attack would follow.

The monster's bone was as hard as anything Ilea had ever hit, most of her energy going right back through her arm as she disengaged.

I don't think I'm doing anything here.

She watched the beast turn and jump – not at her, but over the buildings behind her and beyond, out of her Sphere. Left alone in the darkness, she didn't hear it land, didn't hear or see a single thing with either eyes or Sphere.

Did I injure it? Maybe it just got bored… or frustrated. A shiver went down her spine. *Stop it, body. Get a fucking grip, Ilea.*

At least her Fear Resistance didn't level again. It was the first time she'd been happy about a skill not getting higher.

Not going to chase it. I need a break. Again.

* * *

"The undead's head just vanished," Ilea said, shoveling half of her portion of fried potatoes into her mouth.

"I have replicated it as best I can, based on your description. How accurate is this?" Elfie asked, showing her the sketch he'd drawn. "Any thoughts on what magic it uses?"

The resemblance was eerie. Ilea held up a thumb in approval while she struggled not to suffocate due to her overzealous intake of potato. She coughed and struggled, swallowing twice before she spoke.

"Void, I think. No idea why it's called a Soul Ripper. Maybe there's something else there I'm not seeing. Terok, you might be helpful with your mana sight."

Holding up both hands, the dwarf chuckled awkwardly. "Only if you drag me down there, Ilea. I'd rather pass. Already nearly died against the crazy knights there. I don't need more nightmares to keep me awake."

Fair enough.

"I'd like to see it," Heranuur said, fire dancing around his arms.

"No," Ilea replied. "I'll go down again soon. Shouldn't need more than another ten or twenty until I get to three hundred."

I do hope I actually get an evolution. And a good one at that.

Elfie chuckled. "I had thought you would need years, decades even." His eyes turned hard as he looked toward Heranuur and Neiphato. "Don't even think about it. Not before you can heal as fast as she can."

At the far end of the cathedral, Goldie was working on his bone magic, but Ilea was sure that was because he simply didn't want to join them at their fireplace for dinner.

"You could do the same. Just go in there and fight. Or use your magic against the Miststalkers at night," Ilea suggested.

Elfie shook his head. "My advice to them holds for myself. Curses can heal me, yes, but compared to the health drain or danger posed by most of the creatures roaming these lands, the risks far outweigh the rewards."

"She gets shredded to near death daily," Terok said, pointing at Ilea with his mug.

"How would you know?" she asked.

"By seeing far and flying high. Might want to think about getting binoculars, lassie."

She chuckled. "I might think about it next time I go to Hallowfort." Looking at Elfie, she noted his silver eyes on her. "Speaking of which, did you get your talk with the queen?"

His eyes closed, and he gave a small sigh before he spoke. "I did. And with the fox."

"Find what you were looking for?"

Elfie looked at her for a long moment, then shook his head and continued eating.

"I see," Ilea said. She had an idea by now as to what kind of knowledge he was after, and she remembered Goliath's words.

He probably knows the answers he's seeking already.

"Still want to talk to the king?" she asked, finishing her meal.

"I do. Most human kings would have me hunted down before I even set foot into their cities."

Terok grunted. "You overestimate their security."

Ilea raised her eyebrows, but he just shrugged.

Would actually be interesting to see if he could enter Ravenhall undetected.

Heranuur grinned before drinking from his mug, a red liquid sloshing inside. The blood of an animal or monster mixed with water. Commonplace among elves, Ilea had learned.

"I do not know what wisdom you seek from ancient humans found in tombs, Niivalyr."

Elfie looked at the elf, holding his stare before Heranuur looked away, hissing to himself.

Ancient humans found in tombs, Ilea thought, then she got up and stretched.

"Thanks for the meal. I'm going to find another monster to kill. Wish me luck."

"*Sal var nakuun,*" Elfie said.

She didn't know what it meant, but looking into his eyes, she could make a guess.

Ilea hissed what felt to her like a joyful sound and spread her wings.

SEVENTY-FIVE

Three Hundred

Ilea searched for the undead day in, day out, marking them as she had before, disengaging as soon as another one appeared due to the loud and destructive battling. The strategy of simply being loud herself did bring them to her, but it usually brought more than one.

The more of them she killed, the longer she had to spend on finding them, forcing her deeper and deeper into the dungeon. Avoiding Soul Rippers became normal too, but seeing that they rarely pursued over significant distances, it was easy to stay focused on the knights.

She spent her nights in the dungeon too, continuing her search, but having to disengage after usually a couple of minutes made her progress somewhat slow. At least every kill granted a high amount of experience toward her next levels. In the meantime, Terok and crew continued to hunt the lower-level knights, all still connected to Maro.

Ilea smashed her fist into the chest of the latest undead she'd found, sending him through the stone wall behind, where he finally lay still. The once-man-now-monster was marked on his left leg, meaning it was the one Ilea had already fought four times in the past week.

"We're getting there," Ilea commented as she read through the messages that had accumulated, checking her surroundings constantly. She was deeper in the dungeon than she'd ever been, and more and more Soul Rippers showed up in these parts.

'ding' You have defeated [Undead Rose Knight – lvl 510] – For defeating an enemy two hundred and ten or more levels above your own, bonus experience is granted.

...

'ding' You have defeated [Undead Rose Knight – lvl 513] – For defeating an enemy two hundred and ten or more levels above your own, bonus experience is granted.

'ding' Azarinth First Hunter has reached lvl 295 – Five stat points awarded

...

'ding' Azarinth First Hunter has reached lvl 299 – Five stat points awarded

'ding' Inheritor of Eternal Ash has reached lvl 294 – Five stat points awarded

...

'ding' Inheritor of Eternal Ash has reached lvl 299 – Five stat points awarded

'ding' Blink reaches 3rd lvl 10

'ding' Form of Ash and Ember reaches 3rd lvl 5

'ding' Ash Creation reaches 3rd lvl 7

Ilea checked her status and held her breath. *Two ninety-nine. Come on now.*

She smiled to herself, ready to take the next step.

Spreading her wings, she carefully floated over the houses just low enough for her Sphere to reach the ground. This way, she could move around without producing much noise. The Soul Rippers had a tendency to stick to walls and stay unmoving until she was in range. In the air, most of them wouldn't even notice her.

It was pitch black.

Ripper, Ripper, Ripper, Ripper... Undead. There you go.

Walking alone through a square was a single undead Rose Knight, exactly what she was looking for. Ilea immediately engaged it, not caring about the Soul Rippers somewhat close by. She would try to shoo them away or flee if necessary, as she'd done a dozen times before.

Let's try and keep it contained.

Her wings vanished as she rammed into the knight with all the speed and power she could muster. While the blow didn't even make him stumble, her legs bent under the weight of the blow.

His sword lashed out, Ilea twisting her body as she jumped off him, allowing the blade to hit. She knew the damage would be minimal, a slight dent and a barely cracked bone. Already healing while she danced in the air, Ilea prepared for the now enraged undead's attack.

When she landed on her feet, the knight was already upon her, his blade slashing past her. A blow from her fist flaked off some of the rust on his armor before she disengaged, taking several quick steps back.

Ilea counted the knight's attacks, carefully evaluating when to move in. Another two strikes and she stepped forward, her knee smashing into his thigh. The blow landed, and she didn't stop, ducking under his fist and to the left before striking his back. When his sword came around again, Ilea was already too far away to be in danger.

Come on.

Ilea grinned when the knight let go of his sword at the end of the next slash, the blade flying toward her as she ran at it. She blinked through it before her fists smashed into the creature. His prowess in hand-to-hand combat was miles behind hers, and she delivered hit after hit, avoiding his grabs with calculated dodges and blinks.

When the sword returned to the knight's grasp and Ilea held back at a distance again, the creature started to apply more complicated maneuvers and feints. With her ability to gauge the incoming attacks, his tactics simply delayed the inevitable.

She wouldn't stumble, wouldn't fail. Against an enemy working with the rotten remains of a once masterful swordsman, she would prevail. Now that she could negate its incredible strength and foresee most of its feints.

Still, she was pushed back, the creature slamming through buildings that she jumped over or bypassed using her teleportation magic. Openings were rare, and she was already running out of time.

At least, I should be.

There was still no second knight showing up as the one before her crashed through another set of walls.

No more around in this area then?

She heard the knight smash his blade into a wall before he appeared in her Sphere. As he landed with his blade already digging into the earth where she'd been standing a moment before, her ashen limbs rushed at him but were separated by a powerful swing of his sword.

Ilea prepared herself as the undead screeched at her. *I get it, angry man.* Again and again, her fists smashed into the knight as he tried to hit or grab her with his free hand. *Not happening.* Blinking behind him, she kicked his back, using the momentum to avoid the slash coming at her right after.

Ilea's head spun to the side, but there was nothing there. Her Sphere showed nothing. *I'm hearing things.*

The knight threw his blade again, Ilea dodging it this time before her ashen limbs crashed into him. Twice she hit before finally reaching him, her fist smashing into his stomach before she blinked behind him.

Where's his sword?

Using the circumstances to her advantage, she continued her attack, each blow staggering the undead more and more, one of his legs snapping a moment later and bringing him down.

She ignored his grab this time, knowing the end was near. The steel armor on her leg groaned as he crushed it, but Ilea's reversed healing as well as her ashen limbs and fists continued to pound his life away bit by bit.

Something flashed in her mind. This time she was sure – there had been movement nearby.

Soul Rippers.

Not relenting, she felt a bone in her leg break as one of the creatures entered her Sphere, pouncing at them a moment later. Using her weight and ashen limbs, she pushed herself and the undead knight down, her destructive mana still flowing into him. He grabbed one of her arms now too, both hands grasping her and trying to crush her.

Then, letting go, he pummeled her head, denting her helmet, the metal cutting into her face. Yet she knew he was close to done, the damage done to him extensive. So she tried to catch his blows with her ash, grasping one of his hands before she flew through a house, the knight in tow as a Soul Ripper jumped past.

She saw more of the creatures in her Sphere, her body tense as the knight grabbed at her head. She gritted her teeth, fighting its strength with everything she had. Another strike slipped past and hit her face, breaking her jaw before she punched back.

Ilea could feel the next impact rock through her neck. Part of her wanted to push away, to run and hope the Soul Rippers didn't catch her. And she felt the knight's arm going for her neck again. But Ilea stayed where she was, focusing on the unfeeling monster before her.

Not again.

She punched down three times before the impact of the fourth snapped the knight's head back, his body slumping as several dinging noises filled her mind. She sacrificed mana to heal her face as she blinked up, wings spreading. Her Sphere was crawling with movement, spindly limbs moving everywhere.

Fucking hell.

Ilea felt something on her leg. One of the Soul Rippers had jumped and grabbed onto her. She felt its weight as it dragged her down, felt its struggle as it tried to grab her with its other arm. Ilea cut into its thin arm with her ash, but nothing happened. Its skin was as hard as steel.

I'll go down if this continues.

Another building was coming up and she ascended, dragging the beast up with her before she suddenly snapped to a stop. She yelped when the full force of her wings pulled against her leg. The creature had dug its hind legs deep into the wall of the building below and was pulling, both hands now wrapped around her shin.

"Hey, you know what, fuckface, if you really want it, you can have it."

The armor on her leg vanished before her ashen limbs cut through her skin and muscle, separating her leg at the knee. Ilea immediately blinked upward again and again as her wings flapped to take her away from the horrifying creatures.

She didn't let herself relax until she'd reached the crumbling wall leading to the higher part of Tremor. Blood was pouring from her leg, the wound finally closing when she realized she'd neglected to heal it. She'd focused on her head instead.

Ilea continued toward one of the houses she'd sometimes stayed at and blinked through the wall, replacing her armor with comfortable clothes before she summoned and landed on her bed.

Her vision was blurry, and she realized her hands were shaking. She sent Meditation flowing through her before resting her back against the wall.

"Fucking hell."

She repeated the words three times before her hands stilled. The knight had done serious damage to her other leg and her arm, both now mostly mush except for her bones.

Another set of armor wrecked.

Checking her messages, the first thing she saw made her squint before she started laughing.

Damn long-legged bastards.

'ding' Fear Resistance reaches lvl 9

It took her a minute to calm down completely.

Close call, you damn idiot.

Still, she felt elated. In the end, she'd survived. Maybe she would have survived anyway, even if she hadn't been able to cut off her leg. But it didn't matter.

Lifting herself up, she sat down on the bed cross-legged and summoned one of Keyla's meals, the smell of the warm, spicy dish immediately overshadowing the blood and sweat clinging to her body.

Maro was right. There are evolutions.

Now, let's fucking mutate.

'ding' You have defeated [Undead Rose Knight – lvl 518] – For defeating an enemy two hundred and ten or more levels above your own, bonus experience is granted.

'ding' Azarinth First Hunter has reached lvl 300 – Five stat points awarded, one 3rd-tier skill point awarded

'ding' Inheritor of Eternal Ash has reached lvl 300 – Five stat points awarded, one 3rd-tier skill point awarded

'ding' Azarinth Fighting reaches 3rd lvl 5

'ding' Ash and Ember Manipulation reaches 3rd lvl 5

And both Classes at the same time, fucking perfect.

Trying to spend the third-tier skill points first didn't seem to work, both showing no skills to advance.

Requirements should be met. Maybe it's tied to the evolutions in some way. On with it then.

'ding' Requirements met for Class evolution: Azarinth First Hunter becomes Azarinth Elder. No current skills or stats will be lost, be aware that other evolutions and skills may become unavailable.
You have pushed yourself to the pinnacle of humanity and thus deserve to carry the name of Elder. You have leveled at least five Azarinth skills to the end of the second tier, carry the skill Meditation at the end of the second tier, and have an Azarinth Class at level 300 or higher.
The Elders of the Azarinth Order pave the way to the future. Conquest and expansion are theirs to plan and execute. They have the power to rebuild what was lost. Known to be strategic minds, an Elder leading a group of Azarinth Healers might very well be unstoppable.
Would you like to evolve your Class [Azarinth First Hunter] to [Azarinth Elder]?

How about absolutely fucking not? Conquest and expansion my ass.

'ding' Requirements met for Class evolution: Azarinth First Hunter becomes Beast of Azarinth. No current skills or stats will be lost, be aware that other evolutions and skills may become unavailable.
Your blood lust permeates all. You have leveled at least eight Azarinth skills to the end of the second tier and Destruction and Azarinth Fighting to the third tier, have killed at least 1000 higher-leveled beings, have sustained 1000 heavy injuries, and have an Azarinth Class at level 300.
Far from the path of the once-powerful healing order, the Beasts of Azarinth have chosen to seek their own power and the destruction of life itself. Fueled by hatred and blood, the Beast of Azarinth marches on, unable to find or bring peace. Forbidden death magic corrupts the power once destined to heal and mend.
Would you like to evolve your Class [Azarinth First Hunter] to [Beast of Azarinth]?

Come on guys… It's not that bad, is it? At least it's not a thousand kids…

Ilea at least thought about it due to the mention of death magic. Maybe an Azarinth and death magic combination? If she had to choose between Elder and Beast, the choice was clear.

Corrupts… Does that mean no more healing at all?

'ding' Requirements met for Class evolution: Azarinth First Hunter becomes Azarinth Pioneer. No current skills or stats will be lost, be aware that other evolutions and skills may become unavailable.
Adventure is your second name. You have leveled ten Azarinth skills to the end of the second tier, traveled where no human dares to go, survived natural dangers capable of decimating armies, founded a settlement or discovered a lost city, and have an Azarinth Class at level 300.
The Pioneer has chosen their own path, discovering the forgotten and perfecting their skills and powers. Be it erupting volcanoes, the waves of the ocean or blizzards cold enough to freeze their very blood, nothing will stop their desire for adventure. Powerful regeneration and constitution come with their mantle.
Would you like to evolve your Class [Azarinth First Hunter] to [Azarinth Pioneer]?

Surviving natural dangers and not a mention of resistances? Not even one is needed?

'ding' Requirements met for Class evolution: Azarinth First Hunter becomes Azarinth Destroyer. No current skills or stats will be lost, be aware that other evolutions and skills may become unavailable.
You have no equal in battle. You have leveled ten Azarinth skills to the end of the second tier, have Destruction, State of Azarinth, and Azarinth Fighting in the third tier, killed an enemy above level 500, fought hordes of enemies above your own level and prevailed, and have the Azarinth First Hunter Class at level 300.
The Destroyer is a rare sight to behold. A master of Azarinth magic, each strike is powerful and carries intent. They move over the battlefield with grace, leaving nothing behind. They are the true power of the Azarinth Order or anybody they would choose to join. Their Strength is second to none, cracking even steel with their fists.
Would you like to evolve your Class [Azarinth First Hunter] to [Azarinth Destroyer]?

That's more like it, baby. Fighting, level five hundred beast, and a focus on fighting with fists.

'ding' Requirements met for Class evolution: Azarinth First Hunter becomes

Azarinth Wayfarer. No current skills or stats will be lost, be aware that other evolutions and skills may become unavailable.
The unfathomable. You have leveled ten Azarinth skills to the end of the second tier, have Blink and State of Azarinth in the third tier, killed an enemy above level 600, traveled to another realm and returned, have the Veteran skill at level 5 or higher, speak two languages, and have the Azarinth First Hunter Class at level 300.
The Azarinth Wayfarer has grasped the impossible nature of magic, has crossed the boundaries between realms. True understanding will follow for those unwilling to accept the status quo. They are a master of their surroundings, of space itself.
Would you like to evolve your Class [Azarinth First Hunter] to [Azarinth Wayfarer]?

Space mage… seems pretty far off what I've been doing all this time. How many have missed this possible evolution because they weren't bilingual?
She chuckled at the thought and continued her reading.

'ding' Requirements met for Class evolution: Azarinth First Hunter becomes Azarinth Regenerator. No current skills or stats will be lost, be aware that other evolutions and skills may become unavailable.
More monster than man, you have leveled eight Azarinth skills to the end of the second tier, have Hunter Recovery and State of Azarinth in the third tier, killed ten enemies above level 500, have ten Resistance skills at level 5 or higher, have Pain Tolerance in the second tier, have lost either your head or all your limbs in battle before recovering, and have the Azarinth First Hunter Class at level 300.
The Azarinth Regenerator fears no enemy. Be it ice or fire, they stand against it unmoving. Bearers of the pain they have suffered, unwilling to accept defeat. Virtually unkillable, they are prepared to face whatever may move into their path, their bodies mere weapons, tools to be used.
Would you like to evolve your Class [Azarinth First Hunter] to [Azarinth Regenerator]?

Well, at least it's not called the Azarinth Masochist. Bodies are tools to be used… might as well be.
She smirked before she moved to the next one.

'ding' Requirements met for Class evolution: Azarinth First Hunter becomes Avenger of Azarinth. No current skills or stats will be lost, be aware that other evolutions and skills may become unavailable.
A hunter unmatched, you have leveled ten Azarinth skills to the end of the second tier, have Destruction, Azarinth Fighting, and State of Azarinth in the third tier,killed ten enemies at full power above level 400 while alone, have

five General Skills in the second tier, participated in acts of revenge, finding and killing those responsible, lost limbs in the midst of battle and continued the fight, and have the Azarinth First Hunter Class at level 300.
An avenger stopping at nothing to bring justice to those deserving, judge and executioner, powerful and deadly enough to hunt down any target they deem unworthy. Unstoppable and fueled by the magic of Azarinth, healing any injury that might delay them, their bodies mere arbiters of revenge.
Would you like to evolve your Class [Azarinth First Hunter] to [Avenger of Azarinth]?

Flashes of the Birmingales went through her mind, of Eve lying dead in her bed...

She shook her head, breathing in hard and focusing on the task at hand.

Requirements are pretty high, and finally there's a mention of killing something alone. Healing might be enhanced, and there's at least talk about one's own body.

Ilea saw there was only one option remaining, but the Avenger was probably her favorite for now.

'ding' Requirements met for Class evolution: Azarinth First Hunter becomes Azarinth Sentinel. No current skills or stats will be lost, be aware that other evolutions and skills may become unavailable.
Life and death. You have leveled ten Azarinth skills to the end of the second tier, have Destruction, Hunter Recovery, Azarinth Fighting, and State of Azarinth in the third tier, killed ten enemies at full power above level 500 while alone, faced hordes of enemies above your own level on your own and prevailed, have fifteen or more Resistance skills in the second tier, two or more at the highest level, have helped and healed strangers of various races, unasked for or even in the face of hostility, risked your life for others on multiple occasions, and have the Azarinth First Hunter Class at level 300.
The Azarinth Sentinel has reached the pinnacle of Azarinth magic, mastering its style while not forgetting their roots. A healer at heart, they seek to mend the wounds of those they deem close and strangers alike. True veterans of battle, they have chosen a most peculiar path, savior to one and destroyer to another. Their bodies forged into weapons, their mana overpowers all. They are a force of their own to decide on the fate of beings.
Would you like to evolve your Class [Azarinth First Hunter] to [Azarinth Sentinel]?

Ilea shifted her attention back to her food, the smell of the spicy orange sauce with potatoes and vegetables making her stomach rumble. She looked at the bowl, the rice still steaming even after all that reading.

Did I really heal so many strangers? Risk my life for others?

None of her actions seemed out of the ordinary. This whole world was ridiculous, of course. She'd turned into a survivor here, a murderer, a hunter.

But a savior? Screw that.

She was quite aware that the same line read 'destroyer' as well.

Besides the first couple of possibilities, the rest seemed exceptional.

Destroyer, Wayfarer, Regenerator, Avenger, Sentinel. Each with its own specialty, each with increasingly high demands.

She asked herself whether there would have been another Class if she had ten resistances at the end of the second tier or if the Sentinel description would have simply required ten at that point. Would there have been another Class had she killed ten level six hundred beasts alone? Possibly.

Most of the Classes required her to be at level 300, making it unlikely she'd get anything new at this point. She'd chosen to reach 300 now, and these were her choices.

Sentinel lists the hardest achievements. Pinnacle of Azarinth magic, bodies forged into weapons… What am I, a fucking paladin?

She chuckled and went back to eating, savoring every bite, the taste and smell so wonderful that she entirely forgot about the choice to be made for a few seconds.

Regenerator doesn't seem to grant a lot of offensive potential, and I can't see how more regeneration would change anything drastically at this point. Wayfarer is cool, but with my focus on fighting instead of the study of magic and teleportation, I think I'll pass.

Destroyer seems to be a Sentinel Lite with a focus on strength, and Avenger is pretty vague. How often have I actually needed to be a hunter? I feel like most monsters and people were found easily enough. It could help with the Lily…

Sentinel is the best choice if I look at the requirements.

She scribbled into her notebook, comparing the Classes with bullet points, ignoring all the blabbering about justice, death, and revenge. She had to admit that Sentinel was also the best one with its power descriptions. Other than 'healer at heart', the rest was pretty straightforward.

Well, 'mana overpowers all' is a little weird too. But there's a specific mention of one's body. Maybe it's talking about mana intrusion?

She felt a little queasy, putting her food away as she got up and walked to the hole in the wall, once a window. It was dark outside, the sound of a distant explosion barely audible. She smiled, knowing the others were out there taking out knights.

She found that she wasn't sure which one to pick. *There's a few good options. Hunter unmatched, arbiter of revenge. Hmm. Doesn't quite fit.* Closing her eyes, Ilea tapped her lip with her finger. *Life and death. A force of their own to decide on the fate of beings.*

"A true veteran of battle. Not sure on the savior and destroyer part, but the rest does sound appealing. Not too keen on deciding anyone's fate, but I do want to decide my own," she said to herself, then accepted the Class evolution.

'ding' Class change: Azarinth First Hunter becomes Azarinth Sentinel

Vitality +30
Strength +15
Dexterity +15
Endurance +15
Intelligence +30
Wisdom +20

Body enhancement magic is improved by 300%
All healing magic skills are improved by 200%
Natural health regeneration is increased by 1% per minute
Quantities of food, water, and sleep needed to sustain yourself are reduced

Ilea felt the weight of the decision fall away. Her previous uncertainty was replaced with excitement as she felt newfound power flow through her veins.

She smiled at the improvements to her body enhancements and healing skills. The additional stats were welcome as well, but they were a drop in the bucket compared to what she'd gained through leveling alone.

Skills changed by Azarinth Sentinel:

[Destruction] becomes [Absolute Destruction]
Active: Absolute Destruction – 3rd lvl 9:
Send a destructive pulse of mana into your enemy with every punch or kick. Your Intelligence stat enhances the damage potential.
2nd stage: The amount of mana used per strike can be regulated with a maximum of 100 mana per strike. You may charge each strike whilst unmoving with 100 mana per second to a maximum of 3000 mana.
3rd stage: Due to the healing nature of Destruction, it partially ignores protection against Mana intrusion.
Category: Healing

So if I'm reading this right, the mana per strike has increased from twenty to one hundred, plus I can charge it. While not moving, but still. And the additional hundred percent increase for healing skills should apply here as well. Doesn't seem like it's a multiplier, but it's a good increase. That's already an insane power up. Costs a bunch more mana, but with my regeneration…

She smiled, already itching to test it out on some unfortunate undead.

[Hunter Recovery] becomes [Sentinel Reconstruction]
Active: Sentinel Reconstruction – 3rd lvl 12:
Send a healing pulse of mana into yourself or your ally with a touch. This skill can be channeled.
2nd stage: Your control is increased greatly. You can now focus your healing on specific parts of the body. As long as mana and health remains, your Sentinel Reconstruction will restore your body. Lose your head and see for yourself! Health loss and critical blows are recalculated due to the nature of your healing.
3rd stage: You have healed your body time and time again and know every cell and where it belongs. Sacrifice a large amount of mana to boost your healing to unprecedented speeds. A lack of knowledge about your body may result in heavy damage.
Category: Healing

Ilea noted the mention of healing herself being vastly superior to healing others had been removed, but there was a new line about health loss and critical blow calculation.

I hope that doesn't mean it's worse on myself now.

She would test it later, but with her healing getting another hundred percent bonus from the Class change, she assumed it would at least even out.

How many changes did I get last time? This is ridiculous, she thought as she scrolled a little further. *I sure as hell won't complain…*

[State of Azarinth] becomes [Azarinth Awakening]
Active: Azarinth Awakening – 3rd lvl 10:
Your body glows with the power of Azarinth, increasing your resilience, speed, Intelligence and Strength by 75% [450%].
2nd stage: Your sight, hearing, and sense of smell are also affected by Azarinth Awakening.
3rd stage: You are one with Azarinth. The skill's upkeep has been removed. Instead, you may overcharge it with your life's energy. The amount depends on both skill level and health used.
Category: Aura – Body Enhancement

"Holy fuck." Ilea was nearly shedding tears. Months and months of fighting and training had finally paid off. And it had paid off tenfold. "It boosts Intelligence now?" A four hundred fifty percent increase meant her Intelligence should be above three thousand.

Coupled with Destruction's increases…

Plus, it seemed the base percentage had been increased again, from thirty-five to fifty percent, each level in the skill giving an added boost of half a percent.

What else do you have for me, beloved Sentinel?

[Azarinth Hunter Sphere] becomes [Sentinel Sphere]
Active: Sentinel Sphere – 2nd lvl 20
Perceive everything in a sphere around you while this skill is activated. The higher the level, the further the sphere reaches.
2nd stage: The Sentinel Sphere opens your senses to the arcane, a paramount skill both on and off the battlefield.
Category: Aura – Perception Aura

Well that's the first one to remove some good stuff. No more senses dialing… and I loved just ignoring all the blood and guts around me. No more trap detection and hidden paths either. For a mana sense?

She didn't know how to feel about that at the moment. The sense for hidden things had helped her plenty so far, so suddenly losing that wasn't something she'd planned for.

Makes sense, though, since I'm switching from Hunter to something else. I'll survive it, I guess. I have so far, even without this 'paramount' skill.

[Body of the First Hunter] becomes [Sentinel Core]
Passive: Sentinel Core – 2nd lvl 20:
Your body was changed by magic. All pain is reduced greatly. Your body is 40% [320%] more durable. You heal even fatal injuries without the help of healing magic. Your natural Health regeneration is improved by 120% [960%].
2nd stage: The magic of Azarinth has settled inside your body. Your resistance to magical damage is increased by a static 25% [200%], and your bones are three times as heavy and dense.
Category: Healing – Body Enhancement

"Well fuck me… what are those numbers?"

Ilea started scribbling, but it didn't make sense until she realized that the category had changed from just healing to healing and body enhancement, giving an additional five hundred percent increase in power to the skill.

Three hundred twenty percent more durable… what does that even mean? And magic damage resistance above one hundred percent? Is there, like, a hidden baseline that's now increased twofold instead of a simple twenty-five percent increase?

It had been at fifty percent before, but Ilea was pretty sure the damage she sustained hadn't been halved after getting the skill.

Or was it? Further testing is definitely required.

The high multiplier to her natural health recovery was another bonus. She had to test it, of course, but it should at least equal to a couple of free Health points every second.

[Hunter's Sight] becomes [Sentinel Huntress]
Passive: Sentinel Huntress – 2nd lvl 20:
Huntress turned Sentinel. Your eyes are unmatched, and so is your nose. Perceive the smallest irregularities in your surroundings as well as the ambient mana to find clues about your target's whereabouts.
2nd stage: You gain a sense for the distress in the people around you. Amplify this by sacrificing mana.
Category: Body Enhancement

Ambient mana added as a detection source? And that new second tier might actually do something compared to before. Is it a sixth sense to gauge the mood in a room or something?

"Well, that's a bunch of new stuff to play with," Ilea commented as she continued scribbling into her notebook, deciding to wait with testing until all the changes were through. Already, she felt lighter, stronger, the mana around her body tangible, a blue hue in constant motion.

"Now, what kind of Classes does my ashen side have in store?"

SEVENTY-SIX

The Ashen Side of Things

Ilea started on the messages concerning her ashen Class, but the Sentinel evolution was so distracting, she needed a moment to focus. Her body itched, ready to unleash power she had never felt before.

Perhaps the boost to her Intelligence was responsible, or perhaps it was the improvements to all her body enhancement and healing spells. Either way, the new sensation and what felt like pure arcane energy flowing through her was incredible.

Focus, she reminded herself, meditation surging again. The fat grin on her face was a constant by now.

'ding' Requirements met for Class evolution: Inheritor of Eternal Ash becomes Empress of Eternal Ash. No current skills or stats will be lost, be aware that other evolutions and skills may become unavailable.
The ruler. You have leveled at least five ashen magic skills to the end of the second tier, have Ash Creation and Ash and Ember Manipulation in the third tier, trained with the ruler of a nation, identify as female, and have the Inheritor of Eternal Ash Class at level 300.
The Empress rules over all, her ashen magic an iron fist controlled and used to her advantage. She will conquer and rule. All shall kneel or burn.
Would you like to evolve your class [Inheritor of Eternal Ash] to [Empress of Eternal Ash]?

The flavor text was concise and told her exactly what she needed to know to discard this possibility immediately.

Same with the Elder one… Guess they at least present the shit options at the start.

'ding' Requirements met for Class evolution: Inheritor of Eternal Ash becomes Glutton of Cinders. No current skills or stats will be lost, be aware that other evolutions and skills may become unavailable.
Consumption unending. You have ten skills in Inheritor of Eternal Ash at the end of the second tier, enough food with you to feed a small town, own a restaurant, have risked breaking the law and considered cold-blooded murder to protect a cook, and have the Inheritor of Eternal Ash Class at level 300.
A Glutton of Cinders grows power equally to their weight. Fueled by the lust to eat, they ignore injuries and pain. Their jaw strength has enough force to break through steel. With their supportive elemental magic, few may stand in their way. All will be eaten.
Would you like to evolve your Class [Inheritor of Eternal Ash] to [Glutton of Cinders]?

Fair enough. Guess it's judging Ilea day. Still, the jaw strength is a boon for sure, and I bet there's something in there that would allow me to digest literally anything. Still a better option than Empress.

'ding' Requirements met for Class evolution: Inheritor of Eternal Ash becomes Sharpshooter of Eternal Ash. No current skills or stats will be lost, be aware that other evolutions and skills may become unavailable.
Unseen death. You have ten skills in Inheritor of Eternal Ash at the end of the second tier, the Heavy Archery skill as a General Skill, own a storage item, have killed ten enemies above your own level without being spotted and while alone, and have the Inheritor of Eternal Ash Class at level 300.
An unusual combination of magic and the bow. The Sharpshooter of Eternal Ash has extraordinary sight and firepower to unleash death upon groups of enemies without ever being seen. They stalk the night and work alone. Mercenaries or adventurers, they seek their prey and slay it silently.
Would you like to evolve your Class [Inheritor of Eternal Ash] to [Sharpshooter of Eternal Ash]?

We're getting somewhat serious now. Didn't think my archery training would come up here, but I guess I know now that evolutions can be gained from General Skills, should I ever wish to get something else.

Of course, it didn't fit her in any way, neither personality-wise nor from a skill perspective.

'ding' Requirements met for Class evolution: Inheritor of Eternal Ash becomes Master of Eternal Ash. No current skills or stats will be lost, be aware that other evolutions and skills may become unavailable.
Fire consumes, nothing remains. You have ten skills in Inheritor of Eternal Ash at the end of the second tier, the Ash Creation and Ash and Ember Manipulation skills at the third tier, have killed at least 500 beings of a

higher level using ashen magic, killed members of your own species, been betrayed, and have the Inheritor of Eternal Ash class at level 300.
True mastery comes with control, effort, and time. The Master of Eternal Ash has grasped the true power of ash and ember, wielding them to the fullest of their destructive potential. Widespread and fast spells consume even the toughest enemies in everlasting flame, pierced by lances of ash. The battlefield bows to your power.
Would you like to evolve your Class [Inheritor of Eternal Ash] to [Master of Eternal Ash]?

That's more like what I'm looking for. No mention of body enhancement magic, but it seems like a powerful class with its specialties.

'ding' Requirements met for Class evolution: Inheritor of Eternal Ash becomes Berserker of Eternal Flame. No current stats will be lost, be aware that other evolutions and skills may become unavailable.
Forever battling. You have ten skills in Inheritor of Eternal Ash at the end of the second tier, the Ashen Warrior skill in the third tier, have battled and killed thousands of enemies at a higher level than yourself while alone, sustained critical wounds in battle and continued the fight, have Heat Resistance in the second tier and at least twenty Resistance skills, and have the Inheritor of Eternal Ash Class at level 300.
The Berserker of Eternal Flame is untiring, unkillable, and unforgiving. Their bodies becoming one with the flame, they consume and tear through their enemies, their wounds mere stepping stones on their way to power. Their mind is consumed by fire, their bodies weapons of war.
Would you like to evolve your Class [Inheritor of Eternal Ash] to [Berserker of Eternal Flame]?

Ilea tapped her cheek before she sighed. *Mind consumed by fire.* The line gave her pause. Otherwise, the Class sounded badass. More of a focus on fire, obviously, but she wouldn't terribly mind. That's how she'd started out, burning herself to get the Fire Mage Class back in the Calys mine.

Might need to consult some people in regard to Berserker Classes. Roland did kind of lose it sometimes. Wonder if he's doing alright. Probably not, with all that happened. I hope he and the girl are at least alive.

There was one more evolution she could choose. Before moving on, Ilea also realized there was no mention of any current skills being lost if she chose the previous one.

'ding' Requirements met for Class evolution: Inheritor of Eternal Ash becomes Kin of Ash. No current skills or stats will be lost, be aware that other evolutions and skills may become unavailable.
One of Ash. You have ten skills in Inheritor of Eternal Ash at the end of the

second tier, Veil of Ash, Form of Ash and Ember, Ash Creation, Ash and Ember Manipulation and Ashen Warrior in the third tier, Fear Resistance at level five or higher, have fought beings beyond your comprehension while alone, fought and defeated ten or more enemies above level 500 while alone, trusted your body and the ash around you to prevail when faced with certain death, found beauty in ash beyond destruction, and have the Inheritor of Eternal Ash class at level 300.
Kin to Ash itself, their body is clad in armor, unyielding. Their body smolders with embers, unforgiving.
Would you like to evolve your Class [Inheritor of Eternal Ash] to [Kin of Ash]?

Alright, I guess that has to be the one. The requirements are ridiculous. When did I face certain death and trust in my ash and body?

Several memories flashed in her mind, but none fit. She remembered playing around with Kyrian, his metal and her ash. That was probably the part where she'd found beauty in ash beyond its destructive capabilities.

And my beloved friend Fear Resistance.

Ilea thought about consulting Maro or Elfie, perhaps even Catelyn, but as she thought, she felt ash come to life around her, gently swirling around her. It was her own doing, she realized.

Clad in armor, unyielding.

All her third-tier skills had been mentioned in the last evolution option. Compared to the other good classes, it mentioned one's body twice. The Berserker class seemed good too, but it was too sketchy for her. Her mind was her own, and she would choose her own path, being made neither for war nor for any other specific purpose.

The ash around her continued swaying in the air as if carried by a gentle breeze. Compared to her Azarinth evolution, this one just felt… right.

Let's see what you have in store for me.

'ding' Class change: Inheritor of Eternal Ash becomes Kin of Ash

Vitality +30
Strength +20
Dexterity +20
Intelligence +20
Wisdom +15

Body enhancement magic is improved by 300%
All Ashen magic skills are improved by 100%
All fighting styles using hand-to-hand combat are more refined
Your will is ash and embers

Seems like I made the right choice. Another set of stats as well. And whatever the line about my will means. Another hundred percent… meaning a ton of my Sentinel skills just became, what, fifteen percent stronger? From six hundred percent total to seven hundred.

The start was already promising as Ilea moved on to the more interesting stuff.

Skills changed by Kin of Ash:

[Veil of Ash] becomes [Armor of Ash]
Active: Armor of Ash – 3rd lvl 10:
A shroud of condensed ash to shield you. Hard as steel and forming to your will. The Armor increases your resilience by 125% [1000%]. Halved effects if armor beyond light category is worn.
2nd stage: The strength of your Resistance skills also benefits from the Armor of Ash.
3rd stage: Increases the defensive capabilities of all ash and ember you control. Effects additionally apply to your body itself, halved if armor heavier than light is worn.
Category: Body Enhancement – Ashen magic

I see we're continuing with the ridiculous bonuses. What the hell constitutes light armor? It bummed her out a little. Ilea liked her heavy metal gear. *Half would still be good. Guess I'll have to find out how good this armor actually is. Maybe I can have something well made that's also considered light armor.*

She had a smith to help her out. If ashen armor could replace her current set completely, she wouldn't have to constantly worry about having a smith nearby to repair sets or make new ones.

One thousand percent. Guess that's worth an achievement of sorts. Should I ask someone to explain resilience to me?

Ilea immediately discarded the idea, instead just planning to let different monsters attack her to find out more about her new armor.

Plus my body itself gets the bonus? So, it's basically two thousand compared to the four hundred before?

The description of the first tier had changed significantly as well.

Further testing needed. Again.

[Form of Ash and Ember] becomes [Aspect of Ash]
Active: Aspect of Ash – 3rd lvl 5:
Ember glows within you, raising your resilience, speed, Strength, Intelligence, and Dexterity by 57.5% [402.5%].
2nd stage: The longer you fight in the Aspect of Ash, the deeper roots it gains. Each minute of fighting adds 15% more power to the skill, up to a maximum of 150%.

3rd stage: Familiarity with the skill removes its upkeep. When reaching the maximum second-tier bonus, you may reset it by amplifying your next attack with ash and ember.
Category: Aura – Body Enhancement

There you go. Exactly what I've been looking for.

Intelligence was now a part of the skill as well. The difference in power from the additional two hundred percent from body enhancement bonuses was good enough, but with Intelligence affected, her mana intrusion spells would benefit immensely.

[Ash Creation] becomes [True Ash Creation]
Active: True Ash Creation – 3rd lvl 7:
Create ash in a certain radius around you.
2nd stage: You can control the density of the ash to an extent.
3rd stage: You have proven your dedication. Ash swirls to aid and destroy at your whim.
Category: Ashen Magic

"Well, what happened exactly?"

Ilea noticed the line 'It can be used as a surge to blind or as a shroud to hide' was missing now, but otherwise everything had stayed the same.

Guess I have to find out what the 'true' part means. Maybe it doesn't vanish anymore after a while? Or the properties somehow change?

[Embered Body Heat] becomes [Heart of Cinder]
Active: Heart of Cinder – 2nd lvl 20:
Increase the heat in your body and release it in a blast around you.
2nd stage: The embers run deep. The heat you may reach is only limited by your very life.
Category: Body Enhancement – Ashen Magic

"So that's completely different. No more hiding then with this one… or I guess only from fire beasts."

Ilea was skeptical about how much this one would help, but with the boost to her body enhancement and ashen magic, the damage could be helpful if she was surrounded.

Just burn a dozen demons to a crisp. Doesn't that sound lovely.

At least she wouldn't replace it with any other skills until she tried it.

[Wave of Ember] becomes [Storm of Cinders]
Active: Storm of Cinders – 2nd lvl 20:
Burn the inside of whatever your body hits with a surge of heat and embers or release the attack in a burst of fire and cinders.

2nd stage: The flame burns on. Targets hit will have fire burning through or on them. Time and consecutive attacks will increase the effect.
Category: Ashen magic

Added utility, I guess. Why not?

Compared to Destruction, the skill didn't actually get a damage increase. At least it would be boosted a little by the ashen magic buff.

I'm getting a lot of skill changes. Did I just fuck up my level two hundred evolution, or is this normal?

[Ash and Ember Manipulation] becomes [Ash and Ember Unity]
Passive: Ash and Ember Unity – 3rd lvl 5:
You are one with Ash and Ember. Allies rushing to your aid.
2nd stage: Your understanding grows, allowing you to create greater change in ash and ember.
3rd stage: The elements themselves become extensions of your body, of your will, for as long as they stay in physical contact with you. Ash not connected benefits from passive abilities enhancing your body.
Category: Ashen magic

Well, that's just as ambiguous as before. The new passive benefits are nice, but active skills would have been a game changer. Damage increases though… maybe.

Still not done…

[Body of Ash] becomes [Avatar of Ash]
Passive: Avatar of Ash – 2nd lvl 20:
Increases your reflexes and speed by 50% [400%]. Your ability to avoid damage to your vitals when dodging increases.
2nd stage: Your muscles grow more dense. For each Resistance skill, your body becomes tougher: first-tiers gain a static 5% increase, second-tiers gain a static 10% increase.
Category: Body Enhancement – Ashen magic

Oh man. I guess Resistance farming is on the menu again. For good reason. Damn, with this I could become literally indestructible. Just have to find the rarest magic to fight against. Bummer that it doesn't benefit from the multipliers.

[Ashen Warrior] becomes [Keeper of Ash]
Passive: Keeper of Ash – 3rd lvl 3:
You are one with the fighting style of Ash. Damage inflicted is 71.5% [500.5%] higher.
2nd stage: Adds density to your bones, muscles, and skin to increase strength, speed and damage. Base body weight is doubled.
3rd stage: Reduces stamina consumption by a static 35%.

Category: Body Enhancement

"Never mind the three hundred evolution – I feel like I just underwent a supersoldier experiment. On top of already being one in the first place," Ilea whispered to herself, forming a fist with her hand as she felt the strength flow through her. With these evolutions in place, she wasn't just one step but maybe five steps closer to her goals.

Blinking onto the house's roof, she lay sprawled on her back. She held a hand in front of her face and looked past it into the darkness above. Breathing in, she tried to grasp the extent of the changes. It was like waking up in a new body. Every part of her was different. Not just more powerful, but fundamentally changed. She was overwhelmed by it all.

Still, her stats, and the skills themselves, somewhat helped her cope with the abrupt change. She didn't feel like she was in the *wrong* body, just a better one. She didn't have difficulties moving, nor accessing her abilities.

Yet she definitely felt the differences. A simple squeeze of her arm showed how dense the muscle had become, and, extending her Sphere, she could see the wisps of mana that surrounded her, coming from her auras.

Is this what I wanted to achieve? What I wanted to become? Have I made it?

Ilea felt a little lost, like she'd finished a good book, having fulfilled a task that wasn't necessarily about its completion but the execution.

But I do have a result.

She put her unspent stats into Intelligence and Wisdom, then checked her stats while thinking about what to do next.

Name: Ilea Spears
Unspent stat points: 0
Unspent 3rd-tier skill points [Azarinth Sentinel]: 1
Unspent 3rd-tier skill points [Kin of Ash]: 1

Class 1: Azarinth Sentinel – lvl 300
- Active: Absolute Destruction – 3rd lvl 9
- Active: Sentinel Reconstruction – 3rd lvl 12
- Active: Azarinth Awakening – 3rd lvl 10
- Active: Blink – 3rd lvl 10
- Active: Sentinel Sphere – 2nd lvl 20
- Passive: Sentinel Core – 2nd lvl 20
- Passive: Azarinth Fighting – 3rd lvl 5
- Passive: Sentinel Huntress – 2nd lvl 20
- Passive: Azarinth Perception – 2nd lvl 20
- Passive: Azarinth Reversal – 2nd lvl 20

Class 2: Kin of Ash – lvl 300
- Active: Armor of Ash – 3rd lvl 10

- Active: Aspect of Ash – 3rd lvl 5
- Active: True Ash Creation – 3rd lvl 7
- Active: Heart of Cinder – 2nd lvl 20
- Active: Storm of Cinders – 2nd lvl 20
- Passive: Ash and Ember Unity – 3rd lvl 5
- Passive: Ashen Wings – 2nd lvl 20
- Passive: Eyes of Ash – 2nd lvl 20
- Passive: Avatar of Ash – 2nd lvl 20
- Passive: Keeper of Ash – 3rd lvl 3

General Skills:
- Elos Standard language – lvl 6
- Harmony of the Drowned – lvl 1
- Heavy Archery – lvl 4
- Identify – lvl 8
- Meditation – 2nd lvl 20
- Veteran – lvl 6
- Arcane Magic Resistance – 2nd lvl 1
- Blast Resistance – 2nd lvl 5
- Blood Magic Resistance – lvl 14
- Corrosion Resistance – lvl 13
- Crystal Resistance – lvl 18
- Curse Resistance – 2nd lvl 2
- Dark Magic Resistance – lvl 12
- Death Magic Resistance – lvl 5
- Dust Magic Resistance – lvl 1
- Earth Magic Resistance – lvl 16
- Fear Resistance – lvl 9
- Health Drain Resistance – 2nd lvl 20
- Heat Resistance – 2nd lvl 12
- Ice Resistance – 2nd lvl 2
- Light Magic Resistance – lvl 17
- Lightning Resistance – 2nd lvl 6
- Mana Drain Resistance – 2nd lvl 20
- Mental Resistance – 2nd lvl 13
- Mist Magic Resistance – 2nd lvl 5
- Pain Tolerance – 2nd lvl 4
- Poison Resistance – 2nd lvl 9
- Silver Magic Resistance – lvl 1
- Void Magic Resistance – lvl 7
- Water Resistance – 2nd lvl 1
- Wind Resistance – 2nd lvl 1
- Wood Magic Resistance – lvl 1

Status:
Vitality: 875
Endurance: 233
Strength: 217
Dexterity: 223
Intelligence: 866
Wisdom: 869

Health: 8750/8750
Stamina: 2317/2330
Mana: 8475/8690

Nearly all of her Class skills had different names now, had more powerful aspects since the changes.

You can do it now. Survive the storms, fight the Miststalkers, fight off a bunch of nobles.

And maybe, maybe, I can finally face the Praetorians.

SEVENTY-SEVEN

Testing

Ilea was woken up by light shining through the missing window of her currently chosen apartment in Tremor. Sadly, no birds were chirping, and no busy city life could be heard outside. No distractions.

Her dreams had been filled with howling undead, silent Soul Rippers, and various other horrible monsters straight out of a fantasy novel, game, or film. In the dreams, these weren't beasts she wanted to fight but monsters that she'd run from in terror.

It took her a couple of minutes to shake the feeling, turning in her bed to face away from the sunlight as she grumbled. Eventually, food made its way into her mind.

Sitting up, Ilea realized she wasn't hungry. Of course she wasn't. Most of her eating since reaching the two hundreds had been done because she liked it, not because her body needed it.

Maybe not using armor all the time isn't so bad, she thought, feeling the suns on her skin for the first time in a while. A smile blossomed on her face. *Time for a field test.*

She sacrificed three hundred health to activate her third-tier State of—, no, her Azarinth Awakening aura. The first thing she noticed was that the runes that started to glow on her were blue again.

Welcome back.

Testing her healing, she found her health was back at its maximum after only two seconds.

Feels nearly twice as fast. And now it's the same if I heal others?

She assumed as much. The mention of herself healing more quickly had been removed, after all. Ilea had watched it all through her Sphere, noticing the blue wisps around her intensify as soon as her third tier had activated.

When her second aura, Aspect of Ash, activated, the lines on her body burned a deeper red than usual. Less fiery and flamboyant, more like bright lines of cinders cracking through her skin.

Even though her body was supposedly twice as dense and heavy, she felt lighter on her toes. Shadowboxing on the roof made her chuckle, her fists reaching their intended destination far more quickly than before.

The thing Ilea was most interested in was her Veil, now Armor of Ash. Activating the skill, she felt it instantly. Not like before, where the ash moved on its own and layered itself onto her skin or worn armor. Now she felt as if she had a say in the form it took.

Thinking of the armor Goliath had made, she tried recreating it and found the ash moving to her will. A dark gray, nearly black layer of solid ash resembling her Rose Hunter set quickly formed on her, melding over the clothes she was wearing.

Ilea looked at her arms and grinned. Not a piece was missing. Tendrils of ash writhed around the solid armor, giving it an ethereal touch. She could increase the effect if she wished, Ilea noticed.

That's pretty fucking cool, she thought, looking at herself through her Sphere, ash slowly swirling around her. Moving in it wasn't an issue either, the joints simply adjusting to accommodate every twist and flex.

Likely less durable during movements. Still better than real armor with actual separate pieces though.

Her eight limbs of ash came to life behind her, the tips sharpening before she carefully cut into the stone of the roof. Deep furrows were left behind. *Like fucking steel.* Moving to her armor, she tried to pierce it with the limbs but found it hard to penetrate even a millimeter.

Moment of truth.

Deactivating her armor, she watched in fascination as it quickly disintegrated, similar to her wings. She put on a Rose Hunter set and tried cutting into it. This time, she instantly felt the tip drill into her shoulder, the resistance barely registering.

Cuts through Stonehammer steel as if it were cloth.

She activated her ash armor again on top of her Stonehammer set but couldn't form it to her wishes, the ash simply layering over her steel armor instead. Trying to cut into it, she found it harder. Still, after a couple of seconds of applying pressure, she cut through the ash and then immediately through the steel.

So, until I find something substantially better, I'll stick with clothes or light armor plus my ash. Speaking of which…

Ilea put on some Hand-issue leather armor, one of the two remaining sets she had. She reactivated her ashen armor and found herself once again able to manipulate its look freely.

So I can change the look if it's not heavy?

The good thing about her Veil had been that the higher its level had been, the less mana it cost to maintain. The same was true for her evolved skill, so she kept the armor up.

The ashen limbs behind her swayed slightly, but otherwise, Ilea didn't feel anything massively different about them. Creating some ash in front of her, she formed a sphere, adding more and more as she squeezed it together with her magic.

More and more mana was transformed into pure ash, the sphere already looking solid. She heard one crunch, then another. When she finally couldn't make it any denser, she let it float into her hand. A solid black orb about five centimeters in diameter.

"Doesn't look like ash to me."

Circling it around herself, she let it fall into her hand again. Ilea barely felt the weight, but when she let it fall, it didn't even bounce, instead landing with a solid thump.

Jumping down from the building, she let the ball float next to her. Then, using all the magical power she could put into it, she slammed it into the ground.

Shards of rock flew past her and a cloud of dust formed, her Sphere letting her know the orb had penetrated several meters into the stone floor.

"Damn. Okay, that's pretty fucking cool."

She tried once more, this time forming a lance, again adding as much ash as possible. The result was a projectile one meter fifty in length and around two centimeters in diameter.

Fly.

And fly it did, aimed at the house next to her own. The spear crashed through the front wall, out the back wall, and continued onward. Ilea spread her wings and flew up, just barely seeing the thing vanish into the void after penetrating three houses.

Okay, viable ranged weapon acquired.

Creating two more spears, Ilea wondered if throwing them would be better. Her next experiment revealed that her lack of a throwing skill made that option less than effective. Her magic allowed for a straight shot, while her throw managed to penetrate the first wall but then crashed sideways into the next one.

Just let me throw things please.

Ilea mentally added a throwing ability to her training list.

"Wait… my body should be around twice as dense and heavy. The ash around me is my body, right? Gaining the bonuses from passive skills."

She smiled. *That's why they're so fucking destructive.*

Ilea looked at her arm as she walked to the now half-destroyed house. *Wave of Ember, Storm of Cinders.* She hit the wall with her fist, using the evolved skill, but not as it had been used before.

Embers, magic, and fire shot out of her fist when it connected with the wall, blasting through the portion she had hit.

Looks more like a wave of embers than it did before.

Her Sphere had made the hit look even more spectacular, a large amount of mana surging into the air, creating an explosion of heat in the process.

Blinking onto the house and activating her newfound Heart of Cinder, her body immediately grew hotter, as if a fire had been lit within her. Then it continued to grow, wisps of flame forming on her ashen armor, embers floating away.

Ten seconds later, the floor was getting scorched. Another ten seconds later, she started to lose health, her body burning up from within. Ilea smirked and counter-healed. Even with her impressive healing, the blazing heat outpaced her mana. Soon, her health began sinking again. She even had to turn off her Sphere as the brightness she was giving off nearly blinded her.

When her health was down a thousand points, Ilea released the stored-up heat in a blast around her. Fire erupted, and when she blinked her eyes, eighty percent of the house had simply vanished in a near-perfect sphere around her. Disintegrated to ash. Even the ground she'd been standing on had sunk several meters. Chunks of roof that had been outside the range of the blast fell down all around, a few bouncing off her armor and landing on the ground.

Yeah, I'm going to keep this one.

She hadn't gotten any options for new skills anyway, but more might come up. Now she was interested in the third tier of this one in particular. Ilea tested it again, creating heat for one second, then ten, and then as much as she could until her health started going down.

One second created a shock wave of heat around her. It likely wouldn't do anything major against a powerful enemy but was possibly enough to push away lower-leveled creatures. The ten-second one was already a fiery sphere, expanding quickly and burning up everything in its path.

Probably still more powerful than anything I could produce before the evolutions.

The blast, when it went as far as causing her to lose health, was devastating. Ilea had a hard time grasping the power of it all against stone alone.

I should be able to level my Heat Resistance like this.

Considering her constitution and healing, the blast was likely much stronger than most similar spells could produce. Others might scale through mana, but for her, it was a matter of resisting the heat as it built. Keeping the skill active for longer didn't cost exponentially more mana. Just the same rate for longer.

Ilea was starting to get used to the changes now, feeling nearly as comfortable as before. Having no use for her medium and heavy sets of armor anymore for now, she stored them all, to be sold or gifted at a later time.

Should talk to Goliath about light armor then. His other... creation certainly doesn't count as that.

Blinking to her room, Ilea stored her bed, one of her most prized possessions. Blinking outside again, she spread her wings before making her way down toward the part of the upper city that hadn't been cleared yet. It didn't take her long to find a patrolling knight.

[Knight of the Rose – lvl 305]

"Hey, what a coincidence," she smiled.

Overall, the ashen armor she was wearing felt nearly as comfortable as her Stonehammer set, though she assumed the ashen one being less comfortable had to do with the leather armor she wore beneath.

Fighting naked would probably be the nicest. Though I do like the ability to dismiss my ash and still be clothed.

The knight, his shield held to the side, rushed at her and brought his sword down. The blows had been enough to dent her Stonehammer steel armor in the past. Enough to cut into her too, easily breaking through her Veil when she'd been fifty levels lower.

This time, she simply watched as the weapon came down, trusting in her third-tier Azarinth Fighting, and smiled when the steel smashed into her armored shoulder with a dull thump. *Nothing.* Ilea felt the ash on her and how it pushed against the knight's weapon. The attack damaged her about as much as her own ashen limbs had during her testing. In other words, not at all.

"Oh, Mr. Knight. How the tables turn."

She grabbed the sword before he could react and dragged him toward her. *Absolute Destruction.* Ilea's fist lashed out, smashing into the knight's chest with a fiery bang as bits of blue smoke and mana wisps shot out from the impact site, steel caving in from the sheer force of it.

She had used the full hundred mana. Keeping her hand on the blade, Ilea watched in awe as the knight stumbled back. A moment later, he slumped to the ground.

Overdid it a bit, hmm?

Even with the boost her Destruction had gotten, Ilea hadn't expected to kill one of the knights with a single hit.

Maybe he was damaged... no, wait, they regenerate. I guess the skill evolving and my aura boosting Intelligence will do that, coupled with all the other stuff.

Looking at the sword in her hand, she dropped it. "I don't need this."

'ding' You have defeated [Knight of the Rose – lvl 305] – Bonus experience is granted.

For that? Well, I won't say no. Considering what Maro had said, she'd need quite a bit more to level at this stage. *Undead knights, perhaps. The real deal, this time.*

Ilea spread her wings. "Got a head to get back."

SEVENTY-EIGHT

Missing Pieces

Ilea found her head where she'd left it.

"At least none of those void fuckers found the snack I left behind," she said. Feeling her heart rate quicken, she started meditating, forcing herself to blink a moment later.

The blood on the head had dried, her eyes lifeless and mouth slightly open. She knelt down, reaching out with her hand but hesitating. The armor on her arm receded when she touched her own face, closing the eyes a moment later.

Is it still me? Or did I die here and my healing created a clone?

"That's not a road to go down, Ilea," she muttered.

A moment later, she sighed. *When I lost my head, my awareness split. I chose the body. I didn't die.*

Her chest heated up as she held the head in her hands, staring at it as the ground began to blacken beneath her feet. The hair caught fire first. Ilea shut down her Sphere and closed her eyes, touching the cold forehead to her own. Half a minute passed before a rush of heat exploded from her, the sudden heat and sound the only things she noticed.

When she opened her eyes again, Ilea was happy to find the head had gone. Ash fell to the floor. She attributed the head's lack of Heat Resistance to the fact that it was simply discarded tissue and bone, not connected to her mana anymore.

Glad that's gone.

She reached out with her Ash and Ember Unity, feeling the remaining ash. *Still warm,* she noted. Whether it was her Unity or her True Ash Creation, Ilea knew then that she could banish the ash, turn it back into mana. Not for her to use but simply to give it back to nature.

Her eyes closed again, and after a brief moment, there was nothing left of what she had lost. Then the sound of steps caught her attention, the familiar tapping of steel on stone.

She opened her eyes and watched in silence as the monster turned the corner, seeing her in the small black crater, nothing remaining of the rotten and ancient house that had once stood on the site.

Now, only a woman stood there, clad in a writhing armor of ash. Eight limbs grew from her back, as if conjured from the air itself. She prepared herself, eyes focused on the dead white eye sockets of her enemy.

The knight leaped for her. Waiting for the last moment, Ilea stepped a little to the side, letting the blade cut into her shoulder. The weapon dug into her ash with a dull crack, as if it had hit brittle stone.

She didn't take her eyes off the creature as she used her hand to push the blade as it glided out of her armor. Perhaps if he'd used a sharpened blade, the knight would have reached her skin. As it was, the armor reformed quickly as her own strength battled that of the knight.

She smiled under her ashen helmet, glaring at the undead knight, which had once felt like a near-insurmountable challenge. Ilea had to admit that the monster was stronger. Still, the blade slid out, and her ashen limbs crashed into him.

Storm of Cinders. Ilea watched as blazing heat rushed over the creature, embers lighting the darkness, flames burning. Its skin was singed, its armor scratched, and two ashen limbs even managed to pierce its torso.

She lashed out with her fist, ignoring the knight doing the same. Her blow landed first, blue energy erupting from the impact as her mana sought his very core, shattering his insides.

The counterattack crashed into her chest, but her armor held, her body uninjured. Ilea still held the sword, the knight frantically ripping it free after several failed attempts. The blade flashed, and as Ilea lifted her arm to deflect it, another strike of her fist sent both embers and destructive healing mana into the once proud knight of Rhyvor.

Her ashen limbs switched to mana intrusion as well while her chest started heating up. Two more hits landed before the knight's sword smashed into her side. This time, she felt some damage, but it was nothing serious, the injury already healed before he prepared his next attack.

Then the heat from within her was released, coupled with a strike from all eight ashen limbs. The monster staggered and jumped back, but Ilea simply appeared right in front of it. Her fist, clad in hardened ash, punched into his armored chest, mana flowing into him as he was pushed back.

The blade moved, but Ilea was too close, her left hand hitting his forearm to stop the blow before it even came. Then her other hand shot out, fingers grabbing onto his helmet through the sockets for his eyes.

How does that feel?

She held onto his sword hand, struggling to keep him from attacking as her ashen limbs cut into his neck. Again and again, the knight punched her with his free arm, trying to dislodge her grip but failing to do so. Finally, he managed to rip his right hand free, slashing at her neck with his sword. Ash formed around her arm as she held it up, intercepting the blows time and time again.

Then, with a wet sound, her ashen limbs finished cutting through his neck, piercing the steel mail and ripping through the chain links below. Ilea whipped her hand to the side, the blade stuck in her ash was flung to the ground, and steel clattered on stone as she kicked the knight's body away from under his head. She held on to the helmet, dead eyes below still staring at her.

"That's how it feels. Fuck you too."

'ding' You have defeated [Undead Rose Knight – lvl 510] – For defeating an enemy two hundred and ten or more levels above your own, bonus experience is granted.

Ilea breathed out slowly, feeling the power coursing through her body. The last punches had managed to deal some damage. Her arm had been injured by the sword, but with every passing second, her healing mended the tissue.

She tossed the head toward the body, then turned around as her wings spread behind her.

Now to get that leg back.

She remembered she'd actually lost two legs down here. She felt like going for the first one.

* * *

It was lying there, untouched, a dozen meters away from the Kingsguard guarding the entrance to the palace. Ilea frowned, somehow more annoyed by that fact. The suns felt nice, she noted, taking a moment to appreciate how far she'd come. Previously, the knight before her had been too hard to engage, had cut through her armor with ease. Now she felt like she had a shot.

Still have two third-tier skill points as well.

She kept both for now to gauge the skill changes and see what would be worth advancing. If Maro was to be believed, she'd gain another third-tier point every ten levels after three hundred, meaning if she continued to engage ridiculously higher-leveled beings, she'd accumulate them in a reasonable time.

At least if the experience necessary didn't go up by just as ridiculous amounts. The humans to have reached these levels would be few, and Ilea assumed most did it over decades or even centuries, not in the span of two or three years.

Why bother if you're already set for damn near eternal life at two hundred?

There were various reasons, of course, but extending political power took time and effort. Ilea doubted even an organization like the Golden Lily, shrouded in mystery, had more than a handful of people at her level.

She could activate her third-tier blink anytime to return to her house, then to Ravenhall. She could join the war, if it was still going on, and maybe help tip the balance. She could go and look for the Lily, find the people Eve had been looking for, the people likely responsible for her death as well. She could try any of the challenges she'd postponed. Fighting the Kingsguards and freeing Maro was one of them.

Then there was the Taleen. Even if Christopher had found out more about the teleportation gates, she had a dungeon here that was still mostly unexplored. There could be secrets inside that might help, but if Ilea was honest, it felt more personal now. When Kyrian had been teleported, she'd worried about him, but since then, months had passed. By now he would've escaped or if he was still stuck, he would've found a way to survive long term. And if he hadn't returned to Ravenhall yet, they'd find a way to get to him eventually.

This wasn't just about him now, she realized. It was about her first venture into a Taleen dungeon, about the expedition that she'd explored and fought with down below Dawntree. About the machines they'd fought down in that ruin, the machines that had cursed and nearly killed her.

She'd briefly faced one of them in Iz and just about held her own, but she'd still been afraid. And she knew that even though she tried to deny it, she still felt it, the cold feeling in her stomach, where the scythe had pierced her.Ilea breathed in deep and felt the dense magic flowing through her, the power she'd gained from her time in the north. She savored the thought but decided not to rush it, not to face that challenge immediately. She had new toys to play with, and she wanted to know the extent of her magic before going back into that dungeon.

Maro first. And the Kingsguards.

Ilea jumped down, walking casually toward the knight. His armor glistened in the sunlight, his sword sharp and held at the ready.

Let's see how much damage you do this time.

As soon as he spotted her, the blade flashed. A horizontal strike aimed at her chest. Ilea saw the invisible force moving in her Sphere. She saw the damage before it hit, a big grin on her face.

Then the force crashed into her, pushing her back half a meter, the armor on her chest cut, blood oozing through for a split second before it closed again, the shallow wound healing in mere seconds.

"Not so easy this time," she said, four lances of ash forming above her.

Let's see if these do anything. Damage buffs apply, toughness and density buffs apply. I don't see why they shouldn't pack a punch against this guy.

The knight seemed to evaluate her as he stepped forward. His blade moved through the air in two quick motions. Again, Ilea saw the attacks coming in her Sphere. Very quick, but nothing she couldn't handle. She blinked several meters to her left, the lances now reaching their optimal density and form.

Ilea let her intent be known, and the ash followed her wishes. All four lances barreled toward the knight. She was amazed to see the knight actually dodged three of them, deflecting the last with his greatsword. The three that missed cut into the stone ground, sending rubble flying. The deflected one crashed deep into a nearby pillar.

"Okay, this is already getting boring. Let's get up close and personal."

Ilea sacrificed three hundred health, feeling the power of her auras rushing through her veins.

The power to kill what I need to kill and protect who I want to protect. She grinned. *Maybe the Sentinel stuff wasn't too far off after all.*

She took two steps, then vanished, an invisible blade rushing past her disappearing form. She dashed to the side as the knight slashed at her from a couple of meters away. Ash started forming around her, her limbs poised and ready to strike.

Ilea started storing heat while continuing to sacrifice mana into her third-tier Azarinth Awakening. Dodging another blade by jumping and twisting her body in midair, she reached the enemy. Her limbs rushed out, two small spikes of ash she'd formed also flying in from the side.

To her surprise, the Kingsguard jumped back. Then he started to *run away*.

She followed, his sword slashing her way time and time again as she avoided the blades of mana. Twice they grazed her, the ash quickly reforming. Once, an attack landed on her leg, but her damage foresight had told her all she needed to know. The wound quickly closed again, neither interrupting her pursuit nor stopping her from forming additional lances as well as smaller projectiles in the air around her.

The knight rushed through the streets of Tremor, jumping into houses and through walls to avoid the spears and spikes as well as Ilea herself.

Ilea decided to blink, closing the distance immediately. To her surprise, the knight had turned, sword already rushing at her. *Unavoidable.* In the split second she had, she twisted a little to the side, her limbs and right arm lashing out to use the undead's strike to her advantage.

Activating her Heart of Cinder, the fire swept through the knight and the house. His blade slowed ever so slightly as the heat washed over his armor, buffeting the stone around them before Ilea's attacks hit too.

The sword cut into her shoulder, managed to penetrate to her skin before the knight let loose his ranged attack point blank, the blade still stuck inside her. This time, it cut halfway to the bone, but Ilea's own attack sent mana back into the creature in turn.

The remaining projectiles slammed into his face, turning his head into a pincushion. His free hand struck at her head, but Ilea stayed unmoving, withstanding the force before healing her lightly bruised face.

The knight jumped back, sword ripping out of her shoulder as the armor closed, the wound quickly healing thereafter. Blood dripped from his blade as Ilea continued her attack. The knight was also a triple mark, but neither speed nor skill separated him much from the undead she'd faced earlier.

It had magic and certainly more brains as well as a complete set of armor and healing support from Maro. Which just meant she had to deal with it now. The sharp weapon was an added issue, as Ilea's defenses were definitely more durable against the dull blades of the more feral knights.

She could see it too now, the connection the knight had to the palace, to the king and his unholy necromantic machine. It pulsed with power, mana flowing along the thin invisible strand.

I wonder if I could cut it... with a suitable attack?

Ilea slashed one of her ashen limbs through it but found it simply passed through with no effect. She couldn't touch it.

The fight continued with the Kingsguard using the same tactics. They would clash, it would flee, then it would reengage at random intervals with impossible-to-avoid attacks.

After several repeats of the same exchanges, she grabbed onto his blade as it cut into her yet again. Ilea charged up Absolute Destruction and pumped destructive mana into him but was surprised to find the knight immediately let go of his weapon and jumped back.

"Really?" she asked, ripping the blade out of her side before her skin and ash quickly closed over the wound.

Trying to store the blade in her necklace failed, not that she'd suspected a different result. Feeling a strong pull on the weapon, she resisted, instead sprinting at the knight – blade in hand. Ilea had no intention of using the weapon, but as long as it was in her hand, all he had were his fists.

When she reached him, she smashed her fist into his chest, her ashen limbs delivering their Storm of Cinders a split second after. The blade was ripped from her hand, turning in midair before he clasped it and attacked. This time, she had time to dodge before she could continue her assault, sacrificing more health for her aura.

When she noticed her health dropping from the heat within her, Ilea blinked once again, shifting her body ever so slightly to take the following blade strike in her arm. The blast was released in a dome of fire and cinders, vaporizing all the structures nearby. The knight's silver armor was left smoking, the front black in parts.

The knight stumbled back with one arm raised to shield himself. His sword came free as Ilea blinked to cover the two-meter distance between them. Charging her Destruction for three full seconds, she released it – coupled with the third tier of Aspect of Ash.

The arm covered in ashen armor suddenly exploded with fire, blue mana breaking free even before her fist landed. The recoil from the impact shuddered through her, the punch caving his helmet in before he was sent flying backward. Twice he hit the ground before skidding to a stop. Ilea landed on him with her knees next to his chest.

He raised his blade, but she smashed his arm aside, her other fist repeatedly crashing into the helmet, blue wisps and fiery cinders cascading out with each impact. Her limbs focused on his right arm, cutting into the armor and holding it down as more and more ash formed to keep him in place.

When he was secured, Ilea charged her Destruction for ten seconds before delivering one thousand mana directly into whatever was left of his brain. Her mana was quite low at that point, all the attacks having eaten away at her resources faster than she'd have liked.

The punch squashed his head, killing him and breaking his connection to the center of the palace.

Ilea stood slowly, staggering back a step. She breathed heavily, feeling more alive than she had in months. Then she laughed, the smile on her face warm and fierce.

One more step.

Removing each piece of armor, she stored both the corpse and the gear in her necklace and stood up. Her mana was recovering quickly. The only reason she'd been so aggressive was the fact that the Kingsguards had a way to heal themselves. Otherwise, a slower approach would definitely have been beneficial.

I wonder if the others are that defensive? Trying to run away from me while regenerating. Who does he think he is, me?

The sword was in excellent shape, not a chip showing and of rare quality. Seeing as it only took up a single storage space in her necklace, she decided to keep it.

'ding' You have defeated [Kingsguard – lvl 508] – For defeating an enemy two hundred or more levels above your own, bonus experience is granted.

'ding' Absolute Destruction reaches 3rd lvl 10

'ding' Azarinth Fighting reaches 3rd lvl 6

'ding' Aspect of Ash reaches 3rd lvl 6

Ilea grumbled about the lack of a level up before walking over to her stinking leg and grabbing the awful thing. She charged up Heart of Cinders before blasting the surroundings, turning the rotten flesh to ash.

RIP leg. Your service shall not be forgotten.

"Now, where's the next one?"

SEVENTY-NINE

Approach to Power

"Three hundred and you've already taken one down? Not bad, Ilea," Maro nodded. "Especially for a healer." His grin brightened his face, green eyes sparkling.

"New title, then? Suspected as much. Well, I guess I'm going to be underestimated again," Ilea said, sitting down on a chair and putting the Kingsguard blade away again after showing it to him. "You're not fucking with me, are you?"

[Necromancer – lvl 310]

Maro laughed. "No. For once, I'm not. You identify as a healer. Having told me about both classes leveling, I assume your first class is the healer one. If your second one gets higher, you'll be a warrior or mage again, depending on what it is."

He chuckled before continuing. "Well, speaking of underestimating, I have to give credit where credit is due. I thought I'd be stuck in here for a decade at least. When you talked about the Descent and the Taleen dungeon, I hoped for a couple of years. But to think it took less than a few months..." He shook his head. "Outstanding. And here I thought *I* was crazy."

Ilea smiled, relaxing in her Hand-issue leather armor, which was now rather torn. Nothing that would threaten the integrity of the outfit, but she'd have to change it eventually.

And I have regenerating armor now. That fight would have used up, like, ten sets of my usual ones.

Maro's eyes were focused on her. "You're one of the youngest people I've met who has reached three hundred. And I have a feeling you're going to advance even further."

"How would you know how old I am?" Ilea asked with a smile.

She didn't question his other statement. Now that she could take out the normal knights with ease, she had plenty more challenges waiting for her, and those came with level ups as well.

"A feeling."

"It's already been a long road, even though I'm young. Lots and lots of fighting." She stretched and gave a yawn.

"You don't really need much sleep anymore, do you? Oh... You're tired from all the fighting. Well, I can see that. I appreciate it, you know."

Ilea smirked, leaning her head back to stare up at the white marble ceiling.

"I didn't just do it for you, Maro. You could, however, have given me some info about the magical abilities they have. The one I faced sent mana waves capable of cutting through steel my way."

"Sure you didn't do it for me." He smiled, looking incredibly handsome. "As for their abilities, when I created them, they didn't have such things. Capable swordsmen and women, sure. You'll have to figure the rest out by yourself."

Guess hoping to get a dossier of Kingsguard abilities was too much to hope for.

"Well, now that you're able to take them out, we can visit Lisburg together when I'm out. Catelyn told me most of it's now a place where Awakened dwell. Fine by me, as long as there's something to eat and drink. She did let me know that some of the vineyards still remain," he added with a grin.

"Sure. Sorry I didn't manage to check it out earlier," Ilea said.

He shook his head. "It was a whim. I'd hoped for you to go, not expected it, nor for you to get me out in the first place."

"Can't imagine a more relaxing dungeon exploration team than one with you and Terok," Ilea said, lifting her head to give a very meaningful eyeroll.

He snorted. "Oh, stop it, you love us. Even if you hate us."

How does that even make sense? Ilea asked herself, then realized she was smiling despite his nonsense.

Sitting up again, she asked, "You're not going to visit Elana in Hallowfort? I'm sure she already has plans to implement you somewhere in her takeover of the world."

His lips formed a line, eyes losing some of their joy. "She does. Which is why she's not here and why I won't be visiting her. At least, not immediately. I declined to help. We were a good team, built a kingdom and governed more or less successfully. Decades of work and dedication. I would fight and die for Rhyvor, Ilea, even today. Nearly did in the end. But this is it."

"And here I thought a necromancer at three hundred wouldn't need sleep either."

Maro snorted. "She blames me, I think." His voice went quiet again. "For being stuck with me all this time."

"When you were king and queen?"

"No. In here."

Ilea raised her eyebrows. "Well, as far as I recall, it was her choice. Or was that a lie?"

"It was her choice."

Ilea smiled. "Then that's that. There are always two people in a relationship. I wouldn't overthink it too much."

"Easy for you to say. You didn't get your wife stuck in a vault for a few thousand years."

"You didn't either. You both did it to yourselves."

He smiled at her and nodded. "Easier said than felt."

"I'll take your word for it."

Maro looked at her for a long moment.

"What?" Ilea asked.

"You remind me of an old adventurer friend of mine. On closer inspection, you seem quite different, but there are some things that fit."

"You think she's still around? She might be fun if you think we're similar."

"She was cut apart in an inn by a bunch of mercenaries she offended. Half-drunk, I was told."

"Doesn't sound like me then. I'm uncuttable. Did you kill the mercenaries?"

"Uncuttable? Doubt it. She was pretty tough too. Not expecting an attack can do a number on you. And no. The girl had friends all over. Someone else reached them before me. Nasty scene." His voice had dropped even more.

"Yeah," Ilea said. "Sorry to hear about it."

"It is long past. Have you chosen your new third-tier skills already?"

"I haven't, actually," Ilea said. With all the advancements she'd already gotten, she'd nearly forgotten about them.

3rd-tier skill points available [Azarinth Sentinel]: 1
Skills available for 3rd-tier advancement in [Azarinth Sentinel]:
- Sentinel Sphere
- Azarinth Perception
- Azarinth Reversal

3rd-tier skill points available [Kin of Ash]: 1
Skills available for 3rd-tier advancement in [Kin of Ash]:
- Storm of Cinders

- Avatar of Ash
- Heart of Cinder

Well... they're all fucking amazing. Sphere and Perception would likely give some utility, and Reversal might be offensive power. All are interesting. Never know what you're going to get though. Box of bloody chocolates.

For her second Class, Ilea was favoring either Storm of Cinders or Heart of Cinder. Both could enhance her offensive capabilities substantially.

"Some advice from you, maybe?"

"Bring it," Maro said, smirking in his usual charming way.

"One is a sphere of perception around me. One increases my reflexes and perception passively, and the last one lets me use my healing offensively as well as changing a mana intrusion attack I have, giving it a mana drain on hit."

She quickly explained what her three Azarinth skills did without going into their second stages. Maro seemed to actually give it some real thought. She'd expected him to immediately shoot out an answer, likely some kind of joke. She knew from their previous talks that he was serious quite often, but looking at his face and constant smirk now, it was hard to believe those memories were real.

"I think all those skills sound good. You won't know what the third tier does until you get it. Maybe you could wait a little longer? It's not been long since you hit three hundred, I assume. You could get used to all the changes and then make a decision?"

"And then get used to even more changes? No. Look, I don't intend to stay at three hundred. Soon, all of them will be in the third tier anyway. It's just a matter of choosing the best ones for now, in this very moment."

He met her eyes before responding. "Then it just comes down to what you need. Survivability? Damage? Speed? Maneuverability? Detection? Can your reflexes keep up with all the other gains you have gotten? No? Take that one. Any reason your sphere isn't up to the task anymore? Take that. Need a boost to your healing and the mana intrusion attack? Take that one. If you're not in need of anything specific, take the one you use the most."

"I don't think I'm in need of anything. I use my sphere constantly, as well as my healing and the mana intrusion."

"Well, you still have eyes, as well as your other senses. I don't think reliance on anything like that should come first. There are spells and enchantments that can make perception skills like yours a terrible experience. Trust me. Happened to me once. If the choice is between that and a boost to your healing and mana intrusion, I'd take the latter."

Ilea nodded. "Reasonable points. Or a necromancer trying to deceive me right before he takes over the world."

"True," he admitted. "What about your second class?"

"Defensive skill passively boosting my body as well as speed and perception, mana intrusion skill... well, not purely anymore, and an area attack that targets a sphere around me."

Maro didn't pause for as long this time. "Can you use both mana intrusion spells at the same time?" Ilea nodded. "Then for me at least, it would be clear. If you're not in need of anything else, take the two skills possibly boosting your mana intrusion. You'll get the combined boost of both."

"Hey, that actually makes sense. Why not. I'll get two more again at three ten anyway," Ilea said, then used the points on the respective skills.

'ding' Azarinth Reversal reaches 3rd lvl 1
Passive: Azarinth Reversal – lvl 3rd lvl 1:
You have learned of Absolute Destruction and Sentinel Reconstruction. Now you will learn of their Reversal.
Upon activation, Absolute Destruction will send some of the struck enemy's mana into yourself. No mana will be released on impact, reducing Absolute Destruction's offensive potential to zero.
Upon activation, Sentinel Reconstruction will send a destructive force of channeled mana into yourself or an enemy you touch. The healing aspects are reduced to zero.
2nd stage: You may have both the original and reversed aspects activated at the same time.
3rd stage: Healing, power, resilience, and speed. An Azarinth Healer requires balance. Your respective Destruction and Reconstruction spells have their potency increased by a static 25% of your lowest stat. [100%]
Category: Body Enhancement

So what you're telling me is I should invest in Endurance?

Ilea looked at her ten remaining stat points and put them into Wisdom. Getting more mana she could use for anything would be the most beneficial thing at the moment. Especially now she felt both her defense and offense were covered.

For a while, at least.

'ding' Storm of Cinders reaches 3rd lvl 1
Active: Storm of Cinders – 3rd lvl 1:
Burn the inside of whatever your body hits with a surge of heat and embers or release the attack in a burst of fire and cinders.
2nd stage: The flame burns on. Targets hit will have fire burning through or on them. Time and consecutive attacks will increase the effect.
3rd stage: Storm of Cinders burns away all that stands against it, damaging mana intrusion prevention capabilities of defensive enchantments, as well as natural and manufactured armor.
Category: Ashen magic

"Not bad," she said, releasing the breath she'd been holding.

"What did you get?"

Ilea smiled. "I'm not telling. One was really good though."

Maro pouted. "You're no fun."

"Says the guy stuck in his bloody necromancer machine, forcing me to take care of his undead."

"Nobody is forcing you, Ilea. I would understand anybody unwilling to face creatures two hundred levels higher than themselves. I simply know you well enough by now to know that you welcome such a challenge."

"Wouldn't you?" she asked, and the king gave her a somewhat complicated expression. "Oh, don't disappoint me now. Not after all the stories of your reckless adventures."

"With a team of experts and friends. Prepared and knowledgeable about our foes. I don't intend to lose limbs, Ilea, even if I could recover in mere days. I know you're powerful, but don't overestimate yourself just because you can avoid getting hit."

Ilea walked a little closer and stared into his eyes.

"Last week..." she started, but then she stopped. The part of her that was suspicious reminded her that sharing something like her loss of a head wasn't in her best interest. "I can take care of myself."

She blinked out of the room.

* * *

Ilea decided to lure the knights out into the palace courtyard, as few of them as possible at a time. Some patrolled or stood in twos, making it nearly impossible to face them one on one. The two Kingsguards patrolling the halls upstairs were the first she tried to separate. One carrying two short broad swords, guards on his hands. The other one had a nasty halberd. Creating a tiny nail of ash, she sent it flying at the swordsman.

Right before it hit, the knight vanished, reappearing a couple of meters in front of her. She saw a pulse of mana in her Sphere before his movements suddenly sped up, and Ilea blinked back to avoid the attack.

Shit, something's fucky.

The other knight had of course turned as well, looking at her before swinging his halberd downward. Ilea's eyes widened at the storm of magic that shot her way, noticeable from the destroyed tiles and ceiling even before it reached her Sphere's range.

She couldn't blink again so soon, so she braced herself as the full force of the attack hit both her and the sword knight, both of them flung out through a newly created hole in the wall. She rolled to a stop, checking for injuries and getting ready to face the next attack.

What she found, however, was that her armor had held up and the damage was minor at best and quickly taken care of. She allowed herself a smile and turned toward the knight getting up a couple of meters away.

Blinking next to him, she punched at his head. He suddenly lit up in her Sphere and dodged away, far faster than he'd moved before. Rushing after him, she punched again. This time, she felt a strange magic taking hold, her fist moving at a slower pace than before.

The next moment, she saw his blades darting toward her neck. Ilea's eyes widened, but the strange effect she felt passed just as she ducked down to dodge. She was ready to counter his strikes but found the blades suddenly sped up, moving too quickly for her to blink, and cut into her ashen helmet.

The strikes punched through her ash armor, their impact trembling through her. She reached out with her hands to grasp the blades, the tips having cut into her left cheek and her brow, just barely drawing blood.

Not quite, she thought and grinned, pulling the blades out before jumping back right after. *Not just his body, the magic is affecting me too. But if I can take his hits, even just barely, I'll have a chance.*

The next time he rushed at her, she simply focused on his torso, her chest heating up in the meantime. Her ashen limbs swung out to his sides when he reached her as Ilea's fist went for his stomach.

She ignored the blades moving to pierce her heart and stomach, moving her body slightly as the blades cut into her Veil, adding more shallow wounds. Her own fist landed this time, albeit slowed again, all her mana intrusion skills surging into him before her ashen limbs closed around his back.

The knight removed his blades with movements far too fast for her to react, vanishing a split second later. She watched as another wave of force came her way, a cone of energy ripping the ground open.

Ilea didn't dodge this time, bracing herself as the magic washed over and through her. She gritted her teeth and was pushed a couple meters back.

Weaker the further away I am. Deal with the fast one first. I wonder what type of magic that is. Never seen it before.

She saw the halberd user moving slowly and attacking at range, allowing her to face the swordsman directly. A combination that would've been devastating if not for her insanely high resilience and healing.

I think I can work with this.

Ilea tried and failed to dodge his attacks, some of his strikes cutting deeper. The only reason why she was still in the fight was her vastly improved defenses and her ashen armor. She fought with her defenses and healing in mind, trading blows time and time again.

When the heat in her chest had grown to the point where it started to overwhelm her healing, Ilea waited for the next halberd attack. Seeing the sword warrior teleport away, she spotted the disturbance in her Sphere where he would appear and blinked.

Instantly, she released her Heart of Cinder, and though the knight accelerated, he was unable to escape the expanding sphere. The blast sent him tumbling. Ilea was close behind and grappled him before he could recover.

The two crashed down as Ilea started charging up Absolute Destruction, unmoving as he hacked into her armor with one sword. Each strike was accelerated, hitting the same spot again and again. He was going for her heart, digging fractionally deeper with each hit.

A wave of force was on its way from the other knight when Ilea's slowed fist smashed into the swordsman's helmet, bright magic erupting into it before his rotten skull and helmet burst with dark blood and shrapnel.

A few *dings* entered her mind before she blinked away, avoiding the blast.

EIGHTY

Power Cleaning Montage

'ding' You have learned the General Skill Time Magic Resistance – lvl 1
The intricacies of time magic are difficult to grasp, its secrets hidden forever to most who attempt the plunge. A rare few have managed to bend the elusive force to their will, making it a dangerous tool both for themselves and for their enemies.

'ding' Time Magic Resistance reaches lvl 2

Time magic? Shit.

She was glad the knight hadn't been able to do more than slow her a little and make his own movements faster.

Time magic exists?

Returning to the now, Ilea saw the sword was still stuck in her chest, ash growing around the wound before she grabbed the handle and ripped it out, a spray of blood spattering on the ground.

Actually did manage to pierce my heart. Might've killed me. If I wasn't me.

She sent healing through her body, her heart rebuilt in moments, as was the armor he'd pierced before.

Now, let's see what else you can do, she thought and advanced on the second knight.

Lances of ash formed around her, five of them in total as she walked slowly toward the halberd-wielding member of the Kingsguard, who held his weapon steady.

Ilea shot her spears at him, and he swung his weapon. Starting to run right before the two attacks collided, Ilea blinked to the side and kept her focus on the knight, watching as her lances were stopped in the air and flung aside.

When she reached him, her fist crashed into his back. Another hit landed when the butt of his weapon hit the ground, releasing a spherical force attack. Ilea could have blinked to avoid it, but she didn't. She wanted to see if she could take it.

She braced herself and was pushed back, her armor slowly stripped away millimeter by millimeter before her leather armor was ripped apart too. And then it ended. Pushed back a couple of meters, she reformed her armor, a little annoyed at her destroyed set of leathers. At least her skin hadn't been ripped away too, just badly bruised.

He swung his halberd, releasing another attack from point-blank range. This time she blinked behind him before she started charging up her destruction. Her ashen limbs delivered their Storm of Cinders, focused on his back to strip away whatever mana intrusion defenses his armor held.

Right before he repeated the spherical attack, Ilea punched him with her fist, sending around three hundred mana through his system before she blinked, avoiding the sphere that expanded right after. The ground shook, cracking and splitting.

Her own area attack had again reached the point where her healing couldn't keep up, so she sprinted back at him.

"Let's see how you brush *this* off!"

Blinking past his attack, she released Heart of Cinder. Fire rushed over him, powerful enough to turn the very stone below to ash.

He was pushed forward and stumbled, Ilea closing the distance in an instant, ashen limbs again focused on the spot on his back. She was surprised when they pierced the metal, pushing the knight down into the ground.

Before she could press on, a noise echoed in her mind, letting her know that she'd won.

'ding' You have defeated [Kingsguard – lvl 500] – For defeating an enemy two hundred levels above your own, bonus experience is granted.

'ding' You have defeated [Kingsguard – lvl 503] – For defeating an enemy two hundred or more levels above your own, bonus experience is granted.

'ding' Azarinth Sentinel has reached lvl 301 – Five stat points awarded

'ding' Azarinth Fighting reaches 3rd lvl 7

'ding' Keeper of Ash reaches 3rd lvl 4

"That was fun," she said with a wide smile, storing the corpses of the knights in her necklace.

Don't know why Maro thinks leveling up after three hundred is difficult. Another level done. Easy.

* * *

The second set of patrolling knights was easier to deal with, another halberd and time magic duo. She lost both her eyes to the time warrior in this fight, as well as a bunch of fingers as she tried to pin him down long enough to kill him. Another plus point to her sphere. She took the halberd knight out in the same way as the first.

Level five hundred, she mused, already wondering about her next upgrades. *Get used to what you have now. And train up that Time Magic Resistance in case you ever face something that could just freeze you entirely,* she thought, humming to herself as she looked for her next enemies in the ancient palace.

'ding' You have defeated [Kingsguard – lvl 505] – For defeating an enemy two hundred or more levels above your own, bonus experience is granted.

'ding' You have defeated [Kingsguard – lvl 510] – For defeating an enemy two hundred or more levels above your own, bonus experience is granted.

'ding' Kin of Ash has reached lvl 301 – Five stat points awarded

'ding' Absolute Destruction reaches 3rd lvl 11

'ding' Blast Resistance reaches 2nd lvl 6

'ding' Time Magic Resistance reaches lvl 3

'ding' Time Magic Resistance reaches lvl 4

Ilea moved on to the next Kingsguards, who had an ability to pull her closer and push her away. She remembered Sulivhaan using similar magic and powered through, eventually killing the knights and moving on to the next.

She was on a roll and found that she was enjoying her newfound powers. Immensely.

'ding' You have defeated [Kingsguard – lvl 510] – For defeating an enemy two hundred or more levels above your own, bonus experience is granted.

...

'ding' You have defeated [Kingsguard – lvl 505] – For defeating an enemy two hundred or more levels above your own, bonus experience is granted.

'ding' Azarinth Sentinel has reached lvl 302 – Five stat points awarded

'ding' Azarinth Awakening reaches 3rd lvl 11

'ding' Azarinth Fighting reaches 3rd lvl 8

'ding' Storm of Cinders reaches 3rd lvl 2

'ding' Ash and Ember Unity reaches 3rd lvl 6

'ding' You have learned the General Skill Gravity Magic Resistance – lvl 1
A force of nature, bound and warped by magic itself. Perhaps not noticing the damage dealt to your body, you have developed a way to resist this magic.

'ding' Gravity Magic Resistance reaches lvl 2

The last knight she'd killed had been blasted straight through the small hallway below the throne room and into Maro's little vault.

Meditation started flowing through her, increasing her mana regeneration considerably as she made her way inside. Maro was staring at the body when she entered.

"Last one of them," she said, appearing next to the king.

"Good work," he said and nodded. "Now it's only a matter of time until Terok and the elves clear out the rest."

Ilea smiled. "I'll go and help."

* * *

Ilea was sitting next to a downed knight, sunlight already filtering through from above.

So that doesn't work.

She summoned the second attempt at storing an ash lance from her necklace but found it too had become an assortment of loose ash. The form was right for a split second, but she had to act immediately to reform and harden it again.

At least it was possible now to store her created ash, but if it lost its properties, it wouldn't be a big help. The mana she used to store and summon it was about the same as simply creating new ash.

The elves were nearby, Goldie landing next to her a moment later. "We believe the town is cleared, human. The part the light touches, at least."

"Good. Collect the bodies and bring them to the field in front of the cathedral. I'm sure the king will want to see them."

Seviir nodded and vanished, as did the other elves. Terok walked over, looking over his shoulder.

"No argument or sass. I guess he was impressed with your changes, battle-healer."

He joked, but Ilea could tell the dwarf wasn't exactly at ease around her.

"Relax. I'm the same person," Ilea said, forming an ashen sphere in her hand.

"From what I've seen, and those were only brief glimpses of carnage, no you're not. I still feel good about my two hundred evolution, but now I'm already looking forward to the next one." Terok laughed. "You want to check if Maro is out yet? Maybe we're still missing a couple, but I doubt it. We've been pretty thorough."

Ilea nodded, spreading her wings. Terok ascended next to her, and the two covered the distance to the palace in the span of a couple of minutes. Landing in the courtyard, Terok stopped for a second as he looked around.

"How was it? Fighting the Kingsguard?"

"They had magical abilities that made them different to the normal variants. As long as you can take their blows, they're manageable. Taking them on without getting hit though? I don't think I could do that for a long while. One variant even had time magic."

"Time magic? Fucking necromancers. Good thing we dissuaded Hera and Seviir from diving in."

Ilea nodded. "You could have suggested the undead knights in the dark section too. They're a little easier to deal with," she said, thinking back to when she'd lost her head.

Easier than the Kingsguards, at least. Maybe with four people to distract and fight them, they could take one down.

Ilea doubted they could handle one of the Kingsguards, however. They had improved, that much was true, but compared to the boost she'd gotten, their gains were negligible. If her level of power was needed against the Rose Knights and the Kingsguards, then they needed to keep working.

"The dark section was your territory. Neither wanted to offend you, I suppose," Terok said and chuckled as they reached the throne room.

She smirked when she saw Maro sitting casually on the big throne in his robes. His attire looked heavy, with different sections of silver steel interwoven with the dark red fabric as well as dozens of intricate designs depicting mostly roses. Steel boots as well as gauntlets accompanied it, the latter with segments for each joint of his fingers.

His helmet didn't show his eyes. Instead, there were two rounded silver steel pieces separated by a vertical line going through where his nose would be. The only thing distinct about the steel on the sides was the silver antlers reaching up from each side.

Coupled with the two pieces on his face, there were four protrusions going up and over the full plate helmet. All of it screamed wealth as well as countless hours invested by a capable artisan.

The man clasped his hands together and floated up, not moving a muscle. Ilea was impressed by the magical wings she saw in her Sphere, none of it visible to her eyes.

"Welcome to Tremor, subjects. I, the Red Necromancer King of old, will be the doom you unleashed on this world. Cower before me!"

Maro was being an idiot, spreading his arms as well as some kind of intimidating aura through the hall. Terok actually took a step back, but Ilea just rolled her eyes.

"Welcome back, king. I can see you already found some gear to pay us for all that work," she said, her ashen armor forming around her before she walked toward him. Ashen limbs as well as lances formed behind and above her as she started heating up from the inside. "I'm happy to have a fight. Must feel nice to finally move again."

Maro's helmet vanished before he clapped, a big grin on his face.

"I'm kidding, dear friends. No need to beat up an old man." Jumping down from the dais on which the thrones sat, he approached Ilea and hugged her. "Thank you," he said in a much more sincere tone before he moved on to Terok, hugging his huge steel machine. "Thank you."

He stepped back from them. "Now, as for the gear. I had my storage ring on me when I activated the whole thing, of course. Not that I could have summoned anything with my mana constantly being drawn from me. There are some things I can give you in there."

Terok looked at Ilea. "Why not open the vaults instead?"

"That *is* what you suggested, or do I misremember?" Ilea said.

Maro smiled apologetically. "Yeah, about that. Well, let's just say that I might have focused a little too much on the unbreakable part of those enchantments. And it looks like my keys have been misplaced."

The dwarf sighed, throwing his arms to the sky. "You fucking idiot."

"Hey, at least it held," Maro countered.

Ilea didn't really get it. "You can't open it? Even though you made the enchantments yourself? And you lost the keys?"

"Precisely," the old king said.

Ilea just started laughing. Terok shook his head but joined in a moment later.

"I'll stay true to my word, though. What's in there is yours. I can help you crack them open now that the Kingsguards are gone, but it would take a few weeks. Or, we look for the keys. I do at least have an idea where one set might be."

"Let me guess," Ilea said.

He smiled. "The old friend I mentioned. Yeah."

"Seems like we're going on a small trip to Lisburg."

"Let's not get our hopes up just yet."

"You mentioned a storage ring?" Terok said.

Maro nodded, items appearing in quick succession around him. Some swords, armor, three more sets of robes and helmets, wine in bottles entirely too expensive to consider anything but treasure, a bunch of crates with books and documents in them, food, maps, weird-looking magical devices, skulls, furs, and metal ingots.

Why have a treasury when you keep it all in your ring?

Ilea walked past all the invaluable objects and grabbed a few of the plates with food on them with her ashen limbs. Her ash delivered them to her hands before her armor receded and she started eating.

Terok, in the meantime, was carefully looking through everything, mostly interested in the metal ingots.

"No gold on you?" Ilea asked, and Maro pointed at a pouch on his belt.

"A few gold, if you want it. Enough to survive a couple of weeks or months somewhere. That is, if its worth hasn't changed too much in the past thousands of years. Never cared to carry too much. I'm glad you find the food to your liking, at least," he said with sincerity, bowing lightly. "To think my hospitality has declined so much that guests have to face hundreds of dangerous rogue undead just to feast with me. These halls have fallen for sure."

"Well, you're out now," Ilea said, finishing her first plate and moving on to the next one. It looked like chicken or duck in some kind of honey sauce, definitely prepared with care.

Dude was a king, he probably had an entire army of cooks.

Maro stretched his arms wide and sighed, then stretched. "Yes. It does feel... really good." He touched his boots and rolled his shoulders, then grabbed a plate of his own and started eating.

Ilea looked through some of the books and documents. Most were related to Rhyvor – lists of adventurers and citizens, plans and laws, reforms, and maps of the cities, farmland, dungeons, and monsters.

She wasn't sure if he'd kept anything back. If he knew her at all, he had no need to hide anything, except if he was some kind of sadist torturer and had lied to her through it all. Unlikely at this point, but Ilea still watched her back out of habit.

"Terok, take whatever you want and can carry," Maro offered. "I can store it for you if you don't have an item for that. There should be some rings and necklaces in the treasury, but, well, not until we open it up."

"Why not give him your ring?" Ilea suggested with a mouth full of duck. *Delicious.*

Maro blinked. "That's a good idea, actually. But I ask to keep the ring itself for now as well as my armor. Both combined considerably enhance my survivability. Terok will get his storage item in time."

"A storage ring?" Terok asked, not quite managing to keep his excitement out of his voice. "Works for me!" He continued his examination of the ingots with quite a bit more enthusiasm.

Ilea noted that Maro's beard was looking better than before, as did his gray hair. The man definitely didn't look a couple of thousand years old. His face might have intimidated her a couple of years ago, but now he was just another man.

"Did you… collect the bodies?" he asked, a sad note in his voice.

Ilea nodded, putting the rest of the dishes into her own necklace. She blinked to the center of the hall, then laid out the corpses and their armor.

Maro walked over, leaving his things behind as Terok continued looking through it all.

"Thank you," he said, kneeling down next to the last knight in the line and touching the young man's face carefully. Ilea stood close by with her arms crossed. "I'm sorry."

The words were quiet, not meant for her. One by one, he looked at the corpses before they vanished into his ring.

Ilea cleared her throat when he was done and looked up at the murals on the ceiling. "Are you going to reanimate them again?"

Maro turned, a smile replacing the sadness Ilea had seen on his face through her Sphere just moments prior. "No. I will collect wood and burn them. Before we leave, if that is agreeable to you?"

"I have some left. Did the same with the knights I took down previously. The elves are collecting the remaining bodies and will bring them to the small field near the uppermost cathedral."

"Ha!" Terok exclaimed, rolling an ingot around in his hands. "Marvelous."

Both Maro and Ilea looked at him before the king nodded toward her. "I am forever in your debt, Ilea. I know you had your reasons, but know that you did this old king a service he shall never forget. I won't speak of this again – other than to annoy you, of course."

The king actually went to one knee and bowed his head. Ilea stepped toward him and grabbed his shoulder, pulling him up none too gently.

"You know the consequences of annoying me," she smiled.

Maro started laughing. Deep, resonant laughter. "You're pretty strong for a healer! Ah, we will have that bout. As soon as I have some corpses again that don't remind me of old friends who died thousands of years ago," he said, clapping her back and nearly making her stumble.

Speaking of strength… Guess I'm not the only one with boosts.

"Any plans for Tremor? The Soul Rippers still roam the lower regions."

"Did you face them? After you were downgraded to a healer?"

"No. I don't feel like it at the moment."

"They make you uncomfortable, don't they? Well, I don't blame you. Read enough reports on them. For now, I honestly want to get the fuck out of here. Ah, to be free to speak however the fuck I want to. Fuck. Fuck. Fuck. Fuck the court, fuck the nobles, fuck the king!"

The guy's mood swings faster than I can blink, Ilea thought, yet she couldn't help but be infected by his glee. *Damn hidden charisma stat.*

"I'll take most of the metals if you two don't object. The rest I would sell, but you can decide on that," Terok said as they came back.

"You can keep it all in your ring, Maro," Ilea said. "I don't really care for anything here. We can talk about whatever remains in the vaults once we get them open."

The king nodded. "Thank you." He bowed again and vanished when Ilea tried hitting him for it. "So very aggressive. That could have killed a lesser man," he said, dusting off his robe as he appeared with a twirl.

"I'm not gonna say it," Ilea said, letting her fist drop to her side.

"But he is *not* a lesser man," Terok said with a grin.

"Assholes, both of you," Ilea grumbled.

She was glad to have found these two.

* * *

Ilea handed Maro the fire sphere she'd gotten in Hallowfort before stepping back to join the three elves and Terok. Looking toward the cathedral, she saw Elfie leaning against one of the window frames, arms folded and an unreadable expression on his face.

"Warriors of Rhyvor. You have done your duty, a hundredfold. May you all rest in peace," Maro said, activating the rune to set the massive pyre on fire.

"Humans and their weird traditions," Seviir commented, wincing when Ilea turned toward him with an icy stare.

Maro stepped back as the fire spread, looking up to the sunlight shining into the cave before he lifted his arm. Ilea immediately turned when she felt the mana coming from him. A beam of purple energy shot up and evaporated shortly before hitting the ceiling.

She actually saw Neiphato shiver next to her, the sight of the rather mundane-looking spell apparently enough to cause such a strong reaction. *What was that about?* The spell had seemed powerful, a purity in her Sphere she hadn't seen before, but it was still only a simple beam.

Heranuur just grinned. Terok lifted his hand and shot out a metal spike that exploded into shrapnel when it reached a certain height, and Ilea formed tendrils of ash she sent upward before they dispersed into a thin mist that descended over the city.

Maro took a couple of steps away from the pyre, tears rolling down his face as he watched the corpses of his former comrades and knights finally burn away. They stood there until only ash remained – even, surprisingly, the elves, including Elfie at his window.

Once it was over, Ilea stepped up to the king. "I can make the ash disappear too, if you wish."

He turned to her, tears still on his face as he nodded. Lifting her arm, the ash started rising, twirling upward before Ilea made it vanish. The king looked up, a smile tugging on his mouth.

When it was all done, the elves moved past them and walked to the cathedral. Maro sighed hard before replacing his helmet on his head. Ilea put a hand on his shoulder before walking toward the cathedral too.

EIGHTY-ONE

The Vineyard Caves

"King Invalar. My condolences," Elfie said, bowing slightly.

"Thank you, Niivalyr. It is good to finally meet you in person. And I'm willing to answer any questions you may have. But not yet. I will return in a couple of weeks, and then we can talk."

Elfie hissed and bowed his head lightly. "As you wish, King of Rhyvor. I will prepare accordingly." He turned to Ilea. "We will be either here or near the Taleen dungeon."

Neiphato bowed lightly to both Maro and Ilea. "Good fortune on your travels."

Ilea smiled at him. "To you all as well," she said and spread her wings. "I trust you know where to go?" she asked, looking at Terok, who started floating as well. Maro did the same.

"I do," the dwarf replied.

Elfie looked their way as Ilea and Maro ascended, locking eyes with her before she turned. When they reached the top of the cave and emerged outside, Ilea touched Maro's shoulder.

"The arcane storms are dangerous. Let's check first."

She moved ahead and looked around, seeing some clouds in the distance but nothing immediately around them.

"See that crack there?" Maro looked up at the sky before she tapped his chest to get him to focus. "The crack."

"Yes," he said, focusing on the distant crevice.

"Move as fast as you can," Ilea said, her auras spreading through her before she shot off, blinking time and time again, crossing the distance over the barren land before blinking inside the opening.

Maro appeared a couple of seconds later and Terok later still. He moved down immediately, Ilea waiting with Maro near the top of the crevice.

Ilea gestured toward Terok. "We should move down too. Trust me, you don't want to get caught up in them. Nearly killed me with a single bolt of lightning that hit dozens of meters away."

Maro continued to eye the sky, showing no sign of having heard her.

Ilea waved a hand at him. "Are you coming? You can look at the suns from below as well."

Maro turned to her and nodded, reappearing on the ground below. When Ilea followed, he said, "There are only two suns."

"What do you mean?"

"Before Tremor was deep below a mountain, there were three suns in the skies."

Ilea stared at him.

"You guys coming?" Terok shouted from a short way ahead.

"You're saying an actual sun vanished from the sky? Poof? Just like that?" Ilea asked.

Maro frowned. "I know. It would make more sense to think that Tremor was somehow transported to another realm, but with everything that Catelyn and you have shared, it doesn't make sense. These are the same lands that I once knew, just changed. Destroyed," he said, looking back up.

"Some magical astronomic phenomenon?"

He started pacing. "Catelyn mentioned an event in the past, something the Awakened remember. Her language was cryptic, as is often the case with their history. But it fits... The change to the landscape, the utter destruction. 'When light was no more', she said."

"So, if I'm getting this right, a sun vanished from the sky? And that caused these lands to be destroyed? The north to become what it is now?"

"Yes. As ludicrous as that sounds. But these lands were overgrown with forests. Roads, cities, animals and monsters, lakes and rivers," he said, sitting down on a large rock and staring at the ground.

Ilea looked up at the two suns of Elos, raising her right hand and moving her fingers as if to pluck one of the orbs out from the sky. She looked down when her eyes started to hurt.

"I'm not sure I believe it, even with all the magic I've seen. Are you sure it's the only possibility?"

"No. No, this is far beyond anything I've seen or heard of," Maro said, shaking his head.

"We should go, before Terok explodes from shouting after us," Ilea said, heading after the dwarf.

Maro nodded and followed. "A sun vanishing. Such an event would be talked about for hundreds of years, and every scholar would write about it for another ten thousand."

"I never really informed myself about religions or important events in the past, but I feel like someone would have at least mentioned the disappearance of a sun. I know a bunch of librarians. I can ask about it once I go back south."

"That would be an idea. Will that be soon?"

"I want to go deeper into that Taleen dungeon, see if I can find something useful," Ilea said. "After that, maybe? There's plenty of stuff to do here, and while I'm more powerful now, I still haven't ridden a dragon."

Terok poked his head up from beyond a large rock not too far ahead. "If we keep walking at this speed, we'll arrive in two bloody weeks. I know you don't care about the elf's mood swings, but I'll be the one feeling his wrath when I join the training again," he said and shuddered.

"Terok, do you know anything about Elos having three suns at some point?" Ilea asked.

The dwarf stopped and looked at her. "Sounds like cult talk. No. I mean, there are many claiming ridiculous things, but that one takes the cake. Close to a story I've heard claiming that an elder dragon once placed the suns themselves. No, truth is, all of that shit is made up."

"Well, I know for a fact that Elos had three suns when Rhyvor was not a kingdom of ruin," Maro said, shutting the dwarf up. At least for a moment.

"What? Well, fucking tits. Does that mean the Worldeater Margalon will return and devour us all?"

Ilea rolled her eyes. "Now don't you turn into a cult member immediately. All we know is that either Tremor was moved somehow or one sun really died out."

"Catelyn for one doesn't know exactly how many years ago this change happened," Maro said. "And we know that there are human kingdoms and cities in the south, where the territory is lush with life, forests, rivers, and lakes, which raises a lot of additional questions."

Hadn't even thought about that.

"Well, there's not much we can do about a missing sun. Let's go to Lisburg. If it's the same town, that would make the possibility of Tremor somehow being teleported even less likely."

Maro looked up at the sky before he nodded. "Lead the way, Terok."

* * *

"Should be around here," Terok said as he checked their surroundings.

Ilea started looking with her Sphere and Sentinel Huntress, but the dwarf found something before her.

"Got it. Down here."

He lifted a stone, revealing a small cave opening. Ilea hadn't seen it through her Sphere, but when she concentrated, she noticed a faint glow of magic from the concealing enchantment.

Great, now I have to focus on things like that too.

It felt the same as when Eve had tried to hide from her, but rather than shifts in the air, it was like a shift in the mana around her.

They descended and immediately came upon a massive unnatural tunnel, hundreds of meters wide and at least fifty high. It simply led downward, farther than she could see.

A couple of minutes of running later, they saw light in the distance.

"We've got company," Maro said before around ten warriors and mages in various gear and at various levels appeared around them.

Hidden and concealed spaces above and below, Ilea thought, noting the cracks in the ceiling and feeling the weird mana resonance again.

"Travelers, welcome to the Vineyard Caves. What is your business here?" The being, most certainly an Awakened, was clad in black full plate armor. It had a massive torso but insect-like arms. It carried no weapons.

Ilea was about to speak when Maro took over.

"Guardian of truth, we are friends of the Awakened, seeking shelter in the Vineyard Caves as well as an escape from these unrelenting lands."

"You speak truth, ally of the dead. It is an honor to host you, then." The being turned to Ilea. "Healer of ash, it would be most benevolent of you to lend your powers to those in need. Many have been injured in the Great War."

"Of course, armored one," Ilea said, unable to think of anything else. She didn't want to repeat the ridiculous title Maro had given the being.

Fortunately, it didn't seem offended in the least, bowing slightly before they all vanished again except for one creature that looked like a floating orb of purple energy.

"Pleasssse folloooow," it said into their minds, all of them seemingly familiar with the feeling.

They did so, and an immense gate of wood and stone soon came into view, blocking passage farther down the tunnel. The surroundings also showed more signs of occupation, large stone support pillars rising to the ceiling and pieces of rubble that may once have been ruined structures littering the floor.

The dozen guards arrayed in front of the massive gate relaxed the tight grips on their weapons when the three approached with the floating Awakened. Ilea noted the defensive structures and small wall that had been erected, as well as the fresh blood still clinging to various parts of it and the ground itself. At least an effort to clean it had been made.

"Do beasts wander down here?" Ilea asked the ball.

"If you consssider the cursssed Feynooor to be beasssts," the ball cackled, sending sparks of purple energy off to the side.

[Death Wisp – lvl 221]

"It still sounds ridiculous to me that those creatures found intelligence and now threaten an alliance of Awakened," Maro murmured.

The gates were opened, letting the three travelers pass.

"If you would be sssssso kind, the injured are in the tentssss to the leffft," the wisp said before returning through the entrance. The gates were then closed again by two massive creatures with oxen heads, arms as thick as Ilea's whole form.

Her ashen armor slowly retracted as she took in the valley spreading before her. Purple, blue, yellow, and golden stars scattered the sky, illuminating it all. *Crystals or metals.*

"Do you want to stay together?" she asked the others.

"We can meet back here in around five hours," Terok said and walked off.

Maro shrugged. "I'd prefer some company, if you're not averse to the idea."

"Sure."

The king followed in silence as Ilea made her way to the indicated tents. Fabrics of differing qualities and colors clad the hastily built shelters, from which came groaning noises from various unknown creatures, growing louder the closer they got.

A guard stepped up to them and immediately nodded at Ilea. It looked like a squid on top of a human body.

"Hek sai liup?"

Ilea cocked her head to the side,

The squid face quivered. "Standard… apologies. Are you here to offer your healing?"

She nodded. "Do you not have any healers here?"

The squid looked relieved. "We do, various kinds. Some wounds need more than life energy to be mended. The mana I feel from you is different. Perhaps some might find your presence comforting." It looked over at Maro. "Can you heal the undead?"

"She can do that too." The king simply pointed at Ilea.

"Truly? Then feel free to walk the tents," the squid said. "Those in grave danger from the attack two days ago have perished or have been stabilized. There is no rush. Until they attack again."

Then it said a few more words in a language Ilea didn't know.

* * *

Maro watched on as Ilea took care of several Awakened, many of whom had broken bones, cursed wounds, or were simply unresponsive. The unknown biology of most of them brought additional difficulty, but her healing skill had been boosted so much due to her recent evolutions that most of the injuries were curable.

She watched in fascination as a small black wisp grew in size as she poured healing mana into it, Maro standing to the side with a smirk.

[Undead Terror Wisp – lvl 183]

"I feel... dead again!"

The noise sizzled into her mind as the wisp turned around in the tent before flying off.

"I remember fighting one of them. Never saw an Awakened come out of such a spiteful being," Maro commented as he looked at the flying orb of dark magic.

It took Ilea barely an hour to take care of the ones she could help. There were only three beings with curses and poisons her mana couldn't heal. They wouldn't get worse if a healer replenished their health from time to time, but what they needed was simple rest.

The squid thanked them when they left. "If there is anything you need, just come to me. I will make sure the other Awakened know of your generosity," it said and bowed.

"Where may we find the oldest Awakened in this marvelous town?" Maro asked.

"Hmm... I have not been here for a long time. Best ask around the arena. It is the main focus of the Vineyard Caves. Other than shelter, of course." It laughed with a weird gargling noise.

Maro got some directions before rejoining Ilea, who was already strolling off and checking the wares of several street vendors.

"Found anything interesting?" He looked over the wares on offer from an undead with sunken-in eyes and a dried-out face.

"I have no idea what any of this is," Ilea said, kneeling down and checking the colorful marbles. *Some kind of enchanted stones?*

"Prrrr.... Precious stones!" the undead muttered for the third time since she'd stopped.

"I think it's meant as jewelry," Maro commented. "You know what that is?"

Ilea looked at him, then back to the stones. "Of course. I just thought these might be more than shiny marbles."

She walked to the next vendor. *Poisons.* The same lanky insect-like being sold food too, which didn't seem like a good combination. Ilea smiled when two four-legged furry creatures resembling dogs rushed past, one of them apologizing for brushing her leg.

"This place is fun," she smiled.

Maro stepped next to her, took his helmet off, then made a disgusted noise. "Not worth the copper."

Ilea laughed when she saw the plate of possibly poisoned stew in his hands. "You can't just throw it out now."

She tried some, and while she didn't get poisoned, the taste wasn't to her liking. She took it and handed it to a lich-like being floating past, the thing glancing at her, then at the food before it bowed and took the stew.

"Preciate it, flesh-being," it said in a low-pitched, reverberating voice.

"Enjoy," Ilea said. "They don't give much of a fuck around here," she added when the creature had left. "I like it."

"They're so diverse here with all their differing backgrounds and biologies. Suppose that would change someone's outlook on life," Maro said. "It's incredible to see that Awakened have come together to live in settlements."

"That wasn't the case in your time?"

"It wasn't unheard of, but there was nothing of this size. But with the mana density here, I suppose it's no surprise."

EIGHTY-TWO

Mansion of Bones

The two walked in silence for a while before Maro made a delighted noise, hurrying into a store Ilea identified as a wine seller's shop. Inside, the walls were lined with bottles, but she could tell by the smell alone that this wasn't exactly what the king had been looking for. The place stank of vinegar.

He stood near one of the displays, looking dejected as he held one of the bottles. "I thought with the name remaining that maybe some of the wine had too."

Ilea chuckled. "Well, there are some bottles left in Tremor. Not sure how many Terok and I drank, though," she added a little more quietly.

"It's not really about the wine," he said, more to himself, as they stepped out again, ignoring the shopkeeper's attempts to sell them dubious potions.

The streets weren't cobbled – instead, hard-packed dirt or wood covered the obviously worn sections connecting the buildings. The dwellings varied in design as much as those back in Hallowfort. Each seemed to accommodate a different type and shape of being.

Coming out into a square, the two walked toward a set of wooden railings and found a view overlooking nearly the whole of the cave beyond. Much of the city had remained, ruins now repurposed or integrated into the new homes and dwellings of the various Awakened living here.

There were hills, too, covered in green, but the plants didn't look like vines to her. Still, coupled with the serene beauty of the stones and crystals shining in their various hues, Ilea could understand why the king had liked it so much here.

"You know, even warped as it is, I hadn't dreamed it would retain any of its beauty," Maro said after a while.

"Not overrun by fucked-up creatures like Tremor? I can see that," Ilea said as they sat. She summoned two meals, handing one to the king.

When they were done eating, Ilea stood up and stretched.

"So," she said. "Where do you think that key would be? If it's still here at all."

"Gadrian had a massive mansion. If the geography hasn't changed, it should be near the back of this cave."

"Then let's see what remains," Ilea smiled, offering him a hand to get back up. He laughed and took it.

The two of them flew over the city, the only notable thing they spotted being an arena that, according to Maro, hadn't been there before.

"We could have our bout there," he suggested when they landed near a gravel road leading to the mansion.

"Yeah, if you want to destroy the whole thing."

"Wait." He held up a hand. "I can sense an aura of death coming from this place."

Ilea looked around, only now noticing that the whole area seemed deserted, void not just of people but even plants and insects. It was utterly and completely silent.

"What are you sensing? Monsters nearby?"

"No. Just a feeling."

He walked up to the doors and knocked. They opened a moment later. She felt the mana around her fluctuate but didn't let herself react in any way.

Enchantments?

She wasn't sure. Her arcane sight through her Sphere was still new to her.

A man who looked *almost* human bowed to them. He was dressed in a black suit that was torn in more than one place, and his eyes moved weirdly from side to side, as if they were marbles placed in a doll's head.

Jewelry?

"Welcome, travelers, guests. Visitors are so very rare these... days. Why not come in and join the lord at his banquet? It is almost time for... dinner."

The words came out without his mouth moving. Ilea rolled her eyes and looked at Maro. The king wasn't wearing his helmet, and he smiled brightly as he bowed back.

"We would be grateful to accept such a generous invitation. Much have we heard of the lord's generosity."

He didn't even glance at Ilea before he stepped inside, so she followed close behind. She identified the butler and had to roll her eyes again.

[Human – lvl 30]

What the fuck is going on here? Ilea assumed Maro had an idea, otherwise he wouldn't have accepted the invitation. *So, it's an illusion or something? I doubt anybody would be identified like that. That guy is dead.*

She looked at the creature walking in front of them, leading the two through the dark mansion and up a flight of beautiful stairs. Her Sphere flickered again, and Ilea nearly staggered as she saw the bones and rotten meat around her. The most irritating thing was that she didn't smell any of it. It soon disappeared again.

A fire was burning in the hearth of the great hall, in which a long beautiful table had been set with various foods. A big glass chandelier hung above, candles bathing the room in a warm light as they approached. The 'human' moved a chair, and Maro sat down without a care in the world.

Has he somehow been influenced by a spell? I won't believe that. Guess I'll go with the flow for now.

Ilea sat down beside him. At the head of the table, a figure wreathed in darkness appeared.

[The Undying Lord – lvl ???]

She glanced at it and watched Maro slightly incline his head. When it spoke, she heard it directly in her head.

"A necromancer… and a healer. How amusing. Have you come here to die?"

"We haven't come to fight you, spirit of death," Maro said. A hiss came from the dark figure, its features entirely hidden.

"It is not your choice to make, human. Those walking into my halls, willingly or not, are mine to feed upon," it said.

Ilea was getting tired of listening. She was about to stand when Maro grasped her hand and squeezed lightly.

"My Lord. Before we are to die, may I tell you about a man I once knew? He was the owner of this very mansion. The one who had it built, even."

The dark figure moved forward a little, hands of bone moving out of the shadows.

"Is that why you have come? Yes… I remember him, vaguely. A long time has it been. I was young, then, powerless and wild. A land torn by war yet governed by humans such as yourself. Gadrian was his name, was it not?"

Ilea saw Maro gulp at the mention of the name before the creature continued.

"A formidable mage, despite his injuries and the battles he had fought. His death was quick, if you cared to know. His remains have been rotting in the cellar to this day."

The wood of the table and floor cracked as a burst of deathly mana washed over Ilea.

"He... he was a good friend," Maro said. "One of the few who remained to the very end. Gadrian loved this town, loved the quiet. This mansion was built to capture the best view of the sunset, did you know that?"

The being gave a hollow chuckle. "A tragic story, then, that such a town would fall to monsters and vanish into the earth, the very suns unable to reach it anymore."

"Perhaps. I do believe Gadrian lived his life to the fullest. If either one of us was truly fulfilled, it was him," Maro said and shook his head.

"Is it revenge that you seek?" it asked, the tone casual.

Maro tapped the table with one finger. "I don't know. I guess I wanted to see Lisburg again, find out what happened to Gadrian. It has been so long since I sealed myself away. He would have passed one way or another. To learn about his demise, to find the one who killed him, is more than I had expected to find."

He sounded almost defeated, unsure about how he felt about all this.

"Know that it was not malice but simply my very nature that had me kill him, makes me kill. You, being one of death, would surely understand. Are you here to die too, then?"

Maro stopped his tapping and stood up. "No. I don't know what I expected to find, stepping into the domain of a spirit of death. I'm sorry, but we're not here to die."

The doors swung closed before the room turned from a clean, nicely furnished hall to one of death and blood. Bones littered the wooden floors, rot and viscera coloring the walls. Ilea pushed the plate of meat in front of her a little further away as the spell was lifted.

She turned her head to one side and puked up the food she'd eaten just an hour ago. Maro put his helmet back on his head as the spirit stood up, black mist lifted to reveal a huge skeleton protecting a black ethereal form within. It was two meters in height, the bone grown out enough to form suitable armor, nearly creating something akin to a full plate suit.

"This mansion has been one with death for millennia. Those seeking it come here of their own volition. Rarely do I stray. Know that it is an honor to bring one as old as yourself to rest."

A beam of black energy slammed into a shield of the same color thrown up by Maro.

Ilea summoned a flask of water and cleaned out the taste from her mouth, getting more used to the scene around her.

The creature hissed. "Why do you resist? Every human in my path has acted the same way. Clinging to life with all they had. Let go and rest. You already feel my power, necromancer. You cannot stand against me."

The beam turned purple, as did the shield. Maro seemed unimpressed as

Ilea moved her chair back and stood up, cleaning the filth on the chair from her legs and ass.

"I haven't come alone," Maro said. "Ilea, I know you've done a lot for me. I know, however, that this is beyond me. This I ask you for both myself and the thousands that have died to this creature. I'll invite you to dinner once it's over."

She looked at him and smiled. "You know you don't have to ask. Tricking me into a false feast is a terrible offense."

The beam stopped. "A healer will not stand against me. You have known this to be futile since you stepped into this mansion, necromancer."

It moved its hand toward Ilea before a beam of purple energy smashed into her. She simply stood there, her leather armor rotting through in a mere instant before her skin started to melt. Her ashen armor formed as she spread her arms, intercepting the beam to allow her chest to be covered by ash too.

The wounds reformed quickly as the death magic burned into her ash, moving incredibly slowly through the element. When it stopped, her armor simply reformed, her skin already healed.

"You dare wield ash with such a title? And what is that… healing? It is not of life."

Ilea knew her magic wasn't the same as what most other healers used. It was Azarinth magic… and she felt like something had changed again with her recent evolutions.

She didn't react to what the creature said, her chest heating up slowly as lances formed around her. She jumped onto the table, ashen limbs appearing behind her.

"You've lost murder privileges, death spirit."

"So bold. Come then, human. Perhaps you will be the second one this century to escape with their life."

Ilea watched the bones scattered on the floor around her move to form weirdly proportioned warriors. Each had claws and weapons of bone and charged at both her and Maro as soon as their bodies reformed.

Ignoring the created warriors, Ilea appeared in front of the death creature – only to be engulfed by a massive beam of purple light. The energy shaved into her defenses, but she simply pushed against it, blinking again a moment later before smashing her fist into the lord's leg. Her mana flashed into him as he screamed in pain, vanishing and reappearing in the middle of the hall, floating in midair.

The skeletons around her rushed in, stopped by the ash that formed around her. The lances, having reached peak density, were fired at the death spirit, impacting its bones with a teeth-rattling shattering noise. The bone won out. Ilea spread her wings before the summoned creatures broke through her ash, flying up and toward the mage.

"Will this be the one?" it asked, excitement in its voice as another beam enveloped her. Ilea pushed through as the death magic intensified, slowly eating through her ash before she reached it again. Its hands sped out lightning-fast, making her blink away.

She reappeared with the death spirit's skull already in front of her, its hands grasping again. This time, they found purchase. Ilea smiled as it tried to squeeze, one of its hands around her arm and the other clawing into her chest.

Her healing mana flowed into it, and her ashen limbs smashed into its head to deliver more damage. She held her fist close to herself as she charged up Absolute Destruction, counting the seconds.

When she felt its attack coming, warned by her third-tier Azarinth Fighting ability, she simply continued. Her heart suddenly quivered, pulses of death mana directly flowing into it. The skeleton in front of her showed no emotion, and after the fifth pulse, her heart exploded.

It paused, but when her assault didn't stop, the being moved on to her brain. It was then that Ilea sacrificed five hundred health and punched its chest with a ten-second charge of her mana intrusion ability. Blue energy was visible as it flowed through the bone and into the black mist below.

The death spirit screeched, writhing in pain as it tried to get away from Ilea, who was now the one holding on. Her grin was wide as her heart reformed in an instant, another chunk of mana sacrificed.

I still have more than I expected.

She was already charging up another attack as she stopped a beam assault with her ashen limbs.

"Marvelous. I remember now… the Azarinth," it said, the dark form writhing as blue lines burnt up more and more of it, her reversed Sentinel Reconstruction continuing to push mana into the ethereal form.

She noticed the being wasn't floating on its own anymore, her strength and wings keeping it aloft as the skeletons on the floor looked up, some battering the shield of an unconcerned-looking Maro.

"What do you know of the Azarinth?" she asked, but the being simply exploded in purple light, a flash of magic burning part of her armor before she released her area attack to counter it.

Fire erupted, cinders dancing over the skeleton, and half of the black mist turned to ash. Feeling another attack coming, Ilea delivered a brutal uppercut and released the charged-up attack.

"I thank thee… for granting the blessing of death."

The blue lines became bigger before the rest of the black mist evaporated, the skeleton immediately crumpling to the ground. She held onto it, watching all the other skeletons collapse. The butler too fell down, head rolling away from his torso. Ilea hoped he was fine.

'ding' You have defeated [The Undying Lord – lvl 540] – For defeating an

enemy two hundred and thirty or more levels above your own, bonus experience is granted.

'ding' Azarinth Sentinel has reached lvl 303 – Five stat points awarded

'ding' Kin of Ash has reached lvl 302 – Five stat points awarded

'ding' Absolute Destruction reaches 3rd lvl 12

'ding' Azarinth Reversal reaches 3rd lvl 2

'ding' Armor of Ash reaches 3rd lvl 11

'ding' Death Magic Resistance reaches lvl 6

...

'ding' Death Magic Resistance reaches lvl 12

She landed slowly, placing the massive pile of bones on the table.

Basically a single piece of bone. Hey, I leveled.

"You got the whole kill. Good." Maro smiled as he stepped toward the pile. "Well fought, Ilea."

EIGHTY-THREE

Pyre

"You didn't interfere so I'd get the experience?" Ilea asked, tapping the bones. "Damn, we should have asked him more questions."

"Him? It sounded female to me. Interesting. Didn't seem like a talkative fellow if it wasn't about his beautiful villa," Maro said as he cleaned up the bones with his ring.

"You can use them as minions?" she asked, watching him work. "Don't tell me you planned all of this since the moment we got you out of Tremor."

"I'm hurt that you would think so," Maro laughed. "I like to think of myself as a good strategist, but no. I didn't know what was in here until we stepped onto the premises. Your abilities are such a good counter, I thought I'd risk it." He waved her off. "Don't look at me like that. If he'd done significant damage, I would have intervened."

"You would have just healed if you used your own death magic, right? And losing a heart isn't significant damage?"

He shrugged. "That's not how death magic works. And no, apparently losing a heart isn't significant to you. I would have felt it if it was. You're pretty tough. No wonder you cleaned up the Kingsguards so quickly. Battle-healers… Might be an idea worth pursuing in the future. Though it's stupid to spread oneself so thin at early levels."

"Guess I lucked out with my class then. I won against level fifty people while I was below their level and with only one class."

Stepping over to another pile of bones, Maro made the skeleton vanish before he spoke. "Healing magic of the Azarinth Order, body enhancement abilities, and I assume those people you fought underestimated you due to the healer identification. Probably didn't know what hit them. Healing orders and their experiments... Guess something good had to come out of those lunatics at one point or another."

"You want the big one too?" Ilea asked, noting Maro was done with his cleanup.

"I think you could use some of that to make armor. Just have to find someone capable of molding bone. If your fists couldn't crack it, I think it's safe to say that the quality is good." The king appeared next to Ilea, touching the thing's ribcage. "Yeah, this is prime quality. I'll take whatever's left of it," he laughed.

[Undying Skeleton – Timeless Quality]

"Hmm. What does timeless mean?"

"I've seen it only twice, I think. It can regenerate if you push mana into it. Not as quickly as your ashen armor, but at least you don't have to repair it constantly," the king explained as he looked around the room.

I guess instead of scale it's bone... full circle. She smiled at the thought. The drake scale armor had been one of her favorites. *I hope Goliath can work with this. And I hope it can be made into light armor.* It didn't look light at all. Still, she put it into her necklace, where it took up four spaces on its own.

Maro turned to her. "I'll go downstairs to find Gadrian. Give him a proper burial."

"What about all the other skeletons?"

Maro glanced her way before he walked down the steps, Ilea following after she placed the remains of the butler into her own storage item.

"I didn't know them. Nor did the monsters he created match up. No necromancer worth his salt would waste such a large number of bones."

Downstairs, they came upon a closed double door. "Enchantments," Ilea said as Maro put a hand over them. A pulse of purple mana flowed out, and the door opened.

Maro stepped through without a word. More stairs led down and into another big open hall. No monsters were present, and the glint of gold, silver, and other colors shone through all the death and decay.

"It's all yours, as far as I'm concerned," Maro said. "Just leave the bones. We're looking for a small golden key, by the way. Let me know if you find it."

* * *

It took them two hours to sieve through most of it. Much of it was rotten, old, and useless. When they were done, Ilea checked her necklace.

Four hundred twenty-eight gold coins and thirteen thousand eight hundred twenty-one silver coins, equaling one hundred thirty-eight gold coins once exchanged. Pile of gold treasure of varying worth, detail, and age. Pile of weapons and armor of various qualities.

"Hey, can I have one of your crates?" she asked Maro, who wasn't quite done with his search as he separated the remaining bone piles. He appeared next to her and summoned a crate. "Thanks. Still haven't found him?"

He shook his head and continued, Ilea dumping her gear into the crate as well as most of the weapons. *These all belong in a bloody museum.* She requested another two crates, into which she chucked the treasures, weapons, and armor that weren't completely rusted away or rotten. Most of it was.

She stored the crates in her necklace and started moving through the room again. *Probably gonna sell all that... Wait, no... I can use the armory in my house.* She smiled at the thought. *I mean, at least I don't have bones on my shelves.*

She decided to keep all of it and put it into her own house's little exhibition, which currently mainly consisted of Cless' paintings. Plus, the three crates only took up three units.

Maybe I can give some of the treasures to an actual museum if such a thing exists around here. Some of it's probably as old as time itself, coming from this fucker's... Oh hey, look.

Ilea moved a pile of bones and saw a glint of gold.

"Maro!"

The man appeared beside her as she retrieved the key with a thin tendril of ash.

"That it?" she grinned.

He didn't look at the key, instead kneeling down where she'd found it before he moved some bones away.

What remained was the skeleton of a man. Maro's hands shook as he carefully touched the skull. Ilea stored the key as he touched each bone, storing them safely in his ring. Finally, he held the skull in his hands, his helmet vanishing to reveal a pained expression. The skull went into his ring, and he looked at his empty hands.

Waves of black and purple energy burst forth, the piles of bones around him rotting away. Ilea remained at his side, quickly forming her armor for her own protection. As the waves intensified, his helmet reappeared.

With one last wave rotting away a layer of her ash, Maro looked down and let out a single anguished shout with all his breath. He was heaving when Ilea took a step toward him and put her hand on his shoulder.

"Let's burn this fucker down."

* * *

Ilea added the corpse of the butler to the small pyre they'd built in front of the mansion. Her ashen limbs had ripped through half of the entrance to get enough wood. Summoning her fire sphere, she looked at Maro with a questioning gaze.

"You do the honors," he said, not wearing his helmet.

Ilea stepped toward the pyre before she pushed mana into the sphere. The wood wasn't wet, but the pieces were rather big, meaning it took a couple of minutes of burning before it finally caught. She refrained from using her Heart of Cinder in consideration of the event.

When the fire properly caught, she moved back to Maro. He didn't speak, simply watching the flames dance.

"I'm sorry for your loss," she said.

Ilea noticed that, with time, more and more Awakened gathered close to the estate, though none actually stepped upon the dead land.

"We're attracting a crowd," she said to the king.

"It seems so," he agreed.

"Mind if I set the whole place ablaze?" Ilea asked as the pyre started to collapse.

Maro shook his head slightly, so she stepped toward the ruined entrance. Fortunately, most of the mansion was built with wood. When she was inside, she used Heart of Cinder to dry out and slightly burn the stairs before using her sphere to actually set them aflame.

When the flames started spreading, she activated her ashen armor to avoid losing her last set of leather armor.

Guess I still have a bunch of clothes. Just no light armor.

She released Heart of Cinder in the dining hall and added her tiny flamethrower to the mix.

Should be fine now if nobody stops it.

A good part of the mansion was burning now, so Ilea stepped down the collapsing stairs before exiting, her ashen armor receding.

By now, the crowd had grown, and the previous silence had been replaced by cheers and loud conversation. When Ilea rejoined Maro, she formed a spear of ash before releasing it toward the cave ceiling. He smiled and lifted his arm, adding a ball of darkness that exploded in a flash of wild mana.

The man sighed deeply as he looked up at the crystals above them. Different elemental spells started shooting out from the crowd – only a couple at first, but soon a sea of spells added to the colors of the ceiling.

"When I went under... I didn't expect to come back," Maro whispered. "And now I'm back to bury all the people I knew, the kingdom I helped found. This isn't how it was supposed to go."

Ilea looked up too then. "How *was* it supposed to go?"

"Well, I suppose it could be worse. At least Elana is still around."

"As far as I'm concerned, we just defeated Death. I think you can cut yourself some slack," she said, putting her hand on his shoulder.

"I'm not your grandfather who needs to be comforted, Ilea," he snorted, but he didn't move her hand. "I'm the King of Rhyvor, feared necromancer and legendary womanizer."

"Yep. All that. Still human, though," she said as the spells started to subside. The house was now fully ablaze, chunks of wood and stone falling to the ground.

"So, what are you going to do now, having killed Death itself?"

Ilea looked at him. "Isn't that what *I'm* supposed to ask?"

Maro laughed at that.

The first few people had now started entering the dead land, walking toward the two. The mansion actually burning down had probably convinced them that the lord really was dead. Ilea hadn't really thought about the significance it had held in the dungeon.

"You didn't answer my question," Maro said in a teasing tone.

"I came here to get stronger and to find out more about the Taleen." Ilea paused. "Suppose I came here to get away from some things too. Now, I'm stronger."

"So you'll go find out more about the Taleen?"

"I think so, yes. It might be time to face an old fear."

He smiled. "Seems like we've both reached a crossroads. Though I suppose now that I'm free, I'll have to think about what's next for me."

Before either could say anything more, a being with antlers not unlike Maro's headgear approached, bowing to them. "Humans of ash and death, have you killed the Undying Lord?"

"Yeah, the fucker's dead."

"One of ash, the Undying Lord has been demanding tribute in the form of captured monsters or sentient beings for hundreds of years. Of the few remaining dangers in the Vineyard Cave, the spirit of death remained the greatest. You have done us a service we cannot repay."

Ilea smiled. "Don't worry about it. Glad we could help you get rid of it."

Wanting to leave due to the gathering mass of people, Ilea blinked away. Maro followed a moment later, and they made their way back to the city.

"Back to Tremor now?" she asked, but then she turned when someone – a human – appeared a couple of meters behind her.

The man bowed, smiling at her brightly. "You prevailed against that terrible creature. Thank you."

[Mage – lvl 321]

Whoa, not bad old man.

"Sure thing." She gave him a thumbs-up and turned around. The old man seemed unsure, lifting one hand as if to continue the conversation.

Ilea interrupted him. "Look, I'm not in the mood to talk to random people all day. I didn't reach this level to be held to social expectations. Plus, I'm hungry."

"Ah, yeah. You puked in the mansion. Didn't think you would react in that manner. The young and inexperienced, eh?" Maro said.

The old man chuckled, a joyous sound. "Hmm, yes. Perhaps? Mocking others to avoid one's own pain is quite common for those of a young age. You, my dear friend, should be above such. No offense meant."

Ilea turned again as she processed the man's words, looking first at Maro, then back at the man. They were looking at each other.

"Do you know each other?" she asked.

"Not that I'm aware of," Maro said. "Did you serve Rhyvor?"

"Rhyvor... the old kingdom. Ah, yes... wasn't this ruin a part of it too? I believe some of the records state as such. No. You misunderstand. You have defeated one that sowed death and pain amongst those seeking a peaceful life. That is enough to consider you friends. It's been a while since I met a member of the Hand," he said, smiling at Ilea with a kind expression.

I really need to get Charisma Resistance.

Studying the man more closely now, Ilea saw he was older than he'd first appeared. In his seventies perhaps looks-wise, he wore black pants, sturdy leather boots, and a simple shirt covered by a brown poncho. His face was wrinkled and near bronze in color, and his gray hair – like his whole frame – was thin.

The man held a wooden staff and leaned on it while they talked. She assumed him to be older than he was due to the way he looked exhausted just standing there. If it weren't for the fact that he'd appeared out of nowhere and had a level even higher than hers or Maro's, she'd be sure he was a retired craftsman who had worked hard in his field and now spent his days fishing on his boat in some southern country.

"You know the Hand?" Ilea said.

He waved the question away and started walking, moving at a brisk pace. "I think you wanted food? I'm hungry too. I've lived here for a couple of years. You'll want to avoid most restaurants, being human and all." He laughed. "Come then, young ones. My treat – for taking care of that spirit."

Ilea looked at Maro, who gave her a nod before they followed.

"Ah, the Hand. Few know the Order here," he said, leading them into the city. "We work with missions, and other than expeditions, there is little incentive to come here. Plenty of dangerous dungeons and beasts down south, if that is what someone is looking for. Not many humans here to talk to or cities to enjoy. I doubt you're here on a mission, though. No, I don't think so."

Ilea smiled. "No, I'm not."

"Thank the suns. Almost thought you'd been sent to fetch me. Haha! Well, I suppose this old man would be forgotten at one point or another. Is Verena still alive?"

"Well, after the demon invasion, she vanished. Ravenhall was mostly destroyed, but I think it's in good hands with Dagon and Sulivhaan. The defenses now look much better too."

The man stumbled and fell face-first into the dirt.

"Ah, motherfucker," he exclaimed and groaned. "Apologies…" He got up again, dusting himself off. "Destroyed? By demons? Bloody…" He shook his head. "Oh, don't tell me… that fool!"

Ilea felt mana emanate from him, her Sphere informing her that his level definitely wasn't a joke or illusion. He soon calmed down again, hands shaking as he summoned a pipe. Ilea's sense of smell told her it wasn't tobacco inside. Lighting it with a small silver lighter, he took a deep pull and exhaled.

"Mhm, yes. Adam Strand. It was him, wasn't it?"

Ilea nodded.

"Did you retake the city?"

She nodded again.

"Casualties must have been in the hundreds of thousands? But the Empire – is it still standing?" He looked at her with wide eyes.

"Yes to both. Well, Baralia started a war a while back now, so I'm not sure if the Empire is still there. The demons didn't seem as much of a problem though. You're part of the Order then?"

The man smiled again. "Oh, you'll have to tell me all about that. It is, however, good to hear of Dagon and Sulivhaan taking over the Order. And yes, Lucas is my name, Elder of the Shadow's Hand. At least, as far as I know I still am. Pleased to meet you."

"You're an Elder? Where the fuck were you when all that shit happened? And you *knew* Adam would do something like that?" Ilea said.

Lucas looked at her and took a long drag from his pipe. Her words had seemingly barely fazed him.

"I was here. Adam? I never thought he'd do something so brazen. But nobody else I know has the knowledge and capabilities. Well, one man might, but he has no reason to be in Ravenhall. No, Adam makes sense. It is sad that it went this far. I'm sorry… for that loss, that chaos. I would've helped, had I been there."

"You know why he did it?"

He shook his head slowly. "No. But he must've had a good reason. Something to push him. He cares about the Shadow's Hand, but he also considers himself a pragmatist. They are the worst, thinking they are acting rationally when they are, in fact, entirely consumed by emotion. I have my suspicions, but it is already in the past." He pulled on his pipe again.

Ilea sighed. *He dismissed it so easily.* She still wanted to know why Adam had done what he'd done. And she wanted a rematch, wanted him to take responsibility for what he'd done. It pissed her off, now that she thought about it.

"How did you know she was a Shadow?" Maro asked.

"It's a feeling," Lucas smiled. "There is a certain… panache with young and powerful Shadows. The northern air is nice, isn't it?"

Ilea looked at him and sighed. She realized that the frustration and annoyance she felt was probably not really about Lucas.

"It is," she said. "I'm Ilea, joined a couple years ago. Any reason you're here in the north instead of, you know, doing your duty as an Elder?"

The man looked at her and laughed again, pulling on his pipe. "My dear. The duties of an Elder aren't very well defined. Perhaps it has changed now… Well, it is no concern of mine."

Of course it is, you're an Elder…

So far, the Elders of the Hand hadn't made a particularly good impression on her. Except maybe Verena. *Sulivhaan, Dagon, and Claire make up a much better leadership than whatever these people were doing before.*

They soon found a restaurant that Lucas recommended. He ordered food as neither Maro nor Ilea knew anything on the menu.

"You were the human who fought the spirit last," Maro said suddenly, interrupting the awkward silence.

Lucas smiled, puffing on his pipe. "Hmm, perhaps. Maybe I sought to discourse with the Undying Lord. I'm not keen on fighting anyone, but I suppose that one had a way to make me show the worst of myself. I'm thankful you took that burden from this town. It was one of the few things remaining that maintained the feeling of a dungeon around here."

Ilea sat back, her chair leaning against a wall of ash she'd created. "Why are you here? Just to help out the community?"

"I am sorry I disappointed you, my dear," Lucas said. "I tend to have that impact on people," he added in a quieter tone. "Frankly, I was tired of it all. The constant wars… battles. Awakened are much more relaxed."

Are they really? The Dark Protector had an army and was at war with the Feynor. And here, she had even had to heal injured when she'd arrived. *You're just hiding away up here.*

"I'm here to study the north, the events that changed this environment two to four thousand years ago," Lucas continued, looking at Ilea. "More to the point, I'm here to try and change it back. The trees and vegetation you see growing in this dungeon are the first step. With time, I'm sure at least a part of the magical imbalance can be restrained. Not, perhaps, to the extent it was before, but better at least."

"That event. We believe Elos had three suns before," Maro interjected.

The Elder nodded and pointed his pipe at him. "A theory. Well, many exist, but one can't realistically replace a sun. Trees are the next best thing, as well as water and a working ecosystem. And introducing animals and monsters back into the environment."

Maro shook his head. "No, no. I was there. Before. I have been trapped and unconscious for thousands of years. There were three suns before. These lands were normal, the beasts below level one hundred. At least, outside of dungeons. Lisburg was the pride of Rhyvor, its wine unparalleled."

Lucas puffed away again. "A fascinating perspective. But it does not change the now, not if you don't have a solution to the environmental collapse in this region."

Their food arrived then, and Lucas clasped his hands together.

"But you have come here and defeated an old spirit of death," he smiled. "Let us celebrate that instead of dwelling on chaos, war, and destruction."

Ilea looked at him, not particularly interested in eating right now. Was she also here in the north to avoid problems she could help solve? Was she here because she couldn't handle her responsibilities?

No. She knew she would've died had she gotten more involved with the ongoing war, or with the Golden Lily. Or if she'd rushed into any random Taleen dungeon she'd found. She'd needed a break, sure, but she'd needed power too.

She took a bite of food and looked up at the ceiling.

And now I have that power.

EIGHTY-FOUR

Challenger

After dinner, Ilea asked about the arena they'd seen, and Lucas led them there. When they arrived, she wasn't surprised to find Terok already there, shouting wildly at the warrior currently battling three Burrow Dragoons.

"Oh, you made it here too, I see," Terok said. "And you've found another human. Great."

Ilea smiled, taking a free seat next to him.

"Find that key you were looking for?"

"We did," Ilea said.

"Wonderful, wonderful," Terok said, already back to watching the fight.

"I wouldn't drink that," Lucas said, nodding to Ilea's freshly acquired mug. "Brewing isn't exactly their strong suit."

"I'm well aware of that," Ilea said and took a sip. *Better than Hallowfort at least.* "What's his goal? If he's supposed to kill them, he's not doing a great job."

The three were Dragoons circling an Awakened warrior down in the center of the arena. He was panting and bleeding in several places. The warrior was humanoid in shape, but his limbs were disproportionately thick compared to his body.

"He needs to survive for another two minutes... clock's ticking," Terok explained before shouting some encouragement and pumping his fist in the air.

Ilea couldn't identify the Awakened fighting down there, but his movements and the amount of damage he'd sustained made her assume he was in the low two hundreds, perhaps even lower.

Two tense minutes passed, during which time the Awakened struggled against the three circling creatures, trying to keep them at bay with his spear. One of his legs was nearly severed by a bite he didn't manage to avoid in the last ten seconds.

When a gong boomed over the crowd, a bunch of people jumped down from the stands and slaughtered the creatures, overwhelming them with sheer numbers.

"Disgusting," Lucas hissed.

Terok screamed with joy. "Oh man, that was a close one!" He looked at the three. "Did you see that? Fucking brilliant footwork. I knew Raiden had it in him, but against three Burrow Dragoons? Phew!"

"How much did you bet, Terok?" Ilea asked as she stood up, looking around to see if anybody would even attempt to take care of the bleeding Awakened who had sunk down on the side of the arena, coughing up blood.

"Everything, of course. No reason to doubt my man Raiden," the dwarf replied, giving her a thumbs-up with his steel arm.

"You sound like you know the contestants. Is this not your first time here?" Maro asked.

Terok waved dismissively. "Ah, you lack heart, Maro. Believing in someone is enough sometimes."

Understanding why he was so interested in what was in the vaults now, Ilea blinked down to the Awakened and extended an ashen tendril toward him.

He looked at her with delirious blue eyes and thrust his spear at her. Ilea grabbed the weapon mid-movement and held it to the side.

"I'm a healer. You won. Relax now."

A slight sense of understanding washed over his eyes before he closed them and fell unconscious. She went on to heal his wounds. It turned out the leg had nearly been separated, and he might have bled out.

Suppose he made his choice to join this fight, she thought before she finished healing him and returned to the others.

Lucas' expression had darkened further, and Ilea could tell it had to do with more than just his distaste for blood sport. He seemed tense, mana pulsing about his body.

"What's going on?" she asked Lucas, his expression focused on a point in the distance.

"Something's about to attack the town. Feynor probably." He got up and dusted down his clothes. "I'll have to cut your tour short."

"Feynor? What?"

The old man took a deep breath before shouting in a much more powerful voice than usual, "Breach!"

Ilea watched in fascination as the people around them immediately sprung up and rushed to the exits, many sprouting wings or simply flying up as they readied their weapons.

Lucas sighed. "It's the third time this month already." He shook his head and started floating too.

"You're going to fight? How did you even spot them?" Ilea asked, looking around but neither hearing, feeling, or seeing anything indicating battle or intruders.

"I will try to reason with them while those unable to fight seek shelter. They haven't broken through the main gate before, but this time feels different. All my saplings have been destroyed. At once. You have chosen a bad time to visit this town, it seems."

Ilea cracked her neck. "I have a gift for bad timing."

"Feynor coming? Fuck that, what are we going to do? Is there another exit?" Terok asked.

"Perhaps. Yet I would like to see how the Elder handles this," Maro said, floating up next to him. "I doubt Feynor have the power to stand against Awakened… This should be interesting."

Ilea spread her wings and joined them. "Come on, Terok. You can run away if they really overwhelm the place."

"Of course she wants to fight," he grumbled as he floated up. "I try to sit back and enjoy myself just once and all hell breaks loose."

"Tell me about it," Ilea said. "And I didn't say anything about fighting. It's not my war. But I can still heal people."

Ilea was quite aware she probably wouldn't stick to her word. She was surprised to find herself neither annoyed nor angry by the revelation. It really wasn't her war, but if she and her friends were attacked for no good reason, she'd play her part.

And what will you do? she asked silently, looking at Lucas and Maro as they hurried toward the gate at the entrance, hordes of Awakened speeding in the same destination.

* * *

There was a weird atmosphere when they landed on top of a barracks-like building near the massive gate. Ranks of Awakened stood in formation on the street below, while mages ducked behind barricades that were hastily erected by magic or quick labor.

Weapons at the ready, they waited. The gates remained closed. Lucas moved to the very front, none of the assembled Awakened stopping him.

"You think he can do anything?" Ilea asked Maro, who was standing next to her.

"Depends on the enemy forces, I suppose, and what their goal here is. If they even break through the guardians outside. I don't know much about the political situation, or the Feynor."

"Will you fight them?" Terok asked, constantly switching his attention between the gate, the Awakened, and the two people next to him.

Maro didn't reply, simply focusing on the gates. Ilea wasn't sure either. The elves had left no survivors, going as far as to eat dead humans. She didn't know what would happen if Baralia took Virilya, but while some of the soldiers had ignored civilians, others had killed without restraint.

Let's see what the Feynor are like.

The only thing she knew was that once those gates opened, chaos would ensue.

"They'll attack us no matter what Lucas says. Those dragon-worshiping bastards are ruthless," Terok spat.

"Have you fought them then?" Maro asked.

The dwarf shook his head.

Maro shrugged. "Then let's see where this leads."

Ilea sat down a moment later, her legs dangling over the lip of the stone-roofed structure.

So much for this place being different from the south. So many dungeons and interesting monsters to fight, but it seems like people just can't let each other be.

The pounding on the gates grew louder. The dull thumps and pops of different spells and explosions were also audible but muffled.

"There are at least thirty of them," Maro said. "If we assume only the attack mages are trying to get through the gate now, we should expect at least eighty of them overall."

They shouldn't stand so close together, Ilea thought, looking at the hundred or so Awakened gathered in the big area before the gates. The barracks they were on was around two hundred meters farther back.

She saw how they stood, and she remembered how she'd felt back in Virilya. Not afraid, but confused. And overwhelmed. Now, she found, she felt calm. She breathed, feeling her newfound power flow through her. She'd just faced down a three-mark spirit of death. What danger could these Feynor pose?

"They're terrified," Ilea said.

"Course they are, their home is about to be sacked," Terok muttered.

"Tell me, dwarf, what happens to settlements the Feynor attack?" Maro asked.

"They usually don't leave anything behind. Razed to the ground. They consider anything non-Feynor to be an affront to their own culture. At least, that's what everyone says."

The king nodded and walked to the back of the barracks, holding out his hand before bones started dropping down into the alley below.

"So, you'll fight?" Ilea asked.

"There might be no choice. As much as the old man believes otherwise."

A sudden explosion bent the gates inward. The sheer multitude of torches and glinting reptile eyes revealed beyond indicated quite a lot more than eighty attackers. Still, only a single one walked inside, stepping over the bodies of the outer defenders.

The Awakened collectively held their breath as the figure approached. A small creature compared to most of the people in Lisburg, no taller than Ilea. Squinting, she could make out some details.

It reminded her of a lizardman, though the tail was much shorter, and where they were greenish, this beast was nearer to yellow, gold, or brown. Its head was completely different to the lizardfolk, though, more dragon-like than anything else. Even drakes lacked some of the features the Feynor sported, horns being the most prominent one.

The reptile looked dangerous, powerful, its spear glinting in the golden light. It wore light armor, open in several places to reveal scales. It was too far away for Ilea to identify, but the sheer confidence it exuded suggested its level was pretty high.

Lucas stepped forward. "Welcome, noble warrior, to the Vineyard Caves. May we—"

He was interrupted by the Feynor. "Your kind are not welcome here. Do not speak for these dreadful monsters."

It raised a hand and continued, addressing not the Elder but the people of Lisburg.

"Surrender now, and you shall die without pain. This I swear on the Guardian Dragons of the High Peaks. Be returned to where you came from, released from this world that was not made for you."

Ilea heard the words and sighed. Elves attacking Riverwatch and Salia, killing humans for sport. Baralia laying siege on Virilya for political gain, a show of power, or whatever other reason their king had. And now Feynor threatening to slaughter Awakened.

Why? She knew why. She knew how people were, no matter what they looked like. She'd wanted to get away from this, but here she was. People hadn't changed because she'd gone north. She hadn't changed either. She still hated it, still wanted them to stop their wars, their oppression, their abuse of power.

But while Ilea knew that she held the same opinions, she'd had to flee back in Riverwatch, had to retreat in Virilya. But now? She looked down at her hands, felt her magic flow through her, changed, improved by her evolutions, by all the fighting she'd done.

"Negotiations appear to be breaking down," Terok commented.

Maro snorted. The people around them were getting more and more terrified with each word the Feynor spoke. The creature's sheer arrogance and contempt were damn near graspable even from this distance.

"Terok, if shit goes south, lead people to the arena and barricade yourself in with them," Ilea said to the dwarf, who obviously didn't want to stay there. He nodded quickly, not even glancing at her as he stared at the light of near-infinite torches quietly flickering in the dark tunnel beyond the gateway.

"These people are peaceful, unwilling to take part in your war. Nor do they encroach on your territory. Leave this place, you are not welcome here," Lucas said loudly.

The Feynor nodded as if acknowledging the outburst of an unruly child. "Then you shall die with them."

He raised a scaled arm and shouted something in a hissing language. Dozens of Feynor appeared beyond the gate in an instant, and spells started flying as defensive barriers and walls were erected by the Awakened who quickly spread out, rushing into houses or behind cover as the first spells scoured the earth.

The speed and precision of both the attackers and defenders was a marvelous and terrifying thing to watch. Ilea glanced at a wooden wall forming where Lucas had stood, now obscured by rising smoke, explosions, and fire.

Ice rained down on them as Maro raised a shield. Terok looked at Ilea, and she just nodded, the dwarf vanishing right after nodding back. She watched as Maro lifted his hand, a beam of black opaque energy slamming into a flying ball of fire descending on the defenders. The spell exploded in midair.

More and more of the Feynor flooded in, not yet charging into the city but hunting down any Awakened still remaining near the gate. Outnumbering the defenders by four or five to one, the scaled foes broke through the hastily erected barricades and defenses, then cut into armor, skin, and ethereal bodies. They didn't aim for lethal blows, instead cutting and wounding, maximizing pain.

"What are they doing?" Ilea asked as she stood up, her ashen armor forming as a series of dark orbs slammed into her.

Maro was standing behind his barrier, and she felt his magic intensify, the noise of bone on stone now audible from behind it. Many Awakened were already fleeing or repositioning at this point, not even thirty seconds having passed since the initial breakthrough.

"The gift for surrendering was a painless death. There's no rush when they hold the only entrance, so now they're taking their time," Maro said.

As Ilea shook her head, a Feynor appeared in her Sphere and lunged at her, barbed spear in hand. But he moved so slowly and the thrust of his weapon was weak, the magic around him disappointing. Stepping to the side, she grabbed his neck and squeezed.

[Warrior – lvl 159]

He thrashed and clawed at her armor, spear continuously batted away by a limb of ash before she slammed another one down his throat, severing the spine before exiting through his back. When the creature went limp in her hand, she let go. A skeleton moved up next to her, grabbing the body before taking it to Maro.

"So, you're going all out?" she asked.

He pointed to a line of Feynor tossing fireballs into nearby buildings. "They're already burning down the city. If anything, I owe it to the ruins of Lisburg to stop them threatening to destroy what little remains. What are you going to do?"

Ilea watched as six howling Feynor taunted a downed Awakened, blood seeping from his severed legs as they kicked at him and beat him rather than simply killing him and moving on.

She ground her teeth. "Yeah, I don't think I'll back out of this one. This is going to be messy."

She didn't wait for Maro's reply, blinking twice to reach the group of Feynor. Identifying them quickly, she noted the highest-leveled one was just below two fifty.

"Healer…" one of them spat when she appeared above the dying Awakened, a tendril of ash sending mana into him to stabilize his body.

When two of them moved to attack, her limbs shot out, piercing four of them, though one managed to deflect it.

Her ash extended farther than she'd moved the limbs before, a change from her evolutions she hadn't tested yet. Pushing still farther, her limbs punched out of their heads before retracting again.

One of the two remaining Feynor took a step back and snarled. "You will die, and so will they – in pain, suffering, wishing you were—"

Ilea appeared behind him and punched the back of his head, bones cracking as he shot forward and landed hard on the ground. She followed up by cutting an ashen limb into the wound and liquefying his brain.

She avoided the strike from the last survivor of the group, the one with the highest level. His weapon was clad in crystals. When the blade sliced at her, she just let it hit her, Azarinth Fighting informing her about the negligible consequences of her inaction.

As it bit into her ash, she grabbed his arm, her ashen limbs cutting into his body with quite a bit more difficulty than the others. Still, the end result was the same, his form ripped and torn before his head was impaled by ash.

Ilea yanked the blade out. It had cut surprisingly deep into her ash, more so than some of the Kingsguards had managed. *Must have been confident.* She noted the crystals still growing in her ash but simply ignored them before reshaping her armor.

Locating the Awakened's missing legs in her Sphere, she extended her limbs farther than ever before and grabbed them, retrieving them before she healed the warrior enough so he could at least run. Sending a wave of mana into him, the warrior gasped and coughed.

"Go to the arena, defend it," Ilea hissed, hurrying toward the exit. She saw a group of skeletons rushing by – evidently Maro was hard at work.

Entering the combination of mist, fog, smoke, and steam that had formed near the gate, she trusted in her ash. She watched a group of Feynor cut into the corpse of an Awakened before another one came and hissed something at them. The five muttered darkly but walked further into the city.

This isn't an invasion. It's a slaughter.

Ilea appeared amidst the group, her jaw clenched tight. Memories of Riverwatch, of terrified people running through Virilya came to mind.

No more.

Ten limbs of ash absolutely shredded through the blood-covered creatures, all below two hundred. Bits of gore and decimated limbs were sent flying as her ashen arms swept through a second time. When she was done, they were all dead.

"What did you just tell them?" she asked, appearing close to the one she'd heard talking before the group had moved on.

The smoke around them parted and light broke through, revealing more of the creature before her. His scales were deep red, and he wore a necklace of bones that Ilea was certain came from Awakened.

[Mage – lvl 251]

"A healer... human, even. No, you are more than that. Why are you defending them? Do you not know what they are?"

"They are people, like you are. And you gave them a shitty choice, so here's mine. Leave this place and never return. Or die."

The creature hissed before a curse crashed into her, her life draining as he moved backward. She simply shook her head and kept walking toward him. The power of his spells was impressive, yet his curses were nothing compared to Elfie, his drain nothing compared to the Miststalkers.

"Fool," he said and vanished, appearing nearer the exit, behind the ranks of Feynor that were still pouring in. They moved with military precision, rows of five to ten moving in lockstep with groups of mages arrayed behind to offer ranged support. It seemed the initial push had only been the vanguard, and now the main force was just beginning to make its way into the square in front of the gate.

Ilea followed her quarry, blinking once to reach the middle of the square. She found what looked like a cocoon of wood there, cracked open with a bunch of dead Feynor lying to one side. *Negotiations definitely failed then.* She blinked once more.

The red-scaled mage pointed at her and shouted from deep within the Feynor ranks. A dozen other mages sent beams of arcane energy, fire, and lightning at her in response to his words.

She moved her ash, forming walls in front of her, reforming and shifting to deflect the projectiles. While many managed to get through, Ilea moved quickly to dodge, trying to not exert herself too much as the spells sped past, some grazing, or even striking, her armor.

"Stop this," she said, annoyed. Forming shrapnel from what remained of her ash, she smashed all of it into the shields and defenses of the Feynor frontline. The first row lost at least eight as her ash punched through scales, organs, and bones alike. The ones with higher levels survived, some getting injured while others managed to stop her attack entirely.

She noted the shouts as well as vanguard warriors circling back to move in behind her.

"Good. Now that you're all here, I'll repeat it."

The Feynor mages, now exposed, looked between the collapsing corpses of their frontline and the lances of ash forming above Ilea's head. She nodded, letting them understand the truth of their situation.

"The choice is simple. Leave this place, or die."

Roars filled the cavern air as they attacked in unison. Ilea sent her lances into the mass of Feynor still standing around and beyond the bent gate, some skewering through several of them at once due to how densely packed they were.

Ilea vanished and reappeared among them, twelve ashen limbs on her back slashing through the confused mages and warriors, before she vanished yet again. It was absolute chaos, her Sphere and high reflexes keeping her focused and in control as she methodically made good on her threat.

It was shockingly easy. She only had to use her spells against the higher-leveled ones, Absolute Destruction and Storm of Cinders taking quick care of even level two twenty enemies, their defenses mostly ineffective against her form of attack.

And they call the Awakened beasts. They wouldn't last a day in the Hand with such poor Class synergies and resistances.

Many of them defended rather well against her ashen limbs, but for every one deflecting her blows, there were three that were cut apart. As long as there were dozens of weaker Feynor in the tunnel, she could simply use them as shields or cover against the spells and swords from those more powerful. Ilea had no time to meditate, conserving her mana and using reversed Absolute Destruction whenever possible.

Finally reaching the end of their ranks, nearly sixty meters into the tunnel, she grabbed one of them and formed another shroud of ashen shrapnel. She formed all kinds of sharp edges, compounding the mass and density as much as she could before a cloud of deadly, spinning ash shredded through the half-confused, half-pursuing enemies behind her.

"Flee and I won't pursue!" she called, dropping a dead warrior and gesturing down the tunnel. She slammed an incoming spear to the side before four of her limbs crashed into the offending warrior, denting his armor, one even slicing clean through him.

Nothing compared to a Centurion's throw.

A kick sent him flying, knocking down several more Feynor as they charged her, blades, spears, arrows, and spells flashing.

As she thinned their ranks, Ilea moved back toward the city, more and more spells ripping into her or exploding against her now that the chaos was reduced.

The remaining warriors and mages became increasingly defensive as she slaughtered one after another, so she retreated to seek a little cover from their ranged attacks. While few had pierced her armor even halfway, it would only get worse over time.

When she reached the stone barracks, she noted that there were no corpses around. It was nearly quiet. The enemies around her were regrouping and beginning to march in unison across the square while explosions echoed in the distance. The vanguard was likely wreaking havoc in the more populated parts of town.

Blinking into an apartment, Ilea let the spear of the appearing Feynor strike her. It dug two-thirds of the way into her ash as her limbs cut into his neck. She moved two ashen arms around him to pull him closer before a hard punch rocked his head back, nearly ripping it off.

Three more Feynor appeared while a group of mages sent shards of ice and arcs of lightning in through the windows. She danced between them, her ashen limbs ripping into the new enemies, fourteen limbs now, still as easily controlled as her initial eight.

The heat in her chest started to increase as more and more warriors appeared, thrusting their blades at her while they also deflected her ash. Only elites had remained. Her resources were slowly being drained by the mages outside, and a curse landed that slowed her down and made her feel sick.

Her mind was being assailed by mental magic too, but all of it was manageable thanks to her resistances and healing. Metal spikes, bone shards, and stone splinters were simply dodged or ignored as they slammed into floating ash or her armor.

The warriors' strikes rained in, but not a single one was flagged by her damage foresight as a potentially serious injury. She was the center of the storm, dancing among chaos – but her primary emotion was frustration at the lost resources rather than anything else.

So, she used the time to meditate, deflecting only the most dangerous attacks. As such, the drain on her resources became more and more negligible as time went on, the heat in her chest reaching levels where her health started to drop.

Ilea blinked, appearing near the biggest cluster of six mages as her ash rushed out to envelop them in a thin mist.

My body, no teleportation.

Warriors appeared within her range and rushed at her before she sacrificed five hundred health, activated her third-tier Aspect of Ash, and released Heart of Cinder.

A sphere of fire and heat ripped through them. The power was irresistible even to solid stone – the Feynor bodies stood no chance at all of resisting. All became ash.

Ilea spread her wings and rose to float above the crater. Half of the building she'd been in was missing, and of the two dozen enemies, only one remained. Both his arms were missing as he'd thrust them forward to hurl a spell yet was stood just outside the range of her attack.

His eyes were wide as she floated toward him, sixteen ashen limbs ripping through the defenseless mage before silence returned to the square.

Ilea clenched her fists and screamed, breathing hard before she spread her wings.

You shouldn't have come to this place. I was having such a good day.

EIGHTY-FIVE

Cycle of War

Ilea sighed as she returned the ash to mana, her health returning to the max. She slowly flew toward the arena, soon encountering corpses littering the streets. When her mana was back to two-thirds capacity, she sped up, seeing purple beams in the distance. It seemed many of the Feynor had bypassed her as she'd fought indoors, heading instead to the arena, where the Awakened were making their last stand.

As she drew closer, she saw dozens of spells being hurled toward Maro, who was floating above the arena. His shield was tanking the hits as the mages were returned to dust by what looked like instant retaliatory energy beams with unlimited range.

She landed on the ground just outside the arena. A strange-looking Feynor peered at her with glassy eyes before he turned and leaped at his brethren, fangs bared. *Undead*, she realized as a mass of skeletons overwhelmed a group of shield-wielding Feynor by sheer weight of numbers.

Ilea joined in, finding the biggest groups of Feynor she could as they tried to break into the arena. So far, the siege had been resisted, the Feynors' progress halted by walls of stone, ice, and water as acid, fire, and other spells rained down on them.

Ilea found the groups distracted, landing near them before cutting through the Feynor without restraint. They had made their choice by charging down here, attacking people who had chosen to flee. When the groups were cleared, she blinked inside.

Terok appeared close to her the moment she was visible. "The wounded are in the center. We'll hold them back."

He vanished again, the boom and crash of dozens of spells reverberating through the air without pause.

Blinking to the dozens if not hundreds of groaning or dead Awakened, Ilea spread her limbs, finding she'd reached her maximum controllable number at sixteen, with a range of around ten meters. And then she meditated, stabilizing the Awakened as her mana quickly drained.

There were at least a dozen other healers, but half of them were out of mana and more injured were being brought to them by the minute. Some were bleeding out, missing arms, or burnt so badly their features were barely recognizable.

Ilea fought against the smells, the cries and screams of unimaginable pain. A minute passed, but the injured were still numerous, few of them ready to go back into the fight. Most were stable at this point but would only survive if they suffered no more injuries.

Ilea opened her eyes when a skeleton tapped her head. She had removed her armor to allow for a tiny bit more mana to be focused on her healing. The skeleton pointed at her with one of three fingers on its hand and then up to the necromancer in the air. She nodded and blinked up, wings spreading before she reached him.

For once, Maro wasn't smiling. "Seems most are stable. We need you fighting. They're breaking through my undead there." He pointed toward the chaotic fighting below. "Ilea, we'll need to intercept the reinforcements from the tunnel."

"I took care of most of them. Any that slipped past are here already."

He paused, then nodded. "Good. I saw several units move toward the trees, Awakened are hiding in the forest. Once—"

Several projectiles impacted his shield, making him sway to the side. Ilea reached an ashen limb toward him but found the man uninjured.

"Once you're done here," Maro continued, "go to the forest. We have this under control."

Two purple beams smashed into a Feynor mage two hundred meters away. One moment, the creature was standing on a building preparing another spell. The next, he quite literally evaporated.

Ilea didn't wait any longer, blinking down before she used her wings to speed her descent and landed hard on the ground, sending rubble flying. Her limbs lashed out, cutting through dozens of Feynor and undead alike. She had no way to tell them apart, but if all were dead, her enemies would have fallen. Plus, Maro would have plenty of new corpses to choose from.

Spearing through the last three warriors Maro had asked her to neutralize, she changed direction, her wings moving in the air and redirecting her toward the trees in the distance. *I'm flying faster,* she noted, a change likely brought on by her evolutions. Both her ashen magic, as well as her ash itself, had improved.

Speeding up even more, Ilea reached the edge of the trees half a minute later, landing near the corpse of a Feynor before she ran in. She heard the sound of spells a couple of seconds later, turning toward them. A few moments later, she came upon a group of Feynor. Her Sphere let her know they were terrified.

Feeling the attack coming, Ilea blinked up, watching dozens of wooden roots pierce the warriors and mages before they were ripped apart, blood and guts spraying the ground. The spray managed to reach her even though she was twenty meters up in the air.

Something moved in the trees, and she quickly dove toward it.

An Awakened had just appeared after a teleport as something bashed it, sending it crashing into a tree. Ilea landed before she turned to see none other than Elder Lucas before her. Only now, he was covered in bark and two meters tall, roots extending out of his body and into the ground. Blood and guts littered his form.

A spear of wood was launched at the Awakened, but Ilea intercepted it. The creature looked up at her in fear.

"Are there more Feynor here?"

It shook its head. "He… h… he killed all—"

"Run," she said, turning back as her wings formed a cocoon in front of her, the roots and wooden lances glancing off it.

What the fuck is going on with Lucas?

She was being pushed back by the impacts alone, but none managed to pierce the ash.

"Hey, asshole! It's me, stop this!" she shouted as she appeared before him. She slammed her fist against his protected head but without her mana intrusion skills.

"Aaaah… You…" He lifted his hand, wooden claws forming before another punch sent him stumbling. "Ah… Ilea. I'm sorry… I—"

A previously invisible Feynor suddenly appeared a meter behind the Elder, thrusting a spear toward his back. Ilea just watched as a wooden spike shot out from Lucas, piercing the creature and lifting it up before a beam of light burst the Feynor's head like an overripe melon.

Lucas' tree-form fell to its knees. "I'm… sorry… I…," he started, then wailed, screaming in anguish. He looked up at her, his eyes suddenly focused. "I told… I told them… told them that the people here are peaceful… I told… I told…"

She just stepped next to him and put a hand on his shoulder, ignoring the roots that grew around her and tried to pierce her armor.

"It's alright, Lucas. You tried, and they decided not to listen. It's okay. Calm down for me, alright?"

She pushed healing mana into him, then frowned when she saw a group of Feynor running toward them a hundred meters away. Three Awakened intercepted them a moment later, slaughtering the creatures. As she sighed in relief, the wood around her slowly receded, even the Elder's armor slowly sloughing off.

"Come on, you can rest now," Ilea said, grabbing the man after most of the roots had disappeared. She moved him toward a tree and set him down with his back to it.

"I didn't mean to... I didn't mean to..."

Ilea pushed more healing into him, focusing on his mind. "I'll check on the others. Do me a favor and stay here, alright? I'll send a bunch of Awakened to look after you, Lucas."

He seemed to understand but didn't reply before Ilea quickly blinked, reaching the three Awakened who had killed the Feynor.

"The human wood mage is a hundred meters that way. Can you watch over him?"

They looked at each other before one of them spoke. "We usually let him exhaust his mana before anybody approaches. It's too dangerous."

Ilea hesitated for a moment. "He's already resting, I talked to him. His armor is gone, at least. Keep a distance if you think approaching is a bad idea."

Two of them nodded.

Her wings spread, and she soared upward, heading back toward the arena. Ilea spotted Maro flying in the distance, but he wasn't hovering above the circular structure anymore. Instead, he was moving toward the gates leading out.

An army of skeletons and reanimated Feynor were running below him in unison, combing the houses and alleys to find any survivors from the enemy forces.

She reached him a moment later. "How are the injured?"

Maro turned his head and nodded. "Your healing isn't needed, the arena and surroundings are clear. Terok as well as the elite Awakened are guarding the place. Most survivors have flocked there. Forest?"

Ilea winced. "Lucas killed most of them, lost control... Not like a berserker, but... I've no idea. I could still talk to him, but he did try to attack me. He... ripped them apart. I don't think any Feynor survived there. Might have even been Awakened casualties. Hard to say."

"I see. This fight is over, then. The remaining Feynor will either look for easy targets, attack the arena, or try to flee. I'll move toward the entrance, clear out whatever's left."

Ilea nodded. "Send a beam upward if you need help. I'll check on any wounded I can find on the streets."

She didn't wait for his reply before flying off, checking through the streets and rubble of the houses that had been destroyed by spells. The smells were nearly overwhelming, and Ilea found herself missing the ability to regulate her senses inside her Sphere.

Throwing a bunch of corpses to the side, she found a coughing warrior missing both arms, a gaping wound in his belly. Immediately she went to her knees and started healing, focusing first on the stomach wound and then on his severed arms, the immense blood loss making it a miracle that he'd survived at all. She continued healing, making his arms regrow as he gasped and screamed, the sensation overwhelming.

"You're fine," she said and slapped his cheek lightly before moving on, looking through the rubble. Many of the houses surrounding the arena had been destroyed or at least heavily damaged. There had been more Feynor than she'd realized, the chaos too great to make out their precise numbers.

* * *

Half an hour later, she was reasonably sure no more survivors were hiding amongst the rubble. Not about to collect corpses, she made her way back to the arena, checking the injured again. A few remained, but the healers reassured her that was only because of their lack of mana. In general, the Awakened in the area had thinned out again.

"Terrific smell, eh?" Terok said as he stepped next to her.

"They'll need to be burned soon," Ilea said. Terok nodded, looking at the pile of corpses. The dangers of infection and sicknesses were likely small for the usually high-leveled Awakened but still a reality.

Nearby, Ilea found a few Awakened discussing a set of documents they'd retrieved from somewhere. They looked up at her.

"Ashen healer. You have honored us with your fighting."

Terok joined Ilea at her side. "Did you find out why they attacked?"

"Why? They are Feynor, and we are not. That is all the reason they need. The attack today wasn't isolated either. Several Awakened strongholds will have been attacked, as well as independent settlements. These plans we recovered from the bodies are quite detailed."

"Hallowfort?" Ilea interrupted, and the Awakened nodded.

"It is mentioned in one of the documents, yes."

"Thanks," Ilea said. "Terok, I'll be going."

"Fuck, I'll get Maro and Lucas," Terok said.

"Leave Lucas. Ask Maro if he's willing to help."

He looked at her for a second before nodding. "As you wish."

As Terok vanished, one of the Awakened spoke up. "After you have dealt with the Feynor, we suggest seeking an audience with the Dark Protector. I am sure your deeds here shall result in high favor. The enemy has to be defeated, and we could use your prowess, noble healer."

Ilea shook her head. "I won't. Good luck in your war," she said, spreading her wings and following Terok toward the exit.

* * *

Maro was looking through the corpses in the tunnel with a bunch of Awakened.

"There she is," Terok said as Ilea walked up to them.

"Good work here. Not a single one escaped," the king said.

"I'm beaming with pride. Mass murderer number one." Ilea smiled a bitter smile. "We'll have to cut our vacation short, I fear."

Maro nodded. "I have heard. Elana is in Hallowfort too. I offer my help, of course." He stepped toward her and punched her lightly. "I think you're number two at best for today."

He gave her a wink before he summoned his helmet, the undead and skeletons in the tunnel rushing toward him before they collapsed and vanished into his ring.

"We're just feeding the army of an unstoppable necromancer..." Terok commented.

The king laughed his best evil laugh. "Seriously, I can't control more than a hundred. Not if I want them to be capable," he said. "We're not collecting the Elder? He survived, right?"

"Yes, but I don't want to babysit an unstable wood mage attacking friendlies," Ilea said. "I'm happy to visit once the situation has calmed down."

"Doesn't sound like it will anytime soon. Favor for the Dark Protector and his army has grown after this attack. I hear the settlement's elders have unanimously decided to support him with whatever resources and people they can," Terok supplied. "You two don't want to help out as well, do you?"

Ilea looked at Maro. "Not more than I already have."

The king shrugged. "I'm with you on that."

Terok clapped his metal hands together. "Good. Then let's go."

EIGHTY-SIX

Worthy Opponents

Ilea checked the plethora of messages she'd received during the battle in Lisburg. Most of them were kill notifications, the highest level being a mage at two sixty-one.

'ding' You have defeated [Spearmaster – lvl 151 / Iron Defender – lvl 138]

...

'ding' You have defeated [Soul of Fire – lvl 189 / Sharpshooter – lvl 172]

'ding' Blood Magic Resistance reaches lvl 15

'ding' Dark Magic Resistance reaches lvl 13

'ding' You have learned the General Skill Stamina Drain Resistance
Stamina Drain Resistance – lvl 1:
The more rarely used drain magic focused on Stamina. Its effects are not as immediately noticeable as Health or Mana Drain skills, but the end result is just as devastating. You have learned to resist such spells to an extent.

For all the death and chaos, the yield was certainly lackluster. At least the new resistance boosted her resilience thanks to Avatar of Ash. Probably the biggest change.

The three were silent as they flew toward Hallowfort. Ilea had Terok hold onto her back to allow for a faster flight. Maro could nearly keep up with her, Terok's added weight making little difference. Luckily it was sufficiently dark that no arcane storms were active. When they finally entered the caves above the town, all was quiet.

"Death," Maro said after they found the destroyed gate and headed inside. "I can feel it lingering here."

"Sounds like it's already over," Terok said as the trio emerged into the crystal-lit caves where both the Descent and Hallowfort lay.

Smoke was rising from the town in ominous black clouds. A number of buildings were still smoldering. The bridge had been cut, likely to slow the attackers down.

They landed on the statue holding the settlement, bones piling up as Maro moved them from his ring to the ground, accompanied by the wet sounds of fresh corpses.

There was blood everywhere. Awakened as well as Feynor bodies. Ilea moved a familiar large form to the side, the thick armor punctured in at least fifty places, helmet dented in.

Fuckers. She grabbed the heavy hammer and stored it in her necklace. The weapon was manageable now, unlike the last time she'd lifted it. *May you find peace.*

She moved on, the two behind her following slowly as more and more corpses stood up.

Ilea frowned. "Maro, don't use the Awakened."

When she reached the square where the Hunter's Den was located, she found an injured local holding a wound on his belly with his one remaining hand. He was still breathing. Crouching down, she healed the wolf-like creature. "The Feynor. Where are they? Where are the survivors? Injured?"

He winced, barely conscious as he coughed up blood. Ilea's healing moved quickly to stitch up the cuts and regenerate the lost arm.

"The Abyss... We... are to gather... there. Should an attack... happen... barricade it. More came from... below."

She stood up as soon as he was stable, his arm recovered.

"Thank you... warrior of ash," he smiled.

Ilea nodded a farewell before blinking down the stairs and running toward the inn. It didn't take long for them to reach it, the visible carnage continuing every step of the way.

The inn was warded, her Sphere unable to pierce the walls and her blink unable to take her inside. So she simply kicked in the doors.

The three Awakened holding them closed were flung backward as she stepped inside. Lightning smashed into her chest as she moved in, her advance slowed by dark magic wrapping around her legs before she heard Haiden's voice from further back.

"Hold! She is no enemy!"

The spells stopped, the mages looking at her and then Haiden, confused.

"Do you have healers?" Ilea asked, blinking to the cat, who was wearing light armor for once, his head covered in dark steel. "Where are the Feynor?"

Dozens of Awakened looked at the newcomers with fear and confusion, some with weapons unsheathed, hammers and spears in hand. Others tried to get closer to the walls.

"The injured are in a back room. The city is clear. The attackers coming from the Descent were more numerous than those from above. Catelyn went down there an hour ago," he explained, Ilea following him as he moved to the back room.

"You two, go help the fox while I heal," she called over her shoulder.

Terok motioned to Maro, and as the two rushed down toward the Descent, dozens of dead Feynor and skeletons following the necromancer, Ilea blinked into the back room. Once inside, she was appalled by the smell, the sounds, the overwhelming scent of iron, the wetness of blood on the floor.

Since when am I so squeamish?

A single healer was there as well, an Awakened with reddened eyes, tears still rolling down their cheeks as they moved from person to person, sending whatever little mana they had to stabilize the dozens of heavily injured.

Ilea's ashen limbs moved through the groups, checking on each as she determined which ones it was most important to treat first. Haiden left again when he saw her start.

This is worse than I thought.

She started with those about to die, her mana quickly flowing into them, focusing only to treat the worst of their wounds before moving on to the next. Their health would recover on its own, given enough time, but broken bones, open cuts, infections, as well as fevers and coughs would slow it down, even make it impossible to recover at all.

The battles had been recent, meaning she could take care of missing limbs, ears, eyes, or other body parts. Lacking knowledge of most of their anatomy meant she had to use the reconstruction skill without the advanced methods she could use on herself. The rebuilding was slow, taking much more mana than her own body, or another human's, would require. Still, together with the other healer, she quickly stabilized the group.

The two worked without words. The other healer was at level one twenty, and after seeing Ilea start healing, they sat down and started meditating. Soon, pulses of healing energy flowed through the room, and Ilea saw the health of everyone nearby slowly recover, infections cleansed, and even the blood on the floor start evaporating.

She in turn focused more on the individuals, healing the missing limbs and taking care of the nastier wounds that the pulses mostly ignored or could only start closing before they opened again. Ten minutes later, the worst had been handled, and Ilea started focusing on two or three people at once, regrowing limbs as they coughed and screamed.

They continued working in silence, the pulses vanishing after a couple of minutes but starting again two or three minutes later. It likely used up more mana the more people there were. Ilea was impressed by the number of near-corpses that had been brought into the storage room.

"Good work," she said after a while, clasping the Awakened's shoulder. "Can I leave you alone for a bit?"

The creature looked back at her, eyes focused and hard, before it nodded, another pulse of healing power washing through the room as if to confirm.

Ilea didn't wait, blinking twice to reach the tunnel leading down into the city between Hallowfort and the Descent. There were dozens of warriors and mages near the entrance, poised and ready as they waited for any more enemies to come up.

She jumped down, focused on the magic around her. *Dead, undead, skeletons.* Quickly, she sensed the trail and flew through the darkness, seeing dozens of Feynor corpses all around, only increasing in number the farther in she went.

After a while, some skeletons lay broken too. Soon she saw light flickering in the distance, and after increasing her speed and blinking, she appeared in a big hall. The heat here was suffocating, even for her. Flames still clung to many of the bodies around her, while others had had half of their torsos rotted off.

"There she is," she heard Terok exclaim.

Looking around, she saw the dwarf wincing as he lay unmoving with his back against the wall near the entrance of another tunnel. Appearing before him, she pushed healing mana into him.

He grunted in relief. "There's still a bunch remaining. Catelyn must have run into a trap. Maro moved ahead."

Bringing him back to half health and taking care of the worst of his wounds, she nodded. "Thought you could heal yourself now?"

The dwarf chuckled. "Low-level skill still. Only reason I'm still alive. Now stop being sassy and go."

She nodded and rushed onward.

Corpses littered the way, and the next hall showed a similar picture. When she passed through the next hallway, she could hear fighting coming from farther ahead.

In the next room, Maro was deflecting a Feynor's attacks, his body and arms clad in purple flame, beams shooting out that were in turn dodged by the drake-like being, half its armor already burnt away. Dozens of Feynor were fighting the skeletons as well as their brethren, slain Feynor quickly standing up again to join their enemy.

These groups seemed even more organized than those in Lisburg. Healers as well as barrier mages were present, while the rest carefully herded the undead into corners, taking out Maro's troops with efficient formations that negated their numerical advantage.

Still Maro stood, pushing them back. "Don't interfere. Help the fox, she's one hall ahead," he called without pausing his attacks, without fatigue in his voice.

The Feynor he was facing hissed and appeared behind Ilea, but she simply blinked too, the glint of Maro's beam coming at her the last thing she saw before she ran toward the Feynor guarding the entrance to the next chamber.

Barriers were up, her ashen limbs crashing into them before she sped up and smashed her actual fists into them as well. The ash-softened invisible blockade shattered as her Destruction spread through it. She blinked through right after, ignoring the enemies that remained. The heat increased again, and Ilea started to charge up Heart of Cinder as she flew head-on into the flames.

The next room was more of a natural cavern strewn with ruins and rubble. While there was little actual cover, there were plenty of places that the smaller Feynor could have hidden to spring their ambush.

In the center of the space, dozens of mages and warriors were positioned around a five-meter-tall fox clad in flame, with teeth as long as Ilea's arms. The creature delivered a devastating slash and roared in defiance.

'ding' You have heard a mighty beast's roar. You are paralyzed for 0.5 seconds.

She noticed the change in her body but fought against it, the moment passing before she spread her ashen limbs and stormed into the rear of the mages, who were already struggling against the constant fire raging around them.

Ilea blinked through them, the flames sticking to her armor of ash as she landed on one of the Feynor. The mage was forced to the ground as her ashen limbs crashed into his shields and then the armor below, her fists crashing onto his helmet time and time again.

A sudden burst of ice froze her torso, but her legs remained wrapped around the mage, her ash cracking the ice in the next second before her assault continued. His shields cracked, then burst apart, accompanied by the sound of shattering glass. The mage's helmet buckled under the first punch before a heavy projectile slammed into Ilea's side, sending her spinning toward the jagged cavern wall.

She saw someone appear next to the injured ice mage as she tried blinking. The spear that was still embedded in her side flared with light, preventing her skill from activating before it exploded in green shards that dug into her armor, digging in further and further as they began burrowing.

Ilea shed her armor, moving the shards away with her ash before a new set of armor formed. As two Feynor appeared next to her, she released Heart of Cinder, slowing their weapons. A scythe and a fistful of shining claws sped at her before she blinked again, her armor reformed.

Ice guy, sparkly spear guy, scythe guy, claw guy. Aren't I popular?

The ice mage was already standing again, Ilea reactivating her area skill as she blinked at him and the spear user. This time she ducked, avoiding another spear from the sparkly guy, her limbs lashing out at them as they jumped away. The ice mage vanished as she felt the air around her cool down, her ash freezing over before she blinked.

The fox in the center of it all roared and released a wave of fire, clawing at the warriors still attacking her. The melee fighters were being supported by three mages who were channeling their magic into the warriors to buff their attacks. Another two mages were spreading their magic outward around the group.

There was a barrier spell amongst the other AoE spells she could see hanging in the air. Ilea saw it in her Sphere but couldn't see the effect before entering the area – but she did so anyway.

Curses as well as a mana and stamina drain.

She pushed on, barriers stopping her ash as she formed lances, charging up Absolute Destruction while her limbs weakened any mana intrusion defense. She heard the ice mage scream from behind the barrier, ripping the deformed helmet away before his wounds slowly recovered. Another Feynor was touching him with a scaled hand, hard eyes looking at Ilea.

"Leave and live!" she shouted at them, her fist charging up as she stood unmoving behind the barrier, the mages focusing on the fox.

Ilea unleashed her punch, blue magic flowing through the barrier, which disintegrated into motes of mana. She blinked, spells rushing past her as she slammed into their healer, ashen limbs whirling as they tried to slash through the other mages that vanished or jumped away, raising their shields before she shot her lances at them.

Two avoided the black missiles but one was struck, having concentrated too much on the limbs also coming for him. The lance was stopped by his bones but still sent him sprawling as Ilea pumped her destructive mana into the healer below her.

[Warrior – lvl 305]

Several thoughts flashed through her at once when she saw the scythe-wielder appear behind her, fire washing over them all the instant after. Ilea's armor was barely singed, but the scythe-wielding warrior buckled, screaming as his armor started melting.

The Feynor she held down was burning too, his scales melting but reforming quickly until she smashed her fist down, sacrificing health as eight hundred mana spread into him. Her position was now hidden by the continuous stream of fire from the fox, which allowed her to focus fully on the Feynor below her.

She targeted his neck, slicing again and again before she saw his spine, yet her ash glanced off, unable to get through. Her punches sent more and more destructive mana into him while her reverse Reconstruction worked against his recovery. The Feynor was certainly at her level when it came to regenerating his own body but hadn't shown an instant heal like she could manage with her third tier.

Her Meditation was working hard to recover her mana, but she was already using way too much. His resistance against the flames seemed high too. The scythe-wielder had fled already, his back melted and his screams still audible from somewhere to the side.

Sacrificing health again, Ilea's fist slammed down, Heart of Cinder releasing just as it started to damage her. Any metal the creature had worn was now vaporized and half of the warrior was gone, his brain exposed. His bones were still undamaged, but she didn't stop. She pummeled relentlessly, burning through her mana until, finally, a *ding* rang through her mind. The flames around her immediately turned and sought the screaming scythe-wielder.

Once Ilea was visible again, her body suddenly froze entirely, icicles forming on her ash before she blinked away, appearing next to a Feynor mage that was still struggling to rip out her ashen lance from earlier.

Ilea's mana was down to a third, but she didn't stop. Her mind pushed the lance farther into his body as he screamed. He added health drain to the mix when she moved closer, the ice on her ash cracking before she dodged a spear flying at her.

The projectile exploded when it passed, sending black and green shrapnel into her armor, digging into it once again, but she dared not dispel her ash covering this close to another enemy. Her limbs dealt shallow cuts to the curse mage, denting his armor as she pushed him back.

As the fox roared behind her, the burrowing shrapnel reached her skin before exploding once again, ripping into her flesh as a Feynor appeared behind her. The claw-wielding guy. Ilea turned to face the warrior as his claws ripped into her flesh and ash alike.

[Warrior – lvl 310]

His helmet had been melted onto his face, blinding him entirely. The rest of his body was steaming, half-molten and black, but the attacks weren't any less powerful. Still, her wounds were recovering quickly, her ash reforming as she focused on deflecting his claws and continuing her assault on the curse mage behind her.

Ilea's movements were slow, allowing for meditation between strikes. She waited for an opportunity. When it came, the tiniest overextension, she grabbed onto the warrior's hands and moved him toward an oncoming spear, seeing the projectile stop an instant later.

Fire rushed over the three of them as she heard the fox roar. The scythe-wielder charged over and dug his weapon into the monster's leg, the flames moving up and away from Ilea and her enemies. She watched the claw warrior scream through his molten skin and steel as he wrenched her grappling arms apart, kicking her in the stomach and sending her back, his arms free again.

Her armor reformed before shards of ice crashed into both her and the fox. Ilea found her mana was getting dangerously low. She gritted her teeth and focused. When another spear hurtled toward her, a purple beam intercepted it, sending it crashing into a nearby wall before skeletons flooded in.

They were quickly cut apart by scythes and claws but bought Ilea the time she sorely needed. She stepped toward Maro, and the fox too moved closer, the heat setting his shield and her armor aflame.

"Their healer is down," Ilea said as her own ashen lance slammed into an incoming metal projectile sent by their highest-level mage, his armor black and undamaged.

EIGHTY-SEVEN

Survivors

Ilea noted that Maro was still uninjured. His shield had a purple hue in her Sphere and dozens of connections to the undead and skeletons that still rushed at the enemy group.

Catelyn stepped back, moving closer to them as she panted, blood dripping from various wounds and burning up immediately, slowly healing thanks to Ilea's power.

We need time to recover. How much fucking health do you have, foxy?

Ilea watched the skeletons freeze over. The level two eighty ice mage that had lost his helmet looked mostly uninjured. The two remaining warriors, burnt and steaming, cut through the undead Feynor with scythe and claws, both sharp enough to sever steel and bones.

A barrier mage at level two seventy-five was crawling on the floor, moaning in pain as he grasped his face, scales, armor, and skin that had mostly melted together. The curse and drain mage had stopped draining Ilea's mana, likely because her resistance was causing more problems than it was worth. The lance was still stuck in his side, and he was bleeding from dozens of cuts, limping along the wall as he tried to get some distance.

The fire burning the ground, walls, and ceiling had stopped near the Feynor, and she saw in her Sphere that one of their mages, at three hundred and two, was influencing the flames. The last survivor was the mage in black armor, none of his features showing as he formed three lances of steel around him.

The battle had gone on for a while, both parties now starving for mana, some individuals for health as well. It had cost Ilea heavily in resources, Catelyn likely as well, to take down their healer, but it would be worth it in the end.

"Recover your mana. I'll keep them occupied," Maro said, stepping forward as a tide of his skeletons charged at the Feynor, many of them quickly cut apart or frozen.

A broad purple beam crashed into the fire mage, his own magic trying to cancel the death magic before weapons of bone slashed into him from the swarming undead. They were only minor cuts, but they were enough to distract him, a second beam slamming into the mage's legs while Ilea deflected the steel lances that had been sent flying at the necromancer.

She flung her own projectiles at the injured mages, impaling the barrier mage before he slid away, not dead but certainly taken out of the fight for now. The curse mage managed to deflect her attacks but he stumbled and fell, his previous injury worsening.

It didn't take long for all Maro's creatures to be cut down, but when the last fell, Catelyn stepped forward, releasing a cone of fire that enveloped all but the warriors and the ice and steel mages, who teleported to the side of the hall.

Ilea heard the muffled screams from the barrier and curse mages as well as the fire mage, who tried redirecting the attack but mostly failed. A beam of purple light slammed into him before an ashen lance pierced his head, sending his body tumbling back, crashing to the floor, where he lay dead and unmoving.

Three notifications rang out in Ilea's mind – the mages caught by the fire had all been reduced to molten steel and skin. Ilea had recovered a couple of hundred mana, but still she waited as the remaining warriors approached. Her Heart of Cinder was eating away at her health, but she refused to let it go just yet.

Catelyn moved to the side as quickly as a small fox would move despite her size, dodging a barrage of scythe strikes as the warrior using claws slammed into Maro's shield, ripping away at his defenses while his body started to burn with purple flames. Beams shot out at point-blank range, but the warrior dodged them with incredible speed.

Ilea realized that the metal mage was forming a massive array of needles, hundreds of them floating in the air around him. She in turn formed walls of ash connected to herself, moving them into place just as he released the attack, focused on Maro. The air around her froze as she blinked to intercept the projectiles, and while a chunk of her ash turned to ice before it shattered, hundreds of needles were stopped by her ash or armor.

She felt them dig in but ignored the sensation, instead blinking to the ice mage who vanished immediately, Ilea following with her wings. A beam of freezing mana slammed into her chest, her ash cooling down as crystals of ice formed on her. She didn't blink, waiting until she reached the Feynor.

His eyes bulged in fear, then he vanished again. Ilea blinked to the disturbance she felt in her Sphere, reappearing and sacrificing three hundred health before releasing Heart of Cinder, the attack charged up for longer than she'd ever tried before.

The heat erupted out, slamming into the mage just as he reappeared. It met a flash of blue and was partially rebuffed. Next, her ashen limbs cut into him, her wings driving them both forward before he smashed into the wall, Ilea crashing into him right after.

Whatever shield he'd put up saved his life, but his armor was gone now, as were his shields. She pummeled her fist into him repeatedly, lances of steel clattering into the ashen armor on her back, coupled with dozens of needles, both exploding and digging deeper before once again ripping out chunks of armor, skin, and muscle.

It didn't change the sound of bones cracking under her fist or the wet sound of brain matter being reduced to an unidentifiable sludge. Ilea knew he was dead before the ding in her mind. She deflected two more lances with her ashen limbs, a third one navigating around them before it buried itself in her flesh, finding a spot where her armor hadn't recovered yet.

She stumbled to the side, leaving behind the remains of the dead Feynor smeared inside the cratered wall, as she felt the steel dig deeper and deeper. Dull explosions rent the air as she healed the damage. New tissue formed over the needles that exploded moments later, ripping through what she'd just recovered. The mage was focused on her alone, standing only ten meters away as more and more needles of black steel formed around him.

A group of explosions ripped through her lungs, heart, and other organs as she blinked away. A huge chunk of mana left her as her body returned to normal, ashen armor forming on top as she locked eyes with the mage.

A massive shock wave made them both turn toward the others. Bones and corpses exploded in purple light as both Catelyn and the scythe warrior raced through the debris to avoid the death magic.

The sounds stopped a moment later, purple and orange flames littering what remained of the hall as water dripped down from above. Ilea swallowed hard as she saw the claw warrior standing before Maro, shining talons thrust deep into the necromancer's stomach.

A sudden flare of purple fire pushed the Feynor back a little, bones forming around Maro as a roar filled the cavern. The hair on the back of Ilea's neck stood up as she dashed off to the side, dodging the steel needles whizzing after her.

Ilea reached the mage before she felt the attack coming, her ash pierced by the spikes that extended from his armor with lightning speed. Even as her back was shredded by the needles, her ashen limbs started smashing into his armor.

You should have blinked, she thought with a savage grin, pumping destructive mana into him, his arms holding hers as they struggled against each other, ash against metal. His armor and projectiles against her limbs and walls of ash.

Neither relented, both meditating to recover mana. Whenever his steel was pierced, it reformed and closed up again just as her own ashen armor recovered. The only difference was that his actual wounds didn't heal as quickly.

They stayed entangled for half a minute, his spikes ripping into her defenses, digging into her ash before explosions ripped more and more from it. Her back had opened up already, tissue ripped out and recovering time and time again.

When she finally slammed her ash through the steel covering his head, she cut into one of his eyes before releasing Heart of Cinder, burning much of his steel away and melting part of his face. He stumbled back.

Steel fell to the ground as it slid out of her body, Ilea's wounds slowly recovering as she dropped to her knees, nearly out of mana and focusing only on recovering from her wounds. The Feynor made pained noises, and Ilea grinned at the realization that he didn't have his Pain Tolerance in the second tier.

Another advantage, she thought, her vision blurring before she refocused. *Fight isn't over.*

While she recovered more mana, she didn't let up with her ashen limbs, constantly cutting into his face as he struggled to recover his armor. Her limbs then moved on to his legs and stomach. He shifted to the side to dodge the lances she sent his way, the third one hitting and impaling his left leg.

Ilea stood up, her ash connected to the mage to stop his teleportation magic before she grabbed him by the shoulder. Her armor had now recovered entirely, and his attempts to attack her crashed uselessly into her defenses as she charged up Absolute Destruction. She only had enough mana for five seconds, her third-tier Aspect of Ash wreathing her arm in fire, her sacrifice of three hundred health lighting up blue runes below her ash.

"Good fight," she said.

Her fist landed on his face, and his head cracked backward as her mana wrecked his brain. Her limbs followed, cutting into his neck before she finally ripped off his head, another ding echoing in her mind.

No head recovery? Should work on that.

The hall was filling up with water now, and some parts were already flooded as more and more flowed in from the cracks above. She found Maro covered in wounds and protected by a cage of bones, purple fire dancing around him as he deflected the scythe time and time again. She walked toward them slowly, recovering her mana and healing her wounds.

Catelyn was now small and unconscious, lying below Maro. The claw warrior lay in two halves to the side, and the scythe-wielder didn't look to be in much better shape than the necromancer. The Feynor had discarded his armor at some point, only having his scales for defense now. Both combatants were panting, their attacks slow, the scythe digging into the man with each strike, purple fire flaring before each hit.

Ilea breathed hard, then blinked behind the warrior, who turned before sweeping his blade toward her, but he was stopped by the ash as she grabbed his weapon. He jumped back, effortlessly ripping the pole out of her hands before he sank down to one knee.

Looking around, they heard the ceiling crack, chunks of stone falling down as Ilea extended her limbs, stabilizing both Maro and Catelyn. The latter was in much better shape than the necromancer. Her eyes opened wide as she saw the extent of his wounds. His body was barely alive.

That's a death mage for you.

She grinned, seeing her mana converting directly into health for Maro and Catelyn – and for herself. Her mana was nearly spent, but she had her priorities. She spat a mouthful of blood to the ground, raising her slightly shaking hands. She looked at the Feynor, who was holding his side, where blood seeped out from where his ribs should have been. He stared at them with hate-filled eyes.

Leave, Ilea thought. She didn't know if she had enough left in the tank to beat him. Nor if she could do so before the place filled with water. *Come on. Run.*

The ceiling cracked even more before the warrior burst into glowing green light and rushed at them. A desperate last attack. Her limbs shot out, but the Feynor dodged them with quick movements, his glowing scythe coming for her neck. Ilea wasn't sure she had enough mana for a new head.

Then steel projectiles slammed into the Feynor's chest, knocking him off balance. Ilea's ashen spears pierced his stomach just as he reached her, his blade cutting through her raised arm instead of her neck. She held it there and stared into the Feynor's eyes before a beam of purple light enveloped his head. He staggered back, and Ilea ripped his weapon out and flung it to the side before he slid to a stop.

Ilea sighed, using three ashen limbs to prop herself up. The wound on her arm wasn't closing. Then she looked up at another noise.

Terok had appeared above the warrior, his arm slamming down on the Feynor's head. The hit landed, but the creature's arm darted up and clutched at his fist. The metal groaned before Terok's other arm shifted, a beam of white light cutting into the enemy's head. The arm went limp.

A final ding filled Ilea's mind as Terok stumbled backward, cradling his dented limb as the steel reformed, before he gasped, "We have to get the fuck out of here."

Ilea lacked the strength to speak as she pushed all her recovered mana into the two mages. She grabbed Catelyn with ashen limbs and supported Maro with her shoulder, his arm weakly wrapping around her as they stumbled out of the room.

As Terok held up a shield to deflect the chunks of stone now raining down on them and water gushed out into the hallway, Ilea never stopped healing with whatever little mana she had, any she recovered directly flowing into the other two.

Catelyn was stable when they reached the next room, but Maro's condition didn't change. Ilea collapsed when they came out into the hall, the necromancer falling beside her as she meditated, forcing herself to stay awake as the corners of her vision darkened. Terok stood next to the trio, asking something that Ilea couldn't hear.

Time passed, Ilea's mana recovering as she healed constantly. Her vision slowly faded back to normal and, while exhausted, she was ready again, should there be more enemies waiting.

"Was that all of them?" Terok asked.

"I think so," she said, spitting blood from her mouth. "Why were they here?"

The dwarf shook his head, checking on Catelyn. Maro was on his knees, head hanging on his chest with eyes closed. Ilea felt him exuding mana still, likely in a meditative state.

Her healing was showing results now, albeit much slower than anybody she'd healed previously. There was nothing inherently wrong with his body – at least, not according to her spell. The pulses of purple mana in her Sphere were likely an indication.

When Catelyn's insane health pool was topped off, she started pushing mana into her more aggressively. On the third try, the fox woke up. Coughing lightly, she staggered up and looked around, baring her teeth.

"You're safe. You almost look cute without knowing about that fire form," Ilea chuckled.

The fox lay down and snorted. "You... you saved my life."

"As did those two," Ilea said, her ash still in contact with all three of them. "We should head back in case the Abyss gets attacked."

She stood up and nearly stumbled, catching herself before Terok moved in to help.

"You should rest. Too much mana use. I trust Haiden and the power of that group... They weren't here for the town," Catelyn said, starting to pace around slowly. "We need those corpses. Anything left behind could help..." She looked at the dwarf. "Terok, can you get them out, or are you injured too?"

He looked at Ilea and then shook his head, arm forming into a big sledgehammer. "I'm fine. Only joined the fun in the last moments."

Catelyn nodded weakly. "Why would they target me? Or did we misjudge the Feynors' power? The Dark Protector will run into trouble if some random attack squad has six people above three hundred."

"They attacked the Vineyard Caves too. Didn't see a single one above my level. Amongst hundreds," Ilea supplied, looking at Maro, who had stopped exuding mana. She moved quickly when he collapsed, catching him before he woke up.

"Ah… my dreams have come true. A lovely knight in nothing but her shredded leathers," he muttered.

The strain on his body made to deliver that one lame joke must have been enormous. Typical.

Ilea switched her destroyed leather armor to a shirt and pants. "Thought you were a goner for sure," she said, punching his head lightly.

"Death itself cannot be bested." He coughed, spraying blood onto her shirt and face. "Sorry."

She laughed, moving her ash to clean off the blood.

"Then it was targeted," Catelyn said. "The Vineyard Caves have much closer ties to the army. Why me?"

"Looked like dragon worshipers. Seems like this age didn't change much," Maro said, sitting up and reassuring Ilea he was fine. "You know what they usually like?" He paused. "Fire. Not anymore though, I'll bet. You damn near broke through my shield with your presence alone. What the fuck even are you?"

The fox chuckled, smiling wryly as Terok started to rip out chunks of rock from the collapsed hall. "Well, they just wasted some incredibly strong people. Can't say I dislike it." She turned to Ilea. "What do you want for your help?"

Ilea considered. "Got any more of those Blue Reaper eyes? Those were super tasty," she said drily.

Catelyn narrowed her eyes.

Ilea smiled. "Or your potions! Delicious stuff."

"I withdraw the offer."

"That is so sad," Ilea said and crossed her arms.

"Some armor would be nice," Maro said. "Mine's fucked, and I don't want to use up all the remaining sets I have. Sentimental value."

"That can be arranged, I'm sure," Catelyn smiled. "At least one of you is reasonable."

"I'm interested in those cursed potions too, though, now that Ilea mentions them."

"Ugh. Elana was right," Catelyn said.

"Right about what?" Maro asked.

Ilea laughed, seeing both Maro and the fox smiling.

"What are you going to do about the Feynor?" Ilea asked, serious again.

"This is a heavy loss. I doubt they will try something again soon. All I can do is make Hallowfort more attractive for powerful people and level up myself. Guess my days of dabbling in alchemy are over," Catelyn sighed.

"I need someone to pinpoint their locations. I won't dig out that whole bloody room," Terok said, having paused his work.

"I'll get someone to you. Come, let us return for now. If there were any Feynor left, they would have attacked already," Catelyn said, moving toward the town, guided by three flames floating in the air.

EIGHTY-EIGHT

Cleanup

Ilea wrapped herself in her ashen armor again as the three of them returned, Catelyn announcing the group through the opening before they ascended. The fox addressed one of the warriors when they arrived.

"Galin, go help the dwarf. Follow the trail of blood."

"Sure you're alright?" Ilea asked Maro as the warrior disappeared. The man just shrugged.

"You made it back," Haiden said, coming over to them. "It was all a diversion, I assume, to draw out the one carrying the 'flame's blessing', as one of them put it. I assume that's you."

Catelyn growled and shook her head. "And here I thought they were prioritizing Hallowfort's strategic value."

Elana joined them as well, nodding to the group.

"You killed them all?" Haiden asked.

"We did," Ilea said.

"Good. That makes this simple then. We have several options, but if I know you, Catelyn, you'd rather ignore it."

"Some might see it as a notable challenge to attack us. But there were other attacks too," Catelyn said.

"What do you plan to do then?" Elana asked.

Catelyn sighed. "We will support the Dark Army, at least financially. Plenty of gear will be available from all the dead too. I doubt the Dark Protector will leave such an array of assaults unanswered. The Feynor will be too busy with him to attack us again. In the meantime, we can work on our defenses. Any word from the expedition?"

"Still nothing. One scout returned just before the attack, telling of creatures behaving frantically even in the first layer. We'll have to send more guards and prepare to defend ourselves. I don't have a good feeling about it, Catelyn. Will you three be sticking around?" Haiden asked, turning to Ilea and Maro.

"Terok isn't here," Maro said.

"He must be close by. I'm sure you'll be suitably repaid for the help today."

"We need more information. Plenty of things to work through for now," the fox said. "I'll coordinate with the council. Is Goliath still missing?"

"I assume he's in a Taleen dungeon to the north," Ilea supplied.

"He gave you his obelisk?" Catelyn asked, chuckling. "Of course the old fool would trust you instead of me."

"Can't fault him there. She just saved your furry ass," Haiden said with a purr. "Good to know the old relic is alive."

"I'll organize the cleanup if that's alright. You take care of the defenses," Elana said.

Catelyn nodded.

"We'll move back to Tremor for a couple days after this," Ilea said, looking at Maro.

"We'll need a week at least to get a handle on things. There'll surely be interesting work for you afterward," Elana said, nodding to Ilea and Maro before she walked out.

There was a moment's silence before Catelyn sighed and started floating, looking at Ilea.

"First you bring me cake and now you save my life. Whenever you need me, I'll be there." Her gaze was focused, fire burning in her eyes. She turned to Maro. "No cake from you, but also thank you. I have lots of work now. Let me know when you're back in town."

Then she vanished, leaving Ilea there with the king.

"I'll check the injured again, then head back to help Terok," Ilea said. "After that, off to Tremor?"

He shrugged. "No vacation then. Well, I suppose it feels good to stretch my muscles again. Maybe moving some rocks would be fun too."

"Sure you didn't hit your head?"

She made her way toward the room at the back of the pub with the injured. Maro chuckled at her question but didn't reply, simply following her in silence. Most of the Awakened looked at them when they passed through the main room, nods and approving gestures aplenty.

The weakened healing pulse Ilea felt coming through the thick wooden door made her smile. The healer was still at it. Granted, she'd only been gone for an hour, maybe less. Still, even in that time, it seemed more wounded had been recovered. The creature looked up and inclined their head.

Ilea returned the greeting. "Do you need help? Missing limbs or anything serious remaining?"

The creature nodded, getting up from their meditative position and quickly moving around the room, pointing out those with injuries they apparently couldn't treat.

Ilea moved her ashen limbs, recovering missing organs and limbs as well as simply treating wounds too extreme for the other healer to stabilize quickly. Maro sat down with the creature and joined the healers in meditation while they both worked.

Knowing nothing about the alien biology of the creatures here, Ilea mostly let her skill do its magic, allowing her to check through the notifications from the fights.

'ding' You have defeated [Genesis Regenerator – lvl 305 / Warlord Chieftain – lvl 290]

...

'ding' Your group has defeated [Scythe Ruler – lvl 321 / Guardian of Ki – lvl 318] – For defeating an enemy ten levels or more above your own, bonus experience is granted.

'ding' Azarinth Sentinel has reached lvl 304 – Five stat points awarded

'ding' Kin of Ash has reached lvl 303 – Five stat points awarded

'ding' Azarinth Fighting reaches 3rd lvl 9

'ding' Aspect of Ash reaches 3rd lvl 7

'ding' Curse Resistance reaches 2nd lvl 3

'ding' Heat Resistance reaches 2nd lvl 13

'ding' Ice Resistance reaches 2nd lvl 3

'ding' You have learned the General Skill Olvor Magic Resistance – lvl 1
Olvor Magic Resistance – lvl 1:
A rare form of steel manipulation requiring a strong mind and an abundance of olvor. Like many obscure schools of magic, its powers are varied and flexible, molded by their masters. Your body has suffered heavy damage from such magic, making it a little more resistant.

'ding' Olvor Magic Resistance reaches lvl 2

'ding' Olvor Magic Resistance reaches lvl 3

Ilea finished healing the last of the injured as she invested her remaining stat points into Intelligence, Wisdom, and Vitality.

"Hey Maro, are there multipliers for Wisdom and Vitality?"

He opened his eyes, looking at her as she walked back toward him. He nodded to the other healer and stood up.

"Possibly. One of my Class skills reduces the mana cost of active skills used. That's why I can keep going for so long. It actually increases in potency the lower my health goes."

"That sounds amazing… although I'd just walk around half-dead to get the benefits," Ilea said with a smile. "Any idea what's up with Catelyn's health?"

They walked back toward the shaft leading down to the ruined city above the Descent, landing in the darkness before they continued toward Terok. Neither were bothered by the darkness.

"Maybe she just invested a lot into it. The two warriors we fought had ridiculous health too."

"True that," she said, shaking her head.

He glanced her way. "What is it?"

"Just… one hell of a fight."

He laughed. "Sure was. I'm glad nobody on our side died. I think it was close."

"Yeah," Ilea said and smiled. "Thanks for the help, Maro."

"They threatened to torch Lisburg. Least I can do."

"You're not half bad for an ancient necromancer king, you know."

"Don't go falling in love with me now, I thought you were immune to my charms," he said and moved a hand through his hair. It was somehow more charming even though he was doing it on purpose.

"No wonder she liked you," Ilea said.

He faltered slightly. "I expected a joke there, Ilea."

She grinned. "That's exactly why I didn't give you one."

They continued on their way to help Terok, soon reaching the dwarf and his Awakened helper.

"Need a hand?" Ilea asked, cracking her neck.

"About a hundred, yes. Just start smashing through the rock. You know where the corpses are."

She nodded and got to work. Her ashen limbs cut into the stone with ease, the pressure alone softening them up before chunks were ripped out.

After a while, Terok looked her way and shook his head. "You're embarrassing me. Do I even have a use anymore?"

"I like you as a friend," Ilea said after a while. The dwarf just looked down at his metal arms before continuing his work.

* * *

Bringing out the last corpse, Ilea lowered it onto the pile right outside the tunnel, guarded by Maro, who really should have added some undead to the workforce.

"That's the last one," she said.

The Awakened warrior next to her nodded. "Thank you. For defending this town and for defending the revered alchemist."

Ilea wasn't sure what to think of that title. Catelyn had likely forced it on them.

"Hey, you know most guards here, right?" The Awakened nodded. "I talked to one a while back. Found him dead when we arrived. This was his hammer," she said, summoning the massive olvor battle sledge.

"Tal was their name. A noble warrior protecting Hallowfort for centuries. May they find their way to the next life or rest in peace, should they wish so."

The warrior looked skyward as he spoke.

"What will happen to the hammer?" Ilea asked, twirling the heavy weapon.

"It will be stored and given or sold to somebody. Perhaps melted down, should nobody want it."

"What about family?"

The warrior shook his head. "Tal was a solitary guardian, like many who reside in these parts. Should you wish to have it, I'm sure they would be honored to have their weapon wielded by the ashen savior."

"Ashen savior?" she asked, looking at the olvor weapon, black as the night, acceptably balanced for her height.

"Does the name not please you? My apologies, ashen healer. Yet without you and the king of death, I doubt the outcome today would have been so favorable."

Maro chuckled from the side.

Ilea rolled her eyes. "Don't worry about it. As for the hammer, I'd like to have it. I'll leave some gold with you too."

The warrior immediately shook his head, lifting both hands to stop her. "I refuse. In the name of Hallowfort. It is the least we can do to repay you."

Ilea was about to retort when Maro spoke up. "Take the bloody hammer, you dunce. What is this? Bloody court? Nobles trying to one-up each other with their generosity?"

"Hey, fuck off," she said, looking at the hammer with a smile.

[Quiet – Rare]

An appropriate name, she thought, given by a guard who died defending their home.

Thanks, Tal.

"The answer of an uncultured warrior with no regard for nobility," Maro said, shaking his head in mock sadness.

"Yes, exactly, and the reason you're sticking with me, I assume."

Terok snorted as he exited the collapsed hall. "Just warn me when you start fucking. I don't want to die because of a stray spell going off in your weird battle-foreplay."

"He's married."

"She hasn't bathed in years."

"A lie."

"Why can I never shut up?" Terok asked, holding a finger up to his metal head. "No, keep your witty shit to yourself. I nearly died today. So did you two, as a matter of fact. Why can't you be shell-shocked like any normal person?" Terok mumbled to himself as he walked past.

"Death holds no meaning to its king," Maro commented dryly.

Ilea nodded. "I'm just collecting near-death experiences for my next evolution."

Terok's murmuring became incomprehensible. He was probably cursing.

Ilea held out a fist to Maro, who didn't react. "You're supposed to hit it with your fist."

"Why?"

"It's like a celebratory gesture when a team does something they're proud of."

"So we're a team now?"

Ilea dropped her fist. "Forget it, necromancer."

Terok looked back at them. "To Tremor now, finally? I saw at least two people I owe money to in the Abyss. Maybe your treasury holds something useful."

"I could use the money I have here to pay them," Maro suggested.

Terok waved him off. "They can wait another day, or a week."

"You don't intend to pay them?" Ilea asked with a chuckle.

"Maybe after the story of a brave dwarf saving Catelyn and her helpers has had time to spread far and wide," he said and laughed.

They all joined in, the tension of the day finally fading somewhat.

EIGHTY-NINE

The End of Patience

"So, there are healing classes you can get *without* eating the world's hottest chili?" Ilea asked as they entered the mountain below which Tremor lay.

Maro nodded. They'd been discussing her own Class and how unique it was on Elos.

"Yes, but healing orders have always discouraged non-members from practicing their magic. Not uncommon. In my day, lightning magic was nearly unanimously reserved for nobles, as was anything related to blood or the void. I would assume that still holds true."

"Probably," Ilea said, though she could only remember that one healer on the Taleen dungeon expedition.

Didn't they try to poison me? Or was that Alice's family? Well, I remember that healer was an ass either way.

Trian was a noble, as were Edwin and likely Maria, the three examples of lightning, blood, and void magic she knew of.

Another way humans are jeopardizing themselves. The adventurers in the guild looked at me like a freshly baked muffin when they saw my healer tag.

"Any idea why it's like that? Couldn't any random person learn lightning or blood magic?" Terok asked.

"Well, yes and no," Maro said. "Without knowledge, it's definitely harder. Elixirs help too, especially to get a Class initially. Most influential people wouldn't want commoners practicing their choice of magic. I doubt any of those schools are any better or worse than anything else. Otherwise, all the most powerful adventurers would be nobles."

When they landed in the cathedral, Ilea immediately noticed the piece of paper stuck to the double doors with an expensive-looking dagger. She walked over and read it quickly.

Ilea, if you return to see this, please find me in the Taleen dungeon. I need your help.
The Hunters have not returned on time. There was talk of facing the Great Hall.
They are not ready.

The letters were hurriedly written, and Ilea spread her wings as soon as she'd finished reading. The handwriting was the same as the script in the books Elfie had translated.

"The Great Hall," she said, showing the letter to the others and thinking back to the expedition below Dawntree. The Praetorians had showed up in the throne room of the Taleen ruin. Inside the Great Hall. "If they're going in there as they are, they'll be ripped apart."

"Shit," Terok murmured. "Proud fucking idiots. Go, we'll catch up!"

Ilea nodded, blinking twice before she appeared in the rock formation above the entrance. Checking for storms, she shot off. She didn't know when Elfie had written the message, but it couldn't have been too long ago. He must've waited for a while before returning, and his journey there and back would have taken time as well.

If the young Cerithil Hunters died wanting to prove themselves against something far beyond their capabilities, then that was on them.

But a friend had asked for Ilea's help.

So, she would help.

Ilea ignored the crevices, instead moving in as straight a path as possible, her wings moving stronger and faster than before her evolution.

Let's see if these fuckers are enough to avoid the storms.

A cloud moved dangerously close a couple of minutes later, forming out of seemingly nowhere. She flew to the side, but the cloud was too vast and engulfed her, lightning flashing down a few meters away from her.

Ilea was moving at a high altitude, near where the dark storm hovered. Her Azarinth Fighting picked up the lightning a split second before it struck. The impact smashed into the stone below, a shock wave visibly expanding over the land.

Her ashen armor reformed, seared away by the pure arcane power that had flashed by almost within touching distance. Ilea moved a little lower, giving her more time to react while remaining far enough from the ground to ignore the shock wave of the impact.

'ding' Arcane Magic Resistance reaches 2nd lvl 2

'ding' Arcane Magic Resistance reaches 2nd lvl 3

Another strike came from above, and Ilea blinked to put distance between herself and the dangerous power. The armor on her back was burned through, her wings reforming as she fell for a second.

And then she was out, blinking several times to get distance from the cloud, which continued eastward. Her heart pounding fast, she focused and pushed on.

Not training in there yet. But I can survive.

Ilea sped over the land, concentrating on the destination and slowing down as she blinked through another passing arcane storm. The lightning hit much farther away this time, allowing her to speed through to the safe area in front of the dungeon without further interruption.

When she landed, Ilea found Elfie pacing in front of the entrance with a grim expression on his face. When he noticed her, his mouth twisted in a way she didn't understand.

"How long have they been inside?" she asked, her wings disappearing as she looked around, trying to sense anything.

"Over half a day. I thought they would have learned at this point, that they would listen to me," he hissed, his voice frantic. "Ilea, please, you have to stop them..."

Ilea looked at him for a moment. "I have to stop them? You can go in there too, you know? You've trained them, but you still haven't gone in there yourself."

He looked at her with wide eyes and hissed again, this time at her. "You know very well that I cannot do that, human. I'll be c—" His words died in his throat as he shook his head. "No. No, they chose to ignore me and stayed inside! They are blinded by pride, by—"

"You sent them here," Ilea said as she walked past him.

He glared at her.

"I know they mean a lot to you. I'll help, but I'm just one woman. So, make your choice. Getting into a Great Hall takes some doing, but they may already be dead."

His face twisted again as he gazed at her and then at the entrance, his hand clawing at his own neck so hard that blood started flowing.

Ilea gritted her teeth and moved closer to the dungeon, feeling the magic flowing through her.

"Are you coming or not?"

She didn't say anything else, just shook her head as she turned her eyes from him and sped into the Taleen dungeon.

Her Sentinel Huntress skill quickly picked up the magical signs of the three. They'd certainly grown in the past year. Enough to face Centurions.

But there are more than Centurions where they are headed.

She spread her wings when she reached the Taleen town, blinking and hurtling through the ancient city at full speed. She noted the Taleen Guardians moving below her, all making their way toward the Great Hall. The fleeing expedition had rushed right into the blades of the oncoming Guardians, and it seemed the elves had already triggered a similar reaction.

They're really here then. She gulped.

Green eyes flashed in her mind, memories from long ago. Pain and terror began making their way back before she willed them away. *No*. She refused, simply refused, to be afraid, to let herself be beaten again by those mindless creatures.

This hadn't been planned. She'd wanted to train more, to get more powers, but here she was. She was angry at those idiots for forcing her to go into a fight she'd wanted to prepare for more. A fight she'd wanted to have on her own terms.

She laughed as she rushed through the dimly lit streets.

Prepare more? she asked herself, rounding a corner. *No. You've prepared long enough. The idiot elves aren't the issue, are they?*

You're afraid.

You're still afraid even after all this time, with all this power.

Ilea grimaced, feeling a cold sensation in her stomach. But she didn't stop. She wouldn't let them take any more people from her. Whether they were idiots or not.

She slowed her breathing and focused. "You're not the same anymore, Ilea. You've grown," she told herself, but the words didn't sound quite as convincing as she'd hoped.

She landed on the bridge that led to the Great Hall, the same design as in the dungeon she knew, dozens of Guardians turning her way as she breathed out. Her ashen limbs shot forward, ripping through steel limbs and severing heads as if the machines' carapaces were made of paper. She blinked twice, glancing at the numerous machines on the bridge reduced to scrap, before arriving before the gates. They'd been forced open.

They needed time for that, at least.

She blinked inside, finding fewer machines there, many more already destroyed. Small craters as well as burning pieces suggested at least two destroyed Centurions. The Great Hall was bigger than the one she'd visited before, made of the same white stone but several hundred meters of it. Chairs, tables, and even small buildings crowded the place in addition to the guardians of this forgotten town.

Ilea focused her gaze on the closed green gates at the end of the hall. If she knew Goldie and Heranuur, that's where they'd be. Neither cared about treasure. They just wanted to fight the toughest fucker in the room.

Wasn't she the same at heart? The only difference was that she chose fights that were challenging and fun, while the young elves seemed more bent on proving themselves.

And that's how you get yourself killed. I know when to back down.

And yet here, flying through another Taleen Great Hall, she knew she wasn't being rational. No. She was scared. And now she saw it. Felt it. Couldn't ignore it anymore, couldn't find another excuse.

Ilea found herself smiling. It was strange, in a way. Now that she saw the fear, it was just another challenge. She'd reached her evolutions, fought and killed many three-mark monsters. What was another?

She touched her stomach, felt the cold feeling of the memory she still carried. "Fuck that," she said and breathed in, reaching the gate, where she saw destroyed Guardians scattered on the ground. She touched the closed gates to the throne room and blinked past.

Her Sphere let her see the massive mace coming down toward her. She raised her arms, catching the large weapon before she was pushed down, the ground cracking slightly under the strain of her legs.

Looking up, she saw green light shining down from above. A white throne was centered at the back of the big hall, and eight pillars connected the floor to the ceiling on each side. And above her...

[Taleen Praetorian - ???]

Her breath caught in her chest. Two of them again. The same green eyes, the same scythes and mace. She gritted her teeth, pushing back against the weight and strength of the machine.

"I'll rip you motherfuckers apart."

She glanced behind her when the machine raised its weapon once more.

"I had that..." Heranuur said, coughing up blood as he struggled to stand, a big grin on his face, sharp teeth showing.

Ilea pushed him back with two ashen limbs and started healing, raising her brows when she saw the damage.

"You're out of the fight." She looked around the hall and focused forward again. "You shouldn't be able to stand."

She noted that Neiphato had finally decided to use his second Class, wood continuously growing around the second Praetorian a couple of dozen meters away. The elf was standing before a crouching Seviir, the latter breathing hard, likely trying to recover mana.

He's actually holding it back.

The Praetorian's scythes had difficulty gaining enough speed to cut through Neiphato's wood, more roots continually replacing those being cut as he slowly stepped backward.

"How long can you hold?" Ilea called in his general direction, never letting her mace-wielding foe out of her sight.

The mace swung again, this time horizontally and aimed at her, the air whistling as the weapon neared. Ilea activated Blink before she saw magic emanate from the mace itself, disrupting her spell.

Then the heavy weapon was upon her. One wing intercepted the blow from the side as she held up her arm, the force of the blunt hit traveling through her as she was sent tumbling to one side, skidding to a halt. Her whole side was bruised, and there was even internal bleeding. Her healing got to work.

Neiphato hadn't replied, sweat dripping from his face as he focused on his magic.

Not long then.

"You three are lucky you're alive. Get out of the way if you can't face them."

Ilea was back to full health when the closest Praetorian turned toward her, mace casually held in both hands. Its eyes looked different than those of the Guardians and Centurions. It made it seem like an intelligent insect, studying its prey.

Goldie looked her way, and she knew it was futile.

"Ilea... we worked for months..." He coughed, blood spraying onto the floor. "This is it. If we can't beat them..."

She shot off, the mace coming at her immediately. This time, she ducked under the long handle as the head rushed down behind her.

Even the one using the fat weapon is fast as fuck.

Ilea needed a plan. Quickly. Her limbs smashed into the Praetorian, slamming into a magical barrier as her mana flowed into it. She managed to hit it twice before its mace came around again.

She dodged sideways to avoid the blow. Feeling an attack coming, she blinked back as far as she could, an expanding sphere of green energy burning across the floor.

No visual cue, no activation time either.

The initial hit would have corroded her armor, part of her skin too. As the floor sizzled, Ilea realized whatever that sphere produced was still burning into the white stone.

The one back then never used that ability. Are these different? Might want to avoid it.

Dodging another three hits, she focused on one of its massive steel legs, hitting it with all sixteen limbs, the shield flaring up each time. Storm of Cinders seemed to affect the barriers, slowly burning through them, her destructive mana spreading everywhere her limbs struck.

The mace crashed down again, and though Ilea jumped back twice to avoid the hits, the Praetorian followed with quick movements. Closing in, the creature used its area skill again, corrosion eating into the nearby pillars as Ilea blinked away once more.

At least Heranuur wasn't trying to intervene for now, instead sprinting to the others as his mana recovered, his remaining bruises and injuries healing very slowly. The hall was big enough for plenty of maneuvering, making her speed and teleportation quite effective against whatever the machine threw out.

Those three aren't enough against that one with the scythe.

Ilea continued to lead the machine around the hall as it tried to strike at her with a green mace as big as her chest. Another set of attacks followed, Ilea barely moving out of the way before her limbs smashed into the same leg again, their increased range making it a simple affair.

She already saw the problem, though – her mana was eating into the

Praetorian's defenses, but with the amount she'd already used, it wouldn't be enough. The damaged layers were already recovering. She needed her Destruction too.

Ilea looked to the side when she heard the groaning of wood to see Neiphato staggering back, the scythes slowly pushing through his wood.

Oh, fucking hell.

She moved toward the struggling elf in an attempt to lure the mace Praetorian toward the other machine. The creature was right behind her.

Ashen walls formed in front of Neiphato, the elf scrambling back as one of the two scythes sliced through the ash, somewhat slowed as they slammed into it, before Ilea appeared in front of him.

"If you won't retreat, at least don't get in the way!"

The blade stopped halfway through her wings. The second machine had closed the distance, Ilea's eyes widening as its area attack began. She activated her blink, but the scythe was in her ash, pushing further in and preventing her from moving away.

She hastily formed as much ash as possible. Two of the elves had already teleported away, but Neiphato was still standing there, his hands connected to the wood holding the scythe Praetorian back.

The Praetorian's corrosion magic flashed out. Ilea glanced at Neiphato, trying to push herself past the wood and before him to take some of the damage. She would survive the spell, but he probably wouldn't.

The throne room. A flashback to Inström, one of the Dawntree expedition leaders, being cut through by a scythe came to mind. *It's happening again.*

"Get out!" she shouted.

A crack echoed through the hall, part of the Praetorian's attack stopped by barriers that now shimmered in front of Ilea. The rest of the corrosion ran over her defenses, having already burnt halfway into her armor, before the barriers cracked and shattered.

She glanced back and saw Elfie standing near the still-closed gate, blood running from his mouth, nose, and ears as he held up his hands, claws extended.

Ilea smiled as she met his eyes, bloodshot and strained as they were.

Took you long enough.

NINETY

Engage

Rushing to his side, Ilea grabbed Neiphato, six of her limbs carrying the injured elf as she shoved healing into him. Some of the corrosion had still gotten to him, and she could tell he'd already been injured.

Hera and Goldie were injured too, barely on their feet as they joined Elfie behind his barriers, both having lost some of the fight in them. Neiphato had simply passed out, out of mana as his body slowly recovered.

The scythe Praetorian broke out of the remaining wood and rushed toward them, focusing on Ilea before its blades slammed into a set of barriers brought to life by Elfie.

"What are you… doing…" Heranuur panted as Ilea picked up both him and Goldie with a couple of ashen limbs. They struggled weakly but were too exhausted to put up much resistance.

She made her way to the exit before her remaining limbs slammed into the steel gates. A thrown scythe made it past Elfie's barriers, and one of Ilea's wings moved up to deflect the weapon aside before it crashed into the gates, cutting deep into the steel.

"You're no help here," she said.

The red-haired elf looked at her, eyes going wide. "No… We came… this far," he hissed.

Elfie hissed back, shutting him down. "You were not ready," he said through gritted teeth. "But Cerithil Hunters you are, that I will give you. Now stand down. I taught you better than to rush into a hopeless fight."

Ilea kept pummeling the gates. She saw that Elfie was struggling to reform his barriers as the two Praetorians hammered into them. He stepped back as a scythe moved past his face, only partially deflected by his defenses. The other Praetorian slammed his mace into the barriers with terrible strength, cracks already forming.

Ilea kept healing the three, taking care of the worst injuries before she finally opened a hole large enough to get the unconscious Neiphato through. Guardians would be waiting out there, but she'd rather have the injured elves face the lower-leveled machines than keep them in here.

"You want purpose? Want to prove to your teacher what you've learned after all these months? Then go and protect him. There's a flood of Taleen out there – we can't fight if this place is swarmed," Ilea said to Heranuur.

She saw the conflict in his eyes as he glanced between her and the Praetorians. Finally, he looked at Elfie as he stood with both arms raised, a dome-like barrier protecting them all from the magic of the Praetorians.

Finally, he hissed and grabbed Neiphato. "And what will you do?"

Ilea turned away from him and joined Elfie at his side. "Finish what you started."

Heranuur hissed one more time before he left, Goldie following behind with a hiss of his own. They were defeated, but she wasn't sure they'd really understood.

It didn't matter now. She was here, and so were these machines.

Ilea cracked her neck. "How long until they break through?"

Elfie grinned and went down to one knee. His breathing was ragged, his veins were dark and visible, there was sweat on his brow, and her healing had no effect. She could tell that his whole body was in turmoil, but there was nothing for her healing to fix. Whatever was happening to him, it had to happen.

"You don't look so good, friend," Ilea said as she prepared to fight, cracks forming on the barrier with the Praetorians' next strike.

He hissed. "Then we'd better finish this quickly."

Ilea glared at the cold eyes of the Praetorians and smiled.

Her smile grew as two new figures appeared next to her. One made of metal, one pulsing with purple energy.

"Good to see you made it too," she said, skeletons rising slowly from the floor nearby as metal spikes hovered toward the machines.

Terok laughed as he took in the scene. "This is quite a mess, and here I thought we were done fighting for a while. And in this fight here, I'll make sure to keep my distance."

"A human and an elf fighting together," Maro mused as he slowly walked to her side, purple flames dancing around his heavy robes. "I'm not the only one with a hidden stat, it seems."

"The mace one has a spherical corrosive area spell," Ilea said.

Then the barriers dropped, and chaos returned. Ilea and Terok teleported to the right side of the hall. Ilea formed ashen lances while the other two rushed to the opposite side, the two pairs separating the enemies successfully.

"You thought you could take these alone?" Terok asked as they stood a couple of meters apart, a beam of purple crashing into the distant Praetorian's shield just as Ilea's lances struck the shield of the closer machine.

The Praetorian lifted its mace to block the projectiles before a sphere of corrosion spread out. Ilea simply formed more lances as she started toward the machine, her wings vanishing.

"I mean, you lot already joined in, so I guess I won't find out today. Unless there's still a chance for you to fuck off?" Her sixteen ashen limbs writhed behind her, ready to strike. "I'll try to weaken its shield with my mana intrusion. Can you tell anything about its strength?"

She dove in, leaping over the mace as she twirled, her limbs smashing into the shield. Sixteen uses of Storm of Cinder burned quite a bit of mana. She watched the shield turn red where her limbs had touched it, the cinders sizzling through as she jumped up, her fist delivering Absolute Destruction. Ilea saw blue mana burn into the shield before she blinked away, the sphere of corrosion spreading where she'd just been standing.

"Its strength? Well, it's very large. I mean, you can see it too, right?" Terok said, floating between the pillars as he sent metal spikes right at the spots Ilea had already damaged, "Focus on separate spots, I don't think the enchantment encompasses the whole thing. Might find a gap."

Ilea didn't let up, darting in again as soon as the wave of acid vanished, the ground sizzling and a weird scent assaulting her nose.

"Front two legs first then," she said, her limbs battering the creature's legs as it moved quickly to avoid her strikes, its mace swiping at her time and time again as she dodged and weaved.

The fourth hit was unavoidable. Her blink was disrupted once again, and she could only use her arms to block the metal descending from above. The weapon landed, her arms smashed into her face as she was partially driven into the floor, the stone cracking against her armor of ash.

A wave of air rushed out from the impact, but Ilea was already healing her bruised arms and moving again. She grinned.

I can take their hits. I can fight them.

Her ashen limbs once more delivered their payload into the machine's right front leg, latching on for a moment to add her reversed healing. Maro's beams were closer now, striking the Praetorian in front of her as well, precise and deadly as they burned through the shield, stripping away layer upon layer with their combined efforts.

Four overhead slams she dodged, the fifth one coming from the side sending her tumbling once again, skidding across the floor. The Praetorian followed, moving as quickly as she flew. Maro teleported close as he joined in, targeting its front legs while Ilea formed a set of ashen walls in front of her.

She glanced to the side and saw Elfie retreating with barriers deflecting the scythes striking at him before a sphere of fire flashed in from the hall's entrance, exploding on the Praetorian's shield and giving Elfie precious seconds of reprieve.

Couldn't stand back, could you? she thought, but then she smiled.

The next mace strike crashed into and through her ash, Ilea ducking under the slowed attack just as Storm of Cinders finally broke through the machine's shield.

"Now, Maro, front right!"

A powerful purple beam cut into it as Ilea blinked closer, her fists crashing against the leg that stood as tall as her. Absolute Destruction and Storm of Cinders coupled with her sixteen limbs sucked her mana dry. Some returned thanks to her second-tier Reversal, but the machine had a high defense against it.

She felt an attack coming but didn't let up, getting in another strike at the same time as a purple beam rushed in over her shoulder. She saw a chunk of the leg torn off just as a corrosive sphere struck her, a burning smell filling her nostrils.

Ilea blinked back, the ash on her discarded as fresh armor formed. Still, her face, chest, and thighs had burned through, her skin dissolving as she counter-healed. The Praetorian pursued but nearly fell, the damaged leg snapping when it took a step, its integrity no longer enough for the machine's heavy torso.

The time it needed to adjust was enough for Ilea to recover, though the corrosion continued to burn into her skin behind the newly formed armor. *One leg down, five to go.* She smiled to herself, wondering for a moment why she'd feared them in the first place. *Just another monster to fight and kill.*

She focused her mind again, jumping back to avoid another strike as Maro started working on its second leg.

She fought in a trance now, teleporting through the hall and striking at both machines to distract them from the others and damage their shields. Elfie's curse magic burned through the shields, his barriers deflecting blows aimed at anyone in the group.

Maro got some distance from the Praetorians now with Ilea getting the attention of the mace wielder, precise and bright beams of death magic cutting into shield and steel alike. Another leg snapped, and then another.

Ilea was pushing all of her skills as far as they went, sacrificing health whenever possible to get another boost from her aura. Maro sent his remaining skeletons toward the mace-wielder when its fourth leg snapped, causing the machine to collapse.

"I'll keep it occupied!" he shouted.

The Praetorian had two legs and arms remaining as it dragged its massive body across the floor toward them, the grinding noise overshadowed by the sound of their magics, everyone now focused on the scythe-wielder, spells occasionally flashing in from the entrance as well.

Ilea punched the barrier when she saw a wall of wood growing in front of the machine. A moment later, both the praetorian's scythes were entangled and lodged within. *Already done out there?* she thought as she kept up her attacks.

When the Praetorian managed to rip out one of the scythes, slashing it in her direction, Ilea dodged. Purple beams cut into the creature, curse magic enveloping its torso, metal spikes and explosions ripping into its barriers, the wooden wall groaning as it expanded to keep the machine right there.

Jumping back, Ilea avoided another strike from the scythe aimed at her face. She felt the air pressure change as it flashed by, scraping against her ashen armor. Then, finally, the machine tore itself out from the wood, now able to use both weapons.

It focused on her, building more speed with each swing of its scythes. Ilea was forced to teleport, blinking behind the machine and targeting one of its hind legs. She raised her arms when the Praetorian turned quickly, its movements lithe, before it brought its scythe down into her shoulder, the other blade cutting into her side. Both punched through her ash and skin, digging deeper as its green eyes stared at her.

Ilea felt the coldness of the curse magic spread through her as she pushed against the scythes, one with each hand. Her heart pounded in her chest. She could already see the blade piercing through her just like it had in the past, could see the curse overwhelming her.

But neither of those things happened. She stood and held the blades back with her own strength, her body not relenting against the machine's weapons. While its curse had felt insurmountable in the past, it now felt merely dangerous, her healing already combating the cold sensation. Magic surged into the Praetorian, then its weight shifted when one of its back legs snapped.

Ilea screamed, straining her arms as she forced the blades out of her flesh, her third-tier healing ridding her body of the machine's curse, her wounds closing in an instant. She ducked to dodge the next strike, and the next she deflected.

Yes, stay focused on me.

She laughed out loud, stepping backward with measured movements, learning more about the range and weight of its weapons, adapting to the machine just as it was adapting to her.

Another blade came at her, and Ilea lifted her arm to deflect it ever so slightly, her ashen limbs flying out from her back to slam into the enemy shields. Her eyes shone blue in the dimly lit hall, ash wreathing her body.

I'm not running today.

NINETY-ONE

Taleen Praetorian

Ilea blinked a few meters back to avoid the Praetorian's sweeping strikes. Her mana was low now, so she couldn't keep the machine's attention anymore. She flew up and past as it turned, rushing toward Maro instead, who teleported away.

Ilea blinked again when she saw the machine throw one of its scythes, deflecting it with her arm before it could hit Maro. The strike left a gash that she slowly healed, and though the curse made it difficult, it was still easier than in the past.

"Thanks," Maro said, firing more beams at the machine as it was now focused on Terok. Elfie appeared before the dwarf, his barriers blocking the first two strikes, but the third one cut through, piercing his chest.

Ilea blinked close, grabbing onto Elfie before she pulled him away, flying backward as she healed the deep wound. He hissed, his eyes barely lucid.

"Stay with me now," Ilea said as she healed and dodged at the same time.

She twirled away when another scythe was thrown at her, slowing to prepare for the next attack when she saw the Praetorian's fourth leg snap, the machine falling to the ground like its counterpart still dragging itself through the hall.

Ilea breathed out and landed, focusing on healing Elfie, and while her magic was unable to help with his general condition, it at least worked to close the wound.

He reached up to clasp her hand, looking at her with glassy eyes. "Cursed… I'm… cursed…"

Tears flowed down his cheeks as she held him. Ilea glanced over to see

Maro land nearby, arm raised to send another beam into the chest of the scythe-wielder.

"If fighting to help others makes you cursed, then I'm cursed too," Ilea said.

"As am I," Terok said as he arrived too.

Ilea saw the other elves rushing into the hall, hissing when they saw Elfie.

"He'll survive," Ilea said.

"I'm more worried about them!" Maro said, sending out another beam at the Praetorians as he stepped closer to the group.

As a sudden wave of mana flashed through her Sphere, Ilea felt herself being pushed back a little. The machines were now frantically moving closer to them, dragging themselves on both legs and arms. Another heavy wave of mana washed over them.

Ilea knew what was coming.

"He's stable, get him up," Ilea said as she stepped before the group. Heranuur and Neiphato duly helped the barely conscious Elfie up.

"Get behind me," Ilea said. She glanced at the distant entrance to the throne room. One of the machines was now blocking the way out. When a third massive pulse of mana reached them, the machines stopped moving and looked up.

Ilea turned around, her wings spreading around the group of elves, human and dwarf. Most of Terok's armor moved out, reforming in a dome-like shield behind her back, while Neiphato's roots formed a sphere around them with Maro's shield layered in between.

A pulse of kinetic energy washed over them, cracking the pillars around them, splintering the walls and floor. Ilea felt the heat behind her, saw the approaching wall of energy that burned everything in its path. It moved slowly, almost at a crawl compared to a conventional explosion.

Then the energy reached them, burning through the walls of ash, the shields of wood, metal, and death magic. Ilea healed herself and the others, looking at the half-conscious Elfie, who held out a hand, purple veins lining his face and arms, blood seeping from every orifice.

A barrier enveloped them, cracks webbing through it a moment later before Elfie gritted his teeth, then screamed. Another wave of energy reached them, and the barriers shattered. Ilea's ashen armor was burned through, her skin and muscles evaporating faster than she could recover them, desperately using what mana she had to instantly recreate what was lost.

When she was nearly out of mana, her normal healing took over. Their defenses were gone. Her bones were seared, the back half of her body pretty much gone. Her skills and Classes took over from her mental functions as she fell.

Two soft dings rang somewhere in her mind.

Someone caught her as her sight returned, then her brain reformed before anything else, blood dripping as her organs started recovering. The smell was overwhelming. Everything had been burnt.

She found herself smiling with what muscles were left, looking up at Maro's face with her one working eye, blood pooling below them. One of his arms was burnt to the bone, his teeth clenched against the pain.

"Did... anybody... die?"

Speaking, she found, was difficult, all her recovered mana instantly sent to reform her body.

"We're fine. Thanks to you. Now stop speaking until you've recovered. You're one hard nut to crack," Maro said, purple flames searing his wounds shut as he nearly buckled from the pain, still holding her.

"Seems like more machines are coming," Terok said, his armor mostly gone, a couple of metal lances hovering around him.

Ilea closed her eyes and focused on her healing, hearing Neiphato speak close by.

"We'll deal with them."

Turning her head slightly, she wearily opened her eyes, seeing the three elves ready their weapons, their bodies badly burnt. Taleen Guardians, a few Centurions in their midst, were pouring in as a wooden barrier formed around their group.

Terok grunted as he dragged Elfie inside, while Maro helped her sit down when the bleeding had stopped and her skin had mostly reformed. Bones came forth from his ring, and he animated skeletons with his magic to help the others.

"I'll support you from here, mana is still rather low," he told Neiphato, who nodded as his roots continued to spread around them.

"Now let's see who can get more," Heranuur chuckled, and Ilea knew he had that stupid grin on his face. She heard the cracking of Seviir's bone magic. A chilling sound, she'd found.

She breathed in to find her chest reformed and her lungs back in working order, the partially destroyed rib cage now as strong as before.

"You will lose," Goldie declared, running off alongside Heranuur. Shortly after, the dull sounds of fighting could be heard. Steel and bone against metal, the impacts of projectiles on wood. Ranged Guardians below level two hundred were hardly a concern to her now.

Ilea relaxed, closing her eyes again as she lay on the floor. Her body had recovered, barely a minute after half of it had been missing, with no mana left and her health down to half. She smiled.

Half of my body was missing, but they're down, and we survived.

She sighed happily and checked her messages, trusting the elves to handle themselves against the horde of Guardians.

'ding' Your group has defeated [Taleen Praetorian – lvl 600] – For defeating

an enemy two hundred and ninety or more levels above your own, bonus experience is granted.

'ding' Your group has defeated [Taleen Praetorian – lvl 600] – For defeating an enemy two hundred and ninety or more levels above your own, bonus experience is granted.

'ding' Azarinth Sentinel has reached lvl 305 – Five stat points awarded

'ding' Kin of Ash has reached lvl 304 – Five stat points awarded

"You already look better. Almost worried me there when I held the remaining half of you," Maro said as he looked down at her, his arms crossed and helmet gone. He had a warm smile on his blood- and sweat-covered face.

Sitting up, Ilea's ashen limbs came to life, reaching out toward the three people nearby. Her Sphere was back online too now that she didn't immediately need all the mana for her healing.

She discovered Maro's arm wasn't just burnt, it was damn near gone completely, his insides mangled and fucked up. Nearly half the bones on the right side of his body were broken, some virtually pulverized.

"Do you have some additional pain tolerance skill? That looks gnarly."

He grinned. "Partially. Most do at our level, Ilea. Otherwise, you wouldn't remain standing for very long."

The man closed his eyes when she started healing the damage, his breathing and heart rate slowing. Looking around, Ilea saw Neiphato was mostly fine. He, Terok, and Heranuur had been shielded by her the most. Seviir had been to one side, but she knew he had some sort of self-healing ability. Not the best, but at least it was something. Enough that he was fighting Guardians without much trouble now.

Tough fuckers.

She started healing everyone close by. Terok only had minor bruising, the least injured of the five. Elfie was out cold again, but other than the turmoil she could see in his body, there was nothing to heal.

She continued healing them, her ash cutting through some Neiphato's wood to allow the group a view of the shattered gates, partially blown out by the Praetorian detonations.

Goldie and Heranuur were flying through the chaotic horde of machines, bits and pieces flying around. Only two Centurions remained in the actual throne room, the two elves mostly avoiding them and using the other Guardians as shields against the spears thrown in their direction.

'ding' Absolute Destruction reaches 3rd lvl 13

'ding' Sentinel Reconstruction reaches 3rd lvl 13

'ding' Azarinth Awakening reaches 3rd lvl 12

'ding' Azarinth Fighting reaches 3rd lvl 10

'ding' Armor of Ash reaches 3rd lvl 12

'ding' Aspect of Ash reaches 3rd lvl 8

'ding' Storm of Cinders reaches 3rd lvl 3

'ding' Ash and Ember Unity reaches 3rd lvl 7

'ding' Keeper of Ash reaches 3rd lvl 5

'ding' Arcane Magic Resistance reaches 2nd lvl 4

...

'ding' Arcane Magic Resistance reaches 2nd lvl 7

'ding' Blast Resistance reaches 2nd lvl 7

'ding' Blast Resistance reaches 2nd lvl 8

'ding' Corrosion Resistance reaches lvl 14

...

'ding' Corrosion Resistance reaches lvl 17

'ding' Pain Tolerance reaches 2nd lvl 5

So, the blast was arcane in nature? Maybe a mana core or something powers them. Weird that I never got anything like that from the Centurions. Oh, and Pain Tolerance leveled. I did only activate the second tier in the end. Guess the pain accumulated until now was enough to trigger it.

She looked around to see that all that was left of the destroyed Praetorians was craters and shrapnel. Ilea laughed and laid her head back down on the ground, ignoring the ongoing sounds of battle.

I fought and destroyed them.

She grinned to herself.

Next is facing one on my own. Hmm. Could I do it? I probably need more levels in my defensive skills. And more mana for sure. Plus, they seem to come in twos, so I'll have to be able to fight two at the same time.

She found the thought not only exciting but freeing. As if a weight had finally been lifted. She still remembered how it had felt back in her first Taleen dungeon, running away with a curse wracking her body. But instead of fear coming up when she remembered being pierced by the scythes today, she recalled how she'd resisted, pushed back, continued fighting.

She could face them, couldn't she?

"Is there another cap at level twenty for third-tier skills?" Ilea asked, sitting up again.

Maro leaned over the wooden barricade. "No idea. Haven't gotten that far yet. I'm very close though."

"They're actually doing it," Terok said as he walked a little closer, standing near the barrier. "Hey Maro, can you drop me some of that metal you still have? I feel naked."

Ilea smiled as Maro handed over some ingots. The dwarf's metal eye focused on her. With his disheveled beard, he looked positively rugged.

"I think you look great," she said.

He rolled his one real eye and started funneling mana into the steel.

"Would've been surprised to hear that if I hadn't just seen you half burnt up and near dead. You're ridiculous."

Ilea leaned on the wooden barrier and relaxed, watching the ongoing battle with a smile.

"Maybe a little bit."

NINETY-TWO

Aftermath

The throne room was in ruins, two big craters digging nearly fifteen meters down into the white stone, revealing the ordinary rock beneath. Not even rubble was left behind, most of it having simply turned to dust. The gates had been bent and mangled in the explosions, allowing the Guardians from outside to enter. It seemed, though, that after the initial wave, those waiting farther back in the Great Hall hadn't swarmed toward the throne room.

Now that the Praetorians are dead, maybe they'll return to their normal positions.

An explosion boomed nearby, the shock wave traveling toward the group. Ilea's black hair floated back, settling again a moment later.

Heranuur had downed his Centurion first, the blast sending him flying. He rolled a couple of times before crashing into the wall with a wet thud. He was still alive, though. His laughter was indication enough. Seviir and his Centurion were still battling each other, the only noise remaining in the hall now that most of the machines had been cleared out.

Terok looked over from his impromptu workbench Neiphato had provided. The elf had formed a wooden chair for himself, sitting down with a sigh as he started meditating. Ilea nearly asked for one too before she remembered her own ability to make one out of ash.

She was just about to do so when Elfie gasped, the purple veins still showing on his pale white skin. He was already slim, but the toll this experience and entering the dungeon had taken on him definitely showed. His cheeks looked a little sunken in, and his eyes only opened halfway before he groaned in pain.

He scratched his head before shooting up into a sitting position, eyes wide as he stuttered something to himself.

"Is that normal, Neiphato?" Ilea asked.

The wood mage opened his eyes and smiled. "Oh yes, it is. Very painful. He's going to feel that for the next couple of weeks."

He seemed conflicted but finally looked at Elfie with a focused gaze, then nodded and continued his meditation.

"I... betrayed... everything. All of it..." Elfie said, holding a hand to his face.

Ilea wasn't sure if he was about to rip off his skin or start to cry. What she certainly didn't expect was the manic cackling that followed. Even Maro looked away from the fight to glance at the elf. Then, as quickly as his manic state had come on, Elfie calmed down again, his eyes focusing on Ilea.

"You."

Ilea pointed at herself and looked around in a questioning manner. "Hey, that was your choice." She now did form her chair made of ash and summoned herself one of Keyla's meals as well.

He sat up and sighed, then hissed and put on a sincere expression. "Ilea. For many years, I believe, I have known that this path was inevitable. But I did not expect a human as annoying as you to finally bring me here."

"Hey, I'm not that annoying!" Ilea retorted, pointing a fork at him. "Thank you," Elfie said. "Sincerely."

Ilea smiled. "I know you would've made your choice eventually."

She lifted her fork and took a mouthful of noodles in an egg and cream sauce with pieces of bacon. Garlic and cheese were present too, as well as some other flavors she couldn't place. Definitely some sort of carbonara.

"We all learn in time. Some faster than others," Elfie said, glancing at the still-fighting Seviir. His tone was contemplative.

A boom echoed behind them, another shock wave traveling past a moment later. Moans of pain followed, the clattering of metal falling to the stone floor audible throughout.

"My cue," Ilea said, standing up and taking another mouthful as she blinked twice to reach the deformed body of Seviir, her healing mana immediately reaching him through her limbs. "That was one Centurion," she said in a low volume, taking another bite and chewing.

Ilea realized most of Seviir's injuries hadn't come from the battle just now, especially those on his left side, which was mostly mangled.

Heranuur cackled from nearby as he stumbled toward them. "I win," he said, then collapsed. Ilea extended an ashen limb toward him before commencing more healing.

"Care to tell me now why you couldn't wait to face these machines?" Elfie said, glancing at Neiphato. "You would've died had Ilea not interfered. Had we not interfered."

The meditating elf opened his eyes and gulped. "We... we were not sure, I think. If we made the right choice. We have trained for so long, felt stuck, going from one set of rules to the next. We weren't allowed into dungeons, and once we finally broke free, did the forbidden, you set new rules. I agreed to enter the Great Hall because of this, but for the others, I believe it was a way to prove themselves too. I merely wished to test these machines and retreat, but the others wouldn't let up."

"Way to expose them," Ilea smiled.

"I will share this responsibility," Neiphato said. "And I would've fought and died by their side. There is no need to hide anything. You came to prevent our deaths, and now here we are. I am contemplating what it is that I may learn from this."

"Not being a fucking idiot?" Terok suggested. He'd prepared a few pieces of makeshift armor. Nothing compared to the war machine he'd sacrificed to protect them all, but it was better than nothing.

"We will talk," Elfie said. "I agree that I was too limiting, too harsh, in light of my own reluctance to join you. But now I too am c… Now I too am a Cerithil Hunter."

Neiphato hissed, an approving sound. "You are."

"Wonderful," Terok said. "Can we move on now? I'm sure there's abundant treasure here."

"There should be treasure," Ilea said. "I've been inside a Great Hall before. But don't underestimate the traps. Nearly killed me back then."

I wonder how easily I can shrug off the traps now.

"Good," Terok said, pointing behind him toward the shattered throne, only bits and pieces of which remained. "Then we can start with the hidden room behind this one."

Maro laughed at that. "Had to get your armor done first?"

The dwarf chuckled and started walking toward the wall. "Of course, wouldn't want to get left behind. Although you two deserve most of everything here. Anybody disagree?"

Neiphato waved him off. "Of course not. We'd all be dead without them."

"I do ask to see what we find, at least. To see if it has great relevance to me," Elfie said.

"Let's see what we find then," Ilea said.

They stopped in front of the wall, though Ilea didn't sense anything wrong with it. She didn't know if her old Hunter's Sphere would have let her sense anything. Considering her arcane sight didn't reveal the secret either, she doubted it.

"There are enchantments here. Illusion, strong skill disruption, shielding, and a bunch more, all defensive in nature. Maro, what do you think?"

"I don't see half the things you mentioned," he said, surprising the dwarf, who cocked his head, shrugging a moment later.

Terok turned to the elves, but Heranuur and Seviir were punching each other every couple of seconds, giddy and apparently highly uninterested.

"You two can go clear out more of the Taleen," Elfie suggested, both of them grinning before Ilea interrupted.

"Don't enter any of the side paths from the main hall. I don't want to clean your corpses off a bunch of spikes."

They nodded and vanished, bickering amongst themselves as they left the throne room. Ilea rolled her eyes, Maro watching her with a grin.

"As I was about to ask," Terok said, looking between Neiphato and Elfie, "do you have runic knowledge or experience with enchantments?"

As Neiphato shook his head, Elfie said, "Only elven. Though I can read the Taleen language, if that is any help."

"Seven hundred years and he doesn't know his runes," the dwarf murmured, getting to work.

"While we wait, Elfie, I have something for you that I'd like to have translated and transcribed," Ilea said.

She'd hesitated at sharing it before, perhaps still not ready to trust him. She summoned her big crate of stuff and rummaged through it, her Sphere allowing her to find what she was looking for quickly.

Ilea picked out a little leather-bound diary, worn by age, any color gone from it. Yet it had survived, and now she'd found someone who claimed to know the language.

"I found it on a dwarven skeleton. Taleen, most likely. The gear on him was called Legate Guardian Armor. It's also where I got this." She tapped her storage necklace with the Guardian-like head.

Elfie smiled brightly. "I had been wondering about that necklace but deemed it inappropriate to pry. May I?" He held out a hand before she handed over the small book.

Elfie summoned a table and chair before he carefully opened the book. Ilea felt like he was only missing glasses to top off his look.

Turning the pages, he grumbled and hissed time and time again. "Most of it is faded. It is a diary."

"Any of the most recent entries remaining?" Maro asked.

"Yes. Let's see... *Third cycle, the year eight hundred and sixteen...* Some of the numbers are faded, it might not be exactly that. *Still, I am afraid. Questioning every day if it was the right decision to make, even if it had meant our doom. Surrendering control, long theorized yet hardly tested. The Makers are certain, but I fear for my brothers and sisters, their children, and those to come after. Still, we must fight, must prevail. My duty will soon be irrelevant, replaced by the Guardians assigned. Either that or the enemy will hunt us down, slaughter each and every one of us. May the One without Form prevail. I will guard the Tungsten key with my life."*

He looked up.

"That is one of the later ones. Some more entries talk about hunger, sleep, and approaching death. I suppose survival priorities snuck up on the dwarf. Still, he remained at his post," Elfie concluded. He looked at Ilea with sharp eyes. "I wonder what all of it means. The Makers must have had a plan. This enemy, was it our kind? And did you find this Tungsten key? It was deemed important enough for this dwarf to guard with his very life."

"I did. But I want to hold on to it, in case it can help with finding my friend," Ilea said, summoning it.

"That is… Look at this piece," Terok murmured, having turned at the mention of the key. "Incredible."

"Any idea what we're looking at?"

Elfie shook his head.

"An intricate artifact," Maro said.

"Not just intricate, this is the fucking pinnacle of intricate," Terok said. "I can see hundreds of runes just on the first layer. I'd need my tools, but this is way beyond me, I can tell already."

Ilea stored it again. "I'll see if my enchanter friends can find out something about it, then. Haven't shown it around so far."

Elfie nodded, returning to the book. "It is certainly safer with you. Let us know if you find out anything. I will ask around if I meet other Hunters."

Terok focused on the wall again. "Care to help me with these runes instead? Far less complex, but they're tricky too."

NINETY-THREE

Relaxed Exploration

Ilea thought about the journal entry, about this 'One without Form' the dwarf had mentioned.

Did they surrender control of the Guardians to someone? Or something? Did it not work in the end, given they aren't around anymore?

She listened to Elfie talking with Neiphato, discussing the possibility of them fighting in the Centurion facility.

"Don't fuck with the Awakened smith in the facility. He's a friend," Ilea interjected.

Neiphato nodded. "Our enemy are the Taleen. We will not hurt anybody else should they offer the same courtesy to us. It is a shame, the marred reputation our species has gained over the countless millennia." He looked at Elfie with a serious gaze. "Perhaps that is something to consider too. Being freed of the Oracles lends us power not only to enter dungeons but to question their very rule."

Elfie hissed at that, though whether angry or afraid, Ilea was unsure. Neiphato hissed too, and Elfie averted his gaze as he focused on his diary again.

"It is unavoidable," Neiphato added, his usual timidity nowhere to be found.

And he's using his wood magic now too, Ilea thought.

Terok cried out a moment later, something clicking open. Ilea immediately saw the trap with her Sphere, blinking in front of the dwarf before a spear smashed into her ashen armor, her body not moving an inch as it stopped the weapon.

"I could have taken that," Terok grumbled.

Ilea nodded. "That one, yes. I remember there were some much more dangerous traps in the last Great Hall I was in. Green flames that nearly killed me, acid as well as fire traps that you lot might not be able to deal with as easily."

"Sorry," the dwarf said. "Just surprised."

"What's that?" Maro said, pointing at the altar standing in the middle of the small room they'd found. "Nobody go in, there are enchantments all over the floor. I think..."

"Yeah, big explosion if you walk in there," Terok supplied in a serious tone. "Anything else in there but that?"

They all looked at the diamond-shaped white form set onto the altar. It was about as big as a fist, thin green lines flowing on it as if they were veins.

Elfie stepped closer, pushing Maro to the side as he stuttered, "That... could it be? Neiphato, have you seen one before?"

He turned to look at the brown-haired elf. Ilea was a little concerned about the excitement in his voice. Neiphato shook his head, not understanding where he was getting at.

"I don't know what that is."

"Can we disable the enchantments? If what I think is true, then that could be a gate key... You know about the teleportation network between all the Taleen cities? This was described in the notes I found on a murdered Cerithil Hunter... two hundred years ago. I can't think of anything else."

He looked at Terok in anticipation, but the dwarf shook his head.

"These are highly sensitive runes... I managed to bypass an activation when I opened up the room, but this would take weeks. Even then, I would suggest getting a better rune mage."

"Or I could just blink in and take it," Ilea suggested.

"Or that. I doubt there's more power in them than a Praetorian core detonation."

"Does it explode outward?"

"No. The spell should be contained in the room, to increase its potency."

Elfie was pacing, "The risks are too high, we can't—"

Ilea appeared in the middle of the room, grabbing the thing and placing it into her necklace. As an explosion of green fire flashed around her, she spread her wings before they wrapped her in a cocoon of ash.

Didn't even get through my wings...

She was a little disappointed in the trap, remembering the green flames from before. Perhaps she'd been overestimating the dwarfs. Stepping out of the blazing fire, she gave a thumbs-up to the mortified Elfie.

Beside him, Maro was laughing before he slapped his shoulder. "What the fuck did you expect?"

Neiphato had a sly smile on his face, and Terok was just shaking his head.

"Did you get it?" the dwarf asked.

“Of course I did,” she said and summoned the little piece of tech.

[Taleen Gate Key – Ancient]

“It’s called a Taleen Gate Key, so I suppose that’s exactly what you described.”

Ilea felt strange as she looked at the device. Wasn’t this exactly what she’d been looking for? A clue to find out what exactly had happened to Kyrian? And yet she found that she didn’t feel elated.

On the contrary. She felt dread.

Strange. Gotta think about that one.

“Can I see it?” Elfie asked.

Ilea looked at the artifact, then glanced at the elf. “Sure. But I’ll want it back. This is the kind of thing I’ve been looking for.”

“I understand. Your friend who went missing. But it could be very useful to us as well.”

She handed it to him. “I know. But I know an enchanter who’s somewhat familiar with the gates already. If anyone can figure something out about this key, it’s him.”

“This thing is almost as complex as that other relic you showed us before,” Terok said. “You collect ancient puzzles?”

“Seems like I do,” Ilea said with a smile.

The others looked at the item before Elfie handed it back. “Your enchanter is probably the best bet we have. Make sure to not lose this.”

“I’ll try my best,” Ilea said drily, storing the artifact again. “I’ll let you know if I find out anything.”

“So that’s the treasure?” Terok asked in a disappointed tone. “No offense, but we have enough dangerous dungeons around. A gate or something to even more of those doesn’t excite me.”

Elfie scoffed. “It’s not a gate, it’s merely the key.”

“Even worse then. Ilea, any idea where the treasure room is?”

She smiled. “I might. Or, well, he might.” She pointed at Elfie. “There should be inscribed names describing all the side paths in the Great Hall. You’ll be the guide, I suppose.” He looked at her and inclined his head slightly.

Ilea started to understand it now. Why she’d felt dread when she’d held the key. Exploring the rest of this dungeon, adventuring with the people here, the friends she’d made, it felt so easy. The key was a reminder of all the responsibilities she’d had in the south. All the things she’d wanted to get away from. The war that had started. Adam Strand. Everything that had happened with Trian. Eve.

She didn’t want to face it. She knew she had to, but what she wanted to do was explore more up here in the north, fight more monsters, get more levels.

I'm avoiding it the same way I avoided the Praetorians, she thought with a slight smile. Just that instead of using the excuse of getting more powerful, of reaching level three hundred, she'd set herself the goal of finding something to get to Kyrian. It was so long ago now that she knew he was either long dead or didn't need her help. Not anymore.

Maybe she was being unfair to herself. Reaching level three hundred had been a reasonable goal, hadn't it? And, in the end, it had helped her fight the Praetorians. *But would you have faced them if not for Elfie asking for help?* she wondered, but then she decided it didn't really matter. She was here now.

And now she'd actually found something that could help them figure out more about the Taleen gates, about what had happened to her and Kyrian when Arthur Redleaf used the ancient dwarven technology to teleport them away.

She smiled to herself. *Another goal met. Now that I actually have a lead, I bet he's already back in Ravenhall.*

If she was honest, she didn't want to go back yet. She didn't want to find out what had happened, didn't want to get sucked into more problems and conflicts. Despite the power she'd gained here, she knew what would happen as soon as she arrived in Ravenhall.

And yet she knew she had to go.

She took a deep breath and nodded to herself.

I'll go back. Once I've finished up here in this dungeon, and with the vaults in Tremor. She smiled. *More arbitrary goals. Alright. The main goals I set for myself, I've achieved. Once I feel ready, I'll go back.*

* * *

"It's exciting, isn't it?" Maro asked. "Exploring the unknown."

Elfie looked at him after a moment, realizing he was the one being addressed. "I suppose it is. There are, however, many secrets not hidden within the confines of dungeons, human."

The group was standing in front of the entrance that Elfie has translated as being labeled 'Treasury'.

"True, but in dungeons, you have a pretty good chance of finding *something*."

"Death, usually," Terok supplied, opening the door, the stone sliding down into the floor. Ilea noted that it was an enchantment that activated a mechanical device to slide the stone downward. The Taleen really tried to avoid using exclusively magic.

Ilea took the lead. If she was staying in the north a little longer, she'd make the best of it. Looking at the five Centurions protecting an elevator a hundred meters away, she grinned.

The rest of the group caught up with her, stepping into the hall as well.

Broad stairs led down to a white floor, green ivy growing on the walls to each side, both around ten meters away.

One of the lights was flickering. Ilea wondered if it was intentional to give a sense of dread. *Do you really want to face these ancient warriors? You don't.*

Taking a step forward, Elfie stopped her, grasping her shoulder. "May we? It has been a while since I faced a Centurion."

Neiphato, Heranuur, and Seviir moved forward alongside him as they readied their weapons, the latter two grinning as the wood mage checked the walls.

Ilea took a step down the stairs and sat, summoning another meal before starting to eat. Her armor receded to reveal her white shirt and brown pants, both comfortable and providing the same level of defense as an ornamental flower dress.

I do have dresses, actually.

She thought about it, but this fabric was simply more comfortable, the cut easier to fight in.

Maro sat down next to her and looked at the meal. "Looks good. Benefits of storage items, am I right?"

She smiled with a full mouth as Terok grunted behind them.

"Back to Tremor once we're done here?" he asked, looking at the elves as they charged at the Centurions, weapons and spells at the ready before they clashed.

"Yeah," Ilea agreed. "Elana mentioned some jobs in Hallowfort, but I think it's best for me to return south soon," she added, taking another bite. This time, she'd got meatballs in a dark sauce with mashed potatoes and an added vegetable mix of eggplant and tomatoes on an onion and garlic base. *Very hearty.*

She moved the dish a little further away from Maro, whose gaze was fixated on it. He locked eyes with her and grinned, moving his attention back to the elves.

"Good cook. Smells nice." He paused. "You're going back south with that key you found. Sure you don't want to go immediately? We can handle things here, you know."

Ilea smiled at the mention of the cook.

"She really is. Keyla. I hope she's managed to make her way to Ravenhall. If she has, she'll have a restaurant there." She took another bite. "As for going south, I've thought about it," she said but didn't elaborate any further.

Maro smiled. "I see. It's not just your enchanter friend who's down in the south then." He looked at the ongoing fight. "I'd like to see it too, if you want a companion on your journey."

Journeying south instead of teleporting? Ilea thought. She found she liked the idea.

She knew that the monsters and dungeons here in the north didn't run away. *Miststalkers, Blue Reapers, the Descent, the Cliffs Elfie once talked about.* There were plenty of options for training and fighting.

She would deliver the key to Claire. She also wanted to investigate the Golden Lily. If only to find out exactly what had happened to Eve, who she'd killed, and who had killed her. She wanted to know that much, at least. But thinking about it filled her with dread.

I could hire some people to look into Eve. The Lily will show up once I go looking for them. If they have a bunch of people in my level range, it seems an unnecessary risk to rush it.

Her stomach dropped a little when she thought of Eve, covered in blood in her bed. Still, it felt less intense than it once had. It was the same with Petra Birmingale and everything that had happened to Trian.

The first Centurion exploded, the elves moving back to avoid the blast. The shock wave washed over the waiting trio as Ilea finished her meal.

"I'll stick with these elves for now, I think," Terok said. "They're powerful fighters, and they don't really care about treasures. Perfect group to... help."

Ilea laughed at that. "It was nice adventuring with everyone."

"You say that like it's the last time," Terok said. "I'd offer ale. Feels like an occasion."

Ilea summoned a few bottles. "Southern, not the shit that's brewed up here. No offense."

"We all agree on that," Terok said, grabbing a bottle. "To adventures, and to new friends."

Maro took a bottle and raised it as well. "To getting out of necromantic machines and a dungeon of my own making. And to getting out of the responsibility of kingship."

Ilea smiled, raising her own bottle. "To smashing a bunch of Praetorians."

She wasn't sure what she'd expected when she'd decided to go north. Making friends with dwarves and Awakened had certainly not been on that list, let alone befriending elves or finding an ancient necromancer king. She supposed with her already being friends with the Vultures, the last bit wasn't quite as surprising.

She'd reached her next evolution, and she'd found a Taleen relic. With whatever was left in the Rhyvor vaults in Tremor, she'd have quite an assortment of goods ready to deliver to Claire. *And Maro wants to come to Ravenhall as well,* she thought with a smile, wondering how much crazier their reception would be if Elfie joined them too.

She was proud of him for making his choice to enter a dungeon after all. But now he'd joined the cause of the Cerithil Hunters, a random visit to human lands probably wasn't on the cards anytime soon.

Ilea smiled, taking another swallow of ale and looking at the bottle.

One more reason to go south. I need to restock on food and drink.

I'd like to dedicate this book to trees and shrubbery.

Big thanks as always to Brook and Anthony, for the ton of work on the edits. And to Andrea for bring the audiobook to life.

As a last thing, I'd like to place two personal recommendations here, if you're looking for something else to read. I like these stories, so maybe you'll find them to your tastes as well (:

First, Liches get Stitches, by HJ Tolson. "Reborn as a powerful lich, Maud just wants to be left alone. The neighbouring villagers, paladins and busybodies have other ideas."

And The Calamitous Bob, by Alex Gilbert: "An Isekaied witch finds a golem and baby dragon, then embarks on a quest to resurrect an evil empire."

Thank you for reading this book. Or for just reading this dedication. More to come when more is ready :)

Rhaegar

Portal Books - Newsletter and Group

Portal Books is a digital publishing house that specializes in LitRPG, Dungeon Core, Cultivation and Progression Fantasy. Our mission is to bring you the best possible novels, with professional editing, copywriting and cover design.

We only work with authors who have a real passion for the genres and we think this shows in the novels we publish. We know that the heart of LitRPG is solid games mechanics and ensure every story is based on the kind of game system we ourselves would love to play.

If you'd like to try out stories from the other fantastic Portal Books authors, you can sign up to our mailing list for 80,000 words of FREE LitRPG stories. Whenever we add more, you'll get the update, absolutely free.

https://portal-books.com/sign-up

You can also find us on Facebook. Join our group to stay up to date on all our upcoming books, cover reveals, author interviews, giveaways, promotions and more!

https://www.facebook.com/groups/LitRPGPortal/

We also have a Discord server where you'll have a chance to chat with some our authors, members of the Portal Books team, or our community of readers as a whole!

https://discord.gg/GXBNDGYQqT

To find out more about the cultivation and western cultivation genres, you might find these groups to be of interest:

https://www.facebook.com/groups/WesternWuxia

https://www.facebook.com/groups/cultivationnovels

For more general discussions about the genre, these groups may be useful to you:

www.facebook.com/groups/LitRPGsociety

www.facebook.com/groups/LitRPG.books

www.facebook.com/groups/LitRPGGroup

Best wishes,

The Portal Books Team

www.portal-books.com

Join the Group

To learn more about LitRPG, talk to authors, and just have an awesome time, please join the LitRPG Group.

Published by Portal Books, 2023

www.portal-books.com

Made in United States
Orlando, FL
23 December 2023